Newark
Fort Niagara
Ft. George
Queenston
Lewiston
Niagara Falls
Lundy's Lane
Fort Schlosser
Chippewa R.
Ft. Chippewa
Grand I.
Niagara River
Black Rock
10 miles
Buffalo
Ft. Erie
L. Erie
MW01256873
Ottawa River
St. Lawrence
Montreal
Richelieu River
Lake Memphremagog
La Colle Mill
Isle-aux-Nois
Chateaugay R.
Chrysler's Farm
St. Regis
French Mills
Plattsburgh
Lake Champlain
Burlington
Saranac R.
Vergennes
PPER CANADA
Kingston
Sackets Harbor
York
Lake Ontario
Sandy Cr.
Beaver Dams
Fort Oswego
Oswego R.
see inset
Chippewa R.
Buffalo
Dover
River
VERMONT
NEW YORK
Albany
esque Isle (Erie)
Hudson
PENNSYLVANIA
New York
Pittsburgh
Philadelphia
Atlantic Ocean
0 50 100 150 200
miles

# *Voyage to Honor*

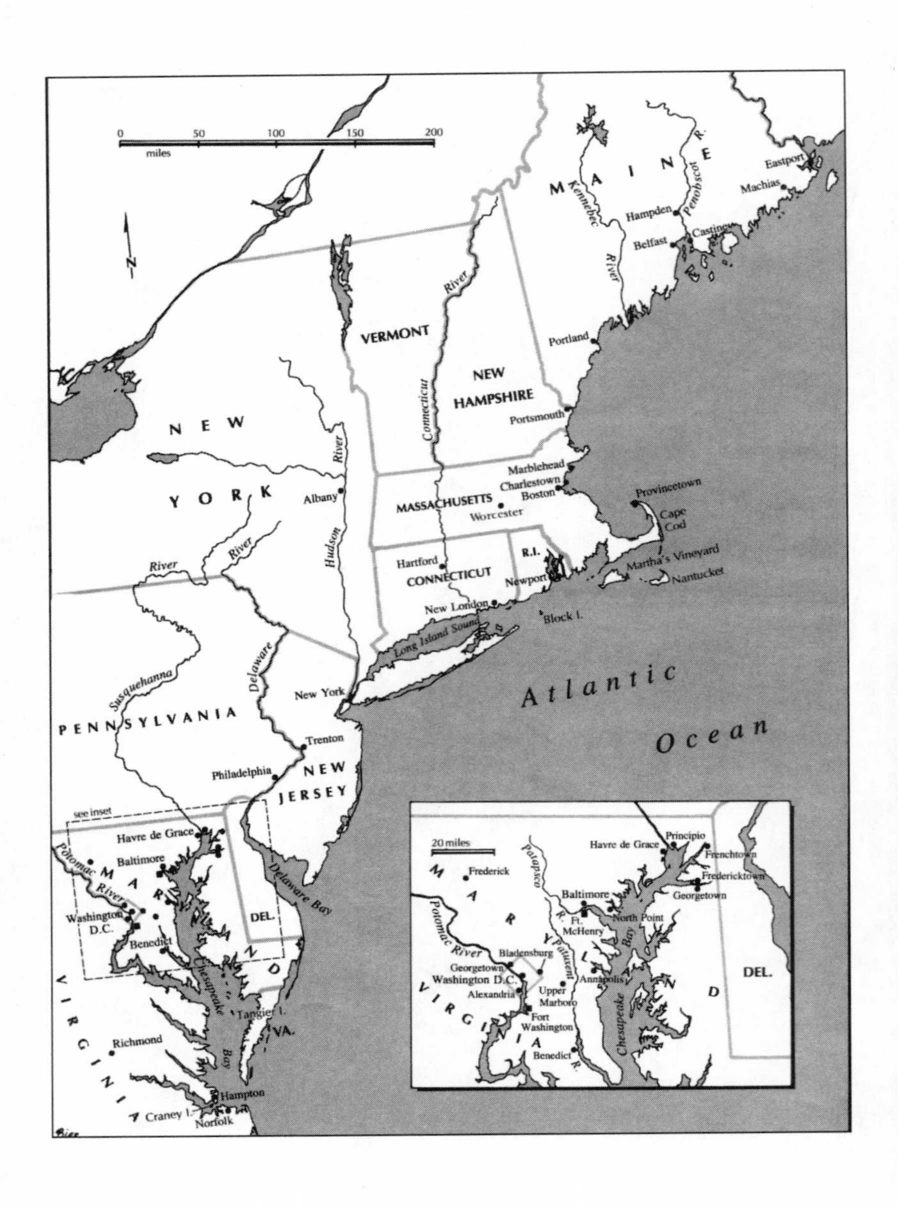

0
50
100
150
200
miles
N
MAINE
Kennebec River
Penobscot R.
Eastport
Machias
Hampden
Belfast
Castine
Portland
VERMONT
NEW HAMPSHIRE
Connecticut River
Portsmouth
NEW YORK
River
Albany
Hudson
Marblehead
Charlestown
Boston
MASSACHUSETTS
Worcester
Provincetown
Cape Cod
R.I.
Hartford
CONNECTICUT
Newport
Martha's Vineyard
Nantucket
New London
Block I.
Long Island Sound
Susquehanna
Delaware
New York
PENNSYLVANIA
Trenton
Philadelphia
NEW JERSEY
Atlantic Ocean
see inset
Havre de Grace
Baltimore
Potomac River
MARYLAND
Washington D.C.
Benedict
DEL.
Delaware Bay
Chesapeake Bay
Tangier I.
VA.
VIRGINIA
Richmond
Hampton
Craney I.
Norfolk
20 miles
Frederick
Patapsco R.
Principio
Frenchtown
Fredericktown
Georgetown
Ft. McHenry
North Point
Bladensburg
Patuxent R.
Annapolis
Alexandria
Upper Marboro
Fort Washington

A HISTORICAL NOVEL
THE WAR OF 1812

Robert H. Fowler

# VOYAGE TO HONOR

STACKPOLE
BOOKS

*For Wade, Alyce, Robert Jr., and Susanna*



Published by
STACKPOLE BOOKS
5067 Ritter Road
Mechanicsburg, PA 17055



Printed in the United States of America

10 9 8 7 6 5 4 3 2 1

First edition



**Library of Congress Cataloging-in-Publication Data**

Fowler, Robert H.
Voyage to Honor / Robert H. Fowler
p. cm.
ISBN 0-8117-0913-2
1. United States—History—War of 1812—Fiction. I. Title.
PS3556.0847V6 1996
813'.54—dc 20 95-52410
CIP

# ACKNOWLEDGMENTS AND EXPLANATIONS

One of the characters in this novel calls the War of 1812 "a messy little war." It certainly has been a messy little war to research and understand. After more than two years of reading scores of histories and talking to many experts on different aspects of the war, I would find it difficult to write a clear, chronological summary of the conflict from the causes, through the actual events, to the ultimate effects of the war.

I have avoided the politics of the war other than demonstrating its unpopularity in much of the country. And I only touch on the largely inconclusive land fighting along the Canadian border, concentrating instead on the war at sea, particularly on privateering out of Baltimore.

This is my fifth historical novel, and I continue to be impressed by the willingness of generous people on both sides of the Atlantic to help with my research. Special thanks are due to:

—Dr. Gerald S. Brinton of New Cumberland, Pennsylvania, retired educator, for lending me many valuable books from his collection devoted to sailing craft and sea history.

—Judy Dillon, librarian for the New Cumberland Public Library, for her help in procuring various volumes through the Inter-Library Loan Network.

—Ralph Hyde, keeper of prints and maps and librarian at the Guildhall Library in London, for guiding me to books and pamphlets about life in London in the early nineteenth century.

—Andrew Griffin, group archivist of St. Bartholomew's Hospitals in London, and his assistant, Caroline Jones, for furnishing information about medical instruction at the hospital prior to 1812.

—Michael Simpson, retired Royal Navy commander and now harbormaster for Newton Ferrers, and Neville Hutchinson of Exeter, England, owner-editor of *English Life* magazine, for their advice about sailing conditions and landmarks along the south Devon coast.

—Peter F. Campbell, English-born, Oxford-educated resident of Barbados and student of that island's rich history, for information about the treatment of prisoners of war.

—John Eck, junior high school teacher from Erie, Pennsylvania, and an avid weekend crewman aboard the restored U.S. brig *Niagara,* and Robert Eaton, historic sites manager for the Pennsylvania Historical and Museum Commission, for their "fly specking" of my account of the Battle of Lake Erie, and Walter Rybka, master of the *Niagara,* for allowing my wife and me to sail aboard the flagship of the Commonwealth of Pennsylvania.

A special thanks is owed Scott S. Sheads, historian at the Fort McHenry National Monument, who guided my reading and checked the final draft of the manuscript. Through luck, the *Pride of Baltimore,* a schooner built along the lines of a War of 1812 privateer, was briefly in the harbor during my first research visit, and Mr. Sheads gave me a personal tour of the craft, which serves as the flagship of the state of Maryland.

A serious historical novelist tries to strike a balance between writing a compelling story with appealing characters on the one hand, and conveying information and insight about the events of the period on the other. Often this means leaving out much of what one has painfully learned or, in some cases, oversimplifying complex issues and events.

Despite my best efforts to get things right, there are bound to be some errors of fact or questionable interpretations in a novel of this length. I found some of these faults in the printed sources I consulted and had to make judgments about which version to accept. However, blame for any factual errors that appear in this novel should be assigned to no one but me.

# Book One

# Part One

# 1 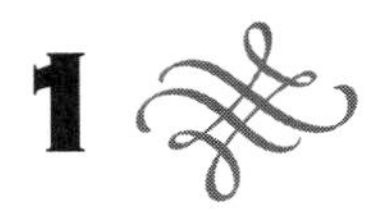

The caulkers, sail makers, shipping clerks, and such who lived or worked along Philadelphia's Delaware River waterfront would never forget that night late in May of 1812. It would live in their memories as the riotous evening they helped Evan Jenkins celebrate his marriage to Primrose Hanrahan.

Some would bear physical scars as well as memories. The celebration, at Evan's own White Swan Tavern on lower South Street, did, as he put it in his Welsh lilt, "get rather out of hand."

At fifty-three, the popular Evan Jenkins was a widower, having lost his wife several years before. No one ever accused Evan of practicing what he called "the evil vice of celibacy," however. If the younger Primrose, herself only recently widowed, had gone against the admonitions of her priest and been freer with her favors, she might have become Evan's mistress rather than his wife.

That would have suited Evan's only daughter, Megan. She regarded Primrose as a simpering, conniving adventuress not fit to tie her dead mother's apron strings and certainly not worthy of stepping into the lady-of-the-house role now filled by herself.

But married they were, and in grand style too, in a fully Catholic ceremony in St. Joseph's Church on Willing's Alley. Primrose had wanted a high mass in the new cathedral, St. Mary's, just around the corner on Fourth Street, but the priest dissuaded her. After all, it was a second marriage for both, and Evan was not a Catholic, although the genial tavern keeper had, with a wink and a nod, signed a paper promising to rear any children in his bride's faith. The priest regarded this question to be of academic interest only. Although Evan had four children—twenty-one-year-old Tom, eighteen-year-old Megan, and the fourteen-year-old twins, David and George—Primrose had remained barren through ten years of marriage to the late Dennis Hanrahan, well-known livery stable proprietor.

The marriage ceremony was a low mass, remarkable only to the Protestants, most of whom had never been in a Roman church.

Evan had hired a convoy of carriages to relay the wedding party down Third and then Spruce Streets to the waterfront and then over to the White Swan. Megan had questioned the propriety of that location, but as Evan said to his son Tom, "I own the frigging place. Why should I pay out good money to my competitors? What's wrong with that silly girl?"

It had fallen to Tom to prepare for the celebration. He had helped their black cook, Rance, roast the carcass of a young steer. He had hired the fiddler, Blind Jack, to provide lively music for the occasion. And he had placed kegs of carefully watered rum in the corners of the White Swan's common room, but when he was not looking, his younger brothers had slipped extra rum into the mix.

By the time the caravan of carriages reached the White Swan, the common room had been transformed into a banquet hall crammed with benches borrowed from neighbors and long tables fashioned from planks laid across sawhorses. The celebration began in orderly fashion, with a long grace by the priest. That was followed by an even longer toast by Evan's best man, Lovejoy Martin, newly come back from his medical studies in London.

Until Lovejoy's unexpected return three days earlier, Evan had intended to have his son Tom stand with him in church. But Tom, who harbored his own reservations about his father's remarriage, gladly relinquished the honor to Lovejoy.

"You're sure now, son, yer feelings won't be hurt?"

"Nay, Pa. Joy will do you a far better job. Lend a bit of prestige, him being so much better educated and from a good family. Besides, ain't he been my best friend since we was in short breeches? And Meggie might take a kindlier view of things with Joy involved."

"If you're certain, then I'll ask him when he comes down for his breakfast. Fine lad, that one. Can't think why he took lodgings here, though, with his family's mansion not half a mile away. Has to do with his father's illness, I expect."

"Better not to pry into that. It's a sore subject. If you like, I'll go rouse Joy up and put the question to him right now."

So now, with the common room jammed from wall to wall with friends and relatives, with the doors barred against the uninvited prostitutes and urchins of the area, and with the windows open to catch the breeze off the Delaware, Lovejoy Martin was rising to his feet and clearing his throat. Wearing a London-tailored black broadcloth jacket and a shirt with ruffled front and cuffs, the twenty-five-year-old Lovejoy did add a touch of prestige. Ramrod straight, of muscular build and standing five feet ten inches tall, the sandy-haired young man looked out over the noisy audience with a gleam in his gray eyes.

He began his toast on a dignified note, praising the priest for his thoughtful grace, and calling the size of the crowd a testimony to the popularity of Evan and Primrose. But he soon dropped the tenor of his remarks to a baser note, telling the delighted assemblage how Evan had first come to Philadelphia in 1777 "as a green youth in the red uniform of a Welsh Fusilier" and how, when Lord Howe evacuated the city, he had deserted King George's service "to become as American as anyone in this room."

"When he joined the Fusiliers he followed the Welsh tradition of 'taking a leek.' Now you may not know this, but when the Fusiliers lined up to march out of the city, Evan asked his sergeant for permission to fall out and go behind a nearby barn to answer a call of nature. There he shed his red uniform and took to his heels. So, you see, he became a soldier for the king by taking a leek and left it by the same method."

After the laughter subsided, Lovejoy slyly alluded to the age difference—some twenty years—between Primrose and Evan, saying that the groom could "show his bride a fresh wrinkle or too."

And he touched upon the bridegroom's marriage to a Catholic. "They say all roads lead to Rome. Our dear friend, Evan Jenkins, has chosen the Primrose path."

A groan arose from the guests, followed by calls for him to "get on with it so we can have our grog."

Lovejoy concluded by commenting on the sign of the White Swan that hung over the establishment's doorway. "I have often thought that the wings of that swan should be extended rather than folded by its sides, for I and many others have found shelter under the welcoming wings of the White Swan. Now with a new bride at Evan's side, let us drink to many more years of good food and drink and jolly companionship. Pray join me in drinking to long health and much happiness for Mr. and Mrs. Evan Jenkins."

Meg Jenkins endured crosscurrents of emotion during the long toast. She winced at Lovejoy's touching on certain sore subjects, but also admired his glib grace of expression. She looked with disgust at the blushing face of her new stepmother and her father's silly grin, then back at Lovejoy, aching for him to take some notice of her.

Tom made a toast heavily laced with how honored and pleased the family was to have his childhood friend, Lovejoy Martin, back from England. A cousin of Primrose's offered one in Gaelic. With each toast, Evan's twin sons came nearer to exploding at the growing effect of their spiked grog.

The first fight broke out when someone at one of the back tables took more roast beef than those at the far end thought fair. Like a mastiff and a terrier, Lovejoy and the smaller, wiry Tom sprang up to separate the battlers and threatened to throw them out.

By this time, the uninvited of the neighborhood had crowded the windows so that air could hardly circulate. This was tolerated until a notorious prostitute, who had brought along her own bottle, raised it and shouted a toast "to my friend Evan Jenkins, the most generous man with which I ever did deal."

An outraged Meg rushed to the window and shut it in the face of the woman and her friends.

Later, after the priest had excused himself, a larger fight broke out between Primrose's cousins and a group of Ulster-descended guests from the Pennsylvania backwoods who insisted on pointedly discussing the Battle of the Boyne in loud voices. Lovejoy had to remove his jacket to separate the battling Celts.

With Blind Jack sawing away at his fiddle, Lovejoy, his arms around the shoulders of Evan and Tom, was bawling out a bawdy song he had brought back from London. He did not see Meg approaching.

"Lovejoy. Someone is at the door, asking for you."

"Tell him to bugger off. I am enjoying myself with the two best friends a fellow ever did have."

"He says it is urgent. I think it is your brother."

"I have no brother."

Tom peered across the common room to the door. "It is Chester."

"He is only my half brother. What does the little lickspittle want with me?"

"He says it's about your father," Meg said.

"Damn! Who told them I was back in Philadelphia? Excuse me."

Chester Peebles was waiting on the sidewalk, a look of resigned disapproval on his face. Slighter and shorter than Lovejoy, he was blond and balding.

Neither man offered to shake hands. "What do you want with me?" Lovejoy asked.

"Father wants to see you."

"What's his hurry?"

"This is not the time to quibble. He has taken a turn for the worse. He has been calling for you all evening. The carriage is here. It would behoove you to come with me."

# 2

As he rode along in silence beside his older half brother, Lovejoy took deep gulps of the soft May air to clear his head. Audiences with Jeremiah Martin had never been easy for Lovejoy, and this one, he knew, would be particularly awkward.

Chester broke the silence, saying in a flat voice, "Father was hurt when he heard you had returned without . . ."

"Why should he be hurt? He is the one who forced me to come back. Stopped my stipend, leaving me no choice but . . ."

"You know what I mean. You've been back for nearly a week. Instead of coming home, you have taken up with that Jenkins crowd."

"Only half a week. I wasn't ready to see him. He cut off my allowance."

"And you know why he did. We had our agent in London make inquiries when you failed to write. The authorities at St. Bartholomew's Hospital told him that you had stopped attending lectures."

Lovejoy made no reply. What Chester said was true. Two years earlier, shortly after he had completed a lackluster course of study in literature and philosophy at the College of New Jersey in Princeton, he had persuaded his father to send him over to St. Bartholomew's famous teaching hospital to learn medicine. He did this partly at the urging of his uncle, Dr. Ephraim McGee, but largely out of a desire to escape his family and to savor life in London.

Lovejoy had not minded the lectures on medicine and physiology, often held at the homes of his teachers. And he had enjoyed "walking the wards" in the wake of his professors and observing their handling of cases. But his stomach for the profession was turned after several weeks when, during his first anatomy lesson, his lecturer, the renowned John Abernethy, had pulled back the sheet from the fresh cadaver of a hanged wife killer and proceeded to slice open the torso with the nonchalance of a butcher at work on a hog carcass. Lovejoy had not been alone among the students who, racked by dry heaves, had fled from the crowded operating theater. The difference was that the others went back. He meant to return to St. Bartholomew's, but each time he approached the hospital the image of the blue-black face of the cadaver and the sickening sight and odor of his exposed viscera dissuaded him. Lovejoy found solace in the theaters, restaurants, strong drink, and women so readily at hand in London.

His life as a popular young American about town ceased without warning earlier that year when he stopped by the office of his father's agent at St. Catherines Docks to pick up his monthly stipend.

"Sorry, Master Martin," the agent informed him. "I have received special instructions from Captain Martin."

Instead of his allowance he got a nontransferable ticket on the next packet from Southampton to Philadelphia.

Lovejoy at first refused to accept the ticket. After several weeks without funds, he had exhausted the charity of his friends. He fell behind in his rent on his rooms in Bishopsgate. His last resort, the married woman who had been so kind and generous to him during her elderly husband's frequent business absences, put it to him straight.

"Lovejoy, it is time for you to face facts. We have had a jolly time together, but all good things must end sooner or later. You have no means of support. I can't spare you any more money without Harold's knowledge. Your father, I gather, is well off back in Philadelphia."

"He is as rich as Croesus, but he has closed his purse and his heart to me."

"He couldn't have closed his heart entirely or he wouldn't have provided for your speedy return."

"You don't know my father."

"But I do know you. My dear boy, whatever made you think you could be a doctor in the first place? You haven't the patience or the compassion. What's wrong with entering the family shipping business?"

"I have an older half brother. He is taking over the business. My father doesn't think I have any commercial sense."

"What about the law?"

"Sitting about all day writing wills and filing documents? As you say, I lack patience."

"You silly boy, that is what solicitors do. I mean you would make a grand barrister. You're well spoken, at least for an American. You cut an imposing figure. Yes, that is what you should do, go home and take up the law. And no, I cannot lend you any more money. And no, I will not go to bed with you again. Now, take that hurt look off your handsome face. You are a darling young man, but it is time for you to grow up. What is over is over."

As they approached the mansion on Arch Street, Chester broke the silence.

"What exactly is Father's trouble?"

"We wrote to you about it. He suffered a slight stroke last Christmas. Left him with slurred speech."

"I thought he had improved."

"He seemed to for a while. He took a turn for the worse when he heard yesterday that you were back in Philadelphia and staying at the White Swan of all places."

"Look, Chester, if you are trying to make me feel guilty for not rushing to the old man's side to beg his forgiveness, you're wasting your time. The Jenkinses have been like a family to me ever since Mother died. I feel at home with them."

"Water seeks its own level, I suppose."

There wasn't time to reply. The carriage had stopped in front of the Martin mansion. Lovejoy choked back his anger and stepped out on the sidewalk.

Looking up at the three-story gray-stone walls, he thought of how like a prison it had become for him since his mother (and Chester's as well) had died five years before, while he was in his first year at Princeton.

"Dear Lovejoy, welcome home."

Lovejoy was shocked at how much his slender, blond half sister, Amanda, now resembled their late mother, Gerta. Amanda, with her husband, Frank, and their two daughters had moved in to look after Jeremiah following his stroke.

She put her arms around his neck and kissed him.

"My, what a man you have become. Look at him, Frank. Isn't my baby brother a handsome devil?"

Lovejoy disentangled himself and shook the hand of his brother-in-law, who said, "Well, the prodigal has returned."

"So he has," Lovejoy said. "Where is the fatted calf?"

"We have missed you terribly," Amanda said. "Especially the children. They have been clamoring to see you ever since you . . ."

"Lovejoy, what a pleasure to see you again."

An elegant-looking man, carrying a black medical bag, was descending the stairs.

"Uncle Ephraim."

After shaking hands, his uncle looked closely into Lovejoy's face.

"I've got a thousand things to ask you about London and St. Bartholomew's, but Jeremiah is anxious to talk to you. Lawyer Bennett is with him just now. Lovejoy . . ." He drew him into the parlor out of the hearing of Amanda and her husband. "Whatever you do, I implore you, don't make him angry. Just inquire after his health. Let him tell you what he wants to say. I gather that it is of great importance. Don't disagree with him, even if it means biting your tongue. And stay off the subject of our troubles with the British. You don't want to bring on another stroke."

"Of course, Uncle Ephraim."

"Good. After you get this family business settled, we must talk about your future. Perhaps St. Bartholomew's was not the right place for you. Perhaps we should have kept you here at the Pennsylvania Hospital. Anyway, don't give up. You have an easy way with people, and that is half the game of being a good doctor."

"I've been thinking about the law, Uncle Ephraim."

"In that case, Bennett is your man. But I'd still like to talk to you. It's awfully good to have you back in Philadelphia. Your father is glad too, although he may find it hard to say so."

With that, Lovejoy followed his sister up the long stairway to Jeremiah Martin's bedroom.

# 3

Since the end of the American Revolution, Jeremiah Martin had become a legendary figure in Philadelphia, up and down the eastern seaboard, indeed throughout the shipping community on both sides of the Atlantic.

Born into a plantation family in Tidewater Virgina, he had run away from home while in his teens and ended up heavily involved in the rebellion against the British, first as an army sutler and later as a privateer. He gained and lost a fortune at sea but recouped his wealth after Yorktown and his marriage to Gerta McGee Peebles, a beautiful young widow with two small children, Chester and Amanda, whom he had raised as his own.

He had known Gerta as a little girl. She was the daughter of a flourishing Ulster Scots-German family from Sherman's Valley, a frontier section west of the Susquehanna River. In his youth, Jeremiah had known many women, but he had loved none as he had the beautiful Gerta. That love had extended not only to her children by her first husband but to all his in-laws, of whom Dr. Ephraim McGee was one.

Lovejoy was their only child, born several years into their marriage. After his birth, Gerta never regained her formerly robust health. Lovejoy sometimes wondered if his father held this against him.

Jeremiah had turned his experiences as a privateer to advantage as a ship owner after the war. Some, especially his competitors, regarded him as ruthless and overbearing; others, including his employees, considered "Captain Martin" a fair man who rewarded loyalty and hard work. So Jeremiah had grown ever richer through the end of the old century and into the new one.

Like many Americans engaged in maritime trade, however, he had suffered during the long conflict between Great Britain and Napoleon's France, as first one side and then the other and, to his fury, his own government imposed restrictions on trade. But Jeremiah Martin had learned long ago not to put all his eggs in one basket and had made other investments with his profits from shipping. Although taking some hard knocks from the Napoleonic Wars, he remained rich and influential.

A vigorous, powerful man two years ago when Lovejoy had departed for England, he had handed his physique on to his son. But whereas Lovejoy had gray eyes and sandy hair, Jeremiah's eyes were hazel and his hair a dark brown, traits he laid to a remote Indian ancestor.

That was the man Lovejoy remembered as he mounted the stairs. On entering the bedroom, he was shocked by his father's appearance. Jeremiah's hair had gone almost as white as the pillows against which he was propped. The ruddy face with its high cheekbones and determined mouth line was slack and sallow. But those hazel eyes retained their old, critical gleam.

His lawyer, a prissy little man named Charles Bennett, stepped away from the bedside so the old man could see who had entered the room.

"Well, sir. You are back." The slurred voice still carried its Virginia accent.

Lovejoy stood at the foot of the bed, waiting for a sign that he should shake hands. None came.

"Yes, Father, I am back."

"And have been back for some days, your brother says."

"Only three days, sir."

"Been carousing, too, judging from your look and smell."

"Chester brought me here from a wedding reception. I was the best man."

"Did you enjoy your life in London?"

"You said I would love the city and you were right."

"I only wish you had learned to love your medical studies as well. It was for that purpose that I expended a considerable sum."

Reminding himself of his Uncle Ephraim's warning, Lovejoy replied simply, "No, Father, I must admit that I did not enjoy very much about my studies. I am sorry to have disappointed you."

"Any notion of what you will do, now you're back?"

"I have been giving thought to reading for the law."

The old man snorted. "Hear that, Bennett? He has been giving thought to entering your profession. Here is a young fellow who just squeaked through Princeton, on whom I wasted several thousand dollars to educate for medicine, and now he is giving thought to reading for the bar."

Lovejoy winced at his father's stinging words. He was grateful to Bennett for saying, "Why, Captain Martin, I expect Lovejoy has the makings of a very good lawyer. I would be happy for him to read for the law in our offices."

"No! He has had his way made smooth for too long. I would not want to fob him off on you."

"No offense, Captain. But my door will be open to him any time, unless you forbid it."

"I do forbid it."

Lovejoy cleared his throat and said, "I was sorry to hear of your illness, Father."

"But not sorry enough to answer our letters."

"And I hope that you will soon be feeling better."

He turned to leave.

"Wait! I am not done with you."

Lovejoy came close to ignoring the command and going back to the White Swan where his friends would still be "carousing," but Bennett motioned for him to remain.

"I was warned not to agitate you, Father. I was afraid my presence was troubling you."

"Stay. We have important business. We'll need more chairs. I want Chester and Amanda here. She can bring her husband, too."

The old man pointed to Lovejoy. "I trust you're not too drunk to summon your brother and sister. And fetch your Uncle Ephraim from next door, as well."

It was nearly midnight before a now cold sober Lovejoy Martin got back to the White Swan. There he found that the guests had all gone home, leaving the common room a jumble of overturned tables and benches and empty grog kegs. Broken cups littered the floor. Rance and the Jenkins twins were sweeping up the debris, while Tom sat trying to console a dejected Megan.

"Where is everyone? What happened?"

"Things got worse after you left. A big fight broke out when a couple of fellows from New Jersey started blackguarding President Madison as a warmonger and, worse than that, for standing up to the British. A sailor called them cowards. Said his ship had been stopped at sea by a British frigate and he had seen one of his best friends taken off, and him with genuine naturalization papers. That is when Pa sent me to fetch the constables. Before they got here, the grog ran out and others started throwing cups. They even smashed poor old Blind Jack's fiddle, but Pa promised he'd pay for a new one."

"What's wrong with Meg?"

Meg suddenly hated Lovejoy, not only for his callous question but for his addressing it to her brother as if she were a child who could not answer for herself.

"Just nerves," Tom said.

She hated her brother as well for not understanding her feelings, and her father too, for becoming so besotted by a shallow, silly woman like Primrose Hanrahan, and, for that matter, David and George for their idiotic laughing.

"You look none too happy yourself," Tom said. "How did you find the Captain?"

"Not well, but not nearly as sick as Chester made out. He just wanted to toll me in for a family conference."

"How did that go?"

"I am not sure. Haven't figured it out yet."

Megan was eager to hear what had happened at the Martin mansion, but clearly Lovejoy was reluctant to speak freely in her presence. She blew her nose and went to upbraid the twins for their horseplay. As she busied herself, she tried to catch the gist of what Lovejoy was telling her brother.

"He says we are as good as at war with England already," Lovejoy was saying.

"His friends in Washington report that any day now President Madison will ask Congress for a declaration of war. Gave that as one reason for forcing me home. But there was a lot more. He is a cunning old devil."

"What a way to speak of your pa."

"You wouldn't understand. Your father is Evan Jenkins, and he is your friend as well as mine. Mine is Jeremiah Martin, who can chew up cannonballs and spit out bird shot. There is a world of difference."

"Our family is not all that happy either. You don't see any of us turning cartwheels over Pa getting married. Meggie's taking it especially hard. Me, I figure if it requires Primrose Hanrahan to make Pa happy, why shouldn't he have her? She is a silly woman, though. She told me and Meggie we should call her 'Mother' now. Thought Meggie would explode. But get to the point, Joy. What did the Captain really want with you?"

"Because of his health and our trouble with England, he wants to settle up his affairs. Divide his estate, as he put it."

"Will you be rich now?"

"I don't think so, but Chester sure as hell will be. The old man is turning over the business to him. Docks, boats, shipyard, the whole lot. All Chester has to do is pay him a fee to live on for the rest of his life. That little ass kisser gets Martin Shipping Company lock, stock, and barrel, and he is only a stepson."

"You mean he cut you and your sister out?"

"No. He is giving Amanda the house and all its furnishings and our farm out at Valley Forge. And then he has other houses and buildings around Philadelphia, which he is signing over to Uncle Ephraim."

"But what about yourself?"

"He is deducting the allowances he sent over to London and the cost of my passage over and back as well as the fees to my lecturers at Barts. Did you ever hear of such cheese-paring stinginess? And just when I could use a bit of cash to make a good impression on a certain someone and her family."

"Surely he wouldn't call you home just to tell you he is kicking you out in the cold?"

"The old fox has something up his sleeve. He wants me to meet this afternoon with his lawyer for what he calls 'your marching orders.' I've a good notion not to see the lawyer."

"You're always welcome here. Pa thinks the sun rises and sets in you. Why don't you squeeze what you can out of your pa. I'll do the same with mine and then let's go into business together."

"Actually, Tom, I've been thinking of settling down and maybe reading for the bar."

"Whatever you decide, the Jenkins family will stand behind you. Ain't that right, Meggie? Boys? Ain't us Jenkinses always ready to help Joy any time he needs it?"

"Meggie would just love to help him, wouldn't you Meggie?"

The twins nudged each other and fell into another fit of laughter at the way their sister blushed.

"You little snots," she hissed. "Mind your mouths or I will tell Pa who spiked the grog. He'll make you pay for Blind Jack's fiddle."

This made them laugh even harder. She threw down her broom and ran up the stairs.

Tom frowned at Lovejoy and asked, "You said something about wanting to make a good impression on somebody. Who were you talking about?"

"I think I have already made my impression on the someone. It's her family I will need to impress. I met her and her mother on the boat coming back from England."

Tom groaned. "Don't tell me you have fallen for still another girl. Is this one serious?"

"It could become so, with a bit of luck."

# 4

Lying in the bed he shared with Tom, Lovejoy took a long time to fall asleep. His mind kept going over and over the meeting around his ailing father's bedside. He had despised the smug look on his half brother's face as Bennett had read their father's instructions. Why didn't anyone else appreciate what a cunning little ass kisser Chester was? He had made Lovejoy's childhood miserable. Chester had a nasty trick of inveigling Lovejoy into some piece of mischief and then distancing himself, leaving his little brother to face Jeremiah's wrath. And the way he curried favor with Jeremiah made Lovejoy sick.

Whereas Chester had resented a new child in the house, Amanda had acted toward him like a junior mother, eager to care for "my baby brother." With Gerta too weak to look after him, she had nurtured him.

Lovejoy knew that he had not been easy to rear. With his father distracted by business, his mother sickly, and his half brother tormenting him, he welcomed his friendship with the Jenkinses.

At first, Evan had allowed him to work around the White Swan, running errands on his pony and sweeping out the tavern. He rewarded Lovejoy with small sums of money and with extravagant stories of his childhood in Wales and his service during the American War of Independence. Lovejoy delighted in his accounts of Lexington and Concord, Bunker Hill, Long Island, the Brandywine and Germantown. The first Mrs. Jenkins had been a large, motherly woman who treated Lovejoy like a son. He had shared the family's grief at her death several years before.

Tom, four years younger, at first had been too little to do more than worship this sandy-haired young prince, but as the relative difference in their ages shrank, Lovejoy and the smaller Tom became familiar sights riding in tandem on Lovejoy's overburdened pony, swimming in the Schuylkill River, and fighting with other boys around the Delaware waterfront.

Jeremiah, remembering his own rowdy youth, saw no harm in the association, even allowing his son to spend an occasional night at the White Swan. "Sleeping over with the Jenkinses," he called it.

In a sense, that was what Lovejoy was doing now: sleeping over with the Jenkins family while estranged from his own. Except that Tom's questions about his shipboard romance were making it impossible to fall asleep.

"Who is she, Joy? You got to tell me."

"Will you swear to keep your mouth shut about it?"

"Yes, but don't leave anything out."

"All right. Coming back from England we hit rough weather right off. Tom, I thought I would die I was so seasick. There were three other chaps in my cabin. One was a young fellow that kept talking about a gorgeous blond traveling with her mother. Finally the ocean calmed down and I felt well enough to venture out on deck. And there she stood. I saw what the fellow meant. She is tall and she has a waist you could almost put your hands around and a figure like you never saw. I couldn't stop staring at her."

"Well, get to the point. What did you do?"

"The purser was a gabby chap and he told me her name. She is Madeline Richter from near Reading. Her father owns several farms and gristmills in Berks County. Must be filthy rich. Purser also said the girl and her mother had been visiting relatives in England."

"That ain't telling me what you did."

"Don't rush me. Her mother is a tough old bird. English born. Had her nose in the air and wasn't about to converse with somebody traveling on a second-class ticket. After she had given me the cold shoulder a couple of times, I was about ready to give up when I had this inspiration."

By now Tom was sitting up in bed. "Well?"

"I gave the purser one of my last dollars to wait until I was standing in earshot of the girl's mother and then to address me in a loud voice as 'Doctor Martin' and say that my suit had been cleaned and was ready in my cabin."

"And that worked?"

"Like a charm. I changed clothes, took a few turns around the deck, and tipped my hat to Mistress High and Mighty, then paused to inquire after her health."

"You are a lying devil, Joy. You ain't no doctor."

"I did not deceive the woman. After she agreed that it was more pleasant now that the bad weather had passed, she wanted to know why a young doctor would choose such troubled times to return to the United States. I told her the purser had misspoke in calling me a doctor. Told her my father had been taken ill and that I had interrupted my medical education to return to his bedside. Surely that is close enough to the truth to satisfy you."

"And that broke the ice?"

"Enough that she treated me to a two-hour litany of complaints about President Madison and the War Hawks trying to pick a fight with the poor, long-suffering English who, by her lights, are all that stands between Napoleon Bonaparte and the freedom of the world. Seems her husband is a hidebound Federalist. After she had worn that subject to the bone, she wanted to know if I played whist and, if so, would I be interested in a game with herself and her daughter. Now, Tom, I am sleepy."

"You can't leave it there, Joy. What happened after that?"

"Mrs. Richter never really let her guard down. I reckon she has had a lot of experience shielding such a beautiful girl from scoundrels like me. But I was allowed to escort the daughter around the ship so long as the mother was on deck at the same time."

"Did you make any time with her?"

"Tom, a gentleman does not discuss such things. Suffice it to say that Mrs. Richter has given me permission to write to Madeline, and not only do I intend to do that but also I shall inquire about a visit with the family in Berks County. Now that is all I will tell you, so shut up and let me get my rest."

There was a good deal more that Lovejoy could have told Tom about Madeline Richter. She turned out to be an intelligent but naive girl with a more outgoing personality than her mother. Like himself, she enjoyed the theater and lamented the fact that she had seen only one play while visiting her mother's parents in London. She had been intrigued by his accounts of living in London.

The close watch Mrs. Richter kept over the daughter only inflamed Lovejoy's ardor. Except for Madeline's hand on his arm as they strolled, there had been no physical intimacy until the evening they dropped anchor in the mouth of the Delaware to take on their pilot for the trip up to Philadelphia. Behind a lifeboat, hidden briefly from the view of Mrs. Richter, Lovejoy had taken Madeline's elbow, swung her to face him, and, with one arm about her, had kissed her on the lips.

Instead of protesting, she had put both her hands on his waist and kissed him back, before breaking away and giggling.

"If mother were to see this she would kill you. And Papa would do worse."

"I am sorry, Madeline. I was afraid I would never have another chance to be alone with you."

"Why not? There is a road between Philadelphia and Reading, is there not? No, Mr. Martin, no more kisses or you will spoil everything. Mother and Papa think everyone is after our money, but she likes you as well as anyone we have met."

"One more kiss."

"Not now. Maybe in Reading. Now let's walk on or Mother will come to investigate."

In the dark of the White Swan room, Lovejoy finally stopped thinking about Madeline Richter and let his mind drift back to his family meeting. He fell asleep wondering what lawyer Bennett would tell him that afternoon.

# 5

The brass plate on the door of the three-story brick building on Pine Street read "Charles H. Bennett, Attorney-at-Law." Lovejoy smiled to think how, when he was growing up, he had thought that Bennett's first name was "Lawyer," for the family always referred to him as "lawyer Bennett."

Lawyer Bennett held himself erect and spoke in a precise way, waving his small, freckled hands to emphasize his points.

"Lovejoy, you heard your father last night. He has decided to distribute what I would call his hard assets among other members of your family. He has other assets, which might be called soft."

"Would that be like money?" Lovejoy asked with rising hopes.

"It would be more like debts owing to your father, personally. He feels that he has expended enough cash on you."

"So he proposes to give me only the debts that are owing him? How much do they come to?"

"The Captain has stipulated that you are not to be informed of the details just yet."

"Is he playing games with me? Trying to make me suffer because I have made a few mistakes?"

Lovejoy rose and paced about the office while the lawyer watched him silently, with narrowed, appraising eyes.

"Well, Mr. Bennett, will I not at least receive a living allowance? Philadelphia may not be as expensive as London, but it still takes money to live here."

"The Captain does not have Philadelphia in mind for you."

"New York, then? I wouldn't mind that so much, providing I had enough to live on."

"He liquidated his interests in New York and Boston during the last embargo."

"Then what is Father's plan for me?"

"Have you ever been to Baltimore?"

Lovejoy groaned. "No, and I have no desire to go there. He might as well send me off to our relatives at Harrisburg. Does he just want to make me suffer?"

"You misjudge your father. I have never known a more just man."

"Then why does he treat me like a poor relation? He showers gifts on his stepchildren and his in-laws but wants to send me off to Baltimore to live on the collection of bad debts."

"Why do you say 'bad debts'?"

"If they were so easily collectible, why has he not converted them to cash as he did in New York and Boston?"

"Captain Martin is not only a just man, he is also fair and wise."

"You should have been his son, Mr. Bennett."

"I have been his attorney and his personal advisor since you were a baby. I have enormous respect for his judgment about business and people. Has it ever occurred to you that your father may expect more from you because you are his only natural-born son? He was more than generous in providing for your education, first at Princeton, and more recently in London."

"I won't be shunted off to Baltimore."

The lawyer smacked the palm of his hand down on his desk and his voice hardened.

"Perhaps it is time that you face up to the facts of your life. You are twenty-five. You have no resources except what your father may be willing to provide. You have no skills that would enable you to live in the style you have enjoyed all your life."

"Did you call me here for another lecture?"

"You look upon your father only as a stern disciplinarian. Perhaps he has been too lax. I watched you grow up without much oversight, consorting with all sorts of riffraff and never buckling down to make proper use of the intelligence you have inherited from your parents. Now, before it is too late, he is offering you an opportunity down in Baltimore. Spurn it if you wish, but be aware that you will be choosing to make your own way in a harsh world during what may be some difficult times. Although I think our grievances against the British somewhat exaggerated, your father feels strongly that we will soon be at war with them. And he may very well be right. There is a reckless mood abroad in much of the country."

Lovejoy was shocked into silence by the lawyer's blunt talk.

"So, there it is, Lovejoy. I can tell Captain Martin that you decline his offer." He paused before adding with raised eyebrows, "I can tell him that you prefer that the Baltimore assets be turned over to your brother Chester."

"I did not say that."

"Or you can take the documents you see on my desk and proceed forthwith to Baltimore."

"I had been planning an important trip out to Reading. This sojourn to Baltimore, would it be for the rest of my life?"

"I know of no such stipulation."

"Why don't you give me the papers and let me tote up the sums that are owed?"

"Your father has directed that I triple seal all these papers and give them to you to be delivered to a friend in Baltimore, together with a letter of instructions to that man. Now, that is as much as I am allowed to tell you. Will you go?"

"I need a few hours to think this over."

"You may have until noon tomorrow. After that, these instruments will become the property of Martin Shipping."

Soon after Lovejoy left, Charles Bennett reported to Jeremiah Martin about their conference.

"He asked a lot of questions, Captain. He doesn't want to go, that is clear, but I think it sank in that he cannot collect his inheritance unless he does."

Jeremiah smiled and ran his hand over the bedcovers.

"Indeed he cannot. And he said nothing else about reading for the bar?"

"The subject never came up."

"Were you serious about his potential for the law?"

"Captain, I know it is hard to see one's own children objectively, but in my view, Lovejoy has much promise. He has the gift of making friends."

"Sometimes they are the wrong sort of friends."

"He also has a quick wit."

"And a lazy one."

"All he requires is to learn how to discipline himself."

Jeremiah laughed. "There is no man better suited to teach him that than Malcolm MacKenzie. So, Charles, what do you think he will do?"

"He has promised to tell me his decision by noon tomorrow. I will let you know as soon as he informs me. Don't be surprised if he refuses. The lad has a lot of pride, Captain. More than I realized."

Chester Peebles and his wife, Rosalind, lived in a small but elegantly furnished house on Elsfreth's Alley. Rosalind was a strikingly beautiful brunette who stood half a head taller than her husband. Chester had met her while studying at Harvard. Her father was a Unitarian minister in Boston, but she had insisted that they join the Episcopal church in Philadelphia. After six years, they still had no children.

As they prepared for bed that night, Rosalind took up the threads of their suppertime conversation, saying, "I still can't understand why Papa Martin did not give us the house."

"I don't begrudge Amanda and Frank getting the house. We got the business. That is what counts."

"You earned the business, Chester. Can't you see that? What else could he have done with it, now he is so ill?"

"I admit that the business is as much of a burden as it is an asset. So, for that matter, is the house."

"What about the farm? He could at least have given us that. I wouldn't mind living here so much if we had a country place."

"I don't begrudge them that either. They have children to enjoy the country."

"Did he have to leave so much to your uncle, who surely is rich enough in his own right? With the rents from those properties, we could afford a new house with plenty of room for entertaining. And adequate household help, as well."

"You have a point there. Unless our flour-shipping venture pays off, we'll have nothing but my salary to live on until . . ."

Rosalind's face took on a brighter aspect. "You mean the money going to Papa Martin will be ours for a new house when he finally dies?"

"Actually, we may need it to reinvest in the business."

Rosalind threw her hairbrush on the vanity and turned toward him. "When you asked me to marry you, there was no talk of reinvesting in the business or living on scraps thrown your way by a stingy old man. Will it always be this way, keeping our noses to the grindstone?"

"We'd be a lot better off if the old man had not lavished so much on sending my baby brother to London to live in grand style, while I remained here slaving away on a modest salary. That I do resent. I wish war with the British had broken out last year when there was so much talk of it. Then dear baby brother would have been trapped in London."

She joined him in bed. He blew out the lamp.

"You said he was making Lovejoy repay the money he spent in London."

"That is just it, Rosalind. Repay the money from what source? There has to be something of value to draw such a sum against."

"And you have no idea what it is?"

"All I know is that baby brother was supposed to meet with lawyer Bennett this afternoon to discuss his future. Whatever the old man is cooking up for Lovejoy, it's not going to come out of my hide or Martin Shipping's. I will put my foot down on that."

"If you stand up to your father, it will be the first time. Now what did you mean when you said 'unless our flour-shipping venture pays off'? Is there any doubt that it will?"

That same night, back on Arch Street, Amanda tucked her children in their beds and peered into Jeremiah's bedroom. Finding him asleep, she joined her husband in their room. Already in bed, Frank watched her fondly as she undressed.

"You don't look happy, Amanda. Something troubling you?"

"Lovejoy visited me this afternoon. I am worried about him."

"I thought you were glad to have the apple of your eye home again."

"That's just it, Frank. He may not be staying at home for long. Father wants to send him away again."

"That doesn't make sense. Send him where?"

"To Baltimore. And he doesn't want to go."

"Baltimore is only a hundred miles away. It is a booming place. A lot livelier than stuffy old Philadelphia. What will he do there?"

"He thinks Father is trying to use him to pull his chestnuts out of the fire before we get into a war with England. He doesn't want to go, and I don't want him to go either."

She blew out the candle and slid into his arms.

"Amanda, you have got to quit fretting about Lovejoy. He is not a baby anymore. He is spoiled. Lord, how I wish I had had his opportunities."

Frank's parents were farmers in Chester County. Moving to Philadelphia as a youth, he had taken a job with a printer. Upon his employer's death, he had borrowed money from Jeremiah Martin to pay off the widow and buy the business.

Jeremiah at first had tried to dissuade Amanda from marrying Frank but finally gave his reluctant consent. With two beautiful blond granddaughters, he had stopped thinking that Amanda could have done a lot better. He had even offered Frank a place in the shipping firm, but his son-in-law sensed Chester's resentment and declined the offer. He was satisfied with his life. Indeed, if Amanda had not insisted on their moving into the mansion following Jeremiah's death, he would have gone on happily living in their modest house near the State House.

He put his face against Amanda's neck and was soon asleep.

Tom Jenkins was waiting back at the White Swan to hear about Lovejoy's conference with lawyer Bennett.

"And you don't want to go? Why not?"

"I haven't lost a damned thing in Baltimore. As I told you, I have my eye on that gorgeous girl in Berks County and shouldn't let any grass grow under my feet where she is concerned. Next, I don't like being sent off like a whipped dog, with my tail between my legs."

"But you don't want to get cut out of everything, either. Maybe this is a big opportunity for you, Joy."

"It doesn't sound that way. I won't know until I get to Baltimore and show the papers to some old Scotsman, Mac something or other."

"Would you go alone?"

"If I go at all. Why?"

Tom put his hand on his shoulder. "Look, Joy, we had a big blowup here while you were gone. My new stepmother ordered me to go and pick up a trunk at her old lodgings. I would have done it gladly if she had asked me in a polite way. So I told her that I was neither her son nor her servant. Pa stepped in and said that I should show her more respect. One word led to another. To make a long story short, I am moving out tomorrow."

"That's too bad, Tom. Anything I can do to help?"

"You can stop acting like a damned fool and go down to Baltimore."

"How would that help you?"

"You could take me with you. I don't want to spend the rest of my life in Philadelphia. From what I hear, Baltimore is a hell of a town."

# 6 

When the coach to Baltimore stopped to change horses at Wilmington, rather than sit jammed against six other passengers any longer, two of them a couple with a fitful infant, Lovejoy and Tom persuaded the driver to let them ride on top with him.

Rocking and swaying through the pleasant late spring landscape, Lovejoy gave up admiring the skilled way of the driver with his four sturdy horses and let his mind wander.

He had been amused by the leave-taking of Tom and his family. Father and son had patched up their quarrel so that they had parted on good terms. Evan had pressed five dollars on Tom and warned him, "If you can't be good, son, at least be careful," and had admonished Lovejoy to "look after this my beloved firstborn."

The twins had requested and been summarily refused permission to go to Baltimore with their brother.

Meg had stood about with a miserable expression on her face while the men shook hands and exchanged rude jokes.

"Here now, Meggie, you've no reason to look so glum," Tom had said. "When we return, I hope we'll find you happily married. Now give us a kiss."

Following her peck on her brother's cheek, Lovejoy said, "Well Meg, if you've any more of those," and was surprised when she threw her arms around his neck and kissed him square on the lips. She was getting to be quite a package, this strange, dark little girl he had known for nearly all her life. The early June sun warming his loins, he smiled to recall the taste of her lips and the feel of her hard little breasts against his chest.

His mind drifted on to the older married woman in London who had been so kind, then to a certain young Drury Lane actress, and to several shop girls. In that department at least, he reckoned, he had got full value for his father's money. And then his thoughts returned to Madeline Richter. He wished there had been more time to get to know her. If this venture in Baltimore turned out well, he would be in a better position to follow up on what he had begun aboard ship.

"What was that?" His attention was drawn back to the driver.

"I was asking what takes you to Baltimore?"

"I am on business . . . for my father."

"You're going to the right place for business. I make this run every week and let me tell you, Baltimore has it all over Philadelphia. Yes sir, if I was a young man starting out, had a proper education and all that, I would take Baltimore in a minute over Philadelphia."

"It is a good deal smaller, is it not?"

"Yes, but she's growing fast. And the people is so different. You got your Irish and your Germans and then, as you will see for yourself, there's many in town that speaks French, Acadians and such. If you ask me, people in Baltimore got more gumption than what they do in Philadelphia."

The driver rattled on and on about the merits of the city until Lovejoy, tired of listening, feigned sleep.

The stage stopped for the night at Perryville. The next morning, they crossed the Susquehanna on a ferryboat, picked up a fresh team at Havre de Grace on the other side, and rolled on south toward Baltimore.

Lovejoy soon saw how accurate the driver's appraisal was. Although Baltimore, with forty-thousand-odd residents, was only half the size of Philadelphia, still it was the third largest city in the country and growing rapidly. But it was more than a question of size. Philadelphia had been planned by disciplined Quakers. Baltimore seemed to have just happened. Whereas Philadelphia's streets ran in an orderly grid between the Delaware and Schuylkill Rivers, Baltimore's formed a haphazard maze wrapped around the wharf-lined inner harbor, called "the Basin" by locals, and spread east to cover Fells Point and south past Federal Hill. And as any Baltimorean would tell you, the harbor was one of the best in the world. The Basin itself was too shallow for deep draft vessels, but there was plenty of room for them to anchor in the harbor enclosed by Fells Point or, if that area happened to be crowded, they could lie to in the mouth of the Patapsco River in the shadow of Fort McHenry while awaiting their turns at the busy wharves of the city.

That afternoon the stage rattled along the Philadelphia Pike and up over Hampstead Hill, from the top of which they were treated to a grand view of the city and the harbors around which it was built. Their driver had explained that he was headed for the Fountain Inn on Light Street, near the Basin. Where were the boys staying?

"We're to see a man named MacKenzie. Here is the address."

The driver looked at the name on the parcel.

"Oh, that's just down the way in Fells Point, near the waterfront. You'd be better to get off here at Market Street and hoof it south, toward the water."

With aching bones and weary eardrums, they bade the driver goodbye and hiked along the broad, dusty street until they found a tavern where they stopped to dine on mutton stew and ale. Then, following lawyer Bennett's instructions, they presented themselves at a small brick building on Bond Street, facing the harbor. "MacKenzie's Ship Chandlery," the sign over the door read.

Malcolm MacKenzie was taking an inventory in the storeroom behind the office when his clerk told him that two young men wanted to see him.

MacKenzie's normally ruddy complexion paled. "Dear Lord, I hope they are not more process servers."

"I don't think so. One is something of a dandy. The other is not so well dressed. They say they are from Philadelphia. The fancy one says his father sent him down here to see you. His name is Martin."

All the way down from Philadelphia, Lovejoy had wondered about the mysterious Malcolm MacKenzie to whom he was to report. He had created an image of an enormous Scotsman with red cheeks and great knobby knees showing beneath kilts. He saw, instead, a round little man with a fringe of gray-blond hair and eyes of deep blue that peered out beneath a thicket of dark eyebrows. Without a trace of a Scots accent, the man asked, "Which of you would be Mr. Martin?"

"I am Lovejoy Martin, and this is my friend Tom Jenkins. You are Mister MacKenzie, I take it."

MacKenzie shook hands with them both, then turned back to Lovejoy.

"And you are the son of Jeremiah Martin, aren't you? I see the resemblance. If you're half the man your father is or used to be . . . Captain Martin is still alive, isn't he? I haven't heard from him for some months."

"Father is not in the best of health, but yes, he is still alive. He has sent me down here to deliver some papers to you."

"Papers? Let's see them."

He left Lovejoy and Tom standing at the counter while he carried the packets to a table by the window, took out a pair of spectacles, and broke the seals, first on the letter of introduction.

MacKenzie's eyebrows went up and down as he labored through the letter. Once he removed his spectacles and stared at Lovejoy. Once he smiled and rubbed his chin. By the time he had finished, his face had grown grim again.

"Now let's see these other papers."

He fanned through the documents, then took pen in hand. After he had scratched out some calculations, he whistled. Turning in his chair to face Lovejoy, he said, "You know nothing of the contents of this packet?"

"I know only that they have to do with some debts owed my father."

"By my reckoning, those debts total very close to fifty thousand dollars."

Lovejoy clapped his hands and put his arm around Tom's shoulder. "Hear that? I'm rich. The old man was just teasing, making me think he was cutting me out."

"Not so fast," MacKenzie said. "These debts first have to be collected."

"How do I do that?"

"You don't. Captain Martin has charged me to do so."

"Will you? And then turn the money over to me?"

"I will collect the money insofar as I am able, but no, I will not turn it over to you. First off, your father offers me ten percent as my collection fee."

Tom said, "That still leaves you forty-five thousand dollars. I wouldn't complain about that."

"Don't count your chickens before they hatch. Your father gives me power of attorney to invest the proceeds."

"Invest in what?"

MacKenzie smiled. "I will tell you in due course. Now then, lads, have you found lodgings yet?"

"We came straight here. We have made no arrangements."

"Then I'll take you home with me. Lovejoy, eh? I expect I know why they named you that. We'll discuss it over supper."

MacKenzie and his wife of thirty-five years, Flora, lived in a three-story frame house on Thames Street, not far from his office. Flora was a tall woman with snow-white hair and dark eyes that looked out upon the world in a no-nonsense manner. Lacking children of their own, they were devoted to each other and to their Presbyterian church. Used to her husband's bringing guests home without warning, she gave Lovejoy and Tom towels and a bowl of water and showed them to a large guest room at the rear of the second floor.

"Expect you will need a rest after two days on the road. We'll call you for dinner in about an hour."

Tom took off his shoes and collapsed across the large feather mattress, while Lovejoy paced across the floor, frowning and, from time to time, peering out the window.

"I swear, Joy," Tom said, "There was never anybody like you for falling in a pile of shit and coming up smelling like a rose."

"Maybe I am getting trapped in a pile of shit."

"I don't call fifty thousand . . ."

"I heard him. But he also said it first had to be collected, and even then he is going to invest it. Invest my money."

"You sure like to look a gift horse in the mouth."

"Then there is the way MacKenzie practically forced us to come home with him. I thought you and I would have a bit of fun tonight. Sample the wine of the district and maybe the girls as well. We're trapped here. And, two to one, they're teetotalers. Notice he keeps a Bible on his desk and she has one open on a stand in the hallway. I'd rather be at a tavern where we could let our hair down."

"I don't know about Baltimore's taverns, but this room is better than anything we have at the White Swan. I wish you would quit complaining and stop stomping about. I want to catch a nap before they feed us."

Downstairs, Flora set the table in the dining room while the family cook, a free Negro woman, prepared supper. Malcolm came in from a visit to the backyard outhouse.

"Well, Flo, what do you think of them?"

"The little dark fellow seems a straightforward lad, maybe rough around the edges. I don't know what to make of the sandy-headed one. A bit too smooth for my taste. Cocky, I'd say."

"Flo, you believe in answered prayers, don't you?"

"You know I do pray."

"And you know of my business reverses. First losing that cargo of flour and then all those foreclosures. And that sad business of Clarence Little's death."

"Dear Mac, I understand how you have suffered. I have prayed for us both to forget our pride and to be thankful for what has been left to us . . . this house and your shop."

"I do not pretend to take your charitable view. No, I have much bitterness in my heart, not so much against the British navy for confiscating a cargo on which I risked so much money. But I harbor much resentment against my creditors, some of whom I regarded as friends, for the way they descended on me like vultures as soon as they heard of my misfortune. As for poor Clarence, well he paid a dear price for misleading me."

"I did try to warn you against overreaching yourself."

"Dear Flo, unless we take risks we cannot succeed."

"Miz Flora," the cook called from the kitchen. "I'se ready to start putting the food on the table."

"Go ahead, Theresa. I'll call the young gentlemen down in a moment." Then, to her husband, "Mac, you must not let bitterness erode your soul. You should pray for grace to meet your disappointments."

"I have prayed, Flo. And my prayers have been answered this very day."

Her face lit up. "God has answered your prayers?"

"Ah, dear Flo, I am not so sure that the Almighty takes that much interest in commercial affairs, but my old friend Jeremiah Martin does, and perhaps we can thank God for that."

Lovejoy had to admit that he could hardly have got a better meal at an inn than the one served him and Tom by Flora MacKenzie and her cook. The crab cakes and fresh bread were so delicious, as were the dried apple turnovers, that he did not miss the strong drink.

Over dinner, MacKenzie told how his father, at age sixteen, following the battle of Culloden, had been exiled along with other Scots rebels by the English and how he himself, at the same age, had signed on as cabin boy aboard one of Jeremiah Martin's privateers out of Philadelphia.

"I did enjoy doing my bit to pay the English out. I owe much to Jeremiah Martin for that opportunity and more. By the way, did he tell you how he came to name you Lovejoy?"

"He had some sort of partner by that name, I believe. Actually, I have often wished he had chosen a plain, honest name like Tom's. I have endured a great deal of teasing over my name. You might say it has brought Joy to some though, eh what, Tom?"

He dug his elbow in Tom's side, then explained, "My friends call me 'Joy'."

MacKenzie laughed. "If you had known the man for whom you were named, you might feel different."

"I only know that he served with my father and was killed."

"His name was Lovejoy Brown. He sacrificed his life for your father and a good many others. There was never a better seaman or a braver man."

MacKenzie proceeded to tell how Lovejoy Brown, a weathered old salt from Marblehead, Massachusetts, had engaged his schooner in a hopeless battle with a British frigate off St. Eustatius in 1781. "He sacrificed his own vessel and his life so your father, aboard our full-rigged brig, could get away safely with crew and cargo to Statia."

"We always figured it was because he liked to have a good time so much," Tom said.

"I gathered that he likes a good time." Then to Lovejoy he said, "Captain Martin has written that you spent nearly two years in London. Is there much talk of war with America over there?"

"I did not follow politics, Mr. MacKenzie. The English take far less notice of us than we do of them. Their attention is fastened on France and Napoleon."

"I despise the British. Imagine, stopping vessels flying our flag and impressing Americans on the pretext that they are British citizens. They thumb their noses at us with impunity, issuing their Orders in Council dictating where we may and may not trade. I can't believe the way the Federalists condone such behavior. They are lickspittles, not fit to call themselves Americans. Let me tell you, the British may come to rue their high-handed attitude toward this country."

Mrs. MacKenzie put her hand on his arm, saying "Dear Mac, you must not get started on politics."

"It is the burning subject of the hour. What's the sentiment in Philadelphia?"

"I only returned a few days ago," Lovejoy said. "Besides, I have little interest in politics."

"Baltimore seethes with Republican sentiment. Yes sir, this is a hotbed of war hawks, all itching for President Madison to declare war.

We do have a newspaper here that takes a contrary view, preaching against war. Calls itself the *Federal-Republican.* The war hawks hate the sheet. I am none too fond of it myself. The rest of the press and nearly all the people are ready for war whenever Mr. Madison gives the word."

Lovejoy had hoped that he and Tom could escape the MacKenzies after supper, but their host insisted on their going to bed early, explaining, "We are going to have a busy day tomorrow, lads, and we must be up at the crack of dawn."

Lovejoy pressed him as to the nature of the business, but he only winked and said, "We'll discuss that in the morning. I want to go over the documents your father sent along once more. I will have a clearer idea of how to proceed in the morning."

In their own bedroom, after saying their prayers, the MacKenzies reviewed the evening.

"Why are you playing cat and mouse with that young man, Mac?"

"He is too eager to get his hands on money. His father warned me in his letter that that might be the case."

"He does have charming manners, but I wonder about the depth of his character."

"Ah, Flo, we mustn't judge him too harshly or quickly. He has spirit. And despite his family's wealth, see the easy friendship between him and this little Tom fellow. Better educated, from a privileged family, and yet he treats his friend as an equal. No, there is good material there to work with."

"Yes, but he is what, twenty-five? Isn't that late for him to be finding himself? Compare him with yourself at that age. Already set up in business, you were."

"Yes, and without that loan from the lad's father, I could still be working as a shipping clerk. If you knew Jeremiah Martin as well as I do, you would understand how difficult it might be to grow up in his shadow. No, Flo, I am reserving my judgment about his son's character. Until he does something to change my mind, I mean to give him the benefit of the doubt. Meanwhile I owe it to his father to do what he has charged me to do."

# 7

Malcolm MacKenzie had never aspired to be as rich as his old Revolutionary War privateering commander. He lacked Jeremiah's willingness to take bold, imaginative, but calculated risks. So while Jeremiah had become a trading titan in Philadelphia, Malcolm had achieved only modest prosperity by patiently plying his profession as a ships chandler in Baltimore, with occasional cautious forays into buying shares of shipping enterprises. As a result, he had never made his way into the circle of some fifty merchants who dominated the commercial and social life of booming Baltimore. Most of these men had built fortunes in such endeavors as flour mills and iron foundries or insurance companies and banking, then branched out into shipping as partners with their peers. From their mansions on the hills to the north of Baltimore, they looked down on mere chandlers like Malcolm or operators of ropewalks or sail lofts as members of "the small beer gentry," to be given due respect, surely, but not to be included in very large undertakings.

Many, like Malcolm, were Presbyterians, but few took their Calvinism as seriously as the MacKenzies. And most of them, again like Malcolm, were avowed Republicans.

Beginning many years before with a loan from Jeremiah Martin, Malcolm had quit his job as shipping clerk to open a ships chandlery. Lacking children and satisfied with their comfortable but unostentatious house, he had ground away year after year selling barrels of beef and pork, flour and cornmeal, and other supplies at a fair profit to ships' owners. Then he judiciously invested those set-aside profits in small shares of ships that defied the British and carried cargoes of highly valued Maryland and Pennsylvania wheat or tobacco to Europe or one of the French possessions in the West Indies.

Malcolm prided himself on not belonging to that flashy tribe of Baltimore speculators called "plungers" or "dashers," men who risked everything on a single ship or cargo without taking out insurance on their ventures. He was proud, too, of the fact that, unlike some other Baltimore merchants, he had declined to get involved in hauling supplies for the British army in Portugal and Spain, despite the profitability of that trade.

Two years before, he had allowed his old friend Clarence Little, owner of a neighboring ropewalk and normally a conservative investor like himself, to persuade him to go into partnership to buy a consignment of three thousand barrels of topgrade flour at ten dollars a barrel and send it off to Bordeaux, where the French were willing to pay nearly triple that price. Malcolm had wanted to send the flour down to Guadaloupe in three separate lots, aboard swift Baltimore schooners that could outrun any British frigate, but Little had prevailed on him to allow the entire cargo to be put aboard a slow brig direct to France. Malcolm had acquiesced only after Little agreed to insure their cost of the flour. It had taken the last of Malcolm's capital to give his friend his half of the premium to be turned over to the underwriters.

Three disastrous events had followed. First came the news that a British frigate had intercepted the brig as it approached the French coast. Already reeling from this intelligence, Malcolm was called the following morning by the police to confirm that the man whose body they had pulled from the harbor, with its throat cut, was his friend and co-investor Clarence Little. Malcolm discovered the reason for the suicide after the funeral, when he went around to the insurance office to enter his claim for the loss of the cargo. Little had taken Malcolm's money and, instead of buying insurance, had paid it to a shipbuilder to start the construction of a trading schooner, one of those swift craft for which Baltimore was noted. A big one, too, of some three hundred tons.

Later, Little's widow found a suicide note to Malcolm explaining that he had hoped to put the two of them into the shipping business in a big way, and begging Malcom's forgiveness for his foolhardiness.

The news of his financial disaster had passed quickly through the business community. Cautious, canny Malcolm MacKenzie was ruined, the word ran. Better get what is owed you before he goes bankrupt. As a result, many suppliers who normally extended credit to his chandlery began demanding cash. He was served with judgments calling for immediate payment for provisions and navigational instruments on consignment in his inventory. Within a few weeks, all that was left to him was his house and a much diminished stock of goods.

Manfully he had swallowed his pride, made good on every obligation, and resigned himself to rebuilding his modest business of selling ships supplies.

Thus Jeremiah Martin's letter and the arrival of Lovejoy could not have come at a better time. The large number of transactions in which his old friend had been involved in Baltimore came as no surprise. He knew that some businesspeople had gone to Philadelphia for loans when they could not find capital in Baltimore. Jeremiah had often solicited his opinion of those loan applicants. But he was amazed at the crafty way Jeremiah had drawn up his instructions for calling in those debts.

Jeremiah Martin's plan was bold and complicated, but basically sound and, for himself, risk free. Vowing to carry it out to the letter, Malcom said a prayer of thanks and fell asleep.

Lovejoy Martin went to bed that night regarding Malcolm MacKenzie as a useful busybody. He supposed he could endure him and his pious wife for a few days. After that, with a pocketful of money, he and Tom would be free to go their own way. He would ask permission to visit the Richter family in Reading. It was early for him to think of marrying and settling down, but then again, it might be a long while before he found another girl as desirable and rich as Madeline.

Hell, he would be rich, too. Perhaps, acting as a silent partner, he would set Tom up in a business and take up law, if not with Bennett then with one of his friends from his Princeton days. He hoped that all the talk of war with England was wrong. With so much money, he could cut quite a swath back in London, especially with a beautiful, blond half-English wife on his arm.

Over breakfast the next morning, Malcolm, to keep Tom occupied, offered him a temporary job in his shop. "As for you, Lovejoy, I want you to put on your best suit and accompany me on some business calls."

Their first stop was at a sail loft on Pitt Street. Malcolm introduced Lovejoy and then launched into a speech he would repeat many times in the next three days.

"No," he said to the owner, "I am not here to order any sails from you, and yes, I do understand why you feel you must insist that any orders I do place must be paid for in advance. I am here on other business. I hold a power of attorney from an old friend, Jeremiah Martin of Philadelphia. Of course you know Captain Martin. You should, for you owe him the sum of twelve hundred dollars, which was due on January first. You cannot pay just now? Well, sir, I have to tell you that I am empowered to take the matter before the court and enter a judgment against you. Yes, I know that cash is in short supply. You should be pleased to hear that Captain Martin has authorized me to allow you to discharge your obligation in kind. By that I mean that we will accept a quantity of good Holland Dutch duck sails. Mind you, we'd have to credit you at your purchase price. And we will have to add the accrued interest on your debt. You don't think you can do that? Well then, let me suggest that you calculate your costs in lawyers' fees in defending yourself in a hopeless case, not to mention the damage to your reputation, for the matter is sure to be reported in the newspapers. You may think me a hard man, but you do see my point, don't you? Ah, good, good. I am glad that we can settle this matter without causing you embarrassment. Yes, this young man is the son of Jeremiah Martin. He will be happy to tell his father of your reasonable approach to this matter. My business? It is going very well, thank you. Most of my problems are all behind me now. If you will just sign this paper, we will be on our way. You can hold the sails until we call for them. Mind you, your best Holland duck. Linen sails will not be acceptable."

By the end of that first day, Malcolm had obtained title to a pair of iron twelve-pounder "Long Tom" cannon, plus carriages, sponges, and rammers, several kegs of gunpowder, a set of navigational instruments, and nearly ten thousand dollars in cash.

After supper that night, Lovejoy questioned his taking so much of the debts in materials rather than money.

"I don't see any benefit, Mr. MacKenzie, in owning all that stuff. I appreciate that you are obtaining things at knockdown prices, but this way we have the burden of selling it all to get our money out."

"You will see the benefit in due course, my boy. By the by, your father's letter mentioned your studying medicine in London. Why did you not continue your studies?"

Lovejoy had to bite his tongue to keep from telling his host to mind his own business. "I wasn't cut out for it. I only wanted to be a doctor because of my uncle."

"Perhaps we can find something you were cut out for."

"With all respect, Mr. MacKenzie, it is not your responsibility to help me find my place in life. I only want to get my money and go my own way."

The next day, with Lovejoy in tow, Malcolm collected six thousand dollars in cash and a score each of pistols, muskets, and cutlasses. By the end of the week, they had settled nearly all the debts, but less than half of the proceeds was in money, the rest in what MacKenzie persisted in calling "kind."

Lovejoy suggested that he turn over all the cash to him and give him a note for the value of the materials.

"Ah, Lovejoy, be not so quick. We have one more, no two more calls to make before our business is done."

Shortly after noon that Friday, Lovejoy followed MacKenzie over to Baltimore Street to a merchant banker's countinghouse. They were greeted in the outer office by a large, red-faced man who was putting on a long coat of fine materials and who at first treated Malcolm in an offhand way, saying, "Well, MacKenzie, what brings you forth from your chandlery?"

"I have a financial proposition for you."

"The last time we had such a discussion, you declined to pledge a mortgage on your home to clear up your obligations. Changed your mind, have you?"

"I am not here to borrow money. Let me introduce Lovejoy Martin. He is the son of a dear friend, someone whose reputation you probably know, Jeremiah Martin."

"Who does not know of him? What brings you to Baltimore, my boy?"

"My father sent me here to consult with Mr. MacKenzie."

"Yes," Malcolm said. "Captain Martin had some debts owing him here. I am helping Lovejoy collect those debts. Now can we go into your office to discuss this matter in private?"

Inside the office, banker Findley closed the door and grudgingly asked them to be seated.

"So, you are Captain Martin's son. I hear that your father has been pulling in his horns. That's a shame. With war brewing, there may be some grand opportunities. But no matter. Now, MacKenzie, just what is your business?"

"I understand that you have advanced Talbot Smith the money to build a schooner."

"You know very well, MacKenzie, that I am not at liberty to talk about such confidential matters."

"Then let us speak in hypothetical terms. Suppose there were a shipbuilder who owes you money. Suppose that he is a bit slow in meeting the payments. Suppose that you found someone willing to buy the debt from you."

"Perhaps you ought to get to the point."

"As you just said to Lovejoy, there may be some grand opportunities if we do go to war. Now if I were owed the sum of fourteen thousand dollars by a man who was slow in meeting his payments, and if someone were willing to take the debt off my hands so that I could invest it better elsewhere, I would jump at the chance."

"MacKenzie, I am not so desperate for capital that I must discount notes owing me. Besides, I never said that it was fourteen thousand."

"Oh, I know the amount. As for a discount, have I asked for one?"

"Then what are you asking for?"

"I am not asking anything of you. I am offering to pay the fourteen thousand that Talbot Smith owes you, plus the overdue interest and an extra two thousand to cover your expenses."

The banker's eyebrows went up.

"Talbot Smith is one of the finest shipbuilders in Baltimore. Our mortgage covers his shipyard as well as the vessel he is constructing. The ship alone would be collateral enough."

"He also is one of the slowest shipbuilders. Come on, Findley, we are talking about cash and your time. How about it?"

Afterward, outside on the street, Lovejoy could no longer hold in check the outrage he felt at the beaming MacKenzie.

"You gave that man nearly all the money we collected this week. You gave it to him for a piece of paper. How dare you do such a rash thing without even consulting me? Damn it, sir, I am not going to put up with this anymore. I want what's coming to me, and I want it right now."

"Calm yourself. I am working for your best interest."

"A lien on a ship is not in my best interest."

"Not ship, schooner."

"Then I don't give a damn for a lien on a schooner. Look, Mr. MacKenzie, I am tired of being manipulated. First my father brings me home from London, where I was perfectly happy. Then he sends me down to this place on the pretext that I am to receive my inheritance. And for the past week, you have been treating me like a child. Now, damn it sir, tell me what this is all about. I can't believe that you would throw our money away on a mere piece of paper."

"My dear boy, you will soon see that I have not thrown our money away. This document, which you call a mere piece of paper, is our passport to a new world. I thought you had some sense of adventure, like your father. Don't disappoint me. Come, lad, come. Take that sullen look off your face. Let's hire a hack and ride out to Lazaretto Point on the Patapsco."

Talbot Smith did not care that few people in the shipping trade around Baltimore liked him. He cared only for turning out top-quality schooners from his small shipyard to suit his own obsessive standards and to hell with anyone else's.

For the past dozen years, he had been specializing in so-called Baltimore schooners, those swift, "sharp built," narrow-waisted craft with twin, raked masts whose crowd of white canvas carried them tripping across the water like dancers.

Although technically a bachelor, he lived with a free mulatto woman in a converted shed on a corner of his shipyard. Himself the illegitimate son of a Baltimore prostitute, he had started his working life as a carpenter's apprentice, then had taken to the sea as an ordinary sailor and had made his way up to second mate. Only a lack of a formal education and a sour disposition prevented his rise to captain of his own vessel. During the so-called quasi-war with France in 1797, he had shipped aboard a privateer and, as prize master, had brought three handsome captures into port. With the extra shares he earned from these prizes, he had purchased a small plot along the Patapsco opposite Fort McHenry and, with a handful of employees, had built a small schooner on speculation. He had taken nearly a year to complete the vessel, putting it together the way he felt all schooners should be built. He had even gone to the extra expense of sheathing the hull below the waterline with copper to prevent sea worms from eating the wood. Some thought this a foolish precaution because the high content of fresh water in the Patapsco discouraged the pests, but as Smith put it, "She'll be sailing down to places where there is worms. If anybody thinks that runs the price too high, then let them buy elsewhere."

After selling that craft at a small profit, he had built another and then another, each larger and costlier than the last. He might have become a rich man if he had done as so many shipbuilders did and turned out a vessel every two or three months under contract. But that was not Talbot Smith's way,

Such a demanding taskmaster would have had trouble keeping enough skilled workers to man a very large operation. By trial and error, he had recruited a handful of loyal carpenters, caulkers and such, enough to get his work done. If one of his men was out sick, Smith pitched in with adze or caulking hammer for he was a master at every craft. Six mornings out of every week, his men found him already at work when they showed up. On Sundays, he usually went fishing, but even then his mind churned away with plans for his next craft, for Talbot Smith, despite his sordid upbringing and his squalid way of life, was a seeker after perfection in his work. God help the lumberman who sent him an order of inferior timber or the foundry that shipped him poorly forged iron fittings.

A lean, leathery man with the eye of a hawk, he terrorized his young employees, running through apprentices at a fearful rate. Any hapless youths who tried to leave his employ before their terms of apprenticeship were up he pursued as relentlessly as a professional slave catcher. Along the waterfront, they called him "Shylock Smith." He did not care what anyone called him as long as they met their obligations the way he met his.

On this Friday afternoon, Smith was overseeing the placement of the final streak of planks on the hull of a very large schooner that he and his men had labored on for nearly a year now. He expected to finish the hull the next morning and then start on the deck Monday.

He did not notice the hack that had been driven onto his property until one of his shipwrights pointed down at Malcolm MacKenzie and Lovejoy.

He handed his hammer to his foreman and climbed down the scaffold.

Still sitting in the hack, Malcolm said with what seemed to Lovejoy a forced cheerfulness, "Well, Talbot, my friend, how are you on this lovely June day?"

"I am well enough, MacKenzie. But very busy. What can I do for you?"

"I am showing this young gentleman around the boatyards of Baltimore. I wanted him to see for himself what a fine shipbuilder you are."

"Is he looking to buy a schooner?" Smith asked.

"You might conclude that. I have agreed to help Lovejoy see what sorts of schooners might be available. For example, is this fine-looking craft spoken for?"

"There is some that have been sniffing about but she won't be ready for another two or three months. They all want things rushed through but I don't work that way."

"As I well know."

"Is the young fellow serious about buying? I got no time for talking if he ain't."

"Talbot, you know that I would not take time off from my business to bring him out here if he were not."

"From what I hear, your business don't require all that much attention these days."

"We are in a bit of a slump just now. Laboring along under yet another of Mr. Madison's embargoes, but this one is only for ninety days. I expect things to be resolved soon. Will you show Lovejoy your plans for this schooner and let him inspect what you have done so far? You will? Good. Why don't you show him your layout here?"

"Shouldn't we discuss this first before we take up this man's valuable time?" Lovejoy whispered between clenched teeth.

"I know what I am doing."

At first grudgingly, but with increasing enthusiasm, Talbot showed them the drying sheds where he seasoned the live and white oak timbers from which the frame and hulls were made.

"They sell me oak they claim is seasoned, but they generally do a piss poor job. If you want anything done right, you have to do it yourself. See there, we have our own lathes. I turn out me own trunnels and belaying pins. Use nothing but the best hickory."

At the saw pit, where the timbers were sawed into planks, he said, "Some builders like to buy their planks ready sawed out, but me, I do it myself here. Then I know they're done proper. You'll never find a knot in a plank on a Smith-built schooner, no, nor a rough adze job either. Smooth as a baby's cheeks I make my hulls."

After a visit to the blacksmith's and the carpenter's shops, he led them back to where the unfinished schooner sat balanced between large beams supporting its graceful bulk like flying buttresses.

"She'll be the biggest and the best I ever did build. She measures 107 feet at waterline and 24 feet acrost her beam. I figure she'll weigh out at close to three hundred tons. And nothing but the finest materials is going into her. How often do you see such portholes along the stern of a schooner? That'll give the captain a fine view from his cabin."

"And you are building her on speculation?"

"Aye. And it will take a pretty penny to buy her, too."

"Have you set a price on her?"

"With a copper bottom, masts and spars in place and ready for her rigging, gunnels pierced with twenty-two gun ports, I'd have to have twenty thousand for her, in cash."

"As much as that?"

"I don't haggle. If the price scares you off, just say so and let me get back to my work."

"I was wondering, Talbot. Is this the same schooner on which Clarence Little made a down payment some months before her keel was even laid?"

"Now what business would that be of yours?"

"Perhaps you heard that Clarence and I financed a shipment of flour to Bordeaux, and the British captured the brig and our cargo."

"You should have took out insurance."

"I did put up two thousand dollars for a premium, but Clarence failed to take out the insurance."

"Maybe you picked the wrong partner."

"That may be. Clarence wasn't trying to defraud me, however. He matched the money with his own and made a down payment on a schooner. His widow says he made that payment to you."

"What if he did?"

"Well, if he did, are not Mrs. Little and I entitled to a twenty percent interest in this schooner?"

"Ha! So that's your game, is it? Sneaking out here with a story about wanting to buy and trying to horn in on my schooner. Well, sir, that down payment was forfeited. I told that woman's lawyer that that was the case, and he seen my point. Now clear out of my shipyard and let me get on with my work."

MacKenzie continued, as if oblivious to Smith's red face and threatening manner. "Would you like to tell me how you raised the additional money after refusing to return our down payment?"

"It is none of your business."

"Then let me tell you. You went and borrowed fourteen thousand dollars from Charles Findley. And you mortgaged your entire shipyard to do so. The shipyard and any vessel that might be under construction is the way the mortgage reads."

"I am telling you, MacKenzie, you are poking your nose into my business and I won't stand for it. Get off of my property or I'll have the law on you for trespassing."

"If I were you, Talbot, I would temper my speech or this property may not remain yours very long."

"What are you getting at?"

"This paper is the mortgage on your property. You are nearly six months in arrears in your payments, which means that the holder of the mortgage has the right to foreclose."

"You're blowing smoke. Findley knows I'll pay soon as I sell this schooner. All the materials is bought."

"Yes, you purchased everything all at once so you could drive a harder bargain with the suppliers. Now you are out of money, aren't you?"

"By God, I ain't going to stand for this no more." He turned toward his living shed and shouted, "Josie!"

His woman opened the door. "What you want, Mr. Talbot?"

"Turn the dog loose."

A moment later a large brindle-colored mastiff came bounding across the shipyard. MacKenzie pushed Lovejoy into the hack and scrambled up beside him.

With the dog circling the hack and barking, Smith picked up a small crowbar and shook it at the pair. "Come back out here again and I'll do worse than set the dog on ye."

MacKenzie smiled. "Talbot, you'd better hear me out. Lovejoy Martin and I have purchased this mortgage from Findley. We have it in our power to take title to this shipyard and have you evicted from the premises. No, I am not jesting. You call off that dog and hear what we have to say or you will find yourself out on the streets of Baltimore."

"I'll get a lawyer and see you in court."

"If I were you, I wouldn't waste my money on a lawyer. Findley has assigned the mortgage to us. It will be a simple matter to take possession of your shipyard and the schooner."

"If this is just a trick to get back the money Little paid in, why don't you say so?"

"It is too late for that, I fear. However, there is a way for you to pay off this mortgage and keep your shipyard."

"I'd burn down every building before I'd let you cheat me out of my shipyard. By God, I'll go in and see Findley myself. Now get out of here and take your dandy young milksop with you."

MacKenzie took up the horse's reins, then paused and said calmly, almost sweetly, "Mr. Findley will not be in his office until Monday morning. I will be in my chandlery until noon on Monday. If you have not come by then to discuss this matter face-to-face in a calm, businesslike way, I shall begin foreclosure proceeedings immediately. And by the by, if you can lay hands on a Bible, let me suggest that you turn to the eighteenth chapter of St. Matthew. Start at the twenty-third verse and read it to the end."

"What's the Bible got to do with you trying to cheat me out of my shipyard?"

"The passage contains the parable of the unmerciful debtor. I urge you to read it and see if you recognize yourself therein. Just remember, if you have not showed up by noon Monday, we foreclose immediately. Now, we'll say good day to you."

"You can go to hell and take your Philadelphia dandy with you. I'll burn this place down before I'd turn it over to you."

"In which case you would end up in prison as a convicted arsonist. Lovejoy is my witness to your threats. Remember, by noon Monday. Good day, Talbot."

The shipbuilder turned and hurled his crowbar against the hull of the schooner. The dog raged in circles around the hack until the terrified horse had drawn it out of the shipyard and on the road back to Fells Point.

Lovejoy had been so fascinated by the interview with the shipbuilder that he had forgotten his objections, but the farther they drove, the more it sank in that MacKenzie was involving him deeper and deeper in a business from which he could see no easy way out. He could not trust himself to speak, he was so angry. MacKenzie pretended not to notice his silence.

Lovejoy contained his rage until after they had returned the hack to the livery stable and were back in MacKenzie's chandlery.

Tom, who was enjoying his job, greeted them at the door, asking where they had been.

"We will talk about it over supper," MacKenzie said. "Now, let's see, Tom, we owe you four dollars for your work this week."

"Mr. MacKenzie," Lovejoy said. "We have got to talk."

"Yes, but let us not talk here. It has been a busy week. Let us repair to my house and reflect on what we have accomplished."

Lovejoy's long-smoldering anger burst like a ruptured abscess. "God damn it, sir. I will not stand for this anymore. You have collected all these debts on my behalf and have spent them on things in which I have no interest."

"Not 'spent,' Lovejoy. Invested. Invested in things of far greater value than that of the debts."

"There you go again, treating me like a village idiot," Lovejoy said in a rising voice.

"No need to shout, my son."

"Don't call me your son."

Tom caught his sleeve. "Joy, take it easy."

"No, I will not take it easy. And I will not go home with this man and sit through another evening of boring reminiscences."

"Lovejoy, you don't understand," MacKenzie said.

"How much money do you have left, Tom?"

"Counting what Mr. MacKenzie gave me, about eight dollars."

"With what I have, that's more than enough. Come on, Tom."

"Wait," MacKenzie said. "Flora will have supper ready."

"Then you can both have double portions."

MacKenzie's expression lost its normally imperturbable expression. "What do you mean to do?"

"Enjoy ourselves until Monday morning. Then I am going to see a lawyer about the way you have pissed away my money."

# 9

Mamie Brown's Calvert House catered to ship officers and owners. Her clientele liked her air of gentility and valued her reputation for discretion as well as the quality of her girls.

Mamie's mother, an ancient quadroon, often sat in the "drawing room" of the establishment with a lap full of knitting, toothlessly smiling at the banter of the clients and the girls. It was rumored that the old woman had been a beauty in her youth and that Mamie's father had been a young blade from one of Virginia's vaunted "first families."

The squatly built Mamie had not inherited her mother's beauty, but she bore herself with a cheerful dignity and governed her "young ladies" with a strict hand. It was a good place to work, if you followed Mamie's rules and "behaved yourself like a lady."

Normally, Calvert House would have been busy on a Friday evening, but with several pro-war meetings being held in the city, her young ladies were sitting around looking bored while a black man picked away at a mournful rendition of "Barbara Allen" on his banjo.

"I think if I hear that damned song one more time I am going to throw up," said Linda Mae, a dishwater blond from York County in Pennsylvania.

"That and 'Robin Adair' is about the only things that dumb nigger knows how to play," replied Dessie, a brunette from the Eastern Shore.

"What kind of talk is that?" Mamie demanded. "You girls know I don't allow strong language in here."

"There ain't no customers around," Dessie said.

"I just don't want you to get in the habit. And another thing, I don't ever want to hear you say that word 'nigger' again, Dessie. You trying to hurt Johnson's feelings? And what about my mama?"

"Aw, Mamie, I didn't mean no harm."

"You say it again and you liable to find yourself out on the waterfront trying to peddle your wares to common sailors that has body lice and ain't had a bath since they left port."

"You want me to apologize to Johnson and your mama?"

"That's all right. I don't think they heard you. But both of you just mind your mouths. Here, Johnson," she called to the banjo player, "go see who is knocking at the door."

Mamie would have turned away two drunken young strangers, but the larger, better dressed chap—the one with the sandy hair—assured her that they had money and that they would be ever so well behaved. Besides, it was a slow night at Calvert House.

"Just remember to behave yourselves. I don't want the plug-uglies from the watch coming in here and shutting me down. By the way, you pay in advance here on your first visit."

"This treat is on me," Lovejoy said.

"That is for both of you? Him too?" She nodded toward Tom, who leaned against the doorsill with a vacant look on his face.

"Especially him. I want him to have first choice."

Tom had only a fuzzy idea of where he was. The last thing he could remember clearly was playing cards at the Blue Eagle Tavern on Fells Point and being assured by Lovejoy that anyone capable of drinking two cups of raw Jamaican rum surely could handle a third.

"If I drink another, I won't be able to play cards anymore."

"Our genial host tells me of a game that you will enjoy a lot more than cards. Here, my good fellow, bring another round."

The faces of Mamie's six girls were a blur in Tom's vision. That of Linda Mae seemed to shimmer with a golden light.

Lovejoy bowed and said, "Ladies, we are honored to be here this evening. We hope that you all are well and in good health."

The girls looked at each other and shrugged.

"Dear ladies," Lovejoy continued, "we all are grateful to Madame Brown for opening her establishment to us. She honors us with her acceptance. Now let me introduce you to my friend. His name is Thomas Jenkins and he is a gentleman right down to the bone. As do I, he hails from Philadelphia, where his father is one of the city's leading innkeepers. There now, is he not a splendid specimen of young manhood?"

The girls laughed.

"Now Mr. Jenkins, look these fair damsels over carefully and decide which suits your fancy. Never mind about me. From what the host of the Blue Eagle tells me, the leavings here are better than the best of any other establishment, isn't that right, Madame Brown?"

Mamie laughed in spite of herself. "You one of them college gentlemen. I can tell."

"You are indeed a perceptive woman, Madame Brown. I plead guilty to the crime of being educated beyond my natural intelligence. Whereas my friend, Tom Jenkins, has a brain that is more than the equal of his learning. Here Tom, take your pick. We haven't got all night. Time is money to these young ladies."

Linda Mae and Dessie looked at the roughly dressed Tom, then at each other, and shrank back into their chairs as if to make themselves invisible to his scrutiny.

Seeing that Tom was staring at the blond, Lovejoy asked her, "What is your name, lovely lady?"

"This is Linda Mae," Dessie said, putting her hand over her mouth to conceal her glee at her co-worker's discomfiture.

"That's right," Mamie said. "And Linda Mae is one of my nicest girls. Very popular, she is."

"Can she not speak for herself?" Lovejoy said.

"Of course I can speak for myself," Linda Mae said. "Does he think I'm ignorant?"

"She can and does speak for herself and well doth she speak, too. 'Her voice was ever soft, gentle and low, an excellent thing in woman.' But please, call yourself not Linda Mae."

"What is he talking about? That is my name. Is he drunk or crazy or both?"

"Linda Mae, you mind your mouth now," Mamie said. "The gentleman is just making polite conversation."

"Well, I don't like nobody making fun of me."

"Let us not call her Linda Mae," Lovejoy said. " 'Her name is Portia . . .' He paused to hiccup. "And, and, and . . . 'Nor is the wide world ignorant of her worth for the four winds blow in from every coast renowned suitors, and her sunny locks hang on her temples like a golden fleece . . . and many Jasons come in quest of her.' "

Dessie whispered to Linda Mae, "The little one likes you, but if you don't want him, I don't mind he's drunk."

"Oh, what the hell," Linda Mae said as she stood up and grasped Tom's hand. "What did you say your name was, mister?"

"You may call him Bassanio," said Lovejoy.

"Linda Mae," Mamie hissed furiously. "I don't want to have to speak to you again about rough language."

"What are you talking about?"

"You said 'hell' and you know it."

Linda Mae rolled her eyes resignedly and drew Tom after her up the stairs. After turning over the last of his money to Mamie, Lovejoy followed with his arm around Dessie.

Technically, Tom was not a virgin. Just before Lovejoy's departure for England, the two friends had visited a bawdy house in Philadelphia's South Side, but it had been a botched affair that caused him more embarrassment than pleasure. Afterward, out in the street, he had thrown up. For weeks thereafter, he had checked himself several times each day, fearing that he had picked up a disease.

But Calvert House was a far cry from that Philadelphia brothel, and true to Mamie Brown's billing, Linda Mae knew her trade. She understood male vanity. Afterward, Tom could not remember exactly what had happened, but once back downstairs, Linda Mae had clung to him in the presence of Lovejoy as though sorry he had to go. Lovejoy was impressed by this show of feigned affection and by the fact that Tom had remained upstairs so much longer than he had with Dessie.

He compared his experience unfavorably with those he had enjoyed in London. His resentment of MacKenzie's handling of his father's Baltimore debts smoldered so fiercely that despite Dessie's best efforts he was disappointed in his performance. He was in a foul mood when they departed Calvert House.

The proprietor of the Blue Eagle was getting ready to close up for the night when Lovejoy and Tom reappeared.

"You look like you found the place. Was I right about it?"

"It was all right," Lovejoy said sullenly. "Let's have another round of rum."

The tavern keeper filled two cups and set them on the bar.

"We'll be closing soon, lads, so drink up."

Lovejoy drained his cup, made a face, and said, "Then let's have another of those."

"You sure you can handle more?"

"I wouldn't ask for it if I couldn't."

"No need to take offense, but it is late, and you lads had more than your share earlier."

"Just pour the rum and save your advice."

The tavern keeper, stung by the insulting tone of Lovejoy's voice, hesitated, then refilled the cup and pointedly recorked the bottle and shut it away in his cabinet.

Tom, stupefied by so much rum and by his experience with Linda Mae, leaned against the bar, staring into his cup. Lovejoy again drained his cup and then slammed it against the bar.

"Another of those, my good man."

"I am not your good man, and I am not serving you any more. Like I told you, we are ready to close up here. So let's see your money. That will be for four cups."

"You are refusing to serve us?"

"That is right, young fellow. Pay up and say good night."

Lovejoy thrust his hand into his pocket, then turned to Tom. "I gave all my money to the woman at that whorehouse. Pay this arrogant publican."

"I don't have any money left, Joy. I'm broke."

"You can't pay?" The tavern keeper came from behind the bar. He was a large man, weighing close to two hundred pounds, with thick, hairy wrists and fists like a pair of clubs.

"You ain't leaving here without paying."

"Now, my good fellow, we can work something out."

"I say you are paying up."

"And I say you can go whistle for your money."

The tavern keeper seized the lapels of Lovejoy's jacket in one huge paw.

"How dare you lay hands on me?" Lovejoy said. And with that, he punched the man on the jaw with his left fist and tore himself free of his grasp.

The tavern keeper stepped back for a moment, wiped the blood from his mouth, then let out a bearlike growl and lunged at Lovejoy. When sober, Lovejoy was an excellent boxer, and he and Tom had had much experience fighting as lads. But this was a powerful man, and Lovejoy's coordination was badly off. He got in one solid blow that bounced off the man's cheekbone and staggered him momentarily. But suddenly those thick arms were around Lovejoy, pinning his hands against his sides. Unable to break the clutch, Lovejoy was lifted from his feet and hurled against the bar like a rag doll. Before he could regain his footing, the tavern keeper gave him a kick in the ribs which knocked the breath from him. A moment later, Tom, belatedly coming to his friend's help, joined him in a heap on the tavern floor.

# 10

Lovejoy awoke with a throbbing head. He forced open one eye. Like a javelin, a shaft of morning sunlight from a high, narrow window pierced his skull. He put his hands over his face and groaned.

"Where am I?"

"We are in jail," Tom said. "Don't you remember?"

"What happened?"

"You got your ass whipped, and so did I. The man at the tavern stomped hell out of us both and then called the watch. Joy, it was bad enough you picking a fight with that big ape, but did you have to go and swing at the watchmen too? They'll never let us out of here."

"I will tell them who we are. They can't keep us here."

Lovejoy tried to sit up but collapsed and held his side.

"My ribs feel like they are busted."

"That son of a bitch kicked you while you were down. I sailed into him, but God, he was strong. Why did you pick a fight with a man like that?"

"I could whip him in a fair fight, and by God I will when we get out of here. Nobody is going to treat me like that and get away with it."

"If you want to take him on again, you're going to have to do it without me."

Nauseated and fighting the pain in his head and side, Lovejoy dragged himself to his feet. Their cell was six by six. Lovejoy rattled the bars on the little window of the heavy oak door. "Help, help! Somebody come and get us out of here."

"Shut up," a voice in the next cell called. "Who do you think you are?"

"I am a gentleman. They have made a mistake."

Derisive laughter echoed from several cells.

"Ooh, listen to that. He's a gentleman."

"And they made a mistake. Oh, the judge will be ever so sorry when he learns they dared arrest a gentleman."

Lovejoy kicked the door of the cell and yelled again for help.

"Ain't you ever been in jail before, young gentleman?" the man in the adjoining cell said with mock concern.

"If it is any of your business, no."

"Well, it is my business when you make so much fuss a man can't sleep, so shut the hell up."

"Go to hell, yourself."

"What are you in here for?"

Tom told him about the incident at the Blue Eagle.

Their neighbor lapsed into a fit of coughing. "Hear that?" he said when he got his breath back. "He picked a fight with Billie Matson at the Blue Eagle. Didn't Billie tell you that he used to be a prizefighter?"

"No, but I could tell he knew what he was doing."

"I would like to have seen that one. Well now, my lad, if you will tell your gentleman friend to keep quiet for a bit, they'll be around with our breakfast. He can explain to the jailers about the terrible mistake that has been made. Until then, keep it quiet in there."

The door at the end of the hallway opened and a jailer entered the cell block, followed by two black trusties, one of whom carried a bucket full of stale bread and the other a pot of cornmeal mush and a stack of tin bowls.

"We should not be in here," Lovejoy said when they reached his cell door. "There has been a terrible mistake."

"From what I hear, there sure as hell has been, and you are the one that made it, starting a fight with Billie Matson."

"Look, please, won't you deliver a message to a friend of ours? His name is Malcolm MacKenzie."

"The chandler? Yeah, I know him."

"Good. Please tell him that Lovejoy Martin and Tom Jenkins are in here and we want him to come and get us out."

"What's it worth to you if I do?"

"I'll give you five dollars."

"Let's see your money."

"I spent all my money."

"Then how can you give me five dollars?"

"Mr. MacKenzie will pay you."

The jailer laughed. "If I carried messages for every drunk in this place, I'd have no time for my family. You can tell the judge you ain't supposed to be in here. Now here's your grub."

Lovejoy took his bowl of mush and hunk of bread and eased his aching body down on the filthy cot.

"Do you think he'll do it?" Tom asked.

"I can't tell."

"After what you said to Mr. MacKenzie about siccing a lawyer on him, maybe he won't want to help you anyway."

"Shut up, Tom. Oh God, I feel awful."

"Look, Joy, if you're not hungry, can I have your grub?"

The next five days and nights were the most miserable either Lovejoy or Tom had ever spent. Locked up in a cell that would have been small even for one person and forced to share a rusty bucket as a chamber pot, they were occupied for most of the first day just in getting over their hangovers. That night they got little sleep as the police brought in one noisy drunk after another. When they awoke the next morning, two other men were sprawled on the floor between their bunks. One was a wiry little sailor arrested for public drunkenness, and the other was a middle-aged man charged with assaulting his wife in public. The former spent the day boasting about women in ports around the world; the latter bored his cell mates with praise for his wife's virtues as a housekeeper and mother to his children.

Not only had neither Lovejoy nor Tom ever been in jail, but neither of them had experienced bedbugs. The sailor identified the cause of the bites that had all four of them itching.

The next morning, after another breakfast of corn mush, the jailers removed the sailor and the wife beater for hearings before the police magistrate.

"What about us?" Lovejoy asked.

"Not today. Maybe tomorrow."

The next morning, it was the same story. The jailers removed more prisoners for hearings and told the two friends that theirs would have to wait. By midweek, Lovejoy and Tom were covered with bedbug bites, their faces matted with whiskers, the stench of the jail soaked into their skins. Lovejoy had fallen into a deep despair.

"Pa says it is always darkest just before dawn," Tom said.

"He was never thrown in jail in a strange city and left there to rot. Look at me. Cast out by my family. Cheated out of my inheritance by a conniving little ships chandler. I haven't got a hope or a friend in this world."

"Why, Joy, you have me."

"Yes, and a hell of a lot of good you are doing me."

Tom lashed back with, "For that matter, you haven't done me much good. If you hadn't hit that tavern keeper, we wouldn't be in this jail. You don't hear me complaining. They can't keep us here forever."

"Oh, shut up, Tom. It was your idea to come down here to Baltimore. 'A hell of a town' you called it. It is hell all right."

Giving up on trying to improve Lovejoy's mood, Tom devoted himself to searching the thin mattresses for bedbugs and squashing them between his thumbnails.

# 11

Lovejoy awoke on Friday morning, the nineteenth of June, to the ringing of church bells and the sound of gunfire. When the jailer came around with their morning food, Lovejoy asked what all the fuss was about.

"Congress has declared war down in Washington. Done it yesterday from what I hear. Whole town is in an uproar. Damned fools running about shooting pistols in the air."

As he choked down the fatty bacon and beans, Lovejoy pondered this news. So his father had been right. The United States of America, that young puppy of a nation, was actually going to war with its mother country, a nation of twice its population and many times its military prowess. That meant the end of his dream of returning to London, with or without a gorgeous wife like Madeline Richter.

A fat man wearing a flat plug hat and short-tailed coat looked through the window in their door.

"Lovejoy Martin and Thomas Jenkins, you are to collect your belongings and come with me."

The officer looked at their unkempt hair and beards. He held his nose. "Follow me, lads, and for God's sake, keep downwind."

Outside the cell block, in the office area, there stood Malcolm MacKenzie, looking pleased with himself.

"Well, my boys, it is good to see you," MacKenzie said.

"It's about time you showed up," Lovejoy replied. "We have been in this hellhole for nearly a week now."

"You have been charged with drunk and disorderly conduct and with assaulting a tavern keeper. Are the charges correct?"

"I suppose so."

"I told the magistrate I feared this was true. I have paid your fine and got you off with a thirty-day sentence to be suspended on one condition."

"What is that?"

"You must go to the Blue Eagle Tavern and apologize to Billie Matson."

"I'll be damned if I will. He laid hands on me first."

"Then you will have to return to your cell for thirty days."

Tom grabbed his arm. "No, Joy. Wait a minute, Mr. MacKenzie. I will apologize for both of us. I can't stand to go back in there."

Seeing that Tom was near tears, Lovejoy shrugged and said, "What the hell. Let's get it over with, and then, Mr. MacKenzie, you and I have some serious talking to do."

"Indeed we do. More serious, perhaps, than you realize."

Matson, whose left cheek was still swollen from Lovejoy's blow, made it easy for the two friends to apologize. "Just don't let it happen again. I don't like fighting. I got enough of that in the prize ring."

He held out his hand. Lovejoy's was lost in his vast grasp. After Tom also shook the tavern keeper's hand, they turned to join MacKenzie in the doorway.

"Not so fast," Matson said. "You owe me a dollar for the rum you drank."

MacKenzie paid him.

"Now lads, I want to take you home and let you shave and clean up. Then we will sit down and talk about a few things that have transpired since your incarceration."

At the doorway of the MacKenzie house, Flora looked at the pair, held a handkerchief to her nose, and ordered them to "go around to the back, to the washhouse. Theresa will bring out hot water and a change of clothes. Goodness, Mac, did you have to leave these poor boys in that place so long?"

Her husband shook his head to silence her and said quickly, "When you are ready, come into the dining room to confer."

When they were changed, they entered the house through the kitchen and went into the dining room, where MacKenzie was sitting at a table littered with drawings and documents. Lovejoy was amazed at the presence of Talbot Smith.

"Sit, sit," MacKenzie said.

When they were settled, he looked at them for a long while, then cleared his throat and said, "Well, lads, the fat is in the fire. We are now at war with Great Britain. The British have always had a powerful navy, but for the past six or so years, since they crushed the French fleet at Trafalgar, they have completely dominated the seas. Of course, their armies have their hands full with Napoleon in Europe. With them so distracted, some people feel that we will be able to whip together enough of an army to take over Canada. I have my doubts about that. No one thinks that our navy's little fleet of frigates and Mr. Jefferson's silly gunboats will be any match for the British navy. But their merchant fleet is quite another matter. That is where our opportunities lie."

"Begging your pardon, Mr. MacKenzie," Lovejoy said. "What has all this war talk got to do with our business? I have no quarrel with the English. I want to know why it took you nearly a week to rescue us. And, besides that . . ." He paused to point at Talbot Smith, "Why is this fellow here? Have you forgotten that he set his dog on us and threatened you?"

"We sometimes say and do rash things when we don't have all the facts at hand. For instance, in our last conversation, you spoke of consulting a lawyer."

"He didn't mean that, Mr. MacKenzie," Tom said quickly. "Joy gets his back up and says things without thinking."

"Stay out of this, Tom. I still don't know what you are up to, Mr. MacKenzie."

But MacKenzie was not to be hurried. "As you know, your father got his start in business as a privateer during the Revolution. He ended up a rich man, with two ships. I know, for I sailed with him during his last year at sea. And Talbot Smith served as prize master aboard a schooner out of Baltimore back in ninety-eight and ninety-nine. He wasn't as successful against the French as your father was against the English, perhaps, but he did well enough for himself, eh what, Talbot?"

"Well enough to afford land and gear to start building schooners the way they should be built."

"Quite so. Back during the latter half of the Revolution, we had the

French and their considerable navy on our side. This time we will be going it alone. However, it will take the British navy a while to move against us. Meanwhile, their merchant ships will be carrying cargo back and forth to the West Indies without close protection. This will give us a golden opportunity to prey on their shipping. I see this, and so does Talbot. So we have concluded that rather than bogging ourselves down in a tedious legal dispute, we will join our forces. He will allow us to bring in extra workmen to lay the decks on our schooner, copper her bottom, step her masts, and install her rigging, while I see to buying provisions for our cruise and recruiting our crew."

Lovejoy shook his head in disbelief.

"Without consulting me, you are risking everything that was to have been my inheritance in a privateering venture?"

"My boy," MacKenzie said, "One ninety-day cruise by a properly armed privateer with a well-led crew can make you a far richer man than you have ever dreamed. Right, Talbot?"

"If there is a quicker way, I ain't ever seen it. For making money and providing entertainment, it sure beats hell out of building ships."

"But I don't know anything about privateering, and besides, it must be dangerous."

MacKenzie laughed. "Not so much more dangerous than tangling with a former prizefighter. You don't need to know the business. You have Talbot, myself, and your father."

"I should have realized that Father put you up to all this. But this fellow," he said, pointing to Smith, "what has he got to do with our affairs?"

"I have persuaded him to close up his shipyard and take command of the *Flora.*"

"What in the hell is the *Flora?*"

"That is the name of the privateer vessel in which you now own an eighty percent interest and that has the potential for making you a very rich young man and should not do too badly for Talbot and myself, each of whom owns ten percent. Now hold your questions, and I will explain everything."

The reconciliation between Lovejoy and Malcom began around the MacKenzies' dining room table that very morning. It was completed the following day as the two talked over cups of strong coffee at the Merchants Coffee House near the waterfront.

"Did the jailer not give you my message?" Lovejoy asked.

"He did."

"And why did you wait so long to set us free?"

"I was terribly busy all week, working on your behalf."

"Look, Mr. MacKenzie, you weren't that busy."

"Please, Lovejoy, let us set aside formalities. Please call me Mac, as do my closer friends."

"Would your closer friends have let you rot in jail for a whole week?"

"Would they threaten to set lawyers on me for trying to help them?"

"So, to keep me safely locked up and out of your way, you did nothing when the jailer informed you . . ."

"I gave the man the five dollars you said you promised him. And then I was distracted by Talbot Smith's visit."

In spite of himself, Lovejoy had to laugh at the evasions.

"You are too clever by half. How did you bring that miserable fellow around to your scheme?"

"After learning from Findley that we held his mortgage and that it lay in our power to take title to his shipyard, he came to my office to plead with me not to seize his business and, you might say, take away his purpose in life. By the way, he followed my advice and read that parable of the unjust debtor. He begged my forgiveness and promised to make the widow Little and myself whole in the matter of the insurance premium. I told him of my plans to turn his schooner into a privateer. His eyes lit up at that. One word led to another, and he ended up baring his heart to me. Much as he loves building his superb schooners, that is not where his true desires lie."

"No? And where would that be?"

"The man would sell his soul to the devil if Satan were to make him master of his own privateering vessel. Talbot has not been as fortunate as you or I. His manners and lack of education have held him back. A sea captain, no matter how rough he may be at sea, is expected to show a bit of polish in port. Yet Talbot has forgotten more about the handling of a ship than many of the captains you see sitting about us conversing politely with their owners ever knew. Unable to advance at sea, he decided to become his own master on land. Always remember this, Lovejoy. When you are dealing with another human being, try to find out what he truly desires. Show him how he can fulfill his dreams while meeting your own ends."

Lovejoy laughed and shook his head.

"Mr. MacKenzie, you are a clever piece of work, you are."

MacKenzie touched his arm. "Please, Lovejoy, if we are to be business partners, let us also be friends. You must call me Mac."

"Very well, Mac."

"It's settled, then. Now, the first thing you should know about privateering is that it is a complicated, expensive, and financially risky business."

"Risky? Then why do people do it?"

"For the gain, of course. As for the risk, generally, to avoid a ruinous loss to any one individual, shares are sold in a venture. This is time-consuming, but it spreads the risk among as many as twenty or thirty investors. Already a number of adventurers are actively seeking backers."

"Tell me more about the possible gain."

"The owners of the vessels—in our case, that would be you, Talbot, and myself—we receive half the proceeds from the sale of captured vessels and their cargoes."

"Only half?"

"Yes. The other half is divided among the officers and crew of the privateer. Their half, in turn, may be split into two hundred or more shares, with ordinary seamen getting one share, bosun's mates three, and so on, up to the captain, who receives fifteen shares."

"What about wages for the sailors?"

"While we might pay recruiting fees, no one gets a salary. Their compensation depends entirely on the success of their venture."

As they talked on and on that afternoon, Malcolm MacKenzie was pleased by how quickly Lovejoy grasped the intricate business of putting together a privateering expedition.

Lovejoy, in turn, was impressed by the depth of MacKenzie's business knowledge and his skill at handling difficult people.

Once he understood that he could gain many times the original value of his father's Baltimore debts, he saw that it would be in his best interest to become MacKenzie's ally rather than his adversary.

"So, Lovejoy. We are to be friends and business associates, are we?"

"Yes, Mac."

"Here, then. Give me your hand and the bargain will be sealed. I will write to Captain Martin over the weekend, telling him of our pact."

Lovejoy frowned at this remark.

"Is it necessary for you to tell him everything . . . you know . . . the business with the tavern keeper and jail?"

"I see no reason for going into that, especially if you, as my business partner, ask that I do not."

"And another point. I haven't mentioned this before, but I have my eye on a young lady whose family would not look with favor on a privateer making war on the British."

"These people are Federalists?"

"To the bone."

"And the girl means a lot to you?"

"She is the only girl I have ever thought of marrying."

"Then we will not advertise your interest in our venture. Who is this fortunate young lady?"

"That will remain my secret. So not a word of this to my father or anyone else."

"You have my word of honor."

They found the sidewalk outside clogged by a mob of men listening to a man with a German accent reading from a newspaper.

"What's going on?" Malcolm inquired of a man on the outskirts of the group.

"It's that damned rag of Hanson's. He is asking for tar and feathers, that one is."

"The *Federal-Republican?* What have they written this time?"

"The bastard Tories have come out against the war. They call the president and the Congress who voted for war dictators and despots. They claim that the French are behind the vote. Practically thumbing their noses at us, that's what they are doing."

The man who had been reading the paper was now haranguing the crowd. "Are ve going to stand for this, my fellow citizens?"

"Hell, no," someone yelled.

"Vell, vot are ve going to do about it?"

"We'll burn his building and ride him out of town on a rail."

Malcolm shook his head and, taking Lovejoy's elbow, led him around the mob out onto the street.

"The owners of the *Federal-Republican* have the courage of their convictions, anyway. The two young men who run the paper would do well to temper their opinions. This is not Boston."

"That lot sound like they mean business," Lovejoy said.

"Probably all talk. Anyway, none of this has anything to do with our enterprise."

Or so it seemed to Malcolm MacKenzie at the time. As he strode back toward his chandlery, he was already composing in his head the letter he would write to Jeremiah Martin the next day. He was also planning the welcoming speech he would make on Monday morning when the crews of the contractors were to show up to help Talbot Smith speed the completion of the *Flora.*

As it turned out, the extra workmen did not appear on Monday morning or several days after. He explained why in his report to Jeremiah Martin, which was similarly delayed.

# 12

*24 June, 1812*

*Dear Captain Martin:*

*I meant to report to you several days ago, but news of Congress's declaration of war has created such an uproar here that it has been difficult to find a quiet time in which to gather my thoughts.*

*I am pleased to inform you that your son has arrived safely in Baltimore, accompanied by his young friend Tom Jenkins, and bringing with him your letter of instructions and the various documents having to do with debts owing you in this area.*

*We have been most successful in collecting those debts as you will see upon perusing the accounts sheet I will append to this letter. . . .*

*To make a long story short, we now hold title to what may very well be the finest, fittest topsail schooner ever built here in Baltimore. It took quite a bit of finagling to bring this off, but the end result is that your son now owns an eighty percent interest in a 300-ton sharp-built schooner to be launched as soon as her main deck has been laid and her hull coppered. I am also appending a list of equipment and materials already purchased and a time schedule for stepping the masts, installing the spars and rigging, and various other stages of construction.*

*We hope to have all necessary papers in hand and a crew of about 100 sailors and landsmen recruited in time to clear the port in mid-August.*

*Captain, I understand your reservations and concerns about Lovejoy, but let me tell you in all honesty that I feel he is a young man of much promise. It has not been easy dealing with a lad of such independent spirit in the way you specified in your instructions. And yes, I do see why you regard him as headstrong and perceive in him signs of cupidity and immaturity, but I think he is beginning to understand how much more he has to gain from the course of action you have mapped out for him than if he were simply to be handed the proceeds of our settlements.*

*Lovejoy has a loyal and worthy friend in Tom Jenkins, to whom, incidentally, I am giving employment in my chandlery. As you know, Flora and I have no children. It is a great pleasure having the two lads as guests in our humble home.*

*The uproar to which I referred earlier has to do with the Federal-Republican newspaper, which has been fulminating against President Madison and the war hawks for some time. Last Saturday, the paper responded to the declaration of war with an editorial calling Congress despots and insinuating that they were acting as tools of Napoleon. Many of our rougher sort of German and Irish immigrants spent Sunday drinking beer and listening to firebrand speeches against the newspaper. That night an enormous gang descended on the newspaper's headquarters on Gay Street and proceeded to pull down the walls of the frame building and to wantonly destroy the contents of the office.*

*I am sorry to say that the mayor of Baltimore and others in authority stood idly by and watched this shameless behavior.*

*Not satisfied with this act of vandalism, the ruffians continued their rampage day before yesterday, that is, Tuesday, by going aboard several vessels suspected of carrying British-bound cargoes and severing stays and lines and ripping off bowsprits and spars.*

*I have it on good authority that the owners of at least two of the damaged ships had surreptitiously applied for one of the notorious Sidmouth licenses the British are issuing to Americans willing to haul supplies to their army in Spain. Some might argue that "all's fair in love and trade," but personally, I abhor this dealing with our ancient enemy, although there is no justification for the lawlessness of the mob, which also pulled down the flimsy dwellings of several Negro citizens rumored to favor the British.*

*While I disagree with the editorial stand of the Federal-Republican, I am embarrassed to see this mob violence going unchecked.*

*The situation was calmer today. The owners of the newspaper have taken what they could salvage from the wreckage of their office and have fled to Georgetown, where, it is said, they intend to continue their campaign against the war. With their employees done with rioting, our contractors were able to begin the work on our schooner today. I am sorry to have lost so much valuable time, but there it is.*

*Finally, Captain, I am more grateful to you than I can find words to express for the opportunity you have given me and for the faith you show in placing so grand a fortune and your son's future in my hands.*

*The prospect of financial gain aside, it is like old times to be once more allied with you in a patriotic adventure in the cause of American freedom. You were a stalwart in our War of Independence with the British, and in your own way, I feel that you once more are demonstrating your devotion to our beloved Republic through this enterprise whose execution you have entrusted to your obedient servant, who hopes that this letter will find you in better health, and who looks forward to your reply and further instructions.*

*Respectfully, your obedient servant,*
*Malcolm MacKenzie*

Lovejoy had never experienced as hectic and exciting a time as he did during the next five weeks, astride his hired horse, carrying messages from Malcolm MacKenzie to this supplier and that, skillfully negotiating prices and delivery dates for provisions and equipment on his own.

Malcolm assumed the official role of "ship's husband" for the complicated enterprise. Leaving Tom to help his longtime assistant run his chandlery, he moved his headquarters out to a small shed at the shipyard, where he spent much of his time settling disputes between a demanding Talbot Smith and the contractors they had engaged to speed up work on the *Flora.* Still, the job proceeded at a rapid rate. Dozens of skilled shipwrights and riggers swarmed over what Lovejoy had first seen as a bare hull, looking much like a beached whale, until, by mid-July, now riding in the water at Smith's wharf, she began to resemble a graceful racehorse of the seas.

As word spread of the remarkable schooner taking shape at Talbot Smith's little shipyard, many prominent Baltimoreans drove out in fine carriages to see for themselves and, having seen, to offer to buy shares in the *Flora's* first cruise.

Malcolm rejected these entreaties with careful courtesy, until one disappointed would-be investor questioned his judgment in selecting "a whoreson who cohabits with a nigger woman" as his captain.

Malcolm lashed back: "Who gives you the right to criticize? Who do you think created that beautiful schooner you see over there? Besides being the best shipbuilder you will ever meet, Talbot Smith has forgotten more about sailing than many of your fancy, social-climbing captains ever knew."

"Well now, MacKenzie, I only meant to make you consider the risk you are running. And I am not alone in my opinion that you are making a huge mistake. There are other schooners in harbor already built, and they are being transformed rapidly into privateers to be captained by respectable men of proven talent."

"Last year, when I was in desperate straits, you and your friends took no thought for my welfare. Well, sir, I have no respect for the opinion of opportunists like you."

"I came out here in a spirit of friendship. You should thank me for my advice."

"I will thank you only to remove yourself from this property forthwith."

As the man drove away, Talbot Smith put his head in the open window of the shed.

"They say a eavesdropper never hears nothing good said of hisself."

"You heard?"

"Aye, part of it anyway. Look, Mr. MacKenzie, I can't help who my mother was. As for Josie, ye know I bought her at auction out of pity and set her free. Fellow bidding against me wanted her for his whorehouse in Richmond. She begged to stay with me, maybe out of gratitude, maybe because she had no place else to go. I don't know. Anyway, we suit each other, and I don't see what business that is of anybody else."

Embarrassed by the shipbuilder's show of emotion, Malcolm said, simply, "I wish you had not heard."

"That is all right. If there's somebody that you'd rather hire, I reckon I could settle for first mate or sailing master."

"No. My mind is made up."

"Well, I am grateful. Now what about this Martin lad? What will Young Mister High and Mighty do after we finish the *Flora?*"

"Have you any ideas on that score?"

"Did I hear it right that the fellow studied to be a doctor in England?"

"Yes, but he did not complete his studies."

"He had to of learned something. And surgeons is hard to come by. I can tell he ain't one to get his hands dirty like ordinary folks, but maybe he wouldn't mind getting them bloody."

"I don't think Lovejoy wants to go to sea."

"How do you know if you don't ask him?"

"For the moment, let's not do that. Now, when will the spars be in place so we can get our fine schooner properly rigged?"

After long days full of activity, Malcolm and Lovejoy sat up late each night, going over the mass of papers that now littered the MacKenzie dining room table. With the help of a lawyer in Washington and the collector of the port of Baltimore, they had obtained their letter of marque and reprisal, signed by Secretary of State James Monroe, within a month after the declaration of war. They also received official instructions setting forth rules of conduct.

Malcolm guided Lovejoy through the tedious business of posting various surety bonds and obtaining a commission from the port collector for a ninety-day cruise.

In response to Lovejoy's complaint of so much red tape, Malcolm replied, "Without all these legalities, we would be regarded as pirates subject to hanging, and not licensed privateers. Believe me, it is well worth all the bother."

Together they went over the Articles of Agreement that members of the crew would be required to sign before the *Flora* sailed. This set forth the rules under which the schooner would operate and specified how half of the proceeds from each British vessel would be divided among the officers and crew.

"This calls for a crew of a hundred. How can we recruit so many in so short a time?" Lovejoy asked.

"That is the next order of business. Here, read this notice that appears in today's edition of the *American Patriot.*"

He handed Lovejoy a newspaper.

> *An Invitation to any brave, experienced seamen and patriotic landsmen desirous of making their fortunes in the service of their homeland:*
>
> *Come join the ship's company of a splendid privateer schooner, the FLORA, now in the final stages of construction by the master shipbuilder TALBOT SMITH, who also will serve as captain of the vessel. The FLORA will depart the port of Baltimore during the first week of August for a*

*90-day cruise against the shipping of our British enemy. Here is your opportunity to share in the proceeds of this well-financed venture and to help your nation right the wrongs we have suffered at the hands of the arrogant enemy. Come to our recruiting rendezvous to be held Saturday next at the Blue Eagle Tavern, Fells Point, where I have agreed to serve as recruiter for this cruise. Free grog is offered.*

*Those signing on will be paid five dollars each as a recruiting fee.*

*—Billie Matson, Recruiting Agent.*

Lovejoy frowned at the sight of Matson's name. "Why, that is the fellow with whom I had that bit of trouble."

"Quite so. He is a popular publican. He'll make us a grand recruiter. I've promised him a dollar for every man he signs up."

The recruiting rendezvous at Billie Matson's Blue Eagle did not take place on July 28 as announced in the *Patriot.* As Malcolm explained in his next report to Jeremiah Martin, the *Federal-Republican* newspaper once again caused a delay in their plans.

# 14

*July 30, 1812*

*Dear Captain Martin:*

*I am remiss in waiting so long to reply to your letter of July 10 in which you inquire about your son and about the progress of our venture. I trust when I explain how busy we have been and tell you of the fresh turmoil that has engulfed our fair city that you will understand and forgive our dilatoriness.*

*It had been my ardent wish to be able to report to you that we have recruited a full roster of officers and crew, but we were forced to postpone our recruiting rendezvous that was planned for day before yesterday. It pains me to tell you, Captain, that Baltimore has been convulsed these past few days by the most shocking mob violence you could imagine, worse, I should think, than that which took place during the French Revolution.*

*In my previous letter, I told you of the vandalism occasioned by publication of inflammatory sentiments against the war by the Federal-Republican. And I mentioned that the owners had removed themselves to Georgetown. Well, sir, not only have they stepped up their attacks on the war, they were foolhardy enough to move back to Baltimore and reestablish an office on Charles Street, this time in a brick building with walls too sturdy to be pulled down.*

*I enclose a clipping from their first issue printed back here in Baltimore so that you can see for yourself the editorial the effect of which was like tossing a lighted match into a powder magazine. As you can read for yourself, in the name of freedom of the press, the piece fairly dared the mobs to attempt to repeat their performance of last month.*

*The evening after this appeared, a gang of ruffians—many of them foreign born—marched upon the building and hurled stones at it until not only the glass in the windows but also the sashes and blinds had been broken. The defiant Federalists, however, had turned the house into a fortress. Upon the mob's refusal to disperse, they fired a volley over their heads, with the result that the ruffians went home and returned with their own firearms. A physician of the neighborhood, a well-known hothead, led the now-armed mob into a fresh assault and was shot dead for his pains. Things settled down to a siege, during which the numbers of the bloodthirsty crowd increased throughout the night. A small troop of mounted militia arrived to reason with the leaders, without success, and then entered the house to try to persuade the Federalists to leave under their protection. The mob wheeled a field piece up and threatened to open fire against the building.*

*I did not know it at the time, but one of the occupants of the offices was General Light-Horse Harry Lee, in town to see to the publication of his memoirs of his heroic Revolutionary War service.*

*By daylight, the size of the mob was reckoned at some two thousand, all crying for the blood of the Federalists, who finally agreed to accept the militia's offer to escort them to the jail, where presumably they could be better protected against the blood lust of the mob.*

*Ah, Captain, I am embarrassed to report what happened thereafter. It will go down as a black chapter in the history not only of Baltimore but also of our Republic.*

*First the mob burst into the now-empty newspaper office and utterly devastated the interior and its contents. That afternoon, the* Whig *came out with an editorial expressing the wish that the mob had put the defenders of the building to death. I enclose a copy of that piece of demagoguery.*

*And then in the evening, a fresh mob marched upon the jail, forced its way therein, and proceeded to beat and torture the Federalists for the next three hours brutally and without mercy. Although only one man was killed, several others were grievously injured and left in a gruesome heap outside the jail door. I was told by a Republican doctor who persuaded the mob to allow him and some fellow physicians to carry the riot victims back into the jail for treatment that General Lee's face and head were so mutilated as to render him unrecognizable and to leave in doubt his ever recovering from his nightmarish experience.*

*And throughout the two days of anarchy, the mayor, the sheriff, and officers of the militia lifted not a finger to suppress the mob.*

*Well, sir, you will undoubtedly read of this shameful business in the Philadelphia papers soon enough.*

*As to our venture, first let me report that Lovejoy has entered into the spirit of the enterprise with zeal and is proving a useful assistant. He has a shrewd knack for handling people. I am pleased by his progress. However, it took all my power of persuasion to keep him and Tom at home during the recent appalling violence, such was their curiosity to witness the events.*

*You have inquired as to the possibility of his sailing with the Flora. Lovejoy is no fool. He understands that once the Flora sails, all he has to do to reap the benefits of her cruise is to sit tight and wait. The relationship between us is going so smoothly now that I am reluctant to approach the subject just yet.*

*Will close and prepare for our rendezvous to be held tomorrow afternoon. Will report to you on the results in a few days.*

*Your respectful servant and old shipmate,*
*Malcolm MacKenzie*

"You want me to do what?"

"I merely inquired if you might be interested in shipping out with the *Flora.*"

"Why would I want to do a stupid thing like that?"

"Keep your voice down, please. You don't want those fine, patriotic lads to hear you."

Malcolm inclined his head toward the group of farm boys being interviewed by Talbot Smith and Billie Matson at the other end of the common room of the Blue Eagle.

"Well, it makes no sense for me to sign up. I have a lot of English friends. I don't hate them. And I told you about that girl from Reading. If I went off on a privateer, it would cook my goose with her family. For me, this is a behind-the-scenes business venture, pure and simple. Besides, I am subject to seasickness."

"You could tell your grandchildren how you went to sea to protect American freedom, as your father did before you."

Tom Jenkins had been sitting quietly at the table in the Blue Eagle Tavern during this conversation. Malcolm turned to him and said, "How about you, Tom? Wouldn't you like to go to sea?"

"I was just thinking about that. But I don't know what I would be good for. I know nothing of sailing."

"You don't need to know anything. Captain Smith requires at least thirty or thirty-five landsmen for boarding parties and to assist the gunner's mate. And you'd be entitled to a full share of the prize money, same as an ordinary seaman."

"I'd be willing if Joy would."

"If you want to get yourself killed, go ahead," Lovejoy said. "Now, Mac, I don't want to talk about this anymore. How many men has our fine feathered publican signed up?"

"I make it sixty so far. We'd have more if Talbot weren't so particular about his requirements. I am well satisfied with his officers, however. His first mate is a good steady fellow of high moral character, and he is backed up by a superb sailing master."

He looked across the room to make sure that Smith was not listening and then said, in a lower voice, "I selected those last two myself. Chose them carefully to make up for what some might see as deficiencies in our captain. The first mate is a stalwart fellow of about thirty, a good family man and a Methodist lay preacher. Being a Presbyterian, I don't see eye to eye with him on the question of free grace, but he is a patient man with calm, easy manners to offset those of Talbot."

"Is that him standing by the door?"

Lovejoy pointed to a square-built chap with a strong chin and mild eyes.

"It is. His name is Phipps. And the slender, gray-haired fellow sitting over there is to be our sailing master. He is Pierre Barineau. He has been teaching school these past ten or twelve years up in Dover, Delaware, but I persuaded him to return to the sea to practice his avocation, which is the study of navigation, for which he has a genius. Furthermore, he is an ardent Republican and he absolutely detests the British."

"And what are his theological proclivities?" Lovejoy asked.

Ignoring the sarcasm, MacKenzie replied, "Barineau is what you might call a rationalist or Deist. His father was a Huguenot, from France. Pierre is a great admirer of our former president Jefferson. Wonderful conversationalist. Great reader of books, including the Bible, though he professes to believe little of it."

"I am glad to know there will be a gentleman of intellectual bent aboard so our learned captain will have someone to converse with," Lovejoy said. "So you're satisfied with your officers?"

"You mean 'our' officers. Actually, I'd prefer that a couple of our prize masters had more seagoing experience. The curly-haired young chap sitting with Barineau has the potential to be a captain, but he needs seasoning. Name's Collins. He and the other prize masters are all bright, willing fellows."

"Who is the tall fellow with the hawk nose and the scar across his face? Looks like a pirate."

"He is to be our gunner's mate. His name is Gandy. He's from Boston. A friend of Talbot's. He hates the British, by the way. As a lad, he spent more than a year in one of their prison hulks back during the Revolution. Knows all there is to know about gunnery."

MacKenzie bent across the table to whisper, "By the way, did I mention that the surgeon aboard a privateer normally receives eight shares, the same as a sailing master or first mate?"

"Hear that, Joy?" Tom said. "He's offering you eight times what I would get."

"Being a surgeon on land or sea is the last thing to appeal to me. I don't like the sight of blood."

"Then there is the position of supercargo. You have demonstrated a knack for business, Lovejoy. That would be useful to Captain Smith. You would see to the details of disposing of prizes in other ports, buying supplies, doing all sorts of things so the captain can keep his attention on handling the ship and its crew. A supercargo receives four shares."

"I don't give a damn if I were to receive the same shares as our miserable little captain. Nothing or nobody can induce me to serve aboard that ship, even if we had a more agreeable master. Now can we drop the subject? When will she be ready to sail?"

"Talbot says three weeks. I say two. The rigging will go quickly. Yes sir, just look at those green young lads over there. They are signing up for the greatest adventure of their lives."

"Yes, in three weeks they will be green with seasickness, leaning over the rail and puking their guts out into the ocean."

Malcolm continued as if he had not heard. "I was just such a lad in seventy-nine when your father recruited me. What a dull life I might have led if I had not swallowed my fears and stepped forward when he advertised for patriotic young men."

"You have told me that story before."

"I haven't heard it," Tom said. "How old were you?"

That night, Lovejoy wrote a letter to Madeline Richter, in which he apologized for not writing sooner. He explained that he had been in Baltimore attending to some business matters on behalf of his father when news of "this dreadful war" had arrived and that this had led to "some time-consuming difficulties." He added that he expected to complete his business mission in a few weeks, after which would it be too much to hope that he might be allowed to come calling on the Richter family?

He also lamented that the outbreak of the war meant that he could not realize his dream of returning to London to complete his medical education. Finally he said that he looked forward to seeing her mother again and to meeting her father.

It was not the letter he wanted to write, but he did not want to overplay his hand so early in what he expected to be a long process of courting. A reply came in two weeks, just as the *Flora* was ready to sail.

*Dear Mr. Martin,*

*What a stilted letter you have written. Are you the same bold fellow who gave me such a lusty kiss that last night aboard ship?*

*Anyway, I have not passed a single hour since we returned home without thinking of you.*

*You ask ever so politely if you might be allowed to pay us a visit. Mama is inclined to say no. She doesn't quite trust you. But Papa, who is a terrible Dutchman, takes a practical view and sees nothing wrong with having you out so as—in his words—to take a good look at the fellow. As for my own wish, it is a hearty yes. I can hardly wait to see you again.*

*We were thinking of the first week of September. Would that suit you? Please write and say yes.*

*Papa has been reading the news about the terrible riots in Baltimore. He is hoping to hear firsthand accounts from "that fellow you met on the ship." And I am dying to hear all about this mysterious business in which you have been engaged. But mostly I just want to see you again.*

*I count the hours until you reply.*

*Fondly,*
*Madeline*

Lovejoy received this letter near noon. He had had time to read it only once before Malcolm hauled him and Tom out to Talbot Smith's wharf, where a crowd of a hundred men and boys stood about with ditty bags over their shoulders, waiting for the shipbuilder to make the customary captain's speech to a new crew.

Perhaps half of the men were wearing wide canvas trousers and other seafaring garb. A large number of the others were dressed in the common clothing of farm boys. At least a dozen of the newly recruited crew of the *Flora* were black.

Smith, himself, wore a brand new woolen captain's suit and a billed cap with gold braid.

Malcolm began the ceremony by praising the company for signing on for the cruise. He restated the general terms of their Articles of Agreement and concluded with, "There is not a better cause to be served than ours, which is to protect American freedom on the seas just as your fathers and grandfathers fought to secure it here on our own soil. There isn't a better vessel in the United States of America than the one waiting here to receive you. And I don't think there is a better sailor than the man who built this extraordinary craft and who has assumed her command. Gentlemen, I introduce to you Captain Talbot Smith, whom I now invite to say a few words."

Lovejoy could tell that Talbot was nervous from the way he was sweating and his hands were trembling. He began in a rasping voice that was barely audible to the men on the edge of the crowd.

"Just look at that schooner there." He pointed to the *Flora* standing at the end of the wharf like a racehorse eager to burst from its starting gate. "I have built many a schooner these past twelve years. There rides the biggest and the best of them. Her hold is full of provisions and ammunition. She carries two Long Tom guns and ten carronades. She's got a full suit of spare sails. All we need is men equal to what I have created."

He paused, with tears in his eyes, and tried without success to clear his throat. “What I want to say . . .” Again he choked up.

The recruits looked awkwardly at each other, waiting for him to resume. Finally, he turned with twisted face to Malcolm, saying, “I’m no good at making speeches.”

Seeing Talbot’s obvious distress and the puzzled looks on the faces of the recruits, Lovejoy seized the shipbuilder’s calloused hand and whispered, “You want me to do this for you?”

At Talbot’s embarrassed nod, he turned to face the recruits.

“Gentlemen,” he began in a loud, clear voice, “you have heard what your captain has said about his ship.”

“It ain’t a ship. It’s a schooner,” one of the older sailors called out.

“Exactly so. It is a schooner,” Lovejoy continued. “And, as Captain Smith has noted, it is one of the best ever built. I can see that we have recruited the best possible crew for the best possible ship . . . I mean schooner. Now let’s see a show of hands of those who have never been to sea.”

He paused to look into the faces of the two score of those with raised hands.

“I have never gone to sea as a sailor, but I have twice crossed the Atlantic between Philadelphia and England, and let me tell you, there is a freedom out there on the bounding main like you would never experience staying at home and following a plow. Yes, you are in for the adventure of your lives. Although I am, like many of you, a landsman, the sea is in my blood. My father took no less than three privateers to sea during our revolution against the perfidious English. He named me for one of his loyal lieutenants who sacrificed his life to save that of my father and others, is that not right, Mr. MacKenzie?”

“Indeed it is. Mine was one of the lives he saved,” Malcolm cried out.

“Then why don’t you come with us?” a sailor shouted.

“I would do so in an instant, but as chief owner I must remain in port to arrange for speedy distribution of your prize monies. Now, speaking of those monies, both your captain and my co-owner, Mr. MacKenzie, are veterans at this game of privateering and they tell me that besides providing you with excitement and adventure it can be a financially rewarding enterprise. So, how about it, lads? Are you ready to make your fortunes?”

This drew a cheer from the crew.

"Are you ready to teach the arrogant British that they can't trample on American rights and get away with it?"

Again the men cheered.

Later, Lovejoy realized that he had got carried away by his own eloquence and wished that he had not said some of the things he had said. He wound up his speech with, "Now lads, Captain Smith wishes you to go aboard this beautiful schooner . . . notice I got it right that time . . . that you go aboard and stow your gear. Then I invite you all to join me at the Blue Eagle for a round of grog and a bit of entertainment."

"What the hell are you doing?" Talbot growled.

"I just want them to sail with some happy memories."

"I hope you know what you are doing."

Soon the Blue Eagle was thronged with the sailors and landsmen. Somewhat like Evan Jenkins's wedding celebration, the party grew increasingly rowdy. When Billie Matson was not serving grog and fending off fights between the crewmen, he was accepting guardianship of prize tickets entrusted to his safekeeping.

Disapproving of the party, Malcolm had taken himself off to his Flo, after making a date with Lovejoy to meet him on the wharf at sunrise to watch their schooner cast off.

Talbot Smith reluctantly showed up at the Blue Eagle and took a corner seat, from which he scowled at the merrymakers.

Lovejoy could not bring himself to like the shipbuilder, but the man looked so lonely sitting by himself that Lovejoy asked if he could join him.

"Suit yourself."

"Don't you want a drink?"

"I don't touch the stuff."

"Why did you come, then?"

"Two reasons. One, I want to make sure they all get back to the wharf in time to catch a little sleep. Hangover or no hangover, drunk or sober, we sail at dawn."

"What's your second reason?"

"I'm sizing up this lot. You can tell a lot about a man when he is in his cups. So don't worry about me. I ain't wasting my time. And come eleven o'clock, Billie and me is closing this place down and hauling everybody back to the wharf."

Having sat down with Smith, Lovejoy could think of nothing else to say to him. He thought that Smith might thank him for taking over his speaking chores, but the shipbuilder simply sat glowering while everyone else enjoyed themselves.

Lovejoy was grateful to Tom for approaching them.

"I wish you was going with us, Joy."

"What do you mean, 'us'?"

"I didn't want to tell you before, but I took Mr. MacKenzie's advice two weeks ago and signed on as a marine. Ain't that right, Mr. Smith?"

"It is Captain Smith, and yes, you are signed up with us."

"Well, that is about the dumbest thing I can think of. What made you do a fool thing like that?"

"I ain't had your opportunities. Things don't get laid in my lap the way they do yours. If I turn this down, I'm likely to hate myself for the rest of my life. With all the money and good education you have, there will be other chances for you. But still, I wish you was coming too."

"What about your pa? I told him I would look after you."

"I wrote to the family telling them I was going. Told them you would be coming too."

"You told them a lie."

"I know, but I figured they'd feel better if they thought we'd be together."

In spite of himself, Lovejoy was touched by Tom's words.

"I hope you don't live to regret it."

Up to that point, Lovejoy had been drinking Billie Matson's grog as a way of celebrating his and Malcolm's success at organizing their venture and of expressing his relief that the long weeks of wearisome activity would soon be over for him. After Tom's revelation, he continued to drink, only now he did so in a spirit of sadness. He dreaded the loneliness he would feel without his friend.

Lovejoy would not remember very much about the rest of the evening. He had a dim recollection of seeing Billie Matson and Talbot Smith conferring in a corner and looking across the room at him. Soon thereafter, he stopped the tavern keeper and purchased a bottle of Jamaican rum, which he shared with Tom. He vaguely recalled upbraiding Talbot Smith and Billie Matson for signing up Tom for the cruise and then challenging Billie to a fight when the tavern keeper refused to tear up the enlistment.

He remembered neither the insulting remarks he made to Talbot Smith, Billie Matson, and Tom, nor finishing off the bottle and demanding and getting a second one.

When eleven o'clock came and Billie ordered all the ship's company to clear out and return to the *Flora,* both Lovejoy and Tom had passed out with their heads on a table.

# PART TWO

# 1 

As a small boy back in Philadelphia, Lovejoy, ill with a fever for several days, had drifted in and out of a delirium in which it seemed that his bed swiveled about while his mother and Amanda stood by whispering.

Now they were back again, speaking in low, gruff voices around his rising and falling bed.

"He's not going to die, is he?"

"Of course not."

Lovejoy groaned. He opened his eyes but could not see in the faint light.

"There ought to be something we can do."

"Now that you're sober yourself, you can go topside with the others. We didn't sign you on to serve as a nursemaid. All right, men, you take his head. You and you each take one arm. Haul him topside."

Lovejoy moaned as rough hands lifted him from his pallet and dragged him up a narrow ladder. Sunlight penetrated his closed eyelids. Dumped on a hard surface, he lay with his hands over his eyes. Now he heard voices and laughter, and the groan of timbers and the slapping of canvas.

"Look there, men," a voice called out. "That is what happens when you drink too much."

Lovejoy drew himself up into a sitting position. Why had the floor become so unsteady? He started to speak, but then his stomach erupted, and he was spewing its foul contents onto the deck of the *Flora.* Once and then twice he vomited. The third time, the sky went black and he collapsed into unconsciousness.

He came to with a shock, sputtering and spitting as seawater was drenched over him from canvas buckets. And again he heard that mocking laughter.

He sat up and opened his eyes. Talbot Smith, hands on his hips, looked down at him without a trace of sympathy on his face. Behind Talbot, a circle of crewmen stood about laughing.

Lovejoy opened his mouth to speak just as another bucket of the Chesapeake's briny water cascaded over his head.

Infuriated, he struggled to his feet, seizing a stay line to keep from falling.

"How dare you? What am I doing on this ship?"

Talbot Smith laughed. "Hear that, lads? He wants to know what he is doing aboard this ship. First off, I'll have ye keelhauled if I hear you call her a ship again. She is a schooner. And you have signed up with your friend here as a landsman."

"I never."

"I have the paper, signed by yourself and witnessed by yer friend Jenkins, here, and Billie Matson."

"Is that right, Tom?" Lovejoy said.

"They called you a coward and you said you weren't, and they dared you to prove it by signing on with me."

"Enough of this chitchat," Talbot said. "Now that ye've come to, I am putting you in the charge of our gunner's mate. He will instruct you and the other landsmen."

"You aren't putting me in anybody's charge. I own this ship . . . I mean schooner."

"Hear that, lads? He is right. But he ain't captain. I am, and I can put him or anybody else in whoever's charge I want."

"You are fired."

"Look, ye spoiled rich man's son, you nor nobody else can fire me until our ninety-day cruise is over and we have returned to port. Until then, my word is law. You have signed on for this here cruise and you will follow my orders."

"I refuse."

"Oh, you refuse, do you? In the old days I would have had you stripped to the waist and flogged. But the times have changed. So all I have to say is that if you don't work on my schooner, you don't eat."

"I am not hungry. Now cut out this charade and put me ashore."

"You will get hungry in time. Until then, say nothing or do nothing to interfere with the operation of this here vessel."

"You can go to hell, you miserable little guttersnipe. I don't know what Malcolm MacKenzie was thinking when he picked you for captain. You don't even know how to address a crowd."

"Joy, careful what you say," Tom muttered.

Talbot's face darkened. For a moment, it appeared that he would strike Lovejoy. Instead, he roared for the bosun's mate to "bind his arms and gag him."

Lovejoy was too weak to resist. With his hands tied behind his back and a rag stuffed in his mouth, he was bound with a rope around the waist to the *Flora's* forward mast.

"All right, men, you see what happens to anybody that refuses an order. Nobody is to speak to this fellow or give him aught to eat or drink without my permission. Now get back to work."

Lovejoy remained tied to the mast throughout the rest of the day, while the other men went through their training drills. He managed to sleep through part of the night as the *Flora* coursed down the Chesapeake under shortened sail. He watched the sun come up over the port rail, and by the time the crew lined up for breakfast, his appetite had returned, along with a great thirst. But no one offered him anything.

They left him there while Tom and the other greenhorns clumsily ran through their gunnery drills. The gunner's mate, the tall, beak-nosed New Englander named Gandy, walked them through the commands: "Cast loose your gun . . . Run in your gun . . . Search the piece . . . Load with cartridge . . . Load with shot . . . Prick and prime . . . Elevate . . ."

Gandy repeated this exercise three times, going through the motions required to load, aim, and fire the stubby carronades.

"Now, lads, we'll try it with live ammunition. Remember what I told you about covering your ears."

"Fire!" he shouted, and applied a lighted linstock to the vent hole of the cannon.

Unable to put his hands over his ears like the gun crew, Lovejoy thought that his head would burst at the explosion just a few feet from where he sat. The cloud of acrid white smoke burnt his nostrils.

Talbot came around later that morning with the bosun's mate, who removed the gag from Lovejoy's mouth.

"Are you ready to assume your duties as a landsman?"

"Go to hell, Smith."

"If that's the way you want it, fine. Give him a cup of water. Leave the gag off as long as he keeps his mouth shut. Just make sure no one speaks to him."

While Lovejoy remained tied to the mast throughout the day, Talbot put his crew through one drill after another. He had the experienced seamen demonstrate to the greenhorns how to raise and lower the *Flora's* sails and shift her booms. The bosun's mate conducted a school in knot tying. The landsmen learned how to use grappling hooks to board other vessels and how to raise cargo nets to repel boarders.

The stage fright that had frozen the shipbuilder's voice on the wharf the previous day was gone. Being on the water and in command of his own vessel transformed him. Like a self-confident bantam rooster, he strode from one end of the schooner to the other making sure that every man was either learning or teaching the many skills that went into operating a privateer.

In spite of his distaste for the little man, Lovejoy was impressed by Smith's knowledge. There was nothing he seemed not to know better even than the veteran sailors on his crew.

By nightfall, the *Flora* was skimming briskly south past Smith Island.

The captain approached him again with the bosun's mate in tow.

"Well, sir, Mr. Martin, have you changed your mind about going to work as you agreed to do in your enlistment?"

"If you weren't so ignorant, Smith, you would know that an agreement signed under duress is not valid. I was intoxicated when I signed that paper. I see we are passing an island over there. If you don't pull in and let me off, you will face dire consequences."

Smith snorted. "Ha. If I let off everybody that signed on while drunk, I wouldn't have much of a crew. As for dire consequences, you keep up your impudent talk and I'll have you gagged again. Now, do you want to eat or don't you?"

In spite of his bravado, Lovejoy dreaded the gag. And he was hungry. He accepted the cup of water from the bosun's mate but refused to ask to be released.

That night, with the *Flora* sailing with shortened sail before a light breeze, he drifted in and out of sleep.

"Lovejoy."

It was Tom, whispering.

"Here, I brought you something."

Lovejoy gulped down Tom's cornmeal cake.

"How long are you going to keep this up, Joy?"

"Until that little son of a bitch comes to his senses and lets me go ashore."

"This time tomorrow we will be at sea. It will be too late."

"I don't give a damn. Have you got anything else to eat?"

"Here's an apple. Wait. I'll cut it up for you."

Tom was stuffing a quarter of the apple in Lovejoy's mouth when the rays of a lantern fell on the pair.

"What the hell is going on here?"

Talbot Smith stood before them in his underwear.

"I gave orders nobody was to speak to this fellow. Ah, so it's you is it, Jenkins? And you've been feeding him, have you. All right, my lad, you asked for it. I'm having you tied to the mast as well, and neither one of you will get a bite to eat until both of you is willing to take his place in our crew."

"But I am willing," Tom said.

"No matter. You both stay here without food until your friend agrees to do his duty."

When Smith was gone, Tom, tied to the mast with Lovejoy, spoke. "Well, Joy, you have got us in a fine fix once more."

"I didn't ask you to sneak up here and feed me."

"That's a hell of a way to thank me for doing a favor."

"I'm sorry, Tom. But you're not telling me to knuckle under, are you?"

"Would it do any good if I did?"

"I think he'll give in and let me go. He knows that if he doesn't I'll never let him sail my schooner on another cruise."

They were silent for a long while. Lovejoy had nearly fallen asleep when Tom spoke again.

"You want to know what your trouble is, Joy?"

"Not really, but I guess you're going to tell me anyway."

"You got too much pride. You set yourself against your father when all he wanted to do was to help you, but you resisted him. Then you resisted Mr. MacKenzie when he was trying to make you a rich man. Pa used to ask me how come I couldn't be as smart as you. If you're so smart, how come we spent the worst week I ever lived through in jail, and how come we are tied up here like a pair of turkeys headed to market?"

Taken aback by the bitterness of the words, Lovejoy said, "Why Tom, I thought we were friends."

"You are my best friend. But with you around, I sure as hell don't need any enemies."

"That is a miserable thing to say."

"What's more, you are your own worst enemy as well."

"Why does everyone keep telling me that?"

"Maybe it's because it is the truth, you bastard."

Having got his feelings off his chest, Tom drifted off to sleep, leaving Lovejoy to brood over his words.

He had assumed that Smith would relent when they reached the mouth of the Chesapeake and allow him to go ashore. He did not believe that the man would take the majority owner of his vessel to sea against his will. But late the next afternoon, when the *Flora* passed the Virginia Capes and spray from the Atlantic was spattering her rising and falling deck, he realized that he had underestimated the captain.

A fresh wave of remorse struck him when he thought of the letter he had just received from Madeline Richter. It remained in his hip pocket, unanswered and, for the time, unanswerable.

By now he had become so hungry that he could have chewed on his leather belt. The smell of the food being ladled out from the cook's galley in the bow nearly overcame him. But still the captain was offering him and Tom only cups of water.

"Joy, I am starving. Why can't you for once swallow your pride and apologize? Life aboard ship ain't so bad."

"Never."

"But we could die."

"Yes, we could. And Smith knows that. What would happen if he went back to Baltimore and reported that he had starved two men to death, one of them being his ship's owner?"

"That thought brings me very little satisfaction."

Lovejoy went to sleep wondering whether Talbot Smith really was willing to let him starve to death. And the captain lay awake for a long while wondering whether he could break the young man's will by denying him food or if he would have to find some other way. Of one thing he was certain: he did not intend to lose this contest.

# 2

At first, Lovejoy thought he was hallucinating. Well out in the Atlantic on a schooner with only men aboard, how could he possibly be hearing the sound of a woman's voice?

"Tom? Lovejoy?"

The *Flora* was sailing south under a cloudy night sky. Except for Tom and himself, no one was supposed to be on deck, other than the helmsman and a lookout in the bow. He strained his eyes trying to see through the darkness.

"Who's there?"

"It's me. Meg."

Feeling certain now that he was suffering another delirium, he closed his eyes.

The voice whispered again, closer this time.

"I heard them talking about how they are treating you. So I sneaked up to give you something to eat. Here."

Even when a fragment of stale biscuit was slid into his mouth, Lovejoy still thought he was hallucinating.

Tom suddenly was awake, too. "What's going on?"

Lovejoy's mouth was too full. But there was the voice again, saying, "Keep quiet. It's me, your sister, Meg. I've brought you some biscuits. Here."

Lovejoy choked down his piece of biscuit. "Somebody is playing a trick on us, Tom."

"Don't be stupid. It really is me."

Lovejoy shook his head to clear his thoughts. "All right, if you are Meg, what is your mother's name?"

"She's dead. Her name was Naomi Evans."

Tom caught on to the game. "How about your stepmother?"

The voice practically spit out, "Primrose Hanrahan, you idiot. She is why I am here."

"But what are you doing here?"

"I couldn't take any more of trying to live under the same roof with that woman. We got your letter, Tom, about you and Lovejoy getting ready to go out on this ship, and I packed up a bag and took my savings and bought a stage ticket for Baltimore."

"How did you get aboard?"

"I bought a cap and some other sailor's garb, got my hair cut off short, and asked questions until I heard about this ship. I slipped aboard while everyone was gone the night before you sailed. I brought along a sack full of biscuits and fruit and found a place to hide in a locker downstairs."

"My God, Meg, you shouldn't have. Keep your voice down."

"What difference does it make now? We are at sea. They can't send me back. From the complaints I hear, they could use a cook."

Lovejoy wished that his head were clearer.

"No, don't let them know you are aboard. Not yet."

"What's going on out there?"

Talbot Smith's voice called from the aft hatch, which led down to his cabin.

"My friend and I were just talking," Lovejoy replied.

"Well knock it off or I will have you both gagged."

"Listen, Meg," Lovejoy whispered after Smith had returned to his cabin, "you must trust me. Slip back to your locker and stay there until we can work out something."

"I don't think I can stand much more of that place. All those men snoring and saying vulgar things. I hear it all. I didn't know men could be such pigs."

"It won't be much longer. Wait, do you have more biscuits?"

She went as quietly as she had come.

"Mama would come back and haunt me if I let anything happen to Meggie. Oh my God, why did she do such a thing?"

"Don't ask me. I suppose she wanted to be with her big brother. My God, Tom, are you crying?"

"What if I am? I feel so helpless."

"Well, you're acting like a baby."

"If you are so damned smart, figure out what we should do."

"If you will quit blubbering, maybe I could. Right now I want to enjoy this biscuit and do some hard thinking."

The next morning, Talbot Smith went through his ritual of inquiring whether Lovejoy was ready to apologize and take his place in the crew of the *Flora*.

"I would like to discuss the matter with you, Captain."

"There is nothing to discuss. Either you accept my authority and follow my commands or you can stay here tied to this mast until you and your friend rot."

"First let me apologize for my rude behavior. I should not have spoken to you as I did in front of your crew. I have spent much time watching your skillful direction of this vessel and reflecting on how fortunate Malcolm MacKenzie and I are to have so talented a sailor in command. I hope that you will forgive me."

Smith pondered his words, looking first satisfied and then suspicious.

"You have a slick way with words. If this is a trick, I'll have you flogged and then tied right back to this here mast."

Lovejoy and Tom had difficulty standing, but they savored their freedom. Smith ushered them, with their wrists still bound, across the deck and down the hatch into his cabin.

Compared with the unpartitioned hold in which the *Flora's* hundred crewmen slept, close packed in hammocks and on pallets, the cabin was a place of luxury, with a desk under the stern portholes, a comfortable bed in a curtained alcove on one side and a table with chairs on the other. It was reached via an only slightly larger officers' compartment that had four double bunks, two on each side and two flanking the passageway to the captain's cabin.

"Speak your piece," Smith said.

"When Malcolm MacKenzie first broached the subject of my sailing with the *Flora*, he offered me the post of surgeon. Said I would receive eight shares and sleep with the officers."

"Aye, and he said you turned him down flat."

"Do you have a surgeon?"

"I couldn't find one who was any more qualified than myself, but we laid in all the medicine and tools any surgeon would require. Even brought along some medical books."

"What about your supercargo?"

"Barineau is a educated man. With his help, I can handle that, too. What is the purpose of all these questions?"

"Would you be willing to accept me as your surgeon?"

"You have already signed on as a marine, for one share."

"I am willing to accept a single share. Now, as to the position of supercargo, Tom here reads, writes, and ciphers as well as anyone I know. He would make you an ideal supercargo."

"He would have to stand helm watches and other such duties while we are under way. Would he be willing to do that and serve for a single share as well?"

Smith ordered all hands to assemble on the deck. He pointed to Lovejoy and Tom, who stood beside him with wrists still bound.

"Listen close. These two men disobeyed me and they have suffered the consequences. They have seen the error of their ways. I'll let Dr. Martin here speak for hisself."

His voice weak from non-use and his knees wobbly from near starvation, Lovejoy began slowly in low tones.

"I am grateful to Captain Smith for allowing me to address you. I am sorry that I spoke to him in such a disrespectful way."

He bowed to Smith, who growled, "Tell them the rest."

"You may not be aware that I spent the past two years in London undertaking a course of medical studies. Because he saw war clouds gathering, my father called me home before I could complete my medical education, but Captain Smith assures me that he has known many a ship's surgeon with far fewer qualifications than myself. And so, I am happy to announce that he has appointed me as your ship's surgeon. He also has given me the privilege of choosing one of your number to serve as my helper. We will make that choice after we become better acquainted with each other. Meanwhile, sick call will be first thing each morning."

"There you are, men," Smith said. "I accept Dr. Martin's apology. We'll let bygones be bygones. But don't none of you never disobey one of my orders again. Now go about your duties, all of you."

"One more thing, Captain," Lovejoy whispered. "Please, could Tom and I have some food, after you untie our hands, that is?"

# 3

Evan Jenkins often said that his daughter Megan had more grit and common sense than all three of his sons put together. Tom was likable and responsible enough. The lad had done well at the dame's school in which he had spent five years, but he tended to drift with events rather than seizing and shaping them to his will. The twins showed little aptitude for learning. As lazy as Tom was dutiful, they were turning into devious little troublemakers.

Meg was another story altogether. If she had been a boy, Evan would have enrolled her in the local dame's school along with Tom. He might even have scrimped enough to send her to college, as upper-class Philadelphians did with their sons. Tom had taught her to read from his schoolbooks. Her handwriting and ciphering were so good that Evan had turned over the record keeping of the White Swan to her.

She had been a quiet child while her mother lived. Only after Mrs. Jenkins's death did her streak of low-key but stubborn assertiveness begin to show. She had taken over the disciplining of the twins until they became bigger and stronger than she. If she had not kept a close eye on her father's drinking, he might have become a sot.

Meg was no conventional beauty, but her small, dark face radiated with a quiet spunkiness that men found appealing. Evan could have married her off to any one of a dozen honest young artisans or clerks who hung about the White Swan. But she had spurned the advances of each.

Meg really had meant to keep her promise to her father that she would try to accept Primrose. But the longer she lived under the same roof as her new stepmother, the unhappier and more withdrawn she became. She was beginning to have second thoughts about some of her local suitors when Tom's letter arrived telling of his and Lovejoy's adventures in Baltimore.

"See here, Primrose, Meggie, boys," Evan had said. "Our lad is going to sea aboard a ship what Lovejoy has bought with his Pa's money. He's going privateering."

"What about Lovejoy?" Meg had asked.

"Tom says he's going also. That puts my mind to ease."

Tom's lie about Lovejoy's planning to join him had not, however, put Meg's mind to ease. She had been comforting herself with the thought that Tom and Lovejoy were on some sort of temporary mission to Baltimore and that if she would only remain patient, they would return to Philadelphia. Not only were they not going to come back, they were about to go to sea for heaven knew how long.

"Is it dangerous what they are going to do?" she asked.

"I reckon so, sure. There is bound to be some fighting. I'd worry if Tom was going alone, but if Joy is with him he should be all right."

"You seem to place more reliance on Lovejoy Martin than I would," Primrose said. "He seems to me like a rather unsteadfast young man."

"What do you know about it?" Meg snapped.

"Why, there is no need to be so touchy, Megan, my dear. I was merely observing that the young man is rather slow in finding his place in life."

"Yes, Meggie," Evan said. "There is no call for you to be so short with your stepmother."

The twins were enjoying the start of what they hoped would be a good row. They were disappointed that Meg met her father's rebuke with silence.

To keep things stirring, David said with affected sweetness, "Don't you see, dear stepmother, Meg's heart starts fluttering at the mere mention of Joy's name."

"Shut up, Davey, I'm warning you," Meg said through clenched teeth.

"Is that true?" Primrose said. "Well, Meggie, you should set your cap for him. Steady or not, he would be quite a catch for our Meggie, would he not, Evan dear?"

"I am not your Meggie. And I reckon you would know all about how to set your cap to catch a man."

George jabbed David in the ribs with his elbow, and both put their hands over their mouths to conceal their amusement.

"Meg," her father said. "Apologize to your stepmother."

"Not in a thousand years," she replied.

At that, Primrose put her hands over her face and cried, "I don't know what more I can do. The girl hates me. All your children hate me."

"Oh no, dear stepmother, David and I don't hate you, do we Davey?"

"Of course we don't. We don't know how we ever got along without you. Yes, definitely, we think Meggie owes you an apology. But she is such a stubborn wench she probably won't."

"Shut up, both of you," Evan roared. "You are just making things worse. Meggie, I insist that you apologize to Primrose."

"Never."

"Then I ask that you leave the table and go to your room. We'll talk about this in the morning."

When morning came, Meg was on the same stage that had carried Tom and Lovejoy south to Baltimore a few weeks before.

Now, huddled behind a bale of Holland duck sails in the dark locker of the *Flora,* disguised as a sailor, she waited as Lovejoy had asked her to. She had no idea how he could help her while he was tethered to that mast, but she trusted him to do something. She hoped it would be soon, for she couldn't remain hidden much longer, having given the last of her cache of food to the boys the night before.

Through the thin wall of the locker, she had heard the crewmen joking about Lovejoy's defiance of the captain and of both his and Tom's punishment. Not knowing of their release, she kept her mind occupied with schemes for getting both them and herself out of their predicament.

Cowering in the dark like a mouse in a pantry, she heard fresh voices in the hold outside her locker.

"And this is where I am to set up my surgery?" Lovejoy was saying.

"Aye. We'll lower that table from the overhead. If conditions is such to allow the main hatch to stay open, you will get some light. The rest'll have to come from lanterns."

"I was hoping that you might have someone with some medical experience to assist me."

"Well, there ain't. The cook would be fine for lugging the wounded below deck. He's big and strong as an ox."

"And equally as dumb, I fear."

"What about your friend Jenkins?"

"He faints at the sight of blood. He will serve you much better as your supercargo. Let me sleep on this question. Now, what is in that locker?"

"We have stored a spare suit of sails in there."

"Do you mind if I take a look?"

Meg heard the door creak open and saw the light from a lantern.

"Is there supposed to be someone in here?"

"Of course not."

"Then who is that behind that bale?" Lovejoy said, mocking surprise. "Why, bless my soul, it's a lad."

And so Meg did appear to be a boy, with her dark hair bobbed off and tucked under a seaman's knitted hat.

"By God," Smith said. "Don't tell me we got a stowaway."

At that, Meg stood up and climbed over a bale.

"Lovejoy," she cried. And before Lovejoy could launch into the reaction he had planned upon pretending to discover their stowaway, she had flung herself into his arms.

Wondering at the sight of a boy showing Lovejoy such obvious affection, Smith demanded, "What in the hell's name is going on?"

She turned her head to look into his face.

"You must be the captain Tom wrote about."

"Tom who?"

"Tom Jenkins. He is my brother."

Only after they reached the deck and Talbot could see more clearly did he realize that the stowaway was Tom Jenkins's sister and not his little brother.

News of a female stowaway brought activity aboard the *Flora* to a halt. Men stopped holystoning the deck or sharpening cutlasses; the lookout in the crow's nest turned his gaze from the horizon to the scene below him; the cook came out of his galley to stare at the slender figure accompanying the captain and their new surgeon toward the aft hatch.

Tom was on the fantail getting a lesson from the quartermaster in steering. Seeing Meg, he turned the tiller back to his instructor and ran to hug his sister.

The captain stood with arms folded across his chest, trying to make sense out of the situation.

"Jenkins, is this really your sister?"

"Yes, sir."

"Did you sneak her aboard?"

"I have no idea how she got here."

Smith turned to Lovejoy. "Then you must be behind this."

"No, Captain. I did not plan to sail with the *Flora*."

"There is something fishy going on here. It's plain that you are well acquainted with this lass."

"Indeed I am, and have been since she was a babe. A finer girl you'd never want to meet."

"A privateer is no place for a female. They bring bad luck." He turned to face the gaping crew. "Get back to work. Ain't you never seen a girl before?"

"Captain," Lovejoy said. "Could I have a word in private with Tom and his sister?"

Smith would have refused their request if he had not wanted time himself to sort out events. "You can use my cabin for a bit. Then I want a full explanation of all this."

He walked to the stern and stared back at the wake of the *Flora.*

It had pleased him to think that he had broken Lovejoy's will. Having publicly humiliated the chief owner of the vessel, he had demonstrated to even the toughest of the men that when Talbot Smith gave an order, it had best be obeyed, and promptly too. Also, he was pleased to have won himself a surgeon. He had not been entirely truthful with Lovejoy about why the *Flora* had sailed without one. Despite the potential financial reward, no Baltimore doctor would stoop to sign on for a cruise with a captain of his low social status. And finally, beneath his bravado, lay a nagging realization that even if Lovejoy did knuckle under and agree to serve as a landsman, he would retain his ownership and thus his power to relieve him at the end of the ninety-day cruise.

Now, just when it appeared that he had smooth sailing ahead, this girl showed up as a stowaway. Even if she had been an ugly crone, she would have been a problem. From long experience at sea, he knew that the farther from port the *Flora* sailed, the randier the crew would become. Where would she sleep? How would she attend to her bodily needs with a hundred sets of male eyes upon her? The best thing he could do would be to put her aboard the first prize they took and send her back to Baltimore.

"Mind your helm," he growled at the quartermaster as he headed for the hatch. He paused to yell up to the lookout in the crow's nest: "Keep a sharp lookout up there. If I see you gaping down again I'll shoot you off your perch and send someone up that can keep his mind on his duty."

In the cabin, while Meg answered Tom's questions about their family and the White Swan, Lovejoy pondered on just what he should do about her. It did not occur to him that Meg had come to join him as much as her brother. He was glad that she had stowed away, for if she had not, he would still be sitting out on the deck, literally tied to the mast and, figuratively, to his own obstinate pride. By making a game of it, he had not minded apologizing to the captain as much as he had expected, for he felt that he was outwitting Talbot rather than capitulating to him. Besides, being a ship's surgeon and sleeping in an officers' quarters bunk rather than a hammock was preferable to serving with the yokel landsmen. As for the job itself, he could handle various stomach ailments and rashes well enough, he supposed. Malcolm MacKenzie had said that privateering depended as much on bluff as on battle. Very likely he would never be called upon to amputate a limb or sew up a saber wound.

If Meg were assigned to him as an assistant, that would put her under his personal protection. Perhaps he might wangle special quarters for her and Tom. And then he would just wait to see what would happen. As for Talbot Smith, he could decide after ninety days just what retribution to take against him, if any. Three days and nights tied to that mast had taught him patience and given him insight into the workings of a privateer and the relationships of the crew. And, much as he hated to admit it, he had gained a grudging admiration for the captain's skill.

"All right, your time is up," the captain said on entering the cabin. "What is all this about?"

Lovejoy had a speech worked out in his head, but before he could deliver it, Meg said, "Captain Smith, sir, could I speak with you in private?"

"Meg, I really think we ought to discuss this situation all together," Lovejoy said.

Meg removed her cap and shook the tangles from her hair in a gesture Lovejoy recognized from the time she had been a little girl refusing to let Tom dominate her.

"I was talking to the captain."

To avoid her supplicating gaze, Talbot lowered his eyes and said, "If the lady wants a word with me in private, she shall have it. Both of you go topside."

# 4

Lovejoy had often been amused by Meg's plucky conduct around her family, the way she acted more like a bossy junior mother than a little sister. He could appreciate how she would have a hard time adjusting to any stepmother. From what she had told Tom in the cabin, she was fleeing from her miserable home situation as much as to her older brother and himself.

The more he thought about it, the more he was pleased that she had stowed away. She had always been a handy person with sick people. She would be an ideal surgeon's assistant. And it would be pleasant to have her around, a relief from the constant company of a gang of rough-cut sailors and green landlubbers. But why was she taking so long talking to the captain?

Tom had returned to his lesson in steering. Lovejoy had taken Madeline Richter's letter from his pocket and had just finished reading it for the third time since his release. He was too far away and too absorbed in his thoughts of the blond beauty to pay attention to what Tom was doing.

"You dirty son of a bitch!" Tom's voice shocked him out of his reverie.

He looked toward the stern just in time to see Tom fling himself on the quartermaster. The man fell backward, leaving the tiller unmanned.

Both Tom and the helmsman regained their feet and began circling each other like a pair of bulldogs. With her rudder free to flop about, the *Flora* lost steerageway. Her sails fell slack and she began wallowing between the waves.

Lovejoy reached the stern too late to stop Tom from wading into the sailor again. He struck the man first with a left and then with a right fist. A head taller than Tom and a good twenty pounds heavier, the helmsman shook off both blows and drew a knife from his belt.

Tom swung again and missed. The helmsman's left hand shot out and seized Tom's collar, and with his right hand he slashed the knife across Tom's chest.

Lovejoy shoved a sailor out of his path and hit the helmsman on the jaw so hard that the man dropped the knife and fell stunned against the rail.

The cut across Tom's chest ran about six inches long but was only skin deep. Lovejoy knelt and pressed his handkerchief against it to stop the bleeding. Suddenly Meg was kneeling beside him, wailing as she cuddled her brother's head.

"What's all this commotion about?" Talbot demanded. "God damn it. Clear the stern. Here, you, take the tiller. Head her to starboard to catch the wind again. Why, the fellow has been hurt. Is this some more of your doing, Dr. Martin?"

"He insulted my sister," Tom offered through teeth chattering from the shock of his wound. "Said he reckoned they would all have to take turns with her."

"Who said that?"

"Him." Tom pointed to the quartermaster, who now sat up holding his jaw.

"Bosun, bind that fellow and tie him to the mainmast. Here, give her a bit more rudder. That's it. How bad is he hurt?"

"He'll need to be sewed up."

With the help of Phipps, the first mate, they carried Tom down to the captain's cabin, stripped off his bloody shirt, and laid him on the table.

With so many eyes on him, Lovejoy refused to let his own distaste for blood stay his hands, shaking as they were. He first gave Tom a generous swallow from a rum bottle and then splashed the rest of the liquid over the wound to cleanse it, causing him to cry out.

"Here, Meg, you thread this needle, same as you learned from your mother. Oh, Tom, do stop moaning. He didn't cut you deep. Don't look if it bothers you so much. That's it, Meggie girl. Let's see if I remember how they did it at Barts. Don't want to pucker the skin. You're lucky, Tom. I won't have to suture the muscles. For God's sake, hold still. I am not enjoying this any more than you are. Now for the second stitch."

Lovejoy knew that one of the secrets of good surgery was to work quickly. He tried to do so now, but as he said to Tom, "Damn, you've got a tough hide. Bet you dulled that fellow's knife. There, Meg, wipe my face, will you? Captain, please don't stand in my light. Just a couple more stitches, Tom, and you'll be ready to start healing."

He drew the needle through the skin for the last stitch and knotted the thread. "I'll just leave a little opening here for drainage. Take the scissors, Meg, and snip the thread."

He straightened up and looked at his friend's lacerated chest, then down at his blood-stained hands and then at Talbot and Meg. Why did their faces seem to be fading away?

"I feel faint . . ."

The first mate caught him before he blacked out completely and lowered him to the cabin deck.

"He told me it was you that couldn't stand the sight of blood," Smith said to an alarmed Tom. "My God, I've gone and signed on a surgeon with a weak stomach."

"What do you expect when you starve someone for three days and nights?" said Meg, who now was holding Lovejoy's head in her lap. "Of course he is weak. You were cruel to treat him so."

"I don't need no lecture from a mere lass. If you'd have stayed at home where you belonged, none of this would have happened."

During her long talk with the captain, Meg had spotted the weak point in his armor. She put a hand over her eyes and pretended to sob.

"Nobody wants me anywhere anymore."

"Now, lass, there is no need to take on so. I meant no harm. It's just that a respectable girl like yourself should be at home with her family."

"I've got no family anymore. Now you look on me as a nuisance when all I wanted was to get away from Philadelphia and be with somebody I cared about. It is not fair. Life is not fair."

"Life ain't fair for most of us, that's true. But then you got fellows like this ship's surgeon what was born with a silver spoon in his mouth. He has had more than his share of fairness, I would say. Look at him. He owns eighty percent of this schooner what I labored over and risked everything I had to build, and he never done a day's hard work in his life. I despised him the minute I set eyes on him."

"Is that why you have gone out of your way to mistreat him?"

"Actually, the fellow has a lot more spunk than I gave him credit for. Don't know what I would have done if he had not given way. And Phipps, you say he stopped the fight?"

"He knocked Overstreet clear across the deck. Never seen such a powerful blow."

"If there is one thing Joy knows how to do," Tom said, "it is how to fight. And he ain't afraid of the devil."

"I reckon there is more to him than I thought. Give me enough time and maybe I can make a man of him."

"Wait, he's seems to be coming around. It is all right, Lovejoy. You just passed out."

Just as Smith feared, the presence of a woman aboard the *Flora* was proving unsettling for the ship's company. He could tell that from the way the men were doing more talking than working. He drew his first mate aside to question him about what they were saying.

"They are wondering where she will sleep."

"So am I, to tell the truth. What else?"

"A few thinks you might have slipped her aboard for your own use, if you take my meaning."

"Why, that is ridiculous."

"Then there are others that says she is your new surgeon's sweetheart. They have took note of the way she looks at him. And they know they were friends back in Philadelphia."

"They may be getting closer to the truth there. How do they feel about young Dr. Martin?"

"Don't take offense, Captain, but they think he's got guts, the way he stood up to you. And after seeing him lay our quartermaster out cold with one lick, I don't think he will lack their respect hereafter. For that matter, neither will you. They know you mean business when you give an order. All in all, it looks like things are shaking down for a good cruise."

"Except for the girl, yes," Talbot said, as he rubbed his chin and wondered what that canny MacKenzie would advise him to do.

The mate said, "I think if you put it to a vote, the men would choose to keep her aboard, to help the surgeon, oversee the cooking or whatever. She's a plucky lass, it is plain to see, and while she surely is no tart, she is easy on the eyes as well."

"But you see how they are neglecting their work."

"Oh, that will pass as they get used to the idea. She could be like a mascot for the *Flora*. Maybe even a useful mascot."

"That may be, but I intend to put her aboard the first prize we take and ship her back to Baltimore."

"What will you do with her meanwhile?"

"Meanwhile is my problem."

Smith had designed the captain's cabin of the *Flora* with only one bed and created pairs of stacked bunks in the adjoining officers' quarters for a first and second mate, a sailing master, ship's surgeon, and four prize masters. Some captains might have included an extra bunk in the commodious cabin for the first mate, but Talbot valued his privacy. Besides, he did not think he would be comfortable with a roommate who never swore and spent his spare time reading his Bible. So, on leaving Baltimore without a surgeon, he had relegated Phipps to a lower bunk in the officers' compartment.

That night he relinquished his cabin to Meg and took the youngest prize master's bunk in the officers' quarters. The prize master, the handsome young chap with curly hair, was none too happy at having to string a hammock in the hold with the crew.

"Get that pouty look off your face, Collins," Smith told him. "As you are our junior prize master, I'll likely send you back on our first capture, saving the others for longer distances after the British get on to our game."

As it turned out, only one person was satisfied with the sleeping arrangements aboard the *Flora* that first night. The captain missed the comfort of his bed and the privacy of his cabin. He managed to fall asleep, but his snoring disturbed the other seven occupants of the officers' compartment through most of the night; Collins, the young prize master, chose to take a blanket up to the deck rather than sleep in a hammock with the men. Only Meg was content. After three days and nights cooped up in a cramped sail locker, she luxuriated in the comfort of the captain's bed. And the wounded Tom was allowed to string a hammock across the other side of the cabin.

First mate Phipps was a level-headed man whose puritanical bent was balanced by a rare understanding and tolerance of human nature. Having four daughters back home on whom he doted, he also understood the effect of winsome young females. He had told the captain that within a week the rank-and-file members of the crew would have taken Meg to their hearts. He was wrong. It took her only two days to win the affection of even the hardest-bitten crewmen.

Foul-mouthed sailors did not entirely reform their manner of speech, but they began looking around to make sure Meg was not in earshot when they felt like swearing.

The quartermaster suffered so much abuse while bound to the mainmast—particularly from the out-of-sorts young prize master— that he soon begged the captain to allow him to apologize to Tom, first for insulting his sister and second for knifing him. The captain released him on probation.

The only drawback to Meg's presence seemed to be the large number of men reporting to Lovejoy each morning at sick call. Some had boils. Unless these were in delicate spots, Lovejoy permitted Meg to lance them. She proved adept at removing splinters and applying salves to rashes. Complaints of bowels that were either locked or too loose were muttered into Lovejoy's ear, as were a couple of confessions of venereal infections.

Lovejoy listened gravely to each man's complaint and then either doled out the potions indicated in Northcote's *Marine Practice* or Lind's *Effectual Means* or turned the luckier patients over to Meg, who drew upon her knowledge of household remedies.

Meg further secured her place in the hearts of the men by teaching the cook, a big Irishman with jet black hair, some of the White Swan's ways of improving the flavor of the food and then standing by at chow time to help him serve the portions.

Lovejoy accused her of having the crew "eating out of your hands, literally and figuratively."

Although Meg liked being considered useful and enjoyed having the captain's cabin to herself at night, the best part of being aboard the *Flora* for her was the companionship of Lovejoy Martin. He stopped treating her like the little sister of his best friend. He asked her opinion about treatments and encouraged her to read the medical texts that Smith had laid in. He complimented her on the dishes she helped the cook prepare. If it were left to Megan Jenkins to decide, this cruise of the *Flora* would last forever.

Seeing the respect with which she was now treated, Tom relaxed and stopped worrying about her safety.

The officers got used to the captain's snoring. The displaced prize master decided that a day or so more of sleeping in a hammock would not kill him.

The only person who was not glad of Meg's presence was the captain, and this was not just because he missed his comfortable cabin. He would get that back as soon as they made their first capture and he could pack his stowaway off to Baltimore.

The captain admired Meg's spunkiness, and she appealed to his protective instincts. But he feared that as a woman she might be jinxing the cruise.

His first mate told him that this was simply a superstition, that such a helpful, decent girl would be more likely to bring them favor from the Almighty.

"Say what you will," Talbot replied. "Here we are a week out of port and we ain't yet encountered our first ship flying the British flag."

# 5

Captain Smith had expected to encounter British ships soon after they cleared Cape Henry at the mouth of the Chesapeake, but, to his frustration, for the next several days, northeasterly winds drove him farther and farther south through heavy seas.

Prevented by cloudy skies from sighting the noon sun or North Star to fix their position, and fearful of running aground on the shoals off Cape Hatteras, he pointed the *Flora* partly into the wind and veered off to the southeast, away from land.

When the weather finally cleared and the sea grew calmer, he and Barineau, his sailing master, were able to get a good sighting of the noon sun. They discovered that they were about two hundred miles off Cape Fear, on the North Carolina coast.

Smith changed his course to east southeast and ordered his lookouts to keep a sharp vigil.

At night, Meg slept soundly in the captain's comfortable bed, with her brother occupying his nearby hammock like a faithful watchdog. Just a few feet away, beyond the officers' compartment bulkhead, the thoughts of a wakeful Lovejoy Martin returned again and again to Madeline Richter and the invitation to visit. He had decided to send a letter back on the first prize they took with instructions for Malcolm to post it on to Reading. He would plead a business emergency and ask permission to delay his visit until the end of November. By then, this cruise would be over. He would be a rich man. He reached in his pocket and ran his fingers over the now dog-eared letter from Madeline. It would be a long wait, but she was worth a bit of patience and conniving.

Meanwhile, he was enjoying his position as ship's surgeon far more than he had ever expected. He had got over his initial seasickness. There really wasn't that much to his job. Between sick calls, he chatted with crew members, played cards with the prize masters, or brushed up on his medical knowledge from the texts Smith had stocked. Occasionally he took over the tiller of the *Flora,* much as the owner of a splendid racehorse might replace a jockey for a few laps just to get the feel of his property and to show off a bit to the stable hands.

That was what he was doing the morning after the weather cleared when the lookout cried, "Sail ho!"

Talbot Smith handed his sextant to Barineau and, with the agility of a monkey, scrambled up the rope ladder to the crow's nest.

"Take the helm, Mr. Phipps," he called to his first mate.

There followed a torrent of commands for the mainsail to be shifted and the *Flora* brought about to an easterly course, as close to the wind as possible to make any headway.

Back on the deck, Smith handed his telescope to Lovejoy.

"You'll just be able to see her topgallants from here. From up there I make her out to be a brig, headed south, with the wind off her port quarter."

"Is she British?"

"Can't make out her colors yet, but we'll intercept her. Mr. Phipps, give the helm to the quartermaster and order all hands on deck. Open the hatches and bring up three rounds for each gun. You, Dr. Martin, better go below and prepare your surgery, just in case. And you, Jenkins, make a record of our lookout's name. He'll receive a half share for spotting her, if she turns out to be a proper prize and if we get her to port."

With the help of the cook and Meg, Lovejoy lowered the table in the hold from the overhead and laid out his surgical instruments on a nearby table. Overhead, he heard the thump of dozens of feet and the voices of the bosuns and the mates relaying the captain's orders.

When he returned to the deck, he found Tom and the other landsmen brandishing cutlasses, pistols, and muskets and listening to the captain telling them what was expected of a boarding party.

"Remember lads, the first man who crosses her rail gets a full share and the second a half share. Scream and shout as you leap. You want to scare hell out of them. Get them to give up quick as you can. We'll try to frighten them into surrendering, but we got to be ready to back up our bluff."

The gun crews were busy loading the carronades. The two twelve-pounder Long Toms had been loaded and run out, ready for firing.

"Ah, Dr. Martin, everything ready below?"

"All ready. She's British, is she?"

"Aye. Here, take my glass and see for yourself."

Like Talbot Smith, Captain Christopher Bledsoe was glad that the northeaster had finally passed and the seas grown calm. The storm had caught him north of Bermuda, on his way from Liverpool to Barbados, heavy laden with a cargo of salt pork, cheeses, woolen cloth, shoes, and hats. With plenty of elbow room between him and the American coast, he had allowed his brig to run before the wind, making good time but, like Smith, sailing blind.

Just as had the captain of the *Flora*, he had shot the sun the day before and changed his course due south. His brig, the *Goodfellow,* had departed Liverpool just before word came that those idiotic Americans had declared war.

Bledsoe had lost a leg just below the knee while serving as a junior officer aboard a frigate at Trafalgar. Each morning, in foul weather or fair, he strapped on his peg leg and took a constitutional stroll about the deck of the *Goodfellow.* He had completed three circuits of the main deck and was about to retire to his cabin when his lookout spotted the *Flora* on the horizon to the southwest.

"Ahead off the starboard bow. She looks to be a schooner. Big one, too."

Unlike Talbot, Bledsoe did not attempt to climb the rigging to verify the sighting. He merely stumped up to the poop deck and gazed through his telescope.

"Damned thing carries so much canvas I don't see how they keep her upright."

"Think she is a Yankee?" his first mate asked.

"I assume so. Seems bent on closing with us. Wonder what they want."

"She is a big one. Looks to run near to four hundred tons. And from the way she rides in the water, she is carrying a full cargo."

Smith fixed his long glass on the brig and added, "She's pierced for eight guns, but her ports are closed, so I can't say for sure."

"How many men?" Phipps asked.

"Looks to be at least thirty. Ah, there, I can make out her name now. *Goodfellow,* Liverpool. Very well. We've got the weather advantage of her now. Let's pass her by to our starboard and then cut close enough to put a shot across her bow. This ought to be easy, but you never can tell."

Smith turned to Meg, who was standing about with a bewildered look on her face. "Miss Jenkins, let me suggest that you go to the cabin and stay there."

"What if someone is hurt? Won't I be needed up here?"

"If that Englishman has any sense at all, no one will be hurt. Until we are sure, I insist that you go below."

Pressing ahead under full sail, the *Flora* easily overtook the lumbering brig. Keeping to the windward, when she was about a ship's length ahead on the brig's port side, Talbot ordered his chief gunner's mate to fire a shot across the *Goodfellow*'s bow from his forward Long Tom.

As the gunsmoke cleared, Talbot shouted through a speaking horn, "Ahoy, *Goodfellow!* Heave to."

"Who are you?" Captain Bledsoe shouted back, and then said softly to his first mate, "I smell a rat. Get ready to put her helm over and set her on a port tack."

"We're the *Flora*, a licensed privateer out of Baltimore. We are at war with you British. Strike your colors and furl your sails."

Talbot thought for a moment that the *Goodfellow*'s crew were preparing to take down her sails and heave to. Before he realized what was happening, however, they were hauling away to shift her mainsails and change course. Too late to react, he saw that the brig was passing the stern of the *Flora* and her starboard gunports were being opened.

The *Goodfellow*'s four starboard nine-pounders fired a ragged salvo. One ball whizzed just past Lovejoy's head. One punched a hole in the *Flora's* mainsail. One missed entirely, but one crashed into the schooner's stern, sending a shudder through the slender craft.

"Meg," Lovejoy cried, and hurtled across the crowded deck to the aft hatch.

The cannonball had carried through the captain's cabin and into the officers' compartment, demolishing a row of bunks.

He found her cowering in the captain's bed with a pillow over her head.

"Oh, Meggie, I was afraid you were killed." He took her in his arms and held her close until she had stopped trembling.

The *Flora* shuddered again, this time from the recoil of her own port-side carronades. This was followed by the sharp reports of musket fire.

Lovejoy picked Meg up and, wondering at her lightness, carried her forward, nearly the length of the vessel, to the sail locker in which she had stowed away.

"Squeeze in between the bales and you'll be as safe as safe can be. Now stay put. I'll come for you when this is all over."

He found the deck of the *Flora* turned into a madhouse. Talbot Smith was raging at himself, at his men, and at the captain of the British brig.

Wham! The *Flora*'s carronades thundered again. A cloud of white smoke drifted across the deck. From overhead, in the rigging, landsmen were peppering away at the *Goodfellow* with their muskets as the *Flora* once more approached her prey, this time from the brig's starboard side.

The *Goodfellow* fired another salvo from her four starboard guns, without doing any damage to the *Flora*.

"Ready with your grappling hooks," Talbot shouted. "Load your pieces and hold your fire until we are well alongside. Stand by to board. Put your helm over hard."

With only a few yards separating them, the two vessels exchanged final broadsides. the *Flora* heeled to starboard from her guns' recoil and the impact of the *Goodfellow*'s cannonballs against her hull. Her bow struck a glancing blow against the beam of the *Goodfellow.* The noise of the two vessels' grating together sounded like a scream of pain. Grappling hooks went flying across the brig's rail. Crewmen hauled away at the lines to snug the schooner up against the brig.

"Fire!" Talbot yelled at the landsmen. Then as the smoke from their muskets cleared, "Boarders away!"

The drills they had been practicing ever since leaving Baltimore paid off. A black former slave from Virginia was the first man to spring upon the deck of the *Goodfellow.* Brandishing a cutlass over his head, he was followed closely by the Irish cook, who was armed with a meat cleaver, and then a surge of the less bold landsmen.

Three English sailors were sprawled on the deck, victims of musket balls. One of their cannon was lying on its side, its carriage splintered. The crew shrank from the boarders, some cowering behind the longboat and others throwing down their weapons and holding their hands over their heads.

On the poop deck, the captain of the *Goodfellow* was waving his arms and shouting, "We strike, you bloody Yankees. We strike."

Talbot had the English captain brought to the deck of the *Flora* and stood glaring at him with arms folded across his chest.

"I know you are a damned fool, but what is your name?"

His captive showed no sign of being intimidated. "I am Captain Christopher Bledsoe and I am master of the brig *Goodfellow* out of Liverpool, bound for Bridgetown in Barbados. Who the hell are you?"

"I am Captain Talbot Smith and I am master of this here schooner which is the *Flora* out of Baltimore."

"Who gave you the right to accost us on the high seas?"

"The Congress of the United States of America, you son of a bitch. Didn't you know we are at war?"

"See here, my good chap, as a master yourself, you should understand. How would it look to my owners if I, a former lieutenant in the British Royal Navy, tamely struck my colors? I had to put up a fight. Or isn't that the way you Yankees play the game?"

"A lot of good it did you. How many men did you lose?"

"Sailors can be replaced. Honor cannot. Don't suppose you would understand that, would you?"

While Smith examined the papers of the *Goodfellow,* the three wounded Englishmen were brought aboard the *Flora* and down to the hold for examination by Lovejoy and Meg.

One man had been hit in the side. The ball had struck a rib and slid along it, coming to rest just under the skin over his stomach.

Another had been shot through the thigh. Fortunately for him, the ball missed the bone and lodged in the muscle.

The third man, a slender little Cockney, had been more seriously wounded. A musket ball had shattered his forearm.

It was a simple matter for Lovejoy to slit the skin over the abdomen of the first Englishman and remove the flattened bullet.

"Now, my friend, if you like you can hold that as a memento while we just suture this little tear in your fabric. Have your needle all threaded, Meggie?"

Both Lovejoy and the sailor with the injured thigh broke into a sweat as he probed about in the wound and snagged the bullet. Meg wiped his face as he worked.

"Are you all right? You look a little pale."

"Why are you worried about him? It me as got hit," the wounded sailor said.

Lovejoy was examining the mangled arm of the third sailor when Captain Bledsoe clumped down to the hold to inquire after his wounded men.

"Don't know why you are dithering about," he said after introductions had been made. "Plain to see you have to amputate."

"You don't mean to cut off me arm, do you?" the sailor said.

"Come, come, Tompkins. There is no way to save that arm. Only thing to do is take her off. Just below the elbow, I'd say. What's the matter, Doctor, didn't you ever do an amputation?"

Lovejoy did not like the man's callous attitude.

"I am not so sure we have to take off the arm."

"Ha! I was in the Royal Navy. Served with Nelson at Trafalgar. That's where I lost my leg. They gave me a dram of rum and a bit of wood to bite on. One of our surgeons had my leg off in less than a minute. You Yanks are too tenderhearted. You don't know medicine."

"It might interest you to know that I studied at St. Bartholomew's Hospital in London."

"That a fact? Thought you looked a cut above this lot of brigands. Don't know why any gentleman would want to serve under that captain of yours. He knows nothing of nautical courtesy. Well, are you going to take off that arm, or would you like me to do it for you? I act as my own surgeon aboard the *Goodfellow*."

"Nobody is going to take off his arm. Meggie, get me out a splint and some bandages. Now, Captain . . . Bledsoe, is it? I would appreciate it if you would go about your business. You are upsetting my patient."

When he had finished, he sat on a stool. His hands shook as he poured himself a cup of rum.

"You're not going to faint again, are you?" Meg asked.

"No, but I think I would have if I had had to amputate that poor fellow's arm. Oh, Meggie, I wasn't cut out to be a doctor. What am I going to do?"

"I reckon you will keep on with your job until you get used to it, Joy.

That is what most of us do in this world, those of us who weren't born with a silver spoon in our mouths."

She took the sting out of her words by putting her hand on his shoulder and adding, "You go topside and get some fresh air. I will clean up down here."

# 6 

While Lovejoy and Meg treated the wounded English sailors, Tom helped Captain Smith inventory the cargo jammed into the *Goodfellow*'s hold.

Later, in the captain's cabin of the *Goodfellow,* they pored over the papers of the brig, and Tom helped prepare the documents that would be required by an admiralty court before the brig and its cargo could be "condemned" and sold at auction.

"Ah, Jenkins, this capture will earn us a pretty penny. A few more such prizes will make this cruise a grand success."

Tom was surprised by the suddenly confidential tone of the man who had kept him tied to the mast for two days and nights.

"I am just glad that we can send my sister back."

"Aye, and I'll be glad to be shut of a woman aboard ship, not that your sister ain't a fine girl, Jenkins."

"There's none finer, and I would say that even if she wasn't my sister."

"Ah, here's Phipps."

"We've put fenders out so we can stay lashed together as long as the sea stays calm," the first mate said. "Carpenters will have to patch up the hole in our stern and your cabin bulkhead."

"How about the prisoners?"

"Each has taken an oath not to offer resistance until after they have been exchanged."

"You think Collins has enough experience to take this brig into Charleston?"

Tom looked up from the papers he was studying.

"Why not Baltimore?"

"Charleston is a lot nearer. It has an admiralty court, and there should be a good market there for this cargo and for the brig herself."

"But you can't just dump my sister off by herself way down there like she was a stray cat. How will she get back home?"

"She ran away from home."

"But if you sent her back to Baltimore, at least Mr. MacKenzie could look after her until this cruise is over."

"Your sister has caused us enough trouble already. The sooner we get her off, the better."

His voice shaking, Tom said, "Please, can't you send this brig back up to Baltimore?"

"The matter is settled. Phipps, tell Collins he will take this prize into Charleston. He will cast off at first light tomorrow. Then tell Miss Jenkins to pack up her gear."

Word that the *Goodfellow*, with her captain and crew, would be sent into Charleston had little effect on the men of the *Flora* until they learned that Meg was to go along too.

"That means we have to go back to eating your slop," the bosun's mate said to the cook.

"I'd take offense at that remark if the thoughts of missing that darling lass did not weigh so heavy on my heart." He sighed, then added, "Anyway, Collins should be glad of the news. He will be able to talk to her without her brother looking daggers."

Meg was as upset as Tom when Phipps told her of the captain's decision, not because of concern over being "dumped" off at Charleston, but because she was enjoying her life aboard the *Flora.*

"I can't go back to Philadelphia," she said later to Tom. "It would kill me to have to put up with Primrose again."

"It will kill me to think of you alone and friendless in a strange port."

"Couldn't you come with me?"

"I asked the captain, but he lost his temper. Said he'd tie me back to the mast if I opened my mouth about it again."

"What does Lovejoy say about this?"

"Don't think he knows yet. He's aboard the brig rooting around in her hold, looking for medical supplies."

"You don't suppose the captain would release him to go back to Charleston?"

When Tom told Lovejoy of the captain's plan to send the *Goodfellow* into Charleston with Meg aboard, Smith was in the cabin interviewing Bledsoe. The two men had stopped their hostile posturing and now were making nautical shoptalk. Bledsoe had just finished telling Talbot of his part in the battle of Trafalgar. Talbot was just beginning the story of how he had constructed his schooner when Lovejoy raged into the cabin, leaving Tom, fearful of the captain's wrath, to skulk outside.

"What's this about sending Meg Jenkins back? You can't do that. I won't stand for it."

"We can't keep a woman on the *Flora* any longer. She is a fine girl, but she has caused enough trouble already."

"But what will she do in a strange port?"

"Collins is a good enough chap. He will look after her."

"He would like that. I have seen the way he looks at her."

"Oh, we are getting jealous, are we?"

"If you won't keep her aboard, at least send our prize back to Baltimore. I will give her a letter for Malcolm MacKenzie. He and his wife would look after her until we return."

Talbot was embarrassed to have his English counterpart witnessing this challenge to his authority. He was upset over the damage to the *Flora.* And he was beginning to be concerned over the effect his decision might have on the morale of his crew. So, curbing his temper, he said evenly, "See here, Dr. Martin, the girl will be safe. If it will make you feel better, I will assign her a half share for her services as a surgeon's assistant."

"That's not good enough. If you send her back at all, it must be to Baltimore. Or else let me accompany her."

"Oh, so that is what this is all about, is it? It's a trick to get out of serving your time on the cruise."

He turned to the English captain. "Look here, Captain Bledsoe, I'll ask you to give us a bit of privacy to work out this little matter between us."

Bledsoe was amused by the scene he had just witnessed. Encountering Tom in the passageway outside the cabin, he drew him to the deck, where Collins and the men selected as his prize crew were being instructed by Phipps in what was expected of them.

"Young fellow," Bledsoe asked, "what is this all about? In the British navy, if a surgeon spoke like that to a captain, he'd be given a taste of the cat before the words were half out of his mouth."

"There is not many surgeons that owns eighty percent of a ship, I reckon," Tom replied.

"Oh? Explain that, and also tell me more about this young woman who seems to be causing so many problems."

"She's my sister . . ." Tom began.

Back in the *Flora*'s cabin, Meg was waiting to hear of Lovejoy's reaction.

"Oh, he is near beside himself, he is," Tom reported. "Went streaking into the cabin and laced right into Captain Smith."

"I want to know exactly what he said."

With a faint smile of satisfaction, she listened to Tom's report of what he had overheard.

"And he really did offer to go back with me? What did the captain say to that?"

"They were arguing about it when the English fellow came out and dragged me off. I reckon they are still going at it hot and heavy. You know how Joy is when he gets his back up."

The *Flora* remained lashed against the *Goodfellow* all that night, and a sleepless night it turned out to be for Lovejoy, Talbot, Meg, and Tom.

Lovejoy had threatened to tie himself to the mast of the *Flora* the next morning if the captain sent the *Goodfellow* off to Charleston rather than back to their home port of Baltimore.

This took the wind out of Talbot's sails, for he had been about to threaten that very thing if Lovejoy did not shut up. Before the captain could reply, Lovejoy had stormed out of the cabin of the *Goodfellow.*

Because of the damage done to the bunks in the *Flora*'s officers' compartment, Talbot shared Captain Bledsoe's cabin aboard the *Goodfellow* that night. He placed an armed bosun's mate at the door of the cabin and set other guards in the forward hold, where the English crew would remain locked away until the brig reached Charleston harbor. Like Lovejoy, he slept little.

Before retiring, he, Phipps, and Barineau, their sailing master, had given Collins charts of the South Carolina coast and instructions on what to do once he reached Charleston.

Collins was a well-spoken, conscientious chap in his early twenties. The only son of a New Jersey farmer, he showed promise of some day commanding his own vessel.

"Charleston is nearer than Baltimore," the captain explained. "It won't be long before British cruisers will be drawn to the mouth of the Chesapeake like iron filings to a magnet. Now, if we sail on toward the Indies, we can catch British ships headed back for England, and they won't know anything about the war. They'll be easier pickings. You are the greenest of my prize masters. You have the makings of a good sailor, but I'd feel mighty uneasy for you to take this brig north around Hatteras and all the way up the Chesapeake. Don't mean to hurt your feelings, lad, but for your first prize it is a lot safer for you to head for Charleston. Any questions?"

"Why, yes. I was wondering what I am to do with Miss Jenkins in Charleston."

"I was going to take that up with you in private. Phipps, Barineau, excuse Collins and me for a few minutes."

Later, Tom drew Collins aside for his own private talk with the prize master.

"I'm holding you responsible for my sister's safety."

"My God, is everybody fretting about her?"

"What do you mean, everybody?"

"The captain threatened to have my scalp if anything happened to her. And so has Phipps."

"I have took note of how you stare at her."

"You think I'd try anything with a girl that is engaged to be married?"

"Meggie? Engaged? Who told you that?"

"The captain said she is to be married to your doctor friend when the *Flora* returns to Baltimore. My view is that she is too good for the lazy layabout. Captain said I was to keep this to myself, but I figured as her brother you would know."

Concealing his puzzlement, Tom said, "I didn't realize the captain knew."

In the *Flora*'s damaged cabin, Meg could not believe what Tom was telling her.

"Why, that is the biggest lie I ever heard. Why would he say such a ridiculous thing?"

"The captain likes you, it is plain to see. He just told Collins that to keep him away from you."

"You don't think it was because of something Lovejoy said?"

"I could ask Joy."

"Don't you dare."

Tom started to tell Meg about Lovejoy's shipboard romance but thought better of it, saying, "With Joy around, nothing is ever dull for long."

While it was still dark, Lovejoy dressed and went topside to sit beside the mainmast and wait for the sun to rise. The fenders between the *Flora* and the *Goodfellow* squeaked from the gentle motion of the calm sea.

The gunner's mate who had the deck watch approached him. "It's kind of early to be starting sick call, ain't it?"

"I am not here for sick call. I just need to think. By the way, would you hand me that coil of line over there? Ah, thanks. Now don't let me keep you from your rounds."

A glimmer of light appeared on the eastern horizon. Lovejoy got up, looped one end of the line about his waist and the other around the mast. Then he sat down to wait. He had lost one test of wills with Smith, and he would be damned if he would lose another.

"What in hell's name are you doing up here?"

Hands on hips, Talbot Smith was standing over him.

"I am once again tied to the mast."

"You're acting like a damned fool. Get up from there."

"I told you last night that if you sent Megan Jenkins off to Charleston, I would do this."

"You know this is mutiny, don't you?"

"Call it what you will. I say I am merely protesting a cruel and unnecessary decision."

"I was just beginning to think you had some common sense."

Smith stood rubbing his chin and looking down at Lovejoy for signs that he might be bluffing. Seeing none, he said, "What would it take for you to quit acting like a spoiled little boy and do your work as surgeon so we can get on with our business, which, in case you have forgot, is to capture British ships?"

"Send the *Goodfellow* up to Baltimore and not to Charleston."

"If I was to do that, you'd quit your bellyaching and carry out your duties as surgeon? Start acting like a real man?"

"You would have no more cause for complaint, I assure you."

"And how would me changing my mind help the girl?"

"I would write a letter for her to give Malcolm MacKenzie. I would ask him and his wife to take care of her."

"Then you had better take that silly line from around yourself before anyone sees you and go write the letter."

Lovejoy sprang up, seized Talbot's hand, and said, "Thank you, Captain, from the bottom of my heart."

"I ain't doing it for you, Dr. Martin. I am doing it for the girl. So go and write your letter."

"Actually, if you're sending the ship up to Baltimore, I have two letters to write."

The *Goodfellow* did not part company with the *Flora* as early as Talbot had planned. Permitting no one to question his change of mind, he spent an hour substituting charts of the Virginia coasts for those given Collins the night before. And he lectured the young mariner on avoiding going aground off Cape Hatteras.

"Sail her to the northeast until you are well clear of the shoals. And Phipps has told you about keeping the Englishmen under lock and key. Let them up on deck two at a time for exercise, but be sure they are well guarded. Now we have took all the small arms off her, but remember, they outnumber you three to one. It will take you longer to get to Baltimore, but at least you will have Mr. MacKenzie to deal with the admiralty court. Dr. Martin is writing a letter to him, having to do with Miss Jenkins, I believe. And don't you forget my warnings about how she is to be treated. And here is something I want you to deliver to my housekeeper. Her name is Josie."

With Tom hanging about, Lovejoy found it difficult to say what he wanted to Meg. He took her hand and smiled at her.

"Well, Meggie girl, you'll have a fine tale to tell your grandchildren some day."

"As will you, I reckon."

"I don't know how I will get along without you, but you will like the MacKenzies, I am sure."

Tom broke in with, "You will never meet kinder people."

Meg looked up at Lovejoy. "You will be all right without me. Just remember that you know more medicine than anybody else. Never let it show if something comes up you think you can't handle. Go ahead and do the best you can. Only try not to faint anymore."

She stood on tiptoe and put her arms around his neck. He lifted her off her feet and kissed her square on the lips.

"They are waiting for her on the *Goodfellow,*" Tom said.

The *Flora* lay to, sails still furled, while Collins and his crew raised those of the *Goodfellow* and put her helm over to catch the wind and start the brig on her northward course.

"Let's get this cruise under way, Mr. Phipps," Talbot roared. "Raise mainsails. Send a lookout aloft. Set her course for south by southwest."

Lovejoy stood against the aft rail. He waved to Meg. She waved back. As the two vessels parted, Meg, with her short hair and baggy canvas sailor's trousers, looked more and more like a forlorn little boy.

The captain came and stood beside Lovejoy. "It is all for the best this way, I reckon. I can have my cabin back now."

"Yes, that is the important thing, isn't it?"

Ignoring his sarcasm, Talbot said, "Here. I'll leave my glass with you for a bit so you don't strain your eyes."

# PART THREE

# 1

Whatever anyone thought of Talbot Smith's superstition about women aboard ship, the *Flora*'s luck quickly took a turn for the better following Meg's departure. Venturing out into the Gulf Stream, two days later she encountered a three-masted ship beating her way on a northeasterly tack. She was the *Cornish Maid,* en route from Jamaica to Bristol with a hold full of mahogany boards, muscavado sugar, and rum, cargo whose value far exceeded that of the creaky, worm-ridden ship herself.

Talbot kept a British ensign flying until he had brought the *Flora* within hailing distance. Seeing that the ship was lightly armed, he ran up his American colors, fired a shot across her bow, and ordered her to heave to.

A younger, more combative captain might have put up a fight. But this captain was no Christopher Bledsoe, and he had only two rusty cannon. An elderly, sickly man, Herbert Jeffries had brought his wife of forty years along for this, his final voyage before retiring. Until this sleek Yankee schooner came racing up alongside like a gray wolf, he and his wife had never been happier.

Captain Jeffries peered through his spyglass at the gunwales of the *Flora* bristling with carronades and then at the mass of rough-looking men bearing cutlasses and boarding axes on the deck of the schooner. He lowered his glass, looked into the frightened eyes of his dear Esmelda, and ordered his mate to strike their colors and lower their sails.

Lovejoy was relieved that he would have no wounds to tend. He went aboard the *Cornish Maid* with Smith and quickly set to work soothing Mrs. Jeffries, who was convinced that she and her husband had fallen into the hands of pirates who would kill the crew and carry her off for their own carnal pleasure.

"Dear lady, pray compose yourself. You have nothing to fear from us. We are civilized people, I assure you."

"Then why do you pounce on us in this disgraceful fashion?"

"Our nations are at war."

"We heard nothing of war in Jamaica. How do we know that this is not a trick?"

"We have newspapers from Baltimore telling of the war."

"Even if that is true, what gives you the right to interfere with us? This is not a warship."

Lovejoy explained about privateering.

"Sounds like nothing but licensed piracy. What do you mean to do with us? Is there some sort of ransom we must pay?"

He explained the process of condemning prizes and selling them at auction.

"And where will this be done? In Bristol, I should hope."

"I fear it must be Charleston, the nearest friendly port."

This drew fresh shrieks. "Oh, Herbert, we are to be kept prisoner. And what will become of the furniture we brought back from Jamaica?"

"I think we might hold any personal possessions out of the auction, don't you, Captain Smith?" Lovejoy said.

"I reckon so. And you'll be exchanged soon as our governments work out a cartel system."

Mrs. Jeffries was not to be so easily soothed. "You Americans are hypocrites. I see nothing civilized about seizing a merchant ship on the high seas and sending innocent people off to prison when they have committed no offense against you."

Talbot turned to face her. "Don't speak to me of hypocrisy. You bloody English have been stopping our ships on the high seas and taking our citizens off to serve on your warships. If that ain't taking innocent people into captivity, I don't know what is. And you've been doing it without there being a state of war declared between us. We just got a bellyful of it. That is what this war is all about, freedom of the seas. You British think you own the oceans and all that sails upon them. Well I reckon you and your husband know now that you don't."

Lovejoy was as surprised as Mrs. Jeffries was shocked by the length and passion of Smith's outburst. He gave Mrs. Jeffries a draught to calm her nerves.

"You are a gracious young man," Mrs. Jeffries said, "but I fear you have fallen in with bad company. That captain of yours is not a gentleman."

Their next capture was not quite so easy, or rewarding. Near noon, heading south, with a strong breeze pushing them along against the Gulf

Stream's current, they sighted a sail on the horizon off their port quarter on a northeasterly course.

Talbot ordered all sail to be bent on and set his course to track that of the target. It took nearly two hours to draw near enough for him to make out that the craft was a large sloop. Another hour passed before they closed enough distance to read the name painted across her stern.

"She's the *Marrianne,* out of St. George's. One of them Bermuda-built sloops. No wonder it has took us so long to catch up to her. They are fast, they are."

By midafternoon, it was obvious that the captain of the sloop was doing his best to outrun the *Flora.*

"We got to catch up with the bastard before dark or he'll get away from us," Smith said to Phipps. "Have your boys double load the forward Long Tom and stand ready to throw a shot in front of them when we draw abreast."

The cannonball arced high up in the air and dropped into the water just off the port bow of the sloop.

As if the shot had been a signal, suddenly the sloop shifted her mainsail and turned her bow sharply to the starboard, causing the *Flora* to overshoot her prey and lose her weather advantage.

Talbot took over the helm himself and raged at his sailors to shift sails and at his gun crews to load their carronades.

Within a half hour, the *Flora* was drawing near enough to open fire with her forward Long Tom again, missing the target. For the first time, the sloop returned fire with a shot from her small stern chaser. The shot sent up a spout of water well ahead of the *Flora.*

By now, Talbot had turned the helm back to the quartermaster and was striding about, grinding his teeth and swearing at his crew and at the sloop.

A bit later, with the distance short enough for the name of the sloop to be read by the naked eye, Talbot ordered his bow chaser to fire again. The shot sailed over the sloop.

Again, a cloud of white smoke burst from the stern of their prey, and a shot dropped close enough to the *Flora* to splash water over her bow.

And again, like a rabbit eluding a pursuing beagle, the sloop changed course, this time to an east-northeasterly direction, sailing very closely into the wind.

The *Flora* slid past her prey before she could reset her sails, but this time Talbot had the satisfaction of firing both his forward and aft Long Toms at the stern of the sloop.

Coming about to the same heading as the sloop, the *Flora,* like her prey, was making scant progress beating against the wind.

"Oh, he's a clever devil, he is. Couldn't quite outrun us, so now he thinks he'll outdodge us."

"We'll catch him, won't we?"

"Unless we run out of daylight. Here, Phipps, let's have some water on the sails. Bear a hand with those buckets."

Slowly, her sails soaked with seawater, the close-hauled *Flora* overtook the sloop again, and Talbot ordered his forward Long Tom to open fire. The response of the sloop was suddenly to set her jib over, swing through the eye of the wind, and veer off on a westerly course, with the wind off her port beam.

This drew a fresh torrent of profanity-laced orders from Talbot, as the *Flora* shifted her heading on a westerly course.

"If he was to dump whatever it is he is carrying, he could get away from us, that's for sure. I got to outthink him."

"We're gaining on her again. Shall we try another shot?"

"Not yet, Mr. Phipps. What I want you to do is stand by with all hands to shift sails. And have your gun crews load the carronades, port and starboard, and then stand by to fire."

"Both port and starboard?" Phipps asked. "What's the sense of that? It'll take every man we got to do that."

"You heard what I said. I'll take the helm. Now it stands to reason that he's gonna change course on us soon as we get within range. He can sail back into the wind as close as he can, but that won't gain him much distance. If he tries to swing her back through the eye of the wind, that would give us time to do likewise and overtake him. Or he can swing to the south again and run before the wind, figuring to gain distance on us before we can change course. I am gonna try something. If I am wrong, he may get away from us. But if I am right . . . I'll take the helm again. All hands stand by."

Lovejoy had been fascinated by the cat-and-mouse game that had been going on for five hours. He glanced at the sun now dipping near the horizon.

"We are within range again, Captain," Phipps yelled.

Talbot suddenly shoved the tiller over and yelled, "All hands, heave!"

That order was followed quickly by: "Bow chaser, open fire!"

Before the echo of the Long Tom had ceased, he ordered first the port and then the starboard carronades to fire. The shot from the stubby cannon came nowhere near the sloop as the smoke from their muzzles floated over the *Flora* like a fog bank, obscuring the crew resetting the schooner's sails.

"Keep it up, damn it," Talbot shouted.

Again and again, every one of the sixteen cannon aboard the *Flora* boomed, hurling shot across the water like a frustrated beast flailing the air and creating a cloud bank so thick that Talbot could not see his own bow.

Coming around to her new heading, the smoke-shrouded *Flora* caught the wind off her port quarter and began gaining speed. Breaking clear of her acrid smoke screen, she seemed to fly across the sea.

"What do you see up there?" Talbot shouted to the lookout, whose view was unobscured by the gunsmoke. "Which way is she headed?"

"She has turned south. She's coming this way."

Within another minute, it was clear that the sloop had done as Smith had anticipated and changed course to run before the wind and, as it were, into the arms of her smoke-shrouded pursuer.

Seeing the trap into which they had fallen, the crew of the sloop were desperately trying to change course again, but agile as their craft was, there was no way for them to dodge the broadside that the *Flora* poured into her.

Chunks of railing flew into the air. The top quarter of her single mast snapped off, dropping her broad topsail to the deck.

A hail of musket balls peppered her deck.

On her stern, a man was waving a large white flag. He dropped it and clutched his arm to his side. Someone else picked up the flag and continued to wave it.

Talbot danced a jig and clapped his hands. "Thought he could outsail Talbot Smith. Well, Dr. Martin, you'd better go below and open your medicine chest. You'll be getting some new patients, I expect."

He picked up his speaking horn and shouted across the water, "Ahoy, *Marrianne*. Do you strike?"

"Yes, for God's mercy, yes," the man who had dropped the white flag shouted back.

This time there was no Meg there to wipe Lovejoy's forehead and to help him bandage wounds. Soon his hands were coated with the blood of the wounded, most of them black Bermudians who had been injured by splinters caused by the brutal battering of the *Flora*'s carronades. Others had been shot down by the American marksmen.

Grinding his teeth to keep down his nausea, Lovejoy, with the cook's help, probed, swabbed, and bandaged for more than an hour.

His last patient was a man whose deep blue eyes contrasted with a sun-bronzed face. One arm hanging limply at his side, he was accompanied by Smith.

"This son of a bitch who calls himself the captain of that there sloop has took a musket ball through his arm. I would just as soon it had been through his heart for all the trouble he has put us through."

Lovejoy had the captain lie down on his table and examined the hole in his snowy white triceps.

"You are lucky, my friend. The ball passed through without striking the bone or hitting your body."

"I was hit while trying to surrender."

"You should of give up earlier," Talbot said.

"We are carrying salt in bins," the captain said through teeth clenched against the pain of Lovejoy's swabbing his wound. "There weren't enough of us to shovel out salt and sail the sloop. Otherwise, I could have run circles around this schooner."

"Ha! You'll never see the day you could run circles around any Baltimore schooner, and this one in particular. I built her myself."

The captain sat up and looked more closely at Talbot.

"Did you for a fact? I built my sloop, too."

Talbot's hostility dissipated at this information.

"How long did it take you?"

As if there were no war, the two captains stayed up until midnight talking about shipbuilding.

Near noon the next day, the *Flora*'s carpenters completed repairs to the sloop's upper mast and finished plugging the holes punched in her hull by the carronades.

As the sloop, now manned by a prize crew, drew away, Talbot said, "Now there goes a man after my own heart."

"It is a shame the fellow lost his sloop," Lovejoy said.

"Don't waste your tears on him. Told me last night he had took out insurance before he sailed. Hopes to put in a low bid at the auction.

May buy his sloop back and pocket the difference from what his insurance pays."

Their next capture was a barkentine slogging her way north with a cargo of indigo and cotton from Surinam. The captain had not heard about the war but said that he was not surprised.

Coming early in the day, the easy capture allowed a quick transfer of the prize crew. The vessel was soon on her way toward the American coast.

"That one was too easy," Talbot said. "We got less than a month left. On our next cruise, the British may be running convoys, and they will be better armed. Let's make hay while the sun shines."

Two days later, they sighted another schooner on a northwesterly tack. Talbot climbed to the crow's nest and spent a long time studying the craft.

He returned to the deck to announce that it was an American vessel.

"Is she flying our flag?" Lovejoy asked.

"She's flying the Union Jack."

"Then what makes you think . . ."

"The British don't build such schooners. Not only is she an American, but I'll lay you two to one she's a clipper out of Baltimore."

*Tomcat,* a two-hundred-ton schooner, had left Baltimore in July as one of the first privateers to clear the port. She had picked up several fishing vessels off the Newfoundland coast before making a sweep south around Bermuda.

Just as Talbot had spotted her as an American, so had her captain spotted the *Flora* for what she was. So he did not try to evade Talbot. Instead, he replaced the Union Jack with the Stars and Stripes and allowed the *Flora* to come alongside.

"Why, it is Talbot Smith, is it not?" the captain shouted.

"Aye, and is it not Phineas Graham?"

"Right. Who's your master?"

"I am."

While this information sank in, Talbot muttered to Lovejoy, "Son of a bitch is one of them high-society captains. Can't believe I am master of my own schooner."

Despite the difference in their social standing, the two men agreed to lash their schooners together and then spent the next two hours discussing their experiences.

Graham recalled that Talbot had been working on a large schooner. After he complimented him on the excellence of his work, Talbot loosened up. *Tomcat* was winding up a successful cruise but had not taken a prize as valuable as either the *Goodfellow* or the *Cornish Maid.* Nor had she been engaged in an exciting chase such as the one the *Flora* had had with the Bermudian sloop.

Amused at the way Talbot was lording it over his better-born colleague, Lovejoy retired to a corner of the deck to write the letters Graham had agreed to carry back to Baltimore.

"Sail ho!" the lookout shouted down to Talbot.

"Where?"

"Just on the horizon, about two points to starboard!"

The captain grabbed his spyglass and scrambled up to the crow's nest.

The *Flora* had been tacking back and forth over calm seas on a generally northeasterly course for several days—"trolling for prizes," Talbot called it.

Returning to the deck, the captain ordered topsails and spirit sails to be furled to slacken the schooner's speed and reduce her visibility.

"I make her out to be a full-rigged ship on an easterly course," Talbot said to Barineau and Phipps. "Can't tell whether or not she be British. Seems headed for our coast, howsomever. Mr. Phipps, raise your British colors and let's see what they do. And send every hand not needed for sailing below decks, out of sight."

An hour later, it was plain to see even from the deck of the *Flora* that the ship was carrying only a light cargo and that she was flying the Stars and Stripes.

"Now that is a curious thing," Talbot said. "They got to have spotted our British colors and yet they're acting like they don't care we're in the same ocean."

"How is she armed?" Barineau asked.

"Here, see for yourself."

He handed the sailing master his telescope.

"One gun fore and one aft, I'd say. Look to be only six-pounders. You suppose they don't know about the war?"

At their approach, the ship lowered her sails without Talbot having to put a shot across her bow.

"Shall we raise our flag to let them know we are American?" Phipps asked.

"Let's keep them thinking we're British. Say," he turned to Lovejoy, "can you talk like an Englishman?"

"I rahther think I might," Lovejoy replied in a voice that sounded as if he had a plum in his mouth.

"Here." He handed him his cap and his speaking horn. "Ask them who they are."

Grinning, Lovejoy took a deep breath and yelled across to the ship in his best imitation of a British accent.

"Ahoy, there, who are you chaps?"

The captain of the ship yelled back, "We are the *Delaware Queen* out of Philadelphia. Who are you?"

Talbot whispered to Lovejoy, "Don't answer. Ask if they know about the war."

"I say, don't you know we are at war with you Yankees?" Lovejoy sang out.

"Yes. We heard back in Cadiz. But it's all right. We have a Sidmouth license. We carried a cargo of flour over for your army in Spain. You don't look to be British navy. Who are you?"

"Son of a bitch is trading with the enemy. All right, Phipps, let's board her."

The crew came boiling up through the hatch and onto the deck. Talbot himself lowered the British colors and raised the Stars and Stripes.

Then, reclaiming his speaking horn, he shouted across the water, "Strike your colors or we'll blow you out of the water."

The captain of the ship did not resist. But he was outraged at being duped.

"Look here, you have no right to board us like this."

"We have a letter of marque and reprisal from the United States government," Talbot replied. "We are fully bonded and acting entirely within the law. You, on the other hand, have been trading with the enemy. Do you deny it?"

"What we are doing is legal. We cleared port before war was declared. If you don't believe me, you can examine our papers."

"You bet your life, I will do just that. Jenkins, Barineau, come with me."

Lovejoy was flattered to be included in the council of war that followed the inspection of the *Delaware Queen*'s papers.

"Her captain has a point, I reckon," Smith said. "She cleared port before Congress declared war. He did not know of the war until after he had unloaded his flour in Spain. He argues that this makes it illegal for us to take him as a prize."

Barineau normally kept his own counsel, but now he spoke up with surprising vehemence.

"He still is operating under a British license. Even though he knew the war was on, he was quick to cite his Sidmouth when he thought he was being challenged by a British rather than an American craft. He is trying to have it both ways, and I for one don't think he should get away with it."

"Who owns her?" Phipps asked.

"A company I never heard of. The Rosachest Company. Isn't that it, Jenkins?"

"Yes, sir. Headquarters are in Dover, Delaware according to her papers."

"What cargo is she carrying?" Lovejoy asked.

"Not very much of anything. Figs and oranges, plus a few casks of Madeira, according to her manifest."

"Her cargo has nothing to do with the question of whether she is a proper prize or not," Barineau said.

"It has a lot to do with whether she is worth the trouble of taking her when the admiralty court may rule against us," Smith replied.

"Is the ship herself likely to bring a good price?" Lovejoy asked.

"She'd bring more if t'werent for the war. She'd be no good for privateering, and I don't see much market for a slow-sailing merchantman until the war is over."

Lovejoy said, "I say let's claim her and take our chances with the court."

Phipps looked at the *Delaware Queen* and at his own diminished crew.

"I don't see how we could man a three-master like that with less than fifteen hands. That's a lot of men for us to give up for a practically empty ship, especially when there is the question of whether she is a proper prize."

"Wait a minute," Lovejoy said. "Her crew are all Americans, aren't they?"

"They seem to be."

"And it would appear that they are experienced sailors, for the most part."

"I would suppose so. They handled her clear across the Atlantic and most of the way back. What are you getting at?"

"Is there anything to stop us from holding a recruiting rendezvous right here at sea?"

It took a moment for Lovejoy's idea to sink in. Suddenly Talbot smote his hands together and then clapped Lovejoy on the shoulder.

"By thunder, our young surgeon is beginning to show a little gumption. Phipps, bring all their hands over here but the captain hisself. Jenkins, bring up plenty of paper and make yourself a desk. Now who's the man to sell them on the idea?"

"Are you asking for a volunteer?" Lovejoy said.

Anyone who might have doubted Lovejoy Martin's powers of persuasion would have changed his mind if he had witnessed the performance that took place during the next half hour. Standing before the very mast where he had been kept bound and gagged early in the cruise, Lovejoy plucked at every chord he thought would resonate with the thirty men of the crew of the *Delaware Queen*.

First he appealed to their patriotism.

"I know you sailed out of Philadelphia in good faith, thinking you were shipping out on a legal trading voyage, but, my lads, you were duped by the mendacious owners of your vessel. They are nothing but war profiteers, trading with the perfidious enemy. We are at war with that enemy now, and it behooves every American who believes in freedom on the sea as well as on land to do what he can to strike a blow for liberty. What better way than to sign up on this splendid schooner that has already taken four enemy prizes and may well take another four before our cruise ends?"

Then he talked about the financial gain offered by privateering.

"Tell me, how much are the unprincipled owners of your ship paying you for taking part in their trading with the enemy?"

"Twenty-two dollars and fifty cents a month," a hard-bitten old salt spoke up. "What are you offering us?"

Lovejoy laughed and turned to Talbot.

"Hear that, Captain Smith? Twenty-two dollars and fifty cents a month. Well, lads, we have already sent prizes back the value of which may well exceed fifty thousand dollars. Now half of those proceeds are to be divided amongst our crew."

"Are you saying we would have shares of what you have already took?" a *Delaware Queen* sailor asked.

"No, but you will have a share in everything we take from this point on, is that not correct, Captain?"

"Aye, it is."

"And could we not include the value of this ship on which they have been serving?"

"I don't see why not."

"Hear that, lads? Here is your chance to become part owners of the *Delaware Queen* herself. Now doesn't that beat twenty-two dollars and fifty cents a month?"

"I got a wife waiting for me back in Philadelphia."

"She'll be just as happy if you come up by stage from Baltimore, especially if you come with a pocket full of money."

"There don't look like you have much room for a crew on this here schooner."

"No, and there won't be much room for you on your old ship, for it will be necessary to keep you locked away in very close quarters on the trip back to Baltimore, if, that is, you are foolish enough to turn down our offer."

The captain of the *Delaware Queen* stood on his own poop deck with his arms crossed over his chest, listening to Lovejoy's discourse. On the threat of being put in irons, he had been forbidden to speak to his own crew.

His expression of disgust turned to one of dismay as Lovejoy ended his appeal with, "Now our supercargo is ready to take your signatures. Let's see which of you are real Americans and which of you are merely lackeys of traitorous war profiteers."

Nearly half of the *Delaware Queen*'s crew—mostly younger men without families at home—lined up to enlist for the rest of the *Flora*'s cruise. There were more than enough of them to make up for the prize crew chosen to man the *Delaware Queen*.

Later, after Tom had come aboard the captured vessel and given the prize master his papers for the admiralty court, the captain detained him.

"Who is the fancy chap with the silver tongue who has stolen my crew from me?"

"He is our ship's surgeon."

"And what might be his name?"

"You are asking too many questions."

"I am going to ask a lot more when I get back. What has just taken place here is little short of piracy on the high seas. My owners and their partners are not going to take this lying down."

"Oh? And who might your owners and partners be?"

"Never mind. You can wait and find out from our lawyers."

During the early part of their cruise, Pierre Barineau, the schoolteacher turned sailing master, had said little on any subject to Lovejoy. He spent most of his spare time reading the books of essays and plays he kept on a shelf over his bunk in the officers' compartment.

Following the taking of the *Delaware Queen*, Lovejoy was surprised when Barineau asked him whether he played chess.

"Not very well, I fear."

"You'd be doing me a favor if you would try a game or two. We could go below to avoid our captain's displeasure at seeing idle hands on deck."

Barineau had a set of chessmen carved from whalebone with bases that fitted into slots on the board so the game could be played in rough seas. He could have ended the first game in less than a dozen turns but chose to drag things out, playing defensively, easily staving off Lovejoy's aggressive moves.

"Want to try another?" he asked when Lovejoy acknowledged defeat.

This time, Barineau, playing white, quickly seized command of the game and trapped Lovejoy's queen in a fork from which there was no escape. Checkmate followed quickly.

It galled Lovejoy to be beaten so easily. He asked for a third game, but Barineau put him off. Taking out a pipe, he loaded it with tobacco and looked into Lovejoy's face for a long while before lighting a taper from their lantern.

"You'd make a good player if you'd learn to think ahead a few more moves. You're too impulsive."

"I haven't had your experience."

"You can tell a man's temperament by the way he plays."

"If that is another way of saying I am impulsive, you should know you are not the first person to tell me so."

"You can learn to play any game calmly and more thoughtfully with discipline. And that goes for the game of life, too."

Lovejoy laughed. "I heard that you were a schoolmaster. You certainly sound like one."

"That is how I make my living. But I am also a student. I have never stopped reading and learning. What about yourself? Do you read much?"

"Not since I left Princeton. Seems to me that time is better spent in experiencing life rather than reading about someone else's experiences and opinions, especially when you are young."

"I see your point, but it is possible to strike a balance. For instance, this privateering cruise is turning into an interesting experience, is it not?"

"I am enjoying it a hell of a lot more than I expected."

"So am I. But I get an extra measure of enjoyment by keeping a journal. I don't mean just the log of the *Flora* but also my own record in which I set down observations far beyond cut-and-dried statements of how many knots we sail in a day or what our estimated noontime positions are. The exercise gives meaning to my experiences. I shall enjoy reading it in my old age."

"My father wrote a memoir of his service in the Revolution. He made me read it when I was in school. It was fascinating."

"My father also served in the American Revolution. I wish he had left such a record. He came over as a servant in Lafayette's entourage and remained in this country when the marquis returned to France. He was not an educated man, but he taught me to love learning and to despise the British."

"Malcolm MacKenzie said you hated the British. Is that why?"

"That is not the entire reason. My oldest boy ran away from home ten years ago. He signed on as a cabin boy aboard a bark sailing out of Baltimore. A British frigate stopped the ship and took off everyone they thought might be English. Most of them were, as a matter of fact, but they took others who were American born. Among them was my son, Phillip. Eventually they freed two men who were able to prove their American nationality. For Phillip, it was too late. He died of a fever. He would have been about your age."

"I am sorry."

Barineau swallowed and continued. "They are such a snobbish race. They tout their alleged individual freedoms while looking down their noses at the rest of mankind. I hate the brutish, callous way they treat their children. And they are such opportunists and hypocrites. Did you not find them so during your stay in London?"

"I had a lot of friends there, at least until my money ran out. I want to go back some day."

"This is very interesting. Enough of my prejudices. Tell me what you liked about your experiences over there."

At first Lovejoy was put off by the sailing master's frankness and his probing questions, but, seeing that the man was genuinely interested, he opened up and told him more about his life in London than he had thus far revealed to anyone.

Barineau laughed at his description of the autopsy. "It does sound ghastly. I have heard that professors of medicine try to shock their students, to see which ones can bear up."

"I fear I failed the test."

"The real test is how you conduct your everyday life. And you seem to be holding your own well enough as ship's surgeon, but I can see that medicine is not your true calling."

"Maybe you can tell me what is."

"I have twice heard you make speeches which, while self serving, still were delivered in a most effective way."

"I did win a prize for debating at Princeton."

"Did you enjoy anything else about your studies there?"

"I acted in a few of Shakespeare's plays."

Barineau grew more animated at this revelation. "Is that a fact? Why, I have three volumes of his plays on my shelf of books, one of his comedies, one his tragedies, and one, histories. Have you a favorite play?"

"I guess that would be *Julius Caesar*. I love Marc Antony's funeral oration."

"So do I. We must have a reading. Maybe we will involve Phipps, as well. You know, divide the play into parts. And say, Dr. Martin, I have been giving some thought to the fact that many of our crew can't read or write. Would you help me persuade the captain to allow me to tutor those who are interested? You would? Grand. Perhaps you would help me instruct them."

"It would help us pass the time. But look here, no more of this Dr. Martin business. My friends call me Joy."

"Now that is a happy name."

Barineau rose and shook his hand. "And my friends call me Pierre."

That night, Barineau sat up late bringing his journal up to date:

> *Our reluctant young ship's surgeon has far more depth than I first thought and more than he himself may realize. His selfishness is only skin deep. At his core, I believe, there is an intelligent man waiting to break out into the open. I think he is beginning to realize that true happiness is only to be found in making oneself useful to other people. We had a wide-ranging conversation today for the very first time. He is a miserable chess player but has a lively mind. We talked for nearly two hours . . .*

"This is a privateering vessel, not a floating schoolhouse."

"I know that, Captain, but there are a good many of our crew who would benefit from instruction."

"Be that as it may, we signed you on to be our sailing master, not schoolmaster. If you liked teaching so much, you should have stayed home."

"Believe me, Captain, I would not neglect my duties as your navigator."

"So you teach them to read. What good will it do them at their ages?"

"Some of the lads are young enough so that it might affect the course of their lives. And even the older men would benefit."

"Reading books is a waste of time."

"You can read, of course, Captain?" Lovejoy said.

"Well enough to get by, if it is any of your business."

"Do you wish that you could not?"

"I never said that."

"We don't want to press our case if your mind is made up."

"What do you mean 'we'?"

"Why, I have offered to help him with his instruction."

"Ha! Never thought a college-educated fellow like yourself would lower hisself to rub knees with poor boys that have to work to make their way in life."

"I am more than willing, but since your mind is made up, we will speak no more of it."

"I didn't say my mind was made up. I just ain't saying yes."

"We understand, don't we, Mr. Barineau? By the way, Captain, would you be willing for us to use your cabin when you don't need it? We were thinking of entertaining ourselves by reading some of Shakespeare's plays."

"You ain't turning my cabin into no theater."

Lovejoy explained what they had in mind.

"Oh, what the hell. You can have an hour this evening, if we don't see a prize before then."

Barineau grinned at Lovejoy as Talbot walked away grumbling about having to put up with "overeducated" men at sea.

# 4

As the friendship between Barineau and Lovejoy deepened, Tom grew increasingly sullen. During the lull in the *Flora's* captures, there was not enough to keep him busy. He felt left out of the conversations that absorbed the other two men. He liked Phipps well enough, but the first mate's piety bored him.

Noticing Tom's black looks, Barineau suggested inviting him to take part in their Shakespearean readings.

To Lovejoy's surprise, Tom's face brightened and he said that he would be pleased to participate if Barineau would explain the story to him.

They invited Phipps also, but he declined their invitation, saying that he was too busy, and besides, he preferred to spend his spare time reading the Bible.

Barineau chose *The Merchant of Venice* for their first reading. He explained to Tom a bit about the history of Venice and its role in late medieval commerce.

"Why, it sounds like Baltimore," Tom said.

"Very much, except that Venice was built on a swamp, and instead of streets, they had, and indeed still have, canals. But it was a booming, bustling center of commerce, just like Baltimore. And you might compare the Adriatic Sea to our Chesapeake Bay."

Once this was all explained and the characters defined, Tom entered into the spirit of the play, taking the parts of Antonio and Lorenzo with enthusiasm.

They were finishing scene 2 of act 1 when Talbot came into his cabin.

"Do you want us to clear out, Captain?" Barineau asked.

"Don't mind me. I am just looking for a duty roster. It's here in my desk, somewhere. Carry on."

By the time their reading had reached the end of scene 3, in which Shylock appears, Talbot had found the papers he was looking for, but he remained at his desk, pretending to study a chart.

When the readers paused at the end of the act to change roles, Talbot cleared his throat and asked, "There weren't a war going on during all this, were there?"

"No," Barineau said.

"Then what was all the worry about them ships not making it back to port?"

Barineau explained about the perils of ship commerce in the days of Venice's glory.

"What kind of ships did they sail in them days?"

"Some were called carracks. They had very high poop decks and a high forecastle. And, I believe, they had a mainmast with one large square sail and a jib extending to the rear. Others were called caravels, with four masts, lanteen rigged, I believe. They had nothing to compare with a Baltimore schooner."

"What about this Jew fellow? What was all the fuss about him charging interest?"

Barineau explained the church's laws against usury, adding that it did not apply to Jews.

"Church or no church, the Jew had a right to take interest. Why should he stick his neck out for somebody that treated him like he was dirt?"

"Don't you think a pound of flesh was a bit extreme?"

"If the fellow didn't want the money, he didn't have to make the bargain. Must have been desperate."

"He was, Captain, he was. But he also was sure that his ships would return safely and he would be able to repay the three thousand ducats."

"He weren't the first fellow to count his chicks before they come home to roost."

Lovejoy put his hand over his mouth to conceal his mirth and said, "No, Captain, nor was he the first person to hatch his plans before his ship came in."

Barineau frowned at Lovejoy, but Talbot, missing the humor, continued. "You know, there is some back in Baltimore that calls me Shylock Smith. Never understood why."

Lovejoy, choking back his laughter, did not dare look at Barineau, as he said, "Nor can I."

The captain puzzled over the question, then asked, "Well, did the fellow's ships get back all right?"

"Why don't you stick around and listen to find out? Maybe you'd like to read a part yourself."

"I don't want to do that, but don't let me stop you. What happened after the fellow signed the bond?"

With Talbot listening, they finished the reading of the play the following night.

"Who was it writ all that?" he asked at the conclusion.

Barineau explained a bit about Shakespeare.

"Fellow was never in business, was he?"

"He is thought to have been in the theater business."

"He would have made a poor merchant if he went about lending money at no interest. And I don't know why he was so rough on the Jewish fellow, Shylock. I have had some dealing with Jews and they have always dealt fair with me. Fairer than many a so-called Christian."

He looked at Lovejoy and added, "Take that banker Findley what sold my mortgage out from under me. Pillar in the Presbyterian church. Takes advantage of his position, he does. Shakespeare should of writ a play about him."

"Of course, none of this really happened," Tom said. "This is just something the fellow Shakespeare made up."

Talbot rose and stretched. "We only got three weeks before we head back into port. Is that enough time for you to teach some hands how to read?"

"If we can enlist Tom to help us, we would have time enough to make a good start."

"Just make sure it don't interfere with their jobs. I'll tell Phipps it is all right."

He paused at the door of his cabin. "You fellows mean to read any more of them plays?"

Barineau looked at Lovejoy. "What would you like to do next? *Hamlet* or *Julius Caesar?*"

"Either of them, or *Macbeth.*"

Rather than conduct formal classes, Barineau, Tom, and Lovejoy decided that each would tutor two of the crew members who responded to their offer of reading instruction.

Lovejoy selected Kevin, the cook, and Toby, the former slave, as his pupils.

"Begin by telling me why you want to read," Lovejoy said as the two men settled beside him on the deck. He looked at the cook.

"There weren't none of my family in Galway that ever could read. Me father drunk most of the time. Me mither, God rest her sweet soul, had ten children, of which I was the second oldest. When me father wasn't beating me up, it was me big brother. I couldn't take no more of that, so I decided to run away to the British navy. But I couldn't sneak off without bidding good-bye to me sainted mither. She give me her little store of egg money what she had been hiding back from me father, God forgive him. She wouldn't let me go until I made her a promise."

"What was that?"

"She made me swear that when I returned I would know how to read and to write, as well. And that is why I want to learn."

"Good, Kevin. I can teach you."

"I come on this voyage to make my fortune. Didn't expect to get this opportunity to learn, as well."

"There is no reason you can't realize your wish to return home with both money and the ability to read and write. You will make your mother proud."

"Yes, that is the first thing I will do, hand my mother a purse of gold and then take out a book and read to her. Then there is something else I mean to do."

"And what is that? Buy a farm for your family?"

"No. The next thing I will do is seek out me big brother and kick the shit out of him."

After he was done laughing, Lovejoy asked Toby why he wanted to learn to read and write.

"Folks says I am a free man, and I reckon I am in a way. Old Master left it in his will that when he died I was to be set free. I appreciate what Old Master done, but I am a long way from being free. He told his friends he looked on me almost as if I was his son. Almost, but not enough to take the time to learn me how to read, and he was a educated man. So, he thought he was setting me free, but how can a man feel free when he can't write his name?"

The cook frowned throughout Toby's story. When it ended, he said, "You ought to count your blessings, boy. Nobody taught me to read, neither. Leastways, you didn't get your ass whipped every day you was growing up, did you?"

"No, but Old Master had the power to whip me or to sell me off to a slave trader, as some of his neighbors did. That was always hanging over my head."

"In the British navy, a bosun's mate would turn your back to ribbons if you looked sideways at him. That's why I jumped ship and come to America. Look, boy, quit complaining. You are just as free as meself. And now you are getting a chance to learn to read, if you got the brains to handle it, that is."

"Why wouldn't I have the brains? See there, that's another way I am still a slave. I am a colored man, and if you think that ain't a handicap, then all I got to say is you ain't never been called nigger by somebody that may not be half the man you is."

"I never called you nigger, Toby."

"No, but you called me boy. And what makes you think I ain't got the brains to learn, same as you?"

Lovejoy, growing impatient, intervened. "There is nothing I can do about your color, Toby, but let's see if we can't break the chains of your illiteracy, and Cookie's too. Do you know your ABC's?"

Talbot would allow them only one hour between watches for their schooling, but Lovejoy was pleased by the progress of his students in their first session.

The following day, he gave them pens and sheets of paper on which he had printed their names. He showed them how to hold their pens. They were laboring away at copying their names when the lookout cried, "Sail ho!"

Talbot remained aloft with his telescope for a long while until Lovejoy, growing impatient, shouted up, "What do you see, Captain?'

"Climb up here and look for yourself."

Lovejoy was bothered almost as much by heights as he was by the sight of blood, but he managed to haul himself up to the narrow ledge that served as the crow's nest.

With a trembling hand, he took the telescope and pointed it in the direction Talbot indicated.

"I count one, two, three . . . why, Captain, it looks like an armada, and they're headed this way."

"I don't know about no armada but it sure looks like a convoy." He shouted down to Phipps, "Bring us to a new heading. Make it east by northeast. And set out the spirit sails."

"Those ships must be British. Aren't you taking us out of the path of what could be some very rich prizes?"

"That is exactly what I am doing."

Talbot snatched his telescope back and studied the distant sails of the approaching convoy.

"There must be ten or twelve of them. Now, you go below and leave this to me."

# 5

Until a few weeks earlier, Captain Wilberforce Harper had considered himself a fortunate man. As the commanding officer of HMS *Petrel*, a British frigate, he had enjoyed patrolling off the French coast to help keep Napoleon landbound and unsupplied with bounty from the New World. The last duty he ever would have asked for would have been to serve as an escort for a mixed lot of merchant tubs on a journey from London to the West Indies.

At least he had a further assignment that was more to his liking. After delivering his lumbering charges to the British navy base on Antigua, he was to take the *Petrel* up to the mouth of the Chesapeake and there rendezvous with other British ships to blockade the American coast. The American navy didn't amount to much, but the Yankees were supposed to have built themselves several excellent frigates. Sometimes he wished that there were a much larger American fleet. A victory over a foe of worthier steel might win him yet another promotion before he retired.

It irked Captain Harper that he had to hold back the *Petrel* and the faster merchant ships so as not to get too far ahead of the slower vessels in his convoy. And the slowest of these was the *Maiden Princess,* a bark laden with ammunition for the Royal magazines on Antigua.

The *Petrel* was kept busy shifting from one position in the convoy to another, like an anxious shepherd watching over a flock of careless sheep. When Harper wanted to change the convoy's course, the *Petrel* had to race to the van of the fleet, raise the proper signals, and lead the way to the new heading. At daybreak each morning, Harper climbed to the crow's nest and looked about to count his flock and see which might have wandered off during the night. Several times he had had to signal the other ships to lay to until the *Maiden Princess* caught up.

Ideally, the convoy would have been larger, and there would have been four warships herding it along: one in the van, one on either flank, and one bringing up the rear. But back in mid-July, when news of the Americans' reckless declaration of war reached London, nervous insurance underwriters had immediately increased rates for unescorted voyages to the New World. Within two weeks, the Admiralty had issued orders to provide naval escorts for British shipping. There hadn't been time to call in all the ships necessary to form this convoy in the proper way. The *Petrel* had to take this duty alone.

They had spotted several sails since departing the southern English coast. One was flying Spanish colors, the others British. All were headed toward home and showed no disposition to close the distance between themselves and the convoy.

So, when a lookout shouted "Sail ho," and a lieutenant sent aloft to confirm the sighting reported that it was a schooner on the horizon ahead, Captain Harper took a wait-and-see attitude.

When the lieutenant reported that the schooner was flying British colors and had changed course and put on fresh sails to avoid the convoy, he simply ordered the lookout to keep a close watch on the craft and held the *Petrel* and her flock on the same course. He was not about to leave his convoy unprotected and chase a vessel that probably could outrun him anyway.

Actually, Harper was more concerned about the gray-blue clouds that lined the horizon to the southeast than the possibility that his lookout might have sighted an American craft under false colors. Except for a brief spell of heavy seas, the weather had been favorable so far. He dreaded a storm that might scatter the convoy. Those clouds to the south did not look too serious, but Harper was a cautious man, so he went below and reviewed his instructions for handling a convoy in a storm.

Two miles behind him, the *Maiden Princess* plodded along at the rear of the convoy. The captain of the bark often wished that his owners had allowed him to sail without an escort. It was such a struggle to keep pace with the convoy, and he really thought that all the fuss about American privateers was ridiculous.

At least he had good company on this voyage. He shared his commodious cabin with two young doctors sent out to Antigua as contract surgeons by the Royal Navy, but he did not mind. They were irreverent, high-spirited young chaps who regaled him with stories of their medical studies and their service at a London hospital for the poor.

Bored with their inactivity, they concentrated on treating the ailments of the bark's crew. Never were sailors so well served medically, nor better entertained. One of the young doctors, the chubby, ginger-haired one, had brought along a mandolin, which he played to accompany the repertoire of bawdy songs that he and his swarthy comrade liked to sing.

The captain of the *Maiden Princess,* like that of the *Petrel,* was concerned about the darkening sky to the south. He had lived through one hurricane several years before and never wanted to experience another. He doubted that his bark, weighted down as she was with a hold full of kegs of powder and crates of cannonballs, could survive a real hurricane.

As it turned out, the clouds did not represent the leading edge of a hurricane, but near sundown, they did bring with them a fresh breeze and a rain squall.

The captain watched first the shortened sails of the *Petrel* and then those of the other ships disappear into the rain ahead. Finally, the sea around the *Maiden Princess* grew choppy, and rain drenched her decks.

Clad in oilskins, the captain remained on the quarterdeck beside the helmsman, keeping a close watch ahead so that the bark did not blunder into a sister ship. The two young doctors took refuge in the cabin as the *Maiden Princess* groped her way along through the drenching rain.

The two were at the point of pouring themselves a dram of rum when they heard shouting overhead, followed by gunshots. The *Maiden Princess* suddenly lurched amid a tremendous, crunching thud. The ginger-haired doctor was thrown from his stool. His taller, dark-haired colleague dropped their rum bottle and fell across the cabin table, knocking it over.

Regaining his feet, the chubby young doctor looked out a stern porthole. The color drained from his face as he said to his comrade, "Good God, Jennings. We have collided with another ship. I told you our captain did not know his business."

Within seconds they heard more voices shouting overhead and then the thump of what seemed to be dozens of footsteps, followed by cries of "Yield!"

The sound of scuffling and shouting continued for only a minute or so until they heard their captain crying, "We strike, damn your eyes."

The two young men barred the cabin door and then shoved the captain's desk against it. They cowered there for ten minutes, until someone tried the door.

"Who's in there? Open up."

The ginger-haired doctor put his finger to his lips and whispered, "Sounds like a bloody Yankee."

"Open up or we'll break down the door."

The pair remained huddled behind the overturned desk until they heard the voice of their captain.

"Better do as they say, young gentlemen."

They set the desk upright and lifted the bar. The door burst open, and several rough-looking Americans, one a huge black man armed with a cutlass, and another a fellow brandishing a meat cleaver, rushed into the cabin. They were followed by a wiry little man sporting a captain's cap. They did not see the well-dressed chap with sandy hair, carrying a black bag, who remained outside with the captain of the *Maiden Princess,* who was guarded by two Americans with pistols.

"Who are you people?"

The wiry little man pushed his way past his own men and declared, "We are privateers operating under a license issued by the United States government, and this here vessel has just been surrendered to us. Who are you?"

"We are medical doctors, and you have no right to interfere with us."

"You don't look much like doctors to me."

"Well, we are."

"You are still our prisoners. Now stand aside so's we can examine this here bark's papers. Where's Jenkins? Get him in here. Let their captain in, so's he can show us his documents. Get a move on. It'll be dark soon, and we don't have time to waste here. Phipps, are you out there?"

"Yes, Captain."

"Well, bear a hand and get your prize crew organized. We don't want that frigate to double back and catch us with our pants down. And get these here so-called doctors out of the way."

Lovejoy stepped back from the doorway so that his face was hidden in the shadows. He whispered to Toby and Kevin, who were now standing outside with him.

As the two doctors left the cabin, each was seized and blindfolded.

"What the hell is going on?"

"You are prisoners. We cannot allow you to see any more than you have already seen. Here, Toby, Kevin, lead these miserable sawbones over under that lantern and sit them down. I have some questions to put to them."

When the two were seated, Lovejoy stood before them with his hands on his hips.

"So, you claim to be physicians. What are your credentials?"

"We don't have to tell you," the swarthy one said.

Lovejoy winked at Kevin.

"Did you bring the castor oil, Cookie?"

"I did, sir."

"Well, much as I hate to do it, we'll have to pour it down their gullets if they won't tell us just what their claims to medical knowledge may be."

"Hell, Jennings, there's no harm in telling him. We both studied medicine at St. Bartholomew's Hospital in London. Now will you remove this blindfold?"

"Not yet, but we will withhold the castor oil as long as you answer our questions. Now we can't have people going about claiming to possess medical knowledge when, for all we know, they may be nothing more than ignorant bonesetters or ambitious barbers as quick to open an honest citizen's purse as they are his veins. If you are not a pair of rougish quacksalvers, tell me, who were some of your lecturers at Barts?"

Lovejoy had to bite his knuckles to keep from laughing as the two recited the familiar names of John Abernethy, James McCartney, and Richard Powell.

"How do I know that you aren't making up those names? I won't be convinced unless you can answer me some questions to test whether you learned anything from the gentlemen you have named."

"What do you want to know?"

"I would like to know what you do if a patient complains of a a pain in his right lower abdomen.

"That would be cramp colic. First off, you wouldn't give him a purgative. Just keep him cool and hope it passes."

"What if a mother brings you a child with convulsions?"

"I'd recommend a bath in cool water and maybe a light dose of silver nitrate. Should take care that it doesn't swallow its tongue."

"What if a feverish patient comes to you coughing and complaining of acute pain in the chest?"

Lovejoy went down a list of several illnesses before he asked, "What about the pox?"

"Do you mean gonorrhea or syphilis?"

"Start with the clap."

"I would treat the patient with an application of sandalwood oil or mercury and forbid him to have sexual intercourse until the infection cleared up."

"Oh? Have either of you ever had the clap?"

"Not I," replied the dark-haired one.

Lovejoy jabbed the shoulder of the ginger-haired doctor.

"What about you?"

"None of your business. Why do you want to know?"

"I will ask the questions here. Now, I have heard that in London, students from—where did you say you studied, Barts? That they frequented a house of ill repute conducted by one Nellie Mungo, in Soho."

"Some of the fellows might have gone to Nellie's, I suppose, but who the hell are you? I am getting tired of these questions."

"I think you are lying. I think you have had the pox yourself, and I'll wager you caught it at Nellie's."

Jennings leaned toward his partner and whispered, "Who is this bounder?"

"How do you know about Nellie's place?"

Before Lovejoy could think of a response, Talbot came out of the *Maiden Princess*'s cabin and interrupted the mock inquisition.

"Look here, Dr. Martin, why are these men blindfolded?"

Lovejoy shook his head and put his fingers to his lips.

"I was hoping to discover where they store their medicine kits. They would be useful to us."

Tom, who was just behind Talbot and missed Lovejoy's signal, said, "Why, Joy, there is two chests full of medicine and such in the cabin."

Jennings tore the blindfold from his eyes and, before Toby or Kevin could stop him, lifted that of his comrade.

"God take me for a fool, it really is Lovejoy Martin. I knew I had heard that voice before."

Lovejoy now was doubled over from laughing so hard.

"What in hell's name is going on?" Talbot asked. "We got no time to be playing jokes here."

Holding his sides, tears coursing his cheeks, Lovejoy gasped, "I know these two blackguards, Captain. I studied medicine with them in London."

Neither "Ginger" Pelham nor "Taffy" Jennings ever thought that the prank was nearly as funny as did their old fellow medical student, "Joy Boy" Martin, although both would tell much embellished versions of the incident afterward. And they definitely saw nothing humorous in what Talbot said when he interrupted the three young men's display of pounding one another on the back and shaking hands.

"We got about fifteen minutes before Barineau and his prize crew have to get this bark under way for Baltimore. So finish up with your reunion so's we can lock your friends up with the rest of this here crew."

"You can't take us to Baltimore," Ginger said. "We have contracts to fulfill on Antigua. See here, Martin, this fellow is not serious, I hope."

Talbot ignored the two Englishmen.

"This is the most valuable cargo that we have took. This tub is carrying enough gunpowder and such to supply our government for the next year. It won't do us near as much good in Charleston as it will in Baltimore. It won't be easy sailing this here thing that far off, so's I want to put my best navigator in charge. And that is Barineau. So you got fifteen minutes with your friends."

The three young men spent the next ten minutes breathlessly bringing one another up to date on what they had been doing in recent months.

The two Englishmen could not believe not only that Lovejoy was serving as a ship's surgeon but that he was doing so on an American privateer of which he was the major owner.

"You never seemed to give a hang about anything but having a good time," Jennings said. "How did you get involved in this silly war, which we all know you Yanks are going to lose?"

"It's too complicated to explain," Lovejoy said.

"If you are the owner, why can't you overrule that rude little man and let us continue to Antigua?" Ginger asked.

"Yes, my family strapped themselves to provide me with my medicines and instruments. You weren't serious about taking them, were you?" Jennings said.

"Of course not. There should be pen and paper in the cabin. I will dash off a note to our agent in Baltimore saying that your personal possessions are not to be condemned."

"That is small comfort, but thanks anyway," Ginger said.

Inside the cabin, Lovejoy handed a hurriedly scrawled note to Jennings and said, "Count your blessings, chaps. You are lucky our captain has decided to send you up to Baltimore and not Charleston or Wilmington. I am asking our agent to see that you are well treated until you can be exchanged. By the way, Ginger, if they allow you any freedom in Baltimore, ask your way to Mamie Brown's Calvert House. It's as good a place as Nellie Mungo's, and you won't catch the clap there."

"I never had the clap. It was only a rash."

"If you say so, Ginger. Now, there is no time to write anything else, but tell our agent—his name is Malcolm MacKenzie—that I am enjoying my duty and that I expect to see him before the end of November. He will give you a helping hand, I am sure."

"Thanks for that much anyway, Martin. Anything we can do for you in Baltimore, if that is to be our fate?"

"Well, there is a girl who probably is staying with the MacKenzies . . ."

"Ah yes, with Joy Boy Martin, there would always be a girl," Ginger said. "Well, what is it you want her to be told?"

In the growing dark, the deck of the *Maiden Princess* had become a madhouse as Barineau and his bosun's mate hurriedly acquainted themselves with the rigging of the bark. The schoolmaster stopped long enough to shake Lovejoy's hand and hear his request that his two friends be treated well on the voyage to Baltimore.

"Captain Smith needn't know this, but I'll lock them away with the others for the first day to give them a taste, and then maybe let them share the cabin again. Do they play chess?"

"Probably. Look here, Pierre, I am going to miss you."

"And I you, Lovejoy. By the way, I didn't have time to pack my books. You'll look after them for me, won't you?"

"Of course. Are you nervous about having to captain this tub all the way back to Baltimore?"

"To quote our friend Shakespeare, 'Fortune brings in some boats that are not steered.' "

"I don't know that one."

"It's from *Cymbeline*. You will find it on my bookshelf."

"Cut out your gabbing and get back over here, Dr. Martin," Talbot shouted from the deck of the *Flora*. "All right, Mr. Barineau, you are the captain of that there prize. We'll see you in Baltimore in three or four weeks. Now cast off."

After Lovejoy had scrambled back to the deck of the *Flora,* Talbot said, "You had your reunion with your friends?"

"Yes, they are jolly good fellows. I told Barineau there is no harm in them and they are lots of fun."

"I told him to keep 'em locked up. Never trust an Englishman. I don't want Barineau to get his mind off navigating that sorry piece of shipbuilding back to Baltimore. I wouldn't let him go if I didn't figure the cargo was worth giving up my best man for it."

"He is a superb navigator, isn't he? The way he brought us about against the wind and then calculated our distances so we could sneak up on the rear of the convoy just before dark fell."

"He done us a good job."

"Did you tell him so?"

"Why give him the big head? Besides, the rain squall was a lucky break for us. If it hadn't been for that, the frigate might of seen us and there would have been hell to pay."

He paused to yell at Phipps, "Raise our sails and let's put some distance between ourselves and that there bulldog of a frigate before they catch on to what has happened."

# 6 

Lovejoy missed Barineau more than he would have thought possible at the beginning of the cruise. The schoolmaster had forced him to think about who he was and what he meant to do with his life. Now there was only Tom and Phipps to talk to, each of whom got on his nerves.

It galled Tom that, although he was doing a good job as supercargo, the captain meant to award him the same single share he would have received as a landsman or ordinary seaman.

He brought up the subject as he was standing a helm watch.

"How much do you reckon my share will be worth, Joy?"

"As I have told you more than once, Tom, it all depends on how much the prizes we have sent in bring at auction, and how many more we take before our time runs out."

"Well, you must have some notion."

"All right, just say everything brings eighty thousand dollars. Half of that comes to forty thousand. Divide by two hundred shares and you get . . ."

Tom scowled and said, "Why, that is only two hundred dollars. And by rights, it should be eight hundred or a thousand. It ain't fair."

"Life's not fair, Tom."

"It sure as hell is fair for you."

"I have to suppose that he will pay me the same single share as you get, whereas surgeons generally get seven or eight shares, same as Phipps will get as first mate."

"You know you'll get eighty percent of the other half."

"Malcolm MacKenzie will rake off ten percent of the owners' shares as his agent's fee. And there are other costs involved."

"Even so, you stand to clear at least twenty-five thousand dollars, and that is only for the first cruise. You might make even more on the next one."

"There will not be a next one for me."

"What will you do with this schooner?"

"Sell it outright, but you mustn't tell our captain. He loves the *Flora* as if she were his baby daughter. Anyway, I reckon she could bring as much as forty thousand dollars."

"There you go. And you get eighty percent of that, making another thirty-two thousand dollars. So what will you do with all that money?"

"I told you long ago about the girl I met aboard ship."

"But you said her family was strong Federalists. How are they going to take to the idea of you privateering against the British?"

"I don't intend to rush right into the subject. Let them learn to love me, and then I will tell them how I was first duped into investing in this enterprise, and then dragooned into serving as a surgeon, and how I got out of the business at my first opportunity. The trick is to feed them the truth in small doses. And my having something in excess of fifty thousand dollars will help the medicine go down."

"Is she really as beautiful as you made out, or were you stretching the truth there, too?"

"Tom, her beauty would take your breath away."

Phipps, assigned the duties of sailing master in Barineau's absence, had come to the stern to check on the compass heading in time to overhear the latter part of this conversation.

"What about you, Mr. Phipps?" Tom asked. "Are you going on another cruise after this one is done?"

"Ask me after we settle up for this one. I'll see how much my shares are worth and discuss the question with my wife. We will pray over it together and then decide."

"My mind is already made up," Tom said. "I like sea life better than running a tavern."

"I would prefer any life to that of running a tavern," Phipps said. " 'Wine is a mocker, strong drink is raging. It biteth like a serpent, and stingeth like an asp.' That's what the Bible says."

"Lovejoy knows our family tavern well. You see anything wrong with the White Swan, Joy?"

Before Lovejoy could reply, Phipps said, "I would be surprised if he did."

"What do you say to that, Joy?"

"Come now, Mr. Phipps, 'Dost thou think, because thou are virtuous, there shall be no more cakes and ale?' "

Phipps scowled. "The devil quotes the Bible to his own purpose."

Lovejoy laughed. "Actually, what I said came from Shakespeare, as does your remark, Mr. Phipps."

Phipps made a gesture of disgust and walked away from the two friends.

"You ought not to tease Mr. Phipps so, Joy. He is a decent fellow."

"I'd like him better if he weren't such a prig."

Lovejoy was careful to avoid revealing his plans to sell the *Flora* when Smith warned of how, on their next cruise, they would have to adjust their method of operating to counter the closer protection the British would provide their shipping.

Cruising far out to sea, north of Bermuda, they took what turned out to be the last of their easy, unsuspecting prizes. She was a hermaphrodite brig, with square rigging on her mainmast and fore-and-aft on her rear. She was laden with a cargo of coffee, cotton, and sugar en route from Surinam to Liverpool. Armed with only two cannon, she hove to and submitted to a boarding party without offering even a token resistance.

The captain had left New Amsterdam before news of the war with the Americans had reached that far-off Dutch-owned, but now English-occupied port. After Talbot had instructed the prize master and the fifteen men he had to give up to handle the vessel, Phipps expressed his concern at the shortage of hands left for sailing the *Flora*..

"Wouldn't you say it is time we headed back to port, Captain?"

"Why? We got two more weeks left."

"I'd be hard put to work this schooner if we had to give up another fifteen men as a prize crew."

"Look here, Mr. Phipps, we already hit one convoy headed out from England. By the time we get ourselves fitted out again, everybody in the islands will know about the war. What do you say to that, Dr. Martin?"

" 'There is a tide in the affairs of men, which, taken on the flood, leads on to fortune.' "

"What in the hell does that mean?"

"It is another way of saying make hay while the sun shines."

"Speaking of the sun," Phipps said. "I don't like how the sky is clouding over. And the sea is beginning to run heavy on us."

"I was speaking metaphorically," Lovejoy said.

"And I am speaking about the real weather. We may need every hand we have if I am any judge of the signs."

As Phipps walked off to consult with his bosun, Talbot shook his head. "You know, Doctor, some men is cut out to run things and some to follow orders. There is another sort which can't run nothing on their own but which can see that the orders of them that can is carried out. Now Phipps there has rizz as high as he ever could. He ain't mean enough to be a captain. Too fearful. All right as first mate but will always need a man made of stronger stuff watching over him. Am I not right?"

"You may be right, Captain. Now tell me what you have in mind for the rest of our cruise."

"I aim to head us east into the Gulf Stream off Cape Hatteras and look for a merchantman headed back for England. Does that make sense to you?"

"I'd like nothing better than to put another fat trout in our creel before we return to Baltimore."

Phipps was right about the approach of bad weather. By noon the sky had grown too cloudy to allow for a shooting of the sun.

For the next three days and nights, as the close-hauled *Flora* slogged along on an easterly course through heavy rains swirling out of the southwest, Phipps kept nervous track of their position by dead reckoning. Every two hours, he held a small half-minute hourglass while a sailor heaved a knotted line over the lee side. This line was attached to a weighted, wedge-shaped wooden plate. By counting the number of knots that ran off a reel in thirty seconds, he calculated their speed and recorded it with the compass heading on a slate. Each noon, using these readings, Phipps and the captain marked their assumed position on a chart.

Lovejoy could tell that neither man had Barineau's navigational skills. He heard frequent disputes between them about what location should be noted on the chart.

At last, when they ran out of the heavy weather and into calmer seas, they were able get a clear noon sighting of the sun. After the two men had gone to the captain's cabin to check their reading against a chart, Lovejoy went down to the adjoining officers' compartment to find a book.

"I thought you knowed something about navigation," he heard Talbot saying in the cabin.

"I never claimed to be a sailing master, but I think I know more than most first mates."

"Then why in hell's name are we a good hundred miles north of where we thought we was?"

Lovejoy sat down quietly at the officers' table to listen.

"I did exactly as Mr. Barineau instructed me."

"Did you allow for extra drift from the storm?"

"I thought you were doing that."

"Jesus Christ, it's no wonder we're way up here when we was supposed to be down here. You been doing a slack job."

"I did as I was taught by Mr. Barineau."

"Barineau would not have got us off of Cape Henry when we is supposed to be off of Hatteras."

"I am not the one that sent him back as prize master."

"No. I am the one, and I done the right thing when I did. Also, I am the one that chose you to serve as first mate, and there I am not so sure I done the right thing."

"It was my impression that Mr. MacKenzie selected me as your first mate."

"By God, are you questioning my authority?"

"I am not defying you. I was setting the record straight. I have had my hands full overseeing what's left of our crew, sailing through rough weather. I don't deserve to be rebuked."

"You've kept your nose stuck in that damned Bible when you should have been seeing that proper readings was being took."

"There is no call for blasphemy against the word of God."

"And there is no call for carelessness. If I had it to do over I would not have allowed MacKenzie to fob off a Bible thumper on me as first mate."

"And if I had it to do over, I would not have signed on to serve under a man who blames others for his own shortcomings. A man who lives in open sin with a colored woman is hardly justified in speaking against the reading of Holy Scriptures."

"By God, I will not stand for such back talk from a jacked-up bosun's mate."

Alarmed at the ugly tone of the confrontation, Lovejoy started to tiptoe out of hearing but, on second thought, turned and rapped loudly on the cabin door.

"Who in the hell is it?"

Lovejoy opened the door. "May I come in?"

"It looks like you are already in. What do you want?"

"I was just curious about our position."

Phipps, his face a sullen red, pushed past him. When he was gone, Talbot said, "We are way off course. Look, this is where we was supposed to be and here is where we have wound up."

He followed this with a tirade against Phipps, to which Lovejoy listened patiently.

"Phipps does get tiresome, but he is a steady fellow."

"Call him what you will, he'll never sail with me again. If I had anybody to take his place I would break him down to ordinary seaman for something he just said to me. He can count hisself lucky he didn't back talk me in front of anybody else or he would be bound and gagged right now."

"Captain, let me suggest that you don't do anything hasty this late in the cruise when you are already shorthanded."

Before Talbot could turn his anger on him, Lovejoy grinned and added hastily, "I speak as one who made some hasty remarks earlier in this cruise, in the hearing of others, and suffered some severe consequences."

Talbot looked at him closely. "You were a bit of a damned fool, weren't you? Hope you don't hold that against me. Had to show my crew that I couldn't be trifled with."

"No, Captain. You taught me a much-needed lesson in humility. Anyway, all's well that ends well, and I would say that this cruise is ending very well indeed."

"It ain't quite over, you know. Now the weather has cleared, and we know where we are, I want to head out to the southeast and keep a sharp lookout for one more prize coming up from the islands. Then we'll have plenty of money to take the *Flora* out again for her second cruise."

# 7

Despite Lovejoy's best efforts at peacemaking, the bad feeling between the captain and Phipps continued to fester, and their mutual hostility became obvious even to the densest of the thirty-odd men who remained aboard the *Flora* as she headed away from the mouth of the Chesapeake, back toward the Gulf Stream. Refusing to speak directly, they relayed their communications to each other through Tom or Lovejoy.

"Jenkins, please notify Mr. Phipps that he should change lookouts every hour. I want fresh eyes to be kept in the crow's nest."

"You may tell the captain that I will do my best to follow his orders, even though we are shorthanded."

"Tell Mr. Phipps that I know how many hands we have. Tell him he can take a turn as lookout hisself, if he feels his men is overworked."

Lovejoy, tired of the tension between the captain and first mate and bored now that he had so few men to attend to, volunteered to take his turn as lookout.

That is how he came to be in the crow's nest two days later when a whitish blur appeared on the eastern horizon. At first he took this to be a small cloud, but after scanning it with his telescope, he sang out, "Sail, ho! Just off the port bow."

Talbot came scrambling up the shrouds to join him.

"Can't make out her colors, but she looks to be a snow-rigged brig."

He yelled down to the deck, "Ahoy, Jenkins. Tell Mr. Phipps to send his landsmen below and arm themselves. Then bring her a'port by two degrees and hold steady."

Then, to Lovejoy, "You'd better take the cook below and lay out your equipment. And tell Phipps to raise our British colors."

Lovejoy started down the shrouds, then paused. "By the way, Captain, you won't forget my half share for spotting our prey, will you?"

The captain looked down into his face for a moment and, for the first time Lovejoy could remember, grinned.

"Only if you sign on for the *Flora's* next cruise. Now get your precious ass below while I see what we have out there. By God, she's carrying enough canvas to cover the Chesapeake Bay. Royals, topgallants, set of studs and a ringtail on her driver. Hope she don't try to run for it. She'd be hard to catch."

With the twenty landsmen below deck preparing themselves for action, Lovejoy saw why Phipps was so concerned by his shortage of seasoned sailors. There were only a dozen real tars on deck.

With the cook in tow, Lovejoy went below and prepared his surgery. After lowering the table and opening his medical chests, they laid out bandages and tourniquets and hung lanterns about, then went topside to see what was happening.

The captain had come down from the crow's nest and sent Tom up to take his place.

"She's carrying British colors, and she is holding steady on her course," Talbot said. "She has to have spotted us by now. Either she thinks we are English or figures she can outrun us."

"Could they not know about the war?"

"If she was sailing up from the south, maybe. But not with her coming from the east. I am going back up for a better look. Tell our first mate he'd better bring up three rounds for each gun and keep his landsmen below again out of sight until I give the word."

Phipps shook his head when Lovejoy informed him.

"We don't have enough men to do this job. Even if she strikes without a fight, we'd have to use a lot of greenhorns for a prize crew. The man has lost his reason. Can't you talk him out of this, Dr. Martin?"

"His heart is set on taking just one more prize."

"His heart is full of sinful pride, and pride goeth before a fall."

"Pride makes problems for a lot of us, Mr. Phipps. I had to swallow mine and apologize to the captain for what I said to him in front of the crew. Remember that?"

"You called him a guttersnipe. And you were right."

"I was wrong to call him that. And I am glad I apologized. Now, Mr. Phipps, I happened to have overheard you throw it up to him about the woman with whom he lives."

Phipps's face turned crimson. "I should not have said that. But did you hear him criticizing me for reading my Bible?"

"Yes. And blaming you for getting us off course during the storm. So maybe your pride is part of the problem."

"You could be right. What should I do?"

"When the captain comes down, take him aside and ask his pardon."

"I will think about it."

Talbot bellowed from the crow's nest. "Tell Mr. Phipps to get cracking or I'll find myself another first mate."

Phipps's jaw hardened as he turned to obey.

"It's my fault for delaying him, Captain," Lovejoy called.

"Well tell him to make that five rounds for each gun. That son of a bitch has tarps over her gunwales. I can't see what guns she carries."

The orders of HMS *Zephyr* called for her to proceed across the Atlantic and take up station off the entrance to the Chesapeake Bay to await the arrival of additional warships for blockading duties.

As Talbot had discerned, the *Zephyr* was rigged for speed. He could not yet see that, behind her concealed ports, she carried sixteen guns, all regular twelve-pounders, and below her decks, out of sight and with muskets at the ready, crouched a platoon of British marines. The *Zephyr's* captain, Augustus Wilsham, had seen the approaching sails of the *Flora* almost as soon as his own had been spotted by Lovejoy Martin. The British flag the *Flora* now flew had not fooled him for a second.

"I will lay you a wager," he said to his first lieutenant. "She is a Yank and she's out of a Baltimore shipyard. Here, take my glass and look for yourself. See how much sail she carries and how sharp built she is. So anxious to close with us she's pinching the wind, too, as only a schooner can do. Ah, come into my parlor, said the spider to the fly."

Aboard the *Flora*, finding it awkward to relay his commands to Phipps through Lovejoy or Tom, Talbot had taken direct charge of the schooner, bellowing orders at his bosun, quartermaster, and gunner's mate as if he had no first mate at all.

Humiliated at being so ignored, Phipps gave up his brief intent of apologizing to Talbot.

"Please inform our captain that if he requires my assistance I will be in the officers' quarters," he said to Tom.

Talbot responded to this message with, "Good riddance. I don't want a man on deck who is afraid to fight."

As the snow, with the wind from her starboard quarter, raced toward them, Talbot maneuvered the *Flora* across her approach and then changed his heading so that the two craft were running before the wind on the same course. He furled his lower sails to slacken speed and allow the other vessel to catch up.

"Are you convinced she is British?" Lovejoy asked.

"She's got to be. And her captain must be the biggest damned fool in the world to take us for one of theirs. Well, we'll know the truth in a few minutes."

When the *Zephyr* got to within a hundred yards, he ordered his forward Long Tom to fire a shot across her bow, raised the American flag, and shouted for all his landsmen to come up from the hold and take up positions as sharpshooters.

"Load your port guns and run them out!"

Aboard the *Zephyr,* with his naked eye, Captain Wilsham could read the name and port of the *Flora* emblazoned across the stern of the schooner. Nonetheless, as he drew alongside, he mounted his raised quarterdeck and shouted through a speaking horn, "Who are you and what do you want?"

"We're the *Flora*, a licensed privateer out of Baltimore, and we order you to strike or we'll blow you out of the water."

"What was that again?" Wilsham shouted, before saying in a lower voice to his lieutenant, "Remove the tarps and run out the starboard guns. Bring up the marines as well."

Talbot had repeated his surrender demand and was waiting for a reply when he realized what was happening.

"Go below," he ordered Lovejoy. "This is going to be a fight. Gunner's mate, open fire. Up there aloft, you landsmen. Aim for that tricky son of a bitch with the speaking horn."

Running alongside each other, barely two ship lengths apart, the two vessels opened fire within seconds of each other. As Lovejoy and the cook tumbled down the ladder to their surgical station, the *Flora* shuddered from the noise of her own broadside and from the impact of twelve-pound British cannonballs slamming against her sturdy oaken sides.

The *Flora*, running with fore and aft sails to the windward of her opponent, was the more maneuverable. However, the *Zephyr* had sixteen regular cannon to the *Flora*'s ten carronades and two Long Toms, and the British marines were slightly more numerous than the *Flora*'s landsmen. As long as they kept the wind behind them, neither vessel enjoyed an edge in speed.

While Phipps sulked in the officers' quarters and Lovejoy and the cook crouched in the hold beside the mess-cum-surgeon's table, overhead the sailors and landsmen of the *Flora* became locked in a desperate slugging match with their British foe.

Had this encounter occurred early in the cruise when he was fully manned, Talbot would simply have put his helm over, laid the schooner alongside the snow, and ordered his landsmen to swarm over the enemy deck. But even in the heat of battle, with his blood up, he knew that the British marines would be more than a match for the men he had available for a boarding party.

He was appalled at the damage being done to his beloved schooner. She had taken at least a dozen balls in her hull, and part of her forward railing had been carried away. But across the way, he could see that at least one British cannon had been knocked over and several holes punched in the lanteen sail rigged behind the rear mast.

One part of him wished to break off the contest and flee for the Chesapeake. But another cried out for him to reduce the Britisher to a hulk and humiliate her captain by hauling him back to Baltimore as a prisoner. The snobs of the city would never again treat Talbot Smith with disrespect if he whipped a British naval vessel in a fair battle.

"Bring up langrage from the hold," he screamed at his gunner's mate. "We got to work on her rigging."

Up in the crow's nest, Tom and three other men were perched with muskets that they were loading and firing so furiously that the barrels had grown too hot to touch. With smoke from the British guns obscuring the *Zephyr's* decks and musket balls singing about their own ears, they could not pick out the British captain or the helmsmen as individual targets. They could only fire their overheated weapons in the direction of the snow's raised quarterdeck.

The first three casualties came down to the surgery all at once. The seemingly worst case had been struck in the side by a splinter from the *Flora*'s rail. Lovejoy pulled out the piece of wood, thrust his finger into the wound to make certain there was no debris, and then stuffed it with cotton wool to staunch the bleeding and quickly bound the sailor's torso with a wide bandage.

"No, you can't go back up there. Lie down over there. What's next, Cookie?"

"It's Toby. He has took a ball in his arm."

"Let's see, Toby, old man."

He took the arm of the giant Negro.

"You can still move your fingers, I see. Let me feel. Ah, yes, the ball lies against the bone. Here, Cookie, give him a wad of cloth to bite on. This may hurt for a moment, Toby, but we ought to get that ball out. Ah, there, the probe has snagged it. Here, Toby, you'll want to keep this as a memento."

When he turned to attend to the third man, a landsman, he thought at first that the fellow had fainted.

"Put smelling salts under his nose, Cookie. That will bring him around."

"Doctor, nothing is going to bring this man around. He is dead."

Ripping off the man's shirt, Lovejoy discovered that a musket ball had made a neat and almost bloodless hole in the upper chest of the landsman.

Lovejoy was helping the cook lay the corpse aside and cover the face with a blanket when a fresh broadside slammed into the hull of the *Flora*. This was followed by a ragged response from the guns of the schooner and, shortly thereafter, by a surge of men down the ladder.

For a moment, Lovejoy thought that he had a half dozen fresh casualties to treat, but then he saw that one man was being carried by the others.

"Henceforth, only two of you need to come down with a wounded man," Lovejoy said sharply. "Now bring him over to the table and then get back up on deck. I am sure the captain needs you."

"The captain needs you, not us," one of the men, the *Flora*'s bosun's mate, said.

"What do you mean?" Lovejoy asked, as he turned to deal with the man who now lay moaning on his surgeon's table.

"It's the captain, you ignorant sawbones," the bosun's mate replied. "A cannonball has hit his leg."

For a moment, as he looked down at the mangled lower leg of Talbot Smith, Lovejoy thought that he was going to faint.

"My God," he said. "Who is in charge up there?"

"Nobody. We are going to have to strike."

"The hell we are. Get your ass back up there and keep the fight going. Cookie, give me a tourniquet and cut away his trousers."

He turned toward the closed door to the officers' quarters. "Phipps," he screamed. "Get out here."

The first mate came immediately.

"Up to the deck, man, and take charge."

Phipps looked down into the chalky white face of Talbot Smith and without a word raced up the ladder to the chaotic deck of the *Flora*.

Aboard the *Zephyr,* one cannon had been hurled from its carriage by an American shot and had crushed the legs of a gunner's mate. The longboat hanging from the stern had been smashed. Several holes now appeared in the lower sails. Among the half dozen crewmen wounded by musket balls was the helmsman, requiring Captain Wilsham himself to seize the tiller.

From that vantage point, he could see that the American schooner was taking a severe pounding as well. God, he wanted to get this battle over with. He cursed his failure to gain the weather gage. That would have allowed him the maneuverability to ram his adversary and give his marines the opportunity to prove their vaunted courage by subduing those damned Americans in hand-to-hand combat. That would have cost him even more casualties, but it would have spared him the embarrassment of delivering a battered HMS *Zephyr* for blockading duty.

Although the smoke swirling over the deck of the *Flora* prevented his seeing exactly what had happened, he soon noticed that the cocky little American captain no longer strode about the schooner's quarterdeck. And the last American broadside had been a ragged affair, inflicting no damage on the *Zephyr.*

But he saw, too, that the schooner had drawn nearly half a ship's length ahead of his own craft, allowing him to bring only the forward section of his starboard guns to bear.

Clearly this situation called for a drastic change of tactics. He called his first lieutenant up from the main deck and instructed him what to do.

The normally phlegmatic Phipps was transformed by the scene that greeted him as he leaped from the after hatch onto the deck of the *Flora*. The four rear guns on the port side were still being loaded and fired, but the crews of the forward section, unable to bring their guns to bear on the enemy, had fallen idle.

Several men had taken shelter behind the galley. Overhead, however, Tom and his fellow sharpshooters were still firing away.

"Raise your sights," Phipps yelled at the men who still stood to their guns. "Aim for their rigging."

"You cowardly scum!" he screamed at the skulkers from the forward guns. "Back to your posts or I will shoot you. Double load with chain and shot. Bear a hand."

The bosun's mate stopped him on his way to the quarterdeck. "Ain't no use, Mr. Phipps. With the captain gone, we got to strike."

Phipps seized the bosun's arm. "We will never strike. Now go make sure we have every scrap of sail up. Get moving, man!"

He then ran to the quarterdeck and shoved the quartermaster away from the tiller.

Below deck, under the faint light of a circle of lanterns, Lovejoy and the Irish cook stood looking down at the form of Talbot Smith.

The captain's right trousers leg had been cut away, exposing the entire limb. A broad-banded screw tourniquet above the knee had stopped the bleeding. The cannonball seemed to have passed between Talbot's legs, carrying away most of the right calf and shattering the tibia beyond the skill of the most experienced surgeon to save the leg.

Lovejoy had stuffed a ball of opium in Talbot's mouth and forced the half-conscious captain to wash it down with a cup of rum. Now he was rereading the section of his surgeon's handbook on leg amputations and wishing fervently that Meg Jenkins rather than the cook were standing by to assist him.

"All right, Cookie, let's make sure we have everything. Curved and straight amputation knives, crooked needle with waxed thread, tenaculum . . . that's the thing with the hook at the end . . . round lint pledgets, long strips of linen, and the woolen cap to cover the stump."

"All laid out, Doctor. And the saw, too."

Lovejoy closed his eyes and for the first time in many a year seriously said a prayer. He prayed for the strength to do what he would have given anything to avoid having to do.

"What's happening?" Talbot moaned.

"A cannonball has messed up your leg."

"I know that, God damn it. What is happening to my schooner?"

"She is in a hell of a fight at the moment, but don't worry. Phipps has taken charge."

"No! Not him." The captain tried to sit up. The cook forced him back on his pillow.

"Don't make this any more difficult, Talbot, please. I am going to have to take off your leg."

"I don't care about that now. What about the *Flora*?"

"Captain, this fight is in the hands of the gods now. And, I am sorry to say, you are in my hands."

"You can't save my leg? You're sure?"

"I'd give my last penny if there were any way to save it. Now lie still."

Lovejoy picked up the rum bottle and took a generous swallow.

"You're scared, aren't you?" the captain said.

"Scared shitless," Lovejoy replied.

"They say surgeons in the British navy can take off a leg in thirty seconds."

"That is what they told us at St. Bartholomew's Hospital."

"I'll make a bargain with you. Do a good job and get me and the *Flora* back safe to Baltimore, and I'll see that you get the eight shares a surgeon generally is entitled to. How about that?"

"What about my half share for spotting that snow?"

"You get that only if we win this fight. Look, Doctor, you know my Josie. If anything goes wrong for me, you'll see she is looked after, won't you?"

"Of course I will."

"Well then, what are you waiting for? Get on with it."

Overhead at the tiller of the *Flora*, Phipps did not hear the captain's first cry as the great curved knife sliced through skin, arteries, veins, and muscle clear down to the leg bone. But when the huge surgeon's saw rasped through the leg bone, the scream from below sounded above the noise of gunfire and shouting. Knowing what it meant, Phipps shuddered and said his own prayer for Talbot Smith and for his beloved schooner. Also he asked forgiveness for not having apologized to his captain.

# 8

Up on the crow's nest with his two fellow snipers, at first Tom wished desperately to be back in Philadelphia working for his father or anywhere else out of danger. But then he became so caught up in the excitement of the battle that he forgot the heat of his gun barrel and the pain in his shoulder from the weapon's kick and his own fear of death.

Balls from the muskets of the British marines sang around his ears and through the topsail above and the mainmast jibs below or ricocheted from the mast itself. He and his two companions took turns hiding behind the mast as they loaded their muskets, then exposed their heads and shoulders to aim and fire.

Below, the deck was too shrouded in gunsmoke for them to see the crewmen carrying the wounded captain down to the surgery. Nor did they see Phipps come racing up from below to take command of the schooner.

Tom and his companions could see that they had gained half a ship's length on the British vessel, and they wondered at the way the rate of fire from the port carronades had slacked off. The noise from the guns having abated, they did hear Phipps shouting orders to his sailors to bend on every scrap of sail they could.

Aboard the *Zephyr*, Captain Wilsham, of course, could not hear those same orders, but when he saw that the schooner was drawing ahead of him, he cursed his luck and, after consulting with his first lieutenant, ordered his own sailors to replace the sails he had furled when they were clearing their decks for battle.

By the time the *Zephyr* was once again under full sail, the *Flora* had gained enough of a lead so that the British guns could no longer be brought to bear on her.

Phipps's mind raced over his choices. He would prefer to race eastward to the refuge of the Chesapeake, but shorthanded as he was, and with the wind behind them both, he was not sure how long he could maintain a lead over his adversary.

Being the more maneuverable, the *Flora* could reverse course and sail much closer into the wind than the *Zephyr,* but this would carry them away from the Chesapeake. Besides that, the maneuver would slow their speed and probably bring them back under the fire of the longer-ranged British guns.

The gunner's mate approached Phipps.

"What are we running for?" he demanded. "We been giving as good as we have took."

"They have us outgunned."

"Yes, but we been getting off three shots with our carronades to their two. As long as we stay in close enough range and keep the weather gage, I say we got a chance of whipping their asses."

"I know what I am doing. Now get back to your gun crews."

Phipps realized that there was some merit in the gunner's mate's advice. If he allowed the *Zephyr* to catch up, there was the chance that his carronades, although fewer in number, might inflict even more damage than the *Flora* would suffer from the longer-ranged but slower-firing British cannon. At a greater distance, however, the British would enjoy a clear advantage.

The gunner's mate still stood before him, hands on hips.

"Well, Phipps, what are you going to do?"

"I am going to keep ahead and to the windward. My job is to get this schooner and what's left of the crew back to port. Your job is to follow my orders. And by the way, it's Mr. Phipps."

Meanwhile, Wilsham, seeing that he could do no better than maintain the distance his prey had gained, decided that it was time to play his remaining trump card.

Turning to his first lieutenant, he said, "Have all gun crews switch to the port batteries and bring up bar and chain shot."

Then he shouted to the sailors who stood by with mainsail lines in their hands, "All hands, haul!"

Once the sails had been shifted, he put his helm over and waited for the *Zephyr* to turn partly into the wind.

Phipps might have been able to make a counter change of course if his attention had not been diverted by his confrontation with the gunner's mate. By the time he saw that the British ship was passing his stern, it was too late to do more than pray that he could continue to outrun his pursuer.

In the crow's nest, Tom saw the *Zephyr* make her slow turn to the starboard. And he saw the flash of her portside cannon and billows of smoke. Although nobody would believe him later, he even saw a bar shot arcing high up from the deck of the British vessel and heading, it seemed, directly for the crow's nest.

"Look out," he cried, as he bent his head between his knees. Like a twelve-pound dumbbell, the bar shot struck the spar holding the *Flora*'s main topsail. The splintered spar was ripped from its collar, and the sail fell across the crow's nest, covering Tom and his fellow sharpshooters.

In freeing himself from the fallen sail, Tom knocked his musket off the crow's nest. All around him, British bar shot and chain shot lashed through the rigging of the schooner.

Tom scrambled down the shrouds back to the deck.

A second broadside from the British ship sent more missiles whizzing through the sails and between the masts of the schooner.

The *Flora* had gained two ship's lengths on the *Zephyr* while the British ship was making its turn to the starboard, against the wind. This would have enabled the schooner to elude her pursuer had it not been for the loss of the topsail. Phipps saw his disability at a glance.

The gunner's mate again stood before him, hands on hips.

"Well, *Mr.* Phipps, sir. Looks like we got no choice but to fight it out with them."

Phipps seized the man's blouse and pulled him forward. "Put every man on your starboard guns. Double load with chain shot. Get moving."

With that he shoved the gunner's mate away from him and turned to his bosun's mate.

"Shift your mainsail about. On the double."

When he saw the damage his bar shot had done to the *Flora*'s topsail, Captain Wilsham smote his hands together.

"Now it is just a matter of time. We have the weather gage. We can overtake them and stay just beyond the range of their carronades and pound them until they give up."

He was still congratulating himself on the success of his maneuver when he observed, to his amazement, that the American schooner had abruptly changed course to the north.

"What the hell are they trying to do, ram and board us?"

Below deck, sweat streaming down his face and his hands trembling, Lovejoy finished suturing the blood vessels and sewing the flap of skin over the stump of the captain's leg.

"Now we'll just slip this cap over the end. . . aah, there, thank God he passed out. All right, Cookie, get him by the shoulders and we'll carry him to his bed."

"What should I do with his leg?"

"Over there, under the blanket with that poor fellow."

After they had lain the captain in his bed and placed a pillow under his stump, they returned to the operating table.

"Where's Toby?" Lovejoy asked.

"I reckon he went topside to join in the fun."

The hours of drill that the gunner's mate had put the *Flora's* sailors and landsmen through paid off during the next few minutes as the schooner crossed the bow of the *Zephyr*.

They fired off their first broadside as they approached the path of the snow. Working with mechanical fury, the men drew back their stubby weapons, swabbed the barrels, rammed home first the powder bags and then the chain shot, and then manhandled the weapons back to point directly starboard while the crew chiefs ran pricks down the touchholes to puncture the bags and pour in the priming powder.

"Fire!" the gunner's mate cried.

At the touch of the slow matches, the six starboard carronades and the two Long Tom's belched flame and smoke. Now the *Zephyr*, momentarily unable to bring its own guns to bear, seemed at the point of ramming the *Flora* amidships.

"Reload! Shift to the right!" the gunner's mate screamed at his men. "Fire!"

This was the moment Phipps had feared when he had planned this desperate maneuver, the moment when his stern would be exposed to a raking fire at close range from the British starboard broadside.

It took a while for the smoke from that third broadside to clear away enough for them to see the damage that their own three broadsides of chain shot had wrought and to understand why the enemy's guns did not punish the *Flora* for her bold move. The mainsail of the snow and its spar had fallen to the deck, preventing the British crew from servicing the starboard guns. And the bowsprit of the British vessel had been splintered.

Belowdecks, Lovejoy was sitting on a bench with his head in his hands, dreading a fresh wave of wounded, when he heard a cheer from overhead.

"Come on, Doctor, let's see what's up," the cook said.

On deck, the men were pounding one another on the back and jumping up and down and waving their fists at the crippled British ship.

"By God, Joy, we've whipped their asses to a fare-thee-well," Tom said. "You should have been up here to watch the fun."

"I would rather have been here than what I was doing."

The gunner's mate, a look of triumph on his face, approached the first mate. "Mr. Phipps," he said, with no trace of sarcasm this time.

"Don't you want to circle around and put a couple of broadsides into their stern?"

"They are still dangerous. I think we will let well enough alone. What do you say, Dr. Martin?"

Lovejoy looked back at the British ship wallowing almost dead in the water. He looked around at the *Flora's* smashed railings and debris from torn rigging. He thought about Smith lying maimed in his bed below, and the body of the dead sailor.

"You are the acting captain," he replied. "But as ship's surgeon, I think that every man deserves a double portion of rum."

"I think we'll hold back on the rum. We got a topsail to replace and a schooner to get back to Baltimore. I need sober men for the job."

# 9

It was the next morning before Talbot Smith had recovered enough from the shock of his amputation to comprehend Lovejoy's account of what had happened.

Lying flat in his bed with the stump of his leg propped up on a pillow, his face drawn and pale, he asked to be told again about the outcome of the fight.

"So Phipps didn't do such a bad job, after all?"

"I was below most of the time, but from what everyone says, Talbot, the only man that could have done any better is yourself."

"And he had the gumption to cross the Britisher's bow?"

"He did indeed, and from all I have heard, your gunner's mate and his gun crews performed marvelously well. With just three broadsides, using double-shot langrage, they cut the Britisher's rigging to ribbons. You were wise to have him drill his men so hard."

Smith closed his eyes, then made a face.

"Thought I told you to take off my leg. Why are you trying to save it?"

"But I did take it off."

"Then why is the damned thing hurting me so bad?"

"They call it 'referred pain.' It's sort of an imaginary thing."

"You wouldn't think it was imaginary if it was you lying here."

He raised his head feebly to stare down at his stump. "What did you do with my leg?"

"I was waiting for you to tell me."

"You say we lost one man?"

"Yes, Sam Ricks. And we are lucky to have got off so lightly. We must bury him this morning. Phipps says he will do the honors."

"Then let Phipps bury my leg, too. Save an extra cannonball and put my leg in the bag with the poor fellow's body."

"I am sure Phipps would be glad to do that. He is a good man, you know, Talbot. Good in more than one sense of the word. And, by the way, I think he wants to ask your pardon for insulting you. He is waiting until you feel like talking."

"No need for nobody to apologize to nobody. Just tell him to get us home. That will be apology enough. I can't wait to see how much our prizes has brung."

"Neither can I, Talbot. I see you making another face. You want an opium pill or a dram of rum?"

"No. I will tough it out. Tell me again, how much damage did those bastards do to my schooner?"

The legend of the *Flora's* fight with the British snow began to develop as soon as the two vessels were out of sight of each other. The men who had deserted the forward guns to hide behind the galley forgot their cowardice. To hear the bosun's mate describe the action, one would never have suspected that he was the same man who counseled Phipps to surrender.

They were sobered by the burial at sea of the sailor killed by the British sniper, but they soon cheered up when the outline of Cape Henry, at the mouth of the Chesapeake, appeared.

With a blanket around his shoulders against the November chill, Lovejoy stood in the bow of the *Flora* watching the flat landscape of the Virginia peninsula slide by. He was bone tired. He had gone without sleep far into the first night after the fight, treating the injuries of men who had delayed coming to him in the heat of battle. Tom's blistered left hand had to be coated with salve and bandaged. The quartermaster had received a lacerated scalp from a falling block and tackle. A powder monkey had suffered an arm fracture caused by a flying section of railing. Already exhausted from having to amputate the captain's leg, he continued patching up these and other less serious wounds for hours and, despite Phipps's orders, doling out drams of rum when he thought it necessary.

He was weary in spirit. It chilled him to think how close he and the *Flora*'s crew had come to ending up as British captives. His stay in the Baltimore jail had instilled in him a fresh appreciation of that word "freedom." And he had heard stories of how miserably captured Americans had fared in British prison hulks during the War of Independence.

It sobered him to think of how, in their eagerness to take one more prize, he and the captain had jeopardized not only their own freedom but also a schooner worth perhaps forty thousand dollars and—who knew?—perhaps the considerable value of the prizes they had sent into port.

Well, he thought, all's well that ends, if not well, at least pretty good. He was a rich man, no doubt about it. True, he had been enriched through the connivance of his father and Malcolm MacKenzie rather than through his own doing. But this was not the same Lovejoy Martin who had left Baltimore three months before. Tempered by his experiences, he felt ready to decide his own fate. He had wanted to quit this foolish war even before their encounter with the British man-of-war. Now he was certain that the last thing he would ever do would be to return to sea. Whoever chose to carry on this pointless quarrel with the British, he hoped that they would resolve the issue soon. He missed London.

What a swath he and a beautiful blond wife, rich in her own right, could cut there. Madeline had said that she loved the city. They could own a house both there and in Philadelphia. Perhaps a country estate as well. Let Chester keep the shipping business. He himself was clever enough to pick up an understanding of the law in a few months of study with an established attorney. As for medicine, well, he had got a bellyful of that profession. As that married woman back in London had asked, whatever had made him think he was cut out for medicine? It was strange, he had not thought of her for weeks.

What would she say about his character if she knew how he had swallowed his revulsion and sewn up wounds and amputated a leg, and how he had won the respect of a crew of rough-cut privateers? And what would Meg Jenkins say when he told her that he had performed an amputation without growing faint? No, Lovejoy Martin was not the same playboy he had been in London, nor the ungrateful, resentful son who had been too blind to realize the opportunity his father had presented him with. Henceforth he would be his own man.

Lost in his thoughts, he did not notice that Tom had joined him until his friend asked, "What are you smiling about, Joy?"

"About life, Tom. Isn't it wonderful to be alive?"

"I'd smile, too, if I was going to be as rich as you."

Just south of the Baltimore Basin stood a knoll called Federal Hill. From atop this eminence, observers could see—far down the mouth of the Patapsco—vessels coming up the Chesapeake. Spotters would then run up signal flags indicating what they saw approaching so that owners and other interested persons could prepare to meet the craft.

Malcolm MacKenzie was in his office conferring with Pierre Barineau when a messenger entered, saying, "The *Flora's* been sighted!"

The two men quickly threw on their overcoats and hired a hack to drive them down to the pier at Talbot Smith's shipyard.

Josie came out of her little house as they approached.

"Oh, thank the good Lord," she said when Malcolm told her the news. "I hope he is all right."

"When I left them, he and all his crew were in excellent health and spirits," Barineau said.

MacKenzie said softly, "Yes, but their spirits may not remain so high when they hear about the *Goodfellow.*"

"No need to go into that until after they are settled in. Ah, there she comes. Beautiful sight, don't you think?"

Against Lovejoy's advice, Talbot insisted on being carried up to the deck of the *Flora* and, wrapped in a blanket, being seated in a chair while propping his stump on a stool.

Lovejoy was the first man to jump onto the wharf. In as few words as possible, he told Malcolm and Barineau about their encounter with the British warship and of Talbot's injury.

When Josie heard what had happened and saw Talbot's pain-racked face, she began wailing. Malcolm put his arm about her shoulders to comfort her and to prevent her from leaping onto the schooner's deck.

Then Phipps came ashore to relate his estimate of what would be needed to make the *Flora* seaworthy again after her pounding from the British guns.

At last, four of the strongest sailors gently lifted the chair in which Talbot sat and carried him onto the wharf.

Josie flung herself on the embarrassed captain.

"That's enough of that, you hear? You go on up to the house and fix my bed for me. Now, you go on. I may not be in one piece but I am alive, by God. Go on now, Josie. No sense in you carrying on like that."

Once Josie had returned to their shed, Talbot looked up into Malcolm's face.

"It was a good cruise up until I bit off more than I could chew with a snow that turned out to be British navy. Anyway, we're back now. I want to get her put back into good shape as soon as we can."

Catching Malcolm's eye, Lovejoy frowned and shook his head.

"There is time enough to talk of that later. First thing we should do is to send a doctor out to look you over."

Talbot motioned for MacKenzie to bend low.

"No need for that," he whispered. "Dr. Martin did a first-rate job on me. Fact is, he done a good job throughout, after we got to understand each other. You was right about him. There is more to him than I first thought. I'm glad we took him along."

Waving Malcolm away, he said in a louder voice, "Now then, Barineau, did you have any trouble bringing that tub and its cargo in?"

"We hit some heavy weather but came through in good order."

"What happened to my English medical friends?" Lovejoy asked.

"Those two were quite a pair. I turned them over to Mr. MacKenzie."

"Yes," Malcolm said. "Lovely lads they are, too. They stayed with Flora and me for several days and then we sent them up to Philadelphia to be exchanged."

"And Megan Jenkins. How is she?"

"Yes, what about my sister?" Tom asked.

Barineau and Malcolm looked at each other.

"Do you want to tell them?" Malcolm said.

"Yes, well, you see . . . that brig we sent back, the *Goodfellow*. Nobody knows what happened to it."

"What do you mean, nobody knows?" Lovejoy asked.

"She never came into port."

Smith tried to rise from his chair, then fell back. "That was the first prize we sent back. She was the best thing we took. I should not have listened to you, Dr. Martin. Should have sent her into Charleston."

"You mean my sister is missing at sea?" Tom said.

"All I have been able to find out is that the brig never made it to the Chesapeake," Barineau said. "Look, I have dreaded having to tell you this."

"But they should have been here a good eight or nine weeks ago," Lovejoy said.

"Son of a bitch," Talbot said. "She carried a fine cargo of cheese and all kinds of cloth, shoes, hats, and such. A brig, she was out of Liverpool and headed for Barbados."

"I know," Malcolm said. "Mr. Barineau told me."

Tom's voice suddenly drowned out the others.

"Who gives a damn what cargo she carried? My sister was aboard that brig, and you sit there complaining about losing the cargo. Meggie was worth all the cheese and shoes in the world."

Fists clenched, he stood over Talbot.

"Why did you send her back with a greenhorn like Collins as prize master? You could have sent Mr. Barineau. My sister would be alive and well if you had done that."

"Your sister would have been alive and well if she had not stowed away on my schooner," Talbot replied.

"You are the cold-bloodedest man I ever met up with," Tom said.

"Careful, Tom," Lovejoy said.

"Don't 'Careful Tom' me. You ain't the one that has to tell Pa . . . oh, this will kill him. It may kill me."

"Isn't it possible that Collins sailed the brig into some other port?" Lovejoy asked.

Malcolm took his arm. "As soon as Mr. Barineau got here, we sent inquiries by post to Charleston, Wilmington, and all other possible ports. Incidentally, the craft you sent to Charleston fetched excellent prices. However, we have received no word from any quarter about this brig . . . what was the name again?"

"The *Goodfellow.* She was captained by an Englishman who used to be in the Royal Navy. Arrogant chap, he was. Look, Malcolm . . ." He drew the chandler out of Tom's hearing. "Do you really think they went down?"

"From the reports of other ships coming in during that period, they would have encountered a violent storm off Hatteras. The only other explanation would be that the British recaptured her, but I think that most unlikely."

"She was a wonderful girl. The crew all fell in love with her. I don't know what to do with Tom. He looks ready to collapse."

"We will do what we can for him, poor lad. By the by, Lovejoy, several letters have come down to you the past few weeks. From Reading, they seem to be."

# Book Two

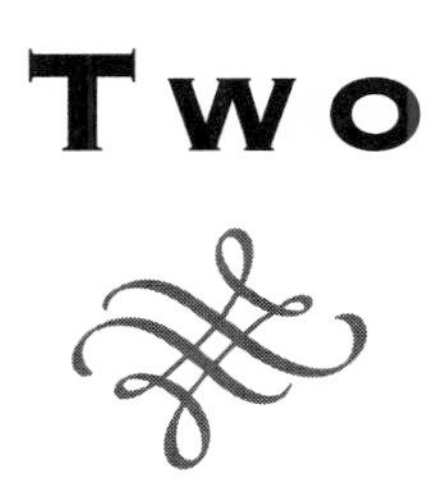

# Part One

# 1 

"Well, darling Lovejoy, was it as bad as you feared?"

"No, Madeline. He put me through a tough catechism but seems satisfied I am qualified to serve as son-in-law to the family Richter. Just as you warned, though, he can be a terrible old Dutchman."

"When can we be married then?"

"He hasn't exactly said yes and won't until he and your mother and, I suppose, yourself all visit Philadelphia to meet my family. I gather your mother put him up to that."

"She would. You don't mind, do you?"

"I started to get on my high horse and tell him he could take me or leave me, and threaten to whisk his precious daughter away in the night."

"Oh, wouldn't that be romantic?"

Madeline looked over her shoulder to see if the old aunt who had been charged by Mrs. Richter with chaperone duties still dozed by the fire, then resumed.

"But of course you said nothing of the sort."

"No, I explained that my father is ill and might not be able to receive them socially but that my sister and her husband would be more than happy to play hostess and host."

"When will that be?"

"The sooner, the better. I've been debating whether to post a letter or go down to Philadelphia myself. I was so anxious to see you again, I have not yet been home, as you know."

"I don't want to let you out of my sight. Stay here through Christmas, at least."

Making sure that her Aunt Elizabeth still dozed, she put her arms around Lovejoy's neck and drew his lips down to hers.

She broke off the kiss to slap his hand.

"You didn't say anything to him about our living in London?"

"No, nor Philadelphia, either."

"And how about your reading for the law?"

"He has it fixed in his mind that I am a doctor. I saw no reason to muddy the waters. Nor did I want him to think I planned to take the apple-of-his-eye daughter away from her family."

"If I thought you weren't going to do just that, I would ask for my letters back and then pack you off to your mysterious shipping business in Baltimore. I am so weary of this stodgy place. You will take me to London, won't you, dear Lovejoy?"

"As soon as this stupid war ends."

"Oh, the war. Did Pa question you closely on where you stand on . . ." Here she sat up straight, put her arms behind her back, and, in imitation of her father, said gruffly, "Dis war vot Mr. Madison has got dis here country into."

"He did, and I told him that I have many friends in England, and that I thought it was foolhardy and unnecessary for us to declare war on the British. But you know, Madeline, your father is a very practical man."

"What do you mean?"

"While he says he voted for De Witt Clinton, he does not seem overly unhappy that Madison has won and will be president for four more years. Thanks to the war, he is enjoying a brisk demand for his flour and wheat. Also, he seemed much more interested in my financial situation than in my politics. Lucky for me I could give him a good report or he just might have sent me packing."

"I would have gone packing with you."

Lovejoy stretched his legs out toward the warmth of the fire and leaned back to get a better view of Madeline Richter. The firelight lent a reddish glow to her hair, making her look more like a strawberry blond than he had remembered. A long silence followed, which she broke by saying, "Lovejoy, you seem somehow different than I remembered you from aboard ship."

"As I told you, I have been through some trying circumstances since last May."

"You act a little sad at times."

"I lost some friends at sea. It is hard to forget them."

"Can't you tell me about it?"

"It is too painful. And talking won't bring them back. No . . ." He stood up with his back to the fire. "Now we must look to the future. And from where I stand, the future never looked better."

He took her hands and drew her to her feet. He had just put his arms around her waist when her aunt yawned and stretched.

"My goodness, gracious me," the old woman said in a Dutch accent. "What time is it getting to be?"

"Ten o'clock, Aunt Elizabeth."

"That's bedtime. Come along with me, Maddy baby. Your young man can take a candle and find his way to his room, I am sure."

Madeline gave him her hand and curtsied. Lovejoy made a mock bow and said, "Sleep well, both of you Miss Richters."

Madeline laughed. "And you, too, Dr. Martin."

As they walked down the hall, the aunt said, "This one seems a nice enough young fellow. What did you say his name was again?"

Lovejoy sat before the fire and stared into the flames.

The interview with Christian Richter had started off with the father saying abruptly, "What's this about you wanting to marry my daughter?"

Seeing that glib words would not sway this self-assured, suspicious Pennsylvania Dutchman, Lovejoy stammered out his declarations of love and his desire to look after Madeline for the rest of his life.

"You ain't the first that has asked for her hand, and you may not be the last neither. Why should she marry you?"

And so the interview had gone with Richter continually knocking Lovejoy off base and, apparently, enjoying the game.

Fed up with playing a defensive role, Lovejoy took advantage of a pause in the barrage of questions and said, "I have a few questions of my own. My father would never agree to my marrying into a family whose means were not, shall we say, commensurate with our own. Not that I require his approval, for I stand on my own two feet. But he will be asking me, I am sure."

"Ain't you seen this house? Not a finer one in Berks County. And chust wait until you see my farms. I got two. More than five hundred acres of good limestone soil, and plenty of tenants to work the land, too. Then there's two gristmills on fine streams. And a sawmill. What has your family got?"

"My father is Jeremiah Martin of Philadelphia. You may have heard of Martin Shipping."

"I have heard of him, sure. Well, now nobody told me that. But ain't he a strong Republican?"

"I don't see what my father's politics has to do with this. Nor for that matter, with all respect, his wealth. When I am done liquidating my shipping interests down in Baltimore, my own worth may exceed fifty thousand dollars."

"That is a lot of money for just a doctor to have. How did you say you came by so much?"

"The nature of my business requires the utmost discretion. However, I assure you that my enterprises are all strictly legal, as, I am sure, are yours."

"Of course, mine are."

"I did not mean to suggest that they are not, but as you said already, marriage is a serious business. Neither of us can be too careful."

Seeing that he had gained the upper hand, Lovejoy fell silent, waiting for Madeline's father to frame his next question.

"I reckon you are wondering what kind of dowry there would be. That is generally what they want to know, even if they beat around the bush all day."

"Mr. Richter, do you know your Shakespeare?"

"I have heard of him, of course. But I leave that sort of thing to the missus. What has Shakespeare got to do with you wanting to marry our Madeline?"

"A line in *King Lear* comes to mind. Lear tells a man who wants to marry his daughter that there will be no wedding gift. The man replies, 'She is herself a dowry.' In other words, if you can't afford a wedding gift for Madeline and me, it doesn't matter one whit."

"I didn't say there wouldn't be nothing for her. I have never stinted in looking after my family. It's just that Mrs. Richter thinks every young fellow in Berks County wants to get his hands on our money. She'll like what you said. How did that Shakespeare business go again?"

Lovejoy congratulated himself on how he had turned the tables in the interview and on how he had been able to avoid revealing his role in a privateering expedition against the British. He had kept his silence, also, when Richter had suggested that Madeline's dowry might take the form of a small nearby farm "beside the main road with a fine stone house and a brick outbuilding that would be chust right for a doctor's office."

There would be time enough to confront that issue.

He smiled at the thought of marrying Madeline and having that luscious beauty all to himself, far from the clinging presence of her parents. Knowledge that she had had other suitors before him only made her more desirable in his eyes.

Her boldness and quick mood changes did take him aback. He wondered whether she had ever written such letters as those waiting for him in Baltimore, or how many evenings old Aunt Elizabeth had sat through in this parlor as a chaperone.

He had not told Madeline the full truth about the cause of his sadness. He could not bring himself to reveal the loss of the *Goodfellow* or the anguish and guilt he felt about Megan Jenkins.

He had given the distraught Tom a letter to carry to Evan, a letter in which he praised Meg's virtues and held out hope that she might yet be found, hope he felt in his heart to be false. He wondered what poor Tom and his grieving family were doing now. As he had written to Evan, there would never be another Megan Jenkins.

He thought, too, of Talbot Smith, sitting on the porch of his shed, under Josie's anxious eyes, as he oversaw the repairs to his beloved schooner. Neither Lovejoy nor Malcolm had had the heart to tell him that there was little chance of his returning to sea as the captain. By the time his stump healed enough for him to be fitted with a peg leg and he had recovered his stamina, the war might be over.

For that matter, Lovejoy had not told Malcolm of his own determination to sell the *Flora* rather than risk her in another privateering cruise. There would be time to put her up for sale after Talbot's shipyard hands had got her back in fighting trim.

The more he thought about it, the more he realized that it made sense for him to take the stage to Philadelphia and inform his family in person of his impending marriage and smooth the way for the visit of the Richters. He would call on the Jenkins family to offer his condolences. And he would meet with his father, the formidable Jeremiah Martin, for the first time in his life as an equal. Now that he had passed so many tests of courage and character, surely the old man would treat him with respect.

Plenty of money either in the bank or soon to be. A beautiful wife from a rich family. His father's approval, and a newfound sense of self-respect. These were, or soon would be, his.

Lovejoy took a candle and made his way toward his bedroom.

# 2

In Berks County, Christian Richter was considered as rich and influential as Jeremiah Martin was down in Philadelphia. But whereas Jeremiah had created his fortune through bold risk taking, both physical and financial, Richter had made his through tenacity and painstaking, native shrewdness.

Like Jeremiah, he had begun his climb up the economic ladder during the American Revolution. Growing up on his family farm with parents who spoke only Pennsylvania Dutch, he discovered early in life that although agriculture might be a good way to provide for one's family, it offered a slow road to wealth.

In the winter of 1777–78, after defeating Washington's army at Brandywine Creek and occupying Philadelphia, Lord Howe needed supplies for his redcoats. Washington's army, huddled in their bleak little huts twenty miles away at Valley Forge, likewise needed food, fuel, and clothing. Whereas Lord Howe could pay the farmers from the hinterland in gold, Washington could offer only Continental dollars and equally questionable promissory notes.

When purchasing agents of the Continental army came around to the Richter farm, they were told that there was only enough flour and cornmeal and bacon on hand to see the family through the winter. When the coast was clear, young Christian then loaded his father's wagon with those same products and drove them down to the Schuylkill River and into the eager hands of the British. He used his first such earnings to purchase more supplies from his neighbors and sell them at a profit in Philadelphia.

By the time the French had entered the war on the side of the Americans, forcing Howe to abandon Philadelphia out of fear that he and his supporting fleet would be bottled up in the Delaware, Christian had amassed enough British gold to buy his first gristmill. From his contact with the British, he had learned to speak English, which opened up new avenues for him among his non-Dutch neighbors after the Revolution.

Methodically acquiring, saving, and investing his growing wealth, he remained a bachelor until 1790, when an English flour importer came out from Philadelphia to Berks County looking for new sources of supply. He had brought along his wife and three daughters for an extended holiday. When he returned to England with a shipload of excellent Berks County wheat and flour, only two daughters accompanied him.

Even if Emily Prentiss had possessed great beauty, her critical nature would have discouraged potential husbands. She was both intelligent and practical enough to realize this but was too stubborn to change. More than one ambitious young man had called on the Prentiss household back in Liverpool but had lost interest in Emily after seeing her two younger sisters.

It was plain to her that Christian Richter needed a wife and, more to the point, that he could afford to keep one in far better style than any of her sisters' suitors could keep them back in England. Whereas they mocked Christian's Dutch accent and his rough manners and plain style of dress, Emily saw in him a man whom a smart wife could develop.

At first, Christian was attracted to the younger sisters, but, seeing how silly they acted, he turned his attention to Emily.

Too clever to throw herself at him, she flattered him by asking questions about his farms and his business interests. By the time he got up his courage to ask for her hand, she had a clear idea of both his present and his likely future wealth.

Could he speak to her father before the family returned to England? Perhaps. But first there would have to be an understanding of what he would do after their marriage.

Hence the grand Georgian house built of the finest brick. Hence the stable with excellent horses both for riding and for drawing a carriage unlike any other in the county. Hence the three servants. And hence their membership in the local Episcopal church rather than the Lutheran one in which Christian had been baptized.

Christian found his wife already in bed when he came upstairs after his interview with Lovejoy.

"What took so long?"

"We had a lot to talk about."

"You did indeed. What answer did you give him?"

"I done chust what you told me to."

"You mean you did what I suggested you do."

"Whatever. Anyway, he will see we get an invitation from his family down in Philadelphia. But say now, Emily, why didn't you tell me his father is Jeremiah Martin . . . the Jeremiah Martin down in Philadelphia?"

"I don't know that name."

"You would if you was in business. One of the richest men in Philadelphia, he is. What's more, the young fellow says he's worth fifty thousand dollars in his own right."

"And he is a doctor, as well."

She reflected on this until her husband had donned his nightgown and sleeping cap and had crawled in bed beside her.

"Did he ask about a dowry?"

"No. I had to bring up the subject. And you will never guess what he said."

After he had finished responding to his wife's cross-examination, Christian Richter turned on his side and drifted off to sleep.

Emily Prentiss Richter did not fall asleep so quickly. She first fretted about leaving her husband's tiresome old maiden sister to oversee the pair. Then she worried about the prospect of going down to Philadelphia to meet Lovejoy's family. She had pictured herself lording it over his family as she scrutinized them with a critical eye. Now she worried about the impression her Dutch-speaking husband would make on this Jeremiah Martin. Could it be that Christian had got it wrong about the man being so rich?

Then there was the question of the wedding itself. Their little Episcopal church was so small. The fine Lutheran church in Reading would be better. Perhaps their own rector would be willing to conduct the service there.

She wished her husband were still awake. She wanted to ask what he had discovered about the politics of the Martin family and whether it was clearly understood that the couple would settle down nearby. Well, let him sleep. She would ask her questions in the morning.

She stayed awake until she heard her sister-in-law and Madeline come up the stairs to their adjoining bedrooms. By the time Lovejoy mounted the stairs with his candle, she had fallen asleep. Thus she did not hear the floorboards creak beneath his feet. Nor did she hear Madeline's door open gently as he passed on his way to the guest bedroom at the end of the hall.

"Lovejoy."

He stopped, turned, and raised his candle.

"In here."

She took his hand and drew him into her room.

"Madeline, what would your parents say?"

"All I want is a kiss to think about when I am in bed."

She was dressed in a long nightgown that fitted up around her neck. Putting one arm about her waist, he felt no undergarments. He kissed her gently. When he tried to pull away, she put both her arms around his neck and, standing on tiptoe, held her mouth pressed hard against his.

Finally, trembling with desire and with fear of discovery by her parents, he pulled away.

"Look Madeline, I spent a good hour trying to convince your father to let us marry. What will he think if he should find me in your room?"

He turned to go, but she pulled him back and eased the door shut.

"Don't you hear Pa snoring away like an old frog? And dear Mama is hard of hearing. One more kiss won't hurt. Here, set that silly candle down and do it properly this time."

Often since he had met Madeline Richter, Lovejoy had ached to possess her. But always he had pictured himself doing so on their wedding night and thereafter as her husband. Even as she continued to cling to him, now pressing her breasts against his chest, he was telling himself that he should stop and betake himself to the guest room before it was too late.

He might have managed to do that, had she not interrupted a kiss and, still holding his hand, leaned over to blow out the candle. In the dark, their kisses grew more passionate. As she led him over to her bed, he was beyond resistance.

It had been four months since Lovejoy and Tom had visited Mamie Brown's establishment in Baltimore, and several weeks before then that he had slept with a girl back in London.

Once unclothed and in bed, he was embarrassed by his haste. Almost the instant he had penetrated her, it was over. Humiliated, he withdrew.

"I got too excited, I suppose."

"Don't apologize. Just put your arms around me. Let me feel your body against mine."

They lay together until the clock on the stair landing chimed the half hour. First Lovejoy and then Madeline felt him quicken again. This time it lasted longer, long enough so that she suddenly arched her back and moaned.

"So that is what it is like."

They slept until they were awakened by the clock striking three.

"My God, Madeline. I had better get back to my room."

"Not yet. Once more."

Afterward he dressed quietly, gave her a final kiss, and, carrying his shoes, tiptoed back to the guest room.

Lovejoy did not understand the emotions that overcame him at breakfast that morning with the Richter family. His earlier conquests had left him feeling triumphant. Now he felt slightly ashamed and disappointed, as though he had spoiled his own dream.

If Madeline felt any shame or disappointment, it did not show. She babbled away to her mother, teased her father about his snoring, and once, when they were not looking, gave Lovejoy a bold wink across the table.

"What did you say?" Lovejoy asked Richter.

"I was chust asking if you like to ride horseback. You do? Then Madeline will ride with you and show you about this farm while I am off on business in Morgantown. And while you are at it, Mad, you might as well ride over to the other farm, too. Show him one of the mills, too. Then, Dr. Martin, you and me, we got to have another little talk tonight."

As Madeline supervised the stable hand in saddling their horses, Lovejoy studied her profile. It was odd how two persons as physically unattractive as her parents could have produced such a stunning girl. She had her mother's strong will and her obvious determination to claim the best of everything, but lacked her hypocrisy. She had a strong dose of her father's plainspokenness, but displayed a mocking sense of humor that was lacking in both her parents. Also, her quick changes of mood baffled him.

She had taken him by surprise last night. Whatever had made him think that she would be a shy virgin he would have to woo long and patiently before she would enjoy lovemaking as much as he did? He felt a surge of jealousy as he wondered whether he had been the first.

"Well, aren't you going to help me mount?"

Lovejoy stooped, caught her by the elbows, and lifted her up onto her sidesaddle.

"Look there, Amos," she said to the stable hand. "Did you see the way he picked me up like I was just a feather?"

"No doubt about it. You got yourself a strong one there."

Lovejoy went through the motions of appearing interested in her explanation of which fields were devoted to which crops and her father's theories of agronomy. At last, he interrupted her to say what was on his mind.

"Madeline, about last night. I really expected to wait until we were married."

"Who cares about that? You liked it, didn't you?"

"Why sure, but what if your folks had found me in your room?"

"I would have told them it was too late for them to pass on whether we should be married or not. The damage had been done. That is the way to go about things."

"Wouldn't your father have been furious?"

"At first. But then I would have asked him whether he wouldn't want to try on a pair of shoes before he paid for them. Look, Lovejoy, you never heard of bundling?"

"What's that?"

"The Dutch allow couples to do their courting in bed on cold nights. They put a bundling board between them, but I don't think that always works, to keep them apart, you know."

"I can't imagine your mother allowing such a thing."

"She is horrified by the custom, but they still practice it hereabouts. Pa's parents courted that way. I have cousins that do too, although we don't have much to do with Pa's kinfolks. We both got carried away last night, that's all. I don't believe in stewing over what is done."

Before he could say more, she struck her riding crop across her mare's flank and galloped away from him.

They visited two tenant farmers' homes, remaining on their horses while Madeline chatted with the wives in their kitchen doorways. They stopped by a barn lot to admire a flock of sheep huddled against the rising wind and visited a huge gristmill where a dozen men labored away at grinding wheat. By the time they returned to the stable, Amos had gone home for his midday dinner.

Lovejoy carried his saddle and blanket into the tack room. He looked back at Madeline as she rubbed down his horse. Was she as uncomplicated as she seemed to be, or was there a mysterious underlayer of personality beneath her matter-of-fact manner? His resolve not to make love to her again until they were married faded quickly as he admired the sensuous way she caressed the horse's mane. As soon as they had put the animal in its stall, he caught her arm and pulled her against him.

"Hey, now, we've got to put my mare away," she said.

"She'll wait."

Minutes later they were in the loft, burrowed deep in the hay, she with her skirts above her waist and he with his trousers down around his ankles. When she arched her back and moaned, her face grew red and as contorted as if she were in pain. Then she relaxed and smiled at him as it became his turn to climax.

"My God, it gets better each time," she said.

Still inside her, Lovejoy raised his upper body and looked down into her eyes, seeking assurance from her that something more than an animal passion existed between them, something that would last through a long lifetime together.

"Lovejoy. Lovejoy Martin. Are you here?"

Someone was calling him from outside the barn.

"My God, Madeline." He withdrew and pulled up his trousers. "Stay here and I will go see who it is. Wait awhile before you come down. Pretend to be tossing hay down to the horses."

"Lovejoy, where are you?"

Shielding his eyes against the sunlight, Lovejoy climbed down the ladder and walked out of the barn. There on a bony old horse sat Tom Jenkins.

"What in hell's name are you doing here, Tom?"

"I took the stage out to Reading and hired this horse. Joy, we have to talk."

Madeline sat up and rearranged her clothes. She would have wanted to marry Lovejoy Martin even if he had not proved such a lover. This was a bonus. She hoped he would never ask her if she had been a virgin. If he did, she would ask him, "How about yourself?" Then, if he admitted that he was not, which was obvious, she would wheedle details of his sexual experiences from him and pretend to be so terribly jealous that he would wish he had never brought the subject up at all. Then she would have that to hold over him after they were married. And she would never have to tell him about her experience with her cousin earlier that year in England or last year with the Scotch-Irish chap who had worked as a business agent for her father until her mother had discerned that the lad was "getting notions" about Madeline and caused his dismissal. Poor George McFairlane. He still made eyes at her when she saw him working at the stage office in Reading. Neither his nor her cousin's awkward performances could compare with Lovejoy Martin's. Besides which, Lovejoy was rich and well traveled.

There, enough time had passed. Who could Lovejoy be talking to out there?

# 3

"I don't understand," Madeline sobbed as Lovejoy threw his clothes into his carpetbag. "Why do you have to go off in such a great hurry?"

"It is too complicated to explain. But I must get back to Baltimore right away."

"What about our visit to Philadelphia?"

"We will do that as soon as possible after Christmas."

"I had my heart set on you spending Christmas here."

"Oh, Madeline, please don't cry."

He looked down into her tear-streaked face and tried to put his arms around her.

She pushed him away, saying, "You got what you wanted and now you are running away from me."

"Never. It is just that I owe it to our lost crew to do what I can to rescue them. I couldn't live with myself if I did not at least try."

"Can't you stay one more night? Pa wants to talk to you again, about us. We have plenty of room for your friend, what's his name?"

"Tom. Tom Jenkins. And he says the stage will leave Reading at three o'clock. There is just time enough for us to make it."

"Can't you at least stay for dinner?"

"Please, Madeline, don't make this any more difficult than it is. I will write to you as soon as I get to Baltimore and find out more details. And I swear to you on my word of honor that I will return as soon as I get things cleared up."

She blocked his way as he started for the door.

"You really do swear?"

"For God's sake, yes. Look, every minute is precious."

"There is a Bible there beside the bed. Put your hand on it."

"Madeline, please. I will miss the stage."

"You will if you and your friend both try to ride on that same sorry nag he brought out here. You won't if I let you borrow my mare. We left her in the barn still saddled, remember? You can leave her at the stage office. Now put your hand on that Bible and swear to Almighty God that you will return and marry me and that you hope you will burn in hell if you do not."

"On pain of eternal damnation, I swear that I will return and marry you."

"All right. You go back on that oath and you will regret it for the rest of your life."

A puzzled Emily Richter was cross-examining Tom Jenkins as Lovejoy came downstairs.

"I really don't understand why you cannot eat before you depart," she said.

"Dear Mrs. Richter. It pains me enormously to rush off like this, and I would not do so if the matter were not of an urgent nature. Please accept my apologies and also my sincere thanks for your hospitality. As I have told Madeline, I hope to return soon after Christmas and escort you and your husband down to Philadelphia to meet my family. Please express my regrets to your husband for my hurried departure."

By the time he had done with fending off Mrs. Richter's questions, Madeline had already lengthened her mare's stirrup straps and was waiting at the stable.

She held herself stiffly as he kissed her.

"You can give the mare to the agent at the stage office. His name is George McFairlane. He used to work for Pa. He will see that we get her back."

He mounted the mare and looked down into her now composed face.

"Good-bye, dear Madeline."

"Good-bye, Lovejoy."

Holding the mare's reins, she leaned close so that Tom could not hear and said, "You took an oath. If you don't keep it, you will be sorry for the rest of your life, I promise you that."

Shocked at the vehemence of her tone, tears brimming in his own eyes, Lovejoy could only nod his head.

"Now give me your hand."

She gripped his wrist and caressed his palm, first with her lips and then her tongue. Then, before he knew what was happening, she turned his hand slightly and bit deep into the fleshy edge, clear down to the bone.

Lovejoy cried out at the pain and jerked his hand away.

"God damn it, Madeline, why did you do that?"

She handed him her handkerchief to stanch the blood.

"There. I have left my mark on you. Show the scar to any woman who tries to steal you. Tell her you have a fiancee in Berks County some call 'Mad.' Any time you are tempted to break your oath, just look at your hand."

She slapped the mare on the rump. Tom's hired nag was already trotting far down the lane. His throbbing hand wrapped in Madeline's handkerchief, Lovejoy dug his heels into the mare's side and cantered up beside his friend.

"So that is the girl?" Tom said.

"Yes, that's Madeline."

"I see what you mean, about her being so beautiful. I am sorry to take you away like this."

"I am going of my own free will."

"What happened to your hand?"

"Never mind. Tell me again what makes you think Megan and our prize crew are still alive."

"You remember Bledsoe, the captain of the *Goodfellow?*"

"Sure. The peg-legged chap who used to be in the Royal Navy. He tried to make me amputate the arm of one of his sailors. Arrogant fellow. What about him?"

"It's complicated. Maybe you can make some sense of it."

They reached the stage office in Reading ten minutes before the coach was to depart for Lancaster, where they were to spend the night before catching an early-morning stage for Baltimore.

The stage agent, McFairlane, was a thin young fellow with a prominent Adam's apple and a shock of red hair.

"I thought that looked like Madeline's mare when I seen you riding up. You say she wants me to return it?"

"Yes. She said you would be glad to do so."

"Sure. But does her mother know she wants me to do that?"

"What difference does it make?"

"Just curious. Who did you say you were?"

"I did not say. Is there room on the Lancaster stage?"

"We can squeeze you in. You been talking business to Old Man Richter, I reckon."

"Yes, of a sort."

"A word of advice. Keep one hand on your pocketbook when you deal with that one. I know. I used to work for the old skinflint. As for his wife . . ."

Lovejoy interrupted to say, "Speaking of business, please accept this to compensate yourself for your trouble of the mare."

"That's no trouble at all. Keep your money, friend. Ah, they are loading the coach. Will you be coming this way again?"

"I expect to, why?"

"Then I will ask you not to repeat what I said about the Richters. I probably misspoke myself."

"You probably did, but fear not. I will say nothing."

The stage was bulging with passengers, and it was too chilly to sit on top with the driver. So Lovejoy and Tom rode wedged in across from each other with several garrulous older men who belabored one another with opinions about the recent presidential election, in which James Madison had won reelection over the Federalist mayor of New York City, De Witt Clinton. One man complained about the rising costs caused by "Mr. Madison's war." Another expressed pleasure at the increased demand for grain by the army. Still another viewed the war as a welcome stimulant for American manufacuring.

Lovejoy closed his eyes and tried to sort out his raging emotions. He had never encountered such fierce passion in a woman as he had in Madeline Richter. There were a hundred things they should have discussed, but everything had been swept away by physical desire. And then there was her making him swear that oath on the Bible. And damn her for biting him so. His hand ached under her blood-soaked handkerchief. One thing was certain, if he could remove her from Berks County, married life with Madeline Richter would not be dull.

Even if Tom had not appeared with his startling news, Lovejoy's emotions would have been in a turmoil at the discovery of how different the real Madeline was from the demure heiress he had imagined her to be. His loins warmed at thoughts of her. He would much rather be back in bed with her than returning to Baltimore, but he had a duty he could not evade. Looking on the bright side, maybe it would be better for them to be separated until close to their marriage date. Perhaps they could settle all the arrangements by letter. She and her parents could meet him in Philadelphia upon his return.

Damn the old farts who kept droning on and on about a war they did not understand, when he wanted to question Tom more closely about the mysterious message that had come to Philadelphia, to his own father, of all people. A message from Barbados.

"Sorry, what were you saying?"

"I vas chust asking what happened to your hand."

"A mare bit it."

"Must have been a wild one, to do that."

"She is an untrained filly."

"What line of work are you two young fellows in?"

"The maritime trade."

"Vell, I hope you made your money while you could. Did you hear the latest trouble what that damned fool Madison has got us into up north? We are getting our asses kicked up there. One disaster after another, it is. And we are stuck with him as president for four more years."

Neither Tom nor Lovejoy had eaten since that morning. No food had ever tasted better than that served to them at the inn in Lancaster where they spent the night.

Over cups of coffee and large servings of apple pie topped with heavy cream, Lovejoy pressed Tom to tell him everything he knew about why he was needed so urgently in Baltimore.

"I had just got back to the White Swan from Baltimore. They were in mourning for poor Megan from what I had told them about the *Goodfellow* not making it back to port, all of them except maybe for Primrose. I could have strangled that bitch for her silly remarks about how what happened to Megan should serve as a warning to girls who run away from home. Anyhow, I was getting ready to return to Baltimore to help get the *Flora* ready for sea when a messenger came asking us to come to see your pa."

"And how did you find Father?"

"He looks feeble, but he was able to sit up and talk to us. Your brother was there too, and the lawyer fellow."

"Tell me exactly what Father wanted."

"He said he had got a message from a lawyer in Barbados saying our prize crew had arrived there in October aboard the *Goodfellow* and that they are being held prisoner in Bridgetown."

"Why did the message come to Father and not me?"

"Your pa said that it was from a lawyer and in code. But whoever sent it was under the impression that you and Megan are engaged to be married and that he, your pa that is, should know about this."

"That is preposterous. I am engaged to marry Madeline Richter."

"I told them how Captain Smith planted that idea to keep Collins from trying to take advantage of Meggie on the way back to Baltimore. I reckon Bledsoe picked it up from Collins."

"How did the *Goodfellow* end up in Barbados instead of Baltimore?"

"According to your pa, the message simply said that Bledsoe had regained control of his ship."

"How does Bledsoe figure in this?"

"He told this lawyer named Fescue to pass the word to your pa that if he did not receive ten thousand pounds sterling by March 1, he will send the entire crew off to England to Dartmoor Prison."

"That is nearly fifty thousand dollars."

"Yes, and your pa says that it is not his place to pay such a sum. He directed me to come and notify you."

"Did Father say what he wants me to do?"

"All he said was to tell you about the message and that the rest is up to you and Mr. MacKenzie."

"I hope you did not tell him where I was and why."

"I had to answer his questions, Joy. He said he might have known it would be something to do with a girl. So there it is. By the way, Pa says he would have been willing to sell the White Swan to help raise ransom money for Megan, but now there is a problem with that."

"What kind of problem?"

"Primrose is in a family way. She has already started laying in things like a cradle and little dresses. Honestly, it is enough to turn your stomach the way she and Pa are acting. And him old enough to be a grandpa. You know what she had the gall to say about Meggie in my presence?"

"Something very diplomatic, I hope."

"Hah! That silly woman said . . ." Here Tom switched to a falsetto voice. "'Well, dear Evan, perhaps I shall bear you another daughter, and a better one, too, I should hope.' Then when we got the news about Meg being alive, she pulled a long face and acted disappointed."

"So, congratulations are in order for you, Uncle Tom. Getting back to Meg, this problem is not for either your father or mine to solve. It is up to me."

"What will you do then, Joy?"

"I don't know yet. First we must get down to Baltimore and consult with Malcolm MacKenzie."

# 4

The streets of Baltimore had grown dark by the time the stage from Lancaster rattled into the station on Light Street. Lovejoy and Tom hired a waterman to row them across the harbor to the wharf at Fells Point. From there they walked to the MacKenzie house on Thames Street.

At the door, Lovejoy said, "Now Tom, let's see how things are going with the *Flora* and the collection of our money from the sale of the prizes before I tell Malcolm what we have learned."

First they had to be greeted by the MacKenzies and then fed a late supper. Then, finally, Lovejoy and Tom were able to sit in front of a fire to consult with Malcolm, who seemed more interested in talking about the war in general than in their prize proceeds.

"While Madison has squeaked by in the election, the fact remains that the war has gone badly for us on land, Lovejoy. It looked so easy last spring. We have a population of—what?—easily more than seven million, while in Canada there are only half a million, and a good part of them speak French and have no great love for the British. On paper, we were to raise an army of thirty-five thousand, and that army was to strike quickly while Napoleon kept the British army occupied across the Atlantic. Ah, there is many a slip twixt cup and lip."

"My mind has been so distracted since we returned from our cruise that I have not paid close attention to the war in the north. What about our accounts?"

"The war has been one debacle after another, for our armies, that is. Here, consider this map. Our General Hull was supposed to establish a base at Detroit and cross over into Ontario. He did so, and seemed on the verge of great success. Many Canadian militiamen were deserting. And then the foolish old man lost his nerve. Became anxious about his supply lines. Held back his men from an attack on Fort Malden, the chief British fort in upper Canada, here on the straits connecting Lakes Huron and Erie. Pulled back across the river. The initiative passed to the British. They crossed to our side and, with the help of a horde of Indians, frightened poor old Hull into surrendering an army of nearly three thousand men. Disgraceful episode. That was in August, about the time we were preparing for the *Flora* to start her cruise."

"I remember there were high hopes at the time for Hull's offensive. There was much talk of our invading Canada and perhaps annexing the country. Now, about our money . . ."

"Yes, it was a black day when news of the surrender reached Baltimore. But the faces of our Republican friends grew even longer when reports came in about our loss of Fort Dearborn, farther west on Lake Michigan. There the British allowed their Indian allies to slaughter scores of men, women, and children. And now we are waiting to hear from our army in New York State. They were moving against Montreal at last report. But I am rattling on and on, and you are tired, from the looks of you. What brings you lads back to Baltimore so soon? Has it aught to do with the young lady you were visiting up in Pennsylvania?"

Lovejoy took a deep breath and, with trembling voice, told him the report he had received, via his father and Tom.

"Why, that is marvelous good news," Malcolm said. "Why did you not tell me this sooner, letting me run on about general affairs? I am overjoyed at this news. Your sister is alive after all, Tom."

"Tell him the rest of the story, Joy," Tom said.

"Ten thousand pounds! And in gold, too," Malcolm exclaimed when Lovejoy had finished. "Even if we sold the *Flora* and sacrificed all our prize monies, much of which has yet to be paid, it would not suffice to meet this demand."

Tom broke in with, "My sister is worth all that and more. I would spend the rest of my life repaying you both."

Malcolm shook his head. "Ah, lads, this is indeed a grave dilemma. Even if you—Lovejoy—Talbot Smith, and I were to agree to pay such an exorbitant ransom, I very much doubt we could raise the money by the first of March. Why would they demand so much for a mere prize crew?"

Again Tom spoke up. "Probably because they think that Captain Martin would cough up the money to save his son's fiancée. You see, Mr. MacKenzie, Captain Smith wanted to protect my sister. So he told the prize master . . ."

When Tom had finished, Lovejoy said, "But even if I were engaged to Meggie rather than Madeline Richter, I doubt very much that Father would sacrifice such a sum."

"I agree," Malcolm said. "He would take the position that being captured and imprisoned is a normal risk in the privateering business. Your gunner's mate and others would tell you the same."

"Let me see our list of prize proceeds."

Malcolm handed him a small ledger.

"I thought there would be far more than this."

"You probably were including the value of the missing brig."

"But we also sent in an American ship sailing out of Philadelphia under a Sidmouth license."

"The *Delaware Queen.* If you had not been in such a hurry to hie yourself off to see your sweetheart, I would have told you that you caused a great deal of difficulty in taking her as a prize. The admiralty court refused to give us a decree of condemnation. Ordered the release of the ship and her crew, and we had to pay the cost of the proceedings."

"Why, that is monstrous. They were trading with our enemy."

"The owners sent down a very persuasive lawyer from Dover who argued that the vessel was trading with Spain, not Britain. And we are not at war with Spain."

"Did we not have persuasive lawyers of our own?"

Malcolm cleared his throat, then said, "Tom, you must be very weary. Let me suggest that you retire while Lovejoy and I discuss our accounts. And again, let me say how pleased I am that your sister was not lost at sea after all. Get some rest. We will think of a way to free her."

After Tom had gone, Malcolm said, "When you stopped that ship, did you not examine her papers, the Sidmouth license in particular?"

"It was not my business to do so."

"If you had, you might have noted that the license was issued to the Rosachest Company, of Dover, Delaware. Have you any knowledge of the owners of that firm?"

"I do not know and do not care. I considered her a proper prize."

"You should care. Our lawyers discovered the significance of the name Rosachest. You have a brother named Chester, Chester Peebles, I believe."

"He is my half brother. Don't tell me . . ."

"And is his wife's name not Rosalind?"

"Rosa-Chest. Oh my God, they have been hauling flour to the British army. He must have done that behind my father's back. Oh, I wish you had persuaded the admiralty court to condemn the ship."

"It would not have damaged them. They owned the cargo, not the ship, which was merely under lease to them."

"Even so, it would have given me great satisfaction to expose him as a traitor. Father would disown him if he knew."

"Perhaps not. Oh, this has caused me much distress, but you see, Jeremiah Martin is listed as surety for the bond of the *Delaware Queen.* When I discovered that, I dropped our claim against the ship. A condemnation would not have damaged the Rosachest Company, but it would have caused your father to forfeit his bond and would have stained his reputation."

Lovejoy rose and paced around the room.

"Would Chester know that you discovered that he was behind the enterprise?"

"Probably not."

"Nor Father, either?"

"Knowing of his illness, I have not communicated with him about this matter. We just dropped our claim. Could it be that in his infirmity he has fallen under the influence of your brother?"

"That is a possibility. Tom said that Chester and our family lawyer were present when he and Evan called on Father. And Chester would have to know that our privateer captured the ship operating under his Sidmouth license."

"Would this Chester be in a position to block any part of a ransom payment, even if your father were so disposed?"

"Yes. Father has turned his business over to him."

"Then whatever we do, it must be without your father's help or even knowledge or, for that matter, Chester's."

"He would be the last person I would want to know our plans."

"So be it. We can solve nothing tonight, Lovejoy. We will attack this problem with fresh minds in the morning."

Dawn found Lovejoy staring at the ceiling, his mind far from fresh. He arose, washed his face in the bowl on the bureau, and dressed as quietly as he could. As he started for the door, Tom awoke.

"Where are you going?"

"To see Talbot Smith."

"Shall I come with you?"

"No. Go back to sleep."

"Do you know what you are going to do about Meggie?"

"I will tell you in good time."

He slipped out the door and down the stairs before Tom could question him further.

# 5

Seven weeks later, on a clear, cold morning early in February of 1813, the *Flora* cast off her lines and drifted away from the wharf of Talbot Smith's shipyard and out into the current of the Patapsco River to begin her second cruise. Lovejoy stood on the stern with Phipps, Barineau, Gandy, Kevin Mahoney, and Tom while crewmen raised the mainsail of the repaired and refitted schooner.

On the wharf, Talbot sat in the wheelbarrow Malcolm MacKenzie had fitted up so that his men could convey him about to oversee the repairs to the *Flora*. Malcolm waved at the departing crew as the schooner took the wind's bit in her teeth and gathered speed. Talbot, bundled in a blanket, simply stared across the water at his graceful creation.

"He would give his other leg and his right arm as well to be sailing with us, wouldn't he?" Lovejoy said to Phipps, who now wore a captain's hat and braided coat.

"He likely would."

"Would you have shipped out with him again?"

"Never."

"I am glad you did not refuse my offer."

"You made it hard for me not to accept. I hope you will not regret naming me to serve as your captain."

"You proved your mettle in bringing us safely back to port before. I do not doubt that you will do even better on this cruise."

Phipps turned to shout at the bosun's mate.

"Raise your topsails."

Then, to the gunner's mate, "All right, Gandy. You may fire off your guns when you are ready."

Starting with the forward Long Tom on the port side, one after another the *Flora*'s cannon fired off a salute to the man who had created the sleek schooner.

"Now, Captain Phipps, I would be grateful if you would assemble your men so that I may address them."

On her first cruise, more than a hundred men had signed on to sail aboard the schooner for a ninety-day cruise. Now there were barely half that number, for in his impatience to get back to sea, Lovejoy had been unwilling to wait for his newspaper notices to attract fresh applicants. Fortunately, he had been able to persuade many of the previous crewmen to sign up again, this time for 180 days.

"Men, we are setting forth on a perilous mission. We will not enjoy the advantages that were ours when we sailed over these same waters last August. The British are fully alert to the danger we pose to their shipping. They will be sailing in well-protected convoys. They will be better armed. We shall have to be more careful in our selection of prizes. But we have the advantage now of experience. We have learned better, have we not, than to challenge a fully armed British naval vessel?"

He waited until the laughter of the veterans died away.

"We have also learned how to work together in harmony. Those of you who have never been to sea before, take this advice: some of the bravest chaps I have ever known are serving as your shipmates. Observe them and learn from them. And among them none is braver than your captain, Hosea Phipps. Although I am the chief owner of this vessel, during this cruise I am merely your ship's surgeon, and as such, like yourselves, I am subject to the orders of this man, who has proved beyond all doubt his abilities as a sailor. Brave fellows all, I present to you Captain Phipps."

Phipps's talk consisted mostly of practical advice. "Remember, when you go aloft, use one hand for the ship and one for yourself. Never show a light at night. I will punish anyone who strikes or even swears at a fellow crewman. If you have any dispute, bring it to me for settlement. If anyone brought any spirits aboard, you will report it to Dr. Martin. You will partake of strong drink only for medicinal purposes and only with his permission or mine. There will be church services every Sunday morning, which I shall conduct. Every man is expected to attend. Now, please bow your heads while we ask the Almighty to give his blessings to ourselves and this schooner."

Barineau, who had stood with crossed arms during Phipps's talk, looked at Lovejoy and shrugged. Lovejoy grinned, closed his eyes, and bowed his head.

Lovejoy had caused the bed in the captain's cabin to be replaced by four bunks. He shared the cabin with Phipps, Barineau and Tom.

On the first night out, midway down the Chesapeake, while Phipps and Tom were out of the cabin, Lovejoy talked in confidence with Barineau. He told the sailing master about his visit to Berks County and his relationship with Madeline Richter, leaving out only their lovemaking.

"So you must have found it very difficult to take leave of your betrothed."

"It was both the hardest thing I ever did and the easiest."

"You will have to explain that."

"Until Tom arrived with his news, my life appeared to have been settled. I was in love with a beautiful girl, and she with me. I was on the verge of winning her father's permission to marry her. While, as it turned out, I was not quite so wealthy as I first thought, still there was more than enough money to launch a new career. It seemed that the strains between my father and me would soon be eased. So, yes, it was wrenching for me to set all that aside, at least for the moment, and return to the sea."

"How, then, was it easy?"

"I realized in an instant that if I did not rise above my own selfish interests and do all that I could to free our prize crew, there would always be that worm of self-reproach gnawing away in the apple of my happiness."

"I brought along a volume of Marcus Aurelius's *Meditations,* in which he says something that is to the point here. You know of him?"

"The Roman philosopher, yes."

"Let me find it for you. Ah, here it is: 'A wrongdoer is often a man that has left something undone, not always he that has done something.' And wait, here is another passage that has meaning: 'Never esteem anything as of advantage to thee that shall make thee break thy word or lose thy self-respect.' "

"That's it. I would have lost my self-respect if I had ignored the plight of our crew. I had to choose between self-interest and self-respect."

"And you chose rightly," Barineau said. Then he paused and asked, "You feel certain that this Miss Richter will still be waiting when you return?"

"I have no doubt whatsoever. See the scar here on my hand? Let me tell you how I came by it."

Near the mouth of the Chesapeake, in the lee of Fisherman's Island off Cape Charles, the *Flora* dropped anchor and signaled for a pilot to come out from the shore.

The pilot, a man whose bronzed face bore the deep marks of fifty years' exposure to sun, rain, and salt spray, briefed them on what to expect upon leaving the Chesapeake.

"British ships as thick as fleas on a dog's back is waiting out there. You're smart to lie to, out of sight here, for they sometimes dash in to try their luck, and there is naught to stop them. And there has been some privateers operating out of Bermuda in these waters. They has took several prizes off us that I knows of. Now the best thing to do is slip through the blockade at night and head straight out to sea. Are you ready for the sea?"

"Indeed we are," Phipps said.

"Good enough. There is no moon tonight, and it's cloudy to boot. You'll have to proceed slowly. Take soundings as you feel your way along. Watch out for shoals here and here." He stabbed at the chart with a calloused finger. "Muffle your bell. Have your leadsman whisper his soundings. Use just one jib sheet. Head west-southwest until you reach this point, then change course and head south by southeast to here. Then you head due east and hope there is enough wind to carry you past the British before dawn. It all depends on the wind. Now, this calls for a dram of rum."

"We don't drink aboard this schooner," Phipps said.

"I'll settle for coffee and my fee of five dollars."

Phipps and Barineau spent a long night feeling their way along through the dark. A sort of firemen's brigade line of sailors standing an arm's length apart quietly passed the leadsman's readings from the bow back to the stern, where Phipps stood with the quartermaster at the tiller. Hourglass and reel of knotted line in hand, Barineau kept a constant check on their progress by dead reckoning.

It was well past midnight when they reached the point where they were to begin their direct run seaward, and only a feeble wind was blowing from the northeast.

"We'll never clear the mouth of the Chesapeake by daylight with just one jib sail," Barineau said. "And we'll be sailing pretty close into this wind at that. We have time to reverse course and wait for a better night."

"Or we could bend on all sail and trust God to carry us through."

Phipps paced around the stern once and then called softly to his bosun's mate, "Raise your topsails and bend on your spirit sails. Crowd on every scrap of canvas. We'll run for it."

The sun rose out of a clearing sky to reveal several British ships, the closest a frigate cruising under shortened sail just a mile to the east. Phipps switched to a southeasterly heading and, with the wind off his port beam, quickly picked up speed. The frigate took up the chase, but after two hours of failing to gain on the *Flora*, gave it up and headed back to its station.

A week later found the *Flora* off the northern headland of Bermuda. She sailed back and forth for several days, watching as vessels entered and left the St. George's harbor. Finally, a trim sloop, heavily loaded, judging from the way she rode so low in the water, left the harbor and tacked first to the north and then toward the east and, at last, under full sail, southward.

George Tradnick had come out from Cornwall twenty years earlier to work as a shipwright's apprentice. He had taken as much pride in building the splendid sloops for which Bermuda was famous as Talbot Smith did in constructing his beloved Baltimore topsail schooners.

On Bermuda, he had married a young Irish schoolteacher who had taught him to read and write and improve his speech. They had saved their money to buy the materials from which he, with the help of friends, had fashioned the ninety-ton *New Hope.* As owner and captain of the sloop, he had carried onions to Jamaica, lumber from Bermuda's fast-disappearing cedar forests to St. Kitts, and passengers to and from Nassau. Now his sloop was laden with gunpowder being transferred from the Royal magazine on Bermuda to the one at Antigua.

His crew of seven Bermudians, all either black or mulatto, liked working for this intelligent and gentle captain. He paid them well by island standards and treated them with respect.

Although the *New Hope* carried several muskets and pistols, Tradnick refused to mount even a single cannon on his sloop. He felt that he could outrun any craft he would ever encounter at sea, and that included the sharp-hulled schooner dogging his tracks as he scurried along with the wind off his starboard beam.

He studied the schooner through his spyglass.

"She's flying our colors, but if she's not a Yankee privateer, I don't know a square from a granny knot," he said to his mate.

The *Flora's* rigging now billowed with every scrap of canvas Phipps could bend on.

"You don't think you ought to let her draw close enough to make sure she isn't one of ours with a message?" the mate asked.

"No, she's got to be American. Good thing for us she's carrying the weight of so many guns. Ah, well, let her have her fun. She can't gain on us at this rate. Tonight, if she don't give up the chase, I'll change course and lose her in the dark."

As the sun sank nearer the horizon, its rays made the sails of the *Flora,* some two miles distant, glow gold and yellow. The sea had turned choppy under a freshening breeze.

Tradnick said, "The fellow hangs on like a bulldog. Now, boys, listen sharp. No one is to show a light. Douse the galley fire. Cover the binnacle. After full dark has fallen, we'll run before the wind for a while and then change course a time or two. By sunup tomorrow, I expect to have lost him. I'll have to stay up here all night with two men at a time to help me check our distances."

Aboard the *Flora,* it became more and more apparent that they could not overtake the sloop before nightfall.

Phipps, Barineau, and Lovejoy withdrew for a council of war.

"There is only one way we can catch her," Barineau said. "Neither of you may like it. Gandy certainly will not."

"You don't mean jettison our cannon?" Phipps said.

"Only our carronades. What do you say, Lovejoy?"

Lovejoy looked at the lowering sun, grimaced, and said, "Who will give the order to Gandy?"

# PART TWO

# 1 

The harbormaster for the port of Bridgetown, Barbados, had been puzzled back in October as he watched a battered brig limp into Carlisle Bay, past Fort Needham, and drop anchor near the careenage at the mouth of the sluggish little Constitution River.

Several holes had been punched through her sails. Part of her railing was missing. And her hull bore patches along the waterline.

He waited on the dock while a peg-legged man laboriously lowered himself into a boat to be rowed to the dock.

"Who might you be?" the habormaster asked as the man thumped his way up the steps to the dock.

"I am Captain Christopher Bledsoe, master of the brig *Goodfellow* out of Liverpool. You will find my papers here in good order. First, would you be a good fellow and send someone to fetch the provost marshal?"

Put off by the captain's overbearing manner, the harbormaster asked, "What do you want with him?"

"I am carrying a dozen American privateers whom I have taken prisoner en route here from Liverpool."

As Bledsoe explained first to the harbormaster, then the provost, and later to anyone who would listen, he had been attacked by an enormous American privateer carrying a horde of landsmen and had capitulated only after a long and bloody fight against awesome odds. But would a former Royal Navy lieutenant who had lost a leg at Trafalgar stay beaten?

"They locked my men in the hold and put a prize crew aboard to sail the *Goodfellow* up to Baltimore. The prize master, the curly-headed young chap standing over there, he wasn't up to his job. Hit heavy weather off Hatteras. Began taking on water where two Yankee cannonballs had struck our hull near the waterline. I persuaded him to release several of my men to help man the pumps and show his crew how to plug the leaks. Simple matter of doubling a swath of canvas and strapping it over the holes with lines run under the keel. Soon as the job was done, I gave the signal, and my lads seized the prize master. I always keep side arms concealed under a locker. With weapons in our hands, it was an easy matter to free the rest of our crew and make prisoners of our captors. Whereupon I turned the brig about and resumed my voyage here."

"I see a girl on your deck," the provost said. "Is she one of your passengers from Liverpool?"

"Hardly. She was a member of the crew of the privateer that foolishly attacked me. Surgeon's assistant, she was."

"Likely looking lass."

"And saucy, too. Smart as a whip in the bargain. But don't get any notions. She is a special prisoner, a most valuable one. She is to be my ticket to a secure old age."

The Town Hall Gaol in Bridgetown was a massive coral stone building with two main floors, a partially sunken basement, and a long attic. It was surrounded by a stout stone wall. Built eighty-odd years before to house the island's legislature and courts, the building also served as the local prison.

Collins and his prize crew were locked away in the basement with prisoners from another American privateer taken in Barbadian waters by a British frigate, who were awaiting transfer to a prison in England. Megan was assigned a small room on the top floor of the building. Once Bledsoe had explained to the chief jailer that she was the prospective daughter-in-law of a prominent Philadelphia merchant and had distributed bribes to the guards, she was treated with respect. Bledsoe arranged with the owner of a local boardinghouse to prepare special meals for her each morning and evening.

At first Bledsoe had been kept too busy to pay Meg much attention. He had to see to having the *Goodfellow*'s cargo of cheese and clothing unloaded and then having her careened so that her hull could be repaired and her railing and sails replaced. And then there was the matter of arranging for a ransom message to be sent to Jeremiah Martin in Philadelphia.

From local merchants, he learned that a man named Martin had once done considerable business hauling Barbadian sugar and rum to Philadelphia. The proprietor of the Bow Bells Tavern recalled that

Martin himself had stayed at his establishment many years before and, if memory served him correctly, he had employed a lawyer, "Old Hiram Fescue," as his local agent.

"Would this Fescue still be living?" Bledsoe had asked.

"Just barely. Keeps his office on Swan Street, when he is sober, that is. Best to call there in the morning. By noon he is usually drunk."

Fescue was an ancient little man with white hair and a nose as bulbous and red as a clown's. At first he had pretended not to remember "this fellow . . . Jeremiah Martin you say his name was?"

The suggestion that there would be a generous retainer finally jogged his memory to the extent that he admitted, "I may have represented such a fellow, but that would have been some time in the past, long before our present troubles with America. I am an old man. Really should give up my practice. Howsomever, I have no truck with Americans anymore, not after the way they have stabbed us in the back while we are engaged in a great war with France. We Bajans are loyal to our sovereign. They don't call us 'Little England' for naught."

"I understand you have practiced law here for forty years."

"More like fifty. Was brought out here by Sir Francis Bolton in sixty-five. Now there was a man. Shrewdest client I ever did serve. Bajan to the bone, but had connections all around the world, he had. Ah, the stories I could tell about that one."

"I would be happy to hear your stories later, but just now I am interested in your connections with Jeremiah Martin."

"I have had so many clients. What might your business be with this Martin?"

Although the old man did not change his expression as Bledsoe explained about Megan Jenkins, his eyes did lose their cloudy glaze at the mention of a large ransom demand.

"The fellow is a Yankee, is he not, and therefore our enemy? Now you say you expect Captain Martin to pay a ransom for this young woman whom you believe is engaged to be married to his son? Here, in the midst of a war, that would be a tricky business."

"Come, come, my good man, nothing is impossible. I am prepared to pay fifty pounds."

"I would have to search my records and my memory. Fifty pounds, you say? Why don't you return tomorrow morning and let's discuss this matter in more detail. This war makes everything so complicated. The

American embargoes were bad enough. Our own government back home has called a halt to the slave trade. Without fresh supplies of Africans, our own slaves get exalted notions of their own value. Won't work like they did when I came here in sixty-five. Sir Francis Bolton brought me out, a green lad fresh from Cambridge and the Inns of Court."

"Yes, yes, my good man. Please do search your records, and I will be back tomorrow morning."

The Hiram Fescue who was waiting for Bledsoe the next morning looked and acted ten years younger. Now he recalled that he had represented Jeremiah Martin "until he started pulling in his horns. Last word I had of him, his health was none too good."

"Could you arrange for a proposal to be sent to him?"

"Captain Martin was a great one for secrecy when I was in his employ. Like Sir Francis Bolton, in that regard. They were distant relatives, as a matter of fact. Sir Francis's grandfather was Captain Martin's great-grandfather. Wrong side of the blanket business. Quite a story about those two."

"Actually, I am much more interested in how to communicate with Captain Martin than in hearing about his genealogy. How would you go about sending him a very confidential message?"

"You just write out in plain English what you want to say. Keep it short and simple, and I will code it into a letter. We'll pass it over to St. Eustatius, where a Dutch friend will see that it gets to Captain Martin, one way or another. Statia is under British occupation now that the French control the Netherlands, but he will find a way . . . for a fee, of course. Make that another fifty pounds. Now, you say this girl is engaged to be married to Captain Martin's son. I wonder which one that would be? He had both a stepson and a younger son of his own, as I recall."

Collins and his fellow captives were brought up from the basement every day and allowed to exercise under armed guard in the high-walled courtyard. At first, the young prize master would call up to Meg to ask how she was being treated. Flattered by his show of concern, Meg looked forward to this ritual. After the prison commandant had ordered the guards to put a stop to these shouted conversations, Collins simply stood under a tree and stared at her window. When the guards were not looking, he would wave and she would return the gesture.

No fool, Meg realized that had it not been for Talbot Smith's lie about her being engaged to Lovejoy Martin, she would not be nearly so well treated. So she kept the truth about their relationship to herself.

Just as she had won the admiration of Talbot Smith aboard the *Flora,* so had she appealed to the protective as well as the acquisitive instincts of Captain Bledsoe. En route to Barbados, he had treated her in an almost fatherly manner.

Once repairs were under way on the *Goodfellow* and he had started his ransom demand on its way to Jeremiah Martin, Bledsoe came around to inquire about her well-being.

"I don't like it here. I would much prefer to be back in America. Why don't you let us go?"

"My dear girl, not until we receive your ransom."

"Please don't call me your dear girl. And what ransom?"

Megan's hopes slumped when Bledsoe told her of his message to Jeremiah Martin. She almost blurted out the truth: that if Martin remembered her at all, it would be as the daughter of a local innkeeper and hardly of a status to be affianced to his son, but she stopped in time and said, simply, "Oh, dear. I hate to think of causing Lovejoy's family any distress."

"From all I have heard, this Captain Martin is rich enough to pay a dozen such ransoms without feeling any distress."

"But what if he does not pay?"

"Ah, then, my dear, you and your fellow privateers will be shipped off to England to Dartmoor Prison and a fate from which I hope you will be spared. There now, my dear child. Don't look so downhearted. I have given your fiancé's family until the first of March to raise the money. Plenty of time for them to do that. Now, about Captain Martin's son. He is the surgeon who worked on my chaps after our battle, is he not?"

"Yes. He studied medicine in London."

"Handsome, well-spoken young man. I still think he should have taken off Tompkins's arm, however."

"The poor fellow's arm is healing, is it not?"

"Aye, but it is of no use to him, or he to me, with one arm dangling at his side. I have given him the sack. Well now, is there anything you require, my dear?"

"Only my freedom," Meg replied.

"As soon as the repairs to the *Goodfellow* have been completed, I expect to haul a cargo of rum over to Antigua and then return here by the first of March to receive the ransom. So you will have to be patient until then. Meanwhile, I trust you are enjoying the meals the black-amoor woman prepares."

"They are good enough."

"Should be for what I am paying her. Well, good day to you."

Besides its oligarchy of sugar plantation owners, many of whose ancestors had come to Barbados in the mid and late 1600s, and its huge population of black slaves, the island was home to several thousand poor whites, held in contempt by both masters and slaves as "redlegs." Most of these spindly-framed, lackadaisical people were descendants of Irish indentured servants or transported English criminals. Those not employed as militiamen to keep the slaves under control or as plantation overseers worked as fishermen or butchers or in some cases, as beggars. As uneducated as the slaves, they were despised by other Barbadians, black and white. They, in turn, treated blacks with contempt.

In addition, the island was home to a population of several thousand "free coloreds," usually persons of mixed blood, many of whom engaged in trades or operated boardinghouses.

The guards at the Town Hall Gaol were redlegs to a man. It was they whom Collins bribed from his little store of coins to provide him with paper and pen so that he could send messages to Meg after officials had stopped his calling up to her window.

Back aboard the *Flora,* Megan had been annoyed by Collins's obvious infatuation with her. If she herself had not been so smitten by Lovejoy Martin, she might have been attracted to the handsome young man. Although of small stature, he was well-knit and blessed with eyes as blue as the tropical skies.

His notes, full of misspelled words and wooden language, stopped when Collins exhausted his little supply of coins. Meg missed getting them.

Since leaving the *Flora* to go aboard the *Goodfellow,* Megan had thought a thousand times of Tom's revelation of Lovejoy's confrontation with Talbot Smith and his tying himself to the schooner's mast to make the captain change his mind about sending the captured brig to Charleston. Although the decision had been a bad one, enabling Captain

Bledsoe to recover control of his brig, still it pleased her to think that Lovejoy had been so concerned for her welfare.

Although she realized that Talbot Smith had deliberately spread the story that she was affianced to Lovejoy as a way of protecting her, she liked to imagine that it might be true. Fortunately, for the sake of her morale, Tom had kept his promise to Lovejoy to keep quiet about Madeline Richter. Ignorant of that relationship, Megan consoled herself with daydreams of somehow escaping captivity and being reunited with Lovejoy and Tom.

Before setting out on the repaired *Goodfellow* to carry a cargo to Antigua, Captain Bledsoe had purchased several secondhand novels for Megan's amusement. She passed the time reading the books: Defoe's *Moll Flanders,* Goldsmith's *The Vicar of Wakefield,* Laurence Sterne's *Tristram Shandy,* and, at her request, a New Testament.

So Megan Jenkins waited out the days in her little cell, reading her novels and her Bible, eating her special meals, chatting with the colored innkeeper, taking walks about the grounds early each morning and late each afternoon, dreaming dreams of Lovejoy Martin, and relishing memories of those pleasant days aboard the *Flora* when she had served as his surgeon's assistant.

# 2

The same harbormaster who had watched the *Goodfellow* limp into port in October was on duty four months later when a graceful sloop dipped her British colors opposite Fort Needham and glided in to anchor some distance from the shore.

A slender, gray-haired man wearing a captain's hat and a sandy-haired young man carrying a black medical bag were rowed toward the dock by a muscular Negro. They were intercepted by a large boat carrying the harbormaster and two armed men wearing the new red uniforms of the Barbadian militia.

"Hold up there. No one allowed to land until you're given permission to do so. Who are you?"

"I am Captain Tradnick, master of the sloop *New Hope* out of Bermuda," the older man said. "Here are my papers. And this is Dr. Jennings, a physician, who is my passenger."

"Doctors are always welcome on this island. As for your sloop, you will be required to anchor over there, close under the guns of Rickett's Fort. Our Royal governor has decreed that all strange vessels are to remain under guard, as it were. We are at war with the Americans, you know."

"Here are my papers. As you can see, we cleared St. George with a load of gunpowder for the navy base at Antigua. With such a cargo, I thought it best to anchor well away from other ships."

"Why have you come here, so far south of Antigua?"

"We encountered a Yankee privateer north of our destination. We carry no cannon. Only way to elude the devils was to make a long run to the southeast, carrying us far off course."

"But why stop here at all?"

"Ah, well, you see, Dr. Jennings wanted to make inquiries about settling here after he completes his term as naval surgeon. And as Barbados was so near to hand. . . . You wouldn't allow us to ride to shore with you, would you? And we'd be grateful if you could recommend an inn."

Seeing that the harbormaster accepted his story, Barineau then turned to Toby and said in his carefully practiced Bermudian accent, "Return to the *New Hope* and make certain none of our boys tries to jump ship. And remind them: no fires."

Then, turning to the harbormaster, "Can't be too careful with a hold full of explosives. And none of my crew will be coming ashore. That's on the advice of Dr. Jennings here."

"Quite so, Captain," Lovejoy said in his pseudo-Welsh-English accent. "Half his chaps have the clap. Felt certain you don't want that carried ashore."

"I should say not. We have enough of that disease as it is."

"Glad you agree with my judgment," Lovejoy said, then changed the subject to inquire about inns in Bridgetown.

After they had climbed into the harbormaster's boat, Lovejoy asked, "By the by, has a brig out of Liverpool, the *Goodfellow,* come into this port?"

"As a matter of fact, she did last October. Why do you ask?"

"I am acquainted with the captain's aunt in London. She told me he was planning a voyage out here. Never met the chap. Aunt says he is minus a leg."

"So he is. Came in with twelve Yankee prisoners. Very proud of himself, he was, and not at all bashful in telling about it."

"Captain Bledsoe is not in port then?" Lovejoy asked.

"No, he cleared out two weeks ago with a cargo for Antigua. You would have encountered him there if you had not had your run-in with the privateer."

Barineau broke in with, "What about his Yankee prisoners?"

"They are being held at the Town Hall Gaol until Bledsoe returns to pick up a cargo of rum and sugar to carry back to Liverpool. He may haul the prisoners back with him."

"And he captured twelve men?" Lovejoy asked.

"Actually eleven. One was a girl."

Barineau and Lovejoy made their way through the varicolored beggars and hucksters who thronged the dock area and walked up Tudor Street to the Bow Bells Tavern.

When they were out of the harbormaster's hearing, Lovejoy said, "We are lucky Bledsoe is not in port. But if he is coming back, we must work fast."

"I was afraid the fellow would insist on going aboard to inspect our cargo. He would have seen in a flash that our lads are not Bermudians. How did my accent sound?"

"Good enough imitation of poor Tradnick's, I suppose, but I doubt it would have fooled a real Bermudian. Well, so far, so good."

They spent the next hour fending off questions from the garrulous innkeeper while eliciting information from him.

"Yes, the Americans are being held in the basement of the building, all except the girl, who I hears is being treated like a princess. Winnie Arbuckle, the fat slut what runs the Bearded Fig Tree, free colored woman, she is, takes over specially prepared meals, so I hears. Don't know whether this Captain Bledsoe has gone sweet on the girl, or what. Yes, Winnie's place is just over on Flowerpot Alley. Lawyer named Fescue? Indeed I do know him. What would your business with him be?"

Lovejoy thought quickly and replied, "His name was recommended to me in London as a good solicitor to assist me should I settle here. Would you recommend him as well?"

"I reckon he was a good enough lawyer in his day, but he is long past his prime. Anyway, you can see for yourself if you go over to his office on Swan Street. Best to wait until tomorrow morning, if you want to find him sober. Would you gentlemen be requiring lodging? I could make room for you."

Lovejoy looked at Barineau and, thinking quickly, said, "We will keep that in mind. May just sleep aboard our sloop."

Outside in the brilliant tropical sunlight, they consulted with each other, then headed for the Bearded Fig Tree, which was a two-storied frame building shaded by a huge tree whose trunk was surrounded by rooted tendrils hanging down from the limbs like flying buttresses.

An enormously fat, beige-colored woman was napping in a wide wooden armchair in the hall of the inn. A barefooted black girl dressed in a short shift stood behind her, lazily wielding a large palm-leaf fan. At the approach of Lovejoy and Barineau, the girl began to fan her mistress with more vigor before saying, "Miss Winnie. We got gentlemens here."

The innkeeper opened her yellow-hazel eyes and appraised the pair shrewdly as Lovejoy inquired about lodgings.

"A doctor and a sea captain man, is that for true? Justly how long would you gone be wanting a room for? You gentlemens minds this is a respectable house. Don't want no gentlemens that gets spranksious and breaks up furniture. And don't go trying to slip no bad women up to your room from off the street out there. And I do be always paid in advance for lodgings. Extra for drink."

Their room occupied a corner on the second floor of the inn. They spent the rest of the afternoon walking about the picturesque town and acquainting themselves with the location of the Town Hall Gaol and the several forts protecting Carlisle Bay.

"Curious island, Barbados," Barineau said as they looked out at the sea. "Not as large as one of our counties in Maryland or Pennsylvania, but a hundred years ago, the British wouldn't have traded Barbados for all of New England. That is how rich this place was. In 1627, the British found the island unpopulated and covered with forests. The Royalists used it as a dumping ground for Puritans. Then, when Cromwell controlled England, he exiled Royalist prisoners here. Both sides 'Barbadosed' Quakers and criminals. That was the term they used. Look about you at all the black and brown faces. If you had stood on this spot a hundred and seventy years ago, you would have seen only white faces."

"According to my father, one of our ancestors, a Quaker he was, came to Virginia by way of Barbados," Lovejoy said.

"As did many American colonists, especially in South Carolina, where the richer ones brought along their slaves. Europe's sweet tooth changed this place from a pleasant land occupied by small farmers—called 'ten-acre men'—and energetic tradesmen. Rich, greedy men started buying up the land and importing Africans to grow cane. Squeezed the little fellow off the land, cut or burnt off the trees to create their huge plantations. More riches for the rich, misery for the uprooted Africans and their descendants, exile for the small white settlers, and sugar for the tea and coffee of England, not to mention rum."

"My Uncle Ephraim, who is a doctor in Philadelphia, practiced medicine here briefly some years ago as a contract doctor to a large plantation. He found the climate so salubrious that he used to send patients here to recover from various ailments."

"The climate may not be so good for our health if we are discovered for what we are. They would hang us as spies, for certain. I counted a good twenty militiamen, all armed."

"We can't back out now, Pierre."

"No, and I wouldn't even if we could."

That evening, Winnie set them down to an excellent supper of stewed chicken and fried flying fish. As they ate, Winnie sat in her armchair and berated the three young women and half-grown boy who padded between the kitchen and the serving room.

"Hey you, little spree-boy. Stop keeping that noise back there and come fill this gentleman's glass. Can't you see him punishing for more wine? Times I wish I had my money back for what I paid for you."

Lovejoy, amused by the woman's colorful speech and imperious management of her staff, praised her cooking extravagantly and generally set out to ingratiate himself with her. By the end of the meal, she and her black servants were laughing at his jokes.

"Oh, you could be a great success on this island. If you come back to stay and be a big doctor man, don't you forget it was Winnie first give you shelter."

Lovejoy pushed his chair back from the table.

"Miss Winnie, we heard a curious story this afternoon. About an American girl held prisoner here."

Winnie's face lost its smile. "How do that young woman concern you?"

"Oh, the man at Bow Bells says you take meals to her."

"That man and his gossip. He just a lick mouth bacra. None of his business what I do. What you getting at, anyway?"

"The harbormaster described her as a pretty girl. Sad thing for her to be in prison."

"She got books to read. I take her good food."

"The man at Bow Bells thought the captain—what's his name—fancies the young lady for himself."

"That Bow Bells man better learn to keep his big mouth shut. Captain Bledsoe is a fine man. He is trying to return that girl to her home. She is a good girl and she gonna stay a good girl. What you care about her anyway?"

"Ah, Winnie, call me a romantic, but the story of her plight has excited my pity."

Winnie's catlike eyes narrowed with suspicion as she sucked her teeth and said nothing.

"Perhaps it would cheer her up if you were to tell her that a new physician is visiting Barbados and that he offers his assistance if she should require any medical attention. And the same goes for you and your staff while I am lodging with you. For instance, is your own health satisfactory?"

It turned out that she suffered from what she called "bad bowels" and frequently endured "a cruel beating in my head."

Lovejoy listened patiently to her recitation, then promised to search through his medicines to see if he might find something that would alleviate her illnesses.

He returned to the subject of Megan, inquiring how her spirits fared in prison.

"This morning I take up her tray and find her looking out the window. I say, 'Child, what you propping sorrow for? What trouble you?' And she say, 'I want to go home.' But she don't need no doctor. She do be in good health."

"Perhaps you would pass a note of encouragement to the young lady. Let her know that someone is concerned about her."

"Big man in charge over there do be kindhearted, but his po bacra guards watches everything I do. I can't go passing no scrip. Them redlegs do be cruel if I do that."

"Not even for a gold sovereign, Winnie?"

She raised her eyebrows at this. "I have to study about that. Ax me in the foreday morning."

The note Lovejoy presented to Winnie the next morning said simply, "I have just arrived from London by a circuitous route and have heard of your sad plight. I know you must long for the *Joy* of freedom. *Joy* is always available for those who have faith. If you should require medical attention, it would give me great *Joy* to attend to you. Yours in Christian *love* and *Joy.* Sincerely, Dr. William Jennings."

Winnie frowned as she read the note.

"What is all this joy talk? You sound like a preacher man."

"Perhaps I do overuse the word, but joy is a great antidote to despair. I am sure the note will lift her spirits. Well, that was a fine breakfast, was it not, Captain Tradnick? There, we had best be about our business."

Leaving Barineau to go out and check on the crew of the *New Hope,* Lovejoy walked slowly away from the Bearded Fig Tree toward Swan Street. He had lain awake much of the night debating just what approach to take with the lawyer through whom Captain Bledsoe had sent a coded ransom message to Philadelphia.

He still had not made up his mind when he reached the one-story building bearing a tarnished nameplate reading "Hiram Fescue, Solicitor." The office door was locked.

As he leaned against a tree to wait, he tried to picture Meg puzzling over the note that Winnie had promised to slip to her with her breakfast. She was a bright girl. Surely she would not miss the meaning, he thought, as he watched a little man with a red nose, wearing a filthy, once-white suit and carrying a cane, shuffle along the street and take a key from his pocket at the door of the office.

"Would you happen to be lawyer Fescue?" Lovejoy said in his fake British accent.

"Do you have an appointment?"

"No, but you come highly recommended."

"Well, sir, I am a busy man. Can't have people pushing in off the street without an appointment. Who are you, anyway?"

"I am a doctor of medicine just arrived on Barbados. If you are too busy to see me, perhaps you would refer me to another solicitor to advise me on investments and other affairs."

Fescue unlocked his door as he pondered the possibility of a prosperous new client.

"What did you say your name was?"

"If you can't see me, why should I identify myself?"

The little man now had the door open and stepped across the threshold. He turned to face Lovejoy.

"Then who recommended me to you, if I may inquire?"

This was the moment Lovejoy had been agonizing over. He took a deep breath and looked into the lawyer's cloudy eyes.

"Jeremiah Martin in Philadelphia."

The blood seemed to drain from the old lawyer's cheeks, making his nose appear even redder. His expression turned from one of crafty suspiciousness to one of alarm.

"Come in, come in," he said.

Once Lovejoy was inside, he closed the door and bolted it.

"Who are you, anyway?"

Megan was starting to read *The Vicar of Wakefield* for the third time when Winnie appeared, accompanied by one of her girls carrying a breakfast tray with a silver cover. A lanky, tow-headed guard in a red uniform unlocked the cell door.

"How you keeping this morning, young missy?" Winnie asked.

"About the same, Winnie."

"Hope you be hungry."

"Actually, I don't have much appetite."

"You not sick, I hope?"

Winnie touched her forehead and then took her hand as if to feel her pulse.

"Don't let that spawgee guard man see this," she whispered. "It's a scrip from somebody staying with us. A doctor man."

Megan slipped the note into the pocket of her dress.

Winnie said in a loud voice, "Cap'n Bledsoe won't like it one bit if he come back and find they let you done be got sick."

"What are you talking in there, woman?" the guard called from the corridor.

"No need to play bad with me, guard man. This young lady don't look good to me."

"We take good care of her. Now you get on out of there, you picky-head madam woman."

Winnie left the cell with massive dignity. Megan eased the note from her pocket and read it, first in confusion and then suddenly with understanding. When the guard came to the door to take away her tray, the food had not been touched.

"I was not hungry. You may have it," Megan said.

The guard grinned and took the tray. When he was gone, Megan sat down and reread Lovejoy's note for the hundredth time.

"Who am I?" Lovejoy said to Hiram Fescue. "Perhaps you ought to sit down. This requires some explanation."

"I detect a touch of the American in your voice."

"I am staying at the Bearded Fig Tree under the name of Dr. William Jennings. I am under contract as a naval surgeon."

Fescue pursed his mouth and scratched his chin as he considered Lovejoy's evasive reply.

"Jennings, you say?"

"Dr. Jennings, but my message is far more important than my name."

"Then tell me the message and keep your voice down. The walls have ears in this place."

"Through an intermediary you sent a coded message by way of St. Eustatius to Captain Jeremiah Martin in Philadelphia. You sent the message on behalf of one Captain Christopher Bledsoe, the master of a British brig, which . . ."

The old man listened carefully until Lovejoy had completed his account of the message, ending it with, "and Captain Bledsoe demands payment of ten thousand pounds sterling by March 1 for the release of one Megan Jenkins and the other eleven prisoners. Now, tell me if I have left out anything."

"Whether I sent such a message or not, what reply does Captain Martin make to such a proposition? Will he pay it?"

"There are certain conditions."

"I am not sure that Captain Bledsoe would entertain any conditions at all. He is not a man to be trifled with."

"Nor is Captain Martin."

"Ah, well I know that. How are you acquainted with him?"

"His son studied medicine in London, as did I."

"Is that the son to whom Miss Jenkins is engaged?"

"That is the report that Captain Martin received. Through an intermediary in Bermuda, where I stopped over en route to this place, he wishes Captain Bledsoe to have the following reply: Deliver the prisoners to St. George on Bermuda, where there will be waiting the ransom money."

Fescue frowned. "The demand specified that the money be brought here to Barbados."

"I am not empowered to negotiate, merely to inform."

"I would like Bledsoe to hear this from your own lips."

"No! Never!"

Lovejoy's rising voice caused the old man to put his finger to his lips.

"Not so loud, my dear fellow. Why do you not wish to report this directly to the captain? He will be returning any day now."

"I am under contract to the Royal Navy. It would be awkward, to say the least, to have to explain my carrying messages from a citizen of a nation with whom we are at war, just as it would be for you, yourself. If I were exposed, I would have to reveal your role. You do see my point?"

"Yet Captain Bledsoe will want to know just how this message was delivered."

"He sent a message in code. Then why do not we concoct a message in writing that will convey Captain Martin's response? You can represent it as having arrived by the same route it was sent."

"You sound more like a lawyer than a doctor."

"You doubt me? I observed you walking up the street. You are suffering from the early stages of cirrhosis of the liver. You should drink more water and less strong spirits. I noted that you halted to rest and put your hand to your breast, which indicates angina pectoris. Chest pains when you exert, correct? You sit uneasily. When you urinate, which probably is quite often, do you not have some difficulty in starting the flow and then, when it comes, does it not do so in a forked stream?"

Fescue's mouth hung open by the time Lovejoy had completed his diagnosis.

"I do not like to mislead Captain Bledsoe."

"I am authorized to pay necessary expenses. Perhaps I could match the fee paid you by the good captain. So, how much is he paying you?"

"A hundred pounds, as a matter of fact, far more I should think than you."

"Done. I will match that amount. Now let's get down to the business of writing a message in which the correct code will be inserted."

"Excuse me," Fescue said, making a face as he arose. "I must use the necessary out back."

"Your prostate gland is bothering you?"

"Yes. Damn nuisance. Back in a moment."

Barineau and Lovejoy sat on the porch of the Bearded Fig Tree, talking in low tones. Barineau was fascinated by Lovejoy's account of his conference with Hiram Fescue.

"And you have no doubt that he will give the epistle you and he contrived to Bledsoe, and that it will do the trick?"

"It gives us something to fall back on if a more direct approach should fail. But we must work quickly, Pierre. It would not do for Bledsoe to return and catch us here. He would recognize us in an instant."

"Did our dusky hostess deliver your message to Megan?"

"Yes, but the guard hurried her out before Meg could read the note. Perhaps, after she takes over her evening meal, she can provide us with a clue as to our next move."

Late that afternoon, Winnie, followed by her black slave girl bearing a tray, presented herself at the Town Hall Gaol, was admitted by the guards at the front door, and laboriously mounted the stairs to the upper floor.

A different guard sat in a chair at the end of the long corridor.

"So, it is you again."

"Yes and don't you go acting like a grumpus back with me like your friend treated me this morning. I just hope that poor young lady ain't got sick."

"She acts lively as a little yellow bird. Been that way since I come to work."

When Winnie entered the cell, Meg arose and threw her arms about her.

"The note. You must tell me about the man who wrote it."

"He put his name to the note. He is a doctor. I told you that."

"Is he handsome? Broad shoulders? Sandy hair and gray eyes? An American?"

"He ain't no American, but otherwise what you say is right."

"Hey, you ain't supposed to stay in there no longer than it takes to set out her food," the guard said from the doorway.

"Here, take this pear and go eat it," Winnie replied. "Cap'n Bledsoe charged me to keep careful watch on this young lady's health. You want me to tell him you interfering?"

"Don't dawdle," the guard said as he took the pear.

"Winnie, please, you must tell him . . . tell him I love him."

"How come you say you love a man you ain't met? You dizzy in the head, girl?"

Megan, realizing her misstep, said quickly, "I mean . . . tell him I love joy. That's it, tell the gentleman I love . . . love joy. That is it. And tell him it would lift my spirits if I could just see him for a few minutes. Tell him . . ."

"What's all the noise you keeping in there?" the guard demanded. "Time's up. Clear out of there."

He seized Winnie's elbow. She pulled herself free of his grasp and moved out of the room. "Cap'n Bledsoe gonna have to be told about this."

"Don't forget, Winnie," Megan called after her. "I love joy."

Winnie had not gained wealth and standing in Bridgetown by being a fool. Her mother, a mulatto slave girl, had caught the fancy of an elderly planter with a sickly white wife. The only child of his extramarital liaison, Winnie had a much older white half brother who had inherited the family plantation and feigned ignorance of her existence. By the terms of her father's will, Winnie's own mother had received her freedom, a small house in Bridgetown, and two hundred pounds in cash. This modest inheritance had been parlayed by Winnie into the Bearded Fig Tree and the ownership of three black female slaves and one male. In her youth, Winnie had had several lovers of various colors. Love of food and money had taken the place of men as she grew older and fatter.

Winnie realized from Megan's reaction to the note that this Dr. Jennings was not who or what he pretended to be.

Thus, while Lovejoy and Barineau dined on yet another of her sumptuous meals that evening, she remained in her own room until after the main course had been served. Even then she kept silent, watching the pair through slitted eyes, listening carefully to the manner of their speech as much as to its content.

"You seem pensive this evening, Miss Winnie," Lovejoy said as the table was being cleared. "I hope you are feeling well."

"I am well enough, thank you for asking, Doctor . . . Doctor. Oh listen to me, I be done forgot what you say your name to be."

"Jennings. William Jennings."

"And where you say you come from?"

"London."

Looking at Barineau, she asked, "And where you say you from, mister captain man?"

"Bermuda."

Winnie sat sucking her teeth and looking at the ceiling. Once the table was clear, Lovejoy moved his chair near her side.

"Look here, you must tell me how the American girl is. What did she say about my note?"

"She acted mighty strange. She say to tell you she loves joy like you say you do. She axed me was you American. You ain't American, is you, Doctor?"

"Of course not. But she said she loves joy?"

"And she wish she could see you."

"Would that be possible?"

"Before I get myself mixed up in this business any more I needs to know just who you is and what you got up your sleeve, cause I think you been telling old Winnie a whole lot of humbug."

"If I tell you everything, would my secret be safe with you?"

"That all depends on what it is."

Lovejoy looked at Barineau, who nodded his assent.

"Winnie, this is a long story . . ."

# 4

"So that is how it be, for true?" Winnie said when Lovejoy had finished telling her almost, but not quite, everything. "Oh, I do wish you had not come here. Why you humbug poor old Winnie? Oh, go away and leave me out of this business."

Barineau, who had kept silent until now, spoke up. "You will not betray us, will you, Winnie?"

"American gentlemens do be more fair and generous than English bacra. But I don't want to get no more mixed up in this business . . . no, no, I won't give you away."

"Up to now you have done nothing except provide us with lodging and carry one note to Miss Jenkins, which no one need ever know about."

"I wish you had kept on lying, that is what I wish."

"I had to head off your voicing your suspicions to someone else. Now as long as you don't do that, we will support your claim of innocence of any involvement."

"What do concern me is what you mean to do to get your lady love out of that place. And what you gonna do when Captain Bledsoe come back?"

"That is for us to think about. Just keep our confidence. Go on pretending to believe that we are who we told you we were."

After the troubled Winnie had taken herself off to bed, Barineau and Lovejoy sat on the porch of the Bearded Fig Tree, talking long into the soft Barbadian night.

"Do you think she will betray us?" Lovejoy asked.

"No. Despite her greediness, I think the romantic aspect of all this intrigue appeals to her feminine nature. I am glad that you did not tell her that you and Meg are not really engaged. Now we must decide on how we go about rescuing her and the others."

"We could slip enough powder off the *New Hope* to blow down a wall of the building," Lovejoy said.

"No, that might injure our people. And it would arouse the militia. How would we get everyone through the town and out to the sloop? Did you hear? Besides the two British regiments already here, the island has enrolled every white and free colored male between sixteen and sixty in the militia."

"We could drug the guard, take his keys, then get Meggie out and slip her down to the dock."

"What about the men in the basement?"

"Bledsoe would accept a reduced ransom for them. The only reason he asks so much is that he thinks Meg is engaged to the son of Jeremiah Martin."

"Too complicated. I say we stick to our original plan. Take *New Hope* back to sea, rendezvous with the *Flora* and wait."

"Whatever we decide, I must try to see Meg in person."

Early the next morning, while Lovejoy and Barineau still slept, in accordance with the new procedure fixed to protect Barbados against American incursions into Carlisle Bay, a ketch from St. Eustatius lay to off Fort Needham, fired a swivel gun to port, and waited to be recognized.

An answering gun boomed from the ramparts of the fort and a signal was raised, indicating that the ketch had permission to approach the dock at Bridgetown.

The harbormaster waited to speak to the captain.

"Easy trip?" he asked as the man picked up two large sacks of mail and tossed them onto the dock.

"Weather was good enough. Would have come in yesterday afternoon, but we ran into a Yankee privateer just over the horizon to the north. Baltimore schooner she was, sort of drifting along like a barracuda watching for fish."

"Did she give chase?"

"Nay, and I don't understand why not. She looked a fast un. To play safe, we tacked away to the west, toward Grenada, and she didn't follow. Took us all last night to work our way back against the wind."

"How do you know she was American?"

"Twas writ across her stern plain enough. The *Flora.* Flying British colors, but there was no mistaking her, the sharp way she was built. Reckon she's waiting for bigger game. By the by, has that brig come back from Antigua? The one with the peg-legged captain?"

"Should be back any day now. Why?"

"I have a special letter for him. Care of old lawyer Fescue."

"You want one of my boys to deliver it?"

"Nay. Chap at Statia give me a guinea to see it in old Fescue's hands safe and sure."

Hiram Fescue had slept badly since meeting Lovejoy. He wished he had notified the provost right off of his suspicions about the fellow claiming to be a British doctor. But then he might have been required to give up the hundred pounds the man had paid him.

It was not that the young man's story did not make sense. No, there was something troublingly familiar about his bearing. The set of his shoulders. The tone of his voice. Yes, and the audacity of his manner.

What if he were to ask the provost to investigate? Besides himself having to give up the hundred pounds, the provost would discover his communicating with an enemy national. Captain Bledsoe would be embarrassed and probably infuriated at the exposure of his scheme of extortion. The fellow's story did hold water, after all. And there was no doubt of his medical expertise.

He paused on the street below his office to wait until the pain subsided in his chest.

He was sitting at his desk, fingering the now sealed bogus message that he and "Dr. Jennings" had concocted, when the captain of the ketch tapped at his door.

"A message for Captain Bledsoe, you say?"

"Aye, to be delivered to yourself. Little Jewish fellow on Statia gave me a guinea. You'll see it is given to the captain when he comes into port?"

Fescue sat for a long while looking at the seal on the letter. He lay that letter beside the one that he and Lovejoy had concocted. The pain in his chest returned then subsided. His hands shook. He picked up first one letter, then the other. At last he struck a fire, lit the candle on his desk, and heated his metal letter opener over its flame.

The seal loosened its hold on the paper without splitting.

His hands shaking more than ever, the old man put on his glasses and opened the letter.

*December 6, 1812*

*Dear Captain Bledsoe:*

*My father has received Attorney Fescue's letter of October 10. He understands the import of your message contained therein but, due to his being too much enfeebled in his health to make a formal reply to Mr. Fescue in his accustomed manner, I am taking it upon myself to inform you both that he has no interest in your proposition. My father and I have reason to suspect that you have been made the subject of a hoax. At this writing, my younger brother is visiting at the home, in the interior of Pennsylvania, of a young woman to whom he is reportedly affianced. The young woman in whose interest you corresponded with my father is known to our family only as the runaway daughter of a common innkeeper here in Philadelphia. My younger brother, it pains me to say, has not always been as discriminating as his family would have preferred in his choice of friendships with persons of either sex. While the young woman in question herself may have given you the false impression that her welfare is of sufficient interest to the Martin family to cause them to take the course of action your message urges, this is not the case.*

*Mr. Fescue may be interested in knowing that, because of the deterioration of his health, my father has turned over the affairs of his shipping company to myself. I know that he holds Mr. Fescue in high regard. For my own part, let me say that when this unfortunate and, in my view, totally unnecessary war between our two great nations has run its course, nothing would afford me greater pleasure than to make Mr. Fescue's personal acquaintance and to resume the relationship that formerly existed between himself and Martin Shipping.*

*Your obedient servant,*
*Chester Peebles Martin*

*P.S. The conditions you have set for the release of the young woman have been made known to her family, but I would be very much surprised if they are in any position to meet said requirements.*

Fescue tried in vain to find a coded message in Chester's stilted words but finally concluded that there was none. The letter must mean exactly what it said: Jeremiah Martin declined to pay a ransom for the girl; the girl's supposed fiancé was engaged to another person; Bledsoe had been hoodwinked. He assumed, rightly or wrongly, that Jeremiah knew of the message.

His mind worked furiously over his dilemma. Which message was correct—the uncoded, written one he had just received, or the one relayed to him by the bold young doctor with the questionable accent? Neither followed the usual protocol of his correspondence with Jeremiah Martin.

With hands trembling more than ever, he reheated the letter opener and managed to reseal the letter. This done, he placed it in a small desk drawer beside the one he and Lovejoy had composed.

"That the craziest thing I ever did hear. You trying to get yourself and poor old Winnie hung?"

"You just have Meg pretend to fall sick while you are there and send your girl rushing out to find a doctor, and I will be waiting nearby."

"They see right through that humbug. They bring their own doctor in. I ain't gonna do nothing like that."

Finally, his shoulders slumping in resignation, Lovejoy said, "Could I at least write her a long letter, explaining everything?"

"That do be dangerous, too."

"You said the guards can't read or write."

"No, but they give the letter to someone that can. No, I can't get mixed up no more in this."

"Will you tell her that I am working to win her release?"

"I will do it if you and this captain man settle up your bill and leave this place tomorrow morning. You gonna bring doom to poor old Winnie."

"All right. When he comes back from his sloop this afternoon, I will tell my friend that we must go tomorrow. Now this is what I want you to tell Miss Jenkins. Tell her that Lovejoy is here and that he is taking the necessary steps to win her release and that of the others. Tell her just to be calm and show no surprise at anything that may happen."

Winnie listened with narrowed eyes until Lovejoy had finished, then said, "And that is all you want me to say?"

"That should be enough to keep her spirits up."

"Don't you want me to tell her you loves her?"

"She knows that, I am sure."

"Yeah, but a woman wants to hear it all the same."

"Very well. Tell her I am very fond of her."

Lovejoy found himself rubbing the scar on his left hand as he concluded his conversation with Winnie and walked down Tudor Street toward Carlisle Bay. The streets of Bridgetown teemed with both white and free colored men of all ages, some in new red uniforms and some in civilian clothes, some shod and some barefooted, some carrying muskets or wearing side arms and some armed only with knives and wooden staffs.

He asked a brown-skinned man, dressed in a red uniform, the reason for the crowd.

"They do be mustering the militia from all over de island this afternoon. De governor gonna address us."

"That is a handsome uniform you are wearing."

"Ain't it, though? Bought it ready-made at Tolliver's store. That man making a fortune for hisself selling uniforms."

As he stood on the dock looking out toward the *New Hope*, Lovejoy started scheming how he might purchase enough uniforms to disguise himself, Barineau, and a few other crewmen and thereby gain access to the prison to free Meg and the others.

There Barineau came now, being rowed across Carlisle Bay toward the dock by Toby. Lovejoy was surprised that he had been able to persuade him to come back ashore at all, for the navigator had favored simply delivering the bogus message to Fescue and then making a run for it. Now he, Lovejoy, would have to do some more persuading.

"Ahoy there, mate," Lovejoy called out in mock greeting as Toby guided the boat to the dock.

Barineau climbed up the stone steps.

"Pierre, I think I have figured out a way to get this business over with in quick order," Lovejoy said.

"What now?"

Lovejoy had just started to explain his idea for disguising themselves as Barbadian militiamen when someone called to him in a high-pitched Cockney accent, "'Ey there, doctor."

A little man in sailor's garb was approaching them.

"I don't believe I know you," Lovejoy said.

"Course you knows me. Ain't you the doctor what wouldn't take off me arm? Ain't I the sailor that is grateful to you for paying no heed to that brute of a Captain Bledsoe?"

"What are you doing here?" was the best Lovejoy could manage.

"Me arm being no use to me just yet, why old Bledsoe put me ashore with ten shillings and no way to earn me way. Might ask you the same question. Wot yer doing 'ere, and you a H'american?"

# 5 

Had the encounter with Tompkins occurred at night, Lovejoy might have knocked the little Cockney unconscious and had Toby haul him off to the *New Hope* to be locked away while he and Barineau remained ashore. But this was in broad daylight on a crowded dock in an enemy land.

Exercising all the control he could muster, he inquired in a low voice about the sailor's maimed arm.

After hearing Tompkins's complaints of continuing pain and lack of strength in the limb, Lovejoy said, "I have a new salve that might strengthen the muscles and relieve the pain. Unfortunately, it is aboard that sloop out there."

"You ain't said wot you doing 'ere on a H'english island."

"The sloop is from Bermuda. I am traveling under special papers. Look, they have fetched me to go back aboard to conduct my daily sick call. If you would care to accompany us, I could tell you all about our business and then treat your arm. It was beastly of Captain Bledsoe to want to amputate."

"That is what the man is, a beast, wot cares nothing for his men. You says the sloop is from Bermuda? Don't reckon they could use a h'experienced seaman aboard her. I'll end up as a beggar if I stays 'ere."

"Actually, the captain has been complaining of a shortage of hands. Come along and you can ask him for yourself."

With four men crammed into it, the *New Hope*'s little boat rode low in the water. Tompkins rattled on and on about his arm and his callous treatment by Captain Bledsoe.

Lovejoy seethed over the frustration the Cockney had caused his plans. But he could not risk leaving a former member of the *Goodfellow*'s crew, no matter how disaffected, free ashore to babble about his identity. He bit his tongue to keep from asking what had happened aboard the English brig after its recapture and just how Meg had been treated on the trip down to Barbados.

When they were about halfway to the *New Hope*, Tompkins paused in his litany of complaints and looked hard at Barineau. "'Ere now, didn't I see you aboard that privateer what took the *Goodfellow?*"

Lovejoy said, "Can you swim?"

"I never learned."

"Then pay close attention. Shut your mouth and keep it shut or we will throw you out of the boat."

"I say throw him out anyway," Barineau joined in.

"Wot's going on 'ere? I thought you was a kind man."

"You will be shown every kindness, if you just close your mouth and keep it closed."

Tompkins's eyes widened in fear.

"The best laid plans . . ." Lovejoy muttered.

After seeing Tompkins locked away belowdecks on their captured sloop, Barineau and Lovejoy argued for a long while without resolving the question of whether they should return ashore, try to procure militia uniforms, and attempt to free their friends.

"Even if you gained access to the building, freed our people, and got them down to the dock, then you have the daunting problem of ferrying them out to this sloop. You saw how near we came to swamping with four of us."

"We could commandeer a larger boat. Look, Pierre, there is a girl waiting in Pennsylvania to marry me. I have a new life to lead back there, and I want to get on with it."

"Your life will end with a British rope around your neck if you continue to tempt fate. Don't push your luck."

"If you are so fearful, I will go ashore alone."

"That does not become you to accuse me of cowardice."

"I am not calling you a coward. You simply are too cautious."

"And you are too impatient. The other plan will work."

Their argument was interrupted by the report of a cannon to the west as a brig saluted Fort Needham and dropped anchor. The harbormaster's boat went skimming out past the *New Hope* to inspect the vessel.

Lovejoy resumed with, "At least can't we go back to hear what Winnie reports on Meg, what she says about my message? And besides, I need to pick up my bag and pay another visit to lawyer Fescue, to make certain he will give my message to Bledsoe."

"I'd prefer to sail right now, but if you will wait until near dark, I will go with you. Now, did you not promise that poor little sailor to look after his arm?"

A bewildered Tompkins was brought up to the deck so that Lovejoy could inspect his injured arm in a better light. Again Lovejoy had to threaten to have him thrown overboard to stop his questions and complaints.

"Here, grasp my two fingers with your hand. You do have some strength there. I will show you a few exercises to tone up the muscles. In time, that arm will be as strong as the other."

Lovejoy was in the midst of his lecture when Tompkins suddenly stood up and pointed with his uninjured arm toward the newly arrived brig, which, following the harbormaster's directions, was shifting to an anchorage under the guns of Rickett's Fort near shore.

"Gor, blimey, if h'it h'ain't the *Goodfellow.*"

"He's right," Barineau said. "Get him back below. Toby, you other men, turn your backs. Don't let them see your faces."

Barineau himself drew his cap low over his eyes and watched the brig tack past, then turn and make its way back toward the anchorage point.

Cursing his luck, Lovejoy remained belowdecks with Tompkins. To pass the time, he completed his examination of the arm and then inquired about events on the *Goodfellow* after Bledsoe had recovered control of the brig. "And Miss Jenkins was treated well?"

"Like a princess, she were. Captain give up 'is cabin for her and threatened anyone as looked sideways at 'er with a flogging."

"How about our men?"

"We kept 'em locked away. Didn't want 'em turning the tables on us, as we did them. If the little prize master chap . . ."

"Collins?"

"Ay, that were 'is name. If 'e 'adn't 'ave been making sheep's eyes at the young lady, 'e might 'ave took note of the leaks sooner, afore the storm when they got so bad 'e 'ad to call on Captain Bledsoe for 'elp. No offense, Doctor, but it were a laugh what the captain pulled off."

Overhead they could hear the sound of the *New Hope*'s capstan being cranked.

" 'Ere, now, wot's going on up there?"

"I don't know. But you are sure Miss Jenkins was not molested by anyone?"

"Like I told you, Doctor, no. That sounds like they is pulling up anchor."

The *New Hope* lurched as her anchor broke free from the floor of Carlisle Bay.

"Stay here while I see what is going on."

Lovejoy ran up the ladder and onto the deck. The crew of the sloop were raising the mainsail. Barineau was standing at the tiller shouting out orders to his crew.

"What is going on?" Lovejoy demanded.

"We are getting under way."

"I have not given my permission."

"I don't need your permission."

"See here, Pierre. Don't forget who owns this sloop now."

"By maritime law, the fellow from Bermuda will own her until an admiralty court has condemned her as a legal prize. And anyway, at sea the decision of a captain takes precedence over what anyone else, owner or otherwise, says. And I say you are going to get yourself captured and hanged if you go back ashore now that that brig is in port."

The two men stood glaring at each other, Lovejoy with his fists clenched at his sides, Barineau with his arms crossed over his chest. Lovejoy started to rage at Barineau for defying him so, then, in frustration, he turned and walked to the bow. He stood there for a long while as the brisk trade wind filled the sloop's sails and bore her quickly away from Barbados.

He remained there, too angry to speak, as the craft skimmed away to the west and he could no longer make out the Town Hall Gaol amongst the buildings of Bridgetown.

# 6

Meg listened carefully, committing every word to memory as Winnie told her what Lovejoy had asked her to say.

"Did he say what he plans to do?"

"He just say for you not to be concerning yourself, that everything gonna be all right. Oh, yes, and he say, now how did he put it?"

Winnie looked into Meg's anxious face, thought for a moment, and said, "He say he beside himself with love for you and his heart burn to have you back in his arms."

Meg frowned. "Did he really? It doesn't sound like Lovejoy."

"Winnie wouldn't tell you no lie. Look here, that man do be risking his life for you, to come in here on a little boat under a British flag. That could get him hung. You think he do that and he don't be punishing with love for you?"

"You will see him again, won't you?"

"I expects him and his captain man friend to eat supper in a while and stay with me one more night."

"Then tell him I love him with all my heart and I trust him to get me safely home."

"All right in there. Time's up," the guard shouted.

Winnie rolled her eyes and patted Meg's shoulder. "I will tell him what you say. Now let your mind rest easy. Just don't never tell nobody I do be carrying messages back and forth."

"Get moving in there."

"I do declare," Winnie said in a louder voice. "I don't know what I gonna tell Captain Bledsoe about how these here guard men do be acting round here."

When Winnie returned to the Bearded Fig Tree, she was amazed to find Hiram Fescue sitting on her porch. He put his fingers to his lips and motioned for her to sit close.

"This doctor that is staying with you," he whispered, "do you know who he is?"

"Why, mister lawyer man, he say he be Dr. Jennings, from London town, back in England . . ."

Fescue waved his hand and shook his head. "I know who he says he is. I mean what is his real identity. I must know."

"How you expect me to know that? I just a poor old woman trying to earn her way . . ."

"Don't try that poor old woman business on me, Winnie. You know as well as I that he is not an Englishman. Don't deny it. If you try to lie, I will denounce you to the provost."

Winnie's eyes widened. She began to sweat and to stutter.

"What make you be cruel to me like that, Mr. Fescue? Who you think him to be, if he ain't a doctor man?"

"Confound it, woman, I am warning you. Tell the truth. He may be a doctor, but he is no Englishman."

"Who you think him to be in that case?"

Seeing that bullying her was not succeeding, Fescue leaned close and said, "Winnie, do you remember Sir Francis Bolton, who owned Bolton Hall Plantation?"

Reluctantly, Winnie nodded. "Everbody remember that old man. But he do be dead many years now."

"Since the end of the American war, thirty-two years, to be exact. Anyway, Sir Francis was my chief client. After he died, I represented a distant American cousin of his, a very rich man from Philadelphia."

He paused to wipe his face and wait for the ache in his chest to subside.

"Now Winnie, I have known you since you first moved into Bridgetown and set up your establishment. We have got to trust each other. I am going to tell you who I think this young doctor really is, and you must tell me whether you think I am correct."

Night had fallen by the time Fescue ended his talk with Winnie. Satisfied that she had told him as much of the truth as she knew, he made his way past throngs of drunken militiamen to his little office. Inside, he locked the front door and lit a candle. He took the two letters from his desk drawer, looked closely at their seals, and then put them back.

He sat there for a long while, staring at the wall and ruminating over what Winnie had told him about the girl's infatuation with young Martin. She had promised to send the young doctor to his office when he returned for his supper, as she expected him to do. Now he understood why the young man had looked so familiar. Except for the color of his hair and eyes, how very like his father he was. And, it would seem, he was just as bold. There were questions to be answered before he would decide which message to present to Bledsoe. He would have to make very certain that he would not become openly involved in whatever scheme was brewing. And, really, a hundred pounds was hardly enough to justify the risks he was taking in not reporting this whole business to the authorities. A thousand pounds would be more like the fee he should demand. Measured against Bledsoe's ransom demand, that was not too much to ask.

If the Chester Peebles message was correct, the young fellow was not really engaged to the girl. What if he should refuse to pay the thousand pounds? But surely he must have some special interest in the girl to take such risks. Ah, well, some considerable increase in his fee could be negotiated, surely, whereas in the case of that arrogant sea captain . . .

It had been many years since he had been involved in such a delicious conspiracy. It took him back to his days with Sir Francis Bolton. He rubbed his hands together and smiled as he practiced what he would say to Lovejoy Martin.

Ah, he could hear someone approaching. He extinguished his candle.

Fescue smiled to think of the surprised look on the face of Jeremiah Martin's son when he confronted him as to his identity, showed him the letter from his brother, and demanded a thousand pounds as his fee for destroying that letter and presenting the other to Bledsoe.

Now someone was rattling his door.

"Coming, my young doctor friend," he said softly.

"I saw your light. I know you are there. Open up."

The old lawyer arose and unlatched his door.

"You Americans are such an impatient . . ." He stopped in midsentence. There stood Captain Bledsoe.

"What took you so long coming to the door?"

"Why, I was expecting . . . oh, sorry. I just drifted off."

"Did we get our answer yet?"

"Yes, yes, we did."

"Well then, out with it. What does it say?"

"Make yourself comfortable. It is here in my desk, still sealed. I will get it out and help you decode it."

Hitherto, the pains in the old lawyer's chest had been merely uncomfortable, a dull ache accompanied by an unpleasant shortness of breath, which faded if he sat quietly. This time the attack felt as though someone had delivered a hard blow to his midsection. He gritted his teeth as he opened his desk drawer and withdrew one of the letters. Confound this nausea. Why was he sweating so? He took a deep breath and turned to face Bledsoe, who now stood with his hand outstretched.

As he leaned forward to hand the letter to the captain, the pain doubled, radiating through his left shoulder and down his arm. He gasped for breath. Sweat soaking his shirt, he blurted, "I seem to be having . . ."

The final words Hiram Fescue would hear before he fell face forward from his chair were those of Captain Bledsoe, demanding, without a trace of pity, "Damn it, man, what is the matter with you?"

# 7

At the time Winnie left with her servant girl the next morning to carry Meg's breakfast to the Town Hall Gaol, Hiram Fescue's body still lay, facedown, in his office. Other than Captain Christopher Bledsoe, no one knew of the old lawyer's sudden death.

If Winnie had known, she might have been even more perplexed by the events and revelations of the past few days.

Looking up from her book, Meg noted Winnie's worried expression as she entered the cell.

"What do be concerning me?" Winnie leaned over and whispered, "You might as well hear this. You and me ain't the only ones that knows about your lover man being on this island."

Meg also was looking worried by the time Winnie had finished telling of her conversation with Fescue the night before.

"Can he be trusted?"

"Have to trust him. He be done figured out the situation, anyhow. I just hopes Captain Bledsoe don't get hold of this. Also I hopes Winnie can trust your sweetheart."

"Oh, Winnie, I am sure Lovejoy would not betray you."

"That don't be all I do be worrying about. He was supposed to stay last night at the Bearded Fig Tree and he didn't show up. Him and his friend do be owing me nine pounds for food and drink. And when I look out at the bay this morning, I don't see that little ship what he came here on. Now I axes you, who gonna pay po' Winnie if he don't come back?"

Dawn found an equally perplexed Captain Christopher Bledsoe in his cabin aboard the *Goodfellow.* He had labored until near sunup over the sealed letter Fescue had been in the act of handing to him when he had keeled over dead. A skilled cryptologist would have solved the puzzle in a few minutes, for Fescue and Lovejoy had deliberately kept this one simple. Still, Bledsoe thought himself very clever when he finally stumbled on to the substitution of letters that was the key to the undated message, which read:

> *Received yours of Oct ten accept your offer but must pay the sum in bermuda not barbados deliver sons fiancee and others to provost st george where letter of credit will be in hands of american agent jeremiah martin*

Bledsoe was elated that apparently Jeremiah Martin was willing to pay the ransom for Megan and her fellow Americans, but he was frustrated by the requirement that he deliver them to Bermuda. He had counted on collecting his ransom and sailing directly back to a financially secure retirement in England.

Well, he told himself as the sun rose over Bridgetown, there was nothing he could do about the matter. With that tiresome old lawyer dead, there was no way for him to communicate with Jeremiah Martin, even if he were willing to risk waiting for a message to be relayed to Philadelphia and an answer back to Barbados. The quicker he got his brig and prisoners to Bermuda, the better.

After delivering Meg her breakfast at the Town Hall Gaol, Winnie, troubled by the failure of Lovejoy to return the night before, was also concerned by the possibility that she might be defrauded of payment for the food and drink consumed by the Americans. Beyond that, she smelled a far deeper trouble. After stewing over the situation, she donned her bonnet and, carrying a parasol, walked over to Swan Street to Fescue's office.

Thus it was a horrified Winnie who discovered the body of the little lawyer, lying on his office floor, his eyes half open and green flies already swarming around his head. And thus it was a distraught, near hysterical Winnie, not Bledsoe, who reported Fescue's death to the provost.

Neither Lovejoy nor Bledsoe was yet aware of certain instructions recently sent to Sir George Beckwith, governor of the island, by Sir John Warren, who, from his headquarters at Halifax, Nova Scotia, was serving as supreme British navy commander in the New World. Warren's jurisdiction ranged from across the Great Lakes to Labrador, clear down the east coast of North America and throughout the West Indies, all the way to Surinam on the South American coast. It was an enormous area to cover, but Warren was being given a huge fleet to carry out his mission: six massive ships of the line, thirteen frigates with thirty-two or more guns, eighteen frigates with eighteen to twenty-four guns each, and a swarm of smaller craft. His mission was to blockade U.S. ports, funnel supplies to the British army still fighting the French on the Iberian Peninsula, and organize convoys against privateers.

His instructions to Governor Beckwith specified that, henceforth, no vessels were to leave Barbados unless as part of a convoy protected by one or more British warships. Warren had also sent instructions to Brigadier General George Horsford, lieutenant governor of Bermuda, to transform certain no-longer-seaworthy vessels into prison hulks. By the end of 1812, Bermudian privateers and British navy vessels had brought in forty-five American ships, and the crews of these prizes had to be housed under guard until they could be either exchanged under cartels for British prisoners or hauled off to English prisons. A natural crossroads in the Atlantic, Bermuda was rapidly becoming a major center in the war with the United States.

Bledsoe learned of the new rule when he called at the provost's to arrange for the transfer of the American prisoners.

"He's not here at the moment," a lieutenant said. "He's investigating a death. An old lawyer was found dead in his office this morning. He has to help the coroner determine whether there was foul play. Is there anything I could do for you?"

"I want to reclaim my prisoners from that privateer."

"What are you going to do with them?"

"Haul them up to Bermuda, if it is any of your business."

"To Bermuda? Then it most certainly is my business to tell you that you will have to join a convoy to leave Barbados."

The lieutenant enjoyed informing this overbearing captain in painful detail of the new rules handed down from the supreme British navy commander. He let him stew over this seeming frustration of his plans before adding blandly, "However, a convoy will be leaving for Bermuda as soon as we have enough ships to form one and an escort becomes available."

"And when in the hell will that be?"

"You may have noticed the warship that came in this morning. She's the *Petrel,* a twenty-four-gun frigate. It will take several days for her to be resupplied and all that."

Bledsoe paused at the door. "The lawyer's death. How was this brought to the provost's attention?"

"Colored woman that runs a hotel found him. Near beside herself, she was that upset. Why do you ask?"

"Just curious. Tell the provost that to spare further expense I want to transfer my prisoners to my brig as soon as possible. They can be fed and housed aboard the *Goodfellow.*"

He started to leave and paused again. "That frigate is the *Petrel?* The captain wouldn't be Wilberforce Harper, would it?"

"Matter of fact, it is. Why? Do you know him?"

Bledsoe left without replying and, his mind churning over all he had learned in the past several hours, strode over to the Bearded Fig Tree. He found Winnie sitting in her accustomed chair and wiping her now puffy eyes.

"They say you found the old man."

"Yes sir, mister captain man. I went to see him and there he laid. Been a long time since I did see a dead. Oh, this do be a terrible thing."

"Why did you go to see him?"

To give herself time to think, Winnie rolled her eyes back, pretending to be overcome by her experience.

"Why did you go to see him?"

"I been thinking about selling off my little spree boy. Wanted to ax Mr. Fescue how to go about it. Oh, Captain, why don't you take that boy off my hand? Carry him to sea wid you. Make you a good cabin boy."

"Last thing I need is a little nigger on my brig. Are you sure that was why you went to see Fescue?"

"What for would Winnie tell you a lie for?"

Bledsoe started to reply but caught himself, and after a moment, said, "No matter. What about Miss Jenkins? Have you looked after her as you agreed?"

"Oh, that young lady do be keeping well, Captain. She do be a fine girl. I been taking her food over faithful."

"Well you need take her nothing else. I will be moving her and the others to my brig."

"I spects you wants to settle up your bill then."

"I am rather busy just now."

"It won't take me but a minute. I been keeping a running list. Just stay right there whiles I gets it."

In his haste to get on with his scheme, Bledsoe barely glanced at the bill presented to him by Winnie and paid her immediately. Only several days later did he realize that the account had been padded by nine pounds.

"Miss Jenkins."

Megan, her eyes closed and luxuriating in a pleasant daydream in which she and Lovejoy were sailing together on a placid tropical sea, did not answer at first.

"Miss Jenkins, are you awake?"

Reluctantly, she opened her eyes to look at the face of the prison commandant peering into her cell.

"Come along, lass," he said in a kindly voice. "Put your things together and be prepared to depart."

"Where?"

"You'll find out soon enough. You have five minutes to get ready. Now pull yourself together, my dear. You are leaving us."

"I haven't had my supper."

"No, and you won't get any in this place. Bestir yourself. My orders are to have you downstairs by five o'clock."

As she put her books and other belongings in her carpetbag, Meg felt like crying. Ever since Winnie had told her the exaggerated version of the feelings Lovejoy had expressed, she had not minded her imprisonment. She had been convinced that Lovejoy would somehow win her release and that they would leave Barbados together. Now she was confused.

In the downstairs entry, she waited as the other prisoners from the *Flora* were brought up from their basement dungeon.

Collins said in a low voice, "Have they treated you well?"

"Quite. How about you and the others?"

"Better than I would have expected. What do you think they mean to do with us?"

"I don't know."

"I am afraid they are taking us back to England. They have a dreadful new prison over there, called the Dartmoor."

The commandant called for the Americans to gather around.

"When you came here in October you were subjected to abuse by the riffraff of the town as you marched up from the dock. We wish to spare you such an indignity this time. Lieutenant Jones is here from the provost's office with an escort of soldiers so that you will not be molested on your way aboard your ship. Lieutenant, I place these American cousins in your custody."

His arms crossed, Captain Bledsoe stood on the quarterdeck of the *Goodfellow* watching the American prisoners climb up the ladder from a barge. In the fast-falling darkness, he motioned for his first mate to lead Meg to his cabin. Crewmen carrying lanterns herded the others belowdecks.

The lieutenant handed Bledsoe a paper.

"Provost says you're to sign this receipt. And he says to remind you not to sail until the frigate is ready and we have enough ships to form a convoy. There is all hell to pay because a sloop from Bermuda slipped off yesterday without permission."

Without replying, Bledsoe scrawled his name and thrust the receipt back into the lieutenant's hand.

"By the way, I almost forgot. Provost says to give you this."

"What the hell is it?"

"It is a letter he found in that old lawyer's desk. Addressed to you in his care."

Impatient to get the lieutenant off his brig, Beldsoe shoved the letter into his pocket without glancing at the address.

"Oh, yes, and he asks that you drop by the office tomorrow. Someone thought they saw you knocking at the lawyer's office door last night. Thought you might help him and the coroner establish the old man's time of death."

"Don't let me keep you any longer, Lieutenant. Better leave while your oarsmen can still see."

"Thanks for your concern. By the way, you never said how you knew the captain of that frigate."

"If it is any business of yours, we served together at Trafalgar. Now good night to you, Lieutenant."

# 8

The letter given him by the provost lieutenant remained in Bledsoe's pocket while he got caught up in instructing his crew on how to go about stealthily preparing the *Goodfellow* for sea.

His resolve to leave that night was stiffened by the knowledge that someone had seen him at the door of Fescue's office. Although he saw nothing wrong in leaving the stupid old man lying there unattended, he did not want to have to explain the circumstances. Obviously the old pettifogger was dead. It had seemed far simpler and wiser not to get involved.

He assumed that slipping away from the anchorage in the moonless night would be a simple matter of easing up the anchor and allowing the ebbing tide to carry the *Goodfellow* gently away from the shore until she was out to sea far enough to risk raising sails. Of course, it would have been an agreeable experience to visit Wilberforce Harper aboard the frigate, but that would only delay and complicate things. No, it was far better to clear out now, convoy rules or no convoy rules.

Weary from having gone without sleep for so long, he ordered his first mate to awaken him when the tide started to turn. Then he treated himself to a long dram of rum and threw himself on his bunk outside the door of his cabin, in which Meg now slept.

He did not remember the letter in his pocket until the mate awakened him shortly after midnight.

"Have your hands stand by the capstan. I will be along in a few minutes. Leave your lantern here with me."

He frowned at the address on the letter, broke the seal, and proceeded to read the message written by Chester Peebles back in December.

In vain he tried to find some hidden message in the letter, which suggested that "you have been made the subject of a hoax," that Jeremiah Martin's son was marrying another girl, that this Megan Jenkins, on whom he had lavished so much attention, in reality was the runaway daughter of a tavern keeper from Philadelphia, and, most distressing, that the Martin family had no intention of coughing up ten thousand pounds for her release.

He got out the letter that the stricken Fescue had been in the act of handing him before dying. He checked the coded message again, then searched the letter from Chester Peebles once more for a similarly hidden code. He broke into a sweat. Why had Fescue given him one letter and not the other? Would he have notified him of the other, if he had not been stricken? If the longer message were correct, he had wasted months of valuable time on some ordinary American prisoners. He would be a laughingstock if he delivered them to Bermuda and the American agent there knew nothing of a ransom.

The mate entered the officers' quarters.

"Are you ready to raise anchor, Captain?"

"Not yet."

"Is something wrong?"

"None of your business. Now get out. I need to think."

It took Bledsoe a while to decide on a plan, but when he did, he acted quickly. Striking his fist against the desk, he bellowed to his mate, "Bring that girl out here right now."

Arms folded over his chest, his peg leg thrust out, and wearing a benign smile, Bledsoe sat and stared for a long while at the confused and sleepy Meg who stood before him, wrapped in a blanket. Then, in a soft voice, he said, "Sit down, my dear. You realize, I hope, that we are trying to deliver you to a point where you can be exchanged."

Meg huddled before him, her hands clutching her blanket and her dark eyes meeting his.

"I had assumed that was the case."

"I understand that you and the young Dr. Martin are to be married."

"Does that make a difference in my being released?"

"No, but I am puzzled about something. Take no offense, but you and he seem to occupy what might be called different stations in life."

"I don't know what you mean."

"He is the son of a very rich man. He is educated. Whereas your father is . . . ?"

"My father owns a tavern," Meg snapped. "It is a respectable establishment. I fail to see your point, Captain."

"I am just trying to understand the situation. Is it correct that you ran away from home to join that privateer?"

"You already know that I left home."

"And at the time were you engaged to Dr. Martin?"

"These are very personal questions. I do not understand their purpose. And why cannot they wait until daylight?"

"Are you well acquainted with the family of your fiancé?"

"Everyone in Philadelphia knows the Martin family."

"You have been received as a guest in their home?"

"No, but Lovejoy has spent much time at ours, and has done so ever since he was a boy. When my father was remarried, Lovejoy stood with him as best man."

"Ah. And Lovejoy has a brother?"

"A half brother, yes."

"And this half brother's name is Chester . . ."

"Chester Peebles. But how do you know that?"

"Oh, my dear girl, I may know far more than you would ever have thought."

Bledsoe looked at Meg for a long while, until she began to fidget under his gaze and asked, "May I return to my bed?"

"Not just yet. Tell me, what would you say if I told you that Dr. Martin is engaged to be married to a young woman somewhere outside of Philadelphia, that, indeed, he may already be settled down and married to her?"

"That is a lie! Lovejoy is not in Pennsylvania. And if he did not love me, why would he have come to Barbados . . . ?" Meg stopped, put her hand to her mouth, and removed it to ask, "Why are you putting me through all these questions?"

Bledsoe's eyebrows went up at her response, but he said simply,

"Read this letter. Take your time and then tell me what you think it means."

Meg turned the note toward the dim lantern light while Bledsoe watched her reaction closely. Tears welled in her eyes. For a moment she feared that she might faint, but she willed herself to remain conscious. She handed the letter back to the captain without speaking.

"Well, what do you make of that?"

"I have nothing to say."

"But you have already said much. Now let me read to you another message."

Bledsoe read the cryptic coded message that had been concocted by Fescue and Lovejoy, paused and asked, "One letter purports to have been written by Jeremiah Martin and one by his stepson. Which am I to believe?"

"I cannot say. I only know that little love is lost between Lovejoy and his brother."

"So you think his letter was written out of spite?"

"That is possible. Now may I go?"

Bledsoe's face hardened. He stood, looked down at Meg, and said in a harsh voice, "All right, lass, let's hear no more evasions. You have let it slip that Dr. Martin came to Barbados to seek your release. Did you see him? Did you speak to him? Where is he now?"

"I have nothing to say."

"Was Winnie Arbuckle kind to you?"

"Yes."

"Did you trust her?"

"She is a good-hearted person."

"Did she tell you about talking to a lawyer named Fescue?"

"No, no, I have nothing to say."

Bledsoe decided to try one more shot in the dark. "This sloop that has been in Carlisle Bay. It departed suddenly day before yesterday. Have you any idea how Dr. Martin might have come by it?"

Megan Jenkins hated lying. So instead of trying to cover up her slips of the tongue with concocted stories as Winnie or Lovejoy might have done, she simply refused to respond to any more of Bledsoe's questions. But he had learned enough to know what to do. So he allowed Meg to return to his cabin and called his first mate to lower a boat so that he could be rowed over to the *Petrel* to awaken his old friend, Captain Harper.

During the two days that the *New Hope* and the *Flora* circled about in the sea lanes between Barbados and Bermuda, even the normally phlegmatic Phipps and the philosophical Barineau grew impatient waiting for the appearance of the *Goodfellow* carrying, they desperately hoped, Meg and the other prisoners.

"We could have taken a half dozen prizes the last week if we did not have this business to attend to," Phipps said.

"What would you do with them?" Lovejoy asked. "It is too far to send prizes back even to Savannah or Charleston."

"We could remove any monies or valuable cargo."

"There will be time for that after we recover our people," Lovejoy said. "Now let's review what to do when she shows up."

Although he was even more eager than his colleagues to complete his mission and return to Pennsylvania, Lovejoy did not doubt that Bledsoe would take the bait and try to deliver the prisoners to Bermuda.

"How can you be so certain?" Tom asked.

"One, Bermuda is on his way back to England. Two, it is a natural cartel depot. Three, and most important, after investing so much time in this project, he would hardly throw away his chances to earn a ransom. No, I have no doubt that he will show up and that our people will be aboard."

"I was hoping you would find a way to get them off while you was in their harbor. You should have let me go with you. I could have thought of some way to get my sister free."

"As I have explained, Tom, we wanted only experienced sailors. As for thinking of something, I had a dozen different ideas, but we ran out of time when the *Goodfellow* showed up back in port. Stop stewing. Everything will turn out well."

"That's easy for you to say. She ain't your sister."

Later, even Lovejoy could not explain his violent reaction to Tom's surly remark.

"God damn it," he snarled. "I know she is not my sister. I am risking everything I own, even my marriage, to rescue her, and to tell the truth, I don't know why I am going to the trouble."

Taken aback by this outburst, Tom replied, "Why, Joy, there is no call for you to talk to me so."

"No, and there is no call for you to complain of my attempts to rescue our people, including your sister. If she had stayed at home, none of this would have happened."

Before further harsh words could be exchanged, Phipps asked Lovejoy to help him select which of the *Flora*'s crewmen to transfer to the *New Hope* when the time came for them to spring their trap on Bledsoe.

The plan that Lovejoy had worked out with Barineau and Phipps was simple. They would crowd as many of their landsmen as possible into the hold of the *New Hope*. Well armed with pistols and cutlasses, Lovejoy and these men would remain belowdecks, out of sight. At the appearance of the *Goodfellow,* Barineau would pretend to be fleeing from the *Flora.* They would maneuver about long enough to attract Bledsoe's attention, then Barineau would run the sloop to within hailing distance, explain that he was unarmed, and ask for sanctuary under the guns of the brig.

Meanwhile, the *Flora* would have broken off the chase as if her captain feared to tangle with the *Goodfellow.* Once alongside, Barineau would order his landsmen to come swarming out of the *New Hope*'s hold and onto the brig.

Out of immediate danger, Lovejoy had time to think about what his life would be like if he had chosen not to undertake this rescue mission. He and Madeline very likely would have been married by now. He could have sold his interest in the *Flora* and, with a pocket full of money, could be safely settling down in Philadelphia, perhaps reading for the law with Charles Bennett. He could see himself showing off his lovely wife to Philadelphia society. But then, what about the Jenkins family? How could he have faced them when their daughter was being held as a British prisoner? He should not have said so to Tom, but damn it, it was her own fault. Even so, he could not bear the thought of her rotting in a prison. And that is what would become of her if Bledsoe learned that she was not really engaged to be married to him. Actually, Meg would make someone a fine wife. No doubt about that. She could do better than Collins, though. Damn Collins, too. It was to protect Meg from him that Talbot Smith had concocted the lie about Meg's engagement.

For the hundredth time, he asked Phipps for his telescope to scan the horizon in the direction of Barbados.

Tom, sitting in the crow's nest of the *Flora,* was on lookout duty when the sails of the *Goodfellow* appeared on the southern horizon. At his cry of "Sail ho!" Phipps climbed up to scrutinize the vessel through his spyglass, then shouted down to the deck for the gunner's mate to fire a portside cannon to attract the attention of the *New Hope* slogging along under half sails two miles to the east.

Hearing the boom of the cannon, Barineau fired off his swivel gun in reply.

"Looks like your scheme may be working," he said to Lovejoy. "Better get your men belowdecks. The game is about to begin."

Phipps, at the helm of the *Flora,* and Barineau, aboard the *New Hope,* maneuvered their two craft along the path of the approaching *Goodfellow*. They were careful to keep the schooner at a distance while running the sloop up into clear sight of the brig.

After studying the *New Hope* from the crow's nest, Bledsoe's first mate reported, "Unless I am much mistook, Captain, it is the sloop what was anchored in Carlisle Bay. She is flying British colors."

"That would be the one that the provost's man said slipped off without permission."

"Aye. And she seems to be running from a schooner."

"I am not surprised. Well then, it is time to lay the cargo nets out along the railing."

"Aye, aye, sir. And shall we load the cannon?"

"I don't think they will be needed, but do so just in case. Then, when the nets are in place, bring the prisoners up from the hold one by one. Make sure that their arms are bound behind them and their legs are hobbled. Then lash them to our masts. And assign a man with a loaded pistol and a knife to stand over each one with weapons at the ready, as we discussed."

"That won't leave enough hands to raise the cargo nets and handle the sails properly. And we surely won't have enough to man the cannon."

"Don't worry about handling the brig. Just keep us on course with short sails. Leave the maneuvering to them."

"And what about the girl?"

"Yes, the girl. She is to be the flame that will draw the moths. Bring the lass from the cabin, gag her, and tie her to the binnacle in easy view. I will stand guard over her myself."

# 9 

Their plan called for Lovejoy, once the *Goodfellow* hove into plain view, to go belowdecks into the *New Hope*'s crowded hold and remain there with his twenty-five hand-picked men. But he quickly grew restive in the cramped quarters, and so, after reviewing what they were to do one more time and again cautioning them to avoid endangering Meg or the other prisoners, he crept back up to the deck to watch the action.

Barineau kept the sloop under full sail while the *Flora* gave mock chase, firing an occasional wild shot from its forward Long Tom. The sloop made a tight turn and sailed back close into the wind, thereby giving the *Goodfellow* time to draw nearer. Phipps allowed the *Flora* to overshoot the course. As the sloop doubled back past him, he fired off a broadside carefully aimed to churn the water just short of its supposed target.

Now the *Flora* had worked her way back onto the trail of the sloop and, likewise sailing close-hauled, appeared to be gaining on its "prey." Meanwhile, the *Goodfellow* plowed ponderously on toward the two craft.

Again, Barineau shifted sails and put his helm over sharply to bring the *New Hope* around to a point where the wind was just off her port quarter, allowing his craft to make maximum speed. Again Phipps allowed the *Flora* to slide past, firing off another mock broadside as he seemed to struggle to bring the schooner about and try once more to overtake the elusive sloop.

Standing on the quarterdeck of the *Goodfellow* beside the bound Meg, Bledsoe smiled as he watched these maneuvers.

"The sloop has raised a distress flag," the first mate said.

"I am not surprised."

"Shall we reply?"

"Fire off our forward port gun and raise the signal that she may come alongside."

"You are taking a big risk, Captain. We don't have enough men to guard the prisoners as you have ordered and put up a proper fight against that schooner."

"To win a game with high stakes, you have to take risks."

The *Flora* continued to fire its forward guns until the *New Hope* adjusted her course to intercept that of the *Goodfellow,* now only a mile distant. At that point, Phipps put his helm over and fired off his starboard broadside at the stern of the sloop, before apparently breaking off the chase and sailing away to the west.

Bledsoe laughed when he saw this happen. Despite his brave words to the first mate, he had feared that he would have to deal with both vessels at the same time. He took up his speaking trumpet and waited until the sloop came to within hailing distance.

"Ahoy there," he shouted. "Who are you?"

His cap pulled low over his forehead and his collar turned up around his chin, Barineau called back in his mock Bermudian accent, "We're the *New Hope,* out of St. George."

"Who was that after you?"

"It's a damned Yankee privateer. We are unarmed. Thought I could outrun him. We need your protection."

"Put out your fenders and come alongside."

He lowered his speaking horn and said to his mate, "Ah, yes. We will take care of them. Have the prisoners sit down and stay there until I order them to stand. This may be even easier than I thought."

As he drew near to the brig, Barineau ordered his sails to be shortened and directed his handful of crewmen to put fenders over the starboard side. Noting how few sailors there were aboard the brig and how her gunports remained closed, he also thought that carrying out his and Lovejoy's plan might be even easier than they had imagined.

As the sloop bumped against the side of the brig, Barineau was surprised by the sight of several grappling hooks being thrown over the rail of the *New Hope.* He had been about to order his own men to do that to the brig, but suddenly his sloop was being snugged up against the brig's side.

Nonetheless, he shouted, "Boarders away!"

In an instant, the hatches in the deck of the *New Hope* flew open and, led by Lovejoy, the concealed men came boiling up from the hold, waving pistols and cutlasses and carrying boarding ladders.

Lovejoy leaped to the sloop's rail and shouted, "Follow me, men!" But when he turned to climb up and over the brig's rail, he was confronted by a wall of cargo netting being hoisted all along the side of the *Goodfellow.* He paused, in confusion. Beside him, Toby sprang up and mounted the rail of the brig. An English sailor jammed the end of a cannon rammer into his stomach, and he fell back onto the deck of the *New Hope.*

Three of Lovejoy's men, sharpshooters armed with frontier-type rifles, started climbing up the sloop's rigging, thinking to pick off the English sailors, but they quickly saw the way Bledsoe had positioned his bound prisoners and held their fire.

"Ahoy, down there!"

It was Bledsoe leaning over the rail of the brig, with one hand grasping Meg's shoulder and the other holding a cocked pistol at her head.

"Is this who you are looking for?"

Lovejoy felt faint at the sight of the girl.

"Yes. Give her up, you bastard. You might as well surrender. We outnumber you two to one."

"Don't be silly. It is you who should surrender. My cannon are loaded and ready to blast you to pieces."

"Do that and our schooner will pounce on you. We took this brig once before, and we can do it again."

"I am far better armed now than I was then. Besides, if either of your craft attacks us, you will put the girl and the other prisoners in jeopardy. You will never take them alive, believe me. Oh, and by the way, a Royal Navy frigate is following us. I expect to see her sails appear any time now."

"Bullshit, Bledsoe. We have you boxed in."

"My dear fellow, don't talk rot. All I have to do is say the word and my men will pour a broadside into you. You try to return our fire, and I will blow the head off this lovely lass."

"There is nothing to stop one of my men from shooting you."

"Nor is there anything to stop my men from doing the same to you, before they cut your friends' throats."

Barineau came close and whispered to Lovejoy. "Even if he is lying about the frigate, he still has us by the short hairs."

Lovejoy waved him away and said to Bledsoe, "Are you prepared to let my people go?"

"Have you brought along the ten thousand pounds? That is the sum your father promised to have ready for us in Bermuda."

"You are a fool, Bledsoe. My father did not promise you such a sum. He doesn't care what happens to our prize crew."

Lovejoy started to tell him of Fescue's role in concocting the false message but, unaware of the lawyer's death and wishing to protect him from retribution, said instead, "I wrote that letter myself, without my father's knowledge, and had it delivered to Barbados. You got it, didn't you? Shall I tell you what it said . . . in code?"

"Never mind, I got it."

Bledsoe started to tell Lovejoy about the other message, the one from Chester Peebles, but said instead, "Are you saying that you tricked me into thinking there will be a ransom waiting in Bermuda?"

"Exactly. You aren't nearly as clever as you think you are."

"Nor are you. By the way, you can save your lies about how that message you say you wrote actually came about. Hiram Fescue is dead now. You must have bribed him."

"Dead? Look here, did you kill that poor old man?"

"He is dead. Never mind by what means. So I will ask you again, have you got my ten thousand pounds?"

"I have two thousand."

"Not nearly enough."

"It is that or nothing."

Bledsoe turned and yelled to his sailors, "Stand by your guns, men."

"What good would it do you to destroy us, assuming that you can do so? You had better take the two thousand pounds."

"I told you, two thousand pounds is not nearly enough."

"It is all that we have. It is better than nothing."

"Do you want the girl either dead or locked up in prison?"

"Why do you think I am going to so much trouble?"

"It seems to me that if you really plan to marry her, ten thousand pounds is not too much for either you or your father or the two of you together to pay."

Trying not to look at Meg gazing down from the rail of the brig, Lovejoy said, "I might as well tell you the truth. We are not to be married, you peg-legged fool. That was a story our captain put out to keep her from unwanted attentions. She is a good girl and I am fond of her, but believe me, we are not engaged. In fact, I am planning to marry another young lady back in Pennsylvania."

At this remark, Meg, who had been forcing herself to remain composed, slumped out of Bledsoe's grasp and fell unconscious onto the deck of the *Goodfellow*. The first mate ran to get a cup of water.

"Fiancée or no, Miss Jenkins appears to have fainted," Bledsoe called down to Lovejoy.

"Damn you! Have you mistreated her?"

"On the contrary, she has been pampered. But that will not be the case if I deliver her to Bermuda. She will be kept aboard a prison hulk along with the rest of your men and, I expect, with you, unless they decide to hang you for a spy or a pirate."

Lovejoy thought furiously. He suspected that Bledsoe might be lying about the approach of a British frigate, but there was no doubt about his ability to destroy the sloop or about the danger to Meg and the other prisoners if either he or the *Flora* attacked the *Goodfellow.*

"Look here, Bledsoe, let's stop acting like two scorpions in a bottle. Give up all the prisoners, take your two thousand pounds, and, hell's bells, we'll escort you to Bermuda."

"I told you, Dr. Martin. The price is ten thousand."

Now it was Bledsoe's turn to sweat. Two thousand pounds was a lot of money, but surely young Martin had to have more than a passing interest in the girl to have taken such risks. He wondered whether the American schooner might be made a part of the ransom. Its value, added to the two thousand pounds, would equal the amount of his ransom demand.

By now, Bledsoe's first mate had loosened Meg's gag and was trying to make her drink the water he had fetched. Unable to bring her back to consciousness, he stood up and looked anxiously at the *Flora,* which lurked two miles to the west, her sails furled and, no doubt, her spy-glasses focused on the drama being played out between the sloop and the English brig. He glanced at the southern horizon, hoping to see the *Petrel.* What if Captain Harper had changed his mind about involving his frigate in Bledsoe's scheme? Sooner or later, the schooner would join in the confrontation, and, well remembering the last encounter with that craft, he dreaded the consequences.

"What if that frigate don't show up? Even if they was willing to give up that schooner, I don't have the men to sail it and this brig. We would be at the mercy of some other privateer. How would we ever go about transferring their people to the sloop and then our crewmen to the schooner?"

"Harper won't let me down. Besides, can you think of a better idea?"

"That old man in Philadelphia don't care about the girl, not enough to put up a ransom. But what if we held his son, instead? He could be worth more to us than a schooner."

Bledsoe took up his speaking horn and leaned over the rail once more.

"Listen carefully, young Dr. Martin. Hand over the two thousand pounds you say you have, and I will release all the prisoners except the girl."

"No. Never!"

"I thought she did not mean all that much to you."

"Never mind what she means to me. My offer is two thousand for all the prisoners."

"What if I were to give them all up in exchange for the two thousand pounds and one other person?"

"One other person? Who?"

"Yourself. Yes, that is my offer. Bring your two thousand pounds aboard. Let us count the money. If it is the correct amount, I will let everyone, including Miss Jenkins, go free except for one person. You must remain in my custody."

"Lovejoy," Barineau said. "You can't do that."

"Give me a moment to consult with my own people," Lovejoy replied to Bledsoe.

"Very well, but don't drag this out. I am losing patience."

"Lovejoy, this is madness," Barineau whispered. "Don't forget what you did on Barbados. They may hang you as a spy."

"Dr. Martin, Dr. Martin . . ."

One of the riflemen was climbing down from the mast of the *New Hope.* He seized Lovejoy's arm and pulled him away from Barineau.

"There is a ship coming up from the south under full sail," he whispered.

Lovejoy handed him his spyglass and said, "See what colors she carries." He turned back to Barineau, who said, "Don't be hasty, Lovejoy. We can keep him boxed in here till hell freezes over. Time is on our side."

"What about the ship that is coming up?"

"It may be one of ours. Keep talking to him while I see for myself."

Meg had regained consciousness soon after the first mate had loosened her gag but had remained quietly in the same spot where she had fallen upon hearing Lovejoy declare that he was planning to marry someone else. But she also heard him refuse Bledsoe's offer to turn over only the male prisoners for two thousand pounds. And now he was being offered herself as well in exchange for his own freedom.

"Help me up, please."

The mate lifted her to her feet. Bledsoe had been too intent on watching the conference between Lovejoy and Barineau to notice that she had come to.

"Don't do it, Lovejoy!" She shouted. "Your brother wrote a letter, too . . ."

Before she could say more, Bledsoe clapped a hand over her mouth. He kept it there until the mate could replace her gag.

"How dare you manhandle her like that?" Lovejoy shouted.

"That is nothing compared to what will happen to her aboard a prison hulk. Come on, Doctor. What do you say?"

While all this was taking place, Barineau had climbed the rigging of the *New Hope,* scrutinized the approaching ship, and now, back on deck, was drawing Lovejoy aside to whisper, "He is not bluffing. It is a frigate, under full sail and bearing down on us fast. Look, why don't we shoot the son of a bitch?"

"We might hit Meg."

"You are running out of time, Dr. Martin. Once our frigate arrives, you and all your men aboard that sloop will join Miss Jenkins and the other prisoners. What are you going to do?"

Before Barineau could stop him, Lovejoy unbuttoned his shirt and removed the money belt from his waist. Holding it over his head, he climbed upon the rail of the *New Hope.*

"Wait, Lovejoy! Don't commit suicide," Barineau said.

Ignoring him, Lovejoy said to Bledsoe, "For myself and this money, you would allow Miss Jenkins and the others to come aboard this sloop and allow it to sail away without interference. Is that the deal?"

"If the money counts out to two thousand pounds, as you say, that is my proposition."

"Then damn your rotten soul, I ask permission to come aboard your brig."

"Permission granted," Bledsoe said with a grin. "Here lads, pull the net back so the good Dr. Martin may join us."

# PART THREE

# 1 

*May 1, 1813—Hamilton, Bermuda*

*Dear Malcolm:*

*I trust that by now the New Hope and the Flora both have arrived safely in Baltimore and that Pierre, Phipps, and Tom and Megan Jenkins will have told you of our many adventures and misadventures at sea and on land.*

*I took some very rash risks in seeking to free Megan Jenkins and our crewmen. But I do not regret doing what had to be done, and thus shall not whine at the price I am now paying.*

*That price is to be held for ransom aboard a prison hulk here in Hamilton Harbor, forced into service as ship's doctor to my fellow American prisoners. My original captor, Captain Christopher Bledsoe, of whom Pierre and Meg can tell you more, has connived to have me kept here until a ransom of 15,000 pounds has been paid to his account. Against my wishes, he has forwarded that demand to my father, whom I doubt would be disposed to pay it, even if my brother allowed the message to reach him. (Ask Megan Jenkins or Pierre why I do not and cannot trust Chester to act in my best interest in this or any other matter.) At any rate, I am assuming that either my father will never see Bledsoe's demand or that, even if he does, he will be unable to assist in my release.*

*Therefore, Mac, I urgently request that you sell my 80 percent interest in the Flora as soon as you can and convert all other debts owing me to cash or letters of credit and see if in that way you cannot raise the required ransom. Rich or poor, I am desperate to get back to Pennsylvania and into the good graces and arms of the girl to whom I am betrothed. So please waste not a moment in the conduct of this business.*

*I have three other requests:*

*Please see that Meg Jenkins is well looked after there in Baltimore. She is a fine girl. I am sure that you and Flo will like her as well as do I. Also see that she receives the eight shares to which I am entitled for my services as ship's surgeon on our first cruise. And please remind Talbot Smith that he agreed to provide Tom with four shares.*

*Secondly, keeping the fact of my presence here from him, please release Captain Tradnick amd allow him to sail his sloop and crew back to Bermuda without causing it to be condemned and sold. Tradnick is a decent fellow. Barineau can tell you of the circumstances by which we gained control of the New Hope. I ask that the English sailor, Tompkins, also be allowed to sail with Tradnick.*

*Finally, Malcolm, please forward the enclosed letter on to Madeline Richter in Berks County, Pennsylvania. I am imploring her to overlook my hasty departure last December and to keep her resolve to marry me. Although my fortunes will be considerably diminished by the time I return, I am determined to make her my wife even if it means an elopement rather than a formal wedding as her family would have wished.*

*Now, here is how to relay the ransom for my release . . .*

*May 1, 1813—Hamilton, Bermuda*

*Dear Meg:*

*It is with a heavy heart that I take pen in hand to write this letter which, I trust, will find you safe and happy in residence with Malcolm and Flora MacKenzie in Baltimore.*

*Upon the arrival of the Goodfellow in Hamilton Harbor, I was delivered into the hands of the authorities by our mutual nemesis, Captain Bledsoe, and forthwith conveyed in irons aboard an old captured French frigate newly arrived in nearly sinking condition to serve as a prison hulk for captured American privateers.*

*While we were still aboard the Goodfellow en route to this place, Bledsoe prepared a letter to be sent to my father in Philadelphia notifying him of my imprisonment and demanding payment of 15,000 pounds sterling for my release. He grew furious at my refusal to add my personal appeal to his letter. Despite his threats of dire reprisals, I stuck to my resolve, reminding him that his original demand had been for 10,000 pounds for you and asserting that my life is of far less value than yours.*

*Bledsoe is a man devoid of any sense of humor or honor. I despise him. At any rate, he sent the letter, sans my endorsement, by one of the cartel craft now operating between Bermuda and Philadelphia and by which I am hoping that this and other letters will be conveyed to my friends in America.*

*So, dear Meg, please do not fret yourself over my fate. I have written instructions to Malcolm MacKenzie regarding the means of effecting my release. Meanwhile, my imprisonment is not as onerous as you might fear. Although Bledsoe left instructions that I was to be kept in irons on a diet of bread and water until ransomed, as soon as his brig had cleared port as part of a regular armada to be convoyed back to England, the commander of this hulk freed me from my bonds and provided me with a dinner from his very own table. He likewise has provided me with a supply of paper and ink for letters such as this. He did this, first, because he is a decent fellow; secondly, because Bledsoe, by his overbearing manner, rubbed him the wrong way in trying to dictate the conditions of my imprisonment and release; thirdly, because representatives of our two governments have signed conventions prohibiting cruel and inhumane treatment of prisoners and, perhaps most important, he heard of my medical training and my service as a ship's surgeon and he needs a doctor for his charges.*

*So, there you are, Meg. I find myself once again dealing with the ailments of several hundred American sailors, the difference being that they are prisoners of war and I am treating them with medicines and equipment supplied by the Royal Navy.*

*I miss your cheerful, helpful presence at my sick calls but do not at all miss the need to sew up battle wounds or to amputate limbs. Rashes, sores, boils, and like infections constitute the chief of my practice aboard this worm-eaten hulk.*

*Dear Meg, it grieved me to part from you in that hectic exchange with Bledsoe without having the opportunity to explain the relationship that exists between myself and the girl to whom you now know I am pledged to marry. Rightly or wrongly, Tom advised me to say nothing to you about Madeline Richter during our pleasant time together aboard the Flora. By now, however, I expect that he has told you all about how I lost my heart to her while returning from England and of my visit to her home upon our return from our cruise last November.*

*Tom met Madeline briefly when he brought me the shocking, but welcome, news that rather than being lost at sea you were being held captive in Barbados. He can affirm my judgment that she has a peerless beauty and many other qualities needed by a wife who wishes to help a man of ambition advance in life. If you were to meet Madeline, you would readily understand that she is the ideal person for me*

*As for yourself, let me say to you directly what I have said to many out of your hearing: There was never a spunkier, more highly principled girl in all the world than Megan Jenkins. I pray that this letter finds you in good spirits and reconciled with your family and getting on with your life.*

*Fondly,*
*Lovejoy Martin*

*P.S. Bledsoe took a malicious pleasure in showing me the letter he received from my brother, Chester, which, he said, he likewise had shown to you. Please tell Malcolm MacKenzie of the contents of that letter so that he will fully appreciate why I do not wish the subject of my imprisonment and terms of my ransom to be broached to any member of my family. Malcolm needs to know this.*

*HMS Argus—Hamilton Harbor, Bermuda*

*Dear Darling Madeline:*

*Through a set of curious and trying circumstances, which I am not at liberty to explain at present, I find myself serving as physician aboard a British vessel here in Bermuda where, unfortunately, I will be detained until the terms of my contract have been fulfilled, hopefully within a very few weeks.*

*It grieves me that you and I are not already married and settled down to the pleasant mode of life I envision for us in Philadelphia. So, I must beg you to be patient for a while longer until I can return and we can go forward with our marriage plans.*

*Dear, dear beautiful Madeline. I console myself during the long nights aboard this vessel by reliving in my imagination those precious hours we spent together on our return passage from England a year ago and again at your home last December. A thousand times I have rehearsed in my mind our ride about your father's farms and the way we groomed my horse in your stable.*

*Tell your father that my proposal of marriage holds as firm as when I made it last December. If anything, even stronger.*

*I go to sleep every night with your face and form in my mind and awaken every morning to delightful thoughts of you. A dozen times a day, I lose myself in reveries of what our life together will be when I am free to join you and to resume our progress to marriage and a long lifetime together. Every hour that we are apart is like an eternity.*

*This war which is the cause of our separation cannot last forever. Once our country is again at peace with England, I propose to take you to London as my wife for a long visit there. Nothing would give me greater pleasure than to introduce you to the pleasures and comforts of that exciting city. We shall eat at the finest restaurants and see plays to our hearts' content. I shall spoil you utterly.*

*Please apologize on my behalf to your dear mother for my abrupt departure last December. The matter which called me away was too urgent and too complicated for me to explain quickly. I shall reveal everything to you when we are reunited. The stories I have to tell will surely captivate you and, in time, our children and grandchildren.*

*This letter is to be forwarded to you by my business partner in Baltimore. You may send your reply back to him, and he will see that it is relayed to me.*

*Please, please, write as soon as you get this and tell me all that you have been doing and thinking during the time we have been separated. I yearn for news of you.*

*Meanwhile, keep well, keep happy, remain patient. We are fated for each other.*

*Your ever faithful*
*Lovejoy*

*Dear Pierre:*

*Well, old friend, as the saying goes, I am in a mell of a hess. As I have explained in letters to Malcolm and Meg Jenkins, Bledsoe delivered me to a British prison hulk here in Hamilton Harbor to be held until an exorbitant ransom is paid. Malcolm can tell you the terms and how I propose to meet them.*

*Bledsoe has departed with his accursed brig as part of a huge convoy bound for England, where he will be waiting like a vulture for receipt of his ransom money. To know that man is to loathe him. It galls me to think of that odious wretch living out his days in comfort at my expense, but I do not see how it can be otherwise.*

*As for myself, when first we met last summer, I am sure you regarded me as an arrogant and self-centered young fop, intent only upon getting his hands on money, with little thought for the welfare of others, headstrong and foolhardy.*

*Truly, Pierre, my experiences of the past year have matured and changed me profoundly and for the better, I trust. High among those maturing experiences has been that of making your acquaintance and forging a friendship with one of your wisdom and good judgment. Often during my moments of despair, I reflect upon our conversations aboard the Flora. I now realize that a life without purpose beyond selfish indulgence is mere empty existence; that to live life to its fullness, one must make oneself useful to other persons, must set aside purely selfish motives, must adjust, if not sacrifice entirely, one's own interests to those of others.*

*Somewhere I have read that the wildest colt makes the best steed. While the spirit of this young stallion remains unbroken, I have been forced into harness as a physician aboard what once was a proud French frigate but now, in British hands, has become a dismasted and worm-eaten old hulk, about as far a cry from the graceful Flora as a broken-down nag would be from a fleet young racehorse.*

*Into its rotting frame have been crammed nearly three hundred captured American sailors. I am kept busy treating their ailments and using my powers of persuasion to see that our captors allow them opportunity for exercise and provide them with healthy diets. They are a rowdy lot, my fellow countrymen, full of mischief and high spirits. They chafe at their imprisonment, as do I, but they keep up their spirits with games of chance and with trying to outdo each other in telling tales of their exploits aboard their privateers.*

*Pierre, I have asked Malcolm to allow Tradnick to be given back his sloop and to be allowed to return to St. George, taking with him his crewmen and that hapless little Cockney sailor. You might caution Malcolm to make no reference to any of them about my presence down here in Hamilton Harbor.*

*I am confident that Malcolm will attend quickly to my desires as regards my ransom and that I soon will be on my way back to Pennsylvania to take up the threads of my life. My first order of business at home will be to visit my dear Madeline and reconfirm my intention to make her my wife, then to start working on recovering some part of the considerable fortune that was mine all too briefly.*

*Now I must lay my pen aside and conduct my morning*

*sick call. I cannot close without thanking you for your friendship and loyalty. Hoping to see you soon,*

*Lovejoy Martin, M.D.*

*June 18, 1813—Baltimore*

*Dear Lovejoy:*

*This will acknowledge receipt of your letter of May 1, which came here by overland post from Philadelphia. Your letter to Miss Richter has been received and forwarded to Reading, per your instructions.*

*Lovejoy, it grieves me to inform you that it is impossible to comply with your request to sell your interest in the Flora as a way of raising your ransom money, and for the simple reason that the schooner remains at sea.*

*The sloop, New Hope, did make it safely through the British blockade, thanks to Pierre Barineau's superb seamanship, but the Flora, by his account, was forced to turn back at the mouth of the Chesapeake to avoid capture. The British not only have cordoned off the mouth of the Chesapeake, they have been conducting raids far up the bay, as far as Frenchtown here in Maryland, where they destroyed several vessels and put the village to the torch. Similar depredations have been made against towns such as Havre de Grace, and we have no navy to protect ourselves in these waters. Thank the Almighty for the stout walls and mighty guns of Fort McHenry, or Baltimore would have suffered a dire fate by now. We hear that the British bear a special hatred for this place which they regard as the spawning ground for the privateers that have caused them so much trouble.*

*Here in Baltimore, commerce has been crippled by the blockade. Only a sharp sailing sloop such as the New Hope, captained by a crew of great skill, can carry anything out of the city via the Chesapeake. Insurance rates have risen to nearly half the value of the craft and cargo. The price of imports such as sugar, salt, and coffee mounts daily as the supply diminishes. By the same token, for lack of sea transport, wheat and flour and other staples of our own exports have become a drug on the market here in Baltimore. The only way to carry them is by wagon train. Roads to Philadelphia and New York are becoming ruined from overuse in the rush to profiteer from shortages there.*

*In a blatant effort to drive a wedge between the middle and southern states and those of New England, the British do not strictly blockade ports such as Boston, where sentiment has always been against this war. There is fear—unfounded, I pray—here in Baltimore that the New England states might withdraw from the union, which would throw this nation into a ruinous civil war.*

*So there it is, Lovejoy. Even if the Flora were in harbor, I fear that its sales value would be somewhat reduced. I hope that Phipps has the gumption to adapt to the changed circumstances of this war. No longer can a privateer succeed by capturing ships and cargoes to be brought into American ports for condemnation and sale. Congress, now in session down in Washington, has voted to pay a bounty on the value of British ships that our privateers destroy at sea and $25 for each British sailor taken prisoner. The game henceforth will be to seize valuable, less bulky cargo such as medicines and weapons as well as specie and sailors, and devil take the hapless carrier. If Phipps is successful, the Flora may earn enough money to cover your ransom, but that will take time.*

*You requested that we free Captain Tradnick and allow him to return to Bermuda with his sloop, his crewmen, and the fellow you took prisoner. Barineau did bring Tradnick and his crew along, but alas, condemnation of the sloop has begun, and I am not certain that I can halt it. We shall see.*

*Flo has taken to Megan Jenkins as she would a daughter. Meggie is a dear, thoughtful girl. I spoke to Talbot Smith yesterday about providing her with your surgeon's shares from our first cruise. He grumbled about this arrangement, but finally agreed. Learning to walk on his new artificial leg and chafing at remaining landbound have not improved his disposition. Tom, of course, is aboard the Flora, so I shall hold his four shares in escrow until his return. And we will be happy for Megan to remain with us until she can be reunited with her brother. So you can set your mind at ease on that score.*

*Pierre Barineau has joined his wife in Dover at the moment. I will give him your letter upon his return. Incidentally, he is full of praise for your courage and for your intelligence. I am sure that he will be most distressed at our inability to respond quickly to your request for 15,000 pounds.*

*My impulse would have been to take this up with your father, but I will obey your wishes not to do so. However, you will forgive me if I explore other possibilities with Barineau upon his return to Baltimore.*

*It just occurred to me that this war began exactly one year ago. It has not gone nearly so well as many thought. Although our privateers have caused the British much distress, they are of no use in protecting our coastal towns. Our navy frigates have enjoyed some successes in individual encounters with British ships, but they do not prevent our enemies from dominating our coastal waters.*

*Our army has made three different attempts to invade Canada and all have been failures to one degree or another, mainly because of poor leadership and the refusal of state militias to accompany the incursions. Only recently have the Congress and President Madison initiated reforms to enlarge our regular army and improve the quality of both its men and its generals. Meanwhile, in Europe, it remains to be seen whether Napoleon can rebuild his armies after their disastrous defeat last winter in Russia. I dread the consequences for this country if the British army were free to add its weight to that of their navy in this war about which I and many of my Republican friends now have second thoughts.*

*I shall send this letter along by special post to Lewes in Delaware, with instructions for it to be sent to you on the next cartel boat for Bermuda. Megan has your letter, as I said.*

*By the by, the young prize master, Calvin Collins, seems much smitten with Megan. He has gone off to visit his parents in New Jersey, but I will be much surprised if Megan has seen the last of that likely young man.*

*Flo sends you her best regards.*

*Your faithful friend,*
*Malcolm MacKenzie.*

*P.S. Megan just handed me a letter to be sent to you. She seemed upset and appeared to have been crying. I think she must be missing her brother very much. Poor girl.*

*June 18, 1813*

*Dear Lovejoy:*

*Thank you for troubling yourself to write to me when you have so many other people to write to and so many important matters on your mind.*

*It was very noble and unselfish of you to go to so much bother on my behalf. I and all the members of my family shall always be grateful to you for what you have done for both Tom and me. And while I am grateful to you for offering me your surgeon's shares from the cruise, I must tell Mr. MacKenzie that I cannot in good conscience accept more than two of those eight shares, which I believe is what a surgeon's assistant normally would receive. You have sacrificed far too much on my behalf already.*

*Since I, along with Calvin Collins and the other prize crew members, have been held prisoner, I can sympathize with what you are going through. You don't really value your freedom until it is taken from you, do you?*

*Although my heart was very heavy at abandoning you to the British, the journey back to Baltimore was pleasant until we tried to enter the Chesapeake. While we had stopped to transfer Captain Tradnick and crew from the Flora to his sloop, we encountered two British frigates. Captain Phipps sailed the Flora between them and fired off his cannon as if he were seeking a fight. When they tried to close in on him, he turned back to sea and they followed, which enabled Mr. Barineau to slip into the Chesapeake. We came dangerously close to falling back into British hands.*

*Mr. Barineau is a wonderful man. He thinks very highly of you, incidentally. He was kept busy dodging British ships on the way up the Chesapeake, but we did have some interesting conversations on the way. I like Captain Tradnick, too. He is a fine gentleman, but he is heartsick at losing his sloop, into which he said he had put his lifetime savings. He and Mr. Barineau got on very well for supposed enemies. I wish we had taken Tom off the Flora with Captain Tradnick. But we did not, and so he never got a chance to tell me about your Madeline. I only knew what your brother said in that letter Captain Bledsoe showed me, whose truth I doubted until I heard what you told Bledsoe before you gave yourself up to him, that and a few things Mr. Barineau told me of what you had spoken about her. So thank you for making it clear in your letter about your feelings and intentions for the future.*

*This Madeline is a lucky girl to have won your heart. I hope that when you get free you will be very happy with her. When you marry, it is important to choose someone who loves you as much as you do them and who will help you fulfill your ambitions in life.*

*Speaking of marriage, ever since Calvin Collins learned that the story that I was engaged to you was just a lie put out by Captain Smith to protect me, he has been pestering me to be his wife. I have been putting him off, but he is a decent young man and it don't look like I can do much better. He is off visiting his parents up in New Jersey at present. With those two shares from the cruise, I won't need to remain here as a burden on the MacKenzies. I shall probably return to Philadelphia and allow Calvin to speak to my pa, as he has been wanting to do ever since we got back.*

*My heart remains heavy when I think back on how much trouble I caused by stowing away on your schooner. You would have to be a female trapped in an unhappy life at home to understand why I did such a bold, stupid thing. Anyway, thank you for coming to my rescue. I am sorry to have caused you so much trouble.*

*Calvin promises me that he will devote the rest of his life to making me happy. I hope that your Madeline will do the same for you.*

*So once you are free from your imprisonment and Tom has returned safely from the sea, we shall all be settled for life, or so it would appear.*

*I have heard that prison hulks are horrible places, but it sounds as though you have fallen into kindly hands there in Bermuda. I am glad that your position as a doctor has been recognized and that you can keep yourself busy looking after your fellow prisoners. It was amusing at first, aboard the Flora, to observe the way you handled your patients. You do have a good way with people. And Mr. Barineau and Kevin have told me of how skillfully you amputated the leg of Captain Smith.*

*Those few days aboard the Flora, working with you, were the happiest of my life up to this point. I only hope that there will be equally happy days ahead for us all.*

*Fondly,*
*Megan Jenkins*

*June 20, 1813—Philadelphia*

*Lt. Richard Wittenstall*
*Commandant, HM Prison Ship, Argus*
*Hamilton, Bermuda*

*Dear Sir:*

*We are in receipt of a correspondence from a Captain Christopher Bledsoe, master of the brig Goodfellow, regarding one of your prisoners, Lovejoy Martin, who happens to be my brother.*

*Some months ago, Captain Bledsoe sought to extort 10,000 pounds from our family as a ransom for a young woman whom he was causing to be held in Barbados and whom he mistakenly thought to be my brother's fiancée but who in reality was the runaway daughter of a common tavern keeper here in Philadelphia. Having no interest in her welfare, my father and I declined to pay that sum, and I am compelled to inform you that, while we harbor a naturally strong interest in the welfare of my brother, we likewise decline to pay the 15,000 pounds Captain Bledsoe now demands for his release.*

*Captain Bledsoe's letter indicated that he had captured my brother in the course of releasing the young woman he had previously held for ransom. I quite naturally sympathize with my brother in his plight but must tell you in all honesty that I share the opinion of many of my friends who regard privateering ventures such as that in which he has been engaged for the past year as little better than licensed piracy and do not wish to encourage it by removing the penalties which must befall those who practice this perfidious business.*

*Captain Bledsoe explained that he intended to go on to England, leaving my brother in your custody. He threatened to have my brother sent back to England for incarceration at Dartmoor Prison if we are unwilling to pay his ransom. If that should turn out to be his fate, naturally I and my father would be most distressed, but he, not we, made the decision to enter into his privateering enterprise, and it is you and your superiors, not we, who must make the decision as to his fate now that you understand that no ransom will be paid for his release.*

*Finally, let me say that I regret the state of war that exists between our two countries and look forward to the end of hostilities and the resumption of normal trade.*

*Your obedient servant,*
*Chester Peebles Martin*

# 3 

*August 1, 1813*

*Dear Malcolm:*

*Your letter of June 18 brings me little joy. I hope that by now the Flora may have been able to return to Baltimore or some other American port and that you have been able to find a buyer for her.*

*Time is running out for me, Mac. I, personally, continue to be well treated, with my own small cabin next to that of the commandant, but conditions aboard this prison hulk grow progressively worse for our prisoners as more captives are brought aboard. The nights are sheer hell for our poor boys. They must remain belowdecks, nearly suffocating, with gunports sealed shut against their escape. Despite the heat of the Bermudian summer sun, their days have been made more nearly bearable as our commandant, at my urging, has allowed old sails to be suspended as awnings over the deck whereon they are allowed until sundown.*

*The talk aboard ship is that soon most of our prisoners will be hauled off to Dartmoor or other prisons in England to alleviate the crowded conditions aboard this vessel. If this should occur, there is the possibility that I might be sent along with them. That prospect chills my blood. I am most anxious to return to Pennsylvania. Please do not delay in doing whatever you can to effect my release.*

*I am much distressed in my mind, also, at my failure to receive any reply from my letter to my fiancée. You did forward it to her, did you not? And I have not yet received any reply from Pierre Barineau. Surely my good friend would not abandon me. And what about the New Hope? Were you able to halt the condemnation proceedings and set Tradnick free? From your letter, I sensed a reluctance to do that, because, I suppose, of the money the sloop would yield.*

*Even Meg Jenkins's letter, which arrived in the same*

*post with yours, did little to ease my mind. I am glad that she found refuge with you but was alarmed at her saying that she planned to allow the prize master, Collins, to speak to her father about marrying her. Collins is a decent sort of fellow, I suppose, but he lacks an education and seems on the whole to be a cut below what Meg could expect in a husband.*

*I would appreciate it if Flo would caution her against throwing herself away on someone of lesser quality than herself.*

*Oh, dear friend, Mac, please do not delay in raising my ransom and getting me out of this pesthole. I have read of how our Negroes were carried to the New World like cattle or swine in the holds of slave ships. That is very much like the condition aboard this hulk, except that we are tied up to a dock. I have read that when those hapless Africans were allowed on deck to exercise, they had to be closely guarded to prevent their leaping into the sea. I fear that I shall have to be similarly restrained if I am sent back to England.*

*The latest batch of prisoners brought aboard this hulk were taken off a Marblehead, Massachusetts, privateer but included one fellow from Philadelphia. He said that the talk along the waterfront is that my father's condition has grown worse and that he is not expected to live much longer. It saddens me all the more to think of his dying before I can reach his bedside and be reconciled with him. I would have liked to have had his blessing before he departs this life.*

*The one bright aspect of my imprisonment is the sense of fulfillment I gain from alleviating the misery of my fellow captives. I do this by attending to their medical needs to the best of my ability, and by somewhat improving their living conditions through my influence with the commandant of this prison. Our warden is an amiable naval officer, a farmer's son from Kent, named Wittenstall. Disappointed at being twice passed over for promotion and hating his assignment aboard this prison hulk, he drinks more than is good for him. However, he is, at heart, a decent chap, and I enjoy my conversations with him, when he is sober, that is.*

*He has assigned a recently captured surgeon's assistant to me as my aide. Amiable young chap who used to work for an apothecary. He and I keep busy.*

*So, that is how things stand with me, Mac. Low in spirits and running out of hope, I write to plead with you to rescue me before it is too late. I can only hope that the hackneyed saying—"it is always darkest just before dawn"—will apply in my case. Please send me word that my dawn will soon break and that I can return home while there is still time for me to repair my relationship with my fiancée and receive my father's blessing.*

*In haste and desperation,*
*Lovejoy Martin*

# Part Four

# 1 

"I say, Dr. Martin, can you spare a moment?"

"Actually, Zeb and I were about to begin sick call."

"I thought you might have something in that black bag to settle a chap's stomach and cure his headache."

"The best cure would be to drink less rum and more water, but try these powders. Wash them down with a cup of good strong tea. Will help you sleep, as well."

"Ah, thank you. Don't rush off. Must ask you something."

"My patients are already lined up on deck, but seeing as how both they and I are your prisoners, your request is my command."

Lieutenant Wittenstall motioned for Lovejoy's surgeon's assistant, Zeb Vanstory, to leave the compartment.

"Do you have a brother?"

"I have an older half brother back in Philadelphia."

"Do you trust him?"

"About as far as I could throw the anchor of this stinking hulk. Now look here, my patients are waiting for me."

"Let your aide deal with them. Oh, what the hell, I might as well show you this damned letter. Came several days ago. Hate for you to see it, but here, read it for yourself and you will understand why I have such a headache."

Lovejoy took the letter and read it swiftly.

"Damn him! The self-righteous little prig. Look here, Lieutenant, I never expected my father to ransom me. But I do have friends in Baltimore working to raise the money."

"So you have told me. But no ransom has shown up yet. And this letter, coming as it does from your family, well, it puts me in an awkward position."

"Am I not making myself useful here?"

"You have performed miracles, keeping this infernal ship free of disease. And your presence has had a calming effect on the prisoners.

Confound it, man, I like you better than I ever thought I would a bloody Yank."

"And I find you tolerable enough, for a Britisher, that is. Now that we have exchanged compliments and you know what a little shit my half brother is, what is so awkward about your position?"

"I have dreaded telling you this, but you see, everyone aboard this ship is to be sent off to England to make room for new prisoners. I would like to keep you here as a doctor for the fresh batch, but this letter makes it impossible."

"Can't you just tear up the letter?"

"My superior officer in St. George knows that the arrangement with Bledsoe calls for you to be shipped back to Dartmoor if your father refuses to pay your ransom. It was out of the question for me to deceive him. I had no choice but to tell him."

"This will be bad news for Bledsoe, too, will it not?"

"Yes, that is some consolation, I suppose . . ."

"Not for me, it is not. This dashes all my hopes."

"Sorry, I didn't mean it that way. It is just that the man was so obnoxious, going on and on about losing his leg at bloody Trafalgar and boasting of how he had pulled off a coup in capturing you and putting himself in the way of a fortune. Why won't your father buy your freedom? Is he not wealthy?"

"It is a long story. And my lads have been kept waiting long enough. How much time do we have here?"

"Not more than a week or so. A troop transport just delivered a battalion of soldiers at St. George. As soon as she is ready, we are to march our prisoners up there to be loaded up and hauled off to Dartmoor. Look here, Doctor, I am awfully sorry."

"It is not your fault, Lieutenant. Now I think you should wash down those powders and take a nap. I will have time enough to think about this after I have seen to my patients."

Back in Philadelphia, Chester Peebles had waited for some time after intercepting Bledsoe's ransom letter to Jeremiah Martin before answering it. He had delayed telling even Rosalind, his wife, about the correspondence until after his reply had been sent on to Lewes to be carried by cartel boat to Bermuda. When he did finally tell her, he was taken aback by her reaction.

"So that is why you have been acting so distracted of late. Why did you do such a rash thing?" she demanded.

"Father should not be bothered, not in his condition. And even if he were in good health, where would he find the ready money? I now control Martin Shipping."

"You could raise the money, could you not?"

"If I wanted to take out mortgages, load ourselves up with debts, I suppose I could. But why would I want to do that?"

"You hate him, don't you?"

"I do not love him, that is for certain."

"Why not? Amanda adores him."

"I despise his arrogant, smug so-called charm. I despise the way people fawn over him because he is handsome and glib. It is not fair for him to have things come to him so easily without effort on his part. Whereas I . . ."

"Yes, yes, I know. Whereas you have been the ever-dutiful son, playing up to the old man, doing his every bidding . . ."

"And reaping the benefits, too, would you not say?"

"Actually, are we that much better off than we were before Papa Martin turned his company over to you? We still live in this same wretched little house."

"Rosalind, please don't get started on that theme again. The British have the Delaware Bay blockaded. We can't get shipping in and out of Philadelphia. Our business is stagnant. You know that. We were lucky that our lawyers were able to free that ship we sent over to Spain. If that admiralty court in Baltimore had condemned her, we would have had to sacrifice the bond, and then the fat would have been in the fire. The old man would have discovered that we obtained that bond with a forged signature. Now the Congress and that idiot Madison have put the quietus on carrying wheat and flour to Spain. We were lucky to squeak by before the ban was imposed. And I shall never forget that it was Lovejoy's schooner that captured that ship we leased."

"We won the case, did we not?"

"Yes, but our lawyer's fees ate deeply into the profits."

"What will happen to Lovejoy if no one pays his ransom?"

"He will spend the rest of the war in a British prison. Perhaps it will teach him humility."

"But was he not to be married?"

"Yes, and there again, he fell into a feather bed. I understand the girl is a beauty, the daughter of a rich old Dutchman out in Berks County."

"Shouldn't you notify that family of his situation?"

"I don't want to advertise the fact that my brother is in the privateering trade. Besides, it is none of our business. This war won't last forever. If she loves him, she will be waiting when he returns from prison."

"But when Lovejoy does come home, will he not demand to know why his family did not raise his ransom?"

"By that time the old man will be dead. It won't matter."

"Lovejoy will hate you."

"He already does."

"And why is that, do you think?"

"You saw the look on baby brother's face last year when we gathered for things to be divided up. When he heard that the company was to be turned over to me, well, I am glad that looks cannot kill."

"So you think he hates you because he feels you stole his father's love?"

"And respect and trust. Yes, he is jealous."

"But that does not explain why you hate him so."

"I already told you. He has had things made so smooth for him, whereas my father died when I was only three, leaving my mother a widow with two small children."

"I never knew your mother, Chester, but from all I hear, she was a lovely woman."

"She was lovely, yes."

"Did she love Lovejoy?"

"He was her pet, just as he is Amanda's. Once he was born, I did not seem to matter . . . Really, Rosalind, I am tired of this discussion."

"No need to be so touchy. At the risk of irritating you, is it true about the opportunities for speculation in Bermuda?"

"That is the talk in the coffeehouses. They say that you could easily triple your money, buying up captured cargoes on the cheap and bringing them to our more northern ports. If only we had the ready capital, Martin Shipping could reap a fortune."

"And how much did you say that British captain demands to free Lovejoy, fifteen thousand pounds? In American money, that would be . . .?"

"About fifty thousand dollars. What are you getting at?"

"This may be a wild idea, but you are a clever man, Chester. You can figure out how to make it work. Hear me out . . ."

St. George's harbor had become so crowded with privateers and other American vessels captured by the Royal Navy that there was scarcely room to anchor them. The docks and warehouses of the town overflowed with confiscated cargoes waiting to be condemned and auctioned. The merchants of Bermuda had bought all the vessels and cargoes that they could absorb with their limited capital, but word of the bargains available there had attracted hundreds of sharp-eyed speculators from England, Sweden, Canada, and even the United States.

To avoid violation of new laws against trading with the enemy, those from America arrived on ships nominally under the flags of neutral countries, and they came, or tried to come, incognito. Many of them sniffed about for opportunities wearing green, smoked glasses, their broad-brimmed hats pulled low over their eyes to avoid recognition by any of the crewmen of captured privateers.

In that glutted market, a vessel could be picked up for half its value. And cargoes of sugar, rum, coffee, and such likewise could be purchased for a third to a half of what they would bring back in America. The trick then was to get the stuff on board your falsely registered ship and haul it past the British blockading fleet.

In Baltimore or Philadelphia, the goods fetched higher prices, but you ran a much greater risk of capture by British frigates, which looked the other way to New England traffic as part of a plan to drive a wedge between the American states.

And that is how Chester Peebles came to St. George, aboard a Swedish-registered but Massachusetts-owned three-master out of Boston. He arrived in the port two weeks after his letter had been delivered to Wittenstall. And despite what he had said in the letter about the Martin family's refusal to pay Lovejoy's ransom, he carried sewn into the lining of his jacket three negotiable letters of credit totaling fifty thousand dollars in value: two, for twenty thousand dollars each from his Uncle Ephraim and his brother-in-law Frank Carpenter, and his own for ten thousand dollars.

It would have been impossible to keep a secret such as Lovejoy's from spreading throughout the three hundred obstreperous, bored American prisoners aboard the *Argus*, or to prevent the reports from growing more and more exaggerated.

"So that is why he looks so down at the mouth, is it, Zeb?" a hard-bitten old salt from New York was saying to the young apothecary's clerk who served as Lovejoy's assistant surgeon.

"Aye, Higgins, it is. He's being held for twenty-five thousand pounds, so I hear. And his family won't pay it. Consider him a black sheep. If I thought it would do any good, I'd sign over my shares from the prizes we sent back before we was captured. What about you, Thomas?"

"I don't know, Zeb. Even if every man aboard this hellhole was to do the same, they couldn't raise enough to pay such a ransom. Why that is a hundred thousand dollars. Besides which, my shares is in trust with our ship's husband back in America."

"I reckon there ain't anything we can do to keep ourselves from being sent off to England, but there ought to be something we could do to save the doctor, after what he has done for us."

The air in the lawyer's upstairs office next to the Globe Hotel in St. George was so close and hot that his prospective client found it difficult to breathe. The sweat had soaked through his shirt and linen jacket. Now he felt a puddle collecting in the seat of his trousers as the lawyer, a portly, balding man, regarded him with watery blue eyes.

"You're not the first American that has come to me wanting to do business under a cloak of anonymity. I shouldn't wonder you'd be embarrassed to reveal your nationality after what your countrymen did to York in Canada. Burnt the provincial buildings, they did. Well, they have sowed the wind and will reap the whirlwind when our army finishes off Bonaparte. You mark my words."

"I have never supported this war. And I am as appalled as any Englishman would be at what our army perpetrated in your Canadian capital. I don't consider myself an enemy of England. In fact, I have supported your cause in Europe by hauling flour to your armies in Spain, at no small risk, I might add."

"One of them Sidmouthers, were you? Well, that game is ended. And now you've come to Bermuda to pick up a bargain or two with the profits from your flour trade, isn't that what you're after?"

"That is not my first order of business, but yes, I see nothing wrong with supplying legitimate needs back in the United States, despite the narrow-minded attitude of our government."

"Nor do I. Now, for God's sake, take off those silly green glasses, and quit beating around the bush. I have a roomful of clients waiting downstairs. You're from Philadelphia, I can tell by your accent. So tell me what your business may be."

"You know the prison hulk, the *Argus*?"

"I do indeed. She is tied up down near Hamilton."

"And her commander is a Lieutenant Wittenstall, I believe."

"What is your interest in the *Argus*?"

"I would like very much to ascertain whether a certain individual is still being held on that vessel or whether he has been sent off to Dartmoor in England."

"So that is your business? You've come to try to win the release of . . . what is he, this prisoner? A relative, or what?"

"All I want to know is if he is still on the vessel, and if so, when he will be sent off to England. Preventing his transfer is the furthest thing I have in mind."

"What would the name of this fellow be?"

"Martin. Lovejoy Martin."

"And your name is? Come, come. You'll have to tell me sooner or later."

"Chester Peebles."

"Very well, Mr. Chester Peebles of Philadelphia. You come back here day after tomorrow about this same time, and I may have the information for you."

"Can't you find out sooner? I will pay for your trouble."

"You don't know your geography of Bermuda very well, do you? It is a good dozen miles or more down to Spanish Point, as the crow flies. But this won't be a crow's flight. I have to hire a man to go down there on a rented horse, which is hard to come by. He may have to grease a palm or two. And then ride back with his report. And so, you see, you must pay both me and my investigator for our trouble and our expenses, in advance, I might add."

"Very well. But if Lovejoy Martin remains on the ship, I must know just when he will be sent off to England. And when I know that for a certainty, and only then, I would like to discuss certain other important business matters with you."

"Well, Barineau, we should be in St. George Harbor by noon tomorrow. I hope you know what you're going to do, once there."

"No, Tradnick, I don't know exactly what I shall do, but I know where I must start."

"The less I know, the better. Remember, if they catch you before you can sneak off the *New Hope,* you stowed away without my knowledge. I'll have questions enough to answer when I show up after disappearing six months ago."

"Your crew won't give me away, will they?"

"MacKenzie's bribe should still their tongues. So, we are agreed that you will remain hidden until nightfall . . ."

"And then I will slip ashore and you will be shut of me."

"You are taking a hell of a risk, you know."

"I have visited Bermuda several times, so I know my way around. From all reports, Bermuda now teems with speculators from every country, including my own. So I assume that an American no longer need hide his nationality on your little adopted homeland or, once ashore, that he will have to explain how he came there. So fear not for me nor for yourself. I will not expose you for carrying an enemy national on a secret mission."

"Actually, I had little choice. MacKenzie said that it was the only way I could recover my sloop and my freedom."

"I will tell you a secret. He would have let you go in any case. Lovejoy requested him to do so. Wrote that he felt bad at having seized the sloop of such an excellent fellow as yourself."

"Did he for a fact? Decent of him. You Yankees are full of surprises, aren't you? Understand, though, Barineau, I have not agreed to get you off the islands, only to keep my eyes peeled for you. Well, there they lie, just on the horizon over there. The Summer Isles themselves. Home sweet home, to me."

In St. George, business had never been better for Ross McFadden and his Seahorse Tavern. Upstairs, every room had been taken by war profiteers who did not balk at his prices even when they had to share quarters with three or four others of their ilk. Downstairs, his common room stayed so busy that he had been forced to hire a pair of black slave girls belonging to an elderly couple to help Mollie cook and serve.

Chester Peebles sat in a corner of the Seahorse nursing a cup of grog while his companion, the Swedish captain of the ship on which he had sailed from Boston, complained of the delays in bidding at the daily auctions of captured goods.

"You mean we got to wait until day after tomorrow?"

"At least until then. Perhaps later."

"Time is money to me and my owners. There was nothing in our agreement about waiting all summer for you to buy a cargo."

"I told you, Captain Olaffsen, I can't start buying until I have a certain piece of information."

"I just hope you ain't dragging your feet because you are waiting to raise the money."

"Believe me, Captain, I have more than enough funds available to fill your hold. I will start buying after a few days. Meanwhile, I am putting my time to good use in acquainting myself with what is available and at what prices. Now then, I have had a busy day. Time for me to turn in."

Olaffsen grumbled "good night" and yelled to Mollie, the barmaid, to bring him another cup of grog.

As closing time drew near, Ross McFadden wondered how to clear out his patrons so that Mollie and her helpers could clean up. At first he did not notice the lean, gray-haired man who was speaking to Mollie. He looked across the smoky, noisy room in time to see her pointing in his direction.

The man made his way through the crowd and waited until McFadden stopped pouring cups of rum to wipe his face.

"Would you be the Ross McFadden who is a cousin of Malcolm MacKenzie of Baltimore?"

The tavern keeper glanced around to see if anyone were listening, then whispered, "Keep your voice down. Make as if you are ordering a drink."

"I would like very much to have a glass of stout."

"Here is your stout. Where is your money?"

Barineau slid a gold sovereign across the counter and said, "Take out one for yourself and keep the change."

McFadden pursed his mouth and whisked the coin into his pocket, then poured himself a glass of stout.

"I have ten more coins like the one I just gave you to exchange for a bit of information. There would be no risk for you at all."

"Just for a bit of information?"

"And nothing more."

"Drink your stout and clear out. After we have closed, come to the kitchen door. I'll hear what you have to say then."

Chester was so nervous sitting in the lawyer's waiting room two days later that he had to fight to keep his hands from trembling. What was taking the man so long to receive him? He, like several others in the room, kept his hat on and his shaded glasses in place. No one looked directly at anyone else.

He let his mind wander back to Rosalind in Philadelphia. She was a clever woman, no doubt about it, and ambitious as well. The business in which he was engaged involved risk, certainly, but in essence, Rosalind's idea was as brilliant as it was simple.

"Don't you see, Chester, you can kill two birds with one stone," she had said. "I know Papa Martin is in no shape, physically or financially, to respond. But show the letter from the prison warden to Mr. Bennett and Amanda and your Uncle Ephraim, and offer to go to Bermuda to see to the release of your brother, if they will find the fifty thousand dollars. You don't have to say anything about the reply you have already stupidly sent. Take the money over, but make sure that you arrive too late to keep Lovejoy from being sent back to England. Then, while there with all that ransom money, you can buy a cargo."

"And haul it back to, say, Boston? Yes, I see. Then I pocket the profits. Explain that I got to Bermuda too late to save precious baby brother from being sent off to England. And return their money."

"You have the idea. I leave it to you to work out the details. Honestly, Chester, sometimes I wonder what would have become of you if I had not married you."

"This would require Uncle Ephraim and Amanda to take out mortgages, perhaps ourselves as well, to raise so much."

"Keep our contribution to the minimum. First see how much they can raise between them . . . No, better still, tell them you can find only ten thousand dollars and leave it to them to raise the rest."

"You mean, prime the pump, as it were?"

"Now you are showing some promise."

"This would mean my having to go up to Boston to find a neutral ship bound for Bermuda. It would mean that we would be separated for several weeks, at least."

"I will try to bear up in your absence. Just don't lose your nerve."

"Mr. Peebles!"

Chester Peebles winced at hearing his name called out for a roomful of people to hear. A sallow, emaciated young man motioned for Chester to follow him up the stairs.

The lawyer sat at his desk, hands clasped in front of him.

"Sit, Mr. Chester Peebles of Philadelphia, sit. We have some very interesting information. I trust you have brought along the rest of the money."

Chester looked at the young man, who remained standing and had a smirk on his face. "Cannot we discuss this in private?"

"Cuthbert must stay. He knows everything I know and more. Take a chair, Cuthbert. Good man. Now then, Mr. Peebles you will be pleased to know that Lovejoy Martin remains aboard the *Argus*. By your expression, one would think this news does not please you."

"Surely there is more to report than that. I could have learned as much myself."

The young man looked offended as he interjected, "I got a lot more and got it straight from the horse's mouth, as it were. From the officer in charge of the hulk hisself."

"Would that be a Lieutenant Wittenstall?"

"You know his name, do you? Perhaps you know as well that the fellow likes his drink. You do not? Then let me tell you it cost me half a night of drinking down at the Blue Moon in Hamilton before I got what you are after. I had that expense and the cost of a night's lodging. That is on top of the hire of a horse . . ."

"Mr. Peebles will pay, I am sure," the lawyer said. "Now get on with what you discovered."

"Somebody should have told me the fellow is a doctor. What's more, the lieutenant is heartbroke at having to send him on to England. Says he has worked wonders seeing after the health of all them poor Yankees aboard his miserable hulk. Says the fellow is being held for a considerable ransom but his family refuses to pay it, and so he is left with no choice but to send him on."

Chester said, "All I want to know is when."

The lawyer motioned to Cuthbert to get on with his story.

"Monday morning, everyone on the hulk is to be marched up here to go aboard the transport that came last week with the new soldiers. They are to be housed on Hen Island that night and then sail the following day, weather and tide permitting."

"And there is no doubt that this is true?" Chester asked.

"There weren't any reason for the fellow to lie to me. But I tell you this, he ain't happy at giving up his prison doctor."

Chester mused over the investigator's information, then said to the lawyer, "Next Wednesday will be August 4. I should like to have an appointment with you that morning to discuss further business, assuming, of course, that the transport sails for England as scheduled on Tuesday, with Lovejoy Martin aboard."

Le Roi Cuthbert, or "Weasel" Cuthbert, as he was usually called, had come out to Bermuda ten years earlier on the advice of a doctor who had warned him that he would die of consumption if he remained in smoke-filled London through another damp winter. By the time Weasel's ravaged lungs had cleared up, he had become addicted to the lazy life of the islands.

Back in the dock district of London, he had eked out a living as a shipping clerk. He had found a similar job in St. George but soon demonstrated a talent as what he liked to call "an investigator." At times, as many as half the adult males of Bermuda were away at sea. Not all the sailors trusted their wives and sweethearts. For a modest fee, Weasel would "keep a discreet eye on her, in your absence, if you take my meaning, and give you an honest report upon your return." Or lawyers would employ him to seek out information about persons either suing or being sued by their clients. He also did occasional stints as a process server. But his forte was "weaseling out information." That plus his ferret-like appearance made his nickname a natural.

It was Weasel's habit, after completing an assignment, to take his fee and treat himself to a bit of relaxation at one of the bordellos that had sprung up on the island. Jingling the coins he had earned from his overnight visit to Hamilton, he was approaching his favorite such establishment, on the southern outskirts of St. George, that evening when a lean, gray-haired man stepped out from behind a tree and said to him in an American accent, "Would you be Le Roi Cuthbert?"

"So I am known. What is it to you?"

"I understand that you conduct investigations on a confidential basis."

"What did you have in mind?"

Barineau drew him out of the street and into the shadow of the tree.

"Could you find out something about a prisoner being held on a hulk down in Hamilton?"

"I dare say I could. It would not be easy, or cheap. In fact, I just . . ." Weasel caught himself in midsentence and said, "Actually, it is almost impossible to do that sort of thing."

"But I am told that you can find out almost anything for pay."

Weasel's brain churned at the prospects of yet another fee.

"Tell me what you are after."

"I want to know if a prisoner named Lovejoy Martin is still aboard. This should be easy for you, because he is serving as a ship's doctor and stands in very well with the commandant there."

"Lovejoy Martin, you say?" Weasel squelched his impulse to grab a quick fee for information he already had, and paused to rub his chin. "Now that is an odd name. Never heard of nobody with such a name. And a doctor in the bargain. That would make my job more difficult, him being as well known as what you say he is to the authorities. Dangerous undertaking it would be for me to go nosing about in such a matter, drawing attention to myself."

"I am prepared to pay ten sovereigns."

"As it happens, I do have a source that I might consult right here in St. George who could confirm whether this . . . what did you say his name was?"

"Lovejoy Martin."

"Yes, whether this Lovejoy Martin is still aboard the *Argus*. That much I might find out."

"The matter is urgent. I must know immediately."

"Then suppose you tell me everything you know about this here

Lovejoy Martin. Then we will meet right back at this same spot, say, at noon tomorrow."

Later, lying in bed with "Queenie" Foster, Weasel found it difficult to keep his mind off the knowledge that two well-heeled Americans, apparently unknown to each other, were so much interested in the same prisoner of war. Over and over he tried to make sense of the information he had gained from Peebles in the lawyer's office and that told to him by the older chap outside Queenie's cottage, and then fit it with what he had been told by the drunken lieutenant down in Hamilton. Should he confide all this to the lawyer who had got him involved in the first place?

"Weasel, is something wrong?" Queenie asked sleepily. "You have been here for two hours, now, and you've only done it once. I can't stay awake like this."

"I have something on my mind, Queenie darling."

"It's all right, long as you understand that you pay by the hour here, not by the piece."

"Go back to sleep. There is no problem about the money."

His mind returned to the question of what use he should make of his information. The smell of money, big money, hung over this entire affair. Hadn't the lieutenant mentioned a ransom of fifteen thousand pounds being demanded and refused? The lawyer had already profited from his own investigation and would reap further gains from the business this Chester Peebles wished to conduct. No, he saw no reason to share what he had learned, not with the lawyer. But what about the two Americans? This Peebles chap obviously was eager for Lovejoy Martin to be sent back to England. The other fellow, while he did not say so directly, seemed the more interested in the welfare of the prisoner. The question was which was better able to pay for information about the other's interest. Yes, that was it. But how to go about exploiting this idea? There would be time enough tomorrow to work all this out.

"Queenie, darling?"

"Yes, Weasel, my love?"

"You can wake up now. I reckon I really ought to be getting my money's worth here."

# 3 

Clear skies stretched over Bermuda at dawn on Monday, August 2, 1813, but by noon, the rays of the sun had grown less bright as wispy cirrus clouds spread from high above the southeastern horizon to directly overhead. Although from a distance the surface of the ocean looked as unruffled as if coated with oil, heavy swells had begun to pound the eastern beaches, loudly enough to echo in the streets of St. George while an impatient Pierre Barineau paced near the bordello where Weasel had told him to wait.

Barineau started at the sound of the voice behind their tree.

"Follow me. Stay well behind and keep your eyes off me." Weasel led him to the rear of the graveyard of St. Peter's Church and sat down behind the tomb of an early colonist.

"You brought money with you?"

"Yes. I assume you brought information."

"Let's see the money."

"Let's hear the information."

Weasel laughed. "You are a cool one, you are. All right, I will tell you this much. Your man is on the *Argus*. Just as you said, he has been working as ship's surgeon, and he is a great favorite of the lieutenant in charge."

"I told you as much last night."

"So you did. What you don't know is that he and all the other prisoners aboard that hulk is to be marched up here today, kept overnight on Hen Island, and put aboard a transport to carry them back to England and dear old Dartmoor. So you have heard my information; now let's see your money."

After questioning him closely about the time the prisoners might be expected to arrive, Barineau counted out the coins but, ignoring Weasel's outstretched hand, kept them in his grasp.

"Would you like to make a great deal more money than this?"

"What did you have in mind?"

"Help me find a way to get Dr. Martin free and see him returned to America."

"You want to get me hanged? I can't get mixed up in that."

"Would a hundred pounds make it seem less dangerous?"

Weasel whistled, then said quickly, "That is a lot of money, but then, his ransom was set at fifteen thousand. That is what the lieutenant said."

"But we, his friends, that is, cannot raise that amount. So we must find another way."

"Look, good sir, them prisoners will be guarded every step of the way from Hamilton by soldiers. There is not a chance in hell of getting him free. And once free, you would have the problem of finding a way to ship him off to America. There is nothing I would like better than a hundred pounds, but there is some things that is more than I can accomplish."

"So, you won't even consider the possibility?"

"You meet me back here, about four o'clock this afternoon, and I will let you know if anything occurs to me. Meanwhile, I would like to have my ten sovereigns for services rendered."

Weasel's mind reeled at the thought of picking up a hundred pounds, but he could think of no way to do what Barineau wanted. A coward at heart, he shrank from taking the kind of personal risks the American seemed to suggest. No, he must stick to his line of work, which was to gather information. He wondered how much his information about Chester Peebles being on Bermuda would be worth to the mysterious American. Or, for that matter, how much Chester Peebles might pay for his information that someone else not only wanted to know about Lovejoy Martin but was seeking ways to set him free.

Yes, he concluded, that was the best he could do. Sell to each interested party everything he knew about the other, and extract every penny he could from each. He would have to do it quickly. In another day or so, this Lovejoy Martin would be on his way to England and his information would be no more marketable than yesterday's catch of fish.

It did not take Weasel long to find Chester Peebles. Wearing his green spectacles, he stood on the outskirts of a crowd listening to the auctioning of a cargo of coffee and sugar from a captured American brig. Standing beside Chester was a square-shouldered blond man with eyes as blue as the Bermudian skies.

Weasel sidled up to Chester and took his sleeve. Chester jumped at the touch.

"I would like a word with you in private."

Chester excused himself and followed Weasel out of the hearing of Olaffsen, across the square, and into the Seahorse.

Once seated at a corner table, Weasel said, "I have more information, which may be of great interest to you."

"What sort of information?"

"Another American gentleman is on Bermuda making inquiries about Lovejoy Martin."

A stricken look came over Chester's face, but he quickly recovered and asked in a level, low tone, "Who is he?"

"I do not know his name, but I know something of his interest and the reasons for said interest."

"Then for God's sake, man, quit beating about the bush and tell me."

"I am not in the business of giving away such information."

"Aren't you in the employ of my lawyer? Are you not honor bound to relate all that you know about this matter? He charged me enough."

"You misjudge me, sir. I am a free agent. I was hired to find out certain information, which I relayed to you. Now I am in possession of further information, gained independent like, on my own. If you don't care enough to pay for what I could tell you, it is no skin off my nose. Just pay for these here drinks and we shall call it quits."

Chester seized his arm. "How much more do you want?"

"Can you go twenty-five pounds?"

"I don't have that amount on me. But if the information is useful, I might pay it."

Weasel's first impulse was to insist that he get his payment in advance, but he decided against overplaying his hand.

"Very well. I was approached last evening by an American gentleman. Wouldn't tell me his name. Seems he served on a privateering vessel with Lovejoy Martin and is looking for a way to set him free."

"Yes. Yes. Go on."

Weasel went on to tell an increasingly agitated Chester more of what he had learned from Barineau, making it appear that everything had been told him the night before. He concluded with, "And this gentleman says that he believes that a brother of this Lovejoy Martin is the reason his family will not ransom him. Says the young doctor mistrusts his brother and has asked his friends to see to his release."

"How would he know such a thing? What is the name of this person who told you all that nonsense?"

"I don't have his name, I regret to say."

"Did you divulge anything of what you had already learned, at my expense?"

"Now, Mr. Peebles, that would be unprofessional. Besides which, he already knew the circumstances under which Dr. Martin finds himself."

"Why did he tell you all this?"

"Did I not make that clear? He was seeking to involve me in a scheme to aid the prisoner in escaping."

"And what answer did you make?"

"I told him that it was a dangerous and hopeless thing he was considering. And then I went looking for you, thinking you would be grateful to me for my trouble."

"But if that was last night, why did you wait so long to tell me?"

"See here now, Mr. Peebles, I don't like all this cross-examination. Is not the important thing the fact that I did seek you out and have relayed this information to you? I should think you would find it most useful."

"Unless you can tell me the man's name and where he might be found, it is of no use at all. Certainly not twenty-five pounds worth. I could enter a complaint to my lawyer about your attempt to extort more money. Or I could inform the authorities that you harbor knowledge of an American privateer on this island."

Weasel winced at the thought of what might happen if word of his duplicity should spread. No longer would he receive assignments from other lawyers. And there would be no way he could avoid telling the authorities of his knowledge. So he quickly changed his tack.

"I should not like a report of my attempt to lend you further assistance to get out any more than you might wish to advertise your desire to see this here doctor shipped off to England as fast as possible so you can get on with your business here. Now, it is not for me to inquire into the motives of my clients. And the last thing I would wish is for said clients to mistrust my own motives. And so I make you this proposition. You pay me ten pounds here and now on the spot, and the other fifteen when I can divine the name and full identity of the American gentleman, together with where he might be found. What you do with the information is your business, so long as you leave my name out of it. Now, is that fair, or is it not?"

Realizing he had been outmaneuvered for the moment, Chester grudgingly doled out ten pounds.

"There it is. You said yesterday that the prisoners will be closely guarded until they are aboard that transport tomorrow."

"Indeed they will be."

"And this American is aware of that fact?"

"I believe that to be the case."

"Very well. I must return to my business. I will leave it to you to find out the name of this American conspirator, whereupon you shall receive an additional fifteen pounds. Is there a less public place than this where we can meet, and at what time? The sooner the better, and not a word of this to anyone."

The threat Chester had made, to report him to one of his lawyer clients or expose him to the authorities, had upset Weasel so much that he had not noticed Barineau watching the doorway of the Seahorse from across the street as he and Chester left the tavern.

Ross McFadden still slept in his room upstairs, leaving it to Mollie to serve his early afternoon customers.

She approached Barineau as soon as he was seated inside the Seahorse. "What will you be 'aving today, sir?"

"A glass of Madeira. Oh, by the way, the two gentlemen who just left. I don't suppose you know them, do you?"

"The skinny, dark bloke is Weasel Cuthbert. Everyone knows him."

"And the other gentleman, the well-dressed one wearing green spectacles?"

"Why, 'e's an H'american gentleman what is staying 'ere as a guest along with a Swedish seafaring gentleman."

"And his name is?"

"'E ain't said 'is name to me, not being what you would term a friendly gentleman. 'Owever, I did 'ear the Swedish fellow, Captain Olaffsen, call 'im Mr. Peoples, I believe it was. Mr. McFadden could tell you 'is name."

"No, no, it is not important. Don't trouble him."

When Molly returned with a glass of Madeira, her customer had disappeared, leaving a shilling on the table.

# 4

By midafternoon, a light cover of clouds had drifted high over Bermuda. The air had grown deathly still and hot. Banana tits and other birds had stopped singing, and dogs and cattle were acting restless. Swells still pounded against the eastern shore.

Down by the docks, Chester Peebles was lost in thought as Captain Olaffsen continued to complain about the delay in buying a cargo and carrying it back to Boston.

"Ain't you listening to what I am saying, Peebles?"

"Yes, of course. But tell me, Captain. If I had certain information of interest to the authorities of this island about an enemy of the British, as an American it would be awkward for me to relay that information personally, would it not?"

"What you talking about? You been acting nervous like a cat about this whole business. I see other Yankees here buying up stuff as fast as it comes up for auction. What is your matter?"

". . . Whereas, if you knew the name and whereabouts of such an enemy of the British, being a citizen of a neutral country, you could divulge this information with impunity. Perhaps even collect a reward."

"What means this impunity?"

"Let me explain. There is a lot I have not felt free to tell you about my affairs. Now, it appears that I must."

Across the square, Barineau stood under a tree observing the pair. They seemed to be arguing. The larger man was shaking his head. The slighter chap was gesturing with his hands and talking rapidly.

Barineau drew his watch from his pocket, then turned and walked rapidly toward St. Peter's Church.

Weasel Cuthbert sat with his back against the tomb, out of sight from the church or the street. He did not like the ugly turn his scheme had taken. He had disliked Chester Peebles from the first, and the American's threats frightened him. Perhaps the best thing would be to "weasel" the name from the other American. Ah, here he came. Now the trick would be to extract both the man's name and additional money in exchange for what he knew of Peebles's interest, then relay that information to Peebles, collect his additional fifteen pounds, and, with his pocket full of money, wash his hands of this entire affair.

"Ah, Captain . . . what did you say your name was again?"

"I did not say. Does anyone know you are meeting me here?"

Weasel was taken aback by the abrupt tone.

"Of course not."

"You are sure?"

The way the American stared into his eyes made Weasel uncomfortable.

"Why should anyone know such a thing?"

"Why, indeed? Well, what have you to tell me? Have you discovered a way I can help my friend?"

"I can't do that, but I do have information that may be of great interest to you."

"Let's hear it."

"I would have to have another ten pounds."

"Consider it done. Let's hear what you have."

"There is another gentleman from America here wanting to know about Lovejoy Martin and when he is to be sent off to England."

"Really? And what would the name of this person be?"

Weasel did not like the American's half smile or his intense scrutiny.

"I would have to see your ten pounds before I could divulge that information."

"Then let me guess his name. It is Chester Peebles, is it not? He hails from Philadelphia, and he is staying at the Seahorse. Don't shake your head. Your eyes tell me that I am right, as do mine, for I saw you talking to him barely an hour ago. I followed you to the Seahorse, you see."

"Look here . . ." Weasel said as he started to rise.

Barineau shoved him back down against the wall of the tomb, knelt, and drew a dagger from his belt. Placing the point of the weapon against Weasel's Adam's apple, he growled, "You are playing a dangerous game, young fellow. If you want to leave this graveyard alive, tell me everything you have told Chester Peebles about me. Don't lie, man."

Weasel shuddered as the dagger's point pressed against his throat. Sweat poured down his face. He gasped for breath.

"I did not tell him your name."

"Of course you didn't. I have taken care to conceal it. But you told him someone was here looking for his brother."

"His brother? He never said it was his brother. Why did he go to all the trouble of investigating where his own brother was being held if he wasn't going to help him?"

Still holding the dagger against Weasel's throat with one hand, Barineau used the other to draw a pouch of gold coins from his waistband.

"They call you Weasel, I understand."

"But my real name is Le Roi."

"Very well, Le Roi Cuthbert, I will give you a choice from which you cannot weasel. You can die here with your throat cut, or you can earn enough money to keep you in luxury for a long while."

"It won't do you any good to kill me."

"But it will give me a good deal of satisfaction. And then I will seek out Chester Peebles and deal with him in the same way."

"Would anyone have to know?"

"I would have no reason to tell anyone."

"And how much money is in that bag?"

In Hamilton, a company of soldiers had been ready since dawn to escort the American prisoners on their march north across the chief Bermudian island to be ferried over to St. George and bedded down for the night on Hen Island. They did not get started until late in the morning, however. Neither their company commander nor naval Lieutenant Wittenstall had been in any condition for an early morning start, having been up drinking at the Blue Moon until after midnight. Nor did either feel well enough to march or even ride a horse, although the army captain had a steed at his disposal. Wittenstall had hired a man with a horse and buggy to haul himself, the captain of the soldiers, and his "good friend Dr. Martin" up to the ferry crossing to St. George.

It was an odd assortment of humanity that trudged along in the merciless Bermuda heat: the buggy leading the way, with the captain's saddled horse tied behind, followed by a squad of British soldiers, then three hundred surly American sailors flanked by other soldiers bearing loaded muskets with fixed bayonets, and an entire platoon bringing up the rear.

The livery stable man, a mulatto with kinky, reddish hair, had trouble controlling his horse.

"He ain't usually so fractious. It do be dis weather."

"What about the weather?" Lovejoy asked.

"Ain't natural. De air do be too still. And listen to dat surf. Animals, they knows when heavy weather a'coming."

Both officers slept, leaving Lovejoy, who rode in the seat beside the driver, to ponder his fate. He had been disturbed at having to leave several very sick prisoners back aboard the *Argus*. He had left medicine behind for them. Wittenstall had permitted him to bring along his medical bag and had written a letter for Lovejoy to present to the captain of the transport.

"I am introducing you as the best doctor I have ever known. And I put in a good word for your assistant, Vanstory. Perhaps they will give you better treatment on your way over."

"Bad treatment or good, it is all the same to me, Lieutenant. They might as well throw me overboard. My life is ruined."

"Never say such a thing. Look here, give me the name of your fiancée's father, and I will write and tell him what a grand service you have provided. Let him know that you are worth his daughter's waiting for. She'll still be there when this war is over. Mark my words, she will."

Lovejoy declined the offer to write but did pocket the letter. Wittenstall really had treated him decently during the three months of his imprisonment. He looked over his shoulder. Despite the lurching of the buggy, the captain still slept, but Wittenstall had awakened and was uncorking a bottle of rum.

"Care for a dram?" he said, holding out the bottle.

"No thank you, Lieutenant. And I suggest you go easy on drinking in all this heat."

When he looked back a few minutes later, the lieutenant had fallen into an even deeper sleep. Lovejoy's assistant, the loyal Zeb, who marched along directly behind the buggy, held up his thumb and winked.

Barineau was a skillful interrogator. After using Weasel's belt to tie his hands behind him, he drew from the little man a full account of his investigations from the time the lawyer gave him his instructions. He pretended not to understand certain points and ran him through his story once again.

"Tell me again how you gained the confidence of this Lieutenant . . . what did you say his name was?"

"Wittenstall. I told you that already. It was at the Blue Moon in Hamilton. Publican there said he come in every evening. I offered to buy him a drink."

"And Chester Peebles. Why were you so surprised when I let it slip that he is a brother of Lovejoy Martin?"

"I told you. He acted like he wanted the man sent off to England. Look, it is hot out here. Can't you put that knife away and untie my hands?"

"In due course. Now tell me once more, and no lies this time, you are to meet Chester Peebles where and at what time?"

# 5

By the time the ragtag procession of American prisoners and their British guards reached the ferry landing over to St. George's Island, it was late in the day. Fitful winds arose to sting the Americans' legs with sand, then died away and sprang up from a fresh direction. The surf continued to pound, and whitecaps speckled the ocean's surface.

The prisoners had to be ferried across the narrow inlet in groups of about thirty. The British army captain had recovered from his hangover somewhat but remained in a foul mood. He crossed on the first boat with his horse and a squad of soldiers. Leaving it to his lieutenant to oversee the ferry crossing, he rode ahead to St. George to alert the transport captain that his passengers were approaching.

As the captain neared the outskirts of St. George, Barineau stepped onto the road and held up his hand. In his best imitation of a Bermudian accent, he asked, "Pardon me, Captain, but would you be knowing where I might find a doctor? We have a very ill person here who requires immediate attention."

"Is it Queenie?"

"Yes, as a matter of fact."

"Look, man, I haven't time to talk to you. Queenie should know where to go for a doctor, I should think."

"Queenie is too desperately ill to talk, I fear. I must get help for her."

"Tell you what you do. We are marching some American prisoners up from Hamilton. There is a buggy carrying a navy lieutenant and an American doctor. See if they can help you."

"Would that be Lieutenant Wittenstall?"

"It would."

"And the doctor's name?"

"Damn if I know. Now turn loose my horse. I must get to the docks before night falls."

"You have been most helpful. Would you tell me your name?"

"Captain Freemantle."

Barineau thanked the officer and reentered Queenie's little cottage. She lay in her bed with her hands and feet bound and a gag in her mouth.

Barineau brought her a glass of watered rum.

"I will loosen your gag and give you this, if you promise not to cry out. One peep out of you, though, and I will be forced to use this."

He brandished his dagger.

"You understand?"

Queenie nodded.

He held the glass while she gulped down the grog.

"Who are you?" she gasped after she had swallowed the last drop.

"I told you. I am a friend of Weasel's."

"Honestly, some of you gentlemen do have peculiar habits, but I am a broad-minded girl and I know how it is with sailors. I just want you to go ahead. Some of me regulars'll be coming by tonight. Want me to talk dirty or tie you up, spank you, or what? Weasel's to be here at six, and you ain't even took off your clothes."

"No, I am not interested in that."

"Do you mean to rob me?"

"I am not after your money. In fact, I shall leave a substantial sum when my business here is done."

Queenie's clients had made many strange demands of her, but this man was beginning to worry her. The tied hands and feet she could understand, but why the gag? At the sight of the coins the man left on her dresser, she relaxed and waited to see what came next.

"You say Weasel recommended me?"

"He recommended you most highly. Don't struggle. I won't hurt you, but I must replace this gag."

Barineau did not answer the first knock at Queenie's door. He waited until a voice called, "Cuthbert? Are you in there?"

"Aye," Barineau replied softly.

"Do you have the information?"

"The information, sir?"

"The name of the fellow. Come on, man. You said you would find out who he is and where he can be found. Open up, I say."

Chester stopped in midsentence as the door opened.

"Look here. Where is Cuthbert?"

Barineau seized his lapel.

"In here, quick. We have everything you want to know."

Once inside the dim interior, it was too late for Chester. Within minutes, Barineau had him bound and lying on the bed beside a now thoroughly mystified Queenie. Barineau stood over him with dagger in hand.

"See here. What is your game?" Chester whimpered.

"You wanted to know who seeks the release of your brother."

Chester dared not deny it.

"So, look closely at me, Chester Peebles. I am your man. And let me tell you this: I may or may not leave this island with Lovejoy Martin, but this much is certain: if I do not, you will not leave Bermuda alive yourself. Do you understand?"

Again, Chester nodded, then trembled and grimaced.

Barineau wrinkled his nose and said, "Oh dear me, Queenie, I am sure our guest did not mean to commit such an indiscretion, and on your nice clean bed, too. Don't worry, Peebles. You can clean up the mess in your trousers later, and you can pay our hostess for the trouble of washing her sheets. Now, let's get down to business. Here you are, making inquiries about your brother but not lifting a finger to win his release. So, why have you come to Bermuda?"

By the time the buggy bearing Wittenstall and Lovejoy reached the vicinity of Queenie's cottage, the sun was setting behind a greenish-gray cloud bank. Fearing the embarrassment Wittenstall would suffer if he showed up drunk, Lovejoy tried without success to arouse the lieutenant from his stupor.

The British soldiers urged the American prisoners, as they stepped off the ferry, to "step lively if you don't want a bayonet up your arse."

On the road outside Queenie's cottage, a sergeant stopped the buggy.

"Which of you is the American doctor?"

The driver pointed to Lovejoy.

"Captain Freemantle says there is a desperately ill woman in there and I am to let you attend to her, but mind you, no dawdling. And don't think to slip away. Two men will be guarding the back door, and I'll be here at the front."

Puzzled, Lovejoy dismounted from the buggy with his medical kit and motioned for Zeb to follow him.

By that time, Barineau had gagged Chester as well as Queenie. It took a moment for the confused Lovejoy to recognize Barineau. Before he could cry out, his friend had put a hand over his mouth and whispered in his ear.

"I don't believe it," Lovejoy said.

Holding a candle, he stood beside the bed and looked into the terrified eyes of his half brother while Barineau told him all that he had wrung from Weasel.

At the end of the recitation, Lovejoy motioned for Barineau to remove Chester's gag.

"Ah, dear brother, what would your Rosalind say if she knew you were in bed with a harlot? Oh, I beg your pardon, miss. Perhaps I should ask what your mother might say if she knew you were entertaining a lowlife, conniving villain in what undoubtedly is a respectable establishment."

"This is not funny, Lovejoy," Chester managed through chattering teeth.

"Neither is being held captive on an overcrowded, fetid prison hulk. Nor is being hauled off to Dartmoor Prison."

"You brought all this on yourself. It is not my place to bail you out of your scrapes."

"Nor is it your place to block requests for my ransom. You wrote to Bledsoe about Megan Jenkins and you also wrote to Lieutenant Wittenstall about me. Don't bother lying. I saw both messages. So, why are you here?"

"I thought I might be of some help. I naturally made inquiries thinking there could be some way to appeal to your captors. There was no way to raise your ransom, you see."

Lovejoy snorted. "The tone of your reply made it seem you were washing your hands of me, actually encouraging the British to send me off to England."

"That was just a bluff. After all, I did come out here. Please, Lovejoy. Stop this foolish business and let us discuss the matter as brothers should."

Barineau took Lovejoy aside. "He is lying. He told the lawyer he wanted to consult with him about a serious business matter but only after you were gone."

"Then what do you think his game is?"

While they conferred, Chester's mind worked furiously. Until Lovejoy appeared, he really had feared for his life at the hands of Barineau, whom he had never met. But whatever Lovejoy's faults, he was no murderer. So, embarrassing as his situation seemed, he assumed that he was in no physical danger. He always had the option of revealing the fact that he had letters of credit for fifty thousand dollars sewn in his jacket lining.

At that point, the sergeant guarding the front of the cottage knocked at the door and yelled, "What's taking so long in there? We got to get all these prisoners to the transport before nightfall."

"Don't dare come in," Lovejoy called back. "I think she may have the plague. I need a bit more time."

At the sound of the British voice, Chester's hopes brightened. He called out, "Help! They are . . ."

In an instant, Barineau's hand was clamped over his mouth. In another, the gag had been jammed back in place. The moment in which Chester could have produced the ransom and gained both his own freedom and Lovejoy's had passed.

Barineau and Lovejoy frantically reviewed their options. While Barineau held the point of his dagger at Chester's throat, Lovejoy and Zeb mixed a tincture of opium and brandy from their medical kit. The gag out of his mouth, Chester sputtered and tried to spit the fiery liquid out, but with the resourceful Zeb holding his nose, he had to swallow his medicine to keep from strangling.

Within a few minutes, the concoction had rendered Chester senseless. All anxiety and strength drained from him.

Again the sergeant was hammering at the door.

"It is starting to rain out here. What is taking you so long?"

"We are just cleaning up the mess," Zeb replied. "Give us another minute or two." Barineau and Lovejoy stripped off Chester's coat and dressed him in Lovejoy's own long linen duster. Lovejoy clapped his own cap on Chester's head while Zeb held him on his feet.

Outside, carrying Lovejoy's medical bag in one hand, with the other firmly grasping the barely conscious Chester's arm, Zeb said to the sergeant, "Here, help me assist him back into the carriage."

His hand protecting his eyes from the lashing rain, the sergeant peered through the dark.

"What's wrong with him?"

"He had a fainting spell. Smell in there is awful. Nearly passed out meself. We did the poor woman all the good we could. There, there, Dr. Martin, see if the fresh air don't help. That's it, just squeeze right in there with the lieutenant."

"All right, Yank, you can just get down from that buggy and walk like the others," the sergeant said to Zeb.

The plan had been for the prisoners to be marched and ferried up from Hamilton and onto Hen Island, a sort of mudflat in the St. George's harbor, to be kept there overnight for processing, but old Bermudian hands had advised the captain of the transport that all signs pointed to the approach of a very serious storm and that he would be smart to clear out of the harbor before it struck. Therefore, plans for the prisoners to be housed overnight on Hen Island were changed. They were to be taken directly to the dock and put aboard so that the transport could depart at first light the next day.

With torches illuminating the dock, soldiers shoved the rain-soaked, dispirited prisoners up the gangway onto the quarterdeck of the transport. There the captain stood, holding his nose at the smell of the long unwashed Americans, while his first lieutenant checked off the names of the prisoners against his manifest list.

Ignoring complaints of thirst and hunger, the transport's contingent of marines herded the prisoners down into a hold and into their bunks.

The inventory had been nearly completed when the buggy bearing Lieutenant Wittenstall and Chester, followed closely by Zeb, rolled up to the dock.

Wittenstall had meant to wish Lovejoy a hearty farewell but was only recovered enough from the rum to clap the man beside him on the arm and slip a small purse into the pocket of his duster.

"Thanks for everything, old man . . . good luck to you," he mumbled.

Before he could say more, Zeb was lifting Chester from the buggy and propelling him up the gangway.

"And is this worthy our American doctor friend? What is wrong with him?"

"Was took ill on the way up."

The captain made a face.

"Seems to have shit his trousers. Has he been ill long? Looks to have lost weight from the way his coat hangs on him."

"We have not been overfed these past few months. And he has been somewhat overworked."

"Is he a competent doctor?"

"None better, sir."

"And yourself?"

"Why, sir, I am Zebulon Vanstory, who has been serving as his assistant."

"Yes, there is your name. We'll put you up in the sick bay, both of you. Hope your man recovers enough to lend a hand on our trip over. Wouldn't give me a proper surgeon for the trip home. Ask the bosun for rags and water and see what you can do to clean your doctor up."

# 6

Despite her promises to the contrary, Queenie kept silent about her experiences of that evening only until noon the following day, when a fellow prostitute dropped by to share a cup of tea and to gossip.

"Ah, Rosie, I thought I had seen and done everything in this here profession, but let me tell you, I never went through nothing like what I did last night. First off, this older man shows up in late afternoon saying he was sent by Weasel Cuthbert. Wanted to play a game, he said. You know, tie me arms and me legs, which was all right so long as he understood it would cost him extra. But then he goes and stuffs a rag in me mouth and waves a knife under me nose.

"Next thing I knows, another gentleman, all elegant dressed he were and wearing green eyeglasses, he shows up and the first gentleman knocks him about, ties him up, and dumps him on the bed beside me and threatens to kill him if he didn't answer his questions.

"As if that wasn't enough, I hears English voices outside, from what I took to be soldiers, and two other men comes in, Americans they were as well, and they joins in abusing the gentleman what was lying beside me all tied up.

"Ah, Queenie, I says to myself, you should have joined a regular house where there is a madam to protect you from situations such as this instead of striking out on your own. But with the gag in me mouth I could say nothing. Anyway, these last two fellows, they forced the gentleman beside me to swallow some sort of potion. Then with soldiers outside shouting in for them to complete their business, they strips the jacket from the one poor gentleman, who was quite overcome with the drink what they had poured in him, and they dresses him in this sort of long white coat, and one of them takes him out into the rain and I seen no more of them two.

"The first gentleman, the one what tied me up, and the one he called Lovejoy—ah, he was ever so handsome, too—they stayed and argued for a long time about what to do. Stayed until near midnight they did, looking out the window and talking in low voices. All the while I hear rain falling on the roof and thinks I would die from the need to relieve me poor bladder.

"At long last, they untied me, and I must say they treated me as gentle as ever I might wish. Gave me extra money with the understanding that I would say nothing of what had took place. I was ready to give them the rough side of my tongue, but they were ever so nice and generous that I thanked them for their consideration."

"What happened then?" Rosie asked.

"They bundled themselves up and went off into the rain while I got to my chamber pot as fast as I could. I haven't seen hide nor hair of them since, nor of Weasel neither. And this storm seems to be getting worse, don't you think?"

Lovejoy and Barineau had to feel their way along in the rainy dark into St. George. Fearing that Chester's identity would be discovered when the opium-brandy tincture wore off, they dared not remain at Queenie's cottage until morning.

They huddled at the doorway of the Seahorse.

"We couldn't go in there even if the door was not locked," Barineau said. "McFadden swore he would turn me in if I returned. And he has no reason to offer you protection, either. So follow me around back."

He scratched at the door of the room that Mollie, the barmaid, occupied in a lean-to at the rear. Getting no answer, he knocked softly at first and then harder and harder.

"Oo's there?" Mollie asked sleepily.

"Open up and see for yourself."

"You are taking a big risk," Lovejoy muttered.

"Better than drowning out here in this rain."

Once the door was open and the candlelight had shone on their faces, she said, "Why, hit's the gentleman what was asking about Weasel Cuthbert. You left without your glass of wine, you did. Do come in out of the rain, my dears."

Although Mollie would have been willing to share her bed, Lovejoy and Barineau spent the rest of the night on the floor.

The next morning dawned with a curious yellowish glow. The rain had let up, but the wind had freshened, sending low-level clouds scudding overhead from the southeast.

"I was glad to give you gentlemen temporary shelter from the weather last night," Mollie said, "but unfortunately, this room ain't big enough for three persons. Besides which, Mr. McFadden would kill me if 'e knowed I was 'arboring unknown persons."

"Let us stay until noon to give us a chance to figure out something," Lovejoy said. "That is not asking too much, is it?"

"I suppose not. Just keep your voices low. Now I must go and punch up the fire and start my day. Oh, dear . . ."

She picked up the coat Lovejoy had taken from Chester.

"This lovely jacket is all wet, and hit do look as if you 'as split the seam down the back. 'Ere, I'll take it in to dry by the kitchen fire. And when the work let's up, I'll sew up that split."

"I am afraid I have got you out of the frying pan and now we're both in the fire," Barineau said after she had left.

"Anything is better than going aboard that transport."

"You know as well as I that our safety is only temporary. Your brother should have recovered by now."

"Who else knows you stayed here besides this tavern wench who seems so much taken with you?"

"Only McFadden."

"What about that chap the lawyer sent to investigate my whereabouts on Chester's behalf?"

"My God!" Barineau said as he smote his forehead. "I clean forgot about him. I really should see about him, but I dare not go out in broad daylight."

Weasel had already been frightened as never before in his life by Barineau's rough questioning at knifepoint. He would have gladly forfeited his fee from the lawyer and the considerable sums he had extorted from both Chester Peebles and Barineau, anything to be free of this American madman. He really had told Barineau everything he knew, had told him twice, even three times over, until the truth had been completely wrung out of him.

"Please sir," Weasel had said as he cowered beside the ancient tomb, "you know all that I know. Cannot you now give me my money and let me go free?"

Ignoring him, Barineau looked at the date on the tomb and saw that the last burial would have taken place a century before. He gripped a corner of the stone cover and, using all his strength, lifted it an inch and slid it over to create a two-foot opening. Inside rested two cedar coffins, still in good repair.

"What are you going to do?" Weasel asked.

"You say Chester Peebles is to come to this Queenie's house at six o'clock?"

Weasel nodded.

"Very well. If he does, and all goes well from my point of view, I will return, free you, and pay the agreed amount for your information."

"What do you mean, free me?"

"I will show you."

With that, Barineau seized the little man and, despite his frantic writhing, crammed him down into the tomb and slid the cover back far enough to leave a tiny opening along one side. He listened briefly to the muffled cries from within the vault, then backed away several feet and listened again. Satisfied that no one in the church could hear Weasel, he had squared his shoulders and set out for Queenie's cottage.

All this had taken place some twenty hours before. By now, Weasel, whose last religious involvement had been at his christening back in a

London Cheapside parish church, had made enough vows to God that, if all were fulfilled, he would have been eligible for sainthood.

Had he been less frail, he might have forced off the cover of the tomb. But he was nowhere near as strong as Barineau. He had long ago given up crying for help. He could only lie atop the coffins, listening to the rain beating on his sepulchre and waiting for light to appear through the sliver of air space Barineau had left him. It was the longest night of his life.

That same next morning, the captain of the British transport arose early and noted with satisfaction that the rain had abated. He ordered all hands to fall out and prepare to depart from Bermuda. He ordered all lines cast off and enough sail raised to shift the transport away from the dock, then turned the helm over to the pilot, who had been hired to guide the ship through the intricate passage leading from St. George's harbor to the ocean.

"Now, Captain," the pilot said, "it ain't my place to advise a sailor such as yourself, but if this was my ship, soon as I gets you clear of Governor's Island, at which point I shall take my little ketch back to land, why, sir, I would bend on every scrap of sail and head off to the northeast as fast as you can. We are in for a big blow here, and you would do well to get clear of land and out of the storm's path."

Annoyed at the pilot's presumptuousness, the captain said, "I have been in storms before, my good man."

"I'd say that if you had ever been in a real hurricane with reefs nearby, with all respect, you wouldn't be here to tell of it."

The captain was wondering whether to put the pilot in his place when his first lieutenant interrupted.

"Captain, that American doctor is making a terrible row down in the sick bay. Like a madman, he is. Claims he is not a doctor at all. Some cock-and-bull story of having been drugged and kidnapped."

"His name was on the manifest, was it not?"

"Aye, sir. And the papers on his person identify him clearly as Doctor . . . let's see . . . Lovejoy Martin. And there was a letter in his coat pocket, addressed to yourself."

The captain took the letter. "What is wrong with the chap?"

"His assistant says he has been having what he calls hallucinations but insists that he is a competent medical man. Says the poor man may have been dosing himself with opium."

"Keep him locked away for the present. Later, perhaps, some good fresh sea air will restore his sanity. Now let's see what this letter is all about."

The captain hurriedly read the note of introduction written by Wittenstall and handed it to his lieutenant.

"Poor fellow. Rich family and they refused to pay his ransom. No wonder he has lost his mental balance. Well then, his previous gaoler thought highly of him and found him useful. We shall show him every kindness and trust that he will come around enough in a day or so to be of use to this ship."

He turned to the pilot. "Shall we let you off here? You'll have no trouble getting your ketch back to harbor, will you?"

Business at the Seahorse opened slowly that day as ships' officers saw to battening down their hatches and double-securing their lines as a precaution against the storm that all the old Bermuda hands said was bearing down on the islands. By late morning, a light but steady rain was falling amid sounds of the distant roll of thunder and flashes of lightning. As the crews completed their tasks, the officers began filtering into the Seahorse, flinging off their oilskins, and demanding their grog.

A weary Mollie returned to her room that afternoon.

"It is a regular madhouse in there," she said. "One of our guests, a Swedish gentleman, 'as been kicking up a fuss about 'is companion, an American gentleman what disappeared yesterday afternoon and ain't come back yet. Very disturbed, 'e is."

"What sort of American gentleman?" Barineau asked.

"Why the same what you was asking about: Mr. Peoples, I told you, only I got the name wrong. Hit's Chester Peebles. Captain Olaffsen fears 'is friend may have met with foul play."

"What is the Swedish chap saying exactly?" Barineau asked.

"Says 'is friend was to meet Weasel Cuthbert out at Queenie Foster's house. Weasel ain't been seen since yesterday neither. If you asks me, I shouldn't worry about them two, not if they are with Queenie. She would look after them, let me tell you, she would, as long as they can pay."

"What is the Swedish fellow doing?"

"Why, 'e's on 'is way in all this rain, gone on foot out to Queenie's to inquire. Oh, by the way, Doctor, here is your coat, all nice and dry. I sewed up the seam. You really ought to get yourself a proper-fitting garment. What's that? Captain Olaffsen's room? Why hit's the first one on the right at the top of the stairs. 'Im and that Mr. Peebles shares it. Stay another night? Well, seeing as hit's raining so 'ard, I suppose there is no 'arm. Now, hit's back to work for me."

As soon as she was gone, Barineau looked at Lovejoy.

"I know what you are thinking. But I have never been upstairs, besides which, McFadden knows me. It would be a great risk."

"Remaining here and doing nothing is a greater risk. Here, give me your jacket, Pierre, and your cap as well. I would only burst the seam of Chester's coat again."

Lovejoy ducked out of Mollie's room, into the drenching rain. By the time he reached the front of the Seahorse, he was soaking wet. The common room was full of ships' officers who, having done all they could to secure their vessels against the storm, were sitting about smoking, drinking rum, and playing cards.

Drawing the collar of Barineau's coat up around his chin, Lovejoy sidled through the crowd, keeping out of McFadden's line of sight, until he reached the stairway. Taking two steps at a time, he mounted to the upper floor and seized the handle of the first door on his right. To his immense relief, he found that Olaffsen, in his haste to get to Queenie's, had not locked his door. Inside the room, however, Lovejoy found the Swede's small sea trunk padlocked. Using Barineau's dagger, he jimmied off the hasp and opened the lid.

Despite his concern over the disappearance of Chester Peebles, Captain Olaffsen was too cautious a seaman not to have followed the example of his nautical peers in preparing his ship for the onrushing hurricane. By the time he had blundered through the rain to Queenie's little house, her friend had left and she had gone back to bed, still puzzling over her experiences of the previous night and terrified by the thunder and lightning. At Olaffsen's knock, she hid the coins left by Barineau and went to the door.

Olaffsen had a hearty way with women, which many found appealing. A combination of flattery and bribery quickly made Queenie forget her promise afresh to Barineau to keep silent about the episode of the previous evening.

"And they carried the little man away, you say?"

"After they had took his coat and put the white one on him. Yes, that is what they done."

"And you are sure they were Americans?"

"As sure as I am that it is raining outside. Look sir, I would be more than happy for you to remain with me. To tell you the truth, I am frightened of storms, and it would be a comfort to me. You needn't pay me a cent."

Olaffsen flung a coin on her bed anyway and plunged back into the storm. Leaning against the wind, he stumbled along to the office of the harbormaster in St. George. After much pleading, he persuaded the assistant there to check the manifest of the prisoners who had gone aboard the transport the previous evening.

"Martin. Lovejoy? He was being held for a special ransom, which wasn't paid. He is on his way to England and Dartmoor."

His mind churning over this intelligence, plus what Chester had belatedly told him, Olaffsen slogged back to the Seahorse to demand whether Chester Peebles had returned in his absence.

"We've not seen hide nor hair of him since yesterday," McFadden said. "I told you that before."

Another of the Seahorse's guests overheard this.

"You are talking about the chap who shares your room? Why, if my ears did not mistake me, I thought I heard him knocking about in there not more than an hour ago."

Olaffsen turned and raced up the stairs and into his room. That is when he discovered the broken hasp on his trunk and the disappearance of Chester's portmanteau.

In Mollie's room, Barineau went over the papers Lovejoy had removed from Olaffsen's trunk and Chester's portmanteau.

"So that is what they are up to. Chester has come to buy up contraband and haul it back to Boston in a Swedish-registered ship."

"Which actually is owned by speculators whom I take to be Boston Federalists. But there is no sign of money in his bag."

Not realizing that the prison transport had already sailed, with Chester aboard, the two men agonized over their next step.

"We dare not remain here. Would Tradnick not shelter us? Maybe even slip us off the island?"

"I wouldn't know where to find him, especially in this storm.

Anyway, I promised we'd make no more trouble for the poor man."

"Surely, they must have discovered Chester's identity by now. They will come looking for us as soon as this storm lets up."

"If I had these papers back in Philadelphia, I could cook his goose. Oh, I wish we could find a small craft and slip away from here."

"In weather like this, and with just the two of us?"

They were still debating at nightfall, when a distraught Mollie returned.

"Oh, there is a mighty row going on out there in the common room. Captain Olaffsen says 'is trunk has been broke into. 'E's accusing Mr. McFadden, myself, and the other guests. Like a wild man, 'e is. Thinks 'is friend, Mr. Peebles, 'as been shipped off to England on that transport, and I was wondering . . ."

"Transport?" Lovejoy interrupted.

"Yes. Hit left 'arbor early this morning."

Barineau raised his eyebrows and grinned at Lovejoy.

"You are certain about the transport, Mollie?"

"If you don't believe me, go ask the pilot what directed them from the 'arbor. Just came in and is treating 'is friends to grog. 'Eard 'im telling them about an American doctor as was acting like a madman on the ship as 'e was leaving 'er."

Lovejoy seized Barineau's hands and clapped him on the shoulder. "This is too good to be true."

His face fell, however, as Mollie continued.

"Anyway, Captain Olaffsen says there is a couple of Americans abroad on this island that is behind 'is friend's disappearance. Wants the militia turned out to catch them. I 'ates to ask you gentlemen, but I wonder if you two h'ain't behind this business."

# 7

Wondering at the long absence of Mollie, McFadden braved the lashing rain to nail down the shutters on the Seahorse. The lightning flashes occurred so quickly that one might have read a newspaper in his common room, where, afraid to venture into the furious weather, his customers sat throughout the night, either sleeping or drinking themselves into a stupor.

In the midst of such a storm, Olaffsen had given up hope of turning out the militia to apprehend the two Americans he now realized were behind both Peebles's disappearance and the ransacking of his room. An empty rum bottle beside him, he slept facedown on his bed throughout the night, oblivious to the shrieking wind and crashing thunder.

It had required all of Lovejoy's eloquence and promises of a handsome tip to persuade Mollie to remain in her room after voicing her suspicions. Whatever notions she might have had of reporting the presence of the two Americans were soon driven out by her terror at the howling wind and the constant crash of thunder and flashes of lightning. She huddled in a corner with Lovejoy's arms about her until, exhausted, she fell asleep.

The wind and rain died away briefly as the eye of the hurricane passed. Mollie slept on, while Barineau and Lovejoy consulted in whispers about what to do now that they knew that the transport had departed with Chester aboard and that his purpose in coming to Bermuda had been to profiteer, not to save Lovejoy.

After the eye of the storm had passed, the winds resumed from a fresh direction. Mollie stirred in her sleep. Barineau said, "It is settled then. That is what we will do."

"Yes. The place will be in a turmoil by morning. Perhaps we can slip away in all the confusion. Somehow we will find a way to get off this island. It is either that or hang."

There had been worse hurricanes in Bermuda's history, most notably that of October 1780, and even more violent storms would occur in future years, but the one that swept over the islands on the late afternoon and night of August 3, 1813, outdid most of the others in devastation because of the large number of ships crowded into the St. George's harbor.

The transport carrying the American prisoners had got well clear of land by the time the vicious winds struck. Those vessels whose captains, such as Olaffsen, had heeded the warnings of native Bermudians to double up their lines and put out extra anchors came through the ordeal best. Fewer pains had been taken with the dozens of captured American vessels, however, and most of these ended up as wrecks against the shore.

The harbormaster's office, many of the warehouses, and some of the homes in St. George lost their roofs. Hundreds of thousands of dollars worth of captured cargoes were ruined by the soaking rain. The damage was less severe down in Hamilton, but the surging sea washed out many of the roads on the main island.

"You made me a promise, gentlemen," Mollie said the next morning. "Said you'd pay me twenty pounds and be gone by daylight."

"And you swore that you would not betray us," Lovejoy said.

"And I shan't, but you must leave before anyone sees you."

"Very well. Here, give us a kiss, Mollie," Lovejoy said.

As Barineau took his turn at embracing Mollie, Lovejoy picked up Chester's jacket and slipped his arms through the sleeves. As he tried to button it, the seam Mollie had repaired gave way.

Lovejoy removed the jacket and handed it to Barineau.

"Here, Pierre, this thing will come closer to fitting you."

Barineau took the garment and frowned at the rent down the back. He put it on and patted the sides.

"What's this?"

Mollie said, "Oh, there is some sort of stiff lining in it. Thought perhaps it were the new style of tailoring."

Barineau removed the coat and ran his fingers inside the split seam.

"What in the hell have we here?" he said, as he removed the three letters of credit, sealed in oilskin, that Chester had brought with him from Philadelphia via Boston.

Ingemar Olaffsen was neither a coward nor a fool. Thus when he was shaken awake in his room by a rough hand on his shoulder and looked up into the faces of two strange men, he did not panic. And after they had fully identified themselves and laid their case before him in urgent whispers, he squelched his initial outrage at their disruption of his plans and consulted calmly with them as to how they might work together rather than against each other.

"You say he had letters of credit sewn into his jacket?"

"Yes, but only one is available for your use. It is his own for ten thousand dollars."

"He made me to think he had much more available."

"Sorry, but two of the letters of credit must be returned. They were obtained under false pretense, we believe."

Olaffsen arose and looked out the window at the debris-laden road beside the Seahorse. He winced at the pain the sunlight caused to his eyes and head.

"And you are Peebles's brother?"

"His half brother, yes."

"You won't take it wrong if I say I did not much like him."

"Nor do I."

"And instead of paying your, what you call it, ransom? he is on his way to prison in your place. Ah, that is good."

"He brought it upon himself."

"Now, you chust tell me again what it is you want we should do to put our chestnuts in the fire together."

Barineau laughed.

"You mean pull them out, I think."

"Whatever. To me, business is business. English or American, a chestnut is a chestnut. I don't want to sail from here with a empty ship. Let's hear what you want we should do."

Once Olaffsen agreed to their plan, events moved smoothly for Lovejoy and Barineau. Amid the confusion and destruction caused by the hurricane, it was easy for the Swede to slip the two men onto his ship, whose anchors had held.

They remained there, out of sight belowdecks, while Olaffsen, using Chester's ten-thousand-dollar letter of credit, shrewdly and quickly purchased commodities packed in barrels that had escaped water damage. Even with his limited funds, he came close to filling the hold of his ship.

Olaffsen himself, at Barineau's insistence, slipped into the churchyard of St. Peter's and slid the cover off the tomb.

He laughed as he reported to his two stowaways about his mission. "Before I could give him your money, he vas out of there and gone like a cat let out of a cage. No, no, he didn't ask who I vas or nothing. Chust run off like he vas afraid I vas going to stick him in again or something. So here is back your money."

The voyage from Bermuda to Boston took only a week. Flying a Swedish flag, the ship was ignored by the lone British frigate it encountered cruising off Cape Cod.

In Boston, Lovejoy gave Barineau his power of attorney to dispose of the cargo, which they reckoned would bring at least thirty thousand dollars, half of which, as agreed, would be paid to Olaffsen for him to share with the leasers of his ship.

"I want you to take the rest of the money down to Philadelphia and put it in the hands of our family lawyer. His name is Charles Bennett. You can tell him everything. He will return the letters of credit to Amanda and Uncle Ephraim. Then I suggest you go down to Baltimore and consult with Malcolm MacKenzie. By now he may have some word of the *Flora* and how she is faring. Who knows? We could all be rich again."

"And you are hell-bent on getting back to Reading?"

"As soon as I can find a good horse and proper clothes."

"Well then, Joy, I wish you the very best. We have been through a lot together."

Lovejoy took Barineau's hand, saying, "Pierre, if I live to be a hundred I can't forget what you have done for me. It was the luckiest day of my life when I met you, next to when I met Madeline, of course."

"Of course. I hope that all will go well with you in Berks County and that I soon will be privileged to meet the beauteous Miss Richter, of whom I have heard so much."

"I don't know where or when we will be married, but nothing would please me more than for you to serve as my best man."

"Agreed. Now let's buy you a proper horse and a new suit."

# Book Three

# PART ONE

# 1

By August of 1813, America's war with the British had taken on an aspect both more promising and more dangerous. Except for the New England ports, the blockade had nearly closed down seaborne commerce and driven up the prices of imported goods. Privateers found prizes more difficult to capture, what with the enemy's now-rigid transoceanic convoy system. British vigilance prevented their getting themselves or their prizes into friendly ports. Under the stimulus of a congressional act compensating them for up to twenty-five percent of the value of destroyed merchant ships and twenty-five dollars for each captured crew member, privateers ventured farther out to sea for their prey, some all the way across the Atlantic. Others sailed far south to seize and burn small craft plying between West Indian islands. At least one audacious U.S. naval captain rounded the Horn and wrought havoc on British whalers in the Pacific.

On land, although the war along the Canadian border had not gone very well for either side, the American army was being improved and enlarged through more generous enlistment bonuses and better training and equipment. But meanwhile, Wellington's success on the Iberian Peninsula and the growing strength of the anti-Napoleonic coalition in central Europe raised the specter of veteran British reinforcements—smarting from the Yankee destruction of York, the capital of upper Canada—becoming available to tip the balance should the war not be resolved quickly in America's favor.

British efforts to capitalize on Indian grievances in the Northwest Territories had caused much distress to the American settlers in that area, but an army of tough Kentucky militiamen, led by William Henry Harrison, had crossed the Ohio River, built a strong fort on the Maumee River, and driven the redskins (led by the charismatic Shawnee chief Tecumseh) and their British officers back into Canada.

All this and more Lovejoy learned in pieces and bits as he relentlessly rode his large gray gelding for five days south from Boston, across Connecticut and lower New York State.

Both he and his steed were exhausted after a fifteen-hour ride from the Hudson River across upper New Jersey to the banks of the Delaware, where they halted at a crowded inn for the night.

After paying a stable hand to feed and water his weary horse, Lovejoy asked the tavern keeper about a bed for the night.

"Every room is took, with three to the bed. Best we can do is offer you a pallet in our loft. You'll have to sleep with twenty sailors that is staying with us for the night."

"Sailors? Here?" Lovejoy asked.

"That's right. That's them at my two common tables. On their way from New York to Lake Erie to join Perry's fleet out there."

"I am so tired I could sleep in the barn if need be. What about supper?"

"Go squeeze in with that lot at the long table and you will be served along with them."

Lovejoy seated himself beside a bearded man whose white shirt and tie set him apart from the sailors at the same table. As he waited for his bowl of stew and mug of ale to arrive, the last thing Lovejoy wanted to do was engage in yet another conversation about "Mr. Madison's war."

"Where you headed, friend?" the man asked.

"Reading."

"Where you come from?"

"Boston."

"Do you for a fact? What line of business are you in there?"

"Actually I am from Philadelphia but have been in Boston," Lovejoy replied. Then, to fend off further questions, he asked, "What about yourself?"

He soon regretted asking the question, for once started there was no stopping the fellow's flow of talk.

"I, or I should say we, for I am in charge of this gang of cutthroat riffraff, we are on our way to Lake Erie. What for? Why to assist Commodore Perry, of course."

Dog tired from five days of hard riding and occupied with the anticipation of his reunion with Madeline Richter, Lovejoy desperately wanted to eat, get a few hours of sleep, and finish the last leg of his journey to Berks County. But his stew was a long time coming, and despite his fatigue, he found much of what the fellow told him to be interesting.

The man explained that a year before, "my dear friend Daniel Dobbins," a trader from the shores of Lake Erie, had gone to Washington and persuaded President Madison and his advisors that Presque Isle would make an excellent base for a flotilla to take control of that strategic body of water. Soon thereafter, government contracts in hand, Dobbins had returned to Presque Isle and started work on two fifty-foot gunboats. Later, Commodore Isaac Chauncey, naval commander of the Great Lake region, arrived and liked what he saw so much that he authorized Dobbins to build two full-sized brigs, "near to five hundred tons each, mind you, plus two more gunboats." A twenty-seven-year-old naval officer commanding gunboats on the Rhode Island coast, Oliver Hazard Perry, wrote to Chauncey asking for a transfer and was readily appointed to see to the completion of the fleet and then command it. He had arrived the previous March with his thirteen-year-old brother and 150 seamen. In April, he had gone down to Pittsburgh to order equipment and supplies for his fleet.

"That is where I enter the picture," the man said. "I own a general store there at the fork of the Ohio and Allegheny. Dan Dobbins recommended me to Commodore Perry. Him and I hit it off so well that I volunteered to lend him a hand."

He went on to explain that hitherto the British had controlled Lake Erie with a fleet of only six small vessels.

"Our luck has improved, howsomever," the man said. "Last April, our army crossed Lake Ontario and raided York, burnt the town, and carried away a lot of valuable equipment for our fleet. What's more, we caused the British to burn a frigate what they had under construction there. Our fellows went back and hit the town again in July."

"I have heard that the British have sworn revenge for York," Lovejoy ventured as the tavern wench set his bowl of stew in front of him.

"I expect you heard that and worse, too, in Boston, which to my way of thinking we should burn to the ground to get rid of the Federalist traitors what inhabits the place."

The man plunged into a recitation of how, by capturing a British fort on the Niagara River, the American army had enabled a fleet of five small American vessels to slip into Lake Erie and join Perry's new brigs and gunboats at Presque Isle.

"You see, there is a grand harbor there, protected by a hook of land. Only drawback is this long sandbar crost the entrance, which makes it too shallow for our two big brigs to get out of the harbor. That is the bad part. The good part is it also prevents British ships from getting in at us. Here, I'll show you . . ."

Aching to be left in peace to eat his stew, Lovejoy nodded while his talkative companion scratched a rude map on the tabletop with his knife.

"Sounds as if they have you bottled up, then."

"Ah, my friend, you don't know Perry or Dan Dobbins. When I left three weeks ago, they was working on a scheme to lift the two brigs over the bar with what the Dutch call camels, which is a sort of float what you fix to the sides of your ship. Fellow named Noah Brown designed them. For all I know, they may already have did that, which is why I am in a hurry to get this bunch out there as fast as I can. Perry sent me and others off to scour the coast for sailors, he is that desperate for seasoned hands."

He leaned near to whisper in Lovejoy's ear, "This ain't the type of humanity with which a gentleman such as ourselves would normally associate, but sometimes you have to make do with what you can get."

As Lovejoy looked down the row of rudely dressed men drinking their stew directly from their bowls and talking with full mouths, he was reminded of some of his fellow captives on the prison hulk in Hamilton Harbor. They had left just over two weeks before, so they would be over halfway across the Atlantic by now. He wondered if Chester's true identity had been established, and how his own faithful medical assistant, Zeb, was faring.

"They don't seem like such a bad bunch," he said.

"You surprise me, for I can tell from your way of eating and talking, not to mention your suit, that you are a gentleman. Just what is your profession?"

"I was training for a medical career but the war cut short my studies."

He instantly regretted his remark, for the man called down the table, "Hear this, fellows. My new friend here is a doctor. Why, that is the best news I have heard in weeks."

"What do you mean?" asked a confused Lovejoy.

"Perry in particular wanted me to bring back at least one surgeon, more if I could find them. He is in desperate need of them. There would be quite a bonus in this if you was to sign up and accompany us. Here, soon as you finish let's go off in a corner. I'll make you a offer you can't afford to refuse."

"If you don't mind, I am about to drop from weariness."

"Then, first thing in the morning. I will meet you here for breakfast. Will you do that?"

"Breakfast, yes. We can talk then."

Lovejoy fell asleep almost as soon as he had taken off his shoes and stretched out on his straw pallet. He did not hear the sailors when they came clomping up the stairs, full of rum and talking at the tops of their voices.

He awoke long before they did, however, and, carrying his shoes, slipped down the stairs in his stocking feet. Without waiting for breakfast, he put on his shoes and went out to the stable, where he saddled up his horse and headed for the ferry that would carry him across the Delaware and back into Pennsylvania.

Several times during the long final day of his journey from Boston to Reading, Lovejoy nearly fell off his horse from fatigue. His mind would drift back to the horror of the British prison hulk and the terrible anxiety he had endured before and during the hurricane. To counter those troubling memories, he forced himself to imagine how it would be when he finally arrived at the Richters' great brick house in Berks County.

His poor horse could no longer manage even a trot. At the plodding rate they were going, it would be dark when he got there. He would dismount, tie his horse's reins to a porch pillar, and knock on the door.

"I have come for Madeline," he would say when Christian Richter appeared.

"Not so fast there, young fellow," Richter would reply. "I don't remember inviting you here."

"Who is there?" Mrs. Richter would call from down the hall.

"It is that Martin fellow from Philadelphia, the one what was here last Christmas and left without paying his respects."

"He has his nerve," Mrs. Richter would say. "Turn him away."

"Who is it?" Madeline would call from upstairs.

"Me, Lovejoy."

There would follow a shriek of joy and she would come racing down the stairs, past her parents and into his arms. Oblivious to the protests of the Richters, she would cover his face with kisses. He would lift her from her feet and swing her around, his arms tightly holding her.

At last the Richters would accept the inevitable and invite him, however grudgingly, into the drawing room and even serve him coffee. Revived, an adoring Madeline seated at his knee, he would offer the family his apologies and his explanation for his sudden departure and his long absence.

Lovejoy's character had undergone considerable improvement since his return from England just before the war. He did not intend to deceive the Richters permanently, yet he saw no need to tell them everywhere he had been and everything he had done all at once. No, he would say that in the course of following up on some urgent overseas commercial business of a confidential nature, he had found himself on the island of Bermuda, where the authorities had pressed him into service as a doctor aboard a British vessel tied up in the harbor. That was it.

Then, when his services were no longer needed, he had availed himself of a trading opportunity. This, he knew, would appeal to Christian Richter's instincts for gain. He had brought a shipload of scarce goods into Boston harbor. Violating Madison's latest embargo: that would speak to the old Dutchman's Federalist heart. Now, with profits in hand, he had returned to renew his request for Madeline's hand in marriage.

Of course, they did not need to know that he did not have nearly as much money as he had led them to think on his previous visit. But he would be able to finance a decent honeymoon. Later, there could well be enormous profits from the *Flora's* continuing cruise. Once he and Madeline were married and he was a rich man again, he would not give a hang whether her parents discovered the true source of his wealth.

With or without her parents' blessings, they would be married as soon as possible. He would summon Barineau to serve as his best man. Then they would go down to Philadelphia so that he could show off Madeline to his family, pay homage to his father, and work out an arrangement with lawyer Bennett about the mess Chester had caused for himself. With advice from Malcolm MacKenzie and the evidence of Chester's malfeasance in hand, there was no reason that he could not take over Martin Shipping himself and become, in time, as rich as his own father had been.

Thus his mind went round and round as his gelding plodded across Lehigh County and into Berks.

It was early evening when he reached the Richter home. He tied his horse's reins to the pillar and rapped at the door, but it was not Christian Richter who answered.

"Who is it knocking at such an hour?"

Lovejoy recognized the voice as that of Madeline's Aunt Elizabeth.

"It is Lovejoy Martin. I was here last December."

"Ach, that one. From Philadelphia you was."

"Won't you open the door? I want to see Madeline."

"She ain't here."

"Where is she then?"

"Down the road at the little house."

"What about her parents?"

"They are down there too."

"They are all down there now?"

"Ain't that what I said?"

He stumbled across the porch, untied his horse's reins, and dragged himself into the saddle.

Living in the much smaller tenant house down the road? Perhaps Christian Richter had been ruined by the collapse of flour and wheat prices, of which he had heard so much on his ride from Boston. So much the better for his own case. They would be grateful for a son-in-law with a bit of ready money plus the prospects of even more, no matter what the source of those funds.

A light shone in the front room of the little stone house. A horse and buggy were tied to a hitching rail beside the porch. Lovejoy tied up his own horse to the rail and mounted the steps at the side of the porch. Passing a lighted window, he looked inside. There she sat. In profile, her face appeared even more radiant than he had remembered it during his long nights on the prison hulk. Her hair shone with a golden glow from the lamplight. Across the room sat her mother, wearing her habitual disapproving expression.

Christian Richter was standing behind his wife's chair, his square figure blocking Lovejoy's full view of a man leaning with his elbow on the mantel.

Lovejoy had puzzled at the presence of the buggy. He assumed that the man talking to Richter was there on business. He looked again at Madeline's profile, took a deep breath, and knocked.

Holding a lamp high above his head, the man who had been leaning against the mantel answered the door.

"What can I do for you, stranger?"

"I am here to see Madeline Richter."

"What about?"

"Just tell her Lovejoy Martin is here."

The man stepped out onto the porch and closed the door behind him. "What do you want with Maddy?"

"I want to see her. I have ridden five days to get here. Please step aside and let me talk to her."

"No, you can't. You can clear out, that is what you can do."

"Who in the hell are you to be telling me to clear out? I want to see Madeline."

"I am George McFairlane. We met at the stage office, remember? I am the fellow who returned Maddy's mare to her."

"I don't give a damn who you are. Step aside so I can see her."

"Get this straight, mister whatever you call yourself. You ain't talking to my wife."

Lovejoy came close to collapsing. He stepped back and put his hand against a porch pillar.

"Your wife? You are lying. She wouldn't do such a thing. Let me talk to her."

"Who is it, George?"

Christian Richter had come to the door. McFairlane motioned for him to step outside, then closed the door and said in a whisper, "It is that fellow Martin."

Richter grabbed the lamp from his son-in-law's hand and approached Lovejoy as if he meant to strike him.

"What business you got coming here like this?"

"I wrote to Madeline. I told her I would be delayed getting back. Didn't she get my letter?"

"Your letter came all right. But she never read it."

"Why not?"

"She was married already. We didn't want to upset her. So now you know that you should clear out of here right now."

"That is what I told him, Mr. Richter."

"Let me get this straight," Lovejoy said in a trembling voice. "I asked for Madeline's hand. You said we might be married. I wrote affirming my intentions. She has not been out of my thoughts for a single hour for nearly nine months. I have gone through hell to get back here. I can't believe that you have allowed her to marry this, this . . ."

"This what?" McFairlane demanded.

"Keep your voice down," Richter said. "Calm yourself. What is done is done. You don't want to upset her, not in her condition."

"What condition?"

Although McFairlane seemed ready to knock him off the porch, Richter suddenly turned sympathetic, taking Lovejoy's elbow and urging him to follow him into the yard.

As they passed the window again, Lovejoy glanced in at the two women inside. Madeline had risen from her chair and had gone over to her mother, where she stood with her hand on the small of her back. She wore a long, full skirt. The lissome waist he had so enjoyed putting his arm about was no more.

"You go back inside and tell them it is a fellow that wants to talk to me on business," Richter said to McFairlane. "Get on with you. I'll take care of this here situation. No, no, they don't need to know no more than that."

When Richter turned to continue his conversation, Lovejoy had sunk down upon the ground, unconscious.

Richter swore. Unable to arouse Lovejoy, he went into the house.

"The fellow is drunk. Passed out in the yard," he said to the women. "We got to carry him into town. He is in no condition to conduct any business tonight. Here, you . . ." He snapped his fingers at McFairlane. "Help me get him in the buggy."

Then, to the women, "Carry on with your talking. No, no, you are not needed at all. Who is it? Fellow in the flour business. Had too much to drink. Come on with you, George."

With the help of his son-in-law, Richter lifted Lovejoy into his buggy. They tied the gelding to the back of the buggy and together conveyed Lovejoy into Reading, where they procured a room for him in the poorest inn in the town.

"I will pay for his lodging and for the boarding of his horse for the night," he told the tavern keeper. "Here is the money. Now fetch me a piece of paper so that I may write a note, which I'll ask you to give him when he comes around."

When Lovejoy awoke the next morning, at first he did not know where he was, or even who he was. Only gradually did the memory of the events of the previous night return. He put his face into the moldy pillow and wept.

Finally he arose and went downstairs, where breakfast was being served. He ate the porridge and drank the coffee mechanically, all the while trying to convince himself that he had merely suffered a bad dream, that if he were to ride back out to the Richter house, everything would happen as it had in his fantasies the previous day.

"You looked to be in pretty bad shape last night. You feeling better this morning?" the tavern keeper asked.

"Not much."

"Mr. Richter said I was to give you this when you came around."

Lovejoy opened the letter. After he had read it, he ground his teeth and struck his fist against the table. The tavern keeper, thinking he wanted service, came over to his table.

"No, I don't want anything else to eat. Do you sell rum?"

"Sure."

"Bring me a bottle. No, make that two."

Alarmed, the man hesitated.

"Look here, Mr. Richter only paid for one night's lodging for you and for breakfast."

"God damn Mr. Richter. I would like to see him in hell, and his bitch of a wife, too. Here's the money. Bring the rum."

By noon, the first of the bottles was empty, and Lovejoy had passed out on his bed upstairs. He awoke in the late afternoon, arose with a piercing headache, reread the letter from Richter, then kicked a chair across the room and smashed the empty bottle against the wall. Hearing the racket, the tavern keeper came up to investigate. He found the door barred.

"Go the hell away," Lovejoy said. "I'll pay you for any damage. And go fetch me another bottle of rum."

The man tiptoed away. Lovejoy drew the cork from his second bottle and poured himself a fresh mug of rum.

Instead of bringing more rum, as Lovejoy had ordered, the tavern keeper dispatched his stable hand to summon Richter. It was growing dark by the time Richter's buggy reappeared in the tavern yard.

"You have got to do something about him, Mr. Richter. He has been wrecking his room up there, cursing and shouting like a crazy man. I got other guests to think about. Who is going to pay for the damage and for the loss of my trade?"

Richter rubbed his chin. He was considering going up and reasoning with Lovejoy himself, but his courage failed him as the tavern keeper continued.

"I would hate to have him hauled off to jail. He looks to be a gentleman. And he says he has plenty of money, so he can't be held for vagrancy."

"Could you keep him long enough to get word to his family in Philadelphia? They are rich. They would come and fetch him."

"Look, Mr. Richter, I ain't running a hospital for drunks or lunatics. You brought him here, and the way I see it, you are responsible for him."

"Let him stay one more night. By tomorrow, he will be sober and reasonable again."

"I should tell you that he has uttered some dreadful threats against you and your missus. After I give him your note he Goddamned you to hell and said he would like to cut your throat."

This was not exactly what Lovejoy had said, but the tavern keeper wanted to get himself off the hook without having to defy the rich and influential Christian Richter.

Richter turned pale.

"Did he now? In that case, I had better go and speak to the sheriff about this here situation."

So it was that by the time the second bottle of rum had worn off, Lovejoy found himself housed in the most comfortable cell the Berks County jail could offer. He remembered nothing of the officers taking the door of his room off the hinges and carrying him out of the tavern. Nor could he remember any time in all his life when he had felt more miserable and hopeless.

A doctor came and examined him. He gave Lovejoy a dose of laudanum and advised the sheriff to remove his belt and under no circumstances to allow him a razor, even though he needed a shave.

In his drug-induced stupor, Lovejoy's mind returned to earlier times of despair. He relived his grief at the death of his mother, his disappointment when his father cut off his allowance to force him to return from London, the humiliation of his and Tom's incarceration in the Baltimore jail as well as being gagged and tied to the mast of the *Flora,* his shock at the news of the capture of Megan Jenkins and the members of his prize crew, and finally, the torment of his long imprisonment in the prison hulk. But the anxiety and despair of all those experiences combined could not compare with what he felt in the Berks County jail for those few days in late August of 1813.

His beautiful, winsome Madeline married to that lickspittle of a stagecoach agent, and with child by him, too. Each time he thought of it, he ground his teeth and groaned, so that the keepers of the jail were convinced that they had a madman on their hands and felt that his family's assistance promised by Christian Richter could not come too soon.

Pierre Barineau arrived in Philadelphia ten days after he and Lovejoy had parted in Boston. A poor horseman, he had taken passage on a series of stagecoaches down through New York, across the Hudson on a ferry, and over New Jersey's deep-rutted roads that led to the Delaware River.

Unlike Lovejoy, he had not purchased new clothing, despite the bills of exchange for nearly twenty thousand dollars he carried in a money belt, in addition to those for forty thousand dollars he was returning to members of the Martin family.

He was pleased by the outcome of his adventures with his young friend, and rather surprised at himself for the risks he had taken. A year before, he had been merely a self-taught intellectual, well into his middle age, not entirely unhappy with his life as a schoolteacher but resigned to an uneventful existence. And now he had seen men killed in battle, run a sloop through a blockade, and snatched a promising young man from under the noses of his British captors. He smiled to think of what his wife would say when he told of how he had handled Weasel

Cuthbert. He would have to leave out some of the details of his encounter with Queenie Foster, however.

Lovejoy had thanked him for his intellectual influence and his courageous actions. "I am a far better man, thanks to you, Pierre," he had said at their parting in Boston,

As ready with words as Barineau usually was, he had not been able to say what he felt for Lovejoy. He could not easily express his feeling of gratitude. Thanks to that bright and engaging—if initially somewhat self-centered—young man, he had been able to escape his dull life as a schoolmaster and now possessed a store of memories on which to draw during his old age, not to mention far more wealth than if he had remained in the schoolroom.

As the coach approached Philadelphia late that afternoon, Barineau reviewed what he would do on his arrival. It was too late in the day to see the Martin family lawyer, so he would stop at the White Swan and meet Tom's father and give Megan a report on Lovejoy's escape from prison. Lovejoy said that it would be a good place to lodge as well.

Tomorrow he would present himself at the lawyer's office and turn over the various papers entrusted to him by Lovejoy. Then it would be off to Dover for a reunion with his wife before reporting on their mission to Malcolm MacKenzie down in Baltimore.

He had done his bit to teach the arrogant British a lesson in humility, he reckoned. With the seacoast of the United States dominated by their navy, the war was over for him, and with a rich and beautiful fiancée awaiting Lovejoy Martin, for his reluctant warrior friend as well. Or so Pierre Barineau imagined as he climbed down from the coach in Philadelphia and inquired the way to the White Swan.

He could hear sounds of a celebration as he rounded the corner onto South Street. The noise wasn't as loud as that created by Evan's wedding dinner fifteen months before, but the common room was nearly as full. Blind Jack again was playing his fiddle.

"Mr. Barineau!" someone shouted as he stood in the doorway, bewildered by the raucous crowd.

Before Barineau could adjust his senses to the mob of sailors, a pair of arms were thrown about his shoulders and he was staring into the face of Tom Jenkins.

Within seconds he was surrounded by Gandy, the gunner's mate of the *Flora*; Kevin, the Irish cook; black Toby; and Calvin Collins, the young prize master; as well as Tom and other crew members. They wrung his hand and pounded him on the back and hurled questions at him faster than he could answer.

Yes, yes, he had managed to free Lovejoy, he told them.

A cheer rang through the room as this intelligence was repeated.

Where was Lovejoy? "Why, off in Berks County, as far as I know. Wait, wait, there is too much to tell you all at once. First, what in God's name are you doing here in Philadelphia?"

Tom spoke for the group. "We came in nearly two weeks ago. Ran out of ammunition and fresh water, besides being battered by a hurricane south of Bermuda."

"I have a story about that hurricane, myself," Barineau said, "but go on."

"Couldn't get through the blockade into the Chesapeake, but Phipps slipped us into the Delaware right past the British at night, and with a splintered foremast. Nearly ran aground, but we made it. Wait until you hear the ships we took . . ."

"Phipps did that?"

"He turned into a regular terror to the British, he did, burning their craft left and right. We brought a hold full of their sailors in with us. Worth twenty-five dollars a head."

"I must congratulate Phipps. Where is he?"

"You wouldn't expect to find such a Methodist here, would you? He's gone down to report to his wife and Mr. MacKenzie in Baltimore."

"And what about the *Flora*?"

"She took considerable punishment from the storm. Needs refitting from stem to stern. Will take a while. Now you are not going to believe this, but Captain Smith came up here by coach soon as he heard she was in port."

"What about his leg?"

"He gets about well enough to oversee the refitting. He is sleeping in his old cabin aboard the *Flora* and driving his workmen mad. You'll have to visit him in the morning."

"I'll do that. And how is Megan?"

"She is upstairs, in bed with a fever. Been mighty sick, poor girl. After she recovers, she is to be married to Collins here."

"Indeed, she is," the prize master said. "Took a bit of convincing, but she finally recognized my qualities."

"Here," Tom said as he took Barineau's arm. "I want you to meet my pa and my two little twin brothers."

Barineau normally was a temperate man, indulging himself in no more than an occasional glass of Madeira or a mug of stout. But it would have taken a far more resolute man even than he to resist the hospitality of Evan Jenkins. On this one night in his life he set aside his habit of moderation and drank and ate and talked and drank some more until he lost all sense of time.

"Wait. Wait, a minute," he said thickly, and held up his hand to stop the flow of questions and boasting of the *Flora's* exploits. What is this celebration all about?"

"Why, those of us here are getting ready to travel out to Lake Erie. Haven't you heard about the fleet we have built out there? They need experienced sailors. And seeing that the *Flora* will be out of commission for a few weeks, we thought we'd go show them freshwater sailors how to fight. We are leaving tomorrow in a hired coach. Why don't you come with us?"

"Ah, lads, the war is over for me. I have a wife to see to and business to conduct with Malcolm MacKenzie."

"I have a girl to marry, soon as she feels better, and I am going," Collins said.

"You must go without me. Anyway, I have a great deal of business to discuss with Lovejoy's family and their lawyer."

"At least you'll have another mug of rum, won't you?" Evan said.

Actually, Barineau had three more mugs before the sailors returned to their bunks aboard the *Flora,* and Tom and Evan helped him up the stairs to bed.

Awakening with a queasy stomach and an aching head, Barineau decided against breakfast the next morning and took time instead to visit Megan in her sick room. Far paler and thinner than he remembered her, she was propped up in bed, drinking a glass of tea as he entered.

"Tom told me you had returned. And you rescued Lovejoy?"

"Yes. It was quite an adventure."

Her eyes glistened as he described most, but not all, of what had happened to Lovejoy and himself.

"And he is well?"

"Quite fit, or he was when we parted."

"And happy, I hope?"

"He was elated at the prospects of, well, you know, seeing his fiancée."

"I know all about that now. You realize that he was the real reason I stowed away on the *Flora*, don't you, Mr. Barineau?"

"I always assumed so."

"It was a silly, stupid thing for me to do. I am sorry for the trouble I caused Lovejoy and yourself."

"All's well that ends well. Tom says you are to be married."

"Once I get over this awful sickness, after he returns with the others from Lake Erie. Perhaps you can come to our wedding."

"It would please me very much to do that. Lovejoy wants me to stand as his best man, also."

Megan smiled. "He is lucky to have a friend such as you."

"And I, him. Now, I mustn't tire you. I have some serious business to take up with the Martin family lawyer. You are happy now, I hope."

"Primrose and I are getting along better now that she has a baby to keep her busy. Did his crying disturb you last night?"

"Nothing could have kept me awake."

"Anyway, it is a sweet little fellow. So Primrose and I have declared a truce. In fact, she spends much of her time on planning my wedding, rather more than I really want."

Charles Bennett, Esq., like many good lawyers, had learned not to show surprise, but it took all his self-control not to reveal his shock at the story told him and the documents shown him by Barineau.

He asked a few questions, frowned, and thought for a while.

"This news of Chester's double-dealing would kill Captain Martin," he said. "His life hangs by a thread. We dared not tell him of Lovejoy's imprisonment. He thinks him to be still at sea."

"Lovejoy said that I should trust you to do what you thought best with the documents and the information they reveal."

"And yet, I think it might be a good idea for you to pay the Captain a brief visit. Would you be willing to do that, keeping quiet about this business regarding Chester, of course?"

"It would be an honor. I will be discreet. Lovejoy has told me much about him. It might please Captain Martin to learn that his son has turned into, well, to my way of thinking, into a hero."

"I am delighted to hear you say that, Barineau. To tell you the truth, I always preferred Lovejoy to his brother."

At the Martin mansion, Barineau and Bennett were ushered up to Jeremiah's bedroom by Amanda. The old man, barely able to speak, grasped his hand and motioned for him to draw up a chair.

He smiled as Barineau told him of Lovejoy's courage and growing maturity, making certain that he said nothing that would upset the old man.

"Wh . . . where is. . . is he?"

"Out near Reading. He is visiting a young lady, a girl from an excellent family."

"Is it . . . s . . . serious?"

"He seems to be very much in love. It sounds like she and he would make a fine match."

"Wh . . . when will . . . I s . . . see him?"

"Very soon, I expect. He is anxious to talk to you. He is very proud of his father, you know."

As tears ran down his cheeks, Jeremiah closed his eyes and swallowed hard.

Amanda, who had been listening in the doorway, cleared her throat and nodded to Bennett. The lawyer touched Barineau's elbow, and the two men tiptoed out of the room.

With the help of his father, Tom had hired a coach and driver with four horses to carry him and the other members of the volunteers from the crew of the *Flora* to Harrisburg, from which point they would catch a stage for Pittsburgh. The coach was to leave shortly before noon.

Having finished his business with Bennett, Barineau intended to see the crew off and then take an early afternoon stage to Dover.

For old time's sake, he went aboard the *Flora* to talk to Talbot Smith and see the signs of the schooner's hard service.

Steadying himself with a cane, Smith pointed out the damage done to his beloved craft.

"Phipps was careless, that is what he was. Left too much sail on the foremast. No excuse for that. Sloppy job of splinting her, besides. And did you take note of the patches along her hull? Sorry workmanship that. She'll need new shrouds and a fresh suit of sails, not to mention replacing her foremast."

"There should be plenty of money to pay for refitting her."

"Aye, there will be. Phipps showed more gumption than I ever give him credit for. Took and burned six Britishers. When I left Baltimore, him and MacKenzie was going over the papers and putting in our claims. By God, now that I am back in working order, I aim to take her out to sea again."

"As you are feeling so well, why aren't you going out to Lake Erie with your boys?"

"They are damn fools. That won't amount to nothing out there. Waste of time. No sir, I am in my element right here with this here schooner. Having a hard time finding Philadelphians willing to work as my lads did down in Baltimore, but I'll get the job done. You say you got young Dr. Martin back safe and sound from Bermuda?"

Barineau, now weary of his own story, gave him a short version of his adventures.

"Saved his ass, did you? Hope he appreciates it. Look here, Barineau, I hope you will sign on again as my sailing master."

"My sailing days are behind me, I fear."

"I thought mine was, too, but here I am. Enough of this gabbing. I have work to do. You tell MacKenzie I need more money. It is outrageous what I am having to pay for everything up here."

Back at the White Swan, Barineau found Evan Jenkins slapping Tom on the back and admonishing the others to "look after my son." The coach driver was chewing his lip at the prospect of conveying such a rowdy lot in his vehicle.

Collins was standing about, looking downcast. Megan had not felt up to leaving her bed to say good-bye to him and Tom. She had squeezed his hand and allowed him a kiss while her stepmother stood in the doorway, damn the silly woman's eyes.

Barineau and Evan and the twins stood waving and watching the coach until it turned the corner and headed for the High Street Bridge across the Schuylkill.

"Won't you have a glass of cheer with me, Mr. Barineau?"

"Ah, Mr. Jenkins, I am not really a drinking man. But I would welcome a bite to eat before I collect my gear and report to the stage office."

"Here now, no more of that Mr. stuff. It's Evan for anyone that has done what you have for my friend Lovejoy Martin and my dear son and daughter."

"And it is Pierre for anyone who has fathered two such fine offspring."

After he finished his bowl of soup, packed up his bag, and said a brief good-bye to Megan and a longer one to her father, Barineau set out walking back to the stage office.

He was in the act of buying his ticket for the trip to Dover when a buggy carrying Charles Bennett and Amanda's husband, Frank Carpenter, rolled up to the stage office.

Bennett leapt down and trotted toward Barineau.

"My God, I am glad I found you."

"What is the matter?"

"This is Frank Carpenter. His wife is Lovejoy's sister, Amanda, whom you met this morning. Tell him what you have there, Frank."

"Why, I had just got home for my dinner when a letter came for my father-in-law. From Reading. The man said it was urgent . . ."

Frank paused to wipe the sweat from his face and Bennett took the letter from his hand.

"So he brought it to me. I opened it."

"A letter from Lovejoy?"

"No. The letter is from the father of the girl you said he expected to marry. Christian Richter. But it concerns Lovejoy. Here, read it for yourself."

# 4

Bennett first proposed that he and Barineau take Frank Carpenter's buggy for Reading early the next morning. Barineau disagreed, saying, "I can make it much faster alone on horseback. I could never forgive myself if he harmed himself while we dawdled back here. You can wait and come by buggy tomorrow."

So, much as he disliked riding horseback, he had hired a large, easy-gaited mare and had set forth immediately.

Reading lay about fifty miles northwest of Philadelphia. The fastest route for Barineau to have followed would have been the Germantown-

Reading Turnpike. Instead, he set out along the Philadelphia-Lancaster Pike, the same route Tom Jenkins and his comrades had taken a few hours earlier.

Despite the smooth, crushed-stone surface of the toll road, the overloaded stagecoach carrying Tom and the other crewmen of the *Flora* made slow progress, often locked in place behind ox-drawn Conestoga wagons on hills and through narrow passages between woods, with halts every ten miles to pay a twenty-five-cent toll.

By the time he reached Paoli to stop and water his horses, the driver had got a bellyful of the sailors, especially the loud-mouthed chap with the Irish accent, who insisted on riding on top beside him and bending his ear about the brave deeds he and his comrades had done at sea. The piratical fellow with the scar across his face who kept complaining about their slow pace irked him. And their singing was driving him mad.

As he approached Paoli, Barineau's buttocks were sore and his legs so weary that he was beginning to question his judgment either in riding horseback at all or in not taking the more direct route via Germantown. His attitude changed in a twinkling, however, when he spotted the Harrisburg-bound stagecoach with his old companions at a watering trough.

"Mother of God, if it ain't Mr. Barineau himself," Kevin called out. "Look there, Tom. See if my eyes deceive me."

With trembling legs, Barineau dismounted, and while his mare drank from the trough, he explained to Tom about Christian Richter's letter to Jeremiah Martin urging him to send someone to take charge of Lovejoy.

"So, she married someone else? I had my doubts about that one, although I never said so to a soul before. Then what must we do?"

"I propose to get him out of jail immediately and wait for the family lawyer to arrive and help me sort things out."

"I am coming with you."

"I thought you would. But what about your crewmates?"

"They can go on to Harrisburg and wait for me there."

"You don't have a horse."

"I can trot alongside you on foot," Tom said. Then turning to his crewmates, he called out, "Hear this, lads. I got something important to tell you."

Except for Collins, they all clamored to detour to Reading with Tom.

But in the end, they accepted Tom's reasoning and reboarded their western-bound stagecoach. "We'll wait for you in Harrisburg. Give Dr. Martin our best," Kevin called out as the coach drew away.

"Time is awasting," Barineau said. "Climb up behind me. We can take turns walking if she gives out on us."

From Paoli, they rode north to pick up an unimproved road that followed the south bank of the Schuylkill River into Berks County, where nightfall overtook them and their overburdened mare. Fearful of getting lost in the dark, they persuaded a Pennsylvania Dutch farmer to allow them to sleep in his barn.

Dawn found them riding tandem once more toward Reading. The keepers had just finished doling out bowls of corn mush to their prisoners when the pair arrived at the jail.

They found Lovejoy lying on his side, staring at the wall of his cell, his bowl of mush sitting untouched beside his bunk.

"Lovejoy, look here. It is I, Pierre Barineau."

"And me, your old friend Tom Jenkins. We have come to get you out of here."

Lovejoy continued staring at the wall, not moving.

"He is not asleep."

Buttoning up his shirt, the sheriff entered the cell block.

"Understand you have come about this Martin fellow." Then frowning at their rough appearance, he asked, "Just who are you?"

Pierre identified himself and Tom.

"I can't let him just go free with any Tom, Dick, or Harry, you know. There will have to be a peace bond posted by someone of substantial wealth. Fellow has made some dangerous threats. I have to have a guarantee that he will be removed from Berks County and never return here."

"His family lawyer and his brother-in-law are on their way. There is no problem with what you require."

"Then come along to my office, and we will discuss this. What's that? Enter his cell? Not sure that is a good idea."

"We have been friends since we wore short trousers," Tom said.

"Enter at your own risk, then. And you, sir, just follow me."

The deputy stood by as Tom stepped into the cell and looked down at Lovejoy.

"Joy, it is me, Tom."

"What are you doing here?"

"Mr. Barineau and I have come to take you home."

"I don't have a home."

"Don't say that. Look, Joy, we heard about your bad luck. Let me tell you something that will cheer you up."

Lovejoy showed no interest in Tom's enthusiastic account of the success of the *Flora,* which he ended by saying, "See there, you are a rich man again. And Captain Smith is in Philadelphia, hell-bent to put the schooner back in good sailing order."

"I don't give a damn for money. Give it all to the crew."

"Odd, you should mention the crew. Guess what me and several of the others is on our way to do."

Lovejoy showed no interest in his friend's mission to join Perry's fleet on Lake Erie.

"So, there it is, Joy. I hear they need surgeons out there as well as sailors."

"Who cares what they need?"

Afterward, Tom could not explain his actions of the next few minutes. "I reckon I sort of lost my reason," he would say.

At any rate, he kicked Lovejoy's bunk so hard he nearly broke his toe and raged in a high-pitched voice, "Who cares what they need? You need to stop lying there feeling sorry for yourself and saying you don't give a damn while some of the best fellows in the world are going out to do their duty for their country and could use your help."

"It is none of your business. Go away."

"The hell it ain't my business. I always looked up to you like I would to a big brother. Followed you around like a puppy. Helped you get out of scrapes. My whole family has been your friends. So don't you go telling me it ain't my business."

By the time Tom had finished this outburst, Pierre and the sheriff had returned to the cell block. The sheriff started to intervene, but Barineau signaled for him and his alarmed deputy to keep out of it.

"You don't know what I am going through. I want to die."

"I know what happened. She married another man. It happens all the time. It ain't the end of the world."

Lovejoy sat up, glowering at his friend through a week's growth of beard.

"It is the end of my world, you fool. Now get out of here and leave me alone."

"Alone to do what? Lie here in a Goddamned jail cell feeling sorry for yourself? I am going to kick your ass if you keep talking like that."

"You don't understand. She is the only girl I ever wanted to marry."

"Maybe you ought to think about all the girls that have took to their beds and cried to their mamas for the way you broke their hearts. Maybe you are just getting paid back for some of that. Besides a pretty face and blond hair, I don't think there was all that much to your precious Madeline anyway."

Lovejoy suddenly was on his feet, his fists clenched.

"You son of a bitch, you don't know what there was between us. She was the girl of my dreams."

"She would have turned into a nightmare, if you had married her. I could see what she was made of at a glance."

Lovejoy advanced toward his friend.

"Get the hell out of here or I will whip your ass."

"You aren't man enough. You are nothing but a crybaby who is used to always getting his own way, especially with women."

Tom ducked Lovejoy's first swing and moved just enough so that his second barely missed his jaw. He could have struck back, for Lovejoy was off guard. Instead, he taunted him with, "You have even forgot how to box."

Again Barineau stopped the sheriff from intervening.

Lovejoy lowered his head and rushed toward Tom, who sidestepped him and shoved him off balance so that he fell against the cell door.

"All your life you have done nothing but use other people. How does it feel to have the shoe on the other foot?"

Lovejoy stood up and dropped his fists. Seeing the crumpled look on his friend's face, Tom lowered his guard.

"Look, Joy, I am sorry I said that."

"I don't want your sympathy," Lovejoy screamed, and before Tom could brace himself, Lovejoy threw two hard punches, a left to the jaw followed by a hard right to the left eye. Tom fell across the bunk. Although he remained conscious, he pretended to have been knocked out.

Lovejoy stood over him, breathing hard, fists still clenched. Tom remained sprawled across the bunk with his eyes closed and blood trickling from his mouth.

Lovejoy's angry expression was replaced by one of concern.

"Tom?"

Tom kept his eyes closed.

"Are you hurt, Tom?"

Getting no response, Lovejoy bent over and put his fingers on Tom's pulse.

"I didn't mean to hurt you like that."

Tom opened one eye and moaned.

"I am sorry I hit you, but you had no business saying things like that to me, feeling as I do."

Again Tom moaned, then waited until Lovejoy bent over to inspect his bloody mouth and swollen left eye. Tom brought his left knee up squarely into Lovejoy's groin, causing him to collapse on the cell floor, writhing on his side in pain.

Tom got to his feet and applied a hard kick to Lovejoy's backside.

And that was when Barineau and the sheriff finally intervened to remove Tom so that he could be taken to a doctor.

Barineau remained in the cell, sitting on the bunk, while Lovejoy sobbed with his hands over his face. This went on for some ten minutes, until Lovejoy took a deep breath and looked at Barineau.

"I suppose you are going to quote me some saying from Montaigne or Shakespeare or maybe even the Bible?"

"There is something that comes to mind from the Apocrypha: 'Now therefore keep thy sorrow to thyself, and bear with good courage that which hath befallen thee.' "

"Bullshit."

"You may be right. So why don't you tell me what hath befallen thee to have put you in such a state."

Lovejoy took the handkerchief Barineau gave him and, after wiping his face and blowing his nose, tied and untied knots with it while he haltingly blurted out the story of his encounter with Christian Richter and George McFairlane.

"That must have been a shock," Barineau said. "Any idea of why she did not wait for you?"

"All I have to go on is a note the old bastard left for me with the tavern keeper. Said he had hired someone to go down to Baltimore and snoop about. Whoever it was discovered all about how Malcolm and I collected my father's debts and bought Talbot Smith's schooner. It must be common knowledge around the harbor, about my involvement.

Anyway, that seems to have cooked my goose with her family. Only I can't believe they would let her marry a nobody like that McFairlane. Or, and this really hurts, that she would want to marry such a fellow."

"I have some news from Philadelphia."

Barineau told him about his sessions with lawyer Bennett and Jeremiah Martin.

"Your father seemed much affected when I told him of your heroism. He is eager to have you back in Philadelphia. And Bennett thinks there will be no problem having you put in charge of the company."

"None of that means anything to me anymore."

"I would be surprised if it did. Anyway, Mr. Bennett and your brother-in-law will be coming to collect you."

"I will not be hauled off to Philadelphia like an invalid sent home to recuperate."

"Be that as it may, you will be required to leave Berks County, never to return. Seems you uttered some threats against the Richter family. A peace bond is being prepared. You are welcome to accompany me to Baltimore to consult with Phipps and Mr. MacKenzie. You don't like that idea, either? You could remain in this jail, I suppose, but you have worn out your welcome here. Seems as though you have not been a well-behaved guest."

This drew a rueful smile from Lovejoy.

"Tom and I haven't eaten since noon yesterday. We will be back later. I expect you may want to apologize to him."

"He should apologize to me. Did you hear what he said?"

"Some of it. Perhaps apologize was the wrong word. Rather, you should thank him."

"What in the hell for?"

"In time you will realize what a good service he did you. By the way, could I have my handkerchief back?"

# 5

There was not a more respected physician in Philadelphia than Ephraim McGee, nor was there a better friend of the Jeremiah Martin family.

Born on the Pennsylvania frontier of a Scotch-Irish father and a German mother, Ephraim and his siblings had been tutored by the young Jeremiah. In 1763, his father, Jason McGee, brought the brash young Virginian home with him after they had served together in the battle of Bushy Run. Jeremiah stayed with the McGee family for only a year, but the relationship never ended.

Later, the precocious Ephraim attended college and medical school in Philadelphia. During the American Revolution, he served briefly as a surgeon aboard a privateer sloop owned and captained by Jeremiah. At the end of the war, his widowed sister, Gerta Peebles, married an adoring Jeremiah and lived happily with him until her death several years ago.

Now in his late fifties, Dr. McGee had been married for many years to a half-Jewish woman, Rebecca d'Balboa. He had left his affiliation with the Presbyterian church and she hers with her father's faith to become Quakers.

It was Ephraim McGee who had encouraged Lovejoy to become a doctor and had arranged for his nephew to study at St. Bartholomew's in London. And it was Ephraim McGee who insisted on accompanying Frank Carpenter and Charles Bennett to Reading when he learned of Lovejoy's predicament there.

The three men arrived in Reading sooner than Barineau had thought possible. Starting at dawn in a light buggy drawn by two horses, they had taken the Germantown-Reading Turnpike.

While Bennett and Carpenter were presenting their credentials to the sheriff, Ephraim consulted with Barineau and the battered Tom about the state of Lovejoy's mind and how best to deal with him.

"Whatever course he chooses, he must be kept occupied," Ephraim decreed. "He must remain too busy to brood about his loss. And I caution you that we should say nothing about there being other fish in the sea and that sort of thing. From what Mr. Barineau says, he really was obsessed with this Richter girl. It will take some time for his wounds to heal."

"As it will mine," said Tom, putting his hand over his injured eye.

The sheriff, overawed by Bennett, expressed himself satisfied by their bonds and led them to Lovejoy's cell, where he again lay on his bunk, an arm over his eyes. After signing a pledge to leave the county and never return, he rode in his rescuers' buggy to the tavern where his gray gelding remained stabled.

While Bennett was negotiating with the tavern keeper about payment for the feeding of the animal and repairing the damage caused by Lovejoy, Frank Carpenter took Barineau's hand and said, "Mr. Bennett has told me what you have been through. I understand now just what Chester was up to, and I want to thank you for returning the money Amanda and I put up for that ransom."

"The same goes for Rebecca and me," Ephraim said. "I never thought a nephew of mine would resort to such a sordid device. But enough of that. We must get you sorted out."

"We can't do it here," Barineau said. "We are to have him out of the county by sundown."

At Bennett's urging, they headed south to a country inn at the village of Adamstown, in the northeastern corner of Lancaster County. Lovejoy sat slumped in the buggy with Ephraim and Barineau, while Tom rode his gelding and Carpenter rode the mare that the saddle-sore Barineau had rented in Philadelphia.

There were a thousand questions Ephraim would have liked to ask Lovejoy, but he wisely refrained from doing more than occasionally glancing at him and inquiring if he was comfortable.

All six men were weary, as were their horses, when they reached the inn. Bennett procured two adjoining rooms. They ate supper in silence. Tom was assigned to accompany Lovejoy upstairs while the other four men conferred over pints of ale.

Bennett acted as moderator.

"In time we will have to do something about Chester. Can't leave him to rot in Dartmoor or wherever the English place him. Always the chance that a ransom will be set on his head. Just have to wait and see."

"Could he end up in prison back here?" Carpenter asked. "That would break Amanda's heart and shame the family."

"Only if you and Ephraim press charges, and, as your family lawyer, I would advise against creating such a scandal."

"What about the shipping business? Who is to handle that?"

Ephraim shook his head. "The most pressing question is to decide what we should do about Lovejoy. I am most concerned about his very obvious melancholy."

Barineau stood up and knocked the ashes from his pipe.

"Excuse me for putting in my oar. I don't have your knowledge of medicine, Dr. McGee, nor yours of the law, Mr. Bennett, nor, for that matter, yours of your family relationships, Mr. Carpenter. But let me tell you this: I would go easy on deciding what 'we should do about Lovejoy.' "

Bennett, taking umbrage at what he regarded as an intrusion by a mere schoolmaster-cum-navigator, said, "Naturally we understand your concern, Barineau, but this really is a matter to be decided by his family and his counsel."

"I beg to disagree with you," Barineau replied.

Bennett started to bristle at this, but Ephraim put up his hand. "I would like to hear what Mr. Barineau has to say."

"The Lovejoy Martin whom I hope is now asleep upstairs is not the same young man you may have thought you knew a year or more ago, and whose fate you are presuming to decide."

"You will have to explain what you mean."

"I met Lovejoy last August when I gave up schoolteaching to return to the sea as sailing master aboard his schooner. At first, he struck me as perhaps the most spoiled, self-centered young fop I had ever met. In fact, I avoided his company."

The three men listened with growing interest as Barineau told of the clash of wills between Lovejoy and Talbot Smith, of Megan Jenkins's appearance as a stowaway, of his eventual popularity with the crew of the *Flora*, of their Shakespearean playacting and their teaching sailors to read and write, all the way through Lovejoy's amputation of the captain's mangled leg.

"So you see, gentlemen, Lovejoy had already grown up by the time we returned from that first cruise. But he demonstrated a rare form of maturity when word came that twelve of our people, one of them the sister of Tom Jenkins, had been captured and were being held ransom on Barbados. If he had not answered that call of duty, he would be married, whether happily or unhappily I cannot say, to the woman whose lost love he now mourns."

By now, even Bennett was eager for him to continue.

Barineau was a natural storyteller. By the time he concluded his tale of Lovejoy's sacrificing himself to save Megan and her fellow prisoners and of their trapping Chester and causing him to go aboard the transport in Lovejoy's place, all thought of sleep had been driven from his listeners' minds.

"So you see, gentlemen, your client, your nephew, your brother-in-law, and my cherished young friend has been transformed into a hero fully capable of deciding his own fate."

"You have left out mentioning another hero who was involved in all this," Ephraim said.

"Who?" Barineau asked.

"Yourself, Mr. Barineau. I am awed by the risks you have taken, the loyalty you have demonstrated on behalf of my nephew."

Meanwhile, Lovejoy lay on his back staring into the dark while Tom slept soundly. He pretended to be asleep when Barineau came up to their room and the other three men went to theirs. Finally his mind stopped returning to the sort of fantasies in which he had engaged during his time aboard the *Flora* and the prison hulk. Instead, he weltered in regrets for having returned to the sea to rescue twelve people who might well have been released anyway in time. If he had not been such a fool, he would now be lying beside that gorgeous girl and not that miserable, low-bred . . . He ground his teeth at the thought of Madeline in the bed and the arms of another man.

On the other side of the room, Barineau also lay awake. He had enjoyed relating the story of his and Lovejoy's odyssey. In time, he thought he might write the story. That would give him an occupation for his old age, surely. But meantime, what should be done about Lovejoy? No, he must take his own advice. The question was, what choices should be presented to Lovejoy. Nothing should be forced on him in his present sad state.

6 

The six men who sat around the tavern table at breakfast the next morning presented quite a contrast in appearance.

Upon awakening, Bennett, Ephraim, and Frank had ordered hot water brought to their room and were now clean shaven. And they were well dressed, as became Philadelphia gentlemen.

Barineau and Tom were dressed in rough clothing. The fine suit Lovejoy had bought hurriedly in Boston had become wrinkled and torn from his five days in the saddle and his three in the Berks County jail. His face bristled with several days' growth of beard. Not trusting Lovejoy with a razor in his dejected state, his two shipmates had forgone shaving themselves.

After they had eaten their breakfast of scrapple, potatoes, and eggs and drunk their coffee, all without speaking, Bennett once again assumed the role of moderator.

"Lovejoy," he said, "Ephraim, Frank, and I must return to Philadelphia. We have our practices to attend to. Besides that, as you must know, there are some rather knotty problems for the three of us to work out in regards to Martin Shipping, what with Chester's absence and his . . . well, I won't go into all that."

Lovejoy looked at the lawyer without replying.

"And Barineau, here, must return to his family and then see to some matters having to do with your privateering venture down in Baltimore with your partner, what's his name?"

"Malcolm MacKenzie," Barineau offered.

"Quite so. As I understand it, your enterprise has proved profitable. Not only do you have awards coming from the government for the destruction of some British ships and the capture of their seamen, you own eighty percent of a schooner now being refitted in Philadelphia. Is that not so, Barineau?"

"Besides the proceeds from our first cruise. Lovejoy is a rich man, no doubt about it."

Lovejoy greeted this statement with a half smile.

"So the question to be answered this morning—and Barineau has pressed upon us the point that you and you alone should decide the answer—the question is whether you would like to return to Philadelphia with us."

"Yes, Lovejoy, return and see your father before it is too late. And Amanda is most anxious about you," Frank said.

Bennett frowned at the interruption.

". . . or accompany your friend Barineau to Baltimore and sort out your business down there, saving a visit home for later. Correct, Barineau?"

"Exactly so. Naturally I would welcome the latter course of action, but the decision must be yours, Lovejoy."

"Quite so," said Ephraim. "The important thing is to plunge yourself into an enterprise that demands your attention. Brooding in idleness is the worst thing you could do."

Up to that point, Tom had sat through the discussion without speaking. Aside from his blackened eye and bruised chin, he was conscious of being the youngest, the poorest and the least educated member of the party. But he was irritated by the pomposity of the lawyer.

"You all are overlooking something," he said.

"Such as?" Bennett asked.

"You have given Joy only two choices. There is a third."

"What do you mean?"

"I was on my way to Lake Erie with some of my shipmates to join Perry's fleet out there, when Mr. Barineau overtook us back at Paoli. My mates wanted to go with us to Reading, but I talked them out of it. They are waiting for me in Harrisburg."

Bennett broke in with, "You have done Lovejoy a great service and I think it would be appropriate to reward you with a purse of money to speed you and your friends on your way to Lake Erie. There would be no objection on the part of the Martin family, would there, Frank?"

"None whatsoever. Tom and Lovejoy have been friends since childhood."

"I am aware of the relationship . . ." Bennett began.

"I ain't making myself clear," Tom replied. "There ain't anybody here, unless maybe it is Mr. Barineau, who is any closer to Joy than me. When you and Captain Martin contrived to send him down to Baltimore and he didn't want to go, it was me that went with him. I did it on trust. I have been thrown in jail on account of him and been bound, gagged, and lashed to a ship's mast because of trying to help him. I am not going to stand by and let you drag him off to do something he don't want to."

"Look here, young fellow," Bennett said. "We recognize your concern, but you really have nothing to do with this."

Tom rose and leaned across the table.

"The hell I don't."

Alarmed at the growing heat of the conversation, Ephraim said, "Exactly what are you getting at, Tom?"

"I say Joy has a third choice, and that is to leave all these business transactions behind and come with me and our shipmates out to Lake Erie."

"In his present condition?"

"He may stay in his present condition if he gets in a rut back in Baltimore and Philadelphia. We hear Perry needs surgeons. Maybe you ought to come too, Dr. McGee."

"I am a member of the Society of Friends, Tom. My conscience would not allow me to take part in a war, even if my age and professional commitments at home would. Still, I am interested in what you propose. Who would be responsible for his safety?"

"I have looked after him often enough in the past, and he has done the same for me and members of my family."

Eyebrows raised, Ephraim glanced at the other men around the table. Bennett, his arms folded across his chest, frowned and shook his head. Frank shrugged his shoulders. Barineau closed his eyes and nodded.

Then Ephraim looked at Lovejoy. For the first time that morning, his face remained lifted from the table. He stared at Tom with glistening eyes.

"So, Lovejoy, what do you say?"

Lovejoy spoke in a low voice, husky from disuse.

"Uncle Ephraim, it seems to me that Frank could oversee what is left of Martin Shipping better than I could. If he needs help, he can call on Malcolm MacKenzie down in Baltimore. And Pierre, you and Phipps and Talbot Smith can work out things with Malcolm as well as I could. Whatever you decide about the prize money and selling off the *Flora* will be all right. I don't care about any of that."

Tom bent over to hear what Lovejoy was saying.

"The only problem is that I have a horse, but Tom doesn't."

Tom broke in. "Oh, Joy, I can walk to Harrisburg. Or we can take turns riding your horse."

Barineau looked at the three Philadelphians. Even Bennett nodded.

Barineau grinned and said, "Then I suggest that Tom take my hired mare. There is money enough in Lovejoy's account to pay the livery stable fellow for her."

"Hot damn," Tom said. "Joy, you and I can ride all the way to Presque Isle and let the other fellows follow by stage. We will get there quicker that way."

Lovejoy smiled and rose from the table.

"We had better get started then."

Weeks, even months would pass before Lovejoy stopped falling into fits of depression. The one antidote he found for his grief was to give free rein to the anger stored up in his very soul against the men he felt more and more to be the authors of his agony. They were Captain Christopher Bledsoe and, to a lesser degree, his half brother Chester. He drew a grim pleasure from imagining Bledsoe's reaction to learning that not only had he, Lovejoy, escaped without a ransom's being paid, but that he had made the arrogant, grasping bastard look like a fool by substituting Chester for himself. As for Chester, well, had he, Lovejoy, not taken his revenge of him? He smiled when he thought of the little pipsqueak lying tied up in bed, with shitty trousers, beside a common whore. All he would have needed to do to free both himself and Lovejoy would have been to disclose the fact of the letters of credit concealed in his coat lining. Chester had been hoisted on the petard of his own greed.

They reached Harrisburg late that day for a reunion with the other crew members, who, on Tom's advice, did not question Lovejoy. Tom entrusted Collins with money to pay for their stage fares west to Pittsburgh and then north to Presque Isle.

The two companions arose early the next morning and led their horses onto the ferry to cross the broad Susquehanna River, then headed along the rich Cumberland Valley to Carlisle and Shippensburg, where they spent the night. From that point they proceeded to Chambersburg, where they picked up a new turnpike that carried them west across the several long, low mountain ranges that separate eastern from western Pennsylvania to Bedford and on to Pittsburgh.

Four days later, they paused atop Squirrel Hill to look down upon the forks of the Ohio, now occupied by a fast-growing town of some six thousand. They and their horses were weary. Although Tom had chattered as they rode along, Lovejoy had remained silent. But now he stood in his stirrups to gaze on the panorama.

"Magnificent," he said. "I have always wanted to see this vista. Did you know that my grandfather, Jason McGee, came out here as a lad in, I think it was 1754, when there was nothing but an Indian village down there on the Allegheny? That is the river to the right. The other is the Monongahela. You are looking at the beginning of the mighty Ohio, where those two rivers join. From that point, you could drift all the way down to the Mississippi and then on to New Orleans."

It was the longest speech Lovejoy had made since Reading.

"We, that is the American colonies and Great Britain, fought a war with the French and the Indians to settle whether all that to the west and north should be English or French."

Tom laughed. "And now it is neither one. It is American."

"So it is. Now, from all I have heard, it is to be decided whether this territory to the north and west of us is to remain American or shall revert to the British. Well, let's go down into the town and prepare ourselves for our ride up to Presque Isle to help settle the question."

So the two companions rode into the bustling town of Pittsburgh that first day of September 1813. There, at a newspaper print shop where they stopped to ask directions, they learned that Presque Isle was not to be their destination after all.

The editor, a fat man with thick spectacles, looked up from a galley proof to ask their business.

"Two sailors, are you? From what we hear down here, Perry can use you and a good many more, but you'll not find him at Presque Isle. He left there about three weeks ago. If you don't believe me, go read the extra edition we published about the news. It's posted over by the door. Read for yourself how our ships slipped over the sandbar at Erie and got past the British fleet. It was a miracle what that man Perry accomplished. Couldn't have done it without the help of the good people here in Pittsburgh, though. Gone where? Last we heard, he had moved his base west to Sandusky Bay at the other end of Lake Erie. Has hooked up with Harrison's army. Keeping an eye on the British fleet across the far end of the lake at Malden. I'll show you on this map."

"Why, that is a good hundred and fifty miles to the west of Erie."

"So it is, and you won't have a smooth turnpike to travel over, either. You got horses, have you?"

"Yes, two good ones."

"Then let me show you the route you must follow, through some very rough country, clear across God-forsaken Ohio, I warn you. Unless you have changed your minds, that is."

# Part Two

# 1

Lovejoy and Tom at first did not appreciate what "a miracle that man Perry accomplished," not only in skillfully slipping his vessels out of the Presque Isle harbor past the British, but in even creating the fleet at all.

They were to learn, too, that although Pittsburgh had proved to be a good source of supplies for Perry, the editor may have given more credit to his fellow citizens than they deserved for their roles in creating the fleet.

Workmen not just from Pittsburgh but from the great cities of New York and Philadelphia and from fledgling towns such as Buffalo on Lake Erie's eastern end and Meadville to the south on French Creek had converged on Erie to swell its original population of about five hundred several times over. There was timber aplenty in the forests around the harbor, but iron, rope, tackle, sails, pitch, oakum, coal, and tools of all sorts, from axes and saws to adzes and caulking hammers, had to be purchased elsewhere and hauled in either by boat, through dangerous waters up the Allegheny River and French Creek or along the treacherous coast of Lake Erie, or by wagon over roads that were primitive by comparison with the smooth, crushed-stone turnpikes of eastern Pennsylvania.

And although the brash, youthful Perry was the guiding genius of both the completion and the subsequent handling of the fleet, he could not have done it without foundations (and keels) laid by Daniel Dobbins, the intrepid lake trader, and some gifted naval architects and shipwrights, or without the backing of Commodore Isaac Chauncey, back at his Sackets Harbor base on Lake Ontario.

The Pittsburgh editor also erred in calling Perry's vessels "ships." The American fleet anchored at Put-in-Bay on that rainy September 8 afternoon consisted of three brigs (two large and one small), five schooner-rigged gunboats, and one sloop. A sixth schooner had been sent back to Erie to fetch supplies.

Neither the two large brigs nor the five gunboats constructed of green timber back at Presque Isle would have met the demanding standards of a Talbot Smith, but, considering the circumstances, their creation really was a shipbuilding miracle.

The vessels were well armed, however. The two large brigs each carried two twelve-pounder Long Toms and eighteen thirty-two-pounder carronades. The seven smaller craft mounted a total of fourteen mostly long-range cannon, firing balls of various weights.

That afternoon of September 8, Perry had stood on the quarterdeck of his flagship, the *Lawrence,* observing his fleet's response to his orders for all hands to report to battle stations and exercise both cannon and small arms. He had enjoyed the crash of the *Lawrence*'s great guns all around him, the crackle of his landsmen's musketry overhead, and the reverberations of similar gunfire from the decks and rigging of his other vessels. The booms of the great guns and the acrid smell of gunpowder had been like a tonic to him. But his feeling of optimism soon dissipated like the white smoke of the guns when he returned to his cabin to go over his duty rosters and review his sick lists.

Perry remained unhappy about Chauncey's failure to send him more experienced sailors and fretted that so many of his crewmen had fallen prey to the illness called "lake fever." Both of his chief surgeons were suffering from the ailment, and care for the sick of the entire fleet had devolved upon a surgeon's mate named Usher Parsons, now stationed aboard the *Lawrence.*

As a ketch carrying Lovejoy and Tom sailed out from the Sandusky shoreline late that afternoon, Perry was joined in his cabin aboard the *Lawrence* by his second-in-fleet-command and captain of the *Niagara*, Master Commandant Jesse Elliott.

"I don't understand Chauncey's game," Perry was saying. "The man accepted my request for command here with alacrity. We have accomplished all and more than he asked of us. Yet here we sit in a position to fight the British any time they want to come out of Malden, and what have we to man our vessels? A motley set of blacks, miltiamen, and soldiers, and mere boys."

"I count more than five hundred men," Elliott said. "And they have responded well to our training, especially the Pennsylvania militiamen and more recently General Harrison's Kentuckians. Our gun drills went smoothly enough aboard the *Niagara*."

"Be that as it may, we should have 750 men. Deduct those sick or otherwise unfit for duty, and we have not many more than four hundred. Meanwhile, I am convinced that Chauncey holds the best of his sailors back to serve his own fleet on Lake Ontario. You are his fair-haired boy. Tell me, does he not wish us to succeed?"

"From what those Canadian deserters say, the British have no more men than we," Elliott said. "Besides which, they are running short of supplies, having to feed Tecumseh's horde of Indians."

"Perhaps so, but look at the quality of our men. Nearly half of them recruited from the militia or army, able to shoot their muskets and rifles but ignorant of nautical matters. Only 160 men claiming to be sailors, and one in four of them either black fellows or runaway boys. And then this damned lake fever."

"Look on the bright side," Elliott said. "Barclay has only six vessels to our ten."

"Our nine, you mean. The *Ohio* is away, remember. And according to those deserters, they have the advantage in cannon, sixty-three to our fifty-four."

"Come, come, Perry, you know that when it comes to the weight of our relative broadsides we hold a decided advantage."

"Only at close range. There is not a more experienced or able officer in the British navy than Barclay. He has spent most of his life at sea. Fought at Trafalgar. Survived the loss of an arm in a later action."

"If he wanted to fight us, he missed his chance the other day when we made our reconnaissance of the Malden area."

"Sooner or later, he has to come out or lose his line of communication to the east. He is a Scot, you know, and a canny one, too. Mark my words: he is waiting until he has the weather gage and then will try to pound us at long range."

"If he is so canny, why did he fail to attack while you were lifting the brigs over the bar back at Presque Isle? I counseled Chauncey against making Erie our base in the first place. You were like a bull trying to scramble over a wall. Barclay could have wiped you out had he been more alert."

"We all have our lapses. But I want none on our part when he finally decides to fight. That is why I have watchers on the islands to signal if they see any movement by Barclay's ships. Now, do we have it settled how we are to handle our vessels?"

"You will go after their largest ship, the *Detroit,* while I attack the next largest, the *Queen Charlotte.* The positions of our two brigs will depend on the relative locations of those two ships."

Perry nodded. "Just remember, we must close with them quickly. We will take some punishment from their long guns at first, but once we come in range with our carronades, we can batter them to pieces. And then, well, our best advice comes from Barclay's old commander, Lord Nelson. He said, 'If you lay your enemy alongside, you cannot be far out of place.' Bear that in mind, Elliott. Close with them quickly. Now I have a further bit of advice for the entire fleet. See this pennant?"

He unfolded a blue flag on which was emblazoned in white letters, "Don't give up the ship."

"I am told that those were the last words uttered by James Lawrence back in June when his frigate, *Chesapeake,* was losing its fight with the British frigate *Shannon.* Lawrence was a dear friend of mine. This brig was named in his honor. And that is why I have made his dying words the slogan for this squadron. It shall fly from my foremasthead as we go into battle."

Fingering the pennant, Elliott squelched his impulse to point out that after Lawrence fell, his men had surrendered the battered *Chesapeake* off the coast of Massachusetts.

"It is growing dark," Perry said. "You should return to the *Niagara.* Keep drilling your men. If Barclay doesn't come out tomorrow, I will call in our commanders for another conference in the afternoon. Anything else you can think of, meanwhile?"

Before Elliott could reply, Perry's little brother, dressed in a midshipman's uniform, entered the cabin to report, "Oliver, there is a ketch come out from Sandusky with two volunteers."

"Who are they?"

"They say they served as landsmen aboard a privateer that is being refitted in Philadelphia."

"I would rather they were ablebodied seamen or doctors."

"Shall I talk to them on my way out?" Elliott asked.

"Yes. Interview them and do with them as you wish. Two landsmen more or less won't matter to us now."

Although he was only four years older than Perry, the round-faced, balding Elliott already appeared middle-aged. He had proved his courage earlier that year by leading a raid across the Niagara River to capture two British vessels, one of which, the brig *Caledonia,* was the third largest in Perry's fleet.

A tension existed between himself and Perry. He considered Perry an upstart. Perry resented the fact that when Elliott had arrived a few weeks before with eleven officers and ninety-one men, he had kept the best of the lot for his own use aboard the *Niagara.*

Elliott scrutinized Lovejoy and Tom as they stood on the quarterdeck of the Lawrence.

"I understand that you have been privateers."

"That we were, sir," Tom said. "And we have ridden clean from Philadelphia to join you."

"And you call yourselves sailors?"

"Actually, I was the supercargo. But they taught me to steer. And I fought as a top man more than once."

"And you," he said to Lovejoy. "What are your skills?"

"Actually he was our . . ." Tom began, but stopped when Lovejoy trod on his toe.

"I was and still am part owner of a schooner that is now being refitted in Philadelphia," Lovejoy said.

"One of those war profiteers that has been draining off our best sailors, are you? There is no money to be made for you here, my good fellow."

"I am not here to make money, sir."

"Expect you have made enough of that from privateering. You don't look well. Don't have the fever, do you?"

"I am very tired, sir. It has been an arduous journey."

"Very well. You," he said, pointing to Tom. "You can stay here aboard the *Lawrence.* As for yourself, mister privateer owner, you can ride back in my boat with me to the *Niagara.*"

Turning to the officer of the watch, Elliott said, "Please inform Commodore Perry that I have given him the better qualified of these two fellows."

"My friend and I don't want to be separated," Lovejoy said.

"This is the United States Navy, not a privateer. Here you follow orders. Down the ladder with you."

# 2 

*Thursday, September 9, 1813,*
*aboard the U.S. brig Niagara*

*Dear Pierre:*

*If you received my brief letter scrawled in haste back in Pittsburgh, you will not be surprised to learn that Tom and I ended up near Sandusky, Ohio, rather than Erie.*

*Upon learning in Pittsburgh that Perry had moved his fleet out here, we set forth on a grueling ride across Ohio over some miserable excuses for roads, through swarms of mosquitoes, staying in the worst imaginable sort of lodgings, wherever nightfall found us.*

*On September 8 we reached Sandusky, a place that has little to recommend it, being only a collection of cabins at the mouth of the river of the same name. The considerable army of General Harrison—mostly militiamen from Kentucky, Ohio, and Virginia—is encamped in and around the nearby Fort Stephenson.*

*Learning that Perry's fleet had recently returned from a reconnaissance of the British base at Malden and was now anchored off South Bass Island, Tom and I left our horses in the care of a livery stable and hired the owner of a ketch to convey us out to the flagship of our fleet, the Lawrence.*

*As we set out from Sandusky harbor, all the vessels in Perry's fleet were exercising their guns. It was an awesome sight to see all that destructive power being unleashed by so many cannon belching flame and smoke, although only in practice.*

*Tom was all for blabbing my record as a ship's surgeon, but I, having got a bellyfull of doctoring, prevailed on him to represent ourselves only as landsmen from a privateer. Despite my protests, Tom was assigned to the Lawrence and myself to the Niagara. The choice was made in a highly arbitrary manner by Lt. Jesse Elliott, master of the Niagara, who conveyed me in his own boat to this brig and handed me over to the tender mercies of his chief bosun's mate, an old salt from the regular navy.*

*It is painful to be separated from Tom, but I suppose it is time for me to quit feeling sorry for myself and stand on my own two feet. I just hope that Tom will be all right.*

*The Niagara, like her sister brig, the Lawrence, measures just over 110 feet long at the waterline and has a beam of about 30 feet. She draws only 9 feet of water. Her foremast stands 113 feet tall; her mainmast, 118. She lacks the beauty and grace of the Flora, but considering the difficulties under which she was built, she is marvelously constructed.*

*As for armament, she carries eighteen 32-pound carronades, nine on each side, with two 12-pounder long guns.*

*I have not counted the crew but estimate them to be about 150 officers and men. The former appear to be stalwart fellows, but the latter would be better suited to serve aboard a privateer like the Flora, since the great majority of them were recruited from the Pennsylvania militia gathered back at Erie to protect the base there and the others from the several thousand soldiers and militiamen General Harrison has under his command in and around Sandusky. Thus we have sailors from New England and New York, a few soldiers from the regular army, and riflemen from Pennsylvania, Ohio, Kentucky, and even Virginia. I am surprised, too, by the large number of Negroes, many of them with experience at sea, and all free men, of course.*

*I was given a hammock and shown where to stow it belowdecks in a space where only a dwarf could stand up straight and so crowded that I can hardly get my breath.*

*On going aboard the Lawrence, I had hoped to meet the commander of this fleet, Oliver Perry, but Elliott whisked me away so fast I was denied the opportunity. From all I hear, Perry is a formidable fellow, not much older than myself, and a regular martinet in imposing discipline upon a mixed bag of humanity which could easily get out of control under a less firm hand.*

*Perry has given standing orders that all men must be*

*clean shaven and clean dressed. So off came my beard this morning and on went a sailor's smock and canvas trousers to replace my once fine clothing.*

*Not knowing what else to do with me, and upon my representing myself as conversant with small arms, they have given me a musket and assigned me to serve as a marksman stationed on the foretop, a platform on the foremast, just over the fore mainsail. I was too embarrassed to mention my dislike of heights.*

*I have been put under the command of a Kentucky militiaman armed with a beautifully crafted rifle he claims his grandfather brought out to Kentucky from Pennsylvania. He is a lean, dark fellow who speaks with a drawl I can hardly understand. Assigned to the same station aloft with us is a wiry, slender Negro chap from New Jersey, chosen for the post, I believe, for his agility at climbing, and a simple-minded farm boy from New York State.*

*I awoke this morning to the shrill whistle of a bosun's call to find a light rain falling. Later in the day, the rain ceased, but fresh breezes kept us rocking at anchor under fast-flying clouds.*

*We have been drilling all day, using up God knows how many tax dollars in gunnery practice. If you thought the deck of the Flora a busy place under the captaincy of Talbot Smith, you should have seen the activity that took place aboard this and others of Perry's vessels today: sail makers replacing sails; gun crews filling and stitching bags with langrage; powder monkeys setting out buckets of sand to be strewn about the deck to keep men from slipping on blood; cooks boiling drinking water.*

*From my assigned position up on the foremast, I can appreciate what a powerful, efficient machine even a brig of 20 guns can be when operated by an energetic crew.*

*There is a great shortage of surgeons here and a good deal of illness. Perhaps it is selfish of me to conceal my own medical training, but in my present frame of mind, I do not wish the responsibility, thank you just the same.*

*Pierre, I fear that I did not properly thank you and the others for your exertions on my behalf back in Reading.*

*Once again you have proved to be a sterling friend. God knows what would have become of me if you, Uncle Ephraim, Lawyer Bennett, Frank, and, of course, Tom had not showed up when you did.*

*I remain dejected over the loss of my love and the dashing of my hopes of marriage. I cannot predict what I will do next with my life. Just now I am following the advice of Uncle Ephraim and plunging myself into an activity untinctured by motive of greed, gain, or even self-aggrandizement.*

*Incidentally, we left word at the stage office in Pittsburgh for the others from the Flora to make their way to Sandusky rather than Erie, leaving the means to their own ingenuity. They have not yet showed up, which is a pity. As experienced seamen, they would be most welcome here.*

*Please share this letter with Malcolm MacKenzie. By the time you receive it, perhaps the long-predicted battle with the British fleet may have occurred.*

*If I have learned anything during the past 15 months, it is that in this uncertain world one can rely on little more than a few staunch persons such as yourself and Tom Jenkins. All else seems to depend on chance and the oftentimes evil intent of others, such as Captain Bledsoe (God rot his soul in hell) and my dear brother Chester, whose mortal frame may well be rotting in Dartmoor Prison for all I know or care. Should I not survive the impending battle, please tell Malcolm that my interest in the Flora and its prize monies should be apportioned among the crewmen who served aboard it with such distinction.*

*Given the circumstances and my condition back in Reading, I have but one regret about my decision to hasten out here with Tom, and that is that I have not yet been reconciled with my father and have not received his blessing in person. I will trust you to let him know that I am sorry to have caused him so much disappointment.*

*The lanterns are being extinguished. I must close.*

*Your ever grateful friend,*
*Lovejoy Martin*

# 3

Even before Lovejoy wrote his letter to Barineau on that evening of September 9, 1813, unbeknownst to anyone in Perry's thrown-together fleet, Robert Heriot Barclay, the young commander of the British fleet, had ordered his six ships to slip their moorings and start drifting down the Detroit River toward Lake Erie.

The three Canadians who had deserted to bring intelligence to Perry several days before had not exaggerated the conditions plaguing Commodore Barclay and Major General Henry Proctor of the British army. Besides Canadian militiamen and British soldiers, some fourteen thousand Indian men, women, and children, followers of Tecumseh, had depleted Fort Malden's supplies of flour and other basic foodstuffs. And the presence of Perry's fleet nearby made it risky to send supply boats back to the British base at Long Point on the northeastern shore of Lake Erie. He could wait no longer. It was time for a showdown with the pesky Americans.

Like Perry, the one-armed Barclay was unhappy with the number and the quality of the crews manning his six vessels. Many of his men had been recruited from among Proctor's British soldiers. Barclay was dissatisfied, too, with the quality of his cannon. Failing to obtain enough bona fide naval guns, he had had to supplement his armament with field pieces of various sizes borrowed from the army. And many of his cannon lacked firing mechanisms. Their gun crews had to be taught to fire their pieces by discharging pistols into the breech vents. Still, it was a formidable fleet that floated silently down the river, and by God, he had put them into good shape. They were freshly painted. He had a fine set of junior officers. His crews were well drilled.

Although the Americans had won more than their share of encounters at sea between their handful of frigates and individual British vessels, this would be the first time that two entire fleets would clash. Therefore, Barclay reckoned that he enjoyed one clear advantage: experience. He was a veteran of several battles with the French, including the epochal Trafalgar.

As Barclay saw it, his just completed flagship, the *Detroit,* with nineteen cannon, and the *Queen Charlotte,* with seventeen, might be outgunned by Perry's two brigs, especially at close range, but then his third and fourth largest vessels, the schooner *Lady Prevost,* with fourteen guns, and the brig *Hunter,* with ten, should easily whip any two or even three of Perry's lightly armed gunboats.

Barclay still smarted from the criticism he had received for relaxing his blockade of Presque Isle back in August long enough for the Americans to slip past him. Well, his critics would sing a different tune after tomorrow, unless the Americans tried to duck back into Sandusky Bay and avoid a fight.

As the sun rose above the now calm waters of Lake Erie the next morning, Tom, having lashed up his hammock and attended to his toilet, sat belowdecks on the *Lawrence* with others of his starboard watch, eating his ration of boiled salt beef. Assigned to the crew of the brig's starboard Long Tom near the bow, he had done so well the day before that the hard-bitten gun captain had praised him to Perry himself. Wouldn't that be something to tell Lovejoy later, he was thinking as he drank the vile liquid the ship's cook called coffee, when the bosun's pipes shrilled and the rat-a-tat of a drum echoed from the deck.

"General quarters. All hands clear for action," a petty officer shouted down the hatch.

On the taffrail, Perry stood staring through his spyglass toward the Bass Islands while his officers and petty officers hurried their men to their posts.

"What's this all about?" an out-of-breath Tom asked as he reported to his gun captain.

"We just got a signal from over there on Gibraltar Point," the gunner's mate said. "The English is coming out."

Several minutes later, a similar scene took place aboard the *Niagara.*

After Lovejoy had climbed the ratlines with his musket and settled himself on the fighting top, he asked the Kentuckian what was going on.

"It do sound like the English has showed themselves. Anyway, this ain't no drill. Here, you, Sambo," he said to the Negro marksman. "Haul your black ass up to the topmast and tell us what you can see."

"Who you calling Sambo? That ain't my name. And I ain't doing nothing for nobody that talks to me so. Send this fine Philadelphia gentleman if you don't want to go yourself."

The Kentuckian laughed. "I forgot. You said you was a free man. So I'll ask you kindly if you please will go up and take a look."

"Why couldn't you have axed me nicely in the first place?"

"I swan, I don't know if I would have volunteered if I had knowed I would be sleeping and eating with a bunch of niggers. What about you, Mr. Philadelphia?"

"The bravest man on our schooner was a black man."

"I reckon they are all right as long as they know their place. Can't stand an uppity one, though." Then he called out, "What do you see up there?"

"Ain't no English ships, but things is stirring on ours."

"Well, stay up there and let us know when you see anything."

It was 6 A.M. when Perry received the signal that the British fleet was approaching from the northwest. At the time, a faint breeze was blowing from the southwest, which meant that Barclay would have the weather gage, such as it was, unless the American vessels could clear a nearby island and find elbow room to maneuver themselves to the windward of their approaching foe.

By 7 A.M., with the *Niagara* in the lead, Perry's fleet was under way. Soon thereafter, the Negro marksman called down, "I sees them now. They is a long ways off, but they is headed our way for sure. I counts six of them."

After two hours of tedious, futile tacking to get to windward of a nearby island, Perry summoned his sailing master to the bow. From his gun station, Tom heard him say that he wanted to give up and bear to the northeast.

"Why, sir, you will be conceding the weather gage. We will be fighting at a disadvantage," the sailing master replied.

"I don't care. To windward or leeward, they shall fight today. Pass the order to the helm and signal the other vessels."

At the time, Tom was unaware of the several great pieces of luck that had befallen Perry already since he had come out to Lake Erie. But he observed at close hand a fresh one.

Before Perry's orders could be relayed to the *Niagara* and other vessels, the wind died away briefly and then resumed, this time from the southeast. In a flash, the advantage of the weather gage had passed from the British to the Americans.

Perry clapped the shoulder of his relieved sailing master. With the wind now off his port quarter, he shifted his course to the northwest, heading obliquely for the British. Adjusting to the inevitable, Barclay brought his six ships into a compact line of battle on a now westward course.

The distance between the two fleets was so great and the wind so light that it would be nearly two hours before the first blows were struck. During that time, to the cheers of his excited crewmen, Perry ran up his "Don't give up the ship" pennant. After making a short speech about the significance of the banner, he ordered a full meal to be served throughout the fleet.

From his vantage point above the deck of the *Niagara,* Lovejoy chewed on his hardtack and watched both the distant British sails and Perry's other vessels. In his dejected state, he felt no fear. But the Kentuckian was growing less self-confident.

"You was at sea, was you, Philadelphia?"

"Yes. Aboard a schooner out of Baltimore."

"See any fighting?"

"More than I wanted to."

"Anybody hurt?"

"Several, including our captain, who lost a leg. How about yourself? Done much fighting?"

"Not as much as I would like to. My brother was killed last December at the River Raisin massacre. Him and others surrendered and the British stood by and let the Indian savages slaughter our people. That is how I come to join up with General Harrison. I was at Fort Stephenson back at the end of July when the bastards attacked there. Tried to make us surrender. We whipped their asses and sent them back across the Detroit River with their tails between their legs. I ain't satisfied, though. Don't know who I hate the worse, the English or the Indians. Anyway, I hope we can even up the score today. That is my story. What is yours?"

"Mine is too complicated to tell."

As the British fleet came into clearer view, Perry saw that Barclay's flagship, the *Detroit,* occupied the second place in the enemy line, and the *Queen Charlotte* the fourth. Accordingly, he signaled Elliott that he was moving the *Lawrence* ahead of the *Niagara.* In the process of making this shift, the American fleet became strung out, with the gunboats

*Scorpion* and *Ariel* in the van while the other smaller vessels straggled two miles behind. The two lines converged slowly.

The more Tom saw of Perry pacing about the stern of the *Lawrence,* the more impressed he was by the cocky Rhode Islander. At one point, Perry, accompanied by his young brother James, slowly walked the length of the brig's sand-strewn deck, down the port side, and then back along the starboard, stopping to chat with the crews of each of his eighteen massive carronades and his forward Long Tom and checking to make sure that cartridges were laid out and cannonballs at hand. He lectured the several young powder monkeys about the necessity of opening the hatches just wide enough to pass ammunition up from the hold and keeping no more than one extra powder charge at a time on deck for each gun.

"All it takes is for a spark to fly down into our magazine or a pile of cartridges on deck and we'd all be blown up, lads."

He stopped at the forward Long Tom and said, "You will fire our first shots. 'Twill take a bit until we can get close enough for our carronades to join in. Make every shot count. Ah, you are the fellow from the privateer. Where is home for you, my boy?"

"Philadelphia, sir. But we sailed out of Baltimore."

"One of those fine topsail schooners they build there?"

"Yes, sir. A three-hundred-ton beauty she is, too."

"If I had her here, I'd send her to circle the British and distract them until I could bring our carronades to bear. I warrant you carried nothing like our thirty-two-pounders on your schooner."

Tom was at the point of telling Perry more about the *Flora* when a man wearing a long apron climbed up the aft companionway.

"All my gear is laid out in the wardroom, sir. I will need some assistants if we incur many casualties."

"I am aware, Parsons. I have designated six stout fellows to carry below anyone needing your attentions, but meanwhile, let me suggest that you not wear that butcher's apron up here. Don't want to demoralize our fellows, do we?"

He turned to shout at his sailing master, "When do you reckon we can close with them?"

"It can't be much longer. Wish we had more wind stirring. The *Tigress* and *Trippe* have their sweeps out but still can't seem to keep up with the *Niagara* and the others."

"I have got as much favor from the wind as I can expect."

"He said a mouthful," the captain of Tom's gun crew muttered. "Perry's luck they call it. Hope it holds this day. All right, mates, wrap your ears if you want to save your hearing."

At Perry's command, the *Lawrence* turned her bow more directly toward the British line while raising signals for the other craft to follow suit.

About a quarter before noon, Tom heard a bugle call from the *Detroit* about a mile to the north. Perry whipped out his spyglass and focused it on the enemy flagship.

From the foremast of the *Niagara,* Lovejoy did not hear the sound of the bugle but he did see the flash of a cannon and a billow of smoke. The opening shot of the battle, from a twenty-four-pounder Long Tom, splashed into the water just ahead of the *Lawrence.*

With the bow of the *Lawrence* now turned more directly toward the British line, Perry held his fire. Ahead of him the schooner-gunboats *Scorpion* and *Ariel,* and behind him the little brig *Caledonia*, followed suit while the *Niagara* and the other four small vessels straggled to the rear.

Five minutes later, another flash and billow of smoke burst from the deck of the *Detroit* and, to the shock of Tom and the other men, a twenty-four-pound shot smashed into the *Lawrence*'s forward bulwarks, spraying deadly splinters of wood amongst the men.

Perry shouted, "Signal the *Scorpion* and the *Ariel* to return fire."

A moment after the two forward gunboats opened fire with their long guns, Perry ordered his starboard Long Tom to join in.

Tom's cannon was already loaded and primed. With a muffler wrapped around his head to cover his ears, the gun captain squatted to sight along the barrel and elevated the piece slightly.

"Fire!" The twelve-pounder leaped back against its breeching lines like a startled stallion. Although Tom had placed his hands over his ears, he was shaken by the explosion.

Tom's gun chief shouted, "Run in your gun . . . Search the piece . . . Load with cartridge . . . Shot the gun . . . Come on, lad, bear a hand with that shot . . . All right, prick and prime her . . . Elevate a bit more there and train her forward. Stand clear. This is the last time I will remind you to cover your ears. Now, fire!"

And so it went for the next quarter hour. Caught up in the rhythm of helping service his own gun, Tom had no idea what they were shooting at nor the effectiveness of their firing. While the crews of the carronades stood by their silent short-range weapons, more and more shot from Barclay's *Detroit* struck the *Lawrence*, ripping through her sails and thudding into her sturdy sides of unseasoned timber.

Belowdecks, in the wardroom that now served as his surgeon's station, Usher Parsons's apron was already splattered with blood as he extracted wooden splinters from the first casualties.

From the foremast of the *Niagara*, Lovejoy got a much clearer picture of what was happening than Tom, who was in the thick of the action. The two lead gunboats were firing away at the van of the British line, while the guns of the *Detroit* and the smaller *Hunter* concentrated their fire at the *Lawrence*. Already a cloud bank of smoke lay about the engaged vessels.

Meanwhile, the *Niagara* remained out of the fight, her assigned adversary, the *Queen Charlotte,* a good mile distant.

Frustrated by the punishment the *Lawrence* was taking, Perry ordered his helmsmen to swing briefly to a course parallel to that of the *Detroit* and ordered his starboard carronades to fire.

The *Lawrence* shuddered at the recoil of its own broadside, but the thirty-two-pound shot threw up geysers well short of their target. The frustrated Perry turned his bow once more into the punishing fire from first the *Detroit* and now the *Hunter.*

So intent was he on passing shot to his fellow gunners that Tom was only half conscious of the British cannonballs whistling over his head and smashing into the hull and through the rigging.

By comparison, Lovejoy became more nervous as he observed the destructive fire of the leading British ships against the *Lawrence*. He was startled as the guns of the *Caledonia* just ahead opened up, firing at the *Queen Charlotte,* followed belatedly by the starboard Long Tom of the *Niagara.*

From that point on, with smoke swirling over the deck below him, he could no more tell what was happening between the two fleets than could Tom. Beside him, the Kentuckian licked his lips and checked the priming of his rifle yet again. The farm boy sat with his hands over his ears and his eyes closed.

By 12:15 P.M., in the wardroom of the *Lawrence*, assistant surgeon Parsons was already falling behind in treating the injured men lined up for his attention.

Alarmed at the damage being done to his flagship, Perry again shifted course to bring himself parallel to the British line and ordered his starboard carronades to loose another broadside and for his marksmen to open fire from the rigging. This time several of the *Lawrence*'s missiles struck their target, and Barclay took the first of his casualties.

At this point, Perry had expected Elliott to bring his own thirty-two-pounders into play against the *Queen Charlotte,* but instead, the *Niagara* hung back well astern, firing only its Long Toms, as if trying to avoid counterfire.

Only after the battle did the Americans learn that one of their long-range shots had struck and killed the captain of the *Queen Charlotte,* leaving his second in command to take his place. Seeing that the *Niagara* seemed reluctant to close with him, this replacement put on sail and moved the *Queen Charlotte* up to bring her seventeen guns into action along with the nineteen of the *Detroit* and the *Hunter*'s ten. Thus the fire of the portside cannon of three British ships became concentrated against the *Lawrence,* which was supported only by the two gunboats in the van of the American line.

Once committed to the battle, Perry held nothing back. His landsmen up in the rigging peppered the deck of the British ship with their rifle shots and musket balls. His starboard carronades, firing at a rate twice as fast as that of the Long Toms, belched out broadside after broadside.

Aboard the *Detroit*, her own surgeons soon found their hands full. Barclay himself was hit in the leg by a musket ball, but he returned to his post quickly from the surgeon's station.

Until that September 10, 1813, the greatest terror Tom Jenkins had ever felt had been that day the previous December when the *Flora* had fought its foolish duel with the British snow, when he had almost been struck by a bar shot. In comparison with the next two hours, that encounter seemed like sparring between schoolboys. The carronade next to him was struck in the muzzle and knocked from its platform. A sailor standing beside Perry himself went down with a long splinter in his side. Further forward, other wounded men sprawled in the now bloody sand, victims of splinters and musket balls. Although his marksmen were galling the British with their sharpshooting, Perry had to call them down from the rigging to take the places of sailors and gunners who were falling faster than they could be hauled below to the wardroom for surgery.

There belowdecks, but above the waterline of the shallow draft brig, a scene of horror was taking place. Six times, British cannonballs crashed through the starboard side and out through the port side. In one case, the body of a midshipman whose broken arm Usher Parsons had just splinted was hurled across the wardroom by a cannonball. A marine officer lay screaming in agony from a hideous hip injury that Parsons was helpless to treat. With blood-caked arms and hands, he sewed up arteries to stop bleeding and bandaged wounds. And while his assistants held his moaning patients down, he sawed off mangled arms and legs.

In the midst of this carnage, Perry slid back the hatch and shouted, "Anybody down there that can stand, send them topside."

Having long ago stopped covering his ears, Tom no longer could hear the commands being shouted or the screams of wounded men. The blasts of the carronades seemed muted. But he could tell that the rate of their fire had slackened. Looking down the line, he saw that several had been knocked off their slides and that one had blown up. As he stared down at the body of one of his own gun crew lying on his back, eyes open and mouth gaping, a second man was struck down by a falling pulley block.

Overhead, the sails of the *Lawrence* hung in tatters. Her masts were shattered and her torn shrouds hung loosely. And still the British continued to batter their target, until only two guns remained in action, Tom's and a carronade.

Tom had just passed a shot to the loader of his gun. A trickle of blood ran from one ear. He sat down, exhausted, to rest for a moment on the deck beside the mangled body of a fellow gunner. Just as his crew chief jerked its lanyard, his gun was struck square in the muzzle by a British cannonball. The impact hurled the gun and its carriage backward, rolling over Tom. He was briefly conscious of a crushing pain, and then nothing.

Perry himself left the quarterdeck to help the crew of his remaining carronade load and fire off its final shot.

Throughout the hellish two hours, the *Lawrence* had towed a cutter. After pulling the gun lanyard and sending his final shot toward the British, Perry ordered his "Don't give up the ship" pennant to be hauled down. He then folded the flag under one arm and ordered the boat to be brought to the port side of the brig.

Two-thirds of his men had been killed or wounded. His flagship lay helpless in the water, unable to return enemy fire. Perry and his little brother James climbed down into the boat. Four sailors rowed them away from the wrecked flagship toward the *Niagara,* which belatedly began to make headway to join the fray.

Seeing the *Lawrence*'s flag hauled down, the British slacked off their cannon fire, even as their marksmen intensified the peppering of the water around Perry's rowboat.

With her cannon no longer firing, the smoke drifted away from the *Lawrence* so that Lovejoy could see clearly the flagship's battered decks and tattered sails.

He and his fellow marksmen watched in amazement as the little boat with Perry and his brother passed through a gauntlet of musket balls to the shelter of the port side of the *Niagara.*

The Kentuckian shook his head at the scene below them. "That little son of a bitch Perry is going to have to either put us into the fight now or make a run for it."

Aboard the British flagship, Barclay, his leg smarting from his bandaged wound, studied the helpless wreck his guns had made of the *Lawrence.* He also looked about him at the damage the Americans had done to his ship with their thirty-two-pound carronade shot and at the number of his sailors who lay dead or wounded.

Like Lovejoy's Kentucky marksman, he did not know whether Perry meant to continue the fight or to save his fleet by fleeing. He desperately hoped that it would be the latter. Even at Trafalgar he had not experienced anything like the violent action of the past two hours.

On the deck of the *Niagara*, whose carronades had not yet been fired and whose crew had suffered only a few casualties from long-range British fire, a strange thing was taking place. Without asking why the *Lawrence*'s sister ship had been so slow to close with the British, Perry assumed command of the brig and dispatched Elliott to take charge of the other smaller craft and bring them up quickly to harass the rear of the enemy line.

The two men shook hands. Elliott climbed down into Perry's cutter to be rowed toward the gunboat *Somers*.

Perry handed his pennant to a bosun's mate to be raised to the foremast of the *Niagara*. Shouting orders left and right, he hurried aft to the stern. In a few minutes, the brig slid past the disabled *Lawrence*, which now lay dead in the water, and, with the wind off her port beam, headed for the *Detroit*.

Responding to Perry's shouted orders, Lovejoy and his fellow marksmen opened a steady fire at the deck of the British flagship. The Kentuckian, whose rifle required more time to load, aimed his shots as coolly as if hunting squirrels. Lovejoy, the farm boy, and the black man loaded and fired their muskets as fast as they could without taking careful aim. Musket balls sang through the rigging and spattered the deck of the *Detroit*.

In their zeal to destroy Perry's flagship, the British had bunched up their vessels so that they no longer sailed in an orderly line. Several of the *Detroit*'s portside guns had been dismounted. In order to bring his relatively intact starboard batteries into play against the approaching *Niagara*, Barclay began the slow and intricate process of wearing round, or swinging his ship through the eye of the wind.

On that September day, bad luck overtook Barclay as quickly as good fortune had come to Perry when the wind had suddenly shifted that morning. A musket ball fired by one of the marksmen in the *Niagara*'s rigging struck his single arm, breaking the bone and sending him in agony belowdecks to his surgeon, just at the moment that his seasoned leadership was most needed.

Aboard the *Queen Charlotte,* the replacement for the fallen captain of that ship had himself suffered a severe wound. Command had passed to a provincial marine officer who knew little of sailing. On seeing the *Detroit* attempt its turn, this greenhorn commander tried to follow suit. And in doing so, the head booms of the *Queen Charlotte* ran afoul of the mizzen rigging of the *Detroit*, locking the two ships together.

After the battle, Lovejoy's Kentucky companion would claim that he had fired the shot that had disabled Barclay. Whoever was entitled to the credit, the two main British ships had been left under the command of junior officers who now found themselves unable to maneuver.

Meanwhile, Perry had put over the helm of the *Niagara* and sailed the brig across the bow of the *Detroit*, breaking the British line. At a range of less than a hundred yards, his starboard batteries lashed away at the two entangled giants with both grape and round shot, while his port broadsides tore into three lesser vessels. So punishing was the fire that the men aboard the *Lady Prevost* abandoned their fourteen cannon and hid belowdecks, leaving their captain, who had been horribly wounded, hanging over the rail, screaming with pain. Perry, seeing this, ordered his larboard guns to stop firing on the helpless schooner.

While the *Niagara* sat in the midst of the British fleet, pounding away with both starboard and port broadsides, Elliott brought up four small American craft to join the action. Like so many terriers tormenting two wounded bulls, they poured cannon and musket fire into the British ships. The *Detroit* also was taking punishment from the *Caledonia, Ariel,* and *Scorpion.*

When the new commander finally broke the *Detroit* free from the *Queen Charlotte,* he was unable to handle the ship. Her masts and spars were too splintered to carry enough sail for her to gain headway. More than fifty of her men lay dead or wounded.

With more than forty of her men dead or wounded, the *Queen Charlotte* was little better off. The junior commander of this British ship was the first to haul down his flag.

The *Detroit*'s colors could not be lowered. Barclay had ordered them nailed to the mast. So his replacement told a crewman to wave a white cloth from a boarding pike.

The final action of the battle of Lake Erie, from the time Perry reached the deck of the *Niagara* until his guns fell silent at the waving of that white cloth, covered little more than half an hour.

Aboard the *Niagara* and the other nearby American craft, a mighty cheer arose as the men realized that the battle was over and that they had won. In the brief time since Perry had left one brig to assume command of the other, control of Lake Erie had passed from British to American hands.

Lovejoy's eyes smarted from the gunsmoke. His right shoulder ached from the kick of his musket. The fingers of his left hand were blistered from the heat of the barrel.

The Kentuckian grinned and clapped him on the back.

"By God, Philadelphia, we done it. We got something to tell our grandchildren about now, ain't we? Here now, what you looking so down at the mouth for? Can't you see we whipped their asses?"

Lovejoy was peering at the remains of the *Lawrence*.

"I am worried about my friend."

"I reckon you got a right to. From the looks of that there ship, if he is alive and well he can count hisself a lucky man."

Within an hour after the battle ended, Perry returned to the *Lawrence* to thank the men for their courageous fight and to inquire about the casualties.

"I count twenty men and two officers killed and about sixty wounded, sir," the lieutenant whom Perry had left in command said. "I was sorry to haul down our colors. You go down into the wardroom and you will understand why I had to stop the slaughter. Parsons has his hands full down there."

"You did the right thing, Yarnell. Now come with me. I will visit the injured and then must write a dispatch to General Harrison to let him know the outcome of the battle."

"Let me congratulate you, sir, on this great victory. We have taken every one of their vessels, have we not?"

"Two of their schooners have made a run for it, but I have sent the *Scorpion* and the *Trippe* to overtake them. Anyway, Yarnell, I accept your congratulations. Now we have a lot of cleaning up to do."

"Are the British captains to surrender to us here or aboard the *Niagara*?"

"I have left word for Elliott to send them here. Bring them to me when they arrive. And see that they are treated with absolute courtesy. They put up a valiant fight, and I want no one to gloat in their presence."

Aboard the *Niagara*, Lovejoy and the other marksmen climbed down the ratlines to the deck. Only two of the crewmen had been killed, but twenty-five men had been injured, nearly all of them after Perry had come aboard.

Lovejoy stood the cries of the wounded until Lieutenant Elliott returned to the brig.

"Sir, these men need medical attention."

"Indeed they do, and the assistant surgeon is too ill to attend to them. They must be moved to the *Lawrence*."

"Is there surgical equipment and medicine available for their treatment?"

"You're the privateer chap, aren't you? Why are you pestering me with these questions?"

"Aboard our schooner, it was necessary that I gain some little knowledge of treating wounds."

"Did you for a fact? Ah well, beggars can't be choosers. Everything you need should be laid out in the wardroom. I will send you down some assistants. What did you say your name was?"

Later in his life, Lovejoy would have difficulty remembering all that he had seen and done during that long month of September 1813. Even those experiences he could recall did not fall into any orderly sequence.

Although the ride across Ohio remained a blur in his memory, he could recollect every moment of his part in the battle of Lake Erie.

His long night of labor by lantern light in the wardroom of the *Niagara*, bandaging wounds, splinting broken limbs, suturing arteries, and, in one case, amputating an arm, all those frantic hours seemed later to have been something he had only dreamed.

Yet he remembered clearly standing by the rail the next morning while Elliott read the burial service and the remains of two crewmen, sewn up in their hammocks with thirty-two-pound shot, were slid into the water.

He would not remember Elliott's praise for his patch-up surgery nor, later, back at Put-in-Bay, watching a cortege of boats ceremoniously carrying the bodies of both British and American officers to be buried in a common grave on South Bass Island.

He would sleep for a few hours, then arise to change the dressings of his patients' wounds, then fall across the bunk assigned him in the wardroom to sleep again.

Two days later, an exhausted Usher Parsons came aboard to inspect the wounded of the *Niagara*.

"Who has been attending to these men?" he asked the black marksman who had been assisting Lovejoy.

"That gentleman from Philadelphia standing over there."

"Look here, sir," Parsons said to Lovejoy. "I never saw a neater job than you have done on that poor fellow's arm. What is your profession?"

"I am part owner of a privateer now being refitted."

"I'd say you missed your calling. Should have been a doctor. Nicely done suturing on that fellow's scalp. By the Almighty, I could have used you aboard the *Lawrence* these past two days. Down in the cockpit, during the battle itself, with cannonballs crashing through our hold, mind you, I cut off six legs. Then yesterday morning I had to amputate two arms. One of them right up against the chap's shoulder. He'll be lucky if he lives. I have got to go back and trepan a poor sailor with a fractured skull. Ugly business. Probably can't save him, but I must try."

"Excuse me, but I have a good friend on the *Lawrence*. I have been wondering how he might be. His name is Tom Jenkins."

"I am not familiar with the name, but look here, the *Lawrence* is to be turned into a hospital ship. We're to transfer your wounded and those from the other ships over to her. Eventually we will sail or have her towed back to Erie. I have asked for a doctor to be sent over from Harrison's army. And a British doctor may be joining me, but until then I will have my hands full. I would count it a great favor if you would come along and assist me. It will give you a chance to see your friend."

Lovejoy would not remember much of this conversation, but he could never forget climbing up the battered side of the *Lawrence* and standing on the scarred deck, looking in vain for Tom.

"Come along below and you will see what I have been doing," Parsons said.

In the faintly lit berthing deck, with a growing sense of dread,

Lovejoy slowly walked along, peering down at each of the patients lying on pallets lined up along the hull.

"How many men did you lose?" he asked.

"I count twenty so far, but I hold out little hope for one or two of my amputees. And it will be a miracle if I can save the chap with the head injury, although I will do my best. Ever do a trepan?"

"I am afraid not. Look, I have not seen my friend above decks or down here."

"What did you say his name was?"

"Jenkins, Tom Jenkins."

One of Tom's wounded fellow gunners, lying propped up on one elbow, overheard this.

"You're talking about the chap from the privateer?"

"Yes."

"He is laying over there next to the wardroom. But he'll not know you. In a bad way, he is."

"Oh," Parsons said. "Is that your friend? Sad case. Was knocked senseless by a gun carriage. Still unconscious, he is. Sorry I didn't recognize the name."

Stooping to avoid bumping his head, Lovejoy hurried to the figure under a blanket. Tom's eyes were closed.

"He's not the man you plan to trepan, is he?"

"No. He has no broken bones beyond a few ribs. He must be terribly injured inside though. Can't say what his chances are."

"He'll live. He's got to," Lovejoy said as he knelt beside his friend.

That night, after Lovejoy had assisted Parsons in the removal of bone fragments from a sailor's fractured skull, he stretched out on a blanket beside the still unconscious Tom and tried to sleep. During the night, a storm swept over the area, causing the *Lawrence* to strain against her cables and roll about so violently that many of the already suffering wounded became seasick. Nearby, the shot-riddled masts of the British ships the *Detroit* and the *Queen Charlotte* collapsed from the whiplash motion of the waves.

Tom remained in a coma the next morning. After assisting Parsons in changing the dressings of the other wounded, Lovejoy sat beside his friend, willing him to keep breathing. At times during the next week, Lovejoy nearly gave up hope. But, except when on duty or sleeping, he never stopped talking in low tones to Tom, reminding him of the days they had ridden about Philadelphia on his, Lovejoy's, pony, or their fishing and swimming in the Schuylkill River, and recalling persons they had known as children.

When he ran out of shared memories to talk about, Lovejoy would recite speeches from Shakespeare and quotes from Montaigne. After that he read passages from a borrowed Bible.

One night, as he was at the point of falling asleep, Lovejoy realized that he had barely thought of Madeline Richter since he had come aboard the *Lawrence.* For a few minutes he reflected on the first time he had seen her aboard ship, then saying good-bye to her on the Philadelphia dock. He was reliving the conversation in which he had asked her father for her hand when he fell into a deep sleep. But she returned to him in a dream, holding out her hands and saying, "Why did you desert me?" He awoke, sweating and gasping for breath.

A week after the battle, as Parsons had feared, the sailor on whom he and Lovejoy had performed a trepan died. Parsons was dejected by the death.

"You go to so much trouble to save a life, and then you have to wonder what was the use," he said.

"Well, look around you at the men who wouldn't be alive if you had not been on duty."

"I suppose you are right. Here, let's see if there is any change in your friend."

He knelt and lifted one of Tom's eyelids.

"Pupil still dilated. I gather you are very close to your friend, Mr. Martin," Parsons said as he felt Tom's pulse.

"We have been like brothers since we were children."

At that point, the army doctor General Harrison had sent to assist stopped to listen to their conversation. Parsons stood up and shook his head.

"How long has he been like this?"

"Ever since the battle."

"After a week, not many recover from a coma."

"I know, Dr. Crow. I know."

Lovejoy suddenly lashed out with, "You don't know anything, neither of you. You are a pair of half-educated sawbones. There have been many cases of people recovering from long-term comas. Why, at St.

Bartholomew's there was a man who had been thrown from a horse. He was unconscious for six weeks and . . ."

"St. Bartholomew's in London?" the army doctor said.

"Yes. And the patient awoke one morning to complain that he was thirsty. They released him the next day."

"What do you know of Barts?" the doctor said.

"He went to school there, you damn fool."

The three men stopped and with open mouths stared down at Tom.

Parsons broke the shocked silence.

"Was that you, Jenkins?"

"Who the hell did you think it was?" Tom mumbled.

The two doctors were slack jawed at Tom's suddenly regaining consciousness. The army doctor started to examine Tom, but Parsons held him back.

"Leave them alone for a moment."

"Why didn't you tell me the fellow had studied medicine in London?" the army doctor whispered as Lovejoy, now kneeling beside his friend, told Tom how the battle had turned out.

"I didn't know it."

Later Lovejoy apologized to the two doctors for insulting them. And he explained that he had studied at St. Bartholomew's only briefly.

"I couldn't stand the sight of blood," he said.

"You seem to have got over it," Parsons said.

"I haven't really. It just isn't my line of work."

"What is, then?" Parsons asked.

"I have got to sort that out later. My first order of business is to see Tom Jenkins well again."

"And that will take a while. If he tries to move about before his ribs have knit, he could puncture a lung. So, we will take the both of you back with us to Erie. But you will have to work your passage. Oh, and by the way, I may not have been to St. Bartholomew's, but I did study under Dr. John Warren in Boston and I hold a license for the practice of physics from the Massachusetts Medical Society."

"Mr. Parsons, I have walked the wards with the great surgeon John Abernethy at Barts, and I don't think he could teach you anything you don't already know from hard experience."

"Then you realize I am not just a half-educated sawbones."

With jury-rigged sails, the *Lawrence* rolled and wallowed her way back to Erie. The fort protecting the harbor fired a seventeen-gun salute to honor Perry's flagship. The next day, Lovejoy assisted Parsons in ferrying over the wounded to Erie by small boat. Tom and the other serious cases were taken to the log courthouse now serving as a hospital.

And there Lovejoy finally found time to write to Evan Jenkins about Tom's injuries and the need to keep him immobilized until his ribs and internal organs had healed. He also wrote to his Uncle Ephraim, Malcolm MacKenzie, and Pierre Barineau.

After dispatching those letters, he went to a local tavern and drank himself into a stupor with some of the sailors from the *Lawrence*. He awakened the next morning in bed with the tavern wench. He looked at her face, slack with sleep, lying on the pillow beside him. Quietly, he slid out of bed and dressed himself. As he started for the door, his bedmate propped herself on one elbow and said sleepily, "You didn't forget to leave the money on the stand, did you, dearie? I must say, you got more than your money's worth out of this girl. Never knew a gentleman to be in such a state of need. But it was ever so nice for me, as well. By the way, who is Madeline? Rather not say, would you? Anyway, even if that is not my name, you'll know where to find me the next time you're feeling like a romp."

Feeling a self-disgust rare for him, Lovejoy made his way through a cold rain to the courthouse to see how Tom was faring.

This experience, too, soon faded from Lovejoy's memory.

# 7

*October 15, 1813—Baltimore*

*Dear Lovejoy*

*Your letter of September 26 reached us here in Baltimore soon after the news of Perry's tremendous victory on Lake Erie. I doubt that London celebrated Nelson's victory at Trafalgar any more enthusiastically than Baltimore did Perry's remarkable achievement. The entire city was illuminated and the streets were jammed with celebrants. Our newspapers report similar celebrations in Philadelphia, New York, and even Boston.*

*We are indeed sorry to learn of Tom Jenkins's injuries. If he has survived with the loss of hearing in one ear and some sore ribs, I suppose he will have to consider himself quite fortunate. At any rate, please give him our best regards.*

*Lovejoy, your presence here in Baltimore is badly needed.*

*Up in Philadelphia, the Flora will soon be ready to go to sea again, and Talbot Smith is determined to take her out once more under his captaincy. But, mindful of your instructions to Barineau, I am loath to make the necessary applications for bonds, licenses, and such. Furthermore, the schooner should not be sold without full agreement to do so by Talbot and myself as well as yourself. Naturally, I would be guided by your wishes, but Talbot is quite another matter. I have not yet dared broach to him the subject of selling the schooner.*

*So, assuming that Tom is out of danger and you can be spared from your medical duties at Erie, I implore you to return to Baltimore as soon as possible. This problem cannot be resolved without you here in person.*

*Barineau told us of the disappointment of your hopes for marriage. My dear Flo and I are sorry about this. Just remember that you have plenty of time to find the right person with whom to share the rest of your life.*

*I am appending a list of the monies due ourselves and the crew from prizes and cargoes condemned and sold as well as bounties for vessels destroyed and prisoners brought back. Even without the value of the* Flora *herself, there should be wealth enough here to enable you to do whatever you wish.*

*By the by, I have received word that your fellow crewmen who had meant to join Perry's fleet returned from the west disappointed at their failure to get there in time for the battle. Their coach driver abandoned them at Bedford.*

*And saving perhaps the best news for last, I have received word that your father's condition is no longer so serious.*

*So there it is, Lovejoy. The sooner you can travel here, the better. Convey to Tom our best wishes. We give thanks to the Almighty that both you and he survived the battle, and that He gave us a sorely needed victory in this vexing war.*

*Your friend and obedient servant,*
*Malcolm MacKenzie*

*October 17, 1813—Philadelphia*

*Dear Lovejoy:*

*Ever since we parted at Adamstown, I have been most concerned about you. Amanda and Frank and Rebecca have shared my anxiety, especially since arrival of the news of the dreadful naval battle out there on Lake Erie. It troubled me deeply to read of the sad loss of so many killed and wounded in both the American and British fleets. We have been praying fervently that your name would not appear among the casualties. Your letter of September 26 came like an answer to our prayers. Thank God that you have come through safely.*

*I am sorry, of course, to learn of young Jenkins's injury but am pleased that he is on the mend. Caution him not to exert himself until his ribs have knit. And if he has internal injuries, as you suspect, it would be best that he remain where he is for a time. Upon his eventual return to Philadelphia, I would be pleased to examine him and render a better informed opinion.*

*Meanwhile, it pleases me to report that your father shows some mild improvement in his condition. He is able to sit up and move around his room, with assistance. And his speech is no longer so slurred. He has been asking about both you and Chester. We have told him about your joining Perry's fleet. His improvement followed news of the outcome of the battle.*

*As for Chester, we have told Jeremiah repeatedly that he is on an extended business trip, which is not entirely false. I don't know how much longer we can keep the truth from him.*

*Meanwhile, Charles Bennett and Frank are overseeing the affairs of the company with, I fear, indifferent results, although many others are profiting from the war. Those who had in stock any foreign goods sell them at great profits. Coffee has risen from 15 cents a pound to 35; sugar prices have trebled. The stoppage of foreign commerce diverts some investment capital into the countryside, where farmers now get good prices for produce to be shipped in neutral vessels out of New England ports or slipped out in American bottoms through the blockade. And domestic manufactories flourish. However, we hear that President Madison intends to ask the Congress to enact a new embargo to prevent our ships from even trying to slip through the British blockade. Foolish man and his foolish war, which he finances through ruinous discounted loans, despite frequent talk of internal taxation.*

*To celebrate Perry's triumph, the first illumination of the city since the commencement of the war took place on September 25 by permission of Mayor Barker, an ardent war hawk. It resulted in much injury to property and persons. Some ruffian threw a stone through our parlor window. The same fate befell other Friends in our meeting because their houses, like ours, remained dark during the revelries of the mob.*

*Bad as these fruits of war may seem to us peace-minded folk of Philadelphia, they are trifling compared with the lot of settlers in the Alabama territory. Enflamed by appeals from Tecumseh to reclaim Indian lands from whites, the Creeks are reported to have slain some 400 men, women, and children at Fort Mims. How great a calamity has befallen our nation. I shudder at the talk of the revenge to be taken against our Indian brethren.*

*Keep well. Return to us soon, we pray.*

*Ephraim McGee, M.D.*

*October 23, 1813—Philadelphia*

*Dear Lovejoy:*

*It was a great relief to get your letters, both the one written at Sandusky before the battle and the more recent one from Erie. You and Tom have as many lives as the proverbial cat.*

*I am hungry to hear your eyewitness account of the Lake Erie battle, and that of Tom Jenkins. I am eager, also, to hear more about the victory of Harrison's army against the British and their Indian allies on Canadian soil three weeks ago. If first reports reaching here are true, we captured 600 British soldiers and killed Tecumseh himself. The papers claim that your great hero, Perry himself, went ashore to observe the battle.*

*Two nights ago, the city of Philadelphia was illuminated, and this for the second time in as many weeks, the first being occasioned by news of the battle of Lake Erie. The war, while going well in the northwest, is far from over, I fear.*

*I have been back in Philadelphia for the past week to look into the refitting of the Flora. Talbot Smith has his precious creation almost ready to return to sea, and he is hell-bent to "take her out while the pickings are still there to be picked."*

*Perhaps by now you will have heard that Collins and the others turned back before they reached even Pittsburgh. They claim that the driver of their coach deserted them. I don't think Collins had his heart in the venture, anyway. He only went to kill time until Megan Jenkins recovered her health enough for their marriage to go forward. She does seem better these days.*

*To return to Talbot Smith, he lives aboard the Flora. He has run through several crews of workmen who can't bear his demanding supervision. However, Collins and the others are pitching in to help. And your friend Evan Jenkins daily goes to the dock to observe the work. In fact, he and Talbot have become fast friends. Your name is often on their tongues, incidentally.*

*I know that Malcolm has implored you to return to Baltimore first to settle the accounts of the Flora and then to decide what is to be done with her. Although less than it would have been a few months ago, her value remains high. Fast sailer that she is, she might be just right for eluding the British blockade on Delaware Bay and carrying a cargo to*

*Europe. If talk of yet another—this time iron-clad—embargo on such trade should turn out to have substance, her only use then would be as a privateer.*

*So, let me add my appeal to MacKenzie's for you to return to the east, the sooner the better.*

*In friendship,*
*Pierre Barineau*

*Oct 24—Philladelfa*

*Dere Dr Martin*

*The Flora is ready to sail agin. Mackinsy is draging his feet about the papers. We need you to get your ass back here & help us straiten out things. Hope you will sail with us. By now you aught to be a purty good sergin.*

*Me and yore frend Evan Jinkins has got to be thick as theves. He thinks the world of you. I have not tole him any better. Aniway get on back here soon or I will take the Flora out papers or no papers.*

*Talbot Smith*

# 8

"Megan, that is the silliest thing I ever did hear of."

"What is silly about wanting to go look after my brother?"

"It is too dangerous. You have been pretty sick yourself."

"But I am much better now."

"Even so, it is a long way out to Erie. We had trouble getting even as far as Bedford. After you travel past Harrisburg, the roads are terrible. And you will have to sleep in places I don't like to think of you staying in."

"Now Calvin, Pa will be with me. Primrose doesn't want him to go, but he insists on doing so. And I will not let him make the trip alone."

"Why can't your brothers go with him?"

"I wouldn't send those two to rescue a sick dog. They are totally irresponsible."

"You promised you would marry me once you got well. If you are well enough to travel three hundred miles and back, then why don't we get married right now? We can go out there together as man and wife."

"Now, wouldn't that make a lovely honeymoon? No, there will be time for a wedding once we get back. I am not marrying anyone until my brother is back here safe and sound."

A long silence followed this statement. Finally Collins said, "I suppose he will still be out there too."

"Who are you talking about?"

"I mean that fellow Martin that calls himself a doctor."

"Look, Calvin, I have told you that there was never anything between Lovejoy and me. I used to have a silly infatuation for him, but I got over that. I really did. So please stop acting jealous. It makes you sound little and mean."

"Whereas Dr. Martin is the grand rich man's son that can do no wrong. Well, let me tell you this, Megan. If you had seen him as we did in Harrisburg, you wouldn't think so highly of him. He acted like a lunatic."

"He risked his life to rescue me and, for that matter, yourself, from the British. He has been looking after my brother Tom faithfully. I don't want to hear anything else against him, or about him. Now, it is getting late, Calvin. We can talk about this again tomorrow, but I have heard enough for tonight."

"Do I get a kiss?"

"If you like. There, now that is enough. Good night."

"Megan, I wish you loved me as much as I love you."

"What makes you think I don't?"

"You just don't act like you do."

"I promised to marry you, didn't I?"

"Yes, sure. After you got well. And now it is after your brother gets well. And after that, what will it be?"

"Stop talking like that. All right, one more kiss. Then you must clear out. I promised Primrose I would help bathe the baby and put him to bed."

"I tell you, Amanda, this whole ugly business grew out of a misunderstanding of some sort. Oh, I feel so humiliated to have to come to you like this."

"No more tears, please, Rosalind. What is it you wish the family to do?"

"Why, pay that dreadful man Bledsoe his blood money so that Chester can return."

"Chester is a civilian. They have no right to hold him prisoner. Lawyer Bennett has promised to write to the State Department about this matter."

"But that will take forever. Meanwhile, they are keeping poor Chester in chains, giving him only bread and water. Meanwhile, my friends keep asking where my husband is. I am weary of having to put up these pretenses. Cannot I at least lay this before Papa Martin? He would understand, I am sure."

"Now, Rosalind, Father knows nothing about this business, and Uncle Ephraim has ordered that we keep him ignorant of the matter."

"Your Uncle Ephraim and your husband were ready enough to dig deep to post a ransom for Lovejoy. Why not for Chester? Must I remind them that Chester himself scraped up part of the ransom for Lovejoy and then went to the considerable trouble of traveling out to Bermuda."

"There is some question of his motives in doing that."

"Surely, you cannot believe such a monstrous lie. Chester would never do a thing like that."

"Well, he has never been very close with Lovejoy."

"He has often been disappointed by Lovejoy's behavior, but Chester has nothing but the deepest affection for his brother."

"If it is any consolation to you, dear Rosalind, Uncle Ephraim has written asking Lovejoy to return here as soon as he can. You know he was in that dreadful battle on Lake Erie and has stayed on to treat the wounded. Upon his return, we can seek his advice as to how to effect Chester's release."

"I did not know he might be coming back to Philadelphia. Then let me speak of another urgent matter, and this cannot wait for his return. I am at a loss as to how to bring this to the attention of Frank or Mr. Bennett."

"Is there anything I can do to help?"

"Yes. You see, at my insistence, Chester signed notes to scrape up our portion of the ransom that was to be paid for Lovejoy's release. He even took out a mortgage on our little house."

"That was generous of you."

"As it was of poor Chester. The point is, to date, the monies have not been returned to us."

"I confess that I am ignorant of the financial aspects."

"As am I. But I do know that I have bills to be paid. Could you not use your influence with Frank to have our ten thousand dollars returned to us?"

"Us?"

"I mean, of course, me. Having no funds makes Chester's absence doubly embarrassing."

"I will mention this to Frank. Now, please compose yourself, Rosalind. I am sure that all this will soon be cleared up and Chester will be returned to you and his family."

"I only wish his family showed as much interest in his release as they did his brother's. But I will say no more about it. Thank you for hearing me out. And you will not forget to mention the return of our ten thousand dollars, I trust. It would grieve me to have to seek representation by a lawyer."

"Well, Mr. Bennett, now that you have had time to study the letter from Chester and this latest ransom demand from Bledsoe, what do you think we should do?"

"It really is up to you, Frank. You, your wife, and her uncle. Are you prepared to raise another forty thousand dollars, this time to rescue someone who allegedly got trapped while trying to defraud you?"

"This letter from Chester curdles my blood. Shut away from all human contact on a diet of bread and water. Kept in chains. That is inhuman. Amanda wept when I told her of what he wrote."

"His version of how he came to be incarcerated does not jibe with Barineau's."

"I wonder if there is any truth to his claim that Barineau and Lovejoy drugged and robbed him without giving him the opportunity to explain his mission."

"Frank, when you have been a lawyer as long as I, you realize that no two persons ever see an event in the same way, especially when there are conflicting self-interests involved."

"We have only Barineau's account."

"It is too bad that we cannot interview the Swedish captain who Barineau says was involved."

"But you said that the documents Barineau delivered were incriminating."

"They indicate that Chester was engaged in a trading scheme. He probably would argue that he was merely killing two birds with one stone, trying to turn a profit while rescuing his brother. The evidence of chicanery is persuasive but not conclusive."

"What do you make of this Captain Bledsoe's letter?"

"By Barineau's account, this is that gentleman's third attempt to extort ransom money from the Martin family. First for the Jenkins girl on the mistaken assumption that she was engaged to Lovejoy, then for Lovejoy himself, and now for Chester. He sounds like a charlatan of the worst kind."

"So what is your advice?"

"First, it does not appear that Chester's life is in immediate danger. He writes to us from a prison near Plymouth called, let's see . . . Old Mill. At least it is not Dartmoor. Bledsoe's letter was sent from his home near Plymouth, so I suspect that he wants Chester kept at close hand. Secondly, I would expect Lovejoy to return soon from Erie. I would like to hear from his own lips the story of what happened on Bermuda and, for that matter, seek his advice on what course to follow. Certainly, we should not raise a fresh ransom without his approval."

Frank Carpenter rose from his seat in Bennett's law office.

"Amanda says that Chester's wife came to see her. She is worried sick about Chester and desperate for money herself."

"Did she refer to the letter she received from her husband in the same cartel post with ours?"

"She told Amanda that it was too personal to be read by anyone else. She also asked Amanda to take up with us the question of the money they put up for Lovejoy's ransom."

"By rights, some of that money should be returned to the accounts of Martin Shipping."

"Quite so. I am unable to take advantage of some trading opportunities because we lack ready capital. Yet, as the sole proprietor of Martin Shipping, Chester did nothing illegal in tapping its funds. And he raised part of the ten thousand dollars by taking a mortgage on his house."

Bennett drew a small ledger from his desk.

"Let's see, Barineau returned your bill of credit and Ephraim's. Instead of Chester's, he delivered eighteen thousand dollars in specie and drafts on Boston banks, so there is a profit there of eighty percent. Does his wife know that?"

"No, and I would just as soon that she did not. Rosalind has a mercenary streak. She had the gall to utter a veiled threat to seek her own legal counsel. Anyway, I have no objection to returning to her the original ten thousand dollars, unless you feel we should wait for Lovejoy's return to do so."

"I see no reason for delay. You can tell Amanda to inform Chester's wife that she has worked her will on these two hard-hearted men of business. I will see to drawing up the papers. So, you really expect Lovejoy to be coming home, do you?"

"Well, Joy, I would hate to see you go, of course, but I understand you have better things to do than hang about this God-forsaken town."

"Tom, if you have any doubts that you are on the mend, I will write and tell them that we must stay here until after Christmas, or however long it takes for you to recover."

"I feel a hundred percent better just in the past week. It no longer hurts when I breathe. And Dr. Parsons says I will be all right, as long as I don't try to lift anything heavy for a while. Of course, he wouldn't want to lose your assistance, but that is his lookout. No, Joy, I would feel terrible if you lost a bundle of money on my account."

"The money really doesn't matter that much to me anymore, but I do have to think about the crew and my fellow shareholders, I suppose."

"I agree. Remember that I am due four shares as supercargo. So there is another reason why I think you ought to go back and straighten out your business."

"I want to think about this overnight. If I do decide to go back, I promise I will return to help you travel back home."

"You needn't go to that trouble. I ought to be in good enough shape to travel on my own in another month or two."

"I forbid you to even think about attempting a trip until you have absolutely recovered. You don't know how near you came to dying."

Tom looked into the fire about which they were huddled in the courthouse meeting hall and pulled his blanket closer around him.

"Speaking of recovering, I hope that you are getting over . . . well, you know, that business back in Berks County."

"You and I are both convalescents, Tom. Your hurt is deep inside your body, and it will take time to heal. Mine is in my soul, and it may take even longer."

"That kind of talk makes me worry about you taking such a long trip by yourself."

"Oh, I will be all right."

"Just don't go doing anything foolish. What is over, is over, you know."

Lovejoy laughed harshly.

"A woman back in London said something like that when I was having to leave for Philadelphia."

"And you got over her?"

"I was in love with myself rather than her. That was nothing compared to what I am going through now."

"Just don't go doing anything foolish."

"You said that already."

# 9

After saying good-bye to Tom and Usher Parsons, Lovejoy boarded an ox-drawn wagon headed for Waterford on the headwaters of French Creek. He was so frustrated by the slow pace of the oxen and the tiresome conversation of the driver that he got off and sprinted the last two miles of the fourteen-mile journey.

After a night spent in a sort of dormitory for wagoners and riverboat men, plagued by the bites of bedbugs and the sound of snoring, he awakened to find that a foot of snow had fallen.

He spent the next two days and nights shivering under a blanket aboard a keelboat moving with the current down French Creek into the Allegheny River and thence to Pittsburgh. There he boarded a stagecoach headed east for Bedford.

At a Bedford inn, he lay awake far into the night debating what route to follow from there: the way urged by an irrational emotion, or the course dictated by common sense. The first way would lead him back to Reading for a confrontation with Madeline and her family; the other back into a business and family rut. Had he made the decision at 3 A.M., he might have ended up once more in the Berks County jail for violating his peace bond. But at 7 A.M. in the gray November dawn, he remembered Tom's admonition not to do anything foolish. After a breakfast of cold mush and potato cakes, he bought a ticket for the stage to Baltimore.

"Flo, Flo," Malcolm MacKenzie called from his front hallway. "Come see who is here."

He released Lovejoy's hand, set down the lamp, and threw his arms around him.

"Oh, my dear boy, I have been worried sick about you."

Lovejoy was too weary to resist the overwhelming hospitality of first Malcolm and then Flo, who stood on tiptoes to kiss his long unshaven chin.

That night, after eating his first hot meal and taking his first warm bath in many weeks, Lovejoy climbed into the feather bed in the MacKenzies' guest room and surrendered himself to unconsciousness.

He did not awaken until midmorning. Hearing him arise to use the chamber pot, an impatient Malcolm called up the stairs that breakfast would be ready in half an hour.

Lovejoy had forgotten the pleasure of eating a home-cooked breakfast on real china, with sterling silver fork and spoon. The MacKenzies watched in amusement as he consumed a platter full of corn muffins slathered with preserves and honey and wolfed down two plates of scrambled eggs and ham.

"You seem to have developed a good appetite," Malcolm said as Lovejoy asked for yet another cup of coffee.

"I am sorry. I am afraid that I have made a pig of myself."

"It is good to see you enjoy yourself. Now, Flo, if you will excuse us, Lovejoy and I have many things to discuss."

It was noon before Malcolm was satisfied that Lovejoy had told him all that he was likely to about his adventures in Bermuda and on Lake Erie. Neither man mentioned the episode in Berks County.

"Well, I would say that you have earned yourself a rest. So I will not tax you with our business concerns just yet."

"We might as well get it over with."

"Then perhaps we should go down to my office and go over the papers together."

It was nearly dark before their conference ended at MacKenzie's chandlery.

"So there it is, Lovejoy. You have several choices. You can cash in your chips now and put the *Flora* up for sale. Or you can take part of your share now and use the rest to finance yet another cruise."

"I thought the bloom was off the rose for privateering."

"It is for the way you conducted your first expedition. But there is much talk of carrying the war right to British shores, to interrupt their trade between England and Ireland or the Baltic states, where it is not practical to use convoys. Our little navy has been bottled up, but our privateers could be very effective."

"What would be the point, if you can't take your prizes into a port for condemnation and sale?"

"Our government is offering generous bounties for every British registered vessel you capture and destroy. And twenty-five dollars for each British seaman captured."

"I have never hated the British. Why would I want to be a party to taking such spiteful revenge upon them?"

"Have you not heard of what the British did to the little town of Hampton down in Virginia last summer? Their soldiers came ashore and raped and pillaged like savages, then put the houses to the torch. Earlier this year, they burned most of Havre de Grace and other towns dangerously near here. They have deliberately stirred up the Indian tribes of both the Northwest and Southwest against our settlers. Surely you have heard of the massacres perpetrated on the River Raisin and at Fort Mims?"

"I have heard."

"I fear there is worse to come. The British are close to defeating Napoleon. Their newspapers contain threats of their bringing veterans of Wellington's army to invade us from Canada and committing fresh depradations against other towns. They bear a particular grudge against Baltimore, you know."

"I have heard all this before, Mac. How will our raiding their coastal waters stop them from doing what you fear?"

"It will be a bargaining chip for peace, one of the few remaining to us, what with our failure to seize Canada and the bottling up of our navy and their stranglehold on our own coast. Our New England merchants have been howling against this war, even talking of seceding from the Union. We can make the British insurance and shipping interests howl even louder for peace."

"Even if I were to agree to send the *Flora* out again, is Talbot Smith really up to navigating her across the Atlantic?"

"He might be if Phipps were willing to serve again as his first mate and Barineau would go along as sailing master, but neither of them is."

"Would Phipps go if we were to make him captain?"

"I think not. He got so carried away listening to his great Bishop Asbury preach here at Lovely Lane Church that he is studying to become a full-time Methodist preacher. And anyway, I don't think he would be willing to serve under Talbot Smith again."

"What about Pierre?"

"He says that he is not interested, but you can ask him yourself when you go to Philadelphia. He is waiting there for your return."

"May I have another night to sleep on this?"

"Of course. But then we really ought to decide what we want to do and act on it. Let me emphasize again that the decision will be yours."

"And he told you nothing about that girl he was supposed to marry?"

"I did not ask, and he did not tell."

"He is not the same young man he was last year when he showed up on our doorstep."

"He has been through some trying times."

"I like him better now."

"I told you, Flo, that we should not judge him hastily."

"So you did. Well, now that he has lost his great love, what do you think he will do?"

"The lad has so many choices, it must be bewildering for him. He has wealth and health, a good education, and that most priceless of assets, youth. And, I think you will agree finally, character."

"And yet he seems sad."

"He is sad. But he will come through, once he settles on what his real purpose in life is to be. I know he will."

Over breakfast the next morning, Lovejoy waited until Flora was out of the room and then said, "Mac, I have not yet made up my mind about the *Flora.* What I would like very much would be for you to accompany me to Philadelphia and help me appraise the situation there."

"You really think I would be of any use?"

"Yes, of great use. You must remember that you, too, have a considerable financial stake in the future of the schooner. And whether we decide to sell or to sail, you will have to oversee the paperwork."

"Sell or sail? That really is the question, isn't it? I am flattered that you want me to go. Do you think it possible that I might visit your father now that his condition has improved?"

They were interrupted by Flora's return from the kitchen with a fresh plate of biscuits.

"Flo, my love, Lovejoy has invited me to accompany him to Philadelphia. What do you think?"

Three days later, the stage carrying Lovejoy and Malcolm rattled into Philadelphia. Stiff from being cooped up in the coach, they walked the few blocks to the White Swan. They were greeted there by Rance, the black cook.

"Why, Mr. Evan, he be done gone off to Erie to look after Tom."

Lovejoy glance around the common room.

"How about Meggie?"

"She has gone with him. They left here a week ago. Miss Primrose is running the place now."

Carrying her baby, Primrose came down the stairs. She stopped and stared as if seeing a ghost.

"Why, Lovejoy. We thought you were with Tom."

He explained his presence, then said, "This is my friend Malcolm MacKenzie from Baltimore. Malcolm, this is Mrs. Primrose Jenkins. Now, Primrose, we would like to rent a room."

"You can have two rooms, if you wish. Our trade has been very slack lately. Well, I must say, you don't look the same as when I last saw you. Been taken down a peg or two, I would say. My goodness, if you were coming back here anyway, why didn't you bring Tom along? You would have saved us all a lot of trouble. I told Evan he had no business traipsing off into Indian country and leaving me here with a baby and those twin boys to run a business establishment. He showed no consideration at all."

She paused to shift the baby to her other hip and continued her lamentation. "I told Evan that if he went off and abandoned me I would never speak to him again, but he wouldn't listen. I think it is the influence of that awful man with the peg leg, your captain, what's his name . . ."

"Talbot Smith."

"Yes, him. He had the gall to tell my Evan that he was a henpecked coward if he didn't go and rescue his own son. Encouraged Megan to go with him. Well, I told Evan that his own son chose to go out there and put himself in danger. I can't see why our life has to be disrupted. And I am none too happy with Megan, going off after being sick so long, when she should be here helping me and getting ready for her wedding. Yes, she is to marry Calvin Collins. What, the baby's name? Why, it is Evan Junior of course, but I am half a mind to have it changed. You really want to hold him?"

"Yes, let me see him."

Lovejoy hugged the baby and handed him back to his mother.

"He is a fine son. Gets his good looks from his mother, wouldn't you say, Mr. MacKenzie? Well then, Primrose, if you have two rooms vacant, we will just take them. Then we have to start making our calls."

"It is about time you got up here to see what I have done," Talbot Smith said after shaking hands with Lovejoy and Malcolm.

Before he could say more, Kevin the cook let out a whoop and shouted, "Hey, boys, Dr. Martin is back."

Soon Lovejoy was surrounded by Toby, Gandy, and other old crewmates, all talking at once and asking questions.

Malcolm stood smiling, with his arms crossed, as he observed the warmth of Lovejoy's reception.

"They seem fond of him," he said to Talbot.

"He babied them, that is why. He is all right as a doctor, but he'd make a damned poor captain."

"Where is Pierre Barineau?"

"Sent him and Collins off to see why our spare sails ain't been delivered. Should be back soon. Wish I had my schooner back in Baltimore, where you could count on decent workmanship."

He interrupted his conversation to shout, "That is enough socializing. Now get back to work. You can talk to Dr. Martin after working hours."

"He hasn't changed, has he?" Lovejoy whispered to Kevin.

"Nay, if anything he has got worse. Curious thing, though, he has took to the two Jenkins boys . . ."

"David and George?"

"Aye, the twins. They run errands for him and plague him to tell them sea stories. Since they work for free, he can't treat them as he does us. Ah, it is a shame you didn't get back in time to see our Megan. She used to bring us down mulled cider to drink. That Collins is a lucky one, I'd say."

"So would I."

"Dr. Martin, I will thank you to stop delaying my crew from their duties," Talbot called out. "Join Mr. MacKenzie and I in my cabin, to go over our accounts."

They were still in the cabin when Barineau and Collins returned. Barineau embraced Lovejoy.

"You got my letter then. My, it is good to see you. I have a thousand questions to ask you about the battle out there, but they will wait."

Collins reluctantly shook the hand offered him by Lovejoy.

"Is Tom Jenkins all right?"

"He has shown great improvement."

"Then he will be able to come back soon?"

"Not soon. Certainly not until early next year, I would say."

"You didn't see Megan then?"

"No, and I am sorry I didn't know that she and her father were coming or I might have delayed my departure a few days."

"Well, I am glad you didn't," Talbot said. "Now, can't we hold the chitchat for later? Time is a-wasting."

# 10

"Father, are you awake?"

"Yes, Amanda."

"Do you feel up to some company?"

"Who is it?"

"It is two people. I will bring them up one at a time."

She left the room before he could say more and motioned down the stairs to where Lovejoy stood with his uncle Ephraim and Malcolm.

"Remember, Lovejoy, not a word about Chester. Just answer his questions in a soft voice. He is better, but we still have to be careful not to excite him."

"I understand, Uncle Ephraim."

That May night a year and a half before, the stairs had seemed to Lovejoy like those leading to a gallows. Now he was filled with a new sort of apprehension. What should he say to the man who had always seemed to him a distant, Jove-like character rather than a tender father?

Amanda was fluffing up Jeremiah's pillow as he entered. Lovejoy walked to the foot of the bed. The old man looked at him as if puzzled. And then his face broke into a smile.

"Lovejoy," he said, holding out his hands.

Lovejoy drew close and took his father's right hand in both of his.

"Well, Father, you are looking much better than when I last saw you."

"I wish I could say the same for you, my son. Amanda, draw him up a chair. No, no, before you sit, turn around. Let me get a better look. You resemble your mother more than I remember. Now sit. Ephraim says you were at Lake Erie."

"Yes, Father. I was in the thick of it. Aboard the *Niagara* herself, as a sharpshooter."

"Were you frightened?"

"Mostly I was just kind of numb."

"I remember that feeling from my own privateering days. Oh, dear, Amanda, bring the lamp closer so I can look at him. See here, they tell me your schooner is in Philadelphia."

"She is, sir. A beautiful craft, too."

"I wish I could visit her. Ephraim keeps me shut up in this room like a prisoner. Isn't it good to see him again, Amanda? Now all the more I can ask is to have Chester back. He has been away so long. Not like him. Have you heard anything of your brother, Lovejoy?"

"Not recently, but Father, I have brought someone else you might be glad to see."

He turned to Amanda. She nodded and went out to the hall.

The entrance of Malcolm MacKenzie and Ephraim ended an awkward silence in which father and son had stared at each other with glistening eyes, each wondering what to say next.

Lovejoy stood aside so that Malcolm could approach the bed.

"Who is this?" Jeremiah asked.

"You don't recognize an old shipmate?"

"Which one?"

"Recall the young Scots lad you took along on your last cruise to Statia in 1780? We were captured and locked up in prison there together."

Jeremiah's eyes narrowed.

"And," Malcolm continued, "you don't remember lending that same lad the money to set himself up in business down in Baltimore after the war? Or employing him later to help with your investments down there? Or, more recently, entrusting your son and your capital to that same old comrade?"

By the time Malcolm had finished, Jeremiah was nodding his head and beaming.

"Is it really you, Mac? Oh, come close, my friend. Why you have got as plump as a Christmas goose. It has been too long, too long."

By now tears trickled down the faces of both men as they clung to each other's hands.

Lovejoy stepped back to stand with his sister and uncle while the two old friends talked.

"He is getting too emotional. We mustn't stay long," Ephraim whispered to Amanda.

"Oh, Ephraim, let them talk. I haven't seen him this happy in months."

Ephraim allowed the two men about ten minutes of reminiscing before he intervened.

"Well, by God, I say we had to go to war with the arrogant, sons of bitches," Jeremiah was saying. "Whether we win or lose, maybe they will face up to the fact that we really are independent of them."

Ephraim put his hand on Malcolm's shoulder.

"You mustn't get Jeremiah started on the war."

"Ephraim doesn't like to hear about the war. He is full of Quaker notions. I still say Madison did the right thing."

"Excuse me for interrupting, but Mr. MacKenzie and Lovejoy have an appointment with Charles Bennett."

Malcolm rose and took Jeremiah's hand again.

"I will be in town for a few days, Captain. Perhaps we can talk again."

"One more thing," Jeremiah said as he released Malcolm's hand. "Thank you for looking out for my son. I was hoping you could help turn him into a man. You may have succeeded."

"I can't take the credit, but he is a man now, no doubt about it. And one you can be proud of, too."

When Lovejoy stepped forward to bid his father good night, Jeremiah's eyes were already closed.

Ephraim put his fingers to his lips and led the men from the room while Amanda drew the covers up over her stepfather's shoulders and extinguished the lamp.

Lovejoy's emotions were already stirred by his visit with his father. Neither of them had broken through their shells of restraint to reveal their deeper feelings for each other, but he had been touched by what his father had said about him to Malcolm MacKenzie. Perhaps that was as close to a blessing as he would ever receive from the formidable Jeremiah Martin. But even it was tainted by the old man's distress at the long absence of Chester.

He had been touched by the respect and affection displayed by the two old shipmates and had also been taken aback by the vehemence of his father's comments about the British. Was not Jeremiah Martin himself mainly of English ancestry? Despite his imprisonment on Bermuda, Lovejoy still harbored an affection for the English and had doubts about the necessity of "Mr. Madison's war." Any antipathy he felt was directed more at Christopher Bledsoe personally than at the captain's nation. After all, except for that conniving bastard's machinations, he would be married and settled down to a happy life with Madeline Richter. The baby she carried in her womb would be his. She would lie at night in his arms, not those of that miserable underling to whom she had given herself.

As he, Frank Carpenter, and Malcolm MacKenzie approached Charles Bennett's law office, Lovejoy would not have thought it possible to detest Captain Bledsoe any more than he already did. But a few minutes later, after being shown Bledsoe's latest ransom demand, he grew so angry that Barineau feared that he would lapse into the state that had landed him in the Berks County jail.

"That miserable, bloodsucking, sorry excuse for a human being. That grasping, corrupt, and thoroughly detestable villain. If I could get my hands on him I would snuff out his life with my bare hands."

"But you cannot get your hands on him," Bennett said. "He is out of our reach. The question is how to respond to him."

"Why the hell respond at all? Why not let him sit and stew, waiting day after day for an answer that never comes?"

Bennett picked up the letter written by Chester from prison and looked at Frank Carpenter. Frank shrugged, then nodded and took the letter from Bennett's hand.

"Now, Lovejoy, I don't want to upset you further, but this is something we cannot keep from you. No matter what your feelings, Chester is still your brother."

"My half brother."

"But still very much a member of our family. He may have done a questionable thing, but the fact remains that he is being illegally held in a British prison, under harsh conditions."

"Hold on there, dear brother-in-law," Lovejoy said. "He did not do merely a questionable thing. He was trying to sell me into slavery as surely as Joseph's brothers did him in the Bible. What's more, he gulled you and Uncle Ephraim into financing his scheme. Why this sudden show of sympathy for a man who is no less guilty of extortion than Bledsoe? Those two deserve each other."

"Before you say more, perhaps you should read this," Frank said as he handed the letter to Lovejoy.

Lovejoy read the letter, then snorted and threw it on Bennett's desk.

"If he were here I would stuff that pack of lies down his throat. Didn't have a chance to explain, my ass. He tried to call the soldiers in. He had plenty of opportunity to tell us about the letters of credit. He was just waiting until I had cleared the island. Prison is exactly where he belongs."

"But this matter will create a scandal if word gets out."

"I hope you are not suggesting that we pay Bledsoe hush money as well as a ransom."

"I am not suggesting anything. This is just something we didn't think should be kept from you. Being held in irons on bread and water. Does he really deserve such a fate?"

During all this, Malcolm MacKenzie had remained silent. Now he cleared his throat and said, "If I may be so bold, Lovejoy asked for this meeting to seek your advice on what to do about the *Flora*. Perhaps I should excuse myself so you can thresh out this family matter in private."

Bennett replied, "Let us give Mr. MacKenzie the floor and save the Chester question for later."

For the next ten minutes, Malcolm recited the history of the schooner and her two cruises and summarized her earnings to date. Then he outlined the options open to the owners, ending with, "So there it is, gentlemen. As Lovejoy has expressed it to me, the question is whether to sell or to sail."

"What about this Captain Smith?" Bennett asked. "He owns ten percent interest, you say."

"So he does. And if the decision were his alone to make, he would set out down the Delaware in the morning, as a privateer."

Frank spoke up. "I am no sailor and not really much of a merchant, but if you could slip her out through the blockade quickly, lightly armed as a letter-of-marque trader with a cargo of flour or other commodity, wouldn't that be a good use for the ship and a way to reverse the fortunes of Martin Shipping?"

Malcolm nodded. "It would have to be done quickly. I am sure you all have heard the reports about a new, far stricter embargo on exports being considered by Congress."

Bennett said, "Quite so, but unless I mistake him, Lovejoy seems more interested in washing his hands of the schooner, in selling her outright."

During all the discussion about the *Flora,* Lovejoy had remained silent. But his mind had been boiling as he thought about the messages from Bledsoe and Chester. Now everyone was looking at him.

"So, what do you really want, Lovejoy?" Bennett asked.

"Yes," Malcolm said. "Perhaps the underlying question is what do you want to do, not just with the *Flora,* but with yourself?"

"He can take over Martin Shipping," Frank said. "That will keep him busy and allow me to get back to the printing business."

"You must not forget that Chester is the proprietor of Martin Shipping," Bennett said. "His father turned the business over to him."

"Let me see that ransom letter from Bledsoe again," Lovejoy said. "He gives his address as Goodwill Cottage, Newton Ferrers. Anyone know where Newton Ferrers is?"

"We assume it is near Plymouth. He makes it sound as though he lives near to where Chester is being held."

"And that is the Old Mill Prison."

"So it is," Bennett said. "What are you getting at?"

"As you just suggested, Mr. Bennett, Talbot Smith should have a say in all this. So I would like to adjourn this meeting so that Mac and I can go and iron this out with him. I will let you know what I want to do for sure in the morning."

In the cabin of the *Flora*, Talbot Smith sat with crossed arms and a frown on his face as Malcolm MacKenzie ran through the same speech he had made shortly before in the lawyer's office.

"It would be a crime against nature to sell this lovely schooner. I don't want to hear about it."

"But you don't have a proper crew."

"That is because you been dragging your feet about the papers. I ain't had a chance to advertise. Besides which, we don't need a huge lot of sailors if we won't be having to send off prize crews. I can find us enough sailors inside a week."

"You don't have a sailing master."

"I would if Barineau here would stop being so stubborn and come aboard."

Barineau smiled and shook his head, then said, "You don't have an experienced first mate, either. Phipps has taken up preaching down in Maryland."

"I got someone who would be better than that Bible thumper by the time we got across the ocean. I could learn him quick."

"Who might that be?"

"Young Collins. He is smart. He is willing to learn."

"He would never go. He is to be married as soon as Megan returns from Erie."

"That won't be until after the New Year. Also, he needs the money. Remember, he would get eight shares as first mate."

Barineau replied, "Captain Smith, sailing the *Flora* as a schooner in these waters and down in the Indies is one thing. Operating in the Irish and North Seas is quite another. You get more storms and you would find yourself in some tight situations. A brig would be better suited for those waters."

"I can handle the *Flora* in any waters anywhere."

Barineau continued with, "You don't have a surgeon. Sailors have learned the facts of life the past year. Without a skilled surgeon, what man in his right mind would want to put his life or limb in peril sailing into dangerous waters right under our enemy's nose?"

"What makes you think he doesn't have a surgeon?"

They all turned to look at Lovejoy. He grinned and said, "Of course, what surgeon in his right mind would want to go along on such a dangerous mission without the best possible sailing master?"

Now Barineau was grinning also. Malcolm raised his eyebrows at Lovejoy.

It took a while before the implication of Lovejoy's remarks sank in for Talbot, but when it finally did, he slapped his hands together and said, "By God, we can make them high and mighty British cry for mercy. Leave it to me to bring Collins aboard."

# 11

Although Collins was ambitious and needed the money, at first he refused Smith's offer to make him first mate.

"Are you daft, lad?" Talbot said. "You will never have another chance like this. Besides the eight shares, your next berth could be as master of your own ship."

"I am to be married. You know that."

"Aye, but the lass is three hundred miles away and not likely to return soon. What better way to pass the time? You will come back with a pocket full of money and a reputation."

"I can't see risking my life and maybe even my marriage while a rich man's son stays behind to become even richer."

"You're speaking of Dr. Martin?"

"Aye."

"Didn't you know that he is going along, too? And he has talked Barineau into it as well."

"Both of them, for a fact?"

Collins's face brightened. "So I would get eight shares. Where would I berth?"

"The choice bunk in the wardroom, I should think."

"And how would the men call me?"

"Why, Mr. Collins. What else? And I'll keelhaul anyone that leaves off the mister."

The next three weeks were some of the busiest Lovejoy and his shipmates had ever spent on land. While Malcolm feverishly wrote applications for licenses and bonds, and Barineau scrounged through chandlery shops for coastal charts of the British Isles, Talbot Smith mercilessly drove his carpenters and hired shipwrights in repairing the spars and topmasts of the *Flora.*

Lovejoy kept himself busy during the day recruiting sailors for the cruise. He paid particular attention to their physical fitness. He spent his evenings discussing medical techniques and practices with Ephraim. And several times he followed his uncle on his rounds of the wards of the Pennsylvania Hospital.

For a few minutes each afternoon, he visited his father. Jeremiah questioned him closely about his service aboard the *Flora,* asking more and more detailed questions.

"And that is how you came to do an amputation?" he said at the end of Lovejoy's story of taking off Talbot's injured leg.

"Yes, sir. But it was only my first. I had to amputate the arm of a sailor aboard the *Niagara,* as well."

"Made you wish you had paid more attention to your medical studies in London, I reckon."

To avoid having to answer questions about certain aspects of his cruise and Chester's whereabouts, Lovejoy encouraged his father to talk about his own days as a Revolutionary War privateer. So gradually, the two men grew closer.

One afternoon, as the time drew near for the departure of the *Flora,* Jeremiah said without warning, "Do you feel I have been too hard on you, lad?"

"I don't hold anything against you, Father, except maybe not paying me enough attention after Mother died."

"I was grieving for her. I still do. That is one reason I don't fear dying. Maybe we can be rejoined. Now, did I hear that you were to have been wed?"

"Yes, sir. But she married another man while I was at sea."

"And you loved her?"

"More than anyone. I still long for her."

"Love. It is a strange thing. Some men love money. Some love power or glory. But the greatest thing is to love another person and for that person to love you in return."

Jeremiah closed his eyes. Lovejoy tiptoed out of the room and went downstairs for his daily romp with the two little daughters of Amanda and Frank before supper.

The day the *Flora* left Philadelphia was cold, but the sun was shining and the winds were calm. Barineau had wanted to delay their departure until the end of December so that he could spend Christmas with his family, but, hearing that all traffic down the Delaware was about to be prohibited, Malcolm urged them to leave.

Despite Ephraim's protests, Frank and Amanda gave in to Jeremiah and had him carried down to the dock in a carriage. All wrapped in blankets, he watched the preparations for casting off.

At the last minute, Lovejoy persuaded Talbot to leave off hectoring his crew and meet his father.

Leaning on his cane, the captain thumped his way down the gangplank and across the dock to the carriage.

"So, you're the great Jeremiah Martin? I have heard tell of you."

"And you are Talbot Smith. I have heard there is no better man in America for building schooners. From the looks of that one, I would say they are right."

"Why, Captain Martin, I take that as a particular compliment coming from you as it does."

"That is not all I have heard. They say you are pretty good at turning headstrong young fellows into real blue-water sailors, even if it means leaving them gagged and tied to the mast."

"He didn't go and tell you that, did he?"

"No. I got it from another source."

Lovejoy frowned at the grinning Malcolm and muttered, "I will get even with you, Mac."

The carriage with the old man remained on the dock until the *Flora* disappeared around the bend where the Delaware changed from a southerly to a southwestern course.

Two nights later, the schooner lay anchored off Lewes while Barineau and Talbot conferred with a pilot. They waited all the next day and night, hoping that no British cruiser would spot them.

"Today will be the day," Talbot said. "We'll get some weather before many more hours. Then we can slip past them in the rain."

"What makes you so sure about the weather?"

"My stump aches like holy hell."

The rain did come that afternoon, and with it came a brisk wind out of the northwest. Following the markings on the chart made by the pilot, under light sail, they eased the schooner out into the Delaware Bay and felt their way past the shoals, until they neared open water. Once darkness fell, Talbot roared for all sail to be bent on. By dawn they were a good 125 miles out to sea.

As Lovejoy laid out his medicine kit for morning sick call, Kevin brought him a cup of strong coffee.

"Doctor, may I be the first to wish you a merry Christmas?"

"My God, it is December 25. Merry Christmas, Cookie."

"I am firing up the stove to cook those turkeys I picked up back at Lewes. I was going to ask you to help me dispatch the poor creatures, but then I remembered how you hate the sight of blood. So I have persuaded Toby to do the honors."

Barineau looked out of the cabin where he was conferring with Talbot and Collins to see who was laughing so loudly.

# PART THREE

# 1

The following are excerpts from the log of the *Flora,* a Baltimore-built schooner of three-hundred-ton burthern operating out of Philadelphia under a congressional commission as a privateer, carrying a complement of ninety men and armed with ten twelve-pound carronades and two twelve-pound Long Toms.

> *Wed., Feb. 2, 1814. Rough seas of past week abated. Under clear skies and flattering southeasterly winds sighted Lizard Point on Cornish coast. Position at noon, Lat. 49.50 N; Long. 5.20 E. Sounding shows 89 fathoms . . .*
>
> *Fri., Feb. 4. Near Eddystone Rocks off Devon coast. Cloudy skies prevented taking noon azimuth. By ded reckoning noon position Lat. 50.12 N; Long. 4.15 E. At 16:30 sighted mail packet out of Plymouth. Flying British colors, hailed vessel and burnt same after removing valuables and six-man crew . . .*
>
> *Sat., Feb. 5. Captured and burnt 100-ton barkentine, "Katie Mae," off unfinished breakwater at entrance to Plymouth Harbor, after setting prisoners adrift near shore in their longboat . . .*
>
> *Sun., Feb. 6. Hailed packet boat approaching Plymouth Harbor. Craft turned about and fled to east . . .*
>
> *Mon., Feb. 7. At dawn British frigate sighted on northern horizon. Same gave chase. Ran close-hauled against a southwesterly wind until 17:15 when pursuing vessel turned back toward Plymouth . . .*
>
> *Wed., Feb. 9. Ran all day on westerly course with wind from port beam. Passed in sight of Scilly Isles to the north. Clouds prevented shooting noon azimuth . . .*
>
> *Wed., Feb. 16. Noon position, Lat. 50.30 N; Long. 5.40 E. 72 fathoms. Fishing ketch out of Barnstaple taken. Removed catch and charts. Released craft and crew . . .*

*Sun., Feb. 20. Noon position, 51.25 Lat; 4.50 E. Long. Captured small brig "Fanciful" out of Bristol after short chase. Removed papers, valuables and 12-man crew before burning craft . . .*

*Fri., Feb. 25. No noon sighting in rainy weather. Est. position 51.25 N; 4 degrees E. Armed sloop sighted approaching Bristol Channel from west. Fired shot across bow at 4 p.m. Sloop, the "Dancer," hove to. Removed rum, other valuable cargo and papers and ten men from sloop and burnt same . . .*

*Sun., March 6. Off St. David's Head on Welsh Coast. By ded reckoning in heavy weather, noon position 51.50 N; 5.30 E. Ran all day close-hauled, under light sail on northerly course against northwesterly wind in intermittent rain . . .*

*Tues., March 8. In Irish Sea, near Holy Island. Noon sighting interrupted by ferry out of Dublin carrying 120 passengers to Liverpool. Removed charts, newspapers and allowed vessel to proceed. Newspapers report Wellington's army advancing on Toulouse in southern France . . .*

*Thurs., March 10. On westerly course, under light sail with following wind, sighted British sloop of war coming out from Liverpool. Allowed craft to approach within range. Seen to be armed with ten six-pounders. Craft turned back and fled to the west toward Liverpool . . .*

*Sat., March 12. At dawn, British frigate, followed by sloop of war seen March 10, sighted 8:00, coming out from Liverpool. Changed course to northeast and bent on all sail to avoid encounter . . .*

*Mon., March 14. Isle of Man off port beam at noon. Position 54.20 N; 4.15 E. Southwesterly winds. Heavy seas . . .*

*Fri., March 18. In North Channel, off Belfast. Position 54.40 N, 5.25 E. Took two small barkentines. Burnt larger vessel, the "Hawkseye" out of Carlisle. Transferred other prisoners previously captured and those from "Hawkseye" to smaller barkentine, "Gypsy," and allowed craft to proceed . . .*

*Wed., March 23. Off entrance to Dublin Harbor. Halted snow "Coleen" carrying linen. Took valuables and papers, placed crew in their longboat near shore and set craft ablaze. Among items taken was a Dublin newspaper which quoted reports from Bristol and Liverpool about "an American schooner sailing under the name Flora" that had burned several small British vessels in the Irish Sea. Released prisoners and ferry passengers related details of our rigging and armament . . .*

*Sun., March 27. Overtook ship "Estelle" out of Bristol at approx. 51 N., 6 E., after brief chase. Manifest showed her to be bound for Barcelona carrying full cargo of uniforms and small arms for Wellington's army. During our search of vessel, British frigate sighted on northern horizon. Abandoned seizure of ship, removing only charts of French coast and navigational instruments. With north-northeasterly wind, set course south-by-southwest. Frigate bent on all sail to follow. 18:00 unable to gain distance on frigate . . .*

"Mr. Barineau, I wish you would quit scribbling in that God damned log long enough to consider what we should do. We got every scrap of canvas up and still can't shake that son of a bitch back there."

"He does have us in a tight corner. Changing to a more westerly course would run us aground on one of the Scillies, that is for sure. And it doesn't make any sense to head east unless we want to end up far out in the Atlantic. Sail any closer to the wind than that and you are heading for the southeastern coast of Ireland, besides possibly passing into range of their broadside while doing so."

Talbot Smith shook his head. "I wish to hell I hadn't listened to our high-minded Dr. Martin and had set that damned ship afire back there."

"Without removing the crew and passengers? Come now, Captain, that would have been inhumane warfare."

"It would have been good common sense. That frigate would have had to stop and take them off. Maybe try to put out the fire. We wouldn't have him hanging on our tail all day. Damn. I never knowed a square-rigger to be such a fast sailer, and you think we are boxed in on this course for the night?"

"We would gain speed if you jettisoned some of our guns . . ."

"Do that and we might as well head for home."

"Our guns have fired only warning shots so far."

"Well I ain't giving them up, not yet. We should have kept every man from every vessel what we took. We set them free, and they went ashore and blabbed everything there was to know about us. Right there in their newspapers it is. The captain of that frigate probably knows our registry, our guns, and even my name. There is no doubt in my mind he was looking for us. I shouldn't have listened to our surgeon. Should have kept them prisoners. They would have been worth twenty-five dollars a head, you know."

"Come now, Captain, you couldn't very well have taken all those passengers off that Irish ferry. And our quarters were getting pretty crowded with the sailors we did capture. Aren't you glad you aren't lumbered with them now? We're nearly out of fresh water, you know."

"Well you sitting down here writing in that log and looking at charts ain't going to help. Come topside and see for yourself how that bastard is gaining on us slow but sure."

Lovejoy was standing on the stern of the *Flora* with a wool cap pulled over his ears and the lapels of his long pea jacket drawn up around his face. Even to his landlubber's eye, he could tell that running before the wind as the two craft were, sooner or later the frigate, with its larger expanse of sail, would overtake the *Flora*. The question was whether the Britisher could come within range for its bow chasers to open fire before darkness fell.

About two miles behind them, the frigate did make a beautiful sight with every sail bent on, heeled slightly from the brisk following wind—beautiful but deadly.

He was joined by Barineau and Talbot Smith.

"Our sailing master, here, thinks we ought to dump some of our cannon."

"I wouldn't like to do that."

"No, and you didn't like the idea of setting fire to that ship back there. What do you like?"

The captain of HMS *Winsome* stood in the bow of his frigate, overseeing the loading of his two forward eighteen-pounder cannon.

"Elevate them as much as you can. And double the powder charge. Then just stand by until we close the range a bit more. The wind will help carry the shot somewhat, I should think. That's it. Yes, yes. Prime them both, then cover the vents so no spray wets your powder. That's it. Well, Mr. Lovell, what do you think?"

His first lieutenant lowered his spyglass and replied, "No doubt about it, Captain. That is her. The *Flora*. She is the schooner that has been causing all the trouble. How many has she destroyed?"

"At least six, that have been reported. She has taken others but released them. Of course, it would have been seven if we had not been following the *Estelle*."

Aboard the *Flora,* Talbot Smith was instructing Gandy, his chief gunner's mate, in the same sort of exercise with their aft Long Tom.

"You got the wind against you . . ."

"I know that, Captain."

"So you want to double up on your load and . . ."

"Captain, if you don't think I know my business . . ."

"No call for you to be so touchy, Gandy."

"No, sir, and no call for you to be giving me orders like I was some landlubber. You leave it to me and my boys. We'll give them tit for tat."

The conversation was interrupted by a flash and a billow of smoke from the bow of the pursuing frigate, now about a mile and a half behind them.

The boom of the eighteen-pounder reached their ears only seconds before the shot, after arcing high overhead, threw up a geyser about a hundred feet behind them.

Gandy removed the apron from the vent of his Long Tom and looked at Talbot.

"Wait."

The second bow chaser of the frigate flashed, and another plume of water shot up even with the stern of the *Flora* but fifty feet to the port side.

“Fire!” Talbot shouted.

Gandy jerked the lanyard and his gun belched forth its nine-pound shot, which sailed high into the air and dropped well ahead of the frigate.

Both of the frigate’s bow chasers fired again. The first shot came close enough to throw spray over the taffrail; the second crashed into the longboat, which hung over the stern of the *Flora*.

“That does it,” Talbot said. “Mr. Collins, shift sail and bring her to a southwesterly course. You, Gandy, keep firing. All other hands, stand by to man the capstan.”

“What are you going to do?” Barineau asked.

“We will have to dump the carronades. You take the helm while I see to getting the job done.”

As if to underline the wisdom of the captain’s decision, a few moments later, shots from both the frigate’s bow chasers splashed into the water just where the *Flora* would have been located if Collins had not so handily brought the schooner to her new heading.

Two hours later, Barineau was back in the cabin, writing once more in the log.

> *. . . 18:30. Shot from pursing British frigate destroyed longboat. Captain changed course to southwest and ordered carronades and cargo to be jettisoned. 19:30, running with wind on starboard beam. At last light, frigate lagging three miles behind . . .*

# 3

Three mornings later, armed only with its two Long Toms and nearly out of fresh water and food, the *Flora* slipped through the British blockade off the coast of France and, flying her American colors, entered the heavily fortified harbor of Brest.

That afternoon, leaving Talbot aboard to inventory their needs, Barineau and Lovejoy called on the American consul in Brest, who also doubled as prize agent.

"So you nearly got caught, did you?" the consul asked, after he had finished examining the logs and manifests of the British vessels destroyed by the *Flora*.

"They would have overtaken us if we had not jettisoned our carronades and most of our cargo," Barineau replied.

"Sounds as if you twisted the British lion's tail rather energetically these past few weeks."

"So we did, Mr. Bass. And we came close to suffering his wrath, too. I only wish we had been able to bring that last ship into Brest for condemnation. She would have fetched a pretty price with her cargo."

"Don't be so sure of that."

The consul bent forward and continued in a low voice, "Time is about to run out on Napoleon Bonaparte. Toulouse has fallen to Wellington. My last word from Paris was that the allies were fast approaching the city. The French may very soon be under a new government, and that government will not want to cause additional offense to the British. Take my advice and get out of here as soon as you can."

"But we need to replace our carronades and replenish our fresh water and victuals."

"After such an escape, you mean to have another go at them?"

Lovejoy, who had remained silent during the conversation, now spoke.

"My mission is not complete, Mr. Bass."

"Well, sir, for a ship's surgeon, you seem mighty eager to put your crew at risk."

"Dr. Martin is not merely our surgeon; he is also the majority owner of the *Flora*," Barineau said.

"Then he seems unduly eager to put his schooner at risk."

"We will worry about the risks, Mr. Bass, if you will direct us to the proper persons, chandlers or whatever, to sell us supplies," Lovejoy said.

"That is no problem. A Frenchman will sell you anything you want if you have the money to pay for it. They are as mercenary a race as you can find on this earth."

"Perhaps we should have explained earlier that Mr. Barineau is himself of French parentage."

Barineau laughed and stopped the red-faced consul from continuing his apologies.

"My father was French. I am thoroughly and enthusiastically American."

"I meant no offense. Now that we have that cleared up, let me suggest that you make no secret of your Gallic blood. They will be less inclined to cheat you. Oh, dear, I have done it again. My day for putting my foot in my mouth, isn't it? Do you speak your father's language?"

"Well enough to get by."

"Then do not hesitate to do so. Things will go more smoothly for you. And don't forget your manners, as I did mine. The French are often offended by our blunt-talking ways."

"Thank you for the warning. We'll have find a way to curb our captain's tongue. Now if you would be so kind as to give us that list of vendors, we would count it a great favor, monsieur," Barineau said with a mock bow.

"And you might also advise us as to a suitable lodging on shore," Lovejoy added. "I could do with a comfortable bed while we are in port, couldn't you, Pierre?"

"What do you mean, Barineau must do the buying?"

"The consul says these vendors don't speak English."

"I like to get the best quality at the lowest price. How am I going to know they aren't cheating me if I can't talk to them?"

"The consul assures us that these vendors are patriotic persons eager to assist the American cause. However, he does advise that we work fast. The French may not be able to hold out against Wellington much longer."

Talbot frowned.

"You still hell-bent to have another go at the British, Dr. Martin?"

"Unless you are afraid to do so."

"Me, afraid? Hellfire, I would like to sail right up the Thames and burn their ships."

"I didn't have anything that ambitious in mind."

"I been thinking. By now they must consider any sharp-built schooner as a privateer. They will be on guard like never before. Will take more than flying a British flag to fool them."

"What is your point?"

"I want you to ask that consul fellow to recommend a shipyard that does quality work fast and cheap."

"What for?"

"When we go back, they'll be looking for a schooner, right?"

"Yes, and that is what we are."

"We don't have to remain a schooner. While you and Barineau was lollygagging on shore, I been doing some figuring. Here, call Barineau down here and let's discuss this with him, and Collins too."

In the end, only Collins protested removing the *Flora*'s main fore boom and rerigging her as a brigantine. And, as Captain Smith was quick to point out, his objection was on personal, not technical, grounds.

"It's because of your girlfriend, ain't it?"

"What if it is?"

"Afraid she won't wait for you?"

"No, but I wrote to her out in Erie that we would be back by spring and here it is April already. We are in France, and instead of heading for home, you want to change our rigging and take us out on another cruise."

"You still interested in your own command someday?"

"You know I am."

"Then take my advice and button your lip. Captains don't whine about a little personal inconvenience."

The American consul had given Lovejoy a letter of introduction to be presented to a "Madame Dubuisson," whom he described as the widow of a French colonel who opened her home occasionally to "persons of good repute."

Madame Dubuisson lived in an ancient three-story house overlooking the harbor. Lovejoy went there expecting to be greeted by one of the grim, elderly French army widows dressed in black whom he had observed on the streets of Brest. His knock was answered by a rosy-cheeked maid, who took his letter and left him standing on the doorstep while she carried it upstairs. Shortly thereafter, the door was opened again.

"You are Dr. Martin?"

At first Lovejoy was too taken aback by the appearance of the woman to reply. True, she was dressed in black. And her dark hair was pulled back and tied in a bun, as seemed to be the custom for French widows. But this woman could not be older than thirty-five. And her complexion was too fresh and her dark eyes too bright for a grieving widow.

"Is my English so terrible that you do not comprehend me? This letter from Monsieur Bass says that you are Dr. Lovejoy Martin."

"Why yes. That I am. Is Madame Dubuisson at home?"

"It is Madame Dubuisson to whom you are speaking. Please enter and let us discuss this question of your lodging. How long shall you be requiring a room?"

Although Barineau was able to conduct purchases of six eighteen-pound carronades and casks of water, pickled fish and pork, and other foodstuffs without involving Talbot Smith, getting the spars and other rigging of the *Flora* changed was a different matter. The owner of the shipyard, a dapper fellow with a bulbous nose and black moustache, was eager for work, especially since Barineau promised him a bonus for a quick completion. But it was impossible to prevent Talbot from interfering.

As it turned out, the shipyard owner's English was almost as good as Barineau's French, but he went along with the charade of pretending to understand only his native tongue.

Talbot followed Barineau about the deck shouting remarks such as, "Tell the God damned frog them spars ain't long enough," or "It's no wonder Nelson whipped their asses at Trafalgar. They don't know how to rig a brigantine proper."

While Barineau dealt with that problem, Lovejoy became better acquainted with the American consul in Brest. Through that gentleman's good offices, he interviewed several locals who had been imprisoned by the British at the Old Mill Prison near Plymouth.

"So you are satisfied that any kind of rescue of your brother is out of the question," the consul said.

"From all I have read and heard, the Old Mill Prison is impregnable. High walls. Situated on a spit of land and well guarded. Besides which, to tell you the truth, my heart is not in risking my skin to save his."

"And why is that?"

"Let's not go into that. Anyway, there may be another way to achieve my purpose. I only hope that you are wrong about the downfall of Napoleon. I wish that this and other French ports might be kept open to us for a while at least."

"Frankly, I have mixed feelings about Napoleon. The British regard him as a demon bent on conquering the world, and in truth he is a highly vainglorious man. But then you have to consider the reforms he has brought to French law and his tolerance of other religions. The man really is a military genius, as well."

"Except that he didn't know when enough was enough."

"Yes. The French have been bled white. And it was not just his stupid Russian adventure. Look around you at the one-armed, crippled old veterans of other campaigns. They have been sacrificed to the glory of France."

"A military dictator does seem an unlikely ally for a country that values personal freedom, as does America."

"Or that part of America that does not own slaves. Be that as it may, I shudder to think what it may mean to us if Bonaparte abdicates and France surrenders. The British are eager to take their revenge on the United States, and they will have the ships and men to do so with the French disposed of. Well, enough of such bleak talk. How do you find your accommodations at Madame Dubuisson's?"

"I have no complaints. None whatsoever."

Indeed, Lovejoy had no cause to complain about the large room in the front corner of the second floor of the Dubuisson house; nor the soft bed, nor the excellent meals he shared with the widow and Barineau, when the sailing master was not too busy helping ready the *Flora* for sea again.

At times he felt left out when Madame Dubuisson and Barineau lapsed into French. After one such episode, he complained to Barineau at being excluded from their conversation.

"She was asking about you. Wanted to know why such a handsome fellow remained a bachelor."

"Really? To tell the truth, I was wondering why such a ripe creature as herself remains a widow."

"Her husband led his regiment into Russia two years ago, and like so many of his comrades, he did not return. There are not many men left and so many widows in this played-out country."

It took a while to break through the formalities, but in a few days, Lovejoy and Madame Dubuisson were on a first-name basis. He found that his attempts to speak French amused her.

One evening, when Barineau was absent, she asked about his family, his education, and his ambitions.

"You do not know what you wish to become of yourself? How can it be that you have no ambition?"

"Once I thought I wanted to be a doctor. Then a lawyer. Now, I don't know what I want."

"Poor Lovejoy. Has it to do with that girl who betrayed you?"

Lovejoy looked up in surprise. "Pierre has been blabbing, hasn't he, Odette?"

"Do not be angry with him. You are fortunate to have such a loyal friend. But yes, he did tell me a little. Was she so beautiful, this girl who did not wait for you?"

Tears in his eyes, Lovejoy nodded.

"I know what it is to lose one's love. Mine lies buried on the road from Moscow. He was as brave as a lion. His soldiers adored him. A magnificent man. I dream of him every night."

"And I dream of Madeline. Not an hour goes by that I do not think of her."

Her eyes glistening, Madame Dubuisson looked for a long while at Lovejoy's pained face. Then she rose and took his hand.

"Lovejoy, it is not necessary that we should grieve tonight. Let us comfort each other."

When Barineau returned that night, the maid met him at the door.

"Where are Madame Dubuisson and Dr. Martin?"

The maid giggled and answered, "They retired early, monsieur."

Despite Talbot's interference, but thanks to Barineau's diplomacy and his prudent payment of bribes and other incentives, the *Flora*, with square-rigged sails now occupying her foremast, had been made ready to return to sea as a brigantine. Besides the switch in her rigging, the name painted across her stern had been changed to read the *Florantine.*

James Bass, the American consul, came to the dock to say good-bye and to wish his countrymen well. His intelligence about the French state of affairs had been accurate. Just the day before, Napoleon had assembled his key supporters at Fontainebleau and announced that he was abdicating.

Lovejoy remained on the dock, holding the hand of Odette Dubuisson.

The owner of the shipyard gloomily kissed Barineau on each cheek and wished him well, saying in French, "The little corporal was good for my business. Now it will be back to building fishing boats for me."

"What is the little frog looking so down at the mouth about?" Talbot asked Barineau, who made a face and shook his head in warning.

Missing Barineau's signal, Talbot blundered on with, "He ought to be smiling after what we have paid him for a half-assed job of rerigging. I have heard that the French like to take advantage of us Americans, and now I believe it."

The shipyard owner squared his shoulders and said to Barineau in loud, clear English, "Please to tell the rude little man with the peg leg that this little frog mourns the abdication of his emperor. Tell the uncivilized little barbarian that had it not been for my nation's coming to America's rescue during your so-called revolution, he would still be a subject of the mad King George the Third of Great Britain. Tell the discourteous . . ."

"I think he gets the idea," Barineau said.

The American consul put his hand over his mouth to conceal his smile. Barineau took out his handkerchief and pretended to suffer a fit of coughing to choke back his own amusement. Talbot sputtered briefly as the Frenchman stared him down, then turned and stumped across the gangplank onto the deck of the brigantine the *Florantine,* where, to cover his embarrassment, he hectored his crew mercilessly as they set the topsails and began casting off the lines.

"If you and Dr. Martin don't want to stay behind, I'll thank you to come aboard, so's we can take in the gangplank," he shouted to Barineau.

By now the consul had given up trying to stifle his laughter. Pleased with himself, the shipyard owner smiled at Talbot and called out, "Bon voyage, mon ami."

Lovejoy looked into his landlady's eyes one last time and took her hands.

"Thank you for everything, Odette."

"It is I who should thank you, Lovejoy. You have given me much happiness to carry in my memory. Promise me that never again will you surrender to despair. And promise me that you will not soon forget this poor widow."

"I could never forget you, Odette."

Ignoring the smirks of the *Flora*'s crewmen, Lovejoy put his arms around the widow and kissed her. She drew back, looked into his face and leaned her head against his chest.

"Mon cher ami. Bon voyage," she murmured, and, oblivious to the scandalized stares of her neighbors, kissed him again.

After they had reached the harbor entrance and sent their French pilot back to shore, Talbot said to Barineau, "How come you didn't tell me that little frog knowed how to speak English?"

"You know how sneaky those Frenchmen are," Barineau replied.

The crew of the *Florantine* spent the next week learning the sailing characteristics and handling of a brigantine.

As Barineau explained to Lovejoy, "With square sails on our foremast, we won't be able to pinch the wind as before. But in a tight spot, we can actually bring her bow into the wind and sail backwards, if need be. In a storm, I think we will find her more stable. And, as the captain figured, our rigging won't give us away as an American privateer at first glance."

"You think we are that well known?" Lovejoy asked.

"In the Irish Sea, I'd say yes. And that is why I am convinced we should try our luck in the English Channel and the North Sea on this cruise."

"I will leave that to you and our captain to decide. Meanwhile, let me see your charts for the Devon coast."

"What for? We aren't going back there."

"It's just an idea for later. Ah, thank you. Now help me locate the town of Newton Ferrers."

"You will find it just a few miles east of Plymouth, on the River Yealm. What have you got in mind?"

"Nothing definite. I noted that our old friend Captain Bledsoe wrote to my family from that place. I would like to think of him sitting about vainly waiting for a reply to his latest extortion demand."

"What about your brother waiting at Old Mill Prison?"

"Eventually, something will have to be done about him, but I have other things on my mind for the present."

"Such as looking at charts of the Devon coast?"

"That and what to do about the cases of clap our men picked up in Brest. I have plenty of mercury on hand, the most common antidote, and a little sandalwood oil, which is recommended by some authorities. Perhaps I will experiment with my treatments."

"Yes, I can see you publishing a learned paper titled 'Martin on The Treatment of Venereal Diseases at Sea.' Too bad the poor lads could not find themselves attractive young widows in Brest like some I could mention."

"Odette Dubuisson would be offended by your coarseness, Pierre, as am I. Here's your chart back. Care for a game of chess before the captain comes down to claim his cabin?"

The *Florantine* spent the next three months cruising through the English Channel far up into the North Sea along the Norwegian coast. And as Talbot Smith had hoped, she found rich pickings there, capturing and destroying fifteen British vessels, mostly coastal craft but including several larger prizes, among them a brigantine hailing from Halifax, Nova Scotia, the *Phoenix*.

His hold filled with captured British sailors, Talbot put his prisoners aboard a Danish snow bound for Copenhagen.

"I know it's like throwing away twenty-five dollars a head, but they are a burden to feed and keep guarded," he said.

For his part, Lovejoy was meticulous in examining each prisoner and treating any who were sick or injured as tenderly as he did members of his own crew. He also interrogated them as to their home ports. Most were from London or other east English ports such as Kingston or Newcastle. Finally, off the Firth of Forth, they overtook a small bark out of Plymouth, manned largely by sailors from that area. And one of these, he learned, a lad of only sixteen, had been reared near Newton Ferrers.

Meanwhile, the worst fears of the American consul at Brest were being realized. With Napoleon exiled to Elba and replaced by a Bourbon king, and France once more at peace with Britain, thousands of Wellington's soldiers trooped to Bordeaux and ports on the Mediterranean to await transportation to North America.

Most of the fifteen thousand soldiers were destined to join General Prevost in Canada. Still smarting from his defeat by Harrison in the battle of the Thames following Perry's triumph on Lake Erie, Prevost now concentrated his attention on Lake Champlain, whose waters stretched from just within the Canadian border to some hundred miles deep into New York State. Their capture of two American sloops at the northern end of the lake in June gave the British at least temporary control of a waterway invasion route into the heart of the United States. The speedy arrival of Wellington's veterans and a few additional ships to carry them would bring the United States to its knees, or so the British reasoned.

This development caused dismay in Washington and a fevered effort to beef up American forces in the area.

Unknown to President Madison and his advisors, however, a more serious threat was posed by a force of twenty-five hundred battle-tested British soldiers and eleven ships about to depart from Bordeaux, for quite another destination.

In the cabin of the *Florantine,* Lovejoy looked closely into the face of the apple-cheeked young English sailor.

"So your name is Henry Alleyne. How old are you, my lad?"

"Sixteen, sir."

"And you are from the town of Newton Ferrers?"

"Actually, sir, I growed up crost the creek from Newton on a farm just outside Noss Mayo what my pa works on for Squire Welling. We don't have much to do with them at Newton Ferrers, but I knows the place well enough."

"Good. Sit down, Henry. Don't be afraid. I have a map here of your part of England. I have a few questions to put to you."

An hour later, Barineau entered the cabin to find the young Devonshireman chattering away freely to Lovejoy.

Three days later, the *Florantine* was passing the Isle of Wight, on a westerly heading. All prisoners except the Devon lad had been transferred to a neutral vessel. Lovejoy and Talbot Smith had spent most of the past two days arguing about what to do next with their schooner-built, brigantine-rigged craft.

"There ain't nothing to be done about getting your brother out of that prison. Besides which, I don't know why you want to bother with him. I'd let him stay there until the war ends."

"Captain, I have no intention of trying to storm the prison. And to tell you the truth, the only reason for bringing him home would be to satisfy my family. What I am after is to get back at that son of a bitch Bledsoe."

"I know you have a grudge against him, but I can't see why you would want to risk me and my schooner and all your shipmates to get even. Now, I don't mind trying our hand for a few weeks back in the Irish Sea. If we ain't going to do that, then I say it is time to head for home."

During this discussion, Barineau had sat quietly, pretending to study his charts.

"If I may interject, I would like to ask a question."

"I reckon you are going to take his side," Talbot said.

"I would like to ask Lovejoy if his motive is to save his brother from prison and his family from a public scandal or to get even with Captain Bledsoe."

"Good question," Lovejoy replied. "Rescue or revenge? Actually, I am thinking of achieving both ends."

"Maybe it is time I reminded both of you educated fellows who is the master of this here vessel," Talbot said. "It is me, and I say I ain't going to do anything as foolish as what you seem to want to do when it ain't going to profit us one whit."

Lovejoy caught Barineau's eye, rubbed his chin as if debating whether to say more, then spoke softly.

"I have never revealed what Captain Bledsoe said about you while he was hauling me up to Bermuda, have I?"

Talbot frowned and replied, "What did he say?"

"He told me I was a fool to have signed on to cruise with a man like you. He questioned your ability to handle a vessel where you did not have the advantage of surprise. He said that in his navy you would never have risen above the rank of bosun's mate."

"He is a fine one to talk," Talbot spluttered. "The damned fool risked his brig and his crew when anybody with a spoonful of brains would of knowed it was hopeless to put up a fight . . . Wait a minute. You are making this up, ain't you?"

"I only wish I were. He also bragged about the way he had made a fool of you by recapturing his brig and your prize crew. But I fear I have told you too much already."

Talbot rose and buttoned his pea coat.

"I am going topside."

After he had left the cabin, Barineau shook his head.

"You really ought to be ashamed of yourself."

"All's fair in love and war."

"Your idea really is harebrained, you know."

"Let me fetch Henry Alleyne up here and have you listen to what he says about the anchorage at Newton Ferrers. The lad used to sail out of there on his uncle's fishing boat."

# 5

The village of Newton Ferrers consisted of a string of fishermen's cottages on the north bank of a shallow tidal creek that joined the Yealm a mile upstream from where the river flowed into Wembury Bay. An ancient church, Holy Cross, and a public house were the stark village's only distinguishing landmarks.

Farther upstream and across the creek lay a rival village, Noss Mayo. The inhabitants of the region made their livings from farming, fishing, and the quarrying and burning of limestone, and, now and then, a bit of smuggling.

Properly speaking, there was no harbor at Newton Ferrers, but large boats could and did find anchorage in "the pool" where Newton Creek entered the Yealm.

All this Barineau and Lovejoy learned from Henry Alleyne as the *Florantine*, flying a British flag, gingerly approached Wembury Bay.

The mist hanging over the general area of Plymouth Sound limited visibility to two miles. There was just enough breeze to enable Barineau to nudge the craft northward into the bay.

Barineau, Lovejoy and Henry Alleyne stood in the bow, straining their eyes for sight of the Great Mewstone, a huge pyramid of rock that marked the boundary between Wembury Bay and Plymouth Sound.

"There you are, sir. I can just make her out off the port bow. Now you needs to keep a sharp eye out dead ahead for Wembury Church what stands on the cliffs to the north. But make sure to stay well this side of the Mewstone. There is shallow water all around the rock."

"Good. Now lad, you are sure there is room and depth enough for us to anchor in the river close in to Newton Ferrers?"

"Aye, sir. Although the tide do make a big difference, I have seen ships near the size of this anchored in the pool."

"Maybe a smuggler now and then?"

"Nay. Too many eyes to see them. They generally sends boats in to one of the beaches to the east, when there is no moon."

"Your father never smuggled, did he?"

"I wouldn't want to say he did, nor will I say he didn't. I don't know what it is you are after, sir. All I asks is that if they do catch you, you makes it plain that I did not volunteer to come with you."

"You have my promise on that and also to pay you ten pounds in gold coins. Ah, would that be your Wembury Church on the cliffs ahead there?"

"Aye, sir. If you'll keep her just off your port bow until you draws even with the Mewstone, then bring your heading sharp to the east, you'll see the mouth of the Yealm. Must keep to the headland on your right. They's a sandbar on t'other side. Then work your way around Misery Point where the river bends and right up to the pool."

Using his captured tide tables and charts and carefully noting the direction and speed of the sluggish wind, with the young Devon sailor at his elbow, Barineau timed their entrance into the mouth of the Yealm for just before sundown. By then, the tide was flowing at a brisk rate into the estuary. By the time the current had carried them up the narrow, winding river hemmed in by high, wooded banks and into the pool or anchorage where the Yealm was joined by Newton Creek, candles were appearing in the windows of the town of Newton Ferrers. Talbot ordered his forward anchor to be dropped. Once the fast inflowing tide had swung the stern of the vessel around, he ordered a smaller aft anchor to be dropped.

"That will hold her with her bow pointed to seawards, I reckon," he said to Barineau. "Now I hope you and Dr. Martin can do what you intend doing by the time the tide ebbs. I would hate to be stuck here facing into a breeze in the morning. Ah, there comes a boat."

"Ahoy, there," a man in a rowboat called. "Who do you be?"

"We're the *Florantine*, out of Halifax, Nova Scotia, bound for Plymouth," Barineau shouted back. "The fog is so thick off out toward Plymouth Sound, we put in here for the night."

"Well, I am the revenue agent, and it is my duty to come aboard and examine your papers and your cargo."

"Welcome aboard."

Wearing Talbot Smith's captain's cap and coat, Barineau escorted the official into the cabin and laid out the papers and log of the Canadian brigantine they had burned two weeks earlier.

"You are not British, then?" the man asked.

"I am an Acadian. From Nova Scotia. Name is Barineau. French name, but I hope you are as loyal to King George as I am."

"These manifests show you are carrying salt fish and lumber."

"We were. Discharged our cargo in London, as you can see by our log. Hoping to pick up dry goods and such in Plymouth and join a convoy back to Halifax. We have heard much talk of Yankee privateers operating in these waters."

Barineau opened the log to the point where he had forged the false entries for recent dates and deliberately set it at a distance from the lantern on the desk.

After squinting in the dim light, the man said, "I suppose all is in order, but I must inspect your hold. Just here for the night, you say?"

"Or until the fog lifts. Care for a drop of rum before you begin your inspection?"

"Only a small dram. Must get home to my family for supper."

"By the by," Barineau said as he poured out the rum, which Lovejoy had laced with a strong dose of laudanum. "You wouldn't happen to know a former captain named Bledsoe, would you?"

"Christopher Bledsoe? Indeed I do know him. He lives just up the way from myself, next to Holy Cross Church. One-legged chap. How do you know him?"

"When I knew him, ten years ago, he had both his legs. Was in the navy. Seems he said he was from Newton Ferrers."

"He lost his leg at Trafalgar and has been talking about it ever since, I reckon. But hold. He only moved here with his wife last year. He's a Liverpudlian. He wouldn't have been from here when you say you knew him."

"Perhaps what he said was he hoped one day to retire here. You know how time dims your memory. Like the rum?"

"Never tasted any quite like this. Odd flavor."

"Here, have a bit more, and tell me how old Christopher is faring these days."

The excise man made a face as he swallowed the rum.

"Instead of me telling you, why don't you just come ashore and see for yourself after I am done with you?"

"Could you tell me exactly where I may find his house?"

"From the landing you pass right along by the public house and follow the creek past the church . . ."

The man's speech grew thicker as he talked.

"I theel thrange. Could I have a glath of water?"

"We are short of water, but there is plenty of rum."

"No, no. No more wum. Here, could I lie down for a moment?"

"As long as you like. Take your time. What did you say your name was?"

"Wobert Webther. What kind of wum ith that?"

"It is our own special brand. Just make yourself comfortable right here on my bunk."

Dark had fallen by the time Barineau and Lovejoy were rowed the short way to the shore by Kevin and Toby in the revenue agent's boat. They tied up the boat and walked to the stone cottage where the official had said he lived.

A large woman opened the door. Her look of suspicion quickly turned to one of indignation when Barineau explained that her husband had asked them to tell her that he was being detained in examining their cargo.

"I was afraid he was over at the Old Ship Inn crost the creek a-drinking again. He has never learned to hold his drink. Well, then, we will wait his supper no longer. He can eat cold pease, if he puts his job above his family. What's that? You want to see Captain Bledsoe? I will point out his house to you, but I warn you: expect no hospitality from that one. Thinks himself too good for us common folk. And always going on in the public house about what he done in the navy. What ship did you say you're from? And you are all Canadian, including him?"

She pointed to Toby as she said this.

"He is from Jamaica, a British island in the West Indies."

As they slipped away from the house in the dark, they could hear the woman complaining to her children about their father's lack of consideration.

Bledsoe's house, a two-story affair with a side garden, stood in contrast with the simple fishermen's cottages that lined Newton Creek.

Barineau and Lovejoy stood in the dark, arguing in low tones about whether to take the house by storm or try to lure Bledsoe outside and seize him.

"We really ought to reconnoiter first," Barineau said.

And so they crept into the garden, keeping away from the light shining from the windows of the house. Beside a brick privy, they squatted in the bushes, watching until they saw figures moving in the kitchen at the rear of the house.

Toby volunteered to slip up to the window to spy on the occupants.

He returned in a few minutes.

"The captain with the peg leg is in there and a woman that do look like his wife and a younger fellow, sort of skinny and yellow hair. They eating their supper."

"I'll take a look," Barineau said.

He was back in a moment.

"Lovejoy, I can't believe my eyes," he whispered. "Come along and see for yourself. Keep your head down and look in that window just there."

Shortly after, Lovejoy exclaimed, "Son of a bitch!"

"Keep your voice down. It's him, isn't it?"

Inside the kitchen, Mrs. Bledsoe interrupted the conversation between her husband and Chester Peebles to ask if they had heard a noise outside.

They stopped talking to listen. Hearing nothing, they resumed their conversation. Mrs. Bledsoe opened her kitchen door and peered out into the dark.

Lovejoy and Barineau huddled under the window, and Toby and Kevin remained motionless in the shadow of the privy until the woman closed the door and returned to her kitchen fire.

"Being kept in chains on bread and water at Old Mill Prison, my ass," Lovejoy hissed. "They are treating him like an honored guest. By God, let's seize them both."

"Don't be a fool. We would get ourselves captured."

Inside the kitchen, over mugs of tea and a plate of Mrs. Bledsoe's scones, Chester was saying, "We should be hearing something from Philadelphia any day now. You saw my wife's letter. They believe I am being cruelly treated. My uncle is a Quaker. He has a tender heart. If no one else does, he will send over the money."

"What about your brother?"

"Rosalind said that he had been jailed as a lunatic. Some business about the girl he was to marry throwing him over. She said that he had gone off to Lake Erie, which is three hundred miles from Philadelphia."

"You must write another letter. This time tell them you will be tried as a spy and possibly hanged unless they send over the money immediately."

"I would hate for them to discover that I have lied to them."

"I have agreed to split the ransom with you. That much money surely will salve your conscience."

At that point, Lovejoy and Barineau had retreated from the window and were hiding in the bushes around the family outhouse with Kevin and Toby and were now arguing over what to do.

"Now that you know their game, why not just slip back to our brigantine and return to America?"

"Without repaying them for what they have done to me and our family? Never."

"If it would make you feel better, you can write a note to Bledsoe and give it to the lad for delivery after we set him ashore. That'd plant a thorn in his bosom, and Chester's, too."

"That kind of revenge is too slow, too subtle. My enemy is in that house. No, both my enemies. Let's seize them. Tie up the woman, and haul them both back to America. God damn it, Pierre. This is an opportunity such as we never dreamed of having."

"Don't be a fool. We might have hustled Bledsoe to the boat as planned, but not both of them. Wait, what's going on?"

The kitchen door opened again, and this time Chester stepped through it, carrying a candle. The four men held their breath as he walked out to the backyard privy and stepped inside.

"We will never have a better opportunity," Lovejoy whispered.

"Is he the one you want?" Toby asked.

"Yes," Barineau replied. "Make it quick."

"Who's out there?" Chester called from within the privy.

Before he could say more, the door jerked open and two large men, one black and one white, crowded into the narrow space. Chester was too terrified to cry out at first. By the time he thought to scream, a cloth had been stuffed in his mouth. A moment later, a blow across the back of his neck knocked him unconscious.

Kevin and Toby carried him from the yard down the street, out of hearing of the house. There Barineau stopped them.

"Now set him on his feet. Remove the rag from his mouth. Each of you take an arm and bear him along as if he is drunk. That's it. Now, Lovejoy, put your arm across my shoulder and stumble along with me to the dock as if we, too, are drunk. If anyone accosts us, let me do the talking."

By the time Bledsoe took a lamp into his backyard to see what kept Chester so long, they had rowed the revenue agent's boat back to their schooner-brigantine.The mist had lifted, and a half moon cast a dim light over the river. Lovejoy gave Henry Alleyne his ten gold pieces and wished him well, as Toby and Kevin lifted the excise man down into his boat.

"Just leave the boat tied up to the dock with the gentleman in it," Lovejoy said to the young sailor. "Then you slip away to your home. He will sleep off his drink in good time and return to his cold supper."

"Mayn't I go along with you?" the boy asked.

"Why would you want to do that?"

"I have enjoyed being with you lot. If I goes back home, my pa will want to send me off to work on the breakwater in Plymouth Sound. Or I will have to take a job at the squire's lime kiln. There is no future for me here. Take me with you. I have always wanted to see America."

"Ah, lad, that would be dangerous for you. If we should be captured, they would hang you for desertion."

"What should I say when they asks me at home how I got here?"

"Let your father think up a story for you. 'Twill be easy for an old smuggler, I should think."

# 6

Chester remained bound and gagged in the sail locker until the tide had turned and, under the faint light of a half moon, they had ridden the current back down to the mouth of the Yealm into Wembury Bay and were safely at sea once more.

With the vessel set on a southwesterly course, Talbot ordered his bosun's mate to repaint the name *Flora* on the stern.

During this time, Lovejoy coached Barineau and the others on what to say and what not to say to his brother.

"Let's allow him to explain how he came to be at Bledsoe's house as a guest rather than a mistreated inmate of Old Mill Prison as he represented in his letter. No matter what he says, we must pretend to believe him."

So, at last a frightened and bewildered Chester was brought out from the sail locker and was escorted into the cabin where Lovejoy sat waiting, alone.

It took a few moments for Chester's eyes to adjust to the light.

"Where am I?"

"You are aboard my schooner."

"Is that you, Lovejoy?"

"Indeed it is."

"I thought you were behind this. What are you going to do with me?"

Lovejoy sat for a long time, looking at the anxious, trembling Chester. In spite of himself, he felt pity for his half brother, as well as a sense of triumph.

"Why, Chester, I am taking you home. We have rescued you from that dreadful brute Bledsoe. Are you not grateful?"

"Of course. But how did you know where to find me?"

"Here, sit down. Can you see better now? Sorry about the rough handling you have received, but it was the only way to free you from that awful man. I wanted to go back and seize him, but my companions dissuaded me. However did you come to be in his custody? Did he mistreat you, in any way? You look healthy enough. He must have taken you off the diet of bread and water of which you wrote so eloquently."

Haltingly, improvising feverishly, Chester told an involved tale in which he alleged that he really had been imprisoned but that Bledsoe had arranged to bring him to his home to force him to write ransom notes.

Lovejoy let him talk on and on. When he had finished his elaborate story, very little of which was true and none of which Lovejoy believed, Chester asked, "Why have you gone to so much trouble for me?"

"Let me be honest, Chester. I have done this at our family's request and not from any special love for you. Amanda would like to believe Ephraim's claim that you went to enormous pains to come over to Bermuda to win my freedom. The family persuaded me to exert myself on your behalf."

Chester looked at him with a puzzled expression.

Lovejoy continued, "You see, they convinced me that you really did mean to ransom me. And of course, there were those bills of exchange sewn into your jacket lining. Too bad you did not have time to explain about the money."

"You didn't give me a chance. What happened to the money?"

"Oh, that was returned to Uncle Ephraim and Amanda."

"How did you get off the island?"

"That is a long story. Let's get you fed and cleaned up. It should be a pleasant voyage back home."

Later, Barineau took Lovejoy aside to hear about the interview.

"And you pretended to believe that cock-and-bull story?"

"But he is not sure whether I am sincere. Let's keep him off guard for the present. I will decide how to handle the matter once we are back in Philadelphia."

"Is he not curious as to how we stumbled upon him?"

"He has no idea that we really intended to carry off Bledsoe and hold him as our own form of ransom and revenge. He is dying to know how we learned he was at Bledsoe's house, but I told him that it must remain a secret until after the war ends. Let his imagination gnaw on that one for a while."

"You are a fiend. He knows nothing of our involvement with that Swedish captain, then?"

"No, and let us keep that from him as well. Let him go on thinking that we believe his preposterous story, for the time being at least. Now, what is this about our noble captain wanting to make more captures before we return home? He is so annoyed that we failed to bag Bledsoe, he hardly speaks to me."

"He is dead set on returning to Baltimore rather than Philadelphia."

"I have no objection to that, providing we can slip through the blockade."

"He also wants to cast our net in Bermudian waters for one more prize on the way. He fears you will object, however."

"We might as well humor him. After all, he ventured up the Yealm against his better judgment at my insistence."

"So he did. And he is unhappy that you did not bring Bledsoe away as well as Chester."

"I am none too happy about that myself. But I have been thinking of a way to wreak additional revenge on Captain Bledsoe. Bermuda might fit in very well with what I have been thinking of doing."

Barineau started to go, then paused to say, "Lovejoy, as your friend, let me offer you some advice."

"What will it be this time? Something from Shakespeare or Montaigne?"

"Neither. This is from Milton, and it goes, 'Revenge, at first though sweet, bitter ere long back on itself recoils.' "

"What are you getting at?"

"Don't let a desire for revenge poison your soul. By recovering your brother, you have undone the schemes of our friend Bledsoe. That should be revenge enough."

"I have not undone the damage he or my dear brother Chester have done to my life. Except for them . . ."

"Oh, come now, Lovejoy. The slate has been wiped about as clean as possible. Further acts of revenge will accomplish nothing. What do you have in mind, anyway?"

Lovejoy smiled. "Nothing so very drastic. I will tell you in due course. Just now I am enjoying toying with my dear brother."

Two weeks later, the *Flora* lay to in a calm sea twenty miles north of Bermuda while Talbot and Collins oversaw the replacement of the vessel's spars and square sails on her foremast with her original forward fore-and-aft jib, which had been kept stored along the starboard scuppers.

While she was thus lying helpless in the water, a large fishing ketch approached from the south flying a British flag, as was the *Flora*. Seeing that the ketch was unarmed, Talbot Smith took no precautions other than ordering his two Long Toms to be loaded with grape and for his landsmen to stand by with muskets and pistols concealed along the gunwales.

"Ahoy," the captain of the ketch called, once he was within hailing distance. "What is the matter?"

Once again, Lovejoy's fake British accent was called into service.

"We lost some rigging in a storm," he called back.

"Where do you hail from?"

"We've just come from Plymouth. We're bound for Bermuda."

"Are you now? Let me advise you then. Don't try to get into St. George's."

"Why not?"

"The place is full of navy ships. It is swarming with their sailors and soldiers as well."

"What is happening?"

"They are bound for the Chesapeake."

"What for?"

"To teach the bloody Yankees a lesson."

Lovejoy looked at Barineau and then at Talbot Smith.

"Pump him for more," Barineau whispered.

"How many ships are there?"

"They got one eighty-gun ship and one with seventy-four. They got more transports than you can count. Can I lend you a hand?"

"Should I invite him aboard?" Lovejoy whispered.

"No," Talbot replied. "He'd see we're not British, and we'd have to burn his ketch and take him and his crew prisoner."

"Then I will go to him."

The captain of the ketch assured Lovejoy that he was welcome to come aboard.

It took a few minutes to fill a sack with jars of captured English marmalade and bottles of whisky and for Kevin and Toby to lower the *Flora's* longboat. Aboard the ketch, the captain eagerly accepted the gifts and invited Lovejoy into his cabin.

Lovejoy listened to the captain's description of the arrival of several regiments of Wellington's old soldiers and of how the people of Bermuda had welcomed them with balls and concerts.

"And they are headed for the Chesapeake. What for?"

"There is already a good number of ships and soldiers at Tangier Island. The talk is that this force will stop there and then move up and take Baltimore. Here is a copy of the Bermuda *Gazette and Weekly Advertiser.* You can read it for yourself."

"It is about time something was done about that nest of vipers," Lovejoy said as he pored over the little newspaper.

Satisfied that he had learned all he could from the captain, Lovejoy said, "Well, if we can't get into St. George's, I suppose we could try Hamilton Harbor. But look, I was hoping to send a letter back to a friend near Plymouth. Would you be willing to carry it into St. George's and see that it is placed on the next packet to England? I have brought along writing materials."

After reading over his message, Lovejoy sealed the letter and addressed it to Christopher Bledsoe in Newton Ferrers. The captain accepted the letter and the money and surrendered his copy of the newspaper describing the invasion fleet being marshaled at St. George's.

Back aboard the *Flora,* Talbot Smith waited until Lovejoy had finished his report on what the captain of the ketch had told him and then smote his fist against his desk.

"We got to get that jib boom back in place and haul our asses home with this here news as fast as we can. Them British means business this time."

Later, Barineau asked Lovejoy why he was looking so pleased with himself. Lovejoy told him about the message he had written to Bledsoe.

"I told him what a fool we had made of him by whisking his so-called captive out from under his nose. Who said that revenge is not sweet?"

"It was Milton. And actually, he warned against letting it take over your life, lest it blow up in your face. By the way, how much longer are you going to shun your brother? Not allowing him to eat with the officers: that really does not become you."

"It will do him good to rub elbows with real men. I have set him a task of writing a full account of how he fell into British hands and was carried back to England. He refused to trouble himself until I suggested that he might like to spend the time shut up in the sail locker instead."

"What are you after?"

"I am interested in reading how he explains what happened."

"I just hope you don't get yourself entangled in the web of all these little conspiracies you are weaving."

"Don't spoil my pleasure, Pierre. I don't have much else to relieve my mood of melancholy. There is little for me to live for when you get right down to it."

"Nonsense. We have a country to save. The faster we get back to the Chesapeake with our news the better. So no more morbid, petty talk from you, my friend. And let me caution you not to further humiliate your brother. It is not wise to cause him to hate you any more than you feel he already does."

"Now you are talking nonsense. I have the upper hand over Chester and I intend to keep it. He is powerless to do me harm."

Two weeks passed before the *Flora* arrived off Annapolis, and it was able to do this only through a combination of good luck and superb seamanship on the part of both Talbot Smith and Pierre Barineau.

Now that they had established a large base at Tangier Island, well within the Chesapeake, the British did not keep so many ships blockading the mouth of the bay. Even so, Talbot wisely forwent making a dash past Cape Charles. Instead, he sailed the schooner close enough to a British frigate to attract its captain's attention, then turned back to sea carrying just enough sail to stay out of his pursuer's cannon range. That night, under a light rain, he turned back toward the Chesapeake. By the next morning, the rain was falling in sheets. Under this cover, with Barineau carefully charting their course, he gingerly brought the *Flora* through the outer blockade.

Getting past the British ships at Tangier Island unscathed would have been impossible had it not been for a stiff wind from the north-northwest. The breeze cleared away the rain clouds. The British sent out a brig to challenge the close-hauled schooner beating its way north but found themselves helpless to make headway against the wind.

At Annapolis, Lovejoy had a final conference with Chester before going ashore to carry warnings of the British expedition to Washington.

"I have read what you have written about your experiences on Bermuda and in England."

"I would hope you did. You put me through a good deal of trouble."

"So it was. All I want to say is that I think the entire story is an ingenious work of fiction."

"Look here, Lovejoy. You have treated me like an outcast these past few weeks, not allowing me to eat at the same table with your officers. Now you add insult to the injury you have subjected me to."

"You look here, Chester. And you listen well. I don't believe half of what you have written, but I must admit that I admire your talent for storytelling. Now, this is a family matter and must be kept so. Father remains an invalid. If he knew the truth about what you have done, it would finish him off. Uncle Ephraim and Frank understand that you were playing your own game when you volunteered to ransom me on Bermuda. However, they want to avoid a family scandal, and so do I. Therefore, I shall pretend to believe your story. We shall agree that there was a sad lack of communication and timing between us on Bermuda. And I will not voice my doubts about your explanation of how you came to be at Bledsoe's house rather than in prison."

"In other words, you are calling me a liar."

"You are a liar."

Chester's face darkened and he half rose from his stool.

"You would not dare talk to me like that if you did not have me in your power."

"Don't be ridiculous. I could mop up the floor with you."

"What is the purpose of all this talk, then?"

"I could have you held until my mission to Washington and my business at Baltimore are completed, then return you to Philadelphia personally to make sure that you do not mislead our family. But, on your word that you will commit no more mischief, I will give you funds for your coach fare and let you proceed."

"Very considerate of you, I am sure."

"Have I your word, then?"

"You have my word. I do have a question, though."

"Make it quick. I must get our news to Washington."

"How did you know to find me at Newton Ferrers?"

"I did not know you were there. It was my plan to seize Bledsoe and hold him for ransom for your return. We stumbled on to you, or I should say, you stumbled into me and my men."

"And you have never said how you and your piratical friend managed to get away from Bermuda."

"Perhaps someday, after you have lived up to your word to cause no further trouble, I will tell you everything. Getting off that island was not nearly so easy for me as your getting away from Bledsoe's clutches. Just remember that you are on probation."

Lovejoy was delayed leaving the *Flora* by members of the crew, all of whom, except for Collins, wanted to shake his hand and wish him well. He made them a brief speech praising their courage and assuring them of a quick reckoning and distribution of their shares of the profits from their cruise.

Barineau would not release his hand until he had finished his final word of advice.

"You have behaved nobly, my friend. Continue to do so and you will fulfill the promise I was so slow to recognize in you. Just remember, do not let despair overtake you. It is always out there, like the North Sea that constantly threatens the lowlands of Holland. The Dutch withstand the cold, dark sea through diligent upkeep of their dikes. Similar diligence is required to maintain one's equilibrium in the storms of the spirit."

"I shall keep my dikes under repair, I promise you, Pierre. Thank you again for all you have done."

"Now, don't waste time down there in Washington," Talbot said. "Tell them what they need to know and get back to Baltimore to help me and Barineau with all the damned papers we will have to fill out. And, by the way, what shall we do with that little brother of yours that has put us to so much trouble?"

"Send him on his way to Philadelphia."

"You are making a big mistake. I wouldn't let him out of my sight, brother or no brother. Never trust a fellow with eyes set so close as his is."

Toby rowed Lovejoy to the dock at Annapolis and wished him good luck.

"I hopes you will finish teaching me and Cookie to read."

"I promise to do so, Toby."

At a small hotel, Lovejoy spent the night between clean sheets. Early the next morning, he found a livery stable to supply him with a chaise, complete with horse and driver. Late that day, he arrived in the raw young city of Washington, where he spent a restless night in a boarding-house. After an excellent breakfast, he made his way to the offices of Secretary of State James Monroe.

Monroe listened to his story, asked a few questions, and then read the copy of the Bermuda newspaper.

"This is a most serious matter. I would like you to tell your story to someone else."

"The secretary of war, perhaps?"

"No. That man wouldn't know what to do about your intelligence."

"Then where are we going?"

"To the president's residence. Mr. Madison must hear firsthand what you have to report."

# PART FOUR

# 1 

Weasel Cuthbert sat under a palm tree at Tobacco Beach watching a stream of red-coated British soldiers as they marched down to be loaded onto launches and carried to their transports in Murray's Anchorage off St. George's Island.

He was glad to see that lot leave Bermuda, and all the sailors from Vice Admiral Alexander Cochrane's fleet as well. Perhaps now Queenie Foster would have time for him again. Of course he had made a bit of change pimping for her the past few weeks. Brought her only officers as customers. He hoped she would remember what he had done for her.

Queenie was the only person to whom he had confided the reason that his hair had gone suddenly white during the dreadful hurricane of the previous August. For a time, perhaps out of pity, she had considered giving up her profession and marrying him. But since the arrival of Cochrane's fleet and Major General Robert Ross's tough, horny soldiers, both of them had been kept too busy to carry forward these discussions.

Weasel still had nightmares about the two days and nights he had spent in the tomb behind St. Peter's Church. Sometimes, just as he was about to drift off to sleep, the face of that mad American would appear. Then out would flash that awful knife, and he would hear the man's threatening questions once more.

The word around the harbor was that all those soldiers and ships were being sent to punish the Americans for the dreadful crimes they had perpetrated in Canada. He wished them success.

There wasn't much wind stirring that day, and such as there was blew from the east, making it questionable whether Cochrane's eighty-gun flagship, HMS *Tonnant,* could be maneuvered out the usual channel through the coral reefs encircling the broad anchorage. The word around the harbor was that Joseph Hayward, Bermuda's best pilot, had volunteered to guide the huge vessel through the treacherous North Rock passage, a narrow gap in the reef. So large a ship had never attempted this feat, and many of the residents of St. George, like Weasel, had come to watch.

For many years thereafter, the story would be told and retold on Bermuda of how Hayward managed to ease Cochrane's flagship through the slender passage with barely a foot to spare on either side. The seventy-four-gun HMS *Royal Oak* and the rest of the fleet followed.

With crowds waving their handkerchiefs along the shore, these two powerful ships led three frigates, three sloops, and ten transports westward toward the Chesapeake. Aboard the transports were some three thousand of the best soldiers in the world.

Weasel had no idea where the Americans who had so terrorized him the previous year might be now. He hoped that they would find themselves in the path of that mighty armada whose sails were growing smaller and smaller.

As the sun began to set, Weasel arose, brushed the sand from his trousers, and set out for Queenie's house.

By the time Lovejoy had delivered his message to President Madison and made his way to Baltimore, Chester had already gone on to Philadelphia.

Barineau and Malcolm MacKenzie kept him up past midnight, questioning him about his audience with Madison.

How did the president strike him?

"He is a small gentleman. Looked rather sickly. Very quick of intellect. Polite, as you would expect a Virginian of breeding to be. Wanted to know a bit about me. He warmed up when I told him that I, like him, am a Princeton man. He expressed his sincere gratitude for the pains we took to bring him the news. He said it accorded with other reports he had received. And then he wanted to know all about what we did in the Irish and North Seas. He is very conscious of the effect our privateers are having on British shipping."

"Ah, and well he might be," Malcolm said. "They have proved our most effective weapon against the British. Good thing for us, too. We hardly have a regular navy anymore."

"We have been cut off from general news of the war," Lovejoy said. "Are we yet winning it?"

"Since Perry's great victory on Lake Erie and Harrison's triumph at the battle of the Thames last year, the far Northwest seems secure. The death of Tecumseh has destroyed the Indians' will to fight out there. And we finally have a winning general in the Southwest. Name's Jackson. Andrew Jackson. From Tennessee. Last March he paid the Creeks back with interest for the Fort Mims massacre. Wiped out several hundred of their braves in a battle at a place called Horseshoe Bend in Alabama. Madison has appointed him a major general in charge of Alabama, Mississippi, and Louisiana. As such, he will be responsible for protecting New Orleans and the lower reaches of the Mississippi. There is some fear of British designs in that area."

"But in general, the war is going well for us, is it not?"

"Not really. Despite marshaling troops and probing here and there, the action along the St. Lawrence has been inconclusive. The papers are full of reports that Winfield Scott, one of our new young generals, plans another invasion try, but I hold out little hope for its success. Then one reads of an ominous buildup of British soldiers at Montreal. If the reports are true, this force would rival Lord Howe's expeditionary force that arrived on Long Island during the Revolutionary War in . . . when was it?"

"September of 1775," Barineau said. "And I hope the parallel goes no further than that, for Howe took New York City and chased Washington clear across New Jersey."

"History never really repeats itself, and yet we should learn from the past. What I fear is that the British will move into New York State and down the Hudson Valley. That would separate New England from the rest of the country, with dire consequences."

"Did not the British attempt such an invasion from Canada in 1778?" Lovejoy said. "Burgoyne, wasn't it?"

"So they did."

"And did not that end in disaster for them at Saratoga?"

"It did, but remember that while that campaign was being conducted, Howe moved a considerable army out of New York by sea and landed it far up the Chesapeake. He defeated Washington at the Brandywine and ended up in possession of Philadelphia. And now this intelligence you have brought from Bermuda sounds distressingly similar."

"The president said that he has appointed a general to oversee the protection of Washington and Baltimore."

"He has that. I know the man. His name is William Winder, and he appears to have been selected more for his political value than any military talent. He is a nephew of our governor here in Maryland. Well, we could talk all night of military affairs and, indeed, we nearly have. By every measure, your cruise in British waters was a success. We count twenty-one British vessels destroyed. We haven't toted up their value, but it will be considerable. And you have brought your brother back from captivity. Yet, you do not seem happy."

"I am very tired. A good night's sleep will put me right."

"Quite so. You must be alert in the morning. A correspondent for the *Niles Weekly Register* has learned of your exploits. He wishes to hear of them from your own lips. I have promised to tell him when you arrive."

"I don't really want to see my name in print."

"Why not? What possible harm could come from that?"

"None, I suppose. But I really am tired of this war."

Lovejoy was embarrassed when the article about the cruise of the *Flora* appeared in the widely circulated *Niles Weekly Register.* He avoided mentioning his rescue of Chester, as did Barineau and Malcolm. He praised Talbot Smith for his expert seamanship, knowing how much this would please the captain. He was unprepared for questions about his role in the battle of Lake Erie, but apparently Malcolm had told the correspondent about this, and he could not very well refuse to answer the man's questions. His embarrassment at being painted as a hero faded, however, when he saw how much the laudatory article meant to Talbot Smith.

"Reckon them fellows that thought you was making a big mistake to choose me as your captain ain't so sure now," he said to Malcolm as they surveyed the condition of the *Flora,* now tied up to his shipyard wharf near Lazaretto Point.

Hearing this, Lovejoy concluded that Malcolm had been right. There was no harm in the publication of the article in the *Niles Weekly Register* at all. And so it seemed at the time.

# 2

"You have read what that paper printed about my dear baby brother?"

"Yes, and so have all of our friends. Lovejoy has become quite the hero in their eyes."

"Hero, indeed. All he has done is to charm a half-literate shipbuilder and a self-taught schoolmaster with intellectual pretensions into risking their lives to serve his ends. It made me sick to watch him aboard that ship, playing the grand doctor, buttering up an ignorant lot of riffraff sailors."

"Lovejoy has always been persuasive."

"And lucky. If I could have foreseen this, I might have talked the old man into selling me his Baltimore debts. Then none of our problems would have occurred."

"And the newspaper would be writing of your exploits? Come now, Chester. Anyway, Amanda and Frank seem to think that you should be grateful to Lovejoy for bringing you back from England."

"Grateful, ha! We would have collected half of the ransom from Bledsoe. Besides that, he treated me abominably on the voyage home. I was forced to sleep in a hammock among the lowest sort of scum, and to eat with them as well. And then he put me through the humiliating exercise of writing out my story, as though I were an errant schoolboy. Then, when I had finished it, he mocked my work and called me a liar."

"Well, you are home now, and we must make the best of our circumstances. We are back where we began before you made such a muddle of that trip to Bermuda. Once again we are stuck with waiting for Papa Martin to die. Will he ever?"

"I don't know. He seems better to me. But Rosalind, that is not fair, what you said about Bermuda. You have not been through what I have. Things will come around for us in the end. The old man is delighted to see me again. As for this business between Lovejoy and me, well, it is far from settled. I will repay him."

"How? I would say that he is sitting on top of the world, especially with the publication of this article."

"I will find a way. Believe me. The score between us is far from settled."

"Emily, come in here at once, would you?"

"I was about to go over and help Madeline with the baby."

"That can wait. Now keep your voice down. I want you to read this here newspaper article."

Emily Richter took the copy of the *Niles Weekly Register* and put on her reading glasses. As she read, her mouth dropped open. When she had finished, her husband said, "Imagine something like that."

"I wish the scoundrel had been killed at Lake Erie. Or that the British had captured him and hanged him as a pirate."

"So, you see, what the fellow found out about him down in Baltimore was true, sure enough."

"I should have recognized him for what he was when first we met. I rue the day I allowed him to speak to Madeline."

"Water over the dam. Now put that paper away and hope no one else tells Maddy about it."

"I certainly shall not. Oh, how it galls me to think that we entertained an enemy of my native land here in our own home."

"Just remember. We got to keep this from Maddy. She doesn't know about him showing up last year. And we don't want her to read this neither. Poor girl is unsettled enough these days. Sometimes I wonder if she will ever be the same. And that McFairlane's drinking doesn't help."

Amanda Carpenter sat in a chair beside an open window. In his bed, Jeremiah Martin lay propped up on pillows listening to her read the article from the *Niles Weekly Register.*

When she had finished, he said, "I used to think that what I did in the Revolution was something quite extraordinary, but it does look as though my son may have outdone me."

Amanda smiled. She wondered how much more extraordinary Jeremiah would regard Lovejoy's exploits if he knew how he had brought Chester back from England.

"Lovejoy is a remarkable young man, Father. I am glad that you finally realize that."

A long pause followed. Thinking that her stepfather had fallen asleep, Amanda arose.

"Wait," he said. "Read the article to me again, please."

At the White Swan Tavern, Evan Jenkins burst through the doors, waving a copy of the newspaper.

"Tom! Meg! Primrose! All of you, come out here and see what there is in this paper."

Primrose came downstairs, carrying their baby. Meg, followed by Collins, came out of the kitchen, where they had been talking. Tom, who remained deaf in one ear, had to be called twice.

When they were all assembled in the common room of the tavern, Evan commanded Tom to read the article aloud.

When he had finished, Tom said, "Joy left out a good part of what he did at Lake Erie. What about your cruise, Calvin? Is that pretty much what happened?"

"That makes it sound like he done everything himself. There was a good many other men on that cruise, and it was them that did the real work. But he gets the credit."

Evan replied, "Lovejoy Martin is like a member of this family, and I don't want to hear any cold water being thrown on what he has done. If you are going to join our family, you ought to get that straight."

Before Collins could respond, Evan continued loudly, "The article says that Joy will be coming back here to Philadelphia soon. Let's delay Meggie's wedding until he gets back and then throw a party like this town has never seen before. We can celebrate the return of our hero and Meggie's marriage all at the same time."

Seeing the hurt look on Collins's face, Meg took his hand.

Despite what the newspaper correspondent wrote, Lovejoy did not rejoin his family in Philadelphia in mid-August as he had expected. The business of filing claims for the British craft they had destroyed turned out to be far more time-consuming than they had assumed. Barineau and Lovejoy spent hour after hour in the MacKenzies' dining room, writing out reports on each capture they had made during their six months at sea. As the form for each claim was completed, Malcolm would take it to the clerk of the admiralty court for filing.

They were absorbed in such work when Malcolm returned, out of breath, to report the news that had just burst upon Baltimore.

"The British fleet has arrived in the Chesapeake to join the squadron already at Tangier Island. Their ships have entered the Patuxent River near Washington. They have bottled up Barney's gunboat flotilla.

Rumors are flying that they really mean to attack Baltimore. The city is in such an uproar, it is useless to file any more claims until the crisis has passed. Put away your papers and come with me."

*August 31, 1814*

*Dear Uncle Ephraim,*

*This is the first opportunity I have had to write for nearly two weeks. What I have seen and heard during that time makes me tremble for my country.*

*News of the appearance of an enormous British fleet at the mouth of the Patuxent River burst like a bombshell upon Baltimore on the 19th. Fearing that the force was headed for Baltimore and acting on urgent orders from President Madison himself, Maj. Gen. Samuel Smith, a U.S. senator no less, mustered his Third Division of the Maryland militia into federal service forthwith. He alerted the garrison at Fort McHenry and enlisted the captains and crews of ships bottled up here in plans to oppose any British incursions against this city. And he enlisted every able-bodied male, black and white, slave and free, either in digging breastworks or in drilling with whatever arms they can find.*

*If General Smith rather than General Winder had been entrusted by President Madison with the defenses of the entire Chesapeake region, my story would have a far happier ending.*

*At any rate, my colleagues, Messrs. MacKenzie and Barineau, prevailed upon the captain of our schooner to move the vessel from the wharf of his shipyard at Lazaretto Point, where it would be exposed to British attack. While we were tying her up at Fells Point, I received a summons to report to General Smith.*

*It turned out that he had read that fulsome article and wanted me to organize a small party of mounted scouts to ascertain the movements of the British.*

*I could not refuse that noble and very persuasive old veteran of the Revolution and U.S. senator. I asked only that Pierre Barineau accompany me and that we and our fellow scouts be suitably mounted. My request was granted, and on the morning of the 21st, our column of six mounted men headed south for Washington.*

*At the village of Old Fields, we encountered a scene that would have been comic if it had not had such tragic consequences. Total confusion reigned in our camps there. Several thousand militiamen milled about, without tents or rations beyond what they had brought in their knapsacks. General Winder, who was supposed to be in command, was running about like the proverbial headless chicken. Soon after the first British ship appeared at Tangier Island many weeks ago, he had been charged with arranging a system of defense for the region. Yet he had caused no earthworks of any consequence to be erected. His frantic appeals for more manpower had gone largely unheeded. All he had done was waste time dashing hither and yon, studying the terrain and complaining to Secretary of War Armstrong, who, we are told, felt certain that the enemy would attack Baltimore rather than Washington.*

*By the time I reached the camp, the British fleet had worked its ponderous way as far up the Patuxent as Bendedict, Maryland, beyond which point only their smaller craft could proceed.*

*The fleet of gunboats commanded by brave old Commodore Joshua Barney had taken refuge farther upstream. All the work and expense of creating these silly little craft was in vain. Although Barney proved himself a formidable fighter later on land, his gunboats were as useless as the proverbial teats on a boar hog. With the arrival of the fleet about which I had reported to President Madison, the British now have four ships of the line, some twenty frigates and sloops of war, and a like number of transports carrying close to 5,000 soldiers and marines.*

*Formidable as is this armada, a proper defense could have turned the British effort into a debacle had more able leaders than Winder or Armstrong been in charge.*

*At any rate, a column of about 4,000 British soldiers and some 500 of their marines, led by General Ross, debarked at Benedict and marched northward through heavily wooded country while smaller British vessels made their way up the Patuxent toward where Barney's gunboats had taken refuge.*

*You and I both have heard Father speak of witnessing the harassment of the British column that was sent out from Boston in April of 1775 to Concord, Massachusetts. Just as that column was sent back to their base with their tails between their legs, so we could have ambushed and harried Ross's men back to Benedict and prevented the worst disgrace ever to befall this nation.*

*This was not done. The British were allowed to move up to more open land, causing Barney to blow up his useless gunboats and flee with his sailors to join the ragtag force Winder was collecting at Old Fields.*

*The events of the next few days were to prove the truth that too many cooks spoil the broth. Secretary of War Armstrong, Secretary of State Monroe, and even President Madison himself came out to observe our so-called defenses and, by issuing conflicting orders, to make worse the confusion in which our growing forces had fallen.*

*Altogether, the District of Columbia, Maryland, Pennsylvania, and Virginia militias carry some 90,000 men on their militia rolls. Only the appearance of the British fleet off the mouth of the Patuxent and the president's intervention finally and belatedly produced enough men to offer a credible defense force.*

*Meanwhile, our advance scouts reported that Ross's invaders had halted to rest at Upper Marlborough. The redcoats, enervated by several weeks aboard ship, were exhausted from the heat and the unaccustomed march through the heavily wooded country. Not a few of them are reported to have died from heat exhaustion.*

*Here again, we let a great opportunity pass. If, instead of stumbling about, waiting for still more ill-trained, ill-equipped militia to belatedly answer their nation's call, one strong leader such as Smith or Barney had gathered, say, just the 2,000 men of the District of Columbia militia, the several hundred regulars and marines available, together with personnel from the Washington Navy Yard, and had flung that force against Ross's exhausted column in their camp, surely they would have succeeded in causing the enemy to withdraw to the protection of their fleet. After all, they had accomplished their first objective, the destruction of Barney's fleet of gunboats.*

*But we did not take this bold action and, from Baltimore's viewpoint, perhaps it is just as well that we did not, for surely by now the wrath of the British expedition would have fallen on this city rather than on Washington.*

*Although I sent daily reports of what I saw and heard back to General Smith at Baltimore, in a sense, Baltimore came to our camps in the form of a large battery of cannon under the able command of General Tobias Stansbury and much of the Maryland militia.*

*Soon, our scouts reported that the British were breaking camp at Upper Marlborough and, refreshed by their rest, were advancing upon Old Fields. Instead of moving out to meet them, our odds-and-ends army fell back to the town of Bladensburg, whose name I fear will long live in ignominy.*

*A word or two about the locality. Bladensburg is a pretty village overlooking the east branch of the Potomac, which is little more than a wide creek there. To the west, a wooden bridge crosses the stream. Beyond the bridge, the road forks, one branch leading to Georgetown, the other—alas—eight miles directly to Washington.*

*A ridge overlooks the road to Georgetown, and it was on this ridge that Stansbury established his considerable array of artillery, some twenty cannon in all.*

*By the time the vanguard of the refreshed British column approached Bladensburg, our numbers had grown to 7,000 men, so that we outnumbered our enemy by some 2,000. Posted behind better breastworks and placed under a single, able commander, we once again would have had an opportunity not only to stave off the subsequent disaster but also to inflict a debacle of equivalent scale upon the British, who were now 30-odd miles from their landing site and virtually without artillery support.*

*Alas, we were in disarray. Our men, from various commands, had been hurriedly arranged in three lines facing the west bank of the stream. Our rearmost line was drawn up too far to the west to support the two forward lines. Our good Secretary of State, Mr. Monroe, who fancies himself something of a military man, for what reason I do not know, came along to move our second line back to a point where it could not support our first line.*

*I heard General Stansbury express his dismay at this change. He would have protested had he not thought Secretary Monroe was carrying out the orders of General Winder.*

*By now, the temperature had reached a hundred degrees. Besides Monroe, the president himself and other civilian dignitaries had arrived to watch the proceedings. Indeed, the president came perilously close to falling prisoner to the British, for just as he was at the point of crossing the bridge to Bladensburg, a scout rode up to warn him of the danger.*

*And so, about 1 p.m., in sweltering heat, the battle began.*

*From horseback atop the ridge occupied by Stansbury's guns, Pierre and I watched in fearful awe as a column of British light infantry streamed over a hill beyond the river and down into Bladensburg. Stansbury's guns opened fire as they rushed through the town and toward the bridge, which was defended from the opposite bank by our first line of about 500 Maryland militia.*

*As British soldiers started falling, it looked as though our line might hold, but alas, the fun was only beginning. The British deployed additional men to the north, and these splashed across the shallow stream and opened a destructive fire upon our pickets from the shelter of a woods.*

*At that point, still more British troops came up into Bladensburg and began firing rockets at our artillery position. Although these missiles did little physical damage, I have to admit that they spread much confusion and fear amongst both our men and horses. It was all I could do to keep my steed from bolting as these rockets sizzled and whined about our heads.*

*A growing number of Redcoats having forded the river and got themselves ready to outflank us, and their light infantry having forced their way over the bridge, our first line gave way and withdrew to join our second line, commanded by Stansbury.*

*Here came the British light infantry against our line, first headon and then, as we later learned, around our right flank.*

*General Winder came up and ordered the Fifth Maryland Regiment to counterattack. They chased part of the light infantry back to the bridge, but meantime, British rockets were raining down around our cannon, and our line was being outflanked.*

*Given the stupid way in which our troops had been positioned, I cannot fault our Marylanders for giving way and fleeing to the rear. Many of them, I am sorry to say, fled too far and in the wrong direction—toward Georgetown—to take part in the hardest fighting, which was still to come, back along the road to Washington. Had they withdrawn in orderly fashion to join our third line, again we might well have blunted the British advance and might even have inflicted a serious defeat upon them.*

*Rather than join this exodus toward Georgetown, Pierre and I rode back toward Washington to a hill where Barney had positioned several hundred sailors and marines with five large naval guns in the midst of some 3,000 fresh militiamen.*

*In their zeal to secure the victory, the British light infantry made three headlong attacks upon Barney's position and three times were thrown back with heavy losses.*

*Had the militia fought as bravely and been as stoutly led as Barney's men, Washington could have been saved, but once again, General Winder's ineptness worked to the British advantage. Unaware of Barney's success and finding the British advancing against his left flank, he ordered the militia to retreat.*

*Orderly at first, the retreat turned into a rout and the units into so many mobs. Only Barney's men came out of the battle with honor. Only after their leader fell wounded did those tough sailors and marines leave the field, and Pierre and I with them.*

*And so the way to Washington lay open. The British lost some 500 killed, wounded, captured, or heat-exhausted. The defeat cost our side only a hundred or so casualties, but far more important, it cost us our national honor.*

*By now you will have read in the press of what the British did when they reached our defenseless capital that evening. They put to the torch our Capitol building, the presidential mansion, and the War and Treasury Buildings. Except for a violent thunderstorm during the night, the damage might have been even more severe. They were hoist with their own petard, as it were, when in seeking to set fires at our Greenleaf Point naval base they touched off the explosion of a magazine which killed or injured some hundred of Ross's men.*

*These casualties along with their battlefield losses and their exertions of the past week left the British strength much diminished as they withdrew from our ruined capital. Did guerrillas lay in ambush as they withdrew to their ships at Benedict? Did our cavalry harass their rear guard? Did we take any of the steps the Russians are reported to have taken against Napoleon year before last when he retreated from Moscow?*

*No, we tamely let our enemy escape retribution for his inexcusable actions against our national capital. We even allowed a squadron of his fleet to ascend the Potomac to Alexandria, extract a tribute from that city, and carry off 21 merchant vessels and much material.*

*The British may not find Baltimore such easy pickings if they move against us here, for General Smith and a newly formed Committee of Vigilance and Safety are working night and day to perfect our defenses. My friend Malcolm*

*MacKenzie, a member of the committee, keeps me posted on their efforts.*

*So, Uncle Ephraim, I am back in Baltimore and sick at heart as I return to the business of settling up our latest privateering cruise. As soon as that is done, I will return to Philadelphia. My friends, the Jenkinses, write that their daughter Megan's wedding to the first mate of our schooner is being delayed so that I may attend the ceremony. In my opinion, the girl is throwing herself away on the fellow, but I fear I am a poor person to pass judgment in such matters of the heart.*

*Give my love to your family and Amanda's. Tell Father that I look forward to a reunion with him.*

*Finally, let me caution you to take anything Chester may have told you about our rescue of himself with a grain of salt. I will explain more about that in a few days.*

*Affectionately,*
*Lovejoy*

The British saw their victory at Bladensburg and their capture of Washington in quite a different light from the way Lovejoy Martin and many other Americans perceived the events.

Whereas American Secretary of War Armstrong had felt Baltimore to be the Britishers' primary target from the outset, Admiral Cockburn had wanted Ross's troops to strike first at Washington and then march overland against Baltimore. His superior, the more cautious Admiral Cochrane, thought it imperative to destroy Barney's gunboats first and then move against whichever city seemed the more vulnerable. Their orders from London provided for Cockburn, although junior to Cochrane, to oversee Ross's soldiers and marines as well as his own naval squadron.

Cockburn felt a keen animosity toward the American press for the way it had painted him as a vandal after his raids against Chesapeake Bay towns the year before. He insisted on going ashore with Ross's little army and, once in Washington, had personally overseen the destruction of the offices of the *National Intelligencer,* which he felt had especially vilified him.

In many ways, Lovejoy's criticism of American leadership for failing to take advantage of opportunities was wishful thinking. Although Ross and Cockburn had been surprised at the number of armed militiamen they saw milling about across the river from Bladensburg, they had scorned their quality. In time-honored British tradition, they had thrown their soldiers and marines headlong into the attack. Except for Barney's stubborn defense, they had experienced slight difficulty in winning their victory. The loss of five hundred men, although not taken lightly, was deemed a fair price for repaying the Americans for stabbing Great Britain in the back and for burning York, the capital of upper Canada.

Later, facing criticism both at home and in America for the needless burning of Washington's public buildings, Cockburn would justify the action by saying that he had been unable to find any responsible officials with whom to negotiate for the surrender of the city, as the British later did with the town fathers of Alexandria. President and Mrs. Madison had fled Washington, leaving a dinner on the dining room table in the White House. Cockburn and some of his fellow officers had delighted in eating this food and in helping themselves to the first family's personal belongings as souvenirs, before setting the building on fire.

Oddly, the American will to continue the war was stiffened rather than weakened by the capture of the country's raw, new capital city. Residents of the area blamed the fiasco on Secretary of War Armstrong, a New Yorker with a well-known antipathy for the ruling Virginian clique, as well as on the feckless General Winder. On September 4, Armstrong accepted President Madison's suggestion that he retire as secretary of war and was temporarily replaced by James Monroe.

Meanwhile, in Baltimore, General Smith had blocked Winder's efforts to assume command of the defenses of that city and had relegated him to supervising a force of regulars. Under Smith's firm hand, Baltimore braced itself for what many felt to be an inevitable assault from the British expedition. Fort McHenry bristled with cannon; earthworks had been thrown up to cover every approach to the city; plans were perfected to sink ships and place other obstructions in the channels leading to the inner harbor; and special barges able to bear cannon had been constructed.

General Smith also had at his disposal some fifteen thousand militiamen, some of them from Virginia and Pennsylvania and many of them smarting from their defeat at Bladensburg and spoiling to avenge themselves on the British. And on hand to assist in the defense were Oliver Hazard Perry, the hero of the battle of Lake Erie, together with Commodore John Rodgers and Captain David Porter and several hundred of their sailors and marines from New York and Philadelphia.

By the evening of the tenth of September, a Saturday, Lovejoy and Barineau had completed their documentation of the *Flora's* claims for destruction of British ships during her latest cruise.

A heavy rain was falling on the Baltimore area. Over cups of coffee, they sat around the MacKenzies' dining room table discussing their plans as they waited for Malcolm to return from a meeting of the Committee of Vigilance and Safety.

"What will you do now?" Barineau asked.

"I have a letter from Tom Jenkins urging me to return to Philadelphia to help celebrate Meg's marriage to Collins. It is time for me to see Father and the rest of the family anyway. I plan to take the Monday morning stage. My heart is not in going back, but really, what else is there for me to do?"

"At least you'll never have to worry about money again."

"I feel rather like King Midas in that regard. The more wealth I have, the less I find it satisfying. For that matter, you will hardly be a pauper yourself when all our claims have been paid. What will you do, Pierre?"

"I am grateful for the money, of course, not for its own sake but for the freedom it will give me to do as I please."

"And that is to do what?"

"Enjoy my family and write a history of what we have done these past two years. It has been quite an adventure, hasn't it?"

"Yes, and to tell you the truth, I have had a bellyful of such adventures, and of the practice of medicine."

"So, exactly what will you do?"

"I suppose I will read for the law. Perhaps in time marry a respectable Philadelphia girl and rear a family. But, oh, Pierre, it will never be as I had imagined it a year ago . . ."

"Not over your Berks County girl, even now?"

"I doubt that I ever will be."

"Too bad you never realized what a good wife Megan Jenkins might have made you."

"Meg? Come now, she was and still is like a little sister. Anyway, it is a moot point. Collins has won her heart. And I suppose that he will make her a good enough husband, although he always struck me as a surly chap. Enough of that now. What do you think the British will do next?"

"I hear that the squadron they sent up the Potomac against Alexandria did not escape unscathed."

"Really?"

"Haven't you read the papers? Perry, Rodgers, Porter, and their sailors were summoned to Washington to set up artillery downstream along the Potomac and give the British squadron merry hell as their ships sailed back to the Chesapeake from Alexandria. Our three naval heroes are back in Baltimore now. When the British see the kind of reception they and General Smith have prepared for them here, they may not be so eager to carry out their threats against Baltimore."

"So you don't think our services will be needed here?"

"I'll bet you ten to one that the British will back off when they realize how well defended Baltimore is. And, in any event, there are more than enough men on hand to give them a fight without us. According to the press, the British appear to be negotiating seriously with our peace commissioners over in Ghent. By sacking our capital city, they have won themselves a trump card to play at the peace table. Why risk that advantage by attacking such a well-defended place as this? Ah, here's Mr. MacKenzie. I was offering Lovejoy a ten-to-one bet that despite all the furor the British will not attack Baltimore . . ."

Malcolm interrupted him in midsentence. "Let me stop you from making a foolish wager."

"What do you mean?"

He removed his wet coat and shook the moisture from it before he replied.

"Our committee has word that the British fleet has been spotted heading north past Annapolis. Our scouts report some forty or fifty vessels, including bomb ships and transports."

"Aren't they just bluffing?"

Malcolm hung up his coat and sat at the table.

"I believe this city to be in mortal danger. The British have long yearned to pay us back for the damage our privateers have done to their shipping. If you consider what they did to Washington a disaster, think of what they will do here if our defenses fail. We can survive the sack of Washington. If we lose Baltimore, we will lose this war. The British will dictate a hard peace in Ghent. Mark my words. We face a crisis such as never before has confronted our country."

After some debate between Cochrane and Cockburn as to where they should strike next, the British were now every bit as determined as Malcolm feared to wreak vengeance on America's third largest city and her chief port for privateering. This time their plans called for no tedious maneuvering by Ross's men through uninhabited country, no roundabout excursion for part of Cochrane's fleet. The soldiers would go ashore at North Point, fourteen miles southeast of Baltimore, and march rapidly up the peninsula between the Patapsco and Back Rivers to the city while the fleet of ships, frigates, and bomb ships hammered Fort McHenry into submission. Rarely in history had such a formidable combination of naval and land forces been concentrated against a single city.

And, perhaps, never before had the defenders of such a city so clearly anticipated the plans of an attacking force, or so dreaded the consequences of a defeat.

## 5

Already weary and nerve strained from his long hours of working with Barineau over the documents taken from the *Flora*'s victims at sea, Lovejoy found it hard to fall asleep that rainy night as his mind chewed over Malcolm's pessimistic report. Were Baltimore and the nation really in such serious peril?

He thought back over recent events. He had not entered Washington after it had fallen to Ross and Cockburn, but from far out in the Maryland countryside, he had watched the sky glowing in the night from the fires the British had set and had been appalled by the spectacle. It was hard to imagine only blackened walls remaining of that stately presidential mansion where he had had his interview with Madison and Monroe.

He reflected, too, on how ineffective the militia had proved against the little British army, and how the Potomac fort protecting Alexandria had been tamely abandoned by its garrison. Baltimore might well suffer the fate of Washington. And although he no longer cared about his financial stake in the safety of the city, he hated to think of the loss of the *Flora* or of Malcolm's chandlery and, perhaps, even his house. And the papers and claims over which they had labored would be captured or destroyed.

When he finally fell into a fitful sleep, it was only to dream of a horde of red-coated soldiers sweeping over the breastworks on Hampstead Hill and chasing the militia through the city, and of a vast fleet of British ships hurling broadsides into the ships huddled around Fells Point and of fires ravaging the buildings along the waterfront.

"You look like the wrath of God this morning," Barineau said to him over breakfast.

"I dreamed of the wrath of God all night, or rather of the British."

"I slept like a babe."

"Congratulations. Where are the MacKenzies?"

"They have gone to church. They invited me to go with them to pray for the safety of the city, but I declined. If his predictions are accurate, there is many a British prayer being offered to counter theirs. Puts God in an awkward spot, I should think. Is he on our side or theirs? What do you say?"

"I say it is too early in the morning for philosophizing."

"You did awaken in a bad mood, didn't you? Well, have you decided what you will do tomorrow?"

"If I were convinced the city is in danger, I would stay. But I really owe it to my family to return to Philadelphia."

"My offer of a wager still stands. The British are bluffing. They will never attack Fort McHenry."

"How about a hundred dollars? That was a ten-to-one offer?"

"So I said last night. Now the odds are only two to one."

"Before you change your mind, I will take you up."

Barineau grinned and replied, "The MacKenzies would not approve of bets being laid in their home, especially on a Sunday morning. But make it even odds and I will ignore my scruples."

Shortly after noon, Lovejoy was packing his bag for his departure the next morning. Barineau was downstairs talking to the MacKenzies, who had just returned from church services.

The sound of a blast from a signal cannon posted on Federal Hill echoed across the Basin. Lovejoy raised his bedroom window to listen. Shortly thereafter, bells began to peal from the belfry of Christ Church.

"Lovejoy!" Malcolm called up the stairs. "Come quick."

From that moment on, all thoughts of taking the Monday morning stage back to Philadelphia vanished from Lovejoy's mind. Without asking their compliance, MacKenzie hustled his two guests out of the house and into his hack. They stopped first at the wharf where the *Flora* was tied up.

There they found Talbot Smith stumping about the deck. With him, Lovejoy was surprised to see the gunner's mate, Gandy, loading and priming the schooner's starboard carronades. Toby and several other crewmen were assisting the gunner's mate.

Talbot said, "If them bastards get past the fort, we will make them sorry they ever left England, ain't that right, Gandy?"

"You don't have enough men for a fight. You can't maneuver."

"Gandy has it figured out. Mr. MacKenzie here let the militia take our two Long Toms for their forts, but we will have every carronade double loaded and primed. Then Gandy can move from gun to gun. As for maneuvering, the time for that is past. We have turned this here schooner into one of them floating batteries. You want to stay and help us fight?"

"We have other business," Malcolm said.

From Fells Point, MacKenzie drove his hack around the Basin, stopping often to let militiamen pass on their way to their mustering point at Pratt and Light Streets next to the harbor. Here and there, their path was blocked by the wagons of civilians hauling valuable possessions out of the city.

"Look at all that shipping jammed into this harbor," MacKenzie said. "Millions of dollars worth of ships. The British took twenty-one vessels away from Alexandria, you know. Besides all the privateers and merchant vessels gathered here, there are the three naval ships. The mouths of the British admirals must water at the thought of what a rich prize awaits them in this harbor."

At the Fountain House Inn, they found General Smith himself standing with other officers watching the militiamen gather themselves around their captains. Lovejoy was pleased to see Commodore Perry talking to the militia general and was delighted when the venerable old man motioned for him to dismount from the hack.

"Commodore Perry, this is the fellow I was telling you about. Dr. Lovejoy Martin."

Perry looked at Lovejoy for a moment, puzzled, and then said, "You're the chap that was written up in the *Niles Weekly.* You were with me at Lake Erie, weren't you? Usher Parsons gave you high praise for your medical assistance."

"He served us well in that sad business before Washington," Smith said, "but as a scout, not as a doctor."

"Then press him into service again. We will need every hand we can get until this crisis has passed. If we do our job well, the British may need doctors, but we will not."

"I am at your service, General," Lovejoy said.

"And I, too," said Barineau.

Fort McHenry had been erected some fifteen years before on the site of an old earthwork on Whetstone Point, two miles southwest of the heart of Baltimore. From that strategic site, its guns could fire to the east upon any vessel attempting to enter the narrow northwest branch of the Patapsco, which led into the Baltimore harbor, or the wider Ferry Branch of the river to the west.

The heavy masonry walls of the fort encompassed five arrow-shaped bastions plus an additional detached bastion facing the Lazaretto. This configuration caused some to call it "the star fort." Beneath the parapets of the fort proper, earthen emplacements for artillery lined the high banks of the rivers.

Until recently, the fort had been only lightly manned by a garrison of about a hundred soldiers of the U.S. Corps of Artillery. But when Lovejoy, riding the horse assigned him by General Smith, delivered his first dispatch to Major George Armistead, the regular army commander, he was amazed at the number of men packed into the fort and its nearby earthworks: some thousand in all, including about six hundred infantrymen standing guard on the landward side to protect against a landing party. Everywhere, men were filling cartridges with powder and going through gun drills.

Armistead impatiently took the dispatch and read it.

"If you will be good enough to wait, I will write a reply for you to take back to Senator Smith."

While he waited, Lovejoy strolled to a bastion facing down the Patapsco. A militia lieutenant lent him a spyglass.

With the naked eye, the horizon to the south, where the Patapsco joined the Chesapeake, appeared to be obscured by a forest of bare trees. As Lovejoy adjusted the telescope, there sprang into focus a multitude of British ships' masts.

"You see what we are going to be up against," the lieutenant said as he reclaimed his spyglass.

"Well, are you ready for them?"

"We are now. I wouldn't have said so a year ago, however."

The lieutenant explained how, during March of the previous year, Admiral Cockburn had thrown a scare into Baltimore when his squadron was raiding up and down the Chesapeake. General Smith, as commander of the Third Maryland Militia Division, had been charged by the governor of Maryland with strengthening the defenses of the city. Through cooperation between the U.S. Army Engineers and local militia leaders, a five-foot counterscarp had been dug around Fort McHenry; gun platforms had been built in the line of earthen batteries near the water; and powerful naval guns from a wrecked French warship had been mounted in the fort.

The lieutenant concluded, "The question in my mind is how our militia will stand up to the British foot soldiers this time. I was at Bladensburg . . ."

"Say no more," Lovejoy said. "So was I."

When Lovejoy returned with Armistead's reply, he found that Baltimore's own elite Third Maryland Militia Brigade, some three thousand strong, was marching out to Hampstead Hill, with Smith leading the way.

Beginning at the water's edge just east of Fells Point and stretching northward over Hampstead Hill, the citizenry of Baltimore in recent weeks had thrown up a long line of small earthen forts connected by low breastworks. Lovejoy stood by until Smith had finished talking to Brigadier General John Stricker, commander of the Third Maryland, before handing him Armistead's dispatch.

Smith read the note and rubbed his chin.

"How did the situation at Fort McHenry look to you, Dr. Martin?"

"The place is crammed with men, and they are all very busy."

"Good. I have spent many hours and days striving to bring that place to a state of readiness. It is a curious emotion I am experiencing. I think I would be disappointed if the British did not attack. It would depress me to think that the results of all that expense and labor should not be put to the test. Well, I have done all I can for McHenry. My concern now centers on this side of the river. We must not suffer another Bladensburg. Here, let me introduce you to General Stricker, who will lead our advance guard when the British come ashore, as I assume they will down at North Point. I shall want you and your comrade to act as couriers between me and General Stricker after he moves his brigade forward. General!" He beckoned the commander of the Third Maryland Brigade.

"I would like you to meet Dr. Martin and his friend Mr. Barineau. I am assigning these two men to serve as couriers between our camps tomorrow. Meanwhile, I have much for them to do elsewhere."

As mounted couriers, Lovejoy and Barineau spent the rest of that day and into the night relaying messages from Smith's headquarters on Hampstead Hill to the various militia units either stationed in the surrounding earthworks or camped to the rear as reserves. Barineau carried one message down to the Lazaretto, near Talbot Smith's shipyard, where a large earthworks with three long eighteen-pounder cannon, serviced by more than a hundred men, stood across the Northwest Branch of the Patapsco from Fort McHenry. Lovejoy carried a dispatch far out beyond Federal Hill to another large earthwork, Fort Covington, on the Ferry Branch of the river, west of Fort McHenry.

Each time they returned to his headquarters with their replies, General Smith asked what they had observed. For a man of his age, he displayed an energy and curiosity that seemed remarkable to Lovejoy.

It was long after dark when Smith finally told them to "call it a day. Go get your rest and return here at dawn tomorrow."

That night, Lovejoy was too tired to dream.

# 6 

Well before dawn on Monday, September 12, 1814, the soldiers and marines aboard the twenty British transports anchored off North Point were quietly awakened and ordered to prepare to disembark.

While these hard-bitten veterans of Wellington's army dressed and packed their knapsacks, sailors of the fleet lowered dozens of boats and barges into the water. Transporting several thousand men, plus field artillery pieces and horses, even a short distance by boat was a daunting undertaking.

For several hours, the sweating sailors rowed their small craft back and forth between ship and shore. By 7 P.M., Major General Robert Ross had all his expedition assembled on the sandy beach.

The forty-eight-year-old Irish-born officer felt more confident of taking Baltimore than he had been of seizing Washington. His experience at Bladensburg caused him to hold the American militia in contempt. And this time, such forces as he might find in his path would be distracted by the heavy bombardment Admiral Cochrane planned for Fort McHenry. He had made up his losses with drafts from Cochrane's sailors. They were poor marchers, but he reckoned that they could fight well enough.

So, it was a self-confident General Ross who led his men forward from their landing site, toward America's third largest city. And with him rode the ubiquitous and even more aggressive Admiral Cockburn, eager to personally see to the destruction of "that nest of vipers called Baltimore."

As Ross's troops moved inland, the open fields gave way to flat, wooded country, interrupted by many shallow ponds and small tidal creeks. What cowards these Americans were. They had to know that he was approaching their city. And this terrain offered ideal cover from which skirmishers could harass his column. Where were they? Well, if the cowardly Yankees did not want to fight, he had no objection to yet another easy victory.

Around noon, having advanced four miles without meeting any resistance, Ross halted his column at a plantation house and imposed upon the owners to provide him with dinner. While he and Cockburn were relaxing, their scouts brought in three American dragoons they had captured just down the road.

Ross and Cockburn questioned the men closely, eliciting from them the intelligence that the Third Maryland Militia had taken up a position ahead at Bread and Cheese Creek, where the peninsula was its narrowest.

"Hear that, Admiral?" Ross snorted. "Only militia to oppose us. Good! I don't care if it rains militia. I shall sup tonight in Baltimore, or in hell."

The men who awaited the British column were not just any militia, however. They were members of the Third Maryland Brigade, five regiments of them, and made up mostly of well-drilled Baltimore residents who had much at stake in defending their homes and businesses. And their commander, Brigadier General John Stricker, was no ordinary militia officer; before the day ended, Lovejoy and Barineau would attest to that.

The pair had ridden out the seven miles from Hampstead Hill early that morning to Stricker's advance camp, set up near a small Methodist meeting house. The message General Smith had entrusted to them ordered Stricker to delay the British column as long as possible before falling back to the main defense line along Hampstead Hill at the edge of Baltimore.

Stricker scrawled a reply and gave it to Barineau for delivery to General Smith, saying, "I will ask you to remain with us for the time, Dr. Martin."

So, Lovejoy rode with two regiments down to where a side road joined the North Point Road. There Stricker posted six small field guns, flanked by the two regiments. Two other regiments were left a short way to the rear, and a fifth was half a mile back in reserve on a low hill.

Lovejoy admired the skill with which Stricker made these dispositions.

When his scouts reported the presence of the British column down the road at the plantation house, unaware that three of his men had been captured, Stricker called for volunteers to follow one of his best officers, Major Richard Health, to make contact with the approaching enemy.

As he explained to Health, "The last thing I want is for the British to delay attacking us until dark. A night attack might panic our men. So it will be your job to open the action while there is plenty of daylight left."

Some 250 militiamen volunteered to accompany Health. By 1 P.M. they were cautiously moving south, muskets loaded and primed, with flankers out on either side of the road.

And about that same time, Ross and Cockburn, having finished their meal and their interrogation of the three Americans, mounted their horses and led a small advance party to reconnoiter.

At the approach of this handful of mounted British, Health's volunteers quickly deployed and opened fire. The British advance party returned the fire, and Health, following his orders, began to fall back. But some of his flankers remained concealed in the woods as Ross and Cockburn pushed ahead.

Realizing that a showdown with the militia was at hand, Ross turned his horse around and headed back to bring up his light infantry to press the attack.

From the shelter of the woods, two young Baltimoreans fired at the commander of the British invaders. A rifle ball pierced his arm and penetrated his chest. Ross dropped his reins and slumped over the pommel of his saddle. His horse shied, nearly throwing the wounded general to the ground, but an aide-de-camp steadied him and, with the help of others, eased his commander onto the grass.

The stricken Ross, the man who had humiliated the Americans at Bladensburg and who had been a party to the burning of Washington, the man who had so despised Yankee militia, weakly called for Colonel Arthur Brooke of the 44th Foot to be summoned to take command. Shortly thereafter, the mortally wounded Ross was being hauled on a commandeered farm wagon back toward his landing site. He died before he got there.

Brooke ordered the Royal marines' rocket batteries and his field artillery to come up as his light infantry laid down heavy fire upon Major Health's retreating volunteers.

Once again, Lovejoy experienced British rockets whirring over his head while American artillery blasted away at the approaching redcoats. But Brooke was not as impetuous as Ross had been. While his own hand-drawn artillery pieces returned the American fire, he attempted to move between Stricker's line and the Back River. Stricker quickly ordered up his two reserve regiments to plug this gap on his left flank.

It was one thing to wheel a regiment on the parade ground from a column formation into a line of battle. It was quite another to do this from a country road through woods and underbrush, especially for militiamen facing veteran troops.

Seeing the confused way in which the American reserves were meeting his flank movement, Brooke ordered his men to fix bayonets and charge.

The huzzahs of the light infantry rose above the crash of musketry and the blast of cannon. Even though they were not in the well-ordered line Stricker wished, the men of the two regiments stood their ground, exchanging volley after volley with the British until a fog bank of white smoke obscured the scene. Unable to see their targets, men on both sides aimed their muskets at the muzzle flashes facing them.

Although a few panicked and ran, this time the militiamen did not take to their heels en masse. The forms of fallen British littered the ground on both sides of the North Point Road.

By 2:30, Stricker realized that his line would give way before the more numerous, better-trained British. He had followed the orders given him by General Smith to delay the enemy's advance. He called Lovejoy to his side.

"I am going to fall back before we are overwhelmed. Tell General Smith that we have bloodied their noses. Colonel McDonald's Sixth Regiment is strongly posted back at Cook's Tavern. We will pull back there, rally, and then make an orderly withdrawal to our main lines. Tell Colonel McDonald to stand ready for our arrival. Then hurry back and inform General Smith of my intentions."

At that point, the Americans were unaware of the death of General Ross. From Hampstead Hill, the sounds of artillery could be heard from the direction of the Methodist meeting house. Lovejoy raced his horse back, first to Colonel McDonald, and then to General Smith's headquarters.

"And we stood our ground?" Smith asked when Lovejoy finished his message.

"It was no Bladensburg, General, I assure you. I lost count of the volleys we exchanged with the British, toe-to-toe at twenty yards distance. General Stricker thought that he should withdraw while his casualties were still light."

In the high-strung atmosphere surrounding the militia camps, rumors spread quickly. The Third Maryland Brigade, the flower of Smith's militia, was in retreat. The British were racing toward Baltimore. Surely the city was doomed to experience the fate of Washington.

Near the earthworks on Hampstead Hill there stood a huge rope works, the source of much of the rigging used by Baltimore's privateers. Fearful of the factory's falling into British hands, an anxious militia officer set fire to the building and its tar-soaked materials. Soon an enormous pall of black smoke drifted over the defense works and down over the harbor. This created fresh panic among the already distraught civilians of Baltimore.

Although the smoke from the burning rope works obscured the view of the men on Hampstead Hill, those on Federal Hill, across the harbor, could see a portion of the British fleet making its tedious way up the shallow Patapsco toward Fort McHenry. The larger ships of the fleet dared not venture up the river, for fear of running aground. And so Cochrane had transferred himself and his admiral's flag from the mighty *Tonnant* to the fifty-gun frigate *Surprize.* That vessel and four other frigates dropped anchor in midafternoon about five miles below Fort McHenry. Now five bomb ships and a rocket ship were edging even closer toward the fort.

General Smith had been joking when he said that he feared that the British might not attack Fort McHenry. He was not joking when he ordered naval officers to proceed with sinking merchant vessels to block the channel between McHenry and the Lazaretto.

Aboard the *Surprize,* Admiral Cochrane watched his bomb ships feel their way past the Patapsco shoals northward. There were five of these craft, and they had been specially altered for bombarding coastal fortifications. This had been done by removing their forward masts to make space for two heavy mortars; one was capable of hurling a thirteen-inch bombshell two miles; the other, a ten-inch missile an equal distance. The timbers and decks of the bomb ships had been reinforced to withstand the violent recoil of the mortars. The sixth vessel in his vanguard, the *Erebus,* was a small ship that had been altered to serve as the launching pad for thirty-two-pound Congreve rockets. Admiral Cochrane had been given leeway in his orders to carry the war to American shores. He really had not expected Cockburn and Ross to succeed in taking Washington so easily. Following that triumph, he had considered leaving the Chesapeake to visit similar treatment upon some other coastal city, perhaps returning later to strike at Baltimore. But Cockburn had persuaded him that they should finish the job of scourging the Chesapeake. From the quarterdeck of the *Surprize,* Cochrane could see the tops of the masts of the American vessels that had taken refuge in Baltimore's harbor. The city might not capitulate as readily as Washington, but just think of the rewards that would be his and his fellow officers' if they could blast that fort into submission and seize all that shipping and those stores. Yes, perhaps this was as good a place as any to bring the irksome Yankees to their knees and line his pockets with prize money.

The sounds of the battle of North Point had carried across the peninsula and the waters of the Patapsco. He could see the smoke from the burning rope works. He did not know, at that time, of Ross's death. In fact, he was waiting to receive an answer to a message he had dispatched to the general earlier that afternoon. In it, he had outlined his plans to begin his bombardment early the next morning. As for the defense line the Americans had set up on the outskirts of the city, from what he could observe through his spyglass, "I think it may be completely turned without the necessity of taking it in front."

His message had to be carried by boat to the landing site at North Point and then relayed by horseback to the army headquarters. The answer had to follow the same slow process, in reverse.

About 7:30 that evening, a dispatch boat came up from North Point to return to him his unopened letter to Ross. And so Cochrane learned that the general was dead, and that it was now up to Colonel Brooke, with Admiral Cockburn at his side, to carry the American works and seize Baltimore.

Cochrane quickly redirected the letter to Brooke, together with a postscript in which he reminded Ross's replacement of the "barbarities" the Americans had committed against Canadian communities and urged him to do a more complete job of destroying Baltimore than Ross had done to Washington.

# 7

A heavy rain fell on Baltimore that night. Although the downpour extinguished the fire at the rope works, it did nothing to relieve the anxiety that smoldered in the hearts of many citizens for the safety of their city.

By that time, the more fearful of the residents had fled to the countryside with their wagonloads of heirlooms and other valuables. General Smith ordered those remaining to keep their houses dark and urged them to set buckets of water and sand about to douse fires lest the British fire their rockets into the city.

The rain drenched the militiamen and regulars who stood ready in Fort McHenry. It soaked the tents of the Americans camped on Hampstead Hill and also those of Brooke's redcoats seven miles away at Bread and Cheese Creek.

Despite the loss of General Ross and some three hundred others during the little battle and the discomfort of the drenching rain, the morale of the British ran high. There was much speculation in their camp about the plunder that would be theirs when they took the city the next day, as they surely would.

The morale of the militiamen had improved after they learned how well the Third Brigade had fought. After all, had they not stood up to the British far better than they had at Bladensburg? Had they not withdrawn back here to Hampstead Hill in good order, even taking time to fell trees across the road as they retreated? And did not their artillery, well dug in and much of it manned by seasoned sailors, far outmatch the pitiful battery the British had brought along? Who could forget what Barney's naval guns had done to the British in that brave last stand outside Washington?

So the people of the city, the men of both armies, and those of the British fleet slept through that dreary September night.

Since it was but a short ride from Hampstead Hill to the MacKenzie house, Lovejoy and Barineau returned there to their accustomed beds. With drapes drawn and a single small candle for light, they sat around the MacKenzies' dining room table, drinking cider and munching on cold roasted chicken while Malcolm pumped them for information of what they had seen and done that day.

He told them of the resentment expressed to his Vigilance and Safety Committee by the owners of those ships selected to be sunk as obstructions in the Patapsco.

"They will be compensated, I suppose, but each felt that someone else's vessel would have served as well. I hate to think of what Talbot Smith would do if we tried to confiscate the *Flora*."

"Will the obstructions work?" Lovejoy asked.

"I don't see how a British ship of any size could get into the harbor without first removing them. And that will be impossible as long as the guns of Fort McHenry can pour shot into them as they make the attempt. Even if their army should force its way into the city, as long as McHenry holds, they will have no way to take away our ships as they did at Alexandria."

"So what will they try to do?"

"Eliminate McHenry, what else?"

"Pierre, I think you will owe me a hundred dollars."

"Not till they attack McHenry. Now I am sleepy, aren't you?"

Lovejoy and Barineau were awakened about 6:30 the next morning by a hoarse blast from the direction of Fort McHenry. This was followed by a second explosion. A few minutes later, the same thing happened, first an odd roar, then an explosion of a higher pitch.

They dressed in haste. While they were downstairs, stuffing their pockets with Theresa's cold biscuits, they heard a salvo of blasts that, to Lovejoy's ears, sounded like a naval broadside.

As they left the house to saddle their horses, Malcolm was coming down the stairs in his nightgown, rubbing his eyes.

"What is going on?"

"I don't know for sure, but I think that Pierre is going to owe me a hundred dollars before this day is over," Lovejoy said.

The rain had stopped during the night, but the skies remained overcast. Hampstead Hill reminded Lovejoy of a huge anthill he had once kicked over as a boy. The terrain swarmed with militiamen, most of them staring across at the Patapsco.

An aide to General Smith explained what happened.

"One of their bomb ships fired two shots, but they fell short of the fort. See there, they are moving closer in."

"What was the other firing?"

"That little schooner ahead of the bomb ships fired off a salvo at the fort."

Their conversation was interrupted by two roars from a bomb ship. Lovejoy watched as first one and then another two-hundred-pound bombshell arced high up over the Patapsco and then burst above the enormous American flag flying in Fort McHenry's parade ground. Soon thereafter, the other four bomb ships opened up. The fuses from their bombshells left thin, curved white streaks in the sky, terminating in a flash of light and a puffy cloud. Shortly afterward, the rocket ship began sending its missiles streaking in a flatter trajectory toward the fort. And the schooner boldly joined in with fresh broadsides.

For nearly an hour and a half, the attention of thousands of militiamen and even more residents of Baltimore was fastened on the great fireworks display. The guns of the fort returned the fire, but they were slow to find the range.

When, finally, a shot from one of McHenry's French-made thirty-six-pounders tore through the schooner's mainsail, Cochrane signaled for his bomb ships to fall back to a point just out of reach of the fort's cannon and resume the bombardment from there.

The huge mortars of his bomb ships could hurl their missiles up to two miles. It was an exhausting process to load the wide-mouthed, short-barreled weapons with as much powder as their metal could withstand, then cut the fuses of the bombshells to just the right length, and lower them into the mortars. The force of the propellant charge was so strong, the bomb ships were first thrust two feet down into the water and then set to bucking like unbroken colts when they bobbed back to their normal draft.

Every blast strained the ship's timbers and came near to stunning the crews. Even so, each vessel could belch forth as many as forty or fifty bombshells per hour. Cochrane had five bomb ships and plenty of ammunition. He would see how much punishment the defenders of the fort could bear.

About three hours after his first ranging shots were fired, the British admiral began to wonder about his strategy. Many of his bombshells burst so high above the fort that they did no damage. Others failed to explode or did so wide of their looming target.

Inside the fort, by 10 A.M., Major Armistead decided that it was a waste of ammunition to return the British fire. Even when he double loaded his largest guns and elevated the fronts of their carriages, the shots could not reach the bomb ships. And so his gunners and their protective guard of militiamen hunkered down and prayed that a shell would not burst in their midst.

This cessation in the American gunnery encouraged Cochrane to keep up the bombardment. Hour after hour, the huge shells exploded above and around the fort until an enormous cloud of gunsmoke hung over the Patapsco.

Both Barineau and Lovejoy were kept busy throughout the morning and into the afternoon racing their horses through the streets of Baltimore and Fells Point to deliver dispatches from the ever-vigilant General Smith.

By early afternoon, it once again was raining. As he neared Fort McHenry, Lovejoy leaned forward over his horse's neck as if that might give him better protection from the fragments of the bursting bombshells. Because of the now heavy rain, neither he nor anyone in the fort saw the shell that dropped squarely on the bastion overlooking the Ferry Branch of the Patapsco.

By the time he reached the fort, the damage had been assessed. Two men, a lieutenant and a sergeant, had died instantly. Four men were wounded. It would take a while to put the guns of the bastion back into working order.

Back on Hampstead Hill, General Smith listened closely to his report.

"Claggett and Clemm both dead? A sad loss. I knew them well. But only four wounded. It is a wonder there were not more casualties."

"It is indeed, sir. And Major Armistead asks me to inform you that he is removing his gunpowder from the magazine and spotting the barrels about the fort to avoid a catastrophe. You see, a bomb landed squarely on the roof of his magazine but failed to explode."

"Thank God for that. Fort McHenry might have been destroyed." He paused as an aide entered his tent, saluted, and said, "Sir, the British ships are moving upriver again."

The men in Fort McHenry watched as Cochrane's bomb ships edged closer and closer. Every cannon that could be brought to bear on their course had been loaded and primed. Their gun captains stood with lanyards in hand as the cumbersome craft crept closer and closer. Across the river, the gunners in the Lazaretto fort likewise stood ready. And in the river itself, behind the cordon of obstructions, several American gunboats swung into place to receive the British.

Armistead waited until the enemy craft had moved to within a mile and a half and had dropped anchor and were preparing to start a fresh bombardment. And then he gave the signal to open fire. Any notion the British may have had that the fort had been knocked out quickly faded as the blasts from the bastions, the lower ramparts, the Lazaretto fort, and the gunboats unleashed a rain of cannonballs across the water. A shot plowed into the bow of one bomb ship, springing her timbers and opening a leak. Another punched a hole in the mainsail of a second vessel. Five balls struck a third craft.

Cochrane, seeing the punishment his vanguard took, signaled the bomb ships to withdraw from the range of the American guns. During this maneuver, he received a letter from Brooke, written the previous midnight, telling of his victory over the Third Maryland Militia Brigade and expressing his intent to attack the main works on the outskirts of Baltimore by the following noon.

Yet four hours after the time of the intended attack, there still was no sign of anything happening on that fortified hill Cochrane had been watching all day through his spyglass. Surely, if Ross had still been alive, he would have assaulted the works and forced his way into Baltimore by now. What was holding up Brooke?

# 8 

Colonel Brooke had expected to have scattered Baltimore's militia defenders by now and to have entered the city itself. Certainly, his men had set off that morning from their camps down the peninsula in good spirits. Commandeered farm horses now drew his six little field guns. But the trees felled across the road by the retreating militia had slowed his progress, and the road itself was too muddy from the rainstorm to permit rapid marching.

So it was nearly 10 A.M. before the head of his column reached the Philadelphia Road about four miles east of Baltimore. By now, the bombardment of Fort McHenry had been going on for three hours. That should be diverting the attention of the Americans, Brooke thought. If he kept pushing his men hard, he might still make good on his promise to take the city by noon.

With Admiral Cockburn at his side, urging him on to the attack, he stopped his horse about a mile along the Philadelphia Road to stare in wonder at Hampstead Hill about two miles distant. From a second-floor window of a nearby house, he and Cockburn studied the intricate system of earthworks that crisscrossed the hill. One of his officers counted 120 artillery pieces. Brooke himself estimated that some fifteen thousand militiamen stood ready to meet his attack. And remembering the stiff opposition he had encountered the day before from far fewer militiamen, he wished that he had not sent that optimistic report to Admiral Cochrane.

Obviously, the fleet was doing its best to subdue Fort McHenry. The admiral's advice to attempt to outflank the American works seemed sound to Brooke.

Staying well out of range of the militia's guns, he led a scouting party to the north to see how he might work his men around the left of the defenses and avoid a frontal assault. To his consternation, he discovered that the works had been "refused," that is, they curved northwestward. Furthermore, that section of the defense, he could see, was being reinforced by a stream of militia, as if the bloody Yankees could read his mind.

To attempt an even wider swing around the refused lines would expose his own communications back to his North Point landing site. He could be cut off from his base and surrounded.

Returning to his impatient troops, he surveyed the teeming American lines again. Even Cockburn had to admit that it would cost them too heavily to send their men forward into the face of all those guns. Where had the Americans got so much artillery?

Meanwhile, they could hear and see the bombardment of Fort McHenry going on hour after hour.

Brooke and Cockburn decided that their best chance to take Baltimore would be to wait until after nightfall and then hurl all their men into a bayonet charge. The American cannoneers would be unable to aim their pieces in the dark. And the militia, untrained in night fighting, would probably panic and flee.

They wrote a letter to Admiral Cochrane, explaining their plans and asking him to create a diversion after midnight to draw off some of the militia manning the earthworks on Hampstead Hill. A horseman raced away with this message.

By the time the letter reached Cochrane, the admiral was beginning to develop cold feet about this expedition against Baltimore. He wished that he had followed his earlier inclinations after their success at Washington and had sailed for New Orleans. As long as he stayed out of range of McHenry's guns, he could continue to bombard the fort, but to what purpose? By now, the Americans had blocked the entrance to the harbor with sunken ships. His bombshells could not reach the city itself. Even if Brooke were to take Baltimore, there would be no way to remove the shipping and other treasures from the blocked harbor.

He made all these points in his reply to Cockburn, advising, but not ordering, him and Brooke to give up on the notion of taking Baltimore and return to their landing site.

It was eight o'clock that night before his ambiguous message reached Cockburn two miles from Hampstead Hill. Brooke, unused to high command, was nonplussed by the admiral's advice. But Cockburn pointed out that he and Ross had received a similar message from the admiral on the eve of Bladensburg. They had ignored the advice, and look at the great victory they had won. But Brooke was not Ross. To the disgust of Cockburn, he called his commanders together for a council of war to decide whether to make the 3 A.M. night attack as planned.

Neither Lovejoy and Barineau nor Malcolm MacKenzie returned to their comfortable beds that night. The British bomb ships' continuing bombardment of McHenry would have made sleep impossible, even if General Smith had not requested them all to remain near him. And so the three men sat huddled beneath their oilskin coats to watch the bursts of shells over Fort McHenry.

Shortly after 9 P.M., the bombardment stopped.

"What now?" Lovejoy said.

"Perhaps the British have lost their nerve," Barineau replied.

"I doubt that. General Smith thinks that they may be planning a night attack, which is why he has everyone alerted. Anyway, don't forget that you owe me a hundred dollars."

"I haven't forgotten. And I will bet you another hundred that we will not be attacked here."

"I hate to take so much money off you. At this rate, you will not have much left after we settle our claims with the government."

Malcolm interrupted with, "If the British were to carry these works, there wouldn't be a government to pay any claims. Believe me, my friends, this business is far from over."

Aboard his flagship, Cochrane could not be certain that his message had reached Cockburn and Brooke. He, too, remembered that Ross, at Cockburn's urging, had ignored his advice to return to their ships after causing the destruction of Barney's flotilla of gunboats. If he did not create the diversion they now requested and they attacked and failed, would he not have to share in the blame? Better to be safe than sorry.

He called in one of his most audacious captains and assigned to him the mission of organizing an expedition of some three hundred sailors and twenty barges to be rowed into the Ferry Branch of the Patapsco west of McHenry. Upon a signal, they were to open up with both real and blank charges from their small cannon and muskets, as well as rockets, to make it appear that a landing party was approaching the shore directly south of Baltimore. The mock attack should be made with as much noise as possible sometime after midnight in the hope of causing the Americans to shift some of their militia away from Hampstead Hill before Brooke launched his all-out bayonet attack.

Rain was falling over the area again by midnight. The three friends had run out of anything to talk about. They sat dozing beneath the bed of Malcolm's hack.

Leaning against a wheel of the hack, Lovejoy was dreaming once again of Madeline Richter. It was a troubling dream in which she was holding out her hands to him as if pleading for him to rescue her from some difficulty.

He was startled from his sleep by the crash of fresh firing from the British fleet. The rainy skies flashed with bomb bursts and fiery streaks of rockets.

All through the camps of both the Americans and the British, men awakened and got up to view the most spectacular yet of the bombardments of Fort McHenry. As the explosions continued to rock the city, ordinary citizens either climbed to their rooftops for a better view or, unmindful of the pelting rain, walked out to Federal Hill to join the soldiers who were also watching the bombardment.

The diversion by the fake landing party did not go as Cochrane had planned. About 10 P.M., the loading of the barges had begun, and by midnight, they were all on their way. However, only the first nine barges reached their assigned positions off Forts Covington and Babcock, the two earthworks protecting the southern approach to Baltimore. The others got lost in the rainy dark and blundered into the Northeast Branch of the river, off the Lazaretto.

Thus, when Cochrane ordered a rocket to be fired around 1 A.M. to signal the beginning of a fresh bombardment, most of his boats were in the wrong place. And from the shore, alert American sentries could hear the splashing of oars and see here and there faint lights.

About 2 A.M., first the guns of Fort Babcock and then those of Fort Covington opened fire with both grape and solid shot in the direction of the lights. The men on the barges then began firing off their rockets and blank charges and, in so doing, presented easy targets.

The Americans could never be sure just how many of the boats their shot hit or how many sailors they killed or wounded as they blasted away in the dark.

The men in the eleven boats that had gone astray were luckier. Realizing their mistake, they were able to withdraw unharmed.

Meanwhile, the bomb ships continued to belch their two-hundred-pound shells into the air. The guns of Fort McHenry lashed back more as a demonstration of defiance than for any military advantage. Adding to the pyrotechnic display, lightning from yet another thunderstorm flashed across the skies. If ever there was a right time for Brooke to make his attack, it was now.

About 3 A.M., the word was passed from Colonel Brooke for his four thousand men to pull on their boots, gather up their gear, and fall in. As they watched the flashes of light from the west, they assumed that the rumors they had been hearing were true. They were to attack the American works and once more set a mob of cowardly militiamen fleeing from their bayonets.

Failing to see any signs of an attack on Hampstead Hill, Admiral Cochrane flashed lights to signal his barges to return to their ships. A captain of one of the barges made the mistake of firing a rocket to acknowledge that they were complying. Seeing this, the gunners in Fort McHenry opened fire on the returning boats. Later they would find the wreckage of two of the craft and the bodies of three British sailors.

By 4 A.M., with the remaining boats and crews being taken back aboard his ships, Cochrane ordered the bombardment of Fort McHenry to cease. He assumed that Brooke and Cockburn had come to their senses. And he was right, about Brooke at least.

By the time the first streaks of light appeared on the eastern horizon, instead of assaulting Hampstead Hill, the British troops were marching south along the muddy road that led back to their North Point landing, to the disappointment of many enlisted men as well as Admiral Cockburn. Whether Brooke had saved them from being slaughtered or had thrown away a grand opportunity to smash the Americans and bring the war to a quick close would long be debated back aboard their troop transports.

Unable to see into the minds of their foes, Lovejoy, Barineau and MacKenzie spent the rest of the night waiting for a new bombardment and the expected attack on their positions.

It was after 6 A.M. before enough sunlight filtered through the overcast for Lovejoy to see the outline of Fort McHenry clearly. Her walls still stood, and that gigantic flag still flew from its flagpole. Soon afterward the bomb ships raised their anchors and withdrew to join the other ships.

The attack on Fort McHenry had ended. Before noon, American scouts brought back reports that the British army was well on its way south.

Upon hearing this, Lovejoy took Barineau's hand and said, "Well, Pierre, the slate between us is clear. We both have won our bets."

# Book Four

# PART ONE

# 1

In Philadelphia several evenings later, an exhausted Lovejoy Martin stepped from the stagecoach that had carried him from Baltimore. He was amazed to see that crowds of drunken men and women filled the streets, shouting and singing and firing guns into the air.

He stopped an old acquaintance to ask, "What's the big celebration about?"

"Ain't you heard of our great victory?"

"Of course. I was there at Baltimore in the thick of it. But that was a week ago."

"We already celebrated that one. Now the big news is what happened on Lake Champlain in New York. Macdonough wiped out an entire British fleet at a place called Plattsburgh. Some says it was a bigger victory than Perry's on Lake Erie. And that ain't the half of it. Our militia turned back a big British army before it could reach Plattsburgh. Chased the bastards back to Canada."

Lovejoy had meant to go to his father's house immediately upon his arrival in Philadelphia, but he could not resist stopping by the White Swan on his way.

A noisy crowd filled the common room and spilled out onto South Street. He elbowed his way toward the bar, where Tom and Evan were feverishly filling mugs with ale and grog. Both father and son abandoned their post to greet him.

After they had finished pounding him on the back and shaking his hand, Evan said, "You look like something the cat drug in."

"I have been through an awful lot the past nine months."

"So I have heard from your uncle. Been at Baltimore. Saw the action down there, I expect."

"More than I wanted to. I have had a bellyful of this war."

"After the whipping they got on Lake Champlain, I expect the British may have had a bellyful as well," Tom said. "And speaking of bellyfuls, you look as though you could use some good food yourself. Never saw you so thin and tired looking."

"After a week or two of rest I will be all right."

"There will be time enough for you to rest after Meggie's wedding," Evan said. "Now that you are back, it can be any time. We'll have to wait until all this uproar settles down, of course, but that should be over in a day or so. Then I want to throw a big party, bigger than the one for Primrose and myself. It will serve as a homecoming for you as well as her wedding dinner."

"Where is Meggie?"

"Oh, she and Primrose are off seeing to the making of her wedding dress."

"Congratulate her for me."

"Can we tell her that you will propose one of your famous wedding toasts?"

"Of course. Now that crowd at your bar will wreck this place if you don't hurry up and serve them. And I must go home before I drop from weariness."

At his old house, Lovejoy was greeted just as enthusiastically, if less boisterously, as he had been at the White Swan. Amanda commented on his appearance. Her husband wanted to hear all about the British attack on Fort McHenry, but she stopped his questioning with, "That can wait until tomorrow, Frank. You go next door and tell Ephraim that Lovejoy is home. And before Father goes to sleep, I want him to see Lovejoy. Let's go upstairs quietly. If the girls hear their Uncle Lovejoy's voice, I will never get them back to bed."

Jeremiah Martin was sitting in front of a window with a robe across his knees. He tried to stand when Lovejoy entered the room with Amanda. Amanda eased him back into his chair and said, "Now Father, you mustn't exert yourself or get too excited."

He motioned her away and took Lovejoy's hand.

"Bring him a chair. Sit close, my son. Let me look at you. I can see more and more of your mother in your face. You've been at Baltimore. I must hear all of what you saw there. Is it true the British fired nearly two thousand shells at the fort?"

"Yes, Father. But only about four hundred fell on the fort itself. Many of those did not explode. Anyway, we lost only four dead and about twenty wounded. Our casualties were heavier in our encounter with their army, but not as heavy as the Britishers'."

Lovejoy was surprised at the questions his father asked.

"You seem to have kept up with the war closely."

"He insists on my reading him every word in the papers," Amanda said.

"Messy little war this one has been," Jeremiah said. "But I expect it has been worth it. The British must realize now that we are an independent nation able to stand up for its rights. They are a practical people. There is no profit in their continuing this fight, nor, truth to tell, in our doing so, either. The time has come to make peace. Ah, it is good to have both my sons home again."

Leaving Amanda to help her stepfather to his bed, Lovejoy went downstairs to join Frank.

"So, Chester has settled back into his old routine?"

"Yes. But there isn't much for him to oversee anymore at the company. We have a few government contracts, but the British blockade has put a big crimp in our business."

"And the real reason for Chester's long absence has never come out?"

"No, and I hope that we can keep it that way."

"I promise not to rock the boat, but it does make me sick to hear Father speak of us as *his* sons."

"Chester has been very good about visiting him. He comes almost every day."

"Don't believe half of what he may have told you, Frank. And don't trust him an inch. That is all I will say on the subject."

Hearing Amanda coming down the stairs, Frank said in a low voice, "It upsets Amanda to think that her brothers are not on friendly terms."

A few minutes later, Ephraim McGee came into the house, but seeing how weary his nephew looked, he stayed only long enough to welcome him and offer him help in getting settled.

Lovejoy did not fully appreciate how bone tired he was until he got between the sheets of the narrow bed in his old boyhood room on the third floor. He fell asleep quickly. He awakened briefly the next morning, faintly aware of the door being cracked slightly and of hearing Amanda saying, "There now, girls. You have seen him. There will be plenty of time for a visit after he wakes up." Then he heard his nieces' protests as their mother herded them back downstairs. He fell into a deep sleep that lasted until noon.

Finally awakening, he lay on his back and reflected on all that he had done since leaving home four years ago for London. He concluded that his chief regret was losing Madeline Richter. All the rest of his experiences he could bear. He wondered if he would ever get her out of his heart.

He wondered, too, what he would do with all the wealth he had accumulated from his privateering, or, for that matter, what he would do with himself. Upon bidding him good-bye in Baltimore, Talbot Smith had said, "If the world is anyone's oyster, young Dr. Martin, I reckon it is yours."

"What do you mean, Captain?" Lovejoy had said.

"Look at yourself. Well-educated. From a good family. And now, thanks mainly to myself and others that has risked their lives for your benefit, you've made yourself a uncommonly rich man."

Lovejoy smiled to think of his rejoinder. "To tell you the truth, Captain, I never cared all that much for oysters."

# 2 

Ephraim McGee maintained his medical office on Spruce Street near the Pennsylvania Hospital, on whose staff he served. It was his habit to rise early each morning and meditate for half an hour in the way of the good Quaker he had become. After breakfast, he and his wife, Rebecca, walked together to his office, where he received patients until noon. She interviewed the people in the waiting room, in some cases dealing with minor ailments on her own to leave his time free for more difficult cases.

After returning home for his lunch and a brief nap, he arose refreshed and went to make his hospital rounds, leaving Rebecca to attend to her household duties. By late afternoon, he was back in his office to see patients on his own or to talk with the medical students who assisted him on his hospital rounds.

Ephraim's once blond hair had turned gray, and his waist had thickened with age, but his face looked remarkably youthful for a man of nearly sixty. Odd thing, that. For years he had been known as "the boy doctor." Those were the years he had spent in the shadow of the legendary Dr. Benjamin Rush. A hero of the American Revolution and a medical pioneer, Rush had died the previous year. Ephraim had to share his mantle with several other of Rush's disciples. Only now some referred to him as "old Dr. McGee."

That did not bother Ephraim. In fact, he allowed few outward things to disturb his inward tranquillity. He and Rebecca, regretting her inability to bear children, enjoyed a warm relationship with his late sister Gerta's three children, Amanda, Chester, and Lovejoy, and now with Amanda's two daughters.

Under the care of a less skilled or less devoted doctor, Jeremiah Martin might have died after his first stroke. But Ephraim, living next door to his brother-in-law, had instituted a regimen of light foods, gentle exercise, and protection against emotional upsets.

Dr. Rush would have drawn blood from Jeremiah, as he had done routinely from most of his patients, but early in his career, Ephraim had observed that this practice generally weakened rather than helped the sick. He had become sold, however, on Rush's advanced ideas about the treatment of the insane. Forswearing callous and often violent treatment of "lunatics," Rush had dealt with them gently. Ephraim followed his example.

Ephraim often reflected on the peaceful countenances of his fellow members of the Society of Friends. He wished that he had some way not of converting the mentally ill to Quakerism but of helping them develop the tranquil spirit of his co-religionists.

He had come a long way from the log cabin in which he had been born on the edge of the wilderness just beyond the Susquehanna River to his comfortable house in Philadelphia. Although he bore an Ulster Scots name and had been reared as a Presbyterian, he was actually three-quarters German. And his wife was the daughter of a Sephardic Jew and a Dutch woman from the West Indian island of St. Eustatius. He often pondered on what an interesting mixture their children would have been.

On this morning he was preoccupied by the appearance of Lovejoy. Last night had not been the time to express his concern for his nephew's health, physical or emotional. Besides looking too thin and haggard, he showed signs of melancholy. Well, enough of such musings. Who had come to see him that morning?

It was nearly noon and time for him to return to his home when his wife entered and closed the door behind her.

"A strange young woman wants to see you. Won't give her name. She is very despondent. I think there may be a mental problem. And her face is swollen and bruised. And she has a baby with her."

"Have you asked for her history?"

"All she says is that she must see you in person at once."

"I can't think of any reason not to see her, can you?"

"I suppose not, but Ephraim, she really does seem to be deeply troubled."

"Who recommended me to her?"

"She won't say. Besides her appearance and her manner of dress, there is something else unusual about her."

"And that would be?"

"She arrived at our door on horseback."

"Women do ride horseback sometimes, Rebecca."

"Have you ever seen one riding with a baby strapped on her back?"

"Well, show her in and let me judge for myself."

After eating a late breakfast and answering his sister's many questions, Lovejoy excused himself and walked down to the offices of Charles Bennett.

The lawyer, like everyone else, asked all about his experiences at Washington and Baltimore.

"Having clients who are both Federalists and Republicans, I stay off the subject of politics. I wouldn't want your father to know this, Lovejoy, but I voted for De Witt Clinton rather than Madison in the last election. It seemed to me very foolish to declare war when the nation was so divided on the issue and so ill-prepared to fight. And the way the Republicans have gone about financing the war has been, to say the least, irresponsible. Now, I can see that it would have been wrong of us to try to appease the British. In my view, they have demonstrated a monstrous disregard for American lives in sending Cochrane over here for the sole purpose of devastating our coastal cities."

"As you know, Mr. Bennett, I got dragged into the war by my heels, as it were, but I must agree that there can be no justification for what they did to Washington or tried to do to Baltimore. They would have fired their bombshells into the city itself had not Fort McHenry kept them out of range."

"Now the newspapers are full of speculation as to where their fleet will strike next. The repulse of the British on Lake Champlain may only increase the pressure on Cochrane to punish our seaports. It would not surprise me if he should attack New York or Charleston. Well, sorry to plague you with my opinions. You said you wanted to go over your accounts with me."

After Lovejoy had finished explaining the outcome of his privateering venture, the lawyer put his fingertips together and pursed his lips.

"There is not a richer man of your age in Philadelphia; indeed, few of any age. What will you do with all this wealth?"

"I don't know what to do with my money or, for that matter, myself."

Bennett frowned, then said, "Why not continue as a doctor? You have the means to build your own hospital."

Lovejoy shook his head. "My gorge still rises at the sight of blood."

"Or you could invest in your father's old business. It could use some fresh capital."

"A partnership with Chester? I couldn't bear the sight of him day in and day out."

"While I can understand your feelings, I have to warn you that Frank Carpenter is hoping that you will do just that. Have you thought any more about the law?"

"That is a possibility. But mainly I need to rest up and refocus my thoughts. Meanwhile, there is to be a big wedding at which my presence is required."

Christian Richter stared incredulously at his son-in-law.

"What do you mean she is gone. Gone where?"

"I don't know. I woke up a little while ago and she and the baby was gone. It looks like she took her mare, too. I thought she might've come over here to see her mother."

"Well, she ain't here. This don't sound good. You look like you been drinking again. I warned you about that, didn't I?"

"I might have drunk a bit last night before I went to bed."

"You ain't been mistreating her again, have you?"

"I wouldn't harm a hair on her head, Mr. Richter."

"That ain't what she tells her mother. She says you been drinking a lot lately. Says you slapped her once."

"It was just a little slap. Meant to bring her to her senses. She ain't been the same since the baby was born, you know. Gets funny notions. Says strange things."

"We will talk about that later. Now we don't want to set the neighbors to gossiping. They done enough of that when the baby was born. You get on your horse and ride toward Reading. I will head out the other way. Maybe she just thought a ride would make her feel better. We will say nothing of this to her mother for the time being. When we find her, I warn you, we'll have no more of this here drinking and slapping business. You made a bargain to be a good husband to her, and I will see you live up to it."

"Amanda says you wanted to see me, Uncle Ephraim. She said it was urgent."

"Yes, Lovejoy. Come in. Have you had your dinner?"

"I ate down at the White Swan with Evan and Tom Jenkins. They wanted me to help plan the wedding celebration for Megan. She is marrying the first mate of our schooner."

"Oh? When is that to be?"

"The wedding ceremony will take place on Sunday morning at the old St. George Methodist Church just after their regular service. Since the Methodists don't hold with drinking, especially on Sunday, the dinner will be held at the White Swan the night before. Evan is calling it a welcome-home party for me as well as a wedding celebration. But why did you want to see me?"

"You should sit down to hear this. There. I took on a most unusual patient this morning, a young woman. In fact, my entire day has been devoted to her care."

"She must be an unusual case."

"A mental case. Severe dementia. Unusual in one so young."

"Where is she?"

"In a basement room at the Pennsylvania Hospital, under close scrutiny. She has threatened to take her own life and that of her baby if we don't do something she demands."

"I don't see how I could be of any use to you. Your knowledge of lunacy and its treatment far exceeds anything I may have picked up in London. What are her symptoms?"

"Despondent and hysterical by turns. Obvious evidence of delusions even after I got her calmed down with a sedative. She arrived just before noon on horseback and carrying a year-old baby boy. She is well dressed in an expensive riding habit, but her face is swollen and bears bruises that make it appear that she has been beaten."

"If she is suicidal, surely you have not allowed her to keep the child with her."

"Rebecca has the baby upstairs. It is a handsome little boy. We will care for it until this matter is resolved."

"Well, just who is this young woman, and what do you want me to do about her?"

Ephraim's normally serene expression suddenly looked pained. "Rebecca and I have debated whether to tell you this. You have been under such strain I hesitated to involve you. But Rebecca feels strongly that you have to be told."

"Never mind my feelings. Why are you beating around the bush so? Who is this woman?"

"I don't know for certain, but she claims to be Mrs. Lovejoy Martin."

Lovejoy sat up straight.

"But I am not married. You know that. Is this some sort of joke?"

"There is nothing humorous about this case. None at all. This woman threatens to take her life and that of her baby if we do not find her husband."

Lovejoy groaned and put his head in his hands, then raised his face and said, "What do you want me to do about this?"

"Put on your coat and come with me to the hospital."

A feeling of dread overcame Lovejoy as he followed his uncle through the double doors of the hospital and walked downstairs to a large basement room where a middle-aged matron sat behind a long table with lamps at either end.

Some dozen persons sat or stood in this dimly lit room. In one corner, a middle-aged woman huddled on an upholstered bench with her arms hugging her knees to her breasts, eyes closed, gently rocking on her haunches. In another corner, a young man with acne-pocked face stared up at the ceiling and counted in a stage whisper, "Two thousand, three hundred and six; two thousand, three hundred and seven. . ." A young girl with red hair knelt on the floor, cuddling a doll, her puffy face frozen in a smile while a well-dressed middle-aged couple talked to her in low voices.

"How is our new patient?" Ephraim asked the matron.

"She hardly touched her food. But she is talking. Seems to think she is in some sort of hotel. Been ordering me about, to fetch her this and that."

"This often happens in these cases," Ephraim said. "The patient withdraws from the real world into one of his own imagining and begins acting in bizarre ways."

"She often behaved in an excited manner," Lovejoy said. "Not like any girl I ever knew."

"Sometimes it helps to force them to face the real world."

"And I represent the real world?"

"That, plus we need you to identify her. Remember, just stay calm. No matter what she does or says, show no surprise."

For a moment, Lovejoy had an impulse to bolt from the hospital. He dreaded what he might see. But he followed the matron as she walked down the dark corridor carrying her lamp.

He heard a woman's sobs as they passed one door. A lullaby was being sung behind another.

"What in Christ's name am I doing here?" Lovejoy asked himself. His pulse raced. He removed his handkerchief and wiped his palms and forehead.

"Dear God, if it is her, please don't let her be too dreadful."

Ephraim took the matron's lamp as she unlocked the windowed door. Then he stepped into the room and held the lamp high to illuminate the figure sitting on the cot beneath a barred window.

"Well, Lovejoy. Here she is."

For a moment, Lovejoy feared he would faint. The woman looked more like an older, slovenly sister of Madeline Richter than the elegant girl he had met on the ship coming back from England. One eye was blackened and that side of her face was swollen. Her hair hung lankly over her ears. Her eyes, more restless than he remembered, avoided his face.

"How do you do?" She said in an affected English accent.

Her eyes now directed at the ceiling, she rose and held out her hand with arm fully extended, as though presenting it to be kissed.

Lovejoy took her hand, which was rougher than he remembered. She gestured to the only chair in the room.

"Please, do sit."

She sat back on the cot and began to talk.

"It is so kind of you to come. This can be a grand time of year when the wind is not blowing. I much prefer it when the air is calm. Oh dear, we are so busy here. I apologize for keeping you waiting. And for these other people outside. Some of them are so common, so coarse."

She lowered her voice conspiratorially.

"We must be careful what we say. They eavesdrop, you know. I think they report everything they hear."

She laughed and rolled her eyes.

"It is a pity our flowers are out of bloom. I would like to have shown you the gardens. Of course, they do not compare with ours at home. That is one of the things I so like about England. The gorgeous roses. Goodness, that light is blinding."

She put the back of one hand over her eyes. "I wish my husband were here to meet you. Unfortunately, he is away on business. He is a physician. Do you know my husband?"

For an instant she looked directly at Lovejoy with what he imagined to be a flash of recognition.

"I am not sure that I do."

"He is from Philadelphia. He is a marvelous man. We met in England years ago. And we often visit London. Are you acquainted with London?"

Catching Ephraim's nod, Lovejoy said, "Yes."

"My dear husband studied medicine there."

She laughed loudly.

"I made a Pennsylvania Dutchman out of him and now he oversees my family's milling business. I do wish he were here. He promised he would be back in time to greet our guests. We are planning another trip to Europe, you know. Ah me, so much of the world to see. And so busy. You know how it is with a large family. Goodness . . ." The words tumbled too fast for Lovejoy to follow. "Sometimes I wish we had stopped with two . . ."

Her darting eyes suddenly fixed on the matron standing in the doorway. "My good woman, would you do something about that light? It does so annoy me."

As she chattered, Lovejoy studied her face, thinking how beautiful she had been and wondering if the change in his own appearance explained why she did not seem to recognize him.

Ephraim intervened.

"This is Lovejoy Martin. He is the man you told me you were married to. You came to me because you remembered that he had an uncle who is a doctor. Look at him carefully and tell me if this is the man."

"What did you say, my dear sir?" Madeline asked.

Ephraim repeated himself.

"Who are you, anyway?"

"I am Dr. McGee. Remember? You came to my office this morning with your baby."

"Are you employed here?"

"I am a staff physician."

Madeline turned her eyes toward Lovejoy briefly, then at the ceiling again. "They have difficulty finding proper workers. At home we can still get old-fashioned help, but even they are a dying breed. I would show you around the grounds if the weather were more cooperative. Were you ever in London?"

Tears in his eyes, Lovejoy nodded.

"This weather is so like London's. What month is this?"

"Near the end of September," Lovejoy managed.

"Oh, my goodness. If my husband does not return soon, I shall never speak to him again. My family did not approve of him at first. But he is such a charming man, he won their hearts as he did mine. Are you alone?"

Lovejoy spluttered, "No, I mean yes."

She laughed as though she had just made a witty remark.

"You dear man. Why have they brought you here?"

"I came to see you, Madeline."

"I should not be here at all. It is all a plot, you know."

She looked again at Ephraim. "Who did you say you were?"

"I am Dr. McGee. And this is Lovejoy Martin. Maybe you don't recognize him because he has lost a lot of weight and has gone through some trying experiences. This is the Pennsylvania Hospital. You are a patient here."

Lovejoy was shocked, both by Ephraim's blunt words and by the unsympathetic tone of his voice.

Madeline fell silent. She looked at Lovejoy and smiled.

"My husband is such a sweet, gentle man. He makes me laugh. So very tender and understanding. So considerate."

Ephraim put his finger to his lips, then whispered to Lovejoy, "At first this morning, when she was lucid, she said that her husband beat her and threatened to kill her."

Suddenly, Madeline slumped against the wall and put both hands over her eyes.

"That light. They must do something about it. The service in this place is bad beyond belief. My husband will cause heads to roll around here."

She removed her hands and looked imploringly at the matron. "My good woman, please do me the kindness of going to the manager's office. Tell him I am not happy with my room. I wish a room on the other side of the building, away from so much noise. Off with you. Summon the man at once."

She turned toward Lovejoy and laughed shrilly. "One must show one's teeth to the staff or they will take advantage of one's good nature. I do hope you will stay for dinner. I should like you to meet my husband and my children when they return. Did you have a pleasant drive here?"

Lovejoy's eyes filled with tears. "Yes, yes, a pleasant drive."

"Are you married?"

He shook his head.

"Then you have no children. What a pity. Sometimes I wish I did not have so many. Do you know my husband?"

Lovejoy took a deep breath. "Come to think of it, I did meet him once, but briefly."

"Isn't he a magnificent man? So witty and handsome. A marvelous gentleman. He shares my love of the theater."

"Yes, yes, a marvelous man."

Madeline looked sharply at the matron. "Did I not give you clear instructions to fetch the manager of this establishment? Who asked you to stand here like an equal, eavesdropping on my conversation with this gentleman? Really, you are impudent."

Her voice rose to a high pitch and she gestured excitedly. Ephraim stepped forward and took her hand.

"Mrs. McFairlane, you must compose yourself."

She snatched her hand away. "Mrs. Martin . . ."

"Mrs. Martin, yes. I apologize for intruding on your privacy. We will let you get some rest now. I will see you again tomorrow."

"Tomorrow, yes. I am weary, Doctor. Please, I should like to retire."

She turned and cocked her head in the way Lovejoy had found so engaging. He rose to take her proffered hand.

"So very kind of you to call. I will tell my husband we met."

With the fingertips of her free hand, she explored the scar that still marked the edge of his palm. She frowned, then smiled and turned her face toward him. Lovejoy, on impulse, leaned forward and brushed his lips against hers. She drew away in confusion.

"Thank you. Thank you very much. Come again when the wind is not blowing. When the roses are in bloom."

Ephraim took Lovejoy's elbow. The matron locked the door behind them.

"She did not even recognize me," Lovejoy said.

"I am not sure about that. For a moment maybe. But who knows?"

"It is hopeless?"

Ephraim shrugged. Lovejoy felt like striking his uncle.

"Why did you bring me here and put me through this when it is hopeless?"

"I needed positive identification. And I hoped that seeing you in the flesh might shock her back to reality. Are you sorry you came?"

"I don't know what I feel. Mainly I would like to get my hands on her husband."

"Her husband. Yes. I will dispatch a message to him first thing in the morning."

"Shouldn't the message go to her parents rather than her husband, assuming that what she told you is true, about his mistreating her?"

"I take your point. Through Martin Shipping, Frank can find us a man with a fast horse. Meanwhile, why don't we go home and tell Rebecca about all this? And you really should see her baby. A splendid young boy, he is."

# 4

The message for Madeline's parents, written on Martin Shipping Co. stationery by Ephraim, was carried to Berks County the next day by a company courier at the behest of Frank Carpenter. The courier's lathered horse clopped into the yard of the Richter house in the afternoon just as George McFairlane was leaving.

"I have a letter here for a Mr. Christian Richter," the courier said. "Brung it clear from Philadelphia."

"Mr. Richter is in Reading. Who is the letter from?"

"From Dr. Ephraim McGee. And I am to wait for a reply."

"I am Mr. Richter's son-in-law. You can give me the letter. I handle his business and personal affairs."

"I was give particular orders to put it in the hands of Mr. Richter or his wife and then carry a answer back to Philadelphia. From what I was told, it is a urgent matter."

"You will have to wait a long while for Mr. Richter. Tell you what. Give me the letter, and while you water your horse I will take it in to Mrs. Richter."

"Can you fetch her to the door so's I can put it in her hand personal like?"

"She is in bed, ill and unable to see anyone outside the family. So take your choice. Sit out here till the cows come home or let me carry the message upstairs while you do something about your horse."

The courier looked down into the face of the thin, red-haired chap standing there with his hand outstretched.

"And who did you say you was?"

"I am George McFairlane. I am their son-in-law."

"Here's the letter then. Now where can I water my horse?"

McFairlane told the truth when he said that Christian Richter was in Reading. His father-in-law had gone there to solicit the help of his friend, the county sheriff, in locating his daughter and grandchild. And Mrs. Richter really was in bed, with the drapes drawn, so stricken with anxiety about Madeline and her child that she had refused to receive him, had in fact screamed at him never to set foot in the house again. He lied, however, when he said that he had a power of attorney from his father-in-law. Christian Richter had never held him in much esteem and during the past two days had come to despise him even more than did his wife.

Concealing his curiosity, McFairlane waited until the courier had ridden his horse around the corner of the house and then quietly entered the front door. He slipped down the hall to the study and ripped open the message. The color drained from his face. He clenched his teeth, thought for a moment, and sat down at the secretary desk.

He was scrawling a reply when the door opened and Elizabeth Richter, Christian's older maiden sister, peered in.

"Here now, you ain't supposed to be in here. What are you up to, anyhow?"

"I am handling an urgent matter. Leave me alone."

"Don't you take that tone with me, young fellow. You ought to be out looking for Maddy and the baby instead of hanging about the house. Just wait until I tell Christian about this."

"Tell him whatever you like, old woman. Just clear out and leave me to finish this."

At the bottom of the page, he stopped and thought for a moment, then signed "Christian Richter" and embossed the letter with his father-in-law's own seal.

Then he tiptoed to the door and peered into the hall. Satisfied that the old woman was not hanging about, he slipped back into the study and removed Richter's cash box from its hiding place under a hearthstone.

"So, Ephraim, how did you find her this afternoon?"

"She has withdrawn into a cataleptic state. She lies motionless on her side with her knees drawn up nearly to her chin. Refuses to speak or take nourishment. How is the baby?"

"He is sleeping. Such a darling child. I would keep him forever, if it were allowed."

"Ah, Rebecca, we are a bit long in the tooth to even think about rearing a baby. Besides, the child has wealthy grandparents."

"And you do not think that she will recover to look after him herself?"

"Recovery is rare in cases when there has been such a complete breakdown. It is fortunate that her parents are so wealthy, for she herself will need tender, watchful care for the rest of her life, in my judgment."

"Does Lovejoy understand that is the case?"

"Without bearing down on the point, I have so informed him."

"Do you think he realizes how fortunate he is not to have married her after all?"

"I cannot see into his mind. I rather get the impression that he thinks she would not have fallen into such a state if he had been her husband. He feels much bitterness toward the man she married and toward her family for permitting it."

"Did you really think that taking Lovejoy to see her last night would bring her to her senses?"

"I saw no harm in trying. Beyond that, I thought it might help Lovejoy come to his senses and stop his moping about, yearning for what might have been. It may take some time for it to sink in, but he should be thankful things turned out as they did. A marriage to such a girl could not bring lasting happiness to anyone, including herself."

"I have not seen Lovejoy today. What is he doing?"

"When I looked in on Jeremiah, Amanda said that he had left this morning and hasn't been back all day. Ah, do I hear the baby crying? Fetch him down, Rebecca, and let him play a while."

Lovejoy had not slept at all the previous night. He relived every moment of his relationship with Madeline Richter, from the moment he heard his cabin mate talking about the gorgeous blond girl aboard their ship, through his visit to her home after his first privateering voyage, and his experience in the Berks County jail. He was convinced that she would not have fallen into her present mental state had they been married that first Christmas as she had wanted.

Arising early that morning, he slipped out of the house without eating breakfast and spent the entire day walking back and forth between the Delaware and Schuylkill Rivers past all the scenes of his boyhood. He had even stopped for a while at the grave of his mother in the Presbyterian churchyard.

Finally, physically exhausted, he had made his way to the White Swan, where Rance had already begun roasting a steer and a pig in preparation for the wedding celebration that was to take place the next night. Tom was away on an errand. Without explaining why he was in such a stressed emotional state, Lovejoy sat in the common room drinking mug upon mug of grog while Evan pondered over what could be troubling his friend.

By the time Tom returned, Lovejoy had collapsed across the table. They carried him up to Tom's room, removed his shoes, and laid him across the bed.

"I just hope he don't throw up on my covers," Tom said.

"Maybe you had better go tell his uncle where he is," Evan said. "We got to have him sober and in fit shape for the party. Tell Dr. McGee we'll be glad to keep him here for the night and we'll let him know in the morning how he is."

## 5

After giving the bogus message to Frank Carpenter's courier and seeing the man and his horse on their way back to Philadelphia, George McFairlane returned to the little stone house he shared with Madeline and packed two carpetbags.

Into one bag went an oilskin coat and a change of clothing. Into the other he placed the pair of silver-handled dueling pistols he had removed from over the mantel of Richter's study and two bottles of corn whisky. The money he had stolen from the cash box went into his inner coat pocket.

As he was about to leave, he noticed the copy of the *Niles Weekly Register* lying on the floor, the one that he had caught Madeline reading the night before last. She had tried to hide it when he entered the room, but he had wrested it from her.

"So, that is what your high-toned lover boy has been up to, is it, privateering?" he had snarled after reading the article about Lovejoy. "This came out two months ago, and from the looks of it, you have read it a hundred times. Is that why you have been treating me like dirt? Been mooning over Mr. Martin, have you?"

She had not answered him, had merely turned her face away. Before then he had slapped her on several occasions, but never hard enough to leave any signs. And perhaps even then he might have checked himself if she had not risen to leave the room.

He had seized her arm and whirled her about to face him.

"Why don't you look at your husband when he asks you a question?"

"I do not regard you as my husband. The sight of you makes me sick," she had said. And that was when he had struck her, this time with his fist. After she had fallen, he had kicked her twice and then left the house for the barn, where he kept his whisky hidden. When he had returned, she had gone to bed in the baby's room, as she had done following previous rows. This time, fearful of what her father would do when he saw her face, McFairlane had gone off quietly to their bed and had fallen into a drunken sleep. Upon his awakening the next morning, she and the baby were gone. And he had not known a moment's peace since; indeed, he could not rest until he found her and settled this business about Lovejoy Martin once and for all.

He picked up the newspaper, glanced at the offending story once more, and thrust it into a carpetbag. Soon thereafter he was riding along the Germantown Pike toward Philadelphia.

Lovejoy awoke the next morning feeling as though his skull had been split by a hatchet. He opened his eyes but shut them quickly to stop the stabbing pain of the light. He lay quietly, not daring to move his head, as he listened to the sound of tables and benches being set up in the downstairs common room in preparation for the celebration that night.

Soon after Lovejoy awakened, Tom appeared at the door with a cup of strong coffee and a bowl of sweetened corn mush.

"Go away and let me die," Lovejoy moaned.

"I can't let you die. It would spoil Meg's party. Say, guess who came in late last night after you passed out?"

"Who gives a damn?"

"Mr. Barineau's feelings would be hurt if I told him what you just said."

Lovejoy groaned.

"He came all the way here to attend Meg's wedding. Shall I bring him in to see you when he wakes up?"

"I don't want to see anybody."

Tom set the coffee and bowl of mush on a table near enough for Lovejoy to smell the aroma.

"Look here, Joy. I went around to your uncle's house last night. He was worried sick about you. Said to let him know if you need his help."

"Nobody can help me."

Tom continued as though he had not heard. "And Dr. McGee, he told me about the girl showing up at his office and about your visit with her at the hospital. Now, Joy, I know that this is a hard thing for you to accept. Maybe you can sort it out later, but please don't let it spoil our celebration. We are counting on you to speak. This means more to our family than I can tell you."

"Oh, Tom. How can I go before a hundred or more people and act like nothing is wrong? You don't know what you are asking of me, to act cheerful and witty."

" 'Assume a virtue, if you have it not . . . for use almost can change the stamp of nature.' "

Lovejoy groaned at the sight of Barineau standing in the doorway.

"I have heard what you have been put through, Lovejoy, and I can imagine the emotional upset this is causing you, but Tom is right. The Jenkins family is counting on you to help make their big party a success. No matter what you feel, you cannot let them down. They still talk about your speech at Evan's wedding dinner. It must have been a masterpiece. Let's hear you do an even better job tonight. Come on. Drink that coffee, or Tom and I will pour it down your throat."

Before Lovejoy could respond, Evan Jenkins came into the room.

"Ah, I am glad indeed to see that you have rejoined the living this fine morning. Now then, Lovejoy, we will want you at the head table tonight, of course. I would ask you to serve as master of ceremonies, but seeing as you are to be honored, I have asked Mr. Barineau to perform that duty. Howsomever, we will expect another of your brilliant toasts. And by the by, your Uncle Ephraim has done us the honor of accepting our invitation. This will be a night to remember."

Lovejoy looked up at Barineau. His friend smiled back at him.

"You have me outnumbered, you bastard," Lovejoy muttered as he swung his legs off the bed.

By noon, Lovejoy's head had stopped throbbing. It was so noisy at the White Swan that he could not think, so he returned to his father's house, where he shut himself in his room and worked on the speech he would make that night.

The words came slowly at first but more rapidly as he warmed to the subject. The speech had to serve a double purpose, as a toast to the future happiness of Megan Jenkins and Calvin Collins and as a tribute to his long friendship with the Jenkins family and his appreciation of those members of the *Flora*'s crew who might be present. And a comment about the improvements in the war against Great Britain certainly would be in order.

But even as the composition of the speech commanded his attention, he felt the shadow of that poor demented girl who occupied a cell in the basement of the Pennsylvania Hospital. Surely his uncle Ephraim was wrong in saying that there was no hope for her recovery. Let him get this speech and the celebration dinner out of the way, and by God, he would visit her again. There had to be some way to help her.

"Where have you been so long? Here it is past noon, and I have had no breakfast."

"Don't play the tyrant with me, Chester. I told you yesterday that Carrie May would have this Saturday afternoon off."

"You might have instructed her to leave me something to eat before you went traipsing off. Where have you been, anyway?"

"Wouldn't you just like to know? And wouldn't you be terribly interested if I told you what I have learned this morning?"

"Don't play games with me, Rosalind. I have enough to bear these days without my own wife rubbing salt into my wounds."

"Oh, poor Chester. He turns a scheme that could have made us rich into a disaster, gets himself made a prisoner only to be rescued by the brother he hates, and now has to sleep in the bed he made for himself. No wonder he has such a short temper."

"I am warning you, Rosalind. Don't start in on that subject again. I wouldn't have got into all this if you had not pushed me into it."

"No, you would have lolled about, stewing in your own juices, tamely waiting for your stepfather to die, while your brother does bold, courageous, and, I might add, very lucrative acts. And now you have been reduced to a virtual clerkship while your brother-in-law runs the company."

His face scarlet with rage, Chester rose and started to leave.

"Wait, Chester, don't you want to know where I have been and what I have learned?"

Chester turned about and said, "Well?"

"Sit down. I will pour you a cup of coffee. This will take a bit of time to tell."

"Just don't start in on me again. I have taken all that I can stand. So, what have you got to say?"

"I stopped by Amanda's to inquire after Papa Martin, and Rebecca was there with a baby."

"What baby?"

"You remember the girl from Reading that Lovejoy intended to marry? You will not believe what has happened to her . . ."

The longer his wife's story ran, the more interested Chester became. His coffee grew cold as he leaned across the table to hear what Amanda and Rebecca had told her.

"And you say baby brother is upset about all this?"

"He spent the night getting drunk at the White Swan."

"And what is he doing now?"

"He is back home, working on a speech he is to deliver tonight. You remember the daughter of the tavern keeper, that common girl who ran away and hid on Lovejoy's ship?"

"Of course. Her name is Megan. How could I forget her?"

"She is to be married tomorrow to some sailor. Her father is putting on a great party at his tavern tonight to celebrate her marriage, and Lovejoy is to be the guest of honor. Isn't that absurd? A wedding supper before the wedding takes place?"

"They are a very common family. What is to be done with the Richter girl and her baby?"

"Your uncle Ephraim has sent a message to her parents. Meanwhile, she will stay at the hospital and the baby with Rebecca."

"What about her husband?"

"According to Rebecca, he mistreats her."

Chester drank his now cold coffee.

"You are right. That is very interesting."

"Where are you going?"

"Down to the office. My dear brother-in-law has given me a task that must be completed by Monday morning. I never thought I would be taking orders from a printer, but that is my lot, at least for the present."

"Is that why you are so out of sorts?"

"There is something worse. Frank thinks that it would help if the company were to be recapitalized. Lovejoy is rolling in money from his piracy project. Frank thinks that it would be a good idea if he could bring Lovejoy into the company and expand it into hauling and carrying between here and Harrisburg. That would put me squarely under the thumb of my precious baby brother. I would do anything to prevent that from happening."

"What could you possibly do?"

"I will think of something."

Lovejoy's mood had improved slightly by the time he completed the writing of his speech that afternoon. He felt even better as he stood before a mirror and practiced his remarks.

Barineau was right. He did owe it to the Jenkins family to put on a good performance. There was no profit in his moping about. And besides, after getting over the initial shock of seeing Madeline in her distressed state, he began to wonder if there might not be hope for her after all. Keep her away from that brute of a husband and treat her with kindness, why she might very well recover and become once more the girl of his dreams.

By the time he had bathed and shaved and dressed himself in the suit that Amanda brought him from his father's wardrobe, he began to look forward to an evening he previously had dreaded. Downstairs, his nieces were clamoring for his attention. Finding that his father was napping, he sat and talked to the little girls and Amanda for a long while.

They were still talking when Frank and Ephraim entered the house and asked Lovejoy to step into the hall.

"Shall I tell him?" Frank said.

"No, I will do it. Lovejoy, Frank's company courier has been out to Berks County and back. He rode in this morning with Christian Richter's reply to our message about his daughter."

"Is he coming to take her away?"

"On the contrary, he is sending his son-in-law."

"I can't believe that."

"Here is his reply. Read it for yourself."

Lovejoy groaned and handed the letter back to his uncle.

"You aren't going to allow that, are you?"

"I can only delay it, and then only on medical grounds having nothing to do with her mental state. A husband has the right to remove his wife from a hospital unless her life is in danger."

"I would like to talk to this fellow when he comes."

"I wouldn't expect him for a day or so."

"How is she today?"

"A little better, I would say. A bit withdrawn, but not acting in the hysterical way you witnessed. At least she is eating and sitting up, mainly staring out the window."

"Could I visit her again?"

"Not just now. I would like her to remain calm for a day or so. Besides, you and I have a wedding celebration to attend this evening. Interesting family, the Jenkinses. I am flattered that they invited me. They helped rear you, wouldn't you say?"

The matron on duty in the basement of the Pennsylvania Hospital that afternoon was new on the job. She was younger than her colleagues. And like them, she admired Dr. Ephraim McGee.

She remembered that he had told her that the husband of the new patient, the lovely young woman from Berks County, might be coming to see her. But hadn't he said that it would be next week?

She looked into the face of the red-haired young man standing before her.

"And you are her husband?"

"My father-in-law wrote Dr. McGee that I was coming."

"He did not expect you so soon."

"Soon or late, I am here."

The matron did not like the man's tone of voice, nor the smell of alcohol on his breath.

"I am sorry, but the only person who can release her would be Dr. McGee, and he will not return until tomorrow."

"Where is his office?"

"Just down the street, but he won't be there on a Saturday afternoon."

George McFairlane stood with a belligerent look on his face as he pondered the matron's information.

"He will be here tomorrow? That is Sunday."

"He drops by the hospital every day. On Sundays, it usually is early."

"So, here I am her husband. I have ridden through the night to rescue my wife from this stinking place, and you are telling me I have to wait until tomorrow to see her?"

"You certainly cannot take her away without Dr. McGee's permission."

Seeing that bullying the matron would get him nowhere, McFairlane changed his tone.

"I am so tired and have been sick with worry. It does seem cruel to deny a husband the courtesy of at least seeing his wife. Please, can't you allow that?"

The matron rose. "Let me see if she is awake."

While he waited, McFairlane rubbed his chin. He wished he had taken time to shave. This was a dreadful place. Maybe Madeline would be so grateful to him for getting her out that she might start treating him with more respect. By God, he had put up with enough of her contempt. Hadn't he done her and her family a favor in marrying her?

The matron beckoned to him from the corridor.

"She is awake and seems alert. I have told her that you are here. She wants to see you. But please, I beg you, say nothing that will upset her. I really shouldn't be doing this, but seeing the trouble to which you have gone . . ."

McFairlane stood in the hall, his hands shaking, while the matron unlocked the door of the little room.

"Your husband is here, my dear."

Madeline rose from her cot, her face radiant with expectation.

"Mad. It's me. I am sorry for what happened and I have come to take you home."

The scream that followed his words carried throughout the hospital wing.

Madeline backed away from the door, her hands over her face, screaming and shouting, "You said you were bringing my husband. That is not my husband. Get him out of here. Take him away."

Shocked, the matron put her hand on Madeline's elbow. "Mrs. McFairlane. You mustn't excite yourself."

"Why do you call me by that name? I am Mrs. Martin. Mrs. Lovejoy Martin. Take that dreadful man away at once."

"Maddy," McFairlane said as he stepped toward her.

"No, no. Get him out of here."

The matron pushed McFairlane out of the door and locked it.

Madeline's shrieks followed them back to the reception room.

"I should not have taken you back there," the matron said. "You cannot see her again without Dr. McGee's permission. I hate to think what he will say when I tell him about this."

"She mentioned Lovejoy Martin. Has he been here to see her?"

"I cannot say. Now, I must ask you to leave."

By the time McFairlane reached the hitching post where he had left his horse, a light rain was falling. He removed his oilskin coat from a carpetbag and donned it. Then he pulled out the letter Ephraim had written to the Richters. It was headed, "The Martin Shipping Company, since 1783."

He put the note back in his pocket, mounted his horse, and rode toward the address listed at the top of the letter. By the time he reached the Delaware River docks, the rain was falling steadily.

To offset the damp weather, the Jenkinses had started a blaze in the fireplace of the common room. Again, tables made of planks laid across sawhorses filled the space from wall to wall. Not trusting her twin brothers, Megan had mixed the grog with her own hands and then nailed the barrel tops in place. She had taken Blind Jack aside and instructed him which tunes to play and which to eschew, no matter what inducements might be offered him. She did not intend this wedding dinner to turn out as had her father's to Primrose Hanrahan.

All she had wanted was a quiet wedding in the church where her mother, a faithful Methodist, had worshipped, to be followed—not preceded—by a modest supper with only members of her family and Calvin's in attendance, with no music and no strong drink. But once her father got a notion in his head, who could deter him?

The arrival of Mr. Barineau and his selection as master of ceremonies had lessened her anxiety. He was a thoughtful gentleman who would lend dignity to the affair, help keep it from turning into another disgraceful, drunken fiasco.

As for Lovejoy Martin, well, she would not waste any more time fretting over him. He did not love her. Calvin Collins did. Calvin was levelheaded. He would be faithful to her.

She could not help feeling sorry for Lovejoy. He looked terrible, nothing like the cocky, robust chap who had come back from England two and a half years ago. And that mysterious girl he had expected to marry, could it be true that she had run away from her husband to see Lovejoy, only to end up in the mental ward of the hospital? And, according to Tom, she had brought along her baby.

Well, that scandalous business was no concern of hers. She had sworn to Calvin that she had put Lovejoy Martin out of her mind, and she must do nothing to excite his jealousy. So there could be no show of pity for his distress. Indeed, she would act as if she had neither knowledge of nor interest in this latest scrape of Lovejoy Martin's.

# 7

In the office of Martin Shipping, Chester looked up from his desk and into the face of the red-haired chap who stood before him clad in an oilskin coat.

"You wouldn't be Dr. McGee, would you?"

Wrinkling his nose at the smell of alcohol on the man, Chester said, "He is my uncle, but he is not here. This is a shipping office."

"Where can I find him?"

"Normally he would be in his office on Spruce Street, but he doesn't see patients on Saturday afternoons. You'll have to wait until Monday morning. Now, as you can see, I am busy . . ."

"My business won't wait until then."

"I have no interest in your affairs, my good man."

"Actually, my business is not with him, anyway."

McFairlane put his hand on the corner of Chester's desk to steady himself.

"I am sure that your business is not with me either, and, as I said before, I am occupied."

"Sorry to bother you."

McFairlane paused at the door and turned around.

"Would you happen to know where I could find a fellow named Lovejoy Martin?"

"I might, but first, I would have to know just what you want with him."

"I have a score to settle with the son of a bitch."

"Really?"

Chester stood up and assumed a friendlier expression.

"Take off that wet coat, my good fellow. Have a seat and tell me what is on your mind. You do seem to be in some distress."

Despite the rainy weather, the common room of the White Swan radiated with good cheer and warmth that evening. Blind Jack was playing on his violin. The moderate portions of grog permitted by Meg were just enough to promote conviviality without inciting boisterousness. Rance had done a superb job of roasting both the steer and the pig. As Meg saw that this crowd would be well behaved, she relaxed and began to enjoy her wedding dinner.

Sitting beside her, Calvin Collins shed his usual serious manner and chatted freely with her and with Pierre Barineau, who sat on the other side. He confided to Barineau his plans to seek a master's license so he could captain his own vessel.

Farther down the table, Lovejoy sat with a forced look on his face. His mind bounced back and forth between thoughts of Madeline Richter and her swollen face, shut up in a cell for the insane, and the remarks he had rehearsed for his toast for Meg and Collins.

Barineau led off with an introduction of the persons at the head table. He then told the guests of some of the experiences he had shared with Meg and Collins aboard the *Flora.* He explained the dual purpose of the dinner: to honor the young couple and to "welcome home my loyal friend, Lovejoy Martin, who now will propose a toast for the soon-to-be Mr. and Mrs. Calvin Collins."

Lovejoy rose and looked out over the assemblage. "My dear friends and shipmates," he began, "two and a half years ago, many of you were gathered in this same room with me to celebrate the marriage of Evan Jenkins and Primrose Hanrahan. We were on the eve of our war with Great Britain. Tonight, if reports from across the ocean are not false, we may be on the eve of peace with our old adversary."

Lovejoy continued in that vein for several minutes and then turned his attention to Meg and Collins.

Meg dreaded that he might talk about her stowing away on the *Flora,* but he skirted the manner of her appearing on the schooner, saying only that "through a set of curious circumstances" she had joined the crew as a surgeon's assistant and "in that office proceeded to capture the hearts of all aboard."

He turned to look down into the gleaming face of Meg.

"As I say, she captured the hearts of all during her brief sojourn at sea, but "none more than that of a certain young prize master chosen to sail our first prize back to Baltimore."

Again he turned, this time to look into the face of Calvin Collins. Every eye in the room was directed toward Lovejoy. No one noticed the door of the White Swan open and an oilskin-clad figure slip into the common room.

"Now Calvin Collins had already become a prisoner of love by the time the captain of his prize, a scurvy rogue if ever there was one, turned the tables on our prize crew and regained control of the vessel, making Calvin, Megan, and other members of our prize crew his prisoners of war. Many curious things have occurred during this war, but none more curious that what followed."

The red-haired man slunk around the perimeter of the room, proceeding gingerly, holding on to the wall to keep his balance.

A burst of laughter followed Lovejoy's remark that "Calvin Collins succeeded in escaping his British captors, but, I fear, he shall never break the bonds that Megan Jenkins has forged about his heart. Nor, would it appear, does he have the least desire so to do."

McFairlane had worked his way nearly to the front of the room, but out of Lovejoy's direct line of sight. He unbuttoned his raincoat. The fellow at the shipping office had been right. Lovejoy Martin could be found at the White Swan Tavern on South Street, and there was the bastard standing before this crowd going on and on as if he owned the place. Look at the cocky son of a bitch.

"I have known Megan Jenkins since she was in diapers," Lovejoy was saying as McFairlane left the shadows along the wall and staggered nearer the front of the head table.

"Sit down," someone shouted. "We can't see through you."

"And having known her so long, I feel compelled to warn Calvin Collins of this . . ."

Lovejoy, his face turned toward the prospective bridegroom, did not see McFairlane reach into his raincoat and clutch the silver-plated handle of one of his father-in-law's pistols.

"Yes, I feel it to be my Christian duty to warn Calvin Collins that he is marrying a young woman with a will of iron."

"Sit down, damn it," someone again shouted at McFairlane.

At the far end of the table, Tom noticed the strange figure weaving about now almost in front of Lovejoy. At first he thought that the fellow was just a guest grown exuberant with rum. He rose quietly, meaning to cross over and escort the intruder back to his seat as soon as Lovejoy finished his toast.

Misunderstanding the command to sit down, Lovejoy shot back, still looking at Collins, "How can I sit down until I have completed my task and have warned this honest young sailor that while someday he may realize his ambition to be the master of his own ship, he can never be the captain of his own household, not while Megan Jenkins reigns there. No, indeed . . ."

He turned his attention back to the crowd and continued.

". . . At home he will have to be satisfied with the rank of first mate."

The guests laughed as Lovejoy raised his cup.

"And so, my dear friends, I propose a toast . . ."

He paused to look down into the face of George McFairlane.

"My good man," he said. "Let me suggest that you take your seat and get yourself a mug so that you can join us . . ."

And then he recognized the fellow he had first met at the Reading stage office and had seen later through the window of the little stone house with the pregnant Madeline. By the time it had sunk in that the abusive husband of his beloved stood before him, McFairlane's hand was raising the cocked pistol.

The muzzle of the weapon seemed to explode. Lovejoy's forearm felt as though a hot poker had been laid upon it. He dropped his cup. Down the table, Collins cried out in pain and clutched his shoulder. Megan screamed. While some guests ducked under the table and others started for the door, Tom raced around the end of the table.

Despite the shock of the bullet that had creased his arm, Lovejoy vaulted over the table and flung himself upon McFairlane. The redhead dropped the one pistol and drew the second from his belt. Fending off Lovejoy with his left hand, he cocked the gun. Lovejoy seized his left wrist and was starting to twist the arm when the second pistol fired at point-blank range.

It felt as though someone had struck him full force in the chest as the impact of the bullet knocked him back against the head table. By the time Tom and his brothers had wrestled McFairlane to the floor, Lovejoy had fallen unconscious.

# Part Two

# 1 

Lovejoy regained consciousness briefly and dimly. He was lying on a table in the hospital operating theater, surrounded by mirrored lamps. His jacket and blouse had been removed.

Through his slotted eyes, Ephraim's face appeared above him like that of an angel in the reflection of the lamps. He could hear his uncle saying, "I fear he has lost far too much blood."

"Will he live?" Meg Jenkins was asking.

"I can't be sure until we get the bullet out."

"You must save him. We can't let him die."

"Keep your voice down. He may be able to hear us. What about your fiancé?"

"The other doctor has dressed the wound and put him to bed. Luckily, the bullet missed the bone."

"Lovejoy says that you served as his assistant surgeon on the privateer."

"It wasn't for very long."

"You know your instruments then?"

"Yes."

"Good. Now you keep this compress on the hole in his chest and let's turn him over gently. Ah, yes. I can feel the ball under the skin of his back. Passed clear through the thorax. Oh, dear me, this is serious."

Lovejoy moaned and lost consciousness again.

As it turned out, Ephraim was able to extract the bullet by making an incision in the back and drawing out the flattened lead ball. Meg threaded a needle and helped him close the incision.

Wiping the sweat from his forehead, Ephraim said, "I am relieved that we did not have to probe for the bullet. That might have started a fresh hemorrhage. God knows what damage has been caused to his internal organs. There is nothing more to be done for him except to keep him warm and quiet. Only time will tell."

Meg sat down and put her face in her hands.

"I have caused him so much trouble. I wish the bullet had struck me instead."

"This had nothing to do with you, Miss Jenkins."

Ephraim explained about the unexpected appearance of Madeline Richter at his office.

"Apparently, her husband held Lovejoy responsible for her leaving home. The man is insane, of course."

"And she brought her baby along?"

"Yes. My wife is caring for it."

"How sad. She is in your lunatic ward. Her husband is in jail. And poor, poor Lovejoy . . ."

"I am sorry that this happened at your wedding dinner. I can't imagine how the man knew where to find Lovejoy."

Ephraim was washing his hands and Meg was drawing a sheet over Lovejoy's torso when the matron from the ward for the insane came running down the hall.

"Dr. McGee. Come quickly."

"What for?"

"It is Mrs. McFairlane. She has injured herself."

The matron followed Ephraim along the hall and down the stairs to the basement. "Her husband came soon after I reported for duty. She wanted to see him, but then she went berserk when he appeared. This is my fault. I never should have allowed him . . ."

"How did she injure herself?"

"She seems to have thrust her hands between the window bars and through the glass pane . . ."

Meg sat on a stool beside the operating table. She took one of Lovejoy's hands and pressed it to her lips.

"Lovejoy? Can you hear me?"

Her only answer was his labored breathing.

"You can't die. Even though I am to marry someone else, I can never truly love anyone but you. Dear God, if you will only let him live, I will do anything."

Ten minutes later, when Ephraim returned from the basement ward, she was still holding Lovejoy's hand and praying for his recovery. Ephraim put his hand on her shoulder and said, "Now, my dear young lady, we must have him moved to a quiet room and let nature take its course."

Meg was too concerned about Lovejoy to inquire about Madeline Richter or, at the moment, about Calvin Collins.

"What a dreadful night for you, dear Ephraim. You must be exhausted."

"I have never experienced anything half so terrible, Rebecca. Careful dear, with my shirt. Don't get blood on yourself."

"I am glad you removed your waistcoat. Now here is your nightshirt. Put it on and try to get some rest."

Ephraim crawled into his bed and watched his wife put his shirt, soaked with the blood of both Lovejoy and Madeline Richter, into a basin of water.

She blew out the lamp and slid into bed with him.

"And you are doubtful whether Lovejoy will live?"

"The bullet appears to have passed through the lower lobe of a lung. I feared at first that it might have struck a major artery. If so, he would not have lived long enough to reach the hospital. Such wounds to the lung rarely fail to prove fatal, in my experience."

"And there was nothing you could do to save the woman?"

"By the time I reached her, she was gone. The cell floor was covered with her blood."

"And do you think she intentionally killed herself?"

"Who can say? In her distressed state of mind, she may have thought she was reaching out through the window to freedom. The duty matron herself was so distraught I had to sedate the poor woman and send her home. She blames herself for letting McFairlane see his wife."

"And McFairlane?"

"The Jenkins lad subdued him with the help of his father and brothers and the cook. He was raving mad. He will be tried for attempted murder, at the very least. And if Lovejoy does not survive, for murder."

"And the bridegroom was wounded, too?"

"Yes. The first shot grazed Lovejoy's arm and struck Collins's shoulder. He suffered from shock but is in no mortal danger. But the wedding cannot possibly take place in the morning as planned."

"What is to be done about the dead girl and her baby?"

"In the morning I will ask Frank to send a message to her parents. They will have to come and claim the body. Now I must get a few hours of sleep."

"Could we possibly keep the child?"

"Don't get your hopes up, Rebecca. That decision must rest with the grandparents. Now, please, no more questions. I must get some rest."

When Ephraim returned to the hosptital at dawn, he found Meg asleep in a chair beside Lovejoy's bed and Barineau leaning against the windowsill and staring out at the rising sun.

"Has he stirred at all?"

"Not since I have been here. I don't like the sound of his breathing. Sounds bubbling."

"That's from blood in his lung. He's lucky the shot did not strike him higher or he might drown from his own blood."

Ephraim drew back the sheet and peered beneath the bandage across Lovejoy's chest.

"Not much seepage."

"Do you think he will make it?"

Ephraim put a finger to his lips and motioned for Barineau to follow him into the corridor.

"Coma victims often can hear. Will he recover? It depends on whether fresh bleeding occurs or infection sets in. The only thing we can do is keep him comfortable and offer our prayers."

"I am not much for praying."

"Then I shall have to pray twice as much. Incidentally, Lovejoy seemed to hold you in very high esteem."

"The regard is mutual. He has become like a younger brother to me these past few years. I have enjoyed watching him mature. It would be a grave loss if he should not survive."

Lovejoy drifted in and out of consciousness during the next few days. When he came to, Meg was often standing or sitting by his bed. Once he whispered "Madeline," causing her to withdraw from the room in tears. Another time, when Amanda was visiting his room, he opened his eyes briefly, smiled, and said, "Mama. Where have you been?"

During this time, Christian Richter came to claim his daughter's body and to hear an account of what had happened. Ephraim explained about Madeline's appearance at his office and hospitalization. His face slack with fatigue and grief, Richter listened to the account of the shooting at the wedding dinner, then said, "So, McFairlane tried to kill him?"

"Yes, and very nearly succeeded. Indeed, if Lovejoy does not recover, which at this point remains doubtful, your son-in-law may yet be charged with murder."

"I wish I could say I was sorry . . ."

"Excuse me, Mr. Richter, but let me remind you that you are talking about my nephew."

"I don't care who he is. He has brought ruin and shame to my family. I didn't have the heart to tell my wife that Maddy is dead. It will kill her when I have to tell her. And the fault begins with your nephew."

Richter's face suddenly crumpled and tears ran down his cheeks. Ephraim's indignation quickly turned to sympathy.

"There is too much tragedy involved in all this to dwell on questions of fault. Do you wish to see your son-in-law before you leave Philadelphia?"

"I never want to see McFairlane again. I hope he hangs. He is as guilty as your nephew. They both should be hung for what they done to my Maddy. For that matter, this here hospital and you has some explaining to do. Shouldn't have let him see her."

"I admit that the matron failed to follow my instructions, but she says that your daughter seemed eager to see her husband."

"That's your story. I got to take my poor dead daughter back to Berks County. I got to tell her mother . . ."

Richter put his face in his hands.

Ephraim said, gently, "What about the baby? My wife and I have been looking after him."

"The baby, yes. Well, then, I can't take it home with me, can I? Not just yet."

"My wife has become quite attached to the child. We will be glad to keep him until you or the other grandparents are ready to take him."

"What other grandparents?"

"I thought McFairlane's family might . . ."

Richter looked incredulous.

"McFairlane's family got nothing to do with this."

"I don't understand."

"Then I better set you straight."

Two weeks passed before Ephraim felt that Lovejoy had recovered enough so that he could be moved from the hospital. He remained too weak to speak more than a slurred word or two at a time. Orders had been issued to his visitors not to tell him of Madeline's suicide. The police wanted to interview him about the shooting, but Ephraim would not permit them to do so.

Evan and Tom Jenkins came to the hospital with the twins to carry Lovejoy out on a stretcher to a carriage that brought them to Ephraim's house.

"Now if there is anything else me or my boys can do for him, Doctor, you just say the word," Evan said.

"You can pray for him."

"Oh, we been doing that. But ain't he over the worst of it?"

"He is not going to die, as I very much feared he would at first. Now the question is whether he will ever get completely well. Losing so much blood and coming so very close to dying, that could impair his mind, as it has his speech. Same effect as a stroke, you might say."

"May we pay him a visit from time to time?"

"Not just yet. It is important that he be kept quiet."

"Who is to look after him, then?"

"My wife and I. And his sister."

"That is a great burden to you. Megan was wondering if she might lend you a hand."

"What about her wedding?"

"They have decided to delay that until after Christmas. Give Collins time to get over his wound and for all the fuss about the shootings to die down. Anyway, she asked me to ask you if she could come around every day and be of service."

During the first week of his convalescence, Lovejoy was only dimly aware of his surroundings. He could hear soft footsteps outside his room and, occasionally, the sound of a child's voice. Rebecca, Amanda, and Meg were the only persons Ephraim would allow in his room, and they were charged to speak gently and avoid saying anything that would upset their patient.

With the drapes drawn, Lovejoy could not distinguish between night and day. Ephraim had caused straw to be strewn over the cobblestones in front of the house to deaden the sound of carriage and wagon wheels. Light doses of laudanum made the pain in his chest bearable. The opiate also caused Lovejoy's mind to wander wildy back and forth from his childhood to his days at Princeton and London and up through his experiences as a privateer. Sometimes his mother would appear at his bedside, smoothing his hair and murmuring to him. At other times, he imagined that Madeline had come into his room and slipped into the bed with him.

Two weeks later, Ephraim received a letter from Christian Richter.

*Dear Dr. McGee:*

*You was good enough to offer to look after our grandson until we get over losing our daughter. My wife will want the baby in time, but just now she is not able to get out of bed, she is that tore up about what happened to Maddy. She spends the day crying and won't see anybody.*

*So I reckon that means we will have to accept your offer to keep the little fellow until we are in shape to take him. I said some hard words to you when I come to take our Maddy home, but I have talked things over with our pastor and he has made me see our tragedy in a different light.*

*Anyhow, there ain't nothing we can do to change what has happened. We just have to accept it and go on with our lives.*

*I never said this to anybody, but I liked your nephew well enough that I was ready to give him permission to marry our Maddy and then he up and took off and left her in a sad condition, which is how come we married her off to McFairlane. But I told you that already. No use crying over spilt milk.*

*Anyway, we will come get the little fellow as soon as my wife's health permits. Meanwhile, here is a draft for a hundred dollars to cover your costs of looking after him.*

*Respectfully yours,*
*Christian Richter*

*P.S. I forgot to tell you the baby's name. He ain't been baptized yet, but Maddy had decided to name him after me rather than McFairlane or his real father.*

"How is our patient this afternoon?"

"He seems more alert."

"Any conversation out of him yet?"

"Not more than the usual word or two, but his eyes follow Meg and me about the room. And he smiles sometimes. Here, let me take your coat. Supper will be ready soon."

Ephraim handed Rebecca his topcoat and removed his hat.

"It is bitter cold out there. Ice is already forming on the river. Wouldn't surprise me if we had a white Christmas this year."

He stepped close to the fire and warmed his hands, then turned about to toast his backside.

"And little Chris. Has he been a good child today?"

"He is an angel, but a very active one."

"Where is he?"

"I put him down for a nap about an hour ago."

"Shall I go up and get him?"

"If you want to take responsibility for him, go ahead."

"I will just look in on Lovejoy first."

Ephraim picked up his medical bag and mounted the stairs. At the top, he paused at the sound of voices coming from Lovejoy's room. He listened in disbelief, then called softly down to his wife for her to join him.

Together they tiptoed along the hall to the half-open door of Lovejoy's room. Peering inside, they were amazed to see the baby standing beside Lovejoy's bed. The child was babbling and Lovejoy was grinning.

"Hey, little fellow. What is your name? What are you doing here?"

Lovejoy looked up as Ephraim and Rebecca stepped into the room.

"Uncle Ephraim. Aunt Rebecca. Who is this lovely little child who has come to visit me? Come, help me sit up. No, no I will be fine. Put him up beside me. It is a him, isn't it?"

"Yes. His name is Chris. And he is not supposed to be out of his bed."

"Oh? Chris who?"

"It is a long story, Lovejoy. Too long to go into just now. How are you feeling?"

"Very tired. I feel as though I have been on a long journey. Why are the drapes closed? I would like to see some sunlight."

Rebecca opened the drapes to let the feeble light of the setting winter sun into the room.

"I am hungry. And thirsty. What am I doing here, anyway?"

Ephraim and Rebecca were alternately laughing and crying.

"What's the matter with you two? Why the tears?"

"They are tears of happiness, Lovejoy, believe me. Now Rebecca is going to carry Chris downstairs while I take a closer look at you. There will be time enough to explain everything to you tomorrow, when you are feeling stronger."

That night, Ephraim gave his patient a shot of brandy instead of laudanum. He waited until the next day before he broke the news about Madeline Richter's suicide and the identity of the baby boy.

Lovejoy closed his eyes and put one hand over his face. He lay there with tears streaming for so long that Ephraim wished that he had withheld the truth a while longer.

Lovejoy wiped the tears from his face.

"I should have known. She would never have married such a lout. It all makes sense to me now. She did love me, didn't she?"

"I don't know how anyone could doubt it. Her father said that she waited for your return as long as they dared."

"Where is the baby? Bring him to me."

After that, Lovejoy gained in strength each day. By Christmas, he was able to go up and down stairs freely and to romp on the rug in front of the fire with his son.

Next door, his father's health had improved to the extent that the entire family was able to gather in the dining room for Christmas dinner. Just as little Chris had cheered Lovejoy, so he seemed to reenergize Jeremiah. The sight of the old man lifting his grandson on his lap brought tears to Lovejoy's eyes.

It would be a long while before Lovejoy would be able to take a deep breath without feeling a stab of pain. Nor could he think about Madeline Richter without feeling a similar stab to his heart.

Across town at the White Swan, the Jenkins family also celebrated Christmas with a great feast. Calvin Collins had been called home to the bedside of his ailing mother. Meg sat quietly amid the boisterous talk of her father and brothers. Her prayers had been answered. Lovejoy was recovering far better than she had expected. But she felt lost now that he no longer needed a nurse.

"I am sorry. What did you say, Primrose?"

"Is there any reason to delay your wedding any longer?"

"We can hardly marry until Calvin returns from New Jersey. And we will have a quiet ceremony, without all the fanfare."

# 3

*December 27, 1814—Baltimore*

*Dear Lovejoy:*

*You truly have been through the valley of the shadow of death, haven't you? Flo and I have been praying daily for your recovery, and we rejoice, as do all your friends here in Baltimore, at the news of the improvement in your condition. What has happened to you and others is too terrible to comprehend. I only hope that the experience has not embittered you.*

*Well, the old year is about to depart and a new one take its place. This time last year, you were on your way to cruise the waters off England; the year before that, we were putting the Flora in shape for your adventure at Barbados. I can't help wondering what lies before us during the next year.*

*If you had asked me a few weeks ago, after we had turned the British back from Baltimore with their tails between their legs and won our great victory on Lake Champlain, I would have said that an honorable peace was at hand. But now we are hearing troubling reports of the British gathering fresh naval and army forces at Jamaica for an attack upon Louisiana. Perhaps I should not say "fresh," for the troops and ships are much the same as those that ravaged Washington and tried to do the same here. General Ross has been replaced by a General Pakenham, a brother-in-law of the great Wellington, but Cochrane remains their commanding admiral.*

*However, from all reports, we have a tough, able man in charge of the defenses of the lower Mississippi, namely, General Andrew Jackson, who has demonstrated his military competence by putting down the Indian savages in Alabama and Spanish Florida.*

*It would bode ill for our peace commissioners at Ghent if the British were to take New Orleans and close off our traffic on the Mississippi. They then would hold a powerful trump card. And they do thirst for revenge against us. So, in my view and in the view of many of my friends, this war may go on for yet another year. Which brings me to the subject of the Flora.*

*Lovejoy, Talbot Smith is determined to take the schooner out on a new privateering cruise. I have tried to deter him, but he feels that, in his words, "they'll be better pickings than ever" in the West Indies in the wake of the British fleet set to sail against Louisiana, and he may be right.*

*I have pointed out to him that the decision to sell or sail must lie with you as the chief owner. He has been casting about for the financial backing to purchase your interest in case you do not want to continue owning a privateer.*

*Is it at all possible that you might soon be well enough to come down to Baltimore and settle this business in person?*

*A great deal of money is at stake here. Flo and I would like nothing better than to have you as our guest again. If that is out of the question, then I urge you to write to me of your desires.*

*Please give my best regards to your father, your uncle, and the other members of your family. And do write at your earliest opportunity.*

*Your loyal friend,*
*Malcolm MacKenzie*

*P.S. I assume that Megan Jenkins is now Mrs. Calvin Collins. Please offer the young couple my sincere congratulations.*

# PART THREE

# 1 

"Come in from that dreadful cold. I see in your face the suffering you have endured, Lovejoy. Let me punch up the fire while Flo finds something in the kitchen for you lads."

Over coffee, bread, and cheese, they talked until past midnight. Lovejoy explained how Ephraim would permit him to come to Baltimore for a few days only if Tom were to accompany him.

"So, we expect to complete our business in time to return to Philadelphia before the fifth of February, for Tom must be there to help give his sister away in marriage at long last."

"And what about yourself, Lovejoy?"

"Still as weak as a kitten. Must be careful not to take cold. Aside from recovering my stamina, all I have to look forward to is the company of my son, and that may be a short-lived pleasure."

He told the puzzled Malcolm about little Chris.

"My uncle and aunt are looking after him until the Richters reach a decision about his future. I would like to keep him, but I have no legal claim. There is no doubt about his paternity. That was what inflamed her husband to attack me: jealousy."

"And what about her husband?"

"After I return to Philadelphia, he will stand trial for attempted murder. Although I must testify against him, I have lost my stomach for revenge against anyone. All I want is to put my affairs in order down here and establish a fund so that my boy will be adequately provided for, no matter in whose custody."

"There will be money enough for that and more, especially if you decide to sell the *Flora*. Privateering has been good for you."

"Good for me financially, yes. Otherwise it has caused me and many close to me a great deal of suffering and hardship."

"If it is any consolation, it also has caused our enemy much distress. Have you heard that British insurance companies now charge twenty percent premiums to insure cargoes carried across the English Channel? No wonder they wanted to destroy Baltimore."

"And Talbot Smith wants to have another go at them?"

"He thinks that he can raise most of the money needed to purchase your eighty percent interest. He is trying to persuade Barineau to come along as sailing master and first mate."

"What is your view? You do own ten percent of the schooner."

"The British lines of communication between their fleet and their bases back at Antigua and Barbados may be vulnerable."

"Even if they take New Orleans?"

"Especially if New Orleans falls to them. That would necessitate a great traffic of supply ships. Aside from a chance to further line our pockets, this would be an opportunity to harass the British. So I would not dismiss the idea out of hand."

Wincing at the pain in his chest, Lovejoy coughed.

Tom said, "Look here, Mr. MacKenzie, I promised Lovejoy's uncle that I wouldn't let him get too tired."

"Then we will just fill a bed warmer with hot coals and let you lads go upstairs and get a good night's sleep. Ah, Talbot Smith will be delighted to see you. And so will Barineau."

The next morning, they rode in Malcolm's buggy to the shipyard at whose wharf the *Flora* was tied. Talbot Smith was, indeed, pleased to see Lovejoy and Tom.

"You look like you been keelhauled. I heard what happened to you. Reckon you will ever learn to stay out of trouble?"

"According to Malcolm, you are looking for new trouble yourself. Haven't you pestered the poor British enough?"

"Hah! I won't rest until we make them beg for mercy. I will eat up their shipping down there in the Caribbean. Now, look a here, I can pay you half of the fair value of your shares in the schooner if you will take my note for the rest."

"What if I exchanged half of my interest for your note and retained part ownership, for myself and others?"

Talbot rubbed his chin. Malcolm raised his eyebrows. Lovejoy had not discussed this possibility with him.

"So you would like to stay in the game?"

"Actually, I would like Tom here to have ten percent, his sister to have ten as a wedding gift, and the rest to be reserved in trust for a certain child."

Talbot looked at Malcolm.

"Can that be did?"

"It is complicated, but anything is possible."

"I have set February 8 as my sailing date."

"Then we had better move quickly, if Lovejoy is sure that this is what he really wants to do."

A week later, all the paperwork necessary to transfer Lovejoy's interest in the *Flora* had been completed. He held a promissory note for fifteen thousand dollars in addition to bills of exchange as his share of the proceeds of the schooner's earlier cruises.

His business in Baltimore apparently completed, Lovejoy invited Barineau to join Tom and himself for a farewell dinner at the Old Fountain Inn. Malcolm was to join them there later.

"So, Pierre, you really have accepted Talbot's offer? You are going a-privateering again. Why?"

"He has agreed to assign me shares both as first mate and as sailing master. If we have any luck at all, I will have enough money to found my own school. I am leaving tomorrow to put my affairs in order and say good-bye to my wife."

"That is a large order, serving as both sailing master and first mate."

"Our crew will not be so large this time. Mainly we will be destroying captured vessels rather than trying to man and sail them into port. How about yourself? What will you do now that you have cashed in all your chips?"

"I may have a son to raise. At least, that is my hope."

"And you, Tom?"

"I have a sister to marry off, and then I will look around for a business opportunity. I am hoping Joy will come in with me. I think we could make some big money together."

"I have big money, Tom, and believe me, it doesn't bring happiness. Anyway, there will be time enough to talk about the future once I get my strength built up again. Here, our cups are empty. Let's have another round."

By the time they had finished their next round of drinks, the rum and thoughts of seeing his son again had driven Lovejoy's melancholy into retreat. He and his friends were laughing so loudly that people at other tables were frowning at them.

They were in the act of ordering yet another round when Malcolm crossed the room toward their table. Without removing his greatcoat, he handed Lovejoy an envelope.

"This just arrived in the post from Philadelphia."

"I am in no mood for business, but let's see what it is about."

Lovejoy turned from his friends to open the letter.

*January 28, 1815—Philadelphia*

*Dear Lovejoy,*

*I trust your business arrangements are going well for you down there in Baltimore, and I am hoping that you are taking care not to overexert yourself and are keeping warm and getting plenty of rest.*

*Rebecca and I are feeling very despondent, for we no longer have little Chris living with us. Mr. Richter came yesterday and took the boy away. He said that his wife remains bedridden but that he thinks having their grandson under the same roof will cheer her up and give her a sense of purpose.*

*We would have resisted, but could think of no grounds for doing so. We do miss the little fellow terribly.*

*Rebecca advised me to wait until you return to break this news to you, but I did not want you to have your expectations dashed immediately upon your arrival.*

*We look forward to your return.*

*Sincerely,*
*Ephraim McGee*

# 2

"Joy, I think you are making a big mistake."

"I know what I am doing, Tom. There is nothing left for me in Philadelphia, not anymore."

"But I promised your uncle that I would look after you and bring you back safe and sound."

The two friends stood in front of the Old Fountain Inn, waiting for the Philadelphia stage to depart.

"Here is a letter for you to give to Uncle Ephraim. It explains what I intend to do and why. It absolves you of any responsibility."

"This is about the dumbest thing you have ever done, and I have known you to do some pretty foolish things. You are going to wreck your health."

"On the contrary, it would wreck my health to return to a city with so many painful memories. And sailing off to a warmer climate and breathing refreshing sea air may prove to be just the right remedy for both my body and my spirit."

"My family as well as yours will be mighty disappointed."

"Nonsense. You go ahead and see to Meg's marriage. Without me around, it should go off as planned this time. I seem to bring bad luck to people."

"What about the trial? You are supposed to testify against McFairlane."

"With all the witnesses who saw what he did, surely there will be testimony enough to convict the man. Now, stop arguing and get aboard the stage. You have the papers for Meg's shares in the *Flora*, I hope. Wish her much happiness for me."

By Sunday, February 5, preparations for the *Flora's* cruise to the West Indies had been nearly completed. Talbot Smith had recruited fifty men and boys, most of them experienced sailors. With Malcolm's help, he had procured a full supply of potatoes, flour, and other foodstuffs, as well as ammunition. Although he would not admit it, he was most proud of the fact that both Barineau and Lovejoy were sailing with him, Barineau as first mate and sailing master, and Lovejoy as surgeon and supercargo.

Ironically, now that Lovejoy no longer directly owned an interest in the schooner, Talbot treated him with greater respect, even going so far as to invite him to share his cabin.

That afternoon, as Lovejoy sat in Malcolm's office going over his medical supplies for the voyage, he and the chandler were interrupted by the sound of church bells pealing and cannon firing from Fort McHenry.

The blood drained from Malcolm's face at the sound.

"Dear Lord, don't tell me that the British have returned."

Within a few minutes, as the bells continued to toll and the gunfire echoed over the basin, the streets of Fells Point began to teem with men and women.

Putting on their coats, Lovejoy and Malcolm joined the crowd that had gathered across the street at the Blue Eagle Tavern. Billie Matson was posting a printed bulletin on the door of his establishment.

Lovejoy and Malcolm pushed their way close enough to read the large letters at the top of the bulletin: "JACKSON WHIPS BRITISH AT NEW ORLEANS IN GREATEST VICTORY OF THE WAR."

By that night, the news had spread throughout the city of how, on January 8, the British commander Sir Edward Pakenham had attacked American positions south of New Orleans. From behind their breastworks of cotton bales, Andrew Jackson's riflemen and artillery had killed or wounded some two thousand British soldiers in less than half an hour. Among the dead was Pakenham himself. And Jackson's assorted army of Tennessee frontiersmen, Cajun pirates, and free colored militiamen had suffered only about twenty casualties.

It would be some time before the full story would reach Baltimore and other eastern cities, but this was enough to keep the people celebrating throughout that Sunday night.

Lovejoy awoke early the next morning. He lay in bed reflecting on the news from New Orleans and wondering how the wedding of Megan Jenkins and Calvin Collins had gone off the day before. He hoped that she appreciated the ten percent interest in the *Flora* that he had given her. He thought, too, about little Chris, wondering what the child was doing. It would be up to his Uncle Ephraim to inform the Richters of the provision he had made for the boy. Perhaps, upon his return from the Caribbean, he might be allowed to visit his son.

News of the American victory at New Orleans quickened Talbot Smith's determination to "have a last go at the bastards while there is still time." He would have sailed immediately if all of his crew had been on hand, but many—Barineau included—would not report until the night before their departure.

On Tuesday evening, Lovejoy kissed Flo MacKenzie good-bye, thanked her for her hospitality, and gave their cook, Theresa, a small purse as a gratuity for doing his laundry. Malcolm drove him out to the wharf in his buggy.

"You are sure you want to do this, Lovejoy?"

"It is the only thing for me. If I didn't have this trip to distract me, I might leap into the Patapsco and drown myself."

"Oh, don't speak so. You have much to live for."

"Everyone tells me that. Look, in case anything should happen to me, I have drawn up a will. I would like to entrust it to you."

They shook hands, and Lovejoy carried his seabag down into the cabin he was to share with Talbot Smith. As he was stowing his gear, he heard Barineau's voice on the wharf. A few minutes later, his old friend entered the cabin and seized Lovejoy's hand.

"I am pleased beyond all measure that we are to be shipmates again. I was dreading the prospect of having no one but our beloved captain to talk to for several months. Here, I brought my chess set and a great supply of books. You heard of the battle at New Orleans, I suppose."

"Only the deaf and dumb have not. Such a hubbub."

"The war may well end once the news gets back to England. Meanwhile, we had better get ourselves down to the Caribbean while the getting is good."

Barineau paused and looked closely at Lovejoy.

"Mr. MacKenzie thinks you need cheering up. Says he is worried about your melancholy."

"I haven't got a lot to be cheerful about, Pierre, now that Madeline's parents have taken back my son. All my hopes for the future had hinged on that little boy."

"But nothing is forever. Meanwhile, I have just the right medicine for you. Do you know Burton's 'Anatomy of Melancholy'?"

"I have heard of it."

"I brought along my copy."

Lovejoy groaned. "Not more pious advice, please."

"You will find this a wonderful mixture of wisdom and satire and good common sense. Dr. Johnson's biographer, Boswell, said that he used to get up two hours early to read Burton."

Lovejoy rolled his eyes and said, with a smile, "The Lord deliver me from those who would deliver me from myself."

"Burton has a better thought. He said that many had been relieved of their melancholy by, as he put it, 'exonerating themselves to a faithful friend.' And I am willing to be that friend."

"Give me the damned book and let me read it for myself."

The *Flora* glided away from the wharf on an early tide the next morning. Malcolm MacKenzie and Josie stood watching the schooner slip down the chilly waters of the Patapsco. Soon they had become mere dots, and even the battle-scarred walls of Fort McHenry faded into a blur as a light rain began falling.On previous voyages, Barineau had spent his time studying charts and making observations. Now he found himself in a new role, shouting orders at bosuns and helmsmen and taking them from the captain.

Lovejoy spent most of his time reading the book of philosophy Barineau had given him. The next morning, he conducted a sick call at which every crewman was required to report for a cursory examination. That night, the wind shifted, so Barineau was forced to tack the schooner tediously back and forth to make any headway. Both he and the captain remained on deck throughout the rainy night, leaving Lovejoy alone with his despondent thoughts.

At morning sick call, several men reported sore throats and colds from their unaccustomed exposure to the rain and wind of the past two days. Talbot Smith was in a foul mood at the slow progress of the *Flora* down the Chesapeake. He seemed to hold Barineau responsible for the weather. Noting how tension was building between the two men, Lovejoy began to regret signing up for the cruise.

That afternoon, the skies cleared and the winds shifted so that Barineau was able to press on toward the mouth of the Chesapeake. Lovejoy was sitting in the officers' compartment, eating his evening meal with Talbot Smith, when Barineau, wearing a strange grin, put his head in the doorway.

"Ain't you supposed to be on the quarterdeck?" Talbot growled.

"There is something you should know."

"Well then, spit it out and return to your post."

"Gandy has found two stowaways hiding in the sail locker."

"I put a guard on dock to keep that from happening again."

"They bribed the guard, I think."

"By God, I will have them thrown overboard. Who are they?"

"Why don't I let you see for yourselves?"

Barineau stood aside and ushered into the compartment a man with a cap drawn low over his eyes and the lapels of his sea jacket pulled up to shield his face.

Before the captain could speak, the man whipped off his cap and said, "Can you use a supercargo and a surgeon's assistance on this cruise?"

At first Lovejoy thought that he was hallucinating.

"You devil, Tom. You didn't have to sneak aboard . . ."

"No, but wait until you see who has come with me."

At that, Meg Jenkins stepped into the compartment and took her brother's hand. The captain groaned. Lovejoy stared in disbelief.

"This ought to be our most interesting cruise yet," Barineau said.

# 3

Having huddled in the cramped space of the sail locker with Tom for two days and nights, Meg luxuriated in the comfort of the captain's bunk. Beyond the cabin door, she could hear Talbot berating Tom for bringing her aboard. Now and then she heard a placating word from Barineau. She listened in vain for the sound of Lovejoy's voice.

The captain had ordered the *Flora*'s anchor dropped for the rest of the night "so's we can sort out this God-damned mess this silly girl and her idjit brother have dumped on us."

She was past caring whether anyone besides good old Tom wished her to be on the schooner. Mainly she had just wanted to get away from Philadelphia before it was too late. Bless Tom's heart for understanding and for helping her escape. They could do with her what they wanted now that she was on the schooner. She would cook for the crew. Assist Lovejoy at doctoring. Scrub decks or whatever.

As Tom had pointed out, since she and he were now part owners of the *Flora,* thanks to Lovejoy's generosity, the captain sooner or later would accept their presence on board.

She felt sorry for Calvin, of course. But he had brought this on himself, acting so possessive and jealous. It had started with what he had said the afternoon before they were to be wed.

"Now look here, Megan, you'll have to get used to the life of a sailor's wife. I'll be away at sea a lot. It'll save money if we move in with my folks at first. Later, after we have saved a bit, we will build us a little house perhaps."

She had meant to wait until after the wedding to reveal that Lovejoy had given her and Tom each a ten percent interest in the *Flora,* but decided that this was the right time to tell him.

"He did what?"

"You heard me. Tom and I are part owners of a schooner. We don't have to wait to buy a house."

She would have suggested that he might become the captain of the *Flora* when it returned from its cruise if he had not flown off the handle.

"I don't want a wedding gift from that spoiled rich boy. I am tired of hearing his name."

"It is a gift for me and for Tom. But I am willing to share it with you as my husband."

"You can just give it back to him."

"I can't do that. It would insult him. Besides, how could I? He is going off to sea again."

"Well, it insults me for him to give my wife a gift like that without asking my permission. Oh, I know you and all your family like to lick his boots, but look at the trouble he has brought to us. Got me shot. Ruint our wedding dinner. If it hadn't been for him, you and me would be man and wife by now . . ."

"And you would be off to sea, leaving me at home with your mother?"

"What is wrong with that?"

"Maybe we should get something straight right now, Calvin. I am not going to stay with your parents. And I have no intention of refusing Lovejoy's gift."

"You want to get things straight, do you? Well, let me tell you this. I kept my mouth shut when you spent day after day sitting by his bedside and ignoring me and my wound. I ain't going to keep quiet any longer. I have always despised that man. Just look at the harm he has caused. Ran off and left that poor girl in a family way. Then he comes back and turns into a crazy man because she married somebody else. Then he goes off to Lake Erie and near gets your brother killed. If it hadn't been for that, we could have been married over a year ago. But no, you had to traipse out to Erie, you said to look after Tom, but I have always wondered if it wasn't to be with him again. I hate his guts. I forbid you to keep anything he has give you. And I don't ever want to hear you mention his name again. You understand?"

Tears brimming in her eyes, Meg had responded in a low, level voice. "I understand very well, Calvin. Very well indeed."

"Then you will return that paper to Doctor High and Mighty Martin? And you will not bring up this subject again?"

"I will return the paper. And you will never hear me speak his name again. Now let me suggest that you go back to your lodgings. It is supposed to be bad luck for a betrothed couple to speak on the eve of a wedding, you know."

Puzzled at her sudden, seeming acquiescence, Calvin had glowered at her, then held out his hands.

"I do love you, Megan, more than anything in the world. I am sorry I raised my voice to you so. Can we have a kiss to show there is no hard feelings?"

"No kisses. No more talk. Let's not risk bad luck further."

"Then I will see you at the church in the morning."

"God willing," she had said as she turned to go upstairs.

While Megan was drifting off to sleep to the gentle rocking of the anchored *Flora,* in the compartment next door, Talbot Smith finally wound down his tirade and, at Barineau's urging, Tom explained what had happened back in Philadelphia.

"So you see, it dawned on her what a tyrant of a husband he would be. She said she would jump in the Delaware and drown herself rather than spend the rest of her life with such a man. Actually, she never really loved him anyway, but he kind of wore her down. She had thought she could be content with him until he said what he said. If he had been smarter, he would've kept his mouth shut for another day at least. One thing you can't do with my sister is to forbid her to do something. You remember what a stubborn little girl she was, Joy."

Lovejoy nodded.

"Why in God's name did she have to pick this here schooner to run away to?" Talbot demanded.

"She said she had never spent happier days than those here with all of us. And, Captain, she said she knew you to be a kindhearted man who would understand."

Talbot crossed his arms and snorted.

Barineau smiled and winked at Lovejoy.

The captain said, finally, "All right, Jenkins. You go take the other bunk in my cabin for the night."

"What do you propose to do about this?" Barineau asked.

"I ain't saying until morning. Now get your ass topside and make sure we got lights out fore and aft so's we don't get rammed in the dark."

Barineau motioned for Lovejoy to follow him up to the deck.

After seeing that lanterns were properly burning and that the *Flora*'s anchor was holding, Barineau took Lovejoy's elbow and ushered him into the lee of the galley.

"Our Miss Jenkins once again has put us in a difficult position."

"I am flabbergasted. Why would she do such a rash thing?"

"Maybe we would have to be females to understand. In case you haven't noticed, Lovejoy, Megan Jenkins is a young woman of rare character. She has courage and intelligence and a will of iron. She would have been wasted on a dolt like Collins. She is lucky she realized what she was getting into before it was too late."

"I still don't understand why she would run to us. Or why Tom would help her do such a silly thing."

"You really don't understand?"

"I just said so, didn't I?"

"Then you must be blind. Perhaps it is time someone removed the scales from your eyes."

Tom and Megan slept like babies throughout the night while, in the officers' compartment next door, both Talbot Smith and Lovejoy lay long awake, staring into the darkness, their minds churning. Barineau, by contrast, soon fell asleep. He had got a lot off his chest by talking to Lovejoy, and he now felt at ease.

Several times during their long conversation on deck, Lovejoy had felt like striking Barineau. He had no business saying such things about Madeline. It was cruel. Except for his leaving that Christmas to seek the release of Meg and the prize crew and his being held prisoner on Bermuda, they would have been married for more than two years now. Little Chris would have been born to a happy, legally wed couple. Madeline might have been high-strung and perhaps even hard to live with, but he could have managed her. There was no excuse for Pierre's saying that she would have turned his life into "a living hell." He made it sound as though her death had been fortunate.

As for Meg Jenkins's feelings for him, what basis did Barineau have for saying that she worshipped him and that he was the real reason she had run away to Baltimore? He couldn't very well ask Meg about that, but perhaps Tom would clear up the matter in the morning. There was a lot to be cleared up in the morning. What if the captain should decide to turn back to Baltimore and kick Meg off the schooner? What was the harm of letting her remain? It would be pleasant to have her aboard. After the harsh things Barineau had said to him, he doubted whether it would be possible for them to resume their customary easy relationship. Yes, he was glad that Tom and Meg were aboard. They made his life seem less bleak.

He finally fell asleep thinking of little Chris and wondering whether he would ever be able to gain custody of the boy.

# 4

By the next morning, the skies had cleared and a warm wind was blowing out of the south-southwest. Weary of his bunk in the officers' compartment, Lovejoy went topside to wheedle a cup of coffee from Kevin Mahoney.

"The news is all over the ship about the return of that dear lass Megan Jenkins," the cook said as he handed Lovejoy a cup.

"Yes. You might say history has repeated itself."

"We are all hoping against hope that this time the captain won't send her back. It would be a great pleasure to have her company for the entire cruise."

"I agree, Cookie. It would be a great pleasure."

Talbot waited until after all hands had eaten breakfast and Lovejoy had conducted his sick call before he called a conference in his cabin. Meg sat on her bunk, her hands folded in her lap, her dark brown hair falling down around her shoulders. Tom stood beside her as if to shield her from a fresh verbal assault by the captain. Barineau and Lovejoy leaned against the door while the captain paced back and forth.

"I don't need to tell you what a mess you two have put us in here."

"You told us so last night, Captain," Tom said.

"Well, it just ain't going to work out to let you, or anyway her, go on this here cruise."

"She didn't make any trouble the last time," Tom said. "In fact, she turned out to be a great help to the cook and to Lovejoy."

"I ain't denying that. But circumstances is different this time. We got only about half as many men to be fed and looked after by a doctor, so we don't need her for that. We are going to be sailing into dangerous waters. Besides which, we still have a problem of where she'd sleep. Can't have her bunking with the crew, and by God I need my cabin for myself."

"So what are you saying, Captain?" Barineau asked.

"We got to turn back."

"Clear to Baltimore?"

"Not Baltimore. There is a fresh breeze that will get us back up to Annapolis by tomorrow morning. We can put her off there. Her brother can get off with her or stay on with the crew, as he chooses. No, it won't do any good for you to cry, young lady. My mind is made up. Mr. Barineau, I will thank you to go topside and prepare to weigh anchor and set your course back to Annapolis."

"Just a minute, Captain," Lovejoy said.

"Yes, Dr. Martin."

"I have to tell you that if you put Miss Jenkins ashore, you will have to find yourself a new surgeon for this cruise."

The captain's jaw dropped. Meg put her hand over her mouth. Tom and Barineau stared at Lovejoy during the long silence that followed.

At last, Talbot found his voice, sputtering, "By God, we have been through all this before . . . "

"And this time it will do no good to try to starve me into submission. If Meg goes ashore, I will go too."

"And if Dr. Martin goes, so will I," Barineau said.

"By God, this is mutiny. I can have the lot of you hanged."

"By whom?" Lovejoy replied. "First you would have to have a trial. And that will only further delay your cruise."

The captain's face turned crimson. Lovejoy feared for a moment that the man was about to collapse from a stroke. He turned his back and stared out a porthole until he regained control of his temper.

Facing the group again, he said, "Since you are all so damn smart, what are you proposing we do? But I warn you, I ain't going to sail with a unprotected girl on this here schooner."

"Protected from what?" Lovejoy said.

"From a crew of randy sailors. Have you forgot how Collins lost his head over her? If he hadn't done that, he wouldn't have let that English captain take him by surprise. I got nothing against the young lady, but the sea ain't the place for a unmarried lass."

"What if she were married?"

Again, everyone looked in amazement at Lovejoy.

"Well, she ain't."

"But if she were . . . "

"This is crazy talk. It wouldn't make no difference. Besides, who would she be married to?"

"How about your ship's surgeon?"

At Meg's insistence, the others left her alone with Lovejoy in the cabin. Her face streaked with tears, she stared at him until his eyes dropped.

"This isn't some kind of a joke, is it, Lovejoy?"

"I have never in my life been more serious."

"Then you just feel sorry for me. Is that it?"

"I do feel sorry for you, but that is not it."

"You don't love me. I know that."

"You only think that. Look, I thought I loved Madeline Richter. No, I did love her but it was a sort of obsession. I never really got to know her."

"You fathered her child, so they say."

"True. And I would have married her except for . . . "

"Except for me getting taken prisoner. I am sorry about that."

"Look, Meg, that is water under the bridge. We can't unravel the past. All we can do is start with the present. What I am saying is that I want to go forward from this point with you as my wife."

"You still haven't said you loved me."

"I was trying to explain. There are many kinds of love, I realize that now. With Madeline, I was always on edge. I feel at ease with you, Meg."

"And you call that love?"

Lovejoy knelt beside the bunk and put his head in her lap.

"I need you, Meg. I need you more than I have ever needed anyone."

She put her hand on his head and then ran her fingers through his hair. She started to speak but stopped herself and continued to caress him. At last he raised his face and said, "So what is your answer, Meg? The captain has the power to marry us. He may not like it, but he will have to give us this cabin. We can turn this into a honeymoon cruise."

"No," she said.

"But Barineau said that Tom told him you loved me."

"Tom should keep his mouth shut. I used to worship the ground you walked on. But I wasn't good enough for you. Now, you think you can crook your little finger and I will fall into your arms. You haven't said you loved me. Calvin Collins does love me . . . "

"You're not going back to him, surely. I won't allow it."

"Careful. That is how Calvin lost me, by telling me what he would and wouldn't allow me to do."

"So you don't want to marry me?"

"I need time to think about this. I need to decide whether I want to marry a man who hasn't yet said he loves me with all his heart. No, it is too late to say so now. You go tell the captain I need time to think. And send Tom down here. I have a bone to pick with him."

"Time to think?" Talbot Smith said. "I ain't said I would go along with such a harebrained idea. I'd still have to give up my cabin. Besides, I ain't sure she'd be doing the right thing to marry up with you. Maybe the best thing is to haul you both back to Annapolis."

"That would cost us precious sailing time," Barineau said.

"Once London hears about New Orleans . . . "

"Don't talk to me about wasting time. Anyway, I never married nobody."

"I have the form for you to follow. There is nothing to it. Ah, there comes Tom. Well, Tom, what does she say?"

Tom shrugged and motioned for Lovejoy to join him at the rail, out of hearing of the others.

"She is mad as hell at me. Didn't want you to know how she feels about you. Her feelings are hurt."

"I ask her to marry me and that hurts her feelings?"

"It was the way you went about it. You should have taken her aside and told her you loved her instead of just announcing it like you was doing her a big favor and she had no choice."

"How can I redeem myself?"

"You can start by asking me for her hand in marriage, seeing as how I am her brother. Then go down and talk to her without putting your foot in your mouth."

"What I was trying to say before, Meg, is that the way I feel about you goes deeper than the kind of love most people talk about. I love you, sure, but also I like you and I respect you. You have got more character in your little finger than most girls have in their entire bodies."

"But do you really love me?"

"Right down to the bone, I do love you."

She looked at him for a long while without speaking.

"So how about it? Will you marry me?"

"At last you have got around to asking me properly."

With the *Flora* once again sailing smartly down the Chesapeake, Lovejoy was all for holding the marriage ceremony that very day.

"I will ask Pierre to stand with me as my best man. And I expect you will want Tom to give you away. Is that all right with you, Meggie?"

"That is fine."

"And Cookie says that he can provide us with a grand wedding dinner."

"I am sure he can. But Lovejoy, perhaps we ought to wait a few days, until we are safely at sea."

"Why put it off?"

"I think the captain would prefer waiting until we have cleared land. He has a lot of drills he wants to put his crew through."

"The wedding won't take him that long. All he has to do is read what Barineau gives him."

"And it would be rushing Cookie to prepare a meal on such short notice."

"Nonsense. He is eager to get started. What's the matter? You aren't getting cold feet, are you?"

"Let's just wait three days."

"I am ready now. What is the matter?"

Meg sighed and rolled her eyes. "I thought you knew all about women."

"What do you mean? I don't care about other women. From now on, you are the only woman for me."

"With all your experience, I would think that when a girl puts you off for three days, she wouldn't have to spell out her reason for doing so."

"Oh," Lovejoy said. "Very well then. We will set the date for, let's see, February 14. Why, that is St. Valentine's Day. Oh, Meggie, you have turned me from the most miserable man in the world into the happiest."

# 5

The day set for the wedding found the *Flora* clearing Cape Henry on a calm sea under a clear sky. During the past three days, Lovejoy and Meg had talked longer together and far more intimately than they had during all the years they had known each other.

She told him how she had felt on the death of her mother and her disappointment at her father's refusal to send her to school as he had Tom and the twins. She told him of all the books—mostly novels—she had read and asked him to recommend others.

"I want to improve my mind like you have yours," she said.

Lovejoy revealed to her his own long-suppressed grief at the loss of his mother and his bafflement at never being able to please his father.

He liked the way she listened, her head bent toward his, dark eyes intently watching his lips form his words. He wondered why he had never noticed the graceful shape of her small hands or the delicate contour of her neck.

At first, he had been annoyed at the three-day delay in their wedding. Besides giving them a chance to open their hearts to each other, the respite also served to intensify his desire to hold her trim little body. But she would permit him nothing more than a chaste kiss now and then. He was not allowed in the cabin without Tom's being present. By the day scheduled for their wedding, he ached to possess her. Yet his respect for her character and intelligence increased with each hour of their enforced wait.

With Toby's help, Kevin Mahoney began preparing their wedding feast early that morning. At Meg's insistence, and with the captain's grudging permission, the marriage ceremony was to be held on the open deck late that afternoon, to be followed by the banquet to be shared with the entire crew.

Meg, who never went to bed without praying, had offered a prayer the night before for clear weather. And she had offered thanks to the Almighty for finally granting her wish for Lovejoy to love her as she did him. Now it appeared that all her prayers were being answered.

She felt exultant that at long last Lovejoy had expressed his love for her, but what had really melted her heart had been his confession that he needed her. Perhaps, she thought, it was just as well that all this had not occurred earlier, before that maniac shot him and Calvin. She would have been fearful that his family would not accept her, the daughter of a mere tavern owner. She would have felt inferior, like a usurper in his wealthy family. But the several weeks following the attack had changed all that. Nursing him, first at the hospital and later at Ephraim's home, had given her the opportunity to win the admiration of Lovejoy's family. She and Amanda had become almost like sisters. Certainly she had a lot to learn about social behavior, but she did not doubt her ability to adapt.

With the help of the sail maker, a toothless old tar, she turned a white bedsheet into a simple wedding dress. Gandy, the hard-bitten gunner's mate, worked a gold coin into a handsome wedding ring. By noon, Talbot Smith gave up trying to keep his crewmen's minds on gunnery and sailing drills and gave them the rest of the day off to prepare for the wedding.

Because of this inattention, no one noticed the schooner approaching from the east until it was nearly three miles distant. Flying an American flag, it fired a cannon off its starboard bow, as a signal to parley rather than a challenge.

Chagrined at being caught off guard, Talbot Smith studied the lines of the approaching schooner before ordering Gandy to fire one of his starboard carronades in answer and for the *Flora*'s sails to be shortened.

"She's one of ours, no doubt about it. Now knock off all this wedding nonsense until I sees what they want with us."

The other schooner soon came within hailing distance. Her captain yelled through his speaking trumpet, "Ahoy, is that the *Flora*?"

"It is. Who are you?"

"We're the *Tomcat.* This is Phineas Graham. Where are you headed?"

Lowering his own trumpet, Talbot muttered, "None of his God-damned business where we are headed."

Then he raised the instrument and shouted, "We're going down to the Gulf to try our luck."

"Against whom?"

"Against the British, who else?"

"Haven't you heard the news?"

"What news?"

"The war is over, for God's sake."

"Is this some kind of a joke, Graham?"

"I am serious. They signed the papers on Christmas Eve. We got the news from a packet out of London. That's why we are headed home."

It took much shouting back and forth before Talbot became convinced that the British and American peace envoys in Ghent really had agreed upon terms to be submitted to their respective governments for confirmation.

"Damn it to hell. And I wanted one more shot at the bastards."

Lovejoy stood with Barineau, Tom, and Meg, talking about the situation.

"Christmas Eve, now there is a piece of irony," Barineau mused. "Too bad they didn't wait a few weeks longer. That would have given the news about New Orleans time to reach Europe. It would have stengthened our hand. Imagine that. Two thousand men killed or wounded two weeks after they had already agreed on peace terms. Well, I suppose war really doesn't make much sense anyway."

"So, Captain," Lovejoy said. "Looks as though this cruise is over."

"I reckon you are right. Go ahead, Mr. Barineau, and bring her about. We're heading back to Baltimore. My job is over, it looks like."

"Not quite yet, Captain," Lovejoy said.

"What do you mean?"

"You still have to marry Meggie and me."

"Wait, Lovejoy. Not again. Not just yet."

"Why, Meg, I didn't hurt you, did I?"

"It hurt a little, at first, but it's all right. I loved feeling so close to you. Just give me a few minutes. Oh, I used to dream of lying in your arms like this. Did you know that?"

"How would I know?"

"Wait, now, I want to talk and I can't when you are kissing me."

"What do you want to talk about?"

"What we will do when we get back to Baltimore. And then to Philadelphia. Where we will live. How many children do you think we will have. What will Pa and the twins and Primrose say when they hear we are man and wife."

"That's a lot of questions. Can't we talk about them later?"

"Stop it, Lovejoy. Just hold me close."

"Just once more, and then we will talk all you like."

Afterward, they fell into a deep sleep. Meg awoke first to the dawning sun shining through the stern window. She propped up on one elbow and looked at the relaxed face of her husband.

"He is mine," she said to herself. "After all these years."

She was still staring at him when he awoke. He stretched, smiled, and then took her into his arms.

"Good morning, Mrs. Martin."

"Good morning, Dr. Martin. Lovejoy, I have been thinking."

"More questions?"

"Yes. About your little boy. He is a sweet baby. In case you are wondering, I would love being his mother. He seemed to like me when I was helping look after you. Do you think his grandparents would give him back?"

Lovejoy's eyes welled up. He kissed her gently and said, "I was wondering whether you might be willing, but thought you would resent the fact that . . ."

"That another woman bore him? As you say, that is water under the bridge."

"I will ask lawyer Bennett to look into it as soon as we have settled down. I was afraid you might be jealous or something."

"It is hard to be jealous of a dead woman. But let me tell you this, if you ever look twice at anyone else, you may find yourself staring down a pistol barrel again."

"Really?"

"Really. Talking about babies, did you ever deliver one?"

"No, why?"

"I was wondering if you might want to deliver ours."

"I think I would rather someone else did that, someone such as Uncle Ephraim."

"You are right. After all, you might faint, and I wouldn't be able to help you, would I?"

# *EPILOGUE*

Jeremiah Martin lived on for three years after "Mr. Madison's war" ended. Although he never fully recovered his health, during most of that time he remained well enough to enjoy his family. He was delighted at the birth of Megan and Lovejoy's first child, a boy, which occurred so soon after their return from Baltimore that fingers were set to counting the months. He was further delighted by their naming the boy after himself.

Before this new little Jeremiah had taken his first steps, Christian Richter faced up to the likelihood that his wife would never leave the bed to which she had taken herself upon the death of Madeline. Reluctantly, he agreed to relinquish custody of little Chris to his natural father, which brought fresh joy to the Martin family.

Fearful that his part in directing George McFairlane to the White Swan on that fateful night in October 1814 might come to light, Chester Peebles sold both his interest in Martin Shipping and his Elsfreth's Alley house to Lovejoy. He and Rosalind moved to New York, where he began a new life as an importer and she as a society matron. They learned of Jeremiah's death too late to attend his funeral, one of the largest in Philadelphia's history.

Across the Atlantic, in the village of Newton Ferrers, Christopher Bledsoe was bitterly living out his days on a meager naval pension. At first, he had thought that Chester had fled that night when he failed to return from the privy. He had enlisted the help of the local militia to search for his missing prisoner. Lovejoy's message, forwarded to him from Bermuda, not only ended his hopes of extracting money from the Martin family but also rubbed salt in a wound from which he never recovered.

Beyond the English Channel, in Brest, France, Odette Dubuisson, or, to call her by her new name, Madame LaFontaine, adjusted as best she could to life with the elderly wine merchant she had married the year before. Occasionally, while Monsieur LaFontaine slept, she lay awake and thought about the handsome young American doctor she had housed and comforted in the spring of 1814.

In Bermuda, business dropped off so sharply after the war that Ross McFadden sold the Seahorse and joined his cousin Malcolm in Baltimore. Weasel Cuthbert and Queenie Foster, now man and wife, purchased the establishment with her savings from her old profession. It was not a very profitable enterprise, but, as she told Weasel, "I like working on my feet better than on my back."

On Barbados, the patronage of the Bearded Fig Tree likewise declined with peace. Winnie Arbuckle's girth continued to expand, however. She died of an apoplectic seizure while in the midst of raging at her hapless staff.

In Baltimore, Talbot Smith reluctantly faced up to the facts of postwar life. He sold the *Flora* and returned to building schooners at his shipyard.

Joined by his cousin from Bermuda, Malcolm MacKenzie continued his chandlery business. With the wealth he had gained from privateering, he was no longer considered merely one of Baltimore's "small beer gentry." Despite being asked to serve on bank and insurance company boards in the growing city, he continued his quiet, modest lifestyle with his beloved Flo.

Back in Philadelphia, Tom pooled his earnings with an interest-free loan from Lovejoy to start a business of hauling goods from Philadelphia out to Harrisburg and farm produce from the hinterlands back to Philadelphia.

Calvin Collins married a farm girl and went to sea again, but never realized his ambition to command his own ship.

Lovejoy never again practiced medicine, nor did he study the law as he once thought he might. Instead, he applied himself to building up his father's old shipping business. By the time of Jeremiah's final, fatal stroke, he had reestablished the firm as one of the leading companies of its type in the East. Philadelphia society was slow to accept the daughter of a tavern keeper, but this did not bother either Megan or Lovejoy. Nor did it deter his own acceptance on various philanthropic and civic boards.

He often dropped by the White Swan to share a pint of ale with his father-in-law. And Megan brought both her son and stepson by for visits with Evan, Primrose, and little Evan Junior.

And then there was Pierre Barineau . . .

"Meg, darling. I am home."

In the kitchen, overseeing the preparation of supper, Meg handed little Jeremiah to the cook and, taking Chris's hand, said, "Come, let's go give Daddy a hug and kiss."

Lovejoy picked her off her feet in a vigorous hug, then tossed Chris in the air and kissed him.

"A packet came for you. I think it is from Mr. Barineau."

"Good. I wonder if his school still goes well. Ah, he seems to have sent me yet another book. Pierre was always a great one for stuffing books down my throat."

Ripping off the paper wrapping, Lovejoy opened a small, leather-bound volume.

Meg watched his face as he studied the title page. First he looked surprised. Then he bent his head low, his eyebrows knitted as if in disbelief. When he raised his face, his eyes brimmed.

Without speaking, he handed the book to her. To conceal his emotion, he picked up Chris and carried the boy into the parlor.

Meg opened the book to the title page and read:

*VOYAGE TO HONOR*
*Being an Account of a Privateering Venture*
*in Our Nation's Late War with Great Britain*
*by Pierre Gustave Barineau*

Turning the page, she saw that Barineau had dedicated the book to "Dr. Lovejoy Martin, whom I count as my most cherished and admired friend, and with whom I shared many of the experiences related in this memoir of our struggle to establish the United States of America as a mature nation capable of defending its rights against infringement by other powers."

Meg carried the book into the parlor, where Lovejoy, still holding his son, was staring out the window. She put her arms around his waist and leaned her head against his shoulder. Not trusting their voices, they stood there, gazing silently out the window, until Chris squirmed in Lovejoy's grasp and held out his arms for Meg to take him.

# A READING LIST

*The War of 1812,* by Donald R. Hickey, 1989, University of Illinois Press; *The Perennial Philadelphians, The Anatomy of an American Aristocracy,* by Nathanial Burt, 1963, Little, Brown; *The Republic's Private Navy, The American Privateering Business as Practiced by Baltimore During the War of 1812,* by Jerome R. Garitee, 1977, Wesleyan University Press; *The Navy War of 1812, A Documentary History,* edited by William S. Dudley, 1985, Navy Historical Center; *The Dawn's Early Light,* by Walter Lord, 1972, W. W. Norton; *The Privateersmen,* by Clifford Lindsey Alderman, 1945, Chilton Press; *A History of American Privateers,* by Edgar Stanton Maclay, 1899, Bunt Franklin Co.; *The Rockets' Red Glare,* by Scott S. Sheads, 1986, Tidewater Publications; *The Naval War of 1812,* by Theodore Roosevelt, 1882, G. P. Putnam's Sons; *The Perilous Fight,* by Neil H. Swanson, 1945, Farrar and Rinehart; *The War of 1812,* by Harry L. Coles, 1965, University of Chicago Press; *The Building of Perry's Fleet on Lake Erie, 1812–13,* by Max Rosenbert, 1987, Pennsylvania Historical and Museum Commission; *The Battle for Lake Erie,* by Robert and Thomas Malcolmson, 1990, Vanwell Publishing Ltd.; *Barbadian Dialect,* by Frank A. Collymore, 1955, Barbados National Trust; *The Story of Bermuda and Her People,* by W. S. Zuill, 1973, MacMillan Caribbean; *Bermuda's Story,* by Terry Tucker, 1959, Island Press Ltd.; and *Bermuda from Sail to Steam,* by Henry Wilkinson, 1973, Oxford University Press.

Other Books by Robert H. Fowler

*Album of the Lincoln Murder* (1965)

*Jim Mundy, A Civil War Novel* (1977)

*Jason McGee, A Frontier Novel* (1979)

*The Spoils of Eden* (1985)

*Jeremiah Martin, A Revolutionary War Novel* (1989)

Lake Superior
Sault Sainte Marie
INDIANA TERR.
St. Joseph
Mackinac I.
Lake Michigan
Lake Huron
TERRITORY
MICHIGAN TERRITORY
Detroit River
Thames R.
Moraviantown
Detroit
Ft. Malden
Lake Eri
Fort Dearborn
River Raisin
Frenchtown
Bass Is.
Put-in-Bay
Maumee (Miami) R.
Ft. Meigs
Fort Stephenson
ILLINOIS
Tippecanoe R.
River
Prophet's Town
Wabash
INDIANA TERRITORY
OHIO
Urbana
Fort Harrison
Cincinnati
Ohio River
Bier